UNCLE TOM'S CABIN

UNCLE TOM'S CABIN

or Negro Life in the Slave States of America

◆

Harriet Beecher Stowe

With an Introduction and Notes by
DR KEITH CARABINE
University of Kent at Canterbury

WORDSWORTH CLASSICS

19

Readers who are interested in other titles from
Wordsworth Editions are invited to visit our website at
www.wordsworth-editions.com

For our latest list and a full mail-order service contact
Bibliophile Books, 5 Thomas Road, London E14 7BN
TEL: +44 (0)20 7515 9222 FAX: +44 (0)20 7538 4115
E-MAIL: orders@bibliophilebooks.com

This edition published 1995 by Wordsworth Editions Limited
8B East Street, Ware, Hertfordshire SG12 9HJ
New Introduction and Notes addedd 2002

ISBN 978-1-84022-402-3

Typeset by Antony Gray
Printed and bound in Great Britain by Clays Ltd, St Ives plc

GENERAL INTRODUCTION

Wordsworth Classics are inexpensive editions designed to appeal to the general reader and students. We commissioned teachers and specialists to write wide ranging, jargon-free introductions and to provide notes that would assist the understanding of our readers rather than interpret the stories for them. In the same spirit, because the pleasures of reading are inseparable from the surprises, secrets and revelations that all narratives contain, we strongly advise you to enjoy this book before turning to the Introduction.

General Adviser
KEITH CARABINE
Rutherford College
University of Kent at Canterbury

INTRODUCTION

Uncle Tom's Cabin is arguably the most popular and certainly the most influential novel ever written by an American. Published in March 1852, it sold ten thousand copies in the first week and within a year three hundred thousand had been sold in America and nearly one million in England. It was soon translated into all the major European and continental languages, including Welsh, Polish, Hungarian and Russian. By 1860 Harriet Beecher Stowe was the most famous writer in the world. It spawned numerous stage versions in several languages that were highly edited to emphasise the work's melodramatic and sentimental effects; theatrical, minstrel and vaudeville versions were performed in America until the outbreak of World War II and it also generated in the South a new genre of anti-Uncle Tom narratives, dedicated to refuting her case against the peculiar institution of slavery. More pertinently, in 1861, on the eve of the Civil War, it had sold four and a half million copies. This statistic is truly staggering because the population of the United States was only thirty-two million, including some five million semi-literate slaves, and the book was banned by most Southern legislatures. Thus, if we also discount children, there was one copy of *Uncle Tom's Cabin* for every four or five readers.[1]

The story of the conception, writing and publication of *Uncle Tom's Cabin*, as Ann Douglas remarks, 'is almost as well known as the story the novel dramatises' (p. 7, 1981). This phenomenally successful novel began most inauspiciously. In 1850 Stowe was thirty-nine years old, the harried mother of five surviving children and pregnant with a seventh, married to Calvin Stowe, a poor theologian recently appointed to the faculty of Bowdoin College in Brunswick, Maine. She was one of the ten children of Lyman Beecher, considered the greatest evangelical preacher of his day, and she lived under the shadow of her six brothers who were famous preachers and authors and of her sister Catherine Beecher, the foremost female educator of her generation. Moreover, Mrs Stowe in 1850 was a minor writer of New England sketches and uncontroversial moral tales who had never contemplated writing a novel and who, as she confesses in her 'Concluding Remarks' to *Uncle Tom's Cabin*, had 'for many years of her life ... avoided all reading upon or allusion to the subject of slavery, considering it as too painful to be enquired into, and one which advancing light and civilisation would certainly live down' (p. 409). She was moved to enter the public arena by three events: the passage of, and the Northern response to, the Fugitive Slave Law in September 1850; a direct appeal by her sister-in-law; and by a vision while she was taking communion in church in February 1851. The greatest political problem facing the United States in the 1840s, as the country expanded ever westwards, was whether the new states should accept or reject slavery. The Missouri Compromise of 1850 was essentially a pro-slavery decision and the Fugitive Slave Law commanded citizens 'to aid and assist in the prompt and efficient execution of this law, whenever their services may be required'; moreover, section seven stated that persons who gave shelter, food or assistance to an escaping slave were liable to a fine of $1,000 and six months in prison. The Missouri Compromise gave a new lease of life to the unpopular, radical abolitionists led by William Lloyd Garrison, who since 1831 had demanded the immediate, unconditional, uncompensated abolition of slavery. Stowe shared both her

---

1 Mason Lowance (ed.), *Against Slavery: An Abolitionist Reader*, Penguin Books, London 2000, p. 292. Hereafter, all references appear parenthetically in the text; for full citations see the Bibliography.

father's lifelong distrust of the 'immediatists' and his advocacy of Colonisation, that is the assisted passage of America's black population to Liberia to found an African Christian state. But, whereas her father supported the Compromise, Stowe shared her brother Edward's and her brother Henry's disgust at Senator Daniel Webster's endorsement of it and their outrage at what she later called the 'inexplicable ... dreadful ... apathy of the Christian world of the free North' at the prospect of the trial and return of blacks to slavery (Introduction to *Uncle Tom's Cabin*, cited Fields, p. 145). Stowe's first indignant response, in August, 1850 was to send 'The Slave's Dream' to Gamaliel Bailey, the editor of the moderate anti-slavery journal the *National Era*. This parable recounts the refusal of a farmer to assist some fugitive slaves who are soon recaptured, and Stowe, anticipating the moral stance of *Uncle Tom's Cabin*, invokes not the law of man but that of an avenging voice at the Seat of Judgement thundering, ' "Depart from me ye accursed! for I was an hungered, and ye gave me no meat" ' (Hedrick, p. 206). Meanwhile, her sister-in-law Mrs Edward Beecher wrote to her, ' "If I could use a pen as you can, I would write something that will make this whole nation feel what an accursed thing slavery is" '; and according to her son Charles Edward Stowe, his mother 'rose up from her chair' declaring, ' "I will write something. I will if I live" ' (p. 145). The origin of *Uncle Tom's Cabin*, according to Stowe, occurred in February 1851 when she was taking communion and had 'a tangible vision' of the death of Uncle Tom that stimulated a 'convulsion of tears'. She immediately composed the climax of her tale, the 'victory' of Uncle Tom's death, and read it to her young sons, who too dissolved into tears, 'one of them saying, through his sobs, "Oh! Mamma, slavery is the most cursed thing in the world!" ' (cited Fields, p. 147).

On 9 March, Stowe wrote to Gamaliel Bailey to say that she had begun a 'series of sketches' that would run 'through three or four numbers' of the *National Era*; but, 'written at white heat, they grew into a sprawling, panoramic two-decker novel', appearing in weekly instalments from 5 June 1851 until 1 April 1852 (Hedrick, p. 208) The prospective novel was offered to her sister Catherine's publisher, Phillips, Sampson and Co., who turned it down fearing that an anti-slavery book by a woman would be a poor risk and might alienate a sizeable portion of the Southern trade. Such pusillanimous prejudices explain the biggest howler in the history of publishing, but Stowe herself also greatly underestimated the commercial value of her book. Indeed, expecting that it might buy her a new dress, she signed a contract with her father's publisher, Jewett, forgoing his offer to split profit and risk equally, and accepting instead ten per cent of the sales. The novel was published on 20 March 1852 and despite her modest contract it netted her $10,000 (over $500,000 today!) in the first three months of sales, 'the largest sum of money ever received by any author, either American or English, from the sale of a single work in so short a period of time' (Hedrick, p. 223).

Not surprisingly the novel was greeted with outrage in the South, but the vicious abuse of Mrs Stowe shocks even today. She was accused, as Thomas Gossett thoroughly documents, of traducing the essentially beneficent, paternal institution of slavery for all the usual reasons: she failed to understand that blacks were inferior to whites and that the Bible justified and the American Constitution supported slavery; that on the rare occasions families were split it was usually due to 'the evil conduct of the slaves themselves' (p. 195); that whipping was unfortunately (and occasionally) necessary to ensure order; and that the housed and well-fed slaves, as part of the larger family of the plantation, were essentially better off than the 'wage-slaves' in Northern factories. And, of course, her obtuse claim that slavery was a national sin and her wilful recommendation of the higher law of conscience over that of the law of the land were incitements to Northern interference in Southern affairs that could only end in civil war. Meanwhile, they insisted that she had forfeited the right to be called 'a lady' because she depicted 'scenes of licence and impurity, and ideas of loathsome depravity and habitual prostitution'; and because she had forgotten 'all the sweet and social instincts of her sex', she was now fair game. Thus, William Gilmore Simms raved: 'Mrs Stowe betrays a malignity so remarkable that the petticoat lifts of itself, and we see the hoof of the beast under the table' (p. 190), and condemned her 'to perpetual bedfellowship' with the mulatto George Harris for having the effrontery to describe him as a 'handsome' man (p. 203). The ugliest rejection of the novel came in a package addressed to her from somewhere in the South: 'It contained the severed ear of a black with an accompanying card deriding her defence of the "D—n niggers" ' (p. 211). Fortunately, Calvin Stowe opened the package and disposed of the ear without letting his wife see it. These fierce and disgusting reactions are actually a back-handed testimony to Mrs Stowe's brave, spectacular legitimisation of abolition and of her passionate assertion of a white middle-class woman's right and ability to intervene in the masculine, public world of politics and policy.

In the Northern states and England the novel provoked a storm of competing and contradictory responses among conservative and radical abolitionist groups, blacks and women, with regard to issues of form and genre, and of politics, race and gender that are of great interest because they (broadly) define and anticipate the concerns that vex and divide late twentieth-century critical constituencies, especially the feminists. The anonymous reviewer in the London *Times* (September 1852) sniffily observed: 'We are not ignorant of the mode in which great morals are enforced at our minor theatres, and of the means there taken to impress the imagination and to instruct the intellect by help of domestic melodrama,' and fretted that 'surely there is something more real and substantial in Mrs Stowe's volumes to account for their extraordinary popularity than such absolute and audacious trash' as Uncle Tom's miraculous conversions of the savages, Sambo and Quimbo, into pious, penitent Christians (Ammons, ed., p. 29). Even reviewers who approved of the novel's vigorous critique of the institution of slavery complained either about its excessive sentimentality, especially in the depiction of little Eva, or of its heavy didacticism. Again, *Uncle Tom's Cabin* embodies and reveals the splits in the antislavery groups. Thus the conservative New England clergy lauded the novel because it 'has made the public realise ... the unspeakable wickedness of American slavery' (Gossett, p. 178), and Richard Hildreth, the author of the abolitionist novel *Archy Moore* (1836), claimed that 'but for its admirable realisation of the Christian hero, saint and martyr, it would scarcely have been known out of the small circle of anti-slavery readers' (Gossett, p. 177); but Dr Leonard Bacon, an old friend of the Beechers, also praised both its recognition that 'a distinct *nationality* is ... a natural yearning with the free and enlightened Africo-American' and its advocacy of Colonisation for the African blacks because they were blows against 'the distinctive doctrines and obnoxious measures of the Anti-slavery Societies' (Gossett, p. 178). Garrison was, however, upset by Uncle Tom's 'submission to tyranny' and thought he was 'a disturbing model for a black hero' (Gossett, p. 173); and black abolitionists, such as Martin Delany – anticipating the attacks of James Baldwin and J. C. Furnas a century later – were enraged by Tom's meek submission to indignities, preferring an alternative hero who would 'have buried the hoe deep in the master's skull' (Donovan, p. 18). Again, black and white abolitionists attacked the novel's support of Colonisation, Frederick Douglass famously telling Mrs Stowe, 'The truth is, dear madame, we are *here*, and here we are likely to remain,' and the editor of the *Provincial Freeman*, a black anti-slavery journal, thundered: 'Death or banishment is our doom, say the Slaveocrats, the Colonizationsts and Mrs Stowe!' (Gossett, pp. 172–3). The novel's defiance of the Fugitive Slave Law also divided public opinion; only the radical abolitionists were supportive (and even Lincoln in 1860 was not prepared to go so far), whereas reviewers in both the North and the South were dismayed. In recent times, Stowe's exploitation of the devices and values of the mid-nineteenth-century domestic, sentimental novel has generated a (huge) debate about what Jane Tompkins in *Sensational Designs* (1985) has called 'the politics of literary history' (p. 122), whereby 'the male-dominated scholarly tradition' has excluded *Uncle Tom's Cabin* from the 'canon of American literature', preventing 'even committed feminists from recognizing the *value* of a powerful and specifically female novelistic tradition'. In terms that recall the *Times* review, Tompkins laments that 'twentieth-century critics have taught generations of students to equate popularity with debasement, emotionality with ineffectiveness, religiosity with fakery, domesticity with triviality, and all of these, implicitly, with womanly inferiority' (p. 123). Similarly, modern critics, as we shall see, hold opposing views as to the conservatism or radicalism of the sentimental domestic novel.

It is, I think, no exaggeration to claim that *Uncle Tom's Cabin*, once the most popular and widely debated of all American novels, is still the most controversial in the canon. It has generated radically opposed and contradictory viewpoints because of Mrs Stowe's inconsistent representation of such key issues as slavery, race and gender, which is inseparable from the inherent inconsistencies in her evangelical, utopian agenda.

I

The narrative of *Uncle Tom's Cabin* is a volatile compendium of many different forms – sermon, jeremiad, hagiography, dramatic debate, sentimental tableau, melodrama and allegory: and the omniscient narrator combines the roles of an evangelical preacher, indignant Old Testament prophet, fond sentimentalist, biting satirist, shrewd, realistic observer and analyst of the customs and mores of three different slave regions of the South and orchestrator of a chorus of voices, ranging from the vernacular of the blacks, slave-dealers, Kentuckians and Quakers to the sentimental discourse of Eva and the biblically inflected speech of Uncle Tom. All these voices and forms, together with a plot that 'is an anthology of partings and separations' (Fisher, p. 107) ending with a flourish of reunions so typical of the sentimental romance, are marshalled to prove (in St Clare's words) that the ' "*thing itself* [the institution of chattel slavery] is the essence of all abuse!" ' (p. 207); and because the whole of America is implicated in and responsible for its retention, only the nation's 'repentance, justice and mercy' will prevent, as the novel resoundingly concludes, the onset of 'the wrath of Almighty God' (p. 415).

One unavoidable consequence of Stowe's compendious narrative is that her depiction of her 'African' characters, such as Topsy, Uncle Tom and George Harris, is deeply inconsistent and janus-faced. Topsy, especially for modern readers, is the most successfully realised negro character in the novel. A 'neglected, abused child' (p. 223), whose mischievousness, deceit, drollery and cunning induce in St Clare (in a damning analogy) 'the same kind of amusement in the child that a man might [take] in the tricks of a parrot or a pointer' (p. 234), she becomes the test case for Miss Ophelia's ' "real missionary work" ' (p. 222). The ' "system makes such children" ' (p. 229), as Miss Ophelia correctly notes, and in a series of catechisms we learn that she ' "never had no father, nor mother, nor nothin'. I was raised by a speculator, with lots of others" ' (p. 224); and in response to her teacher's questions, ' "Have you ever heard anything about God, Topsy?" ' and ' "Do you know who made you?" ' she (famously) replies, ' "I 'spect I grow'd" ' (p. 224). Miss Ophelia, after months of training, resorts to whipping her, and when she concedes defeat, Eva the child evangelist resumes the catechism:

'But, Topsy, if you'd only try to be good, you might – '

'Couldn't never be nothin' but a nigger, if I was ever so good,' said Topsy. 'If I could be skinned, and come white, I'd try then.'

'But people can love you, if you are black, Topsy. Miss Ophelia would love you, if you were good.'

Topsy gave the short, blunt laugh that was her common mode of expressing incredulity.

'Don't you think so?' said Eva.

'No she can't bar me, 'cause I'm a nigger! – she'd soon have a toad touch her! There can't nobody love niggers, and niggers can't do nothin'. *I* don't care,' said Topsy, beginning to whistle. [p. 261]

Both Topsy's indifference, which masks her self-hatred, and her sharp perception of Miss Ophelia's reflexive phobia anticipate Joe Christmas's self-loathing and his compulsion to provoke disgust for himself in others in Faulkner's *Light in August* (1932). This realistic exchange reveals a genuine critical intelligence at work; but Mrs Stowe's remarkable awareness of the barriers that separate black and white and of the inconsistencies at the heart of both Miss Ophelia and the anti-slavery impulse itself, is immediately followed by an allegorical cameo and an abrupt change of register that is entirely typical of *Uncle Tom's Cabin*:

'O Topsy, poor child, *I* love you!' said Eva, with a sudden burst of feeling ... 'and I think I shan't live a great while; and it really grieves me to have you be so naughty. I wish you would try to be good, for my sake; it's only a little while I shall be with you.'

... Yes in that moment, a ray of real belief, a ray of heavenly love, had penetrated the darkness of her heathen soul! She laid her head down between her knees, and wept and sobbed; while the beautiful child, bending over her, looked like the picture of some bright angel stooping to reclaim a sinner.   [pp. 261–2]

This is bad writing (*pace* Tompkins) precisely because the 'religiosity' *is* 'fakery': Topsy's complex humanity is sacrificed because she is ecstatically faked as 'a heathen soul' in a standardised missionary cartoon. Thus we move from a vital interaction between realistically conceived characters to an abstract moral drama in which Eva knowingly repeats Christ's promise of the resurrection, 'and again, a little while, and ye shall see me' (John 16:17) and which draws heavily on religious clichés ('ray of heavenly love'). Positive reading of such shifts of discourse invoke notions of 'polyphony', 'resistant orality' and 'fugitive tongues' (Hedrick, p. 210). But even in Dostoevsky there is not, as Bakhtin claims, '*A plurality of independent and unmerged voices and consciousnesses, a genuine polyphony of fully valid voices*' (Bakhtin, p. 6); and in Stowe, as is seen here, plurality and resistance quickly yield to a compliant merging of voices. Indeed, whenever the novel becomes insistently allegorical, Stowe's critical intelligence deserts her and she is oblivious to the condescension ('heathen') and moral blackmail (' "I shan't live a great while" ') at the heart of both her own and Eva's evangelicalism.

This exemplary sentimental tableau is entirely typical of Stowe's art (especially after the introduction of Eva in Chapter XIV) and of her designs upon her reader. She saw her ' "vocation" ' as ' "simply that of a painter ... There is no arguing *with pictures*, and everybody is impressed by them, whether they mean to be or not" ' (Hedrick, p. 208). And, indeed, the heavy allegorical patterning in all the scenes in which the child-evangelist appears prepares us for the presentation in the last third of the novel of Uncle Tom, the black evangelist who also sacrifices his life for others. The melodramatic presentation of moral issues in the antithesis of Eva the 'bright angel' and Topsy the heathen 'sinner' is reworked in the fundamental contrast of the devilish Legree with the Christ-like Tom. The hagiographic depiction of Tom's death at the hands of the brutal Legree is pure Christian allegory whereby '*Uncle Tom's Cabin*' retells the culture's central religious myth – the

story of the crucifixion – in terms of the nation's greatest political
conflict – slavery – and of its most cherished social beliefs – the sanctity
of motherhood and the family' (Tompkins, p. 134). Tom's life is a type
of Christ's. Thus he repeats Christ's words on the cross, ' "Into Thy
hands I commend my spirit!" ' (p. 381); like Christ he forgives his
enemies and he saves his tormentors; and like Christ's, Tom's sacrifice
proves that the meek inherit the earth. They both die to save the
corrupt and the powerful and the 'victory' of their deaths shows they
are more powerful than their tormentors. For, in this novel, the
strident moral patterning asserts that the greatest difference between
human beings is neither between slave and slave owner, nor black and
white, nor man and woman, nor between Northerner and Southerner,
but between the saved and the damned. Dying from this Christian,
eschatological perspective is the supreme form of heroism: as Tom 'the
martyr' announces, ' "*I can die!*" ' (p. 382). And, therefore, Legree's
assault on his helpless black victim expresses his impotence and seals
his damnation. Hence the narrator's rather gloating apostrophe: 'Yes,
Legree . . . thy soul . . . past repentance, past prayer, past hope . . . is
already burning' (p. 383), which supplements Tom's saintly warning to
Legree, ' "But if ye don't repent, yours [his torment] *won't* never end!" '
(p. 382). It won't ever end because this novel insists on the inseparabil-
ity of the sacred and the secular and Legree will spend eternity in hell,
the place reserved by the novel's stark evangelical theology for slave
owners and all who, actively or tacitly, accept the splitting of black
families and their breeding as 'articles' and 'things'; when, in terms of
the sentimental novel's values, the annihilation of the domestic arena is
condoned.

The collusion of the narrator's and Tom's voices and 'the higher
voice' of the scriptures is the central rhetorical strategy of all the
sentimental 'pictures'; and at such moments 'the art' of the novel is
Calvinist, a 'a form of onslaught . . . a great revival sermon, aimed
directly at the conversion of its hearers' (Ann Douglas, p. 245). Such
tableaux are clearly designed to make the reader '*feel right* . . . and the
man or woman who *feels* strongly, heathily, and justly, on the great
interests of humanity, is a constant benefactor to the human race'
(p. 411). Such 'pictures' back all readers into a corner; if we support
slavery or if we are indifferent to it, though we are Christians, we clearly
lack compassion for the lowly of the earth and hence we are damned. If
we see the evil, there is only one line of action possible – that of young
George Shelby who is converted by Tom's sacrifice: ' "Witness, eternal
God! . . . oh witness that, from this hour, I will do *what one man can* to

drive out this curse of slavery from my land!" ' (p. 390). And, forthwith, he becomes 'The Liberator' who frees his slaves and offers to ' "teach" ' them ' "how to use the rights I give you as free men and women" '; they choose, of course, to remain free with their loving master, and 'An aged, patriarchal negro ... lifting his trembling hand, said, "Let us give thanks unto the Lord" ' (p. 406).

Stowe's insistence on the Christian passivity of Uncle Tom and the pious gratefulness of George's black slaves are clearly designed to counter national and especially Southern stereotypes of the blacks as inferior and violent brutes who are incapable of leading free lives. But her rhetorical strategies and manipulation of the conventions of the sentimental novel together with her representation of the blacks have elicited contrary responses. On the one hand, Phillip Fisher argues that the sentimental novel 'is the most radical popular form available to middle-class culture' (p. 91) because 'Sentimentality, by its experimental extension of humanity to prisoners, slaves, madmen, children, and animals, exactly reverses the process of slavery itself which has as its core the withdrawal of human status from a part of humanity' (p. 100). Similarly, Kennneth S. Lynn argues that Mrs Stowe 'brought to the sentimental novel such an unprecedented seriousness of purpose as to turn an escapist genre into an instrument of social upheaval' (p. 37). Moreover, we need to realise that Mrs Stowe's Christian pictures and her intensely millennialist vision of slavery as a national sin that invites an act of divine judgement deeply influenced her age and were most famously articulated in President Lincoln's Second Inaugural Address which viewed slavery as 'one of those offences which, in the providence of God, must needs come ... and until every drop of blood drawn with the lash shall be paid by another drawn with the sword, as was said three thousand years ago, so must it still be said, "The judgements of the Lord are true and righteous altogether." ' And, inspired by such rhetoric, American women sanctioned the sacrifice of their menfolk to ensure that under God all Americans would be free. No wonder, then, that Lincoln, on first meeting Stowe in 1862, alledgedly greeted her half-facetiously: 'So this is the little lady who started this great war.' No novel, from this perspective, ever spoke with such directness and force.

On the other hand, however, locked into her evangelical agenda, Mrs Stowe does not appreciate – given the intractable political realities facing America in 1851 – that both Tom's heroic espousal of non-violence and George's noble manumission of his slaves are purely utopian solutions to the problem of chattel slavery. And, not

surprisingly from the perspective of the blacks struggling for civil and
political rights both in her own age and a century later, Uncle Tom's
triumph is, in James Baldwin's words, 'metaphysical, unearthly', and
he is 'robbed of his humanity and divested of his sex' (p. 13), and
Stowe's 'virtuous rage' is a form of 'theological terror, the terror of
damnation' (pp. 12, 13). Thus, Stowe seems to be unaware that her
pious idealisation of Uncle Tom and George Shelby's slaves inadvertently demeans them because her tableaux can neither encompass nor
represent human complexity. Thus, even though Stowe's rhetorical
strategies, her sermonising and her idealised pictures spoke forcefully
to American mothers and rejuvenated the fading abolitionist cause, to
many post- Second World War readers they were held to have
contributed to 'the wrong-headedness, distortions and wishful thinkings
about negroes in general and American negroes in particular that still
plague us today', and the very name Uncle Tom is now 'a hissing and a
by-word' (Furnas, p. 105).

Uncle Tom's Cabin is, then, compassionate and 'radical' but, also,
deeply conservative, in ways that Fisher and Lynn ignore, on issues of
race and politics; and this contradiction is most evident in Mrs Stowe's
representation and uses of George Harris. In the novel Harris is an
intelligent, resourceful mulatto whose dreadful experiences at the
hands of a 'vulgar, narrow-minded, tyrannical master' (p. 12), who
believes, ' "It's a free country . . . the man's *mine*, and I do what I please
with him" ' (p. 14), powerfully demonstrate that what the whites
experience as law, the blacks experience as madness. Like the abolitionists, he appeals to the tenets of the Declaration of Independence and to
the fight for liberty of the founding fathers of America to justify his
own militant desire for freedom in a country whose laws rob him of
citizenship. He feels, therefore, that he does not belong, and his
willingness to fight for ' "the right . . . to be a man and not a brute; the
right to call the wife of his bosom his wife, and to protect her from
lawless violence" ' (p. 356) invokes the spectre of a slave revolt and the
possibility, voiced by St Clare, that the political revolutions that shook
Europe in 1848 may well occur in America. Harris the atheist,
Republican hero and potential revolutionary, who shoots his pursuers
during his freedom flight to Canada, is clearly both the antithesis of
Uncle Tom, who prays for his tormentors and finds freedom in
heaven, and a threat to the novel's Christian domestic agenda. Their
two plots never intersect, and the Harrises' flight to freedom occupies
only three chapters (XIII, XVII and XXXVII), until George reappears in the
penultimate chapter of the novel ('Results') where his miraculous

conversion in Chapter XIII (to which I will return) is not only reconfirmed, but he is presented as both a triumph and a most unlikely spokesman for the evangelistic values that Uncle Tom incarnates.

At this point, Harris is also coerced to collude in the novel's political agenda of Colonisation and to submit to and articulate the novel's 'romantic racialism'.[2] Stowe was not a racist in any modern sense because she did not believe in the *de facto* inferiority of the blacks and she supported black aspirations to equality and civil rights; rather she believed that races, and indeed people from different regions of the same country, have different and essential characteristics and peculiarities that reflect climate, environment, geography, mores and culture. (Thus, 'Great, tall, raw-boned Kentuckians' are said to have 'the easy lounge peculiar to the race' [p. 97].) Whites and blacks for Kinmont and Stowe manifest different traits because this was part of 'God's plan for the gradual fulfilment of man's intellectual, moral, and spiritual potentialities' (Fredrickson, p. 435). Harris's plan for the future of his 'enslaved African race' in Liberia (p. 400) on the grounds that he is fulfilling God's scheme for 'the African race' which 'has peculiarities yet to be unfolded in the light of civilisation and Christianity, which, if not the same with those of the Anglo-Saxon, may prove to be, morally, of an even higher type' (pp. 401–2), is, therefore, based on the romantic racialist's faith in the moral superiority of the Africans to the cold, self-reliant, industrious, rational Anglo-Saxons. From this perspective, Stowe's fervent vision of Colonisation (which after all recommends segregation as the political solution to the problem of slavery in America) is the inevitable consequence of her 'romantic racialism'. Thus, throughout *Uncle Tom's Cabin*, she casts her Africans as natural Christians because of 'their gentleness, their lowly docility of heart, their aptitude to repose on a superior mind and rest on a higher power, their childlike simplicity of affection, and facility of forgiveness' (p. 167). Such passive, dependent virtues are, however, deeply suspect for two obvious reasons: they damn with ecstatic praise, suggesting that Africans are as much natural slaves as they are natural Christians, and they imply (and the plot endorses) that Africans can only be accepted as

---

2 'Romantic racialism' is George Fredrickson's term (Ammons [ed.], *Uncle Tom's Cabin*, p. 433). He was the first to point out that Stowe's racial stereotyping is virtually identical to that espoused by Alexander Kinmont's *Twelve Lectures on the Natural History of Man* (1839). Kinmont delivered the lectures (1837–8) in Cincinnati, where 'his attempt to combine ethnology and religion in a new system . . . caused a great stir' (Fredrickson, p. 434). Mrs Stowe lived in Cincinnati from 1832–50.

full human beings and as superior to whites if they *are* or *become* Christians. And even as Christians they never qualify as 'Americans' in *Uncle Tom's Cabin*; Stowe always calls her blacks either 'Africans' or 'Ethiopians', thereby dissociating herself from the more militant wings of the anti-slavery movement and the black abolitionists who demanded rights for negroes as men and Americans. Moreover, Colonisation in 1851, as Harris grants (and Stowe, rather shame-facedly, admits) was favoured by ' "our oppressors" ' and was used by conservative forces ' "as a means of retarding our emancipation" ' (p. 401). Africa then serves, as it did historically, as a safety valve for anxieties about miscegenation and slave rebellions (most slave rebellions were led by mulattoes) shared by North and South alike. Thus, Harris's paean – ' "*Our nation* shall roll the tide of civilisation and Christianity along its shores, and plant there mighty republics . . . for all coming ages" ' (p. 401) – is from this perspective, millennialist cant that betrays Mrs Stowe's and her nation's grave anxieties about the emancipation of Africans in America itself.[3] Liberia is then a utopian solution to the prospect of sectional conflict that her very assault on the institution of slavery reinforced; and, concomitantly, 'Mrs Stowe's miraculous plotting, so typical of the sentimental novel, unites all the sundered black families and functions conservatively to suppress the very resistance to slavery her novel advocates. Moreover, this final segregation of the Africans contradicts Stowe's use of the separation of families and the deaths of children to plead with her readers to imagine or relive common human experiences, and to identify with suffering *across* racial and regional divides' (Susan M. Ryan, pp. 760–1).

Stowe's messianic view of history has grave consequences, also, for the novel's sentimental agenda, because the African characters and the African nations evoked at the end lose their individual reality in the God-ordained, cosmic 'drama of human improvement' (p. 167). Further-more, Harris's 'trust that the development of Africa is to be essentially a Christian one' endorses and lays bare the contradictions at the heart of the evangelical missionary impulse, because the spreading of the gospel is not only an evasive political solution to slavery, but it is ineradicably implicated in the spread of imperialism. A sorry fate for Stowe's feminine, maternal world vision, and one that contemporary feminists, such as Tompkins, Elizabeth Ammons and Gillian Brown,

3 In 1851 Colonisation was a marginalised and redundant programme. By 1840 only 1420 negroes had been sent to Liberia and the colony was struggling to survive.

who enlist the cult of motherhood and the matriarchal economy either to challenge 'the patriarchal status quo' or to replace the 'market economy of capitalism', usually ignore.

II

Uncle Tom's Cabin has become over the last thirty years the site of a fervent, complex feminist debate that I can only begin to sketch in an Introduction, concerning the conservatism or radicalism of both the author and of her presentation and vision of women's place and function in the world. Was Stowe a feminist in her time and can she be seen as a feminist now? Lydia Maria Child, a leading nineteenth-century feminist, ally of Garrison and foe of the Beechers, could not praise 'a novel that came out of the orthodox [evangelical] religious tradition of New England' (Gossett, p. 171), whereas modern feminists such as Ammons, Brown, Tompkins and Cynthia Griffin Woolf seize on the radical implications of the evangelical, domestic agenda. Unlike Fisher, who traces the cult and use of the sentimental novel in a line running from Samuel Richardson and Sterne, through Rousseau, Wordsworth, Irving, Stowe, Dickens and Hugo (pp. 93ff), Tomkins and Woolf argue that the sentimental novel is a specifically female form written by, for and about women that flowered in the mid-nineteenth century and that it 'represents a monumental effort to reorganise culture from a woman's point of view' (Tompkins, p. 124) and contains a radical agenda whereby home and mother are 'in no sense a shelter from the stormy blast of economic and political life' (p. 145) because 'the true goal of Stowe's rhetorical undertaking is nothing less than the institution of the kingdom of heaven on earth' (p. 141). In marked contrast, feminists such as Ann Douglas and Susan L. Roberson argue that the sentimental novel, including *Uncle Tom's Cabin*, praises woman's influence within the domestic sphere of Christian example and moral instruction, thereby enforcing a conservative ideology that works against societal change. Ever since Tompkins located her 'radical agenda' in Mrs Stowe's representation of the Halliday family in 'The Quaker Settlement', this chapter has become the site of contention among feminists; so it deserves close scrutiny.

In Chapter XIII the runaways, George and Eliza Harris, have been surprisingly reunited in the Quaker Settlement in Indiana which is part of an underground network that in defiance of the Fugitive Slave Law helps slaves escape to Canada. The chapter contains Mrs Stowe's ideal vision of the family and of the function of 'the Women of America, in whose hands rest the real destinies of the republic':[4]

> The next morning was a cheerful one at the Quaker house. 'Mother' was up betimes, and surrounded by busy girls and boys . . . who all moved obediently to Rachel's gentle 'Thee had better' . . . in the work of getting breakfast . . . a thing complicated and multiform, and, like picking up the rose-leaves and trimming the bushes in Paradise, asking other hands than those of the original mother. . . . Rachel moved gently and quietly about, making biscuits, cutting up chicken, and diffusing a sort of sunny radiance over the whole proceeding generally . . .
>
> While all other preparations were going on, Simeon the elder stood in his shirt-sleeves before a little looking-glass in the corner, engaged in the anti-patriarchal operation of shaving. Everything went on so sociably, so quietly, so harmoniously, in the great kitchen – it seemed so pleasant to everyone to do just what they were doing, there was such an atmosphere of mutual confidence and good fellowship everywhere – even . . . the chicken and ham had a cheerful and joyous fizzle in the pan, as if they rather enjoyed being cooked than otherwise; and when George and Eliza and little Harry came out, they met such a hearty, rejoicing welcome, no wonder it seemed to them like a dream . . .
>
> This, indeed, was a home – *home* – a word that George had never yet known a meaning for; and a belief in God, and trust in His providence, began to encircle his heart, as, with a golden cloud of protection and confidence, dark, misanthropic, pining, atheistic doubts, and fierce despair, melted away before the light of a living Gospel, breathed in living faces, preached by a thousand unconscious acts of love and goodwill, which, like the cup of cold water given in the name of a disciple, shall never lose their reward.
>
> [pp. 130–1]

Tompkins seizes on this utopian depiction of domestic, transforming harmony to argue for 'a new matriarchy' that 'constitutes the most politically subversive dimension of Stowe's novel, more disruptive and

---

4 Tompkins quotes Mrs Stowe's elder sister Catherine Beecher's dedication in her *Treatise on Domestic Economy* (1841), which, according to Tompkins, 'is an instructional book on homemaking' with the millennialist aim of 'world conquest – defined as the reformation of the human race through proper care and nurturing of its young' (p. 143).

far-reaching in its potential consequences than even the starting of a war or the freeing of slaves'. Moreover, Rachel '*is* God in human form. Seated in her kitchen ... the millennarian counterpart of little Eva, [she] enacts the redeemed form of the last supper' (p. 142). Tompkins recognises that an ideal world based on 'household economy' is 'conservative', but maintains that Stowe's 'very conservatism ... is precisely what gives her novel its revolutionary potential', because 'applied universally not just to one segregated corner of civil life, but to the conduct of all human affairs, Stowe means to effect a radical transformation of her society' (p. 145).[5] Then, in a final flourish, Tompkins grasps 'a detail, so innocently placed' (Simeon's shaving) to argue that 'Stowe reconceives the role of men in human history: while Negroes, children and grandmothers do the world's primary work, men groom themselves contentedly in a corner' (p. 146).

'It is clear,' as Josephine Donovan temperately notes, 'that the domestic world, when run properly in accordance with a Christian ethic, is Stowe's political model for how society at large should operate' (p. 45); but I simply cannot see how Stowe's utopian ideology of '*home*' supports an activist, feminist critique and I find Tompkins's reading of this passage particularly blinkered, even perverse. First, she is deaf to tone and to what Roberson calls 'the rhetoric of domesticity' (p.117). The description of the Quaker household is self-consciously charming, full of hyperbolic analogies ('the bushes in Paradise'), nonsensical whimsy (chickens enjoying being cooked!), tired repetition (gentle, gently, quietly, etc.), and pure assertion as to the mother's 'influence' and contentment ('Rachel never looked so truly and benignly happy as at the head of her table' [p. 131]). The huge gap between the tone of the passage and the spiralling weight of Tompkins's argument is most evident in her gross misreading of Stowe's whimsical joke concerning Simeon's shaving, which is 'anti-patriarchal' because of course biblical patriarchs usually have long beards; and where else would he shave but in a 'corner' of the kitchen? Over the table? The pan? Moreover, this 'rhetoric of domesticity', as Roberson notes, belittles the mothers in the novel even when, like Mrs Shelby and Rachel, they connive or assist in Eliza's escape or, like Mrs Bird, they persuade their husbands to break the Fugitive Slave Law, rendering them 'conventionally feminine' (p. 124) and 'erasing or blurring woman's interiority and

5 Brown thinks 'Stowe's critique of American society is . . . more radical than Tompkins realizes' for she 'calls for the reform of kitchens as a precondition to women's reform of market economy' (p. 511).

constructing as the ideal woman a disempowered stereotype or cliché' (p. 132). From this perspective, Tompkins's insistence that this cheerful breakfast is a last supper and a holy communion is grandiose and her weighty analogies inadvertently invoke the very patriarchal tradition that, she argues, Stowe subverts.

Secondly, this domestic scene, like all the others in the book, reinforces the sentimental novel's conservative agenda of 'separate spheres'. Thus, as the remainder of the chapter shows, it is Simeon who speaks for Quaker values when he tells George Harris, ' "Fear not, then, friend . . . it is not for thee, but for God and man, we do it" ' (p. 132). And, of course, like Senator Bird earlier, he organises their escape, leaving Rachel happily ensconced in 'the great kitchen'. Again, Mrs Shelby may remonstrate against the selling of Uncle Tom, but she can do nothing to change her husband's mind, nor is she even consulted; and though she is said to have 'piety and benevolence enough for two', her vision of the power of Christian love is shown to be chimerical compared to the harsh economic realities her husband invokes: ' "I thought by kindness, and care, and instruction, I could make the condition of mine better than freedom. Fool that I was!" ' (p. 33). Moreover, the courageous Eliza is said at the end to be 'more matronly than of yore', and in cutting bread and serving her husband (who is bent on self-cultivation which is denied to all the matrons in the novel) she is 'evidently contented and happy as woman *need* be' (p. 397, my italics). Even though Eliza's situation is highly desirable for an ex-slave, Stowe's '*need* be' is restrictive, confining Eliza to a separate sphere from her husband who is preoccupied with grand plans in the great public world.

Thirdly, this Quaker 'home' is a 'dream' not merely to the runaways but because it functions as an oasis in and a repudiation – rather than a reorganisation – of the world, whose harsh realities Simeon engages when he risks his life to help them escape. Tompkins recognises the scene is idealised, but claims it is not a 'daydream' (p. 142) because the perfected home is 'the prerequisite of world conquest' (p. 143), a formulation that merely embosses Stowe's millennialism and utopianism. Tompkins cannot accept that Stowe's soft-focus representation of domesticity actually supports Ann Douglas's magisterial account of the ways the domestic novel flatters its readers by turning away from the world into self-absorption and idle reverie. And nowhere is this process more evident than in Stowe's ecstatic insistence that the example of a true Christian '*home*' is sufficient to convert George Harris on the spot. Similarly, neither God, man nor woman saves all the runaways in *Uncle*

Tom's Cabin; rather they are saved by Stowe's avid manipulation of the plot, which is in thrall to her fantasy of the power of women and the domestic sphere to transform all the evils we are heir to. *Uncle Tom's Cabin* does not finally endorse a radical form of political activism; indeed, finally, it obfuscates political realities when it unceremoniously (but with great ceremony) transforms all the free Africans into missionaries who prefer to found Christian nations in Africa rather than make a life in America. (Significantly, Stowe in her 'Concluding Remarks' shows the 'capability of the race' when she lists examples of Africans who 'without any very particular assistance or encouragement' [p. 413] have become good tradesmen; but she seems unaware of the contradiction.) Thus the novel's advocacy of separate spheres, its miraculous plotting, its evangelical, missionary ideology, all subvert Tompkins's paradoxical claim that 'Stowe's very conservatism . . . gives her novel its revolutionary potential'. Tompkins paradox is an invention: and her argument for the redemptive force of the Christian home, like Mrs Stowe's, but with far less excuse, idealises and inadvertently demeans women. With sisters like Tompkins, who needs patriarchs?

III

For the remainder of this Introduction I dwell, briefly, on Stowe's orchestration of voices that (temporarily) opposes her drive to make all the voices fit her imperious evangelical agenda. A consideration of dissident voices enables me to do justice to her qualities as a satirist and realistic observer and analyst of the peculiar institution of slavery, qualities that I skimped in my account of her inchoate politics and contradictory representation of race and gender in *Uncle Tom's Cabin*.

As we have seen, Stowe first wrote the victory in death of Uncle Tom in the form of an allegory, and with the advent of little Eva most of the scenes are sentimental and didactic tableaux. When she began the sketches, however, many of the early scenes, in (say) Chapters VIII, XI and XII, are 'pictures' of a very different kind, cast in the form of dramatic debate, punctuated by fierce notations and commentary on her characters' words and behaviour and by sardonic exhortations or addresses to her readers' putative or actual complicity in the evils of slavery she presents. One example must suffice. In Chapter VIII ('Eliza's Escape'), Haley meets his fellow slave-dealers, Tom Loker and Marks, in a tavern and these three 'worthies' discuss 'the peculiar troubles' they encounter in their 'lawful' enterprise. Haley concludes his 'pathetic recital' of Eliza's escape from his clutches with the doleful general observation, ' "This yer young-un business makes lots of trouble in the trade." ' This elicits the following response: ' "If we could get a breed of gals that didn't care, now, for their young uns," said Marks; "tell ye, I think 'twould be 'bout the greatest mod'rn improvement I knows on;" and Marks patronised his joke by a quiet introductory sniggle' (p. 61).

Marks's 'joke', linking the colloquial ' "young uns" ' to the progressive cliché of 'improvement', evinces a black humour worthy of Swift in 'A Modest Proposal', whose speaker blithely advocates the eating of babies as a solution to the over-population of Ireland. Marks and Haley then swap anecdotes about the ' "likely wench" ' who had ' "a young un that . . . had a crooked back" ' and whom ' "she did seem . . . to valley . . . more 'cause '*twas* sickly" ', and of the mother who committed suicide because her ' "stone-blind" ' son was ' "swapped off for a keg of whiskey" ' behind her back. At such moments, Stowe's mastery of dialect for purposes of satire anticipates and rivals Mark Twain. Moreover, as ever during such conversations, the selfish, morally warped characters, as in the fiction of (say) Dickens and Turgenev, are given full vent to condemn themselves out of their own mouths, forcing the reader to become the horrified recipient of tales that demonstrate the grotesque reversal of all civilised values in that they objectify human beings, transforming them into commodities for economic use. Unlike Turgenev, however, who trusts readers of *A Sportsman's Notebook* to recognise the terrible plight of the serfs through and against the placid barbarity of the landowners' voices, Stowe always cuts across the vivid, realistic idiom of her characters in order to hammer home, and implicate the reader in, the message they are patently designed to convey – in this instance that the Fugitive Slave Law is a licensed enormity: 'The catching business we beg to remind them ['our refined and Christian readers'], is rising to the dignity of a lawful and patriotic profession' (p. 67).

Through the unconscious irony of the slave-dealers' brutally jovial dialect, the submerged, pitiable voices of the oppressed are heard (as in Turgenev) indirectly. But Stowe is also impressive when, as in 'The Quadroon's Story' (Chapter XXXIV), she allows the oppressed to speak for themselves and to oppose the novel's evangelical agenda. In this chapter Uncle Tom, near death, is at at his lowest point, anguished and yearning for ' "victory" ' (p. 332), and Cassie, Legree's bitter and vengeful mistress, insists ' "there isn't any God" ' and proceeds to tell her terrible tale of sexual abuse and betrayal and of the secret sale of her children by their white fathers, concluding with her tender murder of her last beloved child because she cannot bear to let ' "a child live to grow up!" ' and be sold. Cassie, intent on the murder of Legree, is presented as another 'lost soul' (p. 340), who must be redeemed. But, for once in the novel, the chapter ends with a character's resistance to both the narrator's and Tom's insatiable compassion. Cassie's matricide anticipates Toni Morrison's *Beloved* and her anguished voice commands our attention. Her fierceness and nascent subjectivity, as with George Harris her male counterpart, are, however, soon repressed as the novel's fantastic plotting reunites her with her lost daughter, Eliza, and the novel's inexorable ideology ensures that her voice is transformed and smothered when she is converted into 'a devout and tender Christian' (p. 399).

Augustine St Clare anticipates the fiction of Turgenev because he is the earliest and most powerful representation in American literature of the figure so familiar in Russian letters, namely 'the superfluous man', who is usually an intelligent, talkative, sensitive, idle member of the gentry who has no civic role to play in an autocratic centralised state and is at once dissociated from, dependent on and sympathetic towards his serfs. Like his Russian counterparts, such as Nezhdanov in Turgenev's *Virgin Soil* (1877), Augustine is ' "a man of honourable and humane feelings" ' (p. 204) who feels that his life ' "is a contemptible *non sequitur*" ' (p. 215) because he hates ' "the using these men and women, the perpetuation of all this ignorance, brutality and vice – just to make money for me" ' (p. 214); but his ' "indistinct yearnings to be a sort of emancipator" ' (p. 215) are thwarted because he lives and suffers in an abominable social system and his intelligent perceptions of the ills that beset his world exacerbate, depress and alienate him from his kin and his peers. Augustine is the most interesting character in the novel because he articulates Mrs Stowe's deepest fears about slavery in America and about the weaknesses of her own evangelical agenda. These fears surface in a remarkable conversation between Augustine and his brother Alfred, who is a racist, autocratic slave-owner who believes that blacks and the *canaille* ' "must be *kept down*, consistently [and] steadily' (p. 248). Augustine cites the French Revolution, the slave rebellion in Haiti and the recent 1848 uprisings in Europe and warns: ' "We are breaking all humanising ties, and making them brute beasts; and, if they get the upper hand, such we shall find them" '; and, ' "if there is anything that is revealed with the strength of a divine law in our times, it is that the masses are to rise, and the under class become the upper one" '. Alfred disdains ' "this millenium of your greasy

masses" ' (p. 249), but the revolt of ' "brute beasts" ' threatens the very
future of America as the home of democracy and of the Christian
American 'home'. Furthermore, the 'divine law' of the early idealistic,
utopian socialists, who are ready like Christ to sacrifice their lives in
order to build the New Jerusalem on earth, appropriates the tropes of,
and thereby threatens to destroy, the very grounds of Stowe's own
evangelical utopian vision. Even more remarkably, Augustine brilliantly questions his author's domineering agenda in ways that anticipate
Karl Marx's case that ideologies follow and are conditioned by the
modes of production of material life. Thus he posits that should
something ' "bring down the price of cotton once and forever, and
make the whole slave property a drug in the market, don't you think we
should have another version of the Scripture doctrine?" ' (pp. 171–2).
Later he scandalises Ophelia when he exclaims, ' "What poor, mean
trash this whole business of human virtue is! A mere matter, for the
most part, of latitude and longitude, and geographical position, acting
with natural temperament" ' (p. 211) – a relativist, sociological position
that denies Stowe's polemical insistence that Christianity is the only
true source of universal human values. Then, just before his very
sudden death, he voices Stowe's despairing belief that even the
immediate emancipation of the 'heathen' blacks would founder because though Southerners ' "are the more *obvious* oppressors of the
negro . . . the unchristian prejudice of the North is an oppressor almost
equally severe" ' (p. 292).

Mrs Stowe, then, through Augustine entertains alternative insights
that indicate the fallacies in her fervent evangelical faith that the
solution to the problem of slavery in America 'must and will become a
purely religious one' and that there is 'no hope' for the anti-slavery
movement 'but in Him' (Charles Edward Stowe, p. 153).[6] Augustine,
however, like George Harris and Cassie, is presented as a lost, heretical
soul who must be redeemed and, thereby, annexed. Thus, he is obliged
to articulate the novel's maternal world vision when he prefaces his

---

6 From a letter (9 July 1851) – shortly after the serialisation of *Uncle Tom's Cabin*
had begun – to Frederick Douglass, who maintained in his *Narrative* (1845) and
throughout his career that 'the church is "pro-slavery" '. As her son Charles
Edward explains, 'This letter gives us a conception of the state of moral and
religious exaltation of the heart and mind out of which flowed chapter after chapter
of that wonderful story' (p. 153). It also highlights the limitations inherent in
Stowe's belief that only a christianisation of America and an acceptance of God's
providence could solve the national problem of slavery.

despair over ' "this whole business of human virtue" ' with his lament that his gentle Christian mother died ' "when I was only thirteen" ': ' "If I had lived to grow up under her care . . . I might have been a saint, reformer, martyr – but, alas! alas!" ' (p. 211). Then he is suddenly murdered and forced in a ludicrous death-scene to submit to and collude in the novel's imperious ideology. Thus, anticipating Uncle Tom's ' "victory" ', he gasps, ' "coming HOME at last!" ', and 'Just before the spirit parted, he opened his eyes, with a sudden light, as of joy and recognition, and said, "*Mother!*" and then he was gone!' (p. 295). The capitals and the italics merely emphasise Stowe's religiosity that (accidentally) ensures a silly and sorry death for one of the most intelligent characters in American literature. But his death, of course, subserves Stowe's imperative drive to Uncle Tom's victorious death that had already been written and ushers in an allegorical, univocal narrative. Thus, Augustine's secular, materialist views, that threatened momentarily to undermine the fantastic base of his author's absolutist evangelicalism, are employed to support its necessity. His doubts, like George Harris's, fuel her glorification of 'HOME', her enthusiastic, unrealistic project of an African 'home' for her (American) blacks and her imperial dream of a christianised Africa. Herein lies, I think, the prime reason for the novel's immense success: Stowe's various Christian projects (which rely on miraculous plotting) are endorsed by coercive rhetorical strategies that co-opt all the opposing voices, thereby enabling her to offer utopian, evangelical solutions to the problem of slavery in America that allow an ecstatic evasion of both the complexity of the human condition and of political, economic and materialist realities.

DR KEITH CARABINE
University of Kent, Canterbury

BIBLIOGRAPHY

Editions of Uncle Tom's Cabin and other works by Stowe

Uncle Tom's Cabin, edited by Elizabeth Ammons, Norton, New York 1994; contains a selection of background materials, early reviews and modern responses

Uncle Tom's Cabin, edited by Jean Fagin Yellin, Oxford World's Classics, 1998

Harriet Beecher Stowe, *A Key to Uncle Tom's Cabin*, John P. Jewett & Co., Cleveland 1853; reprinted Applewood Books, Bedford, Massachusetts, 1998

Harriet Beecher Stowe, *Dred: A Tale of the Great Dismal Swamp*, Phillips, Sampson & Co., Boston 1856; Judie Newman (ed.), BAAS American Library, Ryburn 1992

Harriet Beecher Stowe, 'The Freeman's Dream: A Parable'(1850) in *The Oxford Harriet Beecher Stowe Reader*, edited by Joan D. Hedrick, Oxford University Press, 1999, pp. 57–8

History and Criticism: Collections of Essays, Biographies, Books, General Books

Elizabeth Ammons (ed.), *Critical Essays on Harriet Beecher Stowe*, G. K. Hall, Boston 1980; contains reviews of *Uncle Tom's Cabin* by George Sand, George F. Holmes and from the London *Times* and a mixed collection of subsequent responses to Stowe

Elizabeth Ammons, 'Stowe's Dream of the Mother-Savior: *Uncle Tom's Cabin* and American Women Writers Before the 1920s', in Sundquist (ed.), pp. 155–95

Bakhtin, Mikhail, *Problems of Dostoevsky's Poetics*, edited and translated by Caryl Emerson, Univeristy of Minnesota Press, Minneapolis 1984

Cott, Nancy, *The Bonds of Womanhood: 'Woman's Sphere' in New England, 1780–1870*, Yale University Press, New Haven 1977

Davies, Charles T. and Henry Louis Gates Jr, (eds) *The Slave's Narrative*, Oxford University Press, Oxford 1985; a collection of essays and reviews of slave narratives

Donovan, Josephine: *'Uncle Tom's Cabin': Evil, Affliction, and Redemptive Love*, Twayne Masterworks Studies, Boston 1991

Douglas, Ann, *The Feminization of American Culture*, Knopf, New York 1977

Elkins, Stanley, *Slavery: A Problem in American Institutional and Intellectual Life*, Grosset & Dunlap, New York 1963

Fields, Annie (ed.), *Life and Letters of Harriet Beecher Stowe*, Houghton, Mifflin, Boston 1898

Fisher, Philip, *Hard Facts: Setting and Form in the American Novel*, Oxford University Press, New York 1985, pp. 87–127

Furnas, J. C., *Goodbye to Uncle Tom*, Secker and Warburg, London 1956

Genovese, Eugene D., *Roll, Jordan, Roll: The World the Slaves Made*, Vintage, New York 1975

Goodman, Paul, *Of One Blood: Abolitionism and the Origins of Racial Equality*, University of California Press, Berkeley 1998

Gossett, Thomas F., *'Uncle Tom's Cabin' and American Culture*, Southern Methodist University Press, Dallas 1985

Hedrick, Joan D., *Harriet Beecher Stowe: A Life*, Oxford University Press, Oxford 1994; the best biography

Hildreth, Margaret Holbrook, *Harriet Beecher Stowe: A Bibliography*, Archon, Hamden, Connecticutt 1976

Kirkham, E. Bruce, *The Building of Uncle Tom's Cabin*, University of Tennessee Press, Knoxville 1977

Lewis, Gladys Sherman, *Message, Messenger, and Response: Puritan Forms and Cultural Reformation in Harriet Beecher Stowe's 'Uncle Tom's Cabin'*, University Press of America, New York 1994

Lowance, Mason (ed.), *Against Slavery: An Abolitionist Reader*, Penguin Books, London 2000

Lowance, Mason, Westbrook, Ellen E. and De Prospo, R. C. (eds), *The Stowe Debate: Rhetorical Strategies in 'Uncle Tom's Cabin'*, University of Massachusetts Press, Amherst 1994; contains twelve essays of varying quality

Michie, Helena, *The Flesh Made Word: Female Figures and Women's Bodies*, Oxford University Press, New York 1987

Moers, Ellen, *Literary Women*, Anchor/Doubleday, Garden City, New York 1977

Morrison, Toni, *Playing in the Dark: Whiteness and the Literary Imagination*, Harvard University Press, Cambridge, Massachusetts 1992

Reynolds, David S., *Beneath the American Renaissance: The Subversive Imagination in the Age of Emerson and Melville*, Knopf, New York 1988

Stowe, Charles Edward, *Life of Harriet Beecher Stowe: Compiled from Her Letters and Journals*, Houghton, Mifflin, Boston 1889

Strout, Cushing, *The New Heavens and the New Earth: Political Religion in America*, Harper & Row, New York 1974

Sundquist, Eric J. (ed.), *New Essays on 'Uncle Tom's Cabin'*, Cambridge University Press, Cambridge 1986; contains six essays and a good Introduction

Tompkins, Jane, *Sensational Designs: The Cultural Work of American Fiction*, Oxford Univeristy Press, New York 1985

Weld, Theodore, *American Slavery as It Is: Testimony of a Thousand Witnesses*, American Anti-Slavery Society, New York 1839; Stowe's most important source for the novel

Wilson, Edmund, *Patriotic Gore: Studies in the Literature of the American Civil War*, Lippincott, Philadelphia 1941

Wilson, Forrest, *Crusader in Crinoline: The Life of Harriet Beecher Stowe*, Lippincott, Philadelphia 1941

Yellin, Jean Fagin, *The Intricate Knot: Black Figures in American Literature, 1776–1863*, New York University Press, New York 1972

Criticism: Essays and Reviews

Ammons, Elizabeth, 'Heroines in *Uncle Tom's Cabin*', in *American Literature*, Vol. 49/2, May 1977, pp. 161–79

Askeland, Lori, 'Remodelling the Model Home in *Uncle Tom's Cabin* and *Beloved*', in *American Literature*, Vol. 64, December 1959, pp. 785–805

Baldwin, James, 'Everybody's Protest Novel', in *Notes of a Native Son*, Beacon Press, Boston, 1955, pp. 13–28

Berkson, Dorothy, 'Millennial Politics and the Feminine Fiction of Harriet Beecher Stowe', in Ammons (ed.), pp. 244–58

Brodhead, Richard, 'Sparing the Rod: Discipline and Fiction in Antebellum America', in *Representations*, Vol. 21, 1988, pp. 67–96

Brown, Gillian, 'Getting in the Kitchen with Dinah: Domestic Politics in *Uncle Tom's Cabin*', in *American Quarterly*, Vol. 36/4, 1984, pp. 502–23

Fiedler, Leslie, 'Harriet Beecher Stowe's Novel of Sentimental Protest', in Ammons (ed.), pp.112–16

Fredrickson, George M., 'Uncle Tom and the Anglo-Saxons: Romantic Racialism in the North', in Ammons (ed.), *Uncle Tom's Cabin*, pp. 429–38; excellent on race in *Uncle Tom's Cabin*

Graham, Thomas, 'Harriet Beecher Stowe and the Question of Race', in *New England Quarterly*, Vol. 46/4, 1973, pp. 614–22

Hovet, Theodore R., 'Christian Revolution: Harriet Beecher Stowe's Response to Slavery and the Civil War', in *New England Quarterly*, 47/4, 1974, pp. 527–49

Hughes, Langston, Introduction to *Uncle Tom's Cabin*, in Ammons (ed.), pp. 102–4

Jehlen, Myra, 'The Family Militant: Domesticity versus Slavery in *Uncle Tom's Cabin*', in *Criticism*, Vol. 31, 1989, pp. 383–400

Kerber, Linda, 'Separate Spheres, Female Worlds, and Woman's Place: The Rhetoric of Women's History', in *Journal of American History*, Vol. 75, 1988, pp. 9–39

Lang, Amy Schrager, 'Slavery and Sentimentalism: The Strange Career of Augustine St Clare', *Women's Studies*, Vol. 12, 1986, pp. 31–54

Levine, Robert S., '*Uncle Tom's Cabin* in *Frederick Douglass's Paper*: An Analysis of Reception', in *American Literature*, Vol. 64, 1992, pp. 71–93

Lynn, Kenneth S., Introduction to *Uncle Tom's Cabin*, Harvard University Press, Cambridge, Massachusetts 1962

Nuernburg, Susan Marie, 'The Rhetoric of Race', in Lowance, Westbrook, De Prospo (eds), pp. 255–70

O'Connell, Catherine E., ' "The Magic of the Real Presence of Distress": Sentimentality and Competing Rhetorics of Authority', in Lowance, Westbrook, DeProspo (eds), pp. 13–36

Riis, Arthur, 'Racial Essentialism and Family Values in *Uncle Tom's Cabin*', in *American Quarterly*, Vol. 46, 1994, pp. 513–44

Roberson, Susan L., 'Matriarchy and the Rhetoric of Domesticity', in Lowance, Westbrook, De Prospo (eds), pp. 116–37

Ryan, Susan M., 'Charity Begins at Home: Stowe's Antislavery Novels and the Forms of Benevolent Citizenship', in *American Literature*, Vol. 72/4, 2000, pp. 751–82

Winks, Robin W., 'The Making of a Fugitive Slave Narrative: Josiah Henson and Uncle Tom – A Case Study', in Davies, Gates (eds), pp. 112–46

Woolf, Cynthia Griffin, ' "Masculinity" in *Uncle Tom's Cabin*', in *Amercian Quarterly*, Vol. 47, 1995, pp. 595–618

Yarborough, Richard, 'Strategies of Black Characterization in *Uncle Tom's Cabin* and the Early Afro-American Novel', in Sundquist (ed.), pp. 45–84

Yellin, Jean Fagin, 'Doing It Herself: *Uncle Tom's Cabin* and Woman's Role in the Slavery Crisis', in Sundquist (ed.), pp. 85–105

Zwarg, Christina, 'Fathering and Blackface in *Uncle Tom's Cabin*', in *Novel: A Forum on Fiction*, Vol 22, 1989, pp. 274–87

CONTENTS

AUTHOR'S PREFACE[1]

The scenes of this story, as its title indicates, lie among a race hitherto ignored by the associations of polite and refined society; an exotic race, whose ancestors, born beneath a tropic sun, brought with them, and perpetuated to their descendants, a character so essentially unlike the hard and dominant Anglo-Saxon race as for many years to have won from it only misunderstanding and contempt.

But another and better day is dawning. Every influence of literature, of poetry and of art in our times is becoming more and more in unison with the great master chord of Christianity, 'good-will to man'.[2]

The poet, the painter and the artist now seek out and embellish the common and gentler humanities of life, and, under the allurements of fiction, breathe a humanising and subduing influence, favourable to the development of the great principles of Christian brotherhood.

The hand of benevolence is everywhere stretched out, searching into abuses, righting wrongs, alleviating distresses and bringing to the knowledge and sympathies of the world the lowly, the oppressed and the forgotten.

In this general movement unhappy Africa at last is remembered; Africa, who began the race of civilisation and human progress in the dim grey dawn of early time, but who, for centuries, has lain bound and bleeding at the foot of civilised and Christianised humanity, imploring compassion in vain.

But the heart of the dominant race, who have been her conquerors, her hard masters, has at length been turned towards her in mercy; and it has been seen how far nobler it is in nations to protect the feeble than to oppress them. Thanks be to God, the world has at last outlived the slave trade.

The object of these sketches is to awaken sympathy and feeling for the African race, as they exist among us; to show their wrongs and sorrows under a system so necessarily cruel and unjust as to defeat and do away with the good effects of all that can be attempted for them, by their best friends, under it.

In doing this, the author can sincerely disclaim any invidious feeling towards those individuals who, often without any fault of their own, are involved in the trials and embarrassments of the legal relations of slavery.

Experience has shown her that some of the noblest of minds and hearts are often thus involved; and no one knows better than they do that what may be gathered of the evils of slavery from sketches like these is not the half that could be told of the unspeakable whole.

In the Northern States these representations may, perhaps, be thought caricatures; in the Southern States are witnesses who know their fidelity. What personal knowledge the author has had of the truth of incidents such as here are related, will appear in its time.[3]

It is a comfort to hope, as so many of the world's sorrows and wrongs have, from age to age, been lived down, so a time shall come when sketches similar to these shall be valuable only as memorials of what has long ceased to be.

When an enlightened and Christianised community shall have, on the shores of Africa,[4] laws, language and literature, drawn from among us, may then the scenes of the house of bondage be to them like the remembrance of Egypt to the Israelites[5] – a motive of thankfulness to Him who hath redeemed them!

For while politicians contend, and men are swerved this way and that by conflicting tides of interest and passion, the great cause of human liberty is in the hands of One of whom it is said:

> He shall not fail nor be discouraged
> Till He have set judgement in the earth.
> He shall deliver the needy when he crieth,
> The poor, and him that hath no helper.
> He shall redeem their soul from deceit and violence
> And precious shall their blood be in His sight.[6]

UNCLE TOM'S CABIN

CHAPTER I

In Which the Reader is Introduced to a Man of Humanity

LATE IN THE AFTERNOON of a chilly day in February, two gentlemen were sitting alone over their wine, in a well-furnished dining parlour, in the town of P—, in Kentucky. There were no servants present, and the gentlemen, with chairs closely approaching, seemed to be discussing some subject with great earnestness.

For convenience sake, we have said, hitherto, two *gentlemen*. One of the parties, however, when critically examined, did not seem, strictly speaking, to come under the species. He was a short, thick-set man, with coarse, commonplace features, and that swaggering air of pretension which marks a low man who is trying to elbow his way upward in the world. He was much over-dressed, in a gaudy vest of many colours, a blue neckerchief, bedropped gaily with yellow spots, and arranged with a flaunting tie, quite in keeping with the general air of the man. His hands, large and coarse, were plentifully bedecked with rings; and he wore a heavy gold watch-chain, with a bundle of seals of portentous size, and a great variety of colours, attached to it – which, in the ardour of conversation, he was in the habit of flourishing and jingling with evident satisfaction. His conversation was in free and easy defiance of Murray's *Grammar*,[7] and was garnished at convenient intervals with various profane expressions, which not even the desire to be graphic in our account shall induce us to transcribe.

His companion, Mr Shelby, had the appearance of a gentleman; and the arrangements of the house, and the general air of the housekeeping, indicated easy, and even opulent circumstances. As we before stated, the two were in the midst of an earnest conversation.

'That is the way I should arrange the matter,' said Mr Shelby.

'I can't make trade that way – I positively can't, Mr Shelby,' said the other holding up a glass of wine between his eye and the light.

'Why, the fact is, Haley, Tom is an uncommon fellow; he is certainly worth that sum anywhere – steady, honest, capable, manages my whole farm like a clock.'

'You mean honest, as niggers go,' said Haley, helping himself to a glass of brandy.

'No, I mean really, Tom is a good, steady, sensible, pious fellow. He got religion at a camp-meeting,[8] four years ago; and I believe he really *did* get it. I've trusted him, since then, with everything I have – money, house, horses – and let him come and go round the country; and I always found him true and square in everything.'

'Some folks don't believe there is pious niggers, Shelby,' said Haley, with a candid flourish of his hand, 'but I *do*. I had a fellow, now, in this yer last lot I took to Orleans[9] – 'twas as good as a meetin' now, really; to hear that critter pray; and he was quite gentle and quiet like. He fetched me a good sum, too, for I bought him cheap of a man that was 'bliged to sell out; so I realised six hundred on him. Yes, I consider religion a valeyable thing in a nigger, when it's the genuine article, and no mistake.'

'Well, Tom's got the real article, if ever a fellow had,' rejoined the other. 'Why, last fall, I let him go to Cincinnati[10] alone, to do business for me, and bring home five hundred dollars. "Tom," says I to him, "I trust you, because I think you're a Christian – I know you wouldn't cheat." Tom comes back, sure enough: I knew he would. Some low fellows, they say, said to him: "Tom, why don't you make tracks for Canada?"[11] "Ah, master trusted me, and I couldn't!"[12] They told me about it. I am sorry to part with Tom, I must say. You ought to let him cover the whole balance of the debt; and you would, Haley, if you had any conscience.'

'Well, I've got just as much conscience as any man in business can afford to keep – just a little, you know, to swear by, as 'twere,' said the trader, jocularly; 'and, then, I'm ready to do anything in reason to 'blige friends; but this yer, you see, is a leetle too hard on a fellow – a leetle too hard.'

The trader sighed contemplatively, and poured out some more brandy.

'Well, then, Haley, how will you trade?' said Mr Shelby, after an uneasy interval of silence.

'Well, haven't you a boy or gal that you could throw in with Tom?'

'Hum! – none that I could well spare; to tell the truth, it's only hard necessity makes me willing to sell at all. I don't like parting with any of my hands, that's a fact.'

Here the door opened, and a small quadroon[13] boy, between four and five years of age, entered the room. There was something in his appearance remarkably beautiful and engaging. His black hair, fine as floss silk, hung in glossy curls about his round, dimpled face, while a pair of large dark eyes, full of fire and softness, looked out from beneath the rich, long lashes, as he peered curiously into the apartment. A gay robe of scarlet and yellow plaid, carefully made and neatly fitted, set off to advantage the dark and rich style of his beauty; and a certain comic air of assurance, blended with bashfulness, showed that he had been not unused to being petted and noticed by his master.

'Halloa, Jim Crow!'[14] said Mr Shelby, whistling, and snapping a bunch of raisins towards him; 'pick that up, now!'

The child scampered, with all his little strength, after the prize, while his master laughed.

'Come here, Jim Crow,' said he.

The child came up, and the master patted the curly head, and chucked him under the chin.

'Now, Jim, show this gentleman how you can dance and sing.'

The boy commenced one of those wild, grotesque songs common among the negroes, in a rich, clear voice, accompanying his singing with many comic evolutions of the hands, feet, and whole body, all in perfect time to the music.

'Bravo!' said Haley, throwing him a quarter of an orange.

'Now, Jim, walk like old Uncle Cudjoe, when he has the rheumatism,' said his master.

Instantly the flexible limbs of the child assumed the appearance of deformity and distortion, as, with his back humped up, and his master's stick in his hand, he hobbled about the room, his childish face drawn into a doleful pucker, and spitting from right to left, in imitation of an old man.

Both gentlemen laughed uproariously.

'Now, Jim,' said his master, 'show us how old Elder Robbins leads the psalm.'

The boy drew his chubby face down to a formidable length, and commenced toning a psalm tune through his nose with imperturbable gravity.

'Hurrah! bravo! what a young 'un!' said Haley; 'that chap's a case, I'll promise. Tell you what,' said he, suddenly clapping his hand on Mr Shelby's shoulder, 'fling in that chap, and I'll settle the business – I will. Come, now, if that ain't doing the thing up about the rightest!'

At this moment the door was pushed gently open, and a young quadroon woman, apparently about twenty-five, entered the room.

There needed only a glance from the child to her, to identify her as its mother. There was the same rich, full, dark eye, with its long lashes; the same ripples of silky black hair. The brown of her complexion gave way on the cheek to a perceptible flush, which deepened as she saw the gaze of the strange man fixed upon her in bold and undisguised admiration. Her dress was of the neatest[15] possible fit, and set off to advantage her finely moulded shape. A delicately formed hand and a trim foot and ankle, were items of appearance that did not escape the quick eye of the trader, well used to run up at a glance the points of a fine female article.

'Well, Eliza?' said her master, as she stopped and looked hesitatingly at him.

'I was looking for Harry, please, sir;' and the boy bounded toward her, showing his spoils, which he had gathered in the skirt of his robe.

'Well, take him away, then,' said Mr Shelby; and hastily she withdrew, carrying the child on her arm.

'By Jupiter,' said the trader, turning to him in admiration, 'there's an article now! You might make your fortune on that ar gal in Orleans, any day. I've seen over a thousand, in my day, paid down for gals not a bit handsomer.'

'I don't want to make my fortune on her,' said Mr Shelby, dryly; and, seeking to turn the conversation, he uncorked a bottle of fresh wine, and asked his companion's opinion of it.

'Capital, sir – first chop!' said the trader; then turning, and slapping his hand familiarly on Shelby's shoulder, he added: 'Come, how will you trade about the girl? What shall I say for her? What'll you take?'

'Mr Haley, she is not to be sold,' said Shelby. 'My wife would not part with her for her weight in gold.'

'Ay, ay! women always say such things, 'cause they ha'n't no sort of calculation. Just show 'em how many watches, feathers, and trinkets, one's weight in gold would buy, and that alters the case, *I* reckon.'

'I tell you, Haley, this must not be spoken of; I say no, and I mean no,' said Shelby, decidedly.

'Well, you'll let me have the boy, though?' said the trader; 'you must own I've come down pretty handsomely for him.'

'What on earth can you want with the child?' said Shelby.

'Why, I've got a friend that's going into this yer branch of the business – wants to buy up handsome boys to raise for the market. Fancy articles entirely – sell for waiters, and so on, to rich 'uns, that can pay for handsome 'uns. It sets off one of yer great places – a real handsome boy to open door, wait, and tend. They fetch a good sum;

and this little devil is such a comical, musical concern, he's just the article.'

'I would rather not sell him,' said Mr Shelby, thoughtfully; 'the fact is, sir, I'm a humane man, and I hate to take the boy from his mother, sir.'

'Oh, you do? – La! yes – something of that ar natur. I understand, perfectly. It is mighty onpleasant getting on with women, sometimes. I al'ays hates these yer screachin', screamin' times. They are *mighty* onpleasant; but, as I manages business, I generally avoids 'em, sir. Now, what if you get the girl off for a day, or a week, or so; then the thing's done quietly – all over before she comes home. Your wife might get her some earrings, or a new gown, or some such truck, to make up with her.'

'I'm afraid not.'

'Lor bless ye, yes! These critters an't like white folks, you know; they gets over things, only manage right. Now, they say,' said Haley, assuming a candid and confidential air, 'that this kind o' trade is hardening to the feelings; but I never found it so. Fact is, I never could do things up the way some fellers manage the business. I've seen 'em as would pull a woman's child out of her arms, and set him up to sell, and she screechin' like mad all the time; very bad policy – damages the article – makes 'em quite unfit for service sometimes. I knew a real handsome gal once, in Orleans, as was entirely ruined by this sort o' handling. The fellow that was trading for her didn't want her baby; and she was one of your real high sort, when her blood was up. I tell you, she squeezed up her child in her arms, and talked, and went on real awful. It kinder makes my blood run cold to think on't; and when they carried off the child, and locked her up, she jest went ravin' mad, and died in a week. Clear waste, sir, of a thousand dollars, just for want of management – there's where 'tis. It's always best to do the humane thing, sir; that's been *my* experience.'

And the trader leaned back in his chair, and folded his arm with an air of virtuous decision, apparently considering himself a second Wilberforce.[16]

The subject appeared to interest the gentleman deeply; for while Mr Shelby was thoughtfully peeling an orange, Haley broke out afresh, with becoming diffidence, but as if actually driven by the force of truth to say a few words more.

'It don't look well, now, for a feller to be praisin' himself; but I say it jest because it's the truth. I believe I'm reckoned to bring in about the finest droves of niggers that is brought in – at least, I've been told so; if I have once, I reckon I have a hundred times – all in good case – fat and likely, and I lose as few as any man in the business. And I lays it all to my management, sir; and humanity, sir, I may say, is the great pillar of *my* management.'

Mr Shelby did not know what to say, and so he said, 'Indeed!'

'Now, I've been laughed at for my notions, sir, and I've been talked to. They an't pop'lar, and they an't common; but I stuck to 'em, sir; I've stuck to 'em, and realised well on them; yes, sir, they have paid their passage, I may say,' and the trader laughed at his joke.

There was something so piquant and original in these elucidations of humanity, that Mr Shelby could not help laughing in company. Perhaps you laugh too, dear reader; but you know humanity comes out in a variety of strange forms nowadays, and there is no end to the odd things that humane people will say and do.

Mr Shelby's laugh encouraged the trader to proceed.

'It's strange, now; but I never could beat this into people's heads. Now, there was Tom Loker, my old partner, down in Natchez;[17] he was a clever fellow, Tom was, only the very devil with niggers – on principle 'twas, you see, for a better-hearted feller never broke bread; 'twas his *system*, sir. I used to talk to Tom. "Why, Tom," I used to say, "when your gals takes on and cry, what's the use o' crackin on 'em over the head, and knockin' on em round? It's ridiculous," says I, "and don't do no sort o' good. Why, I don't see no harm in their cryin'," says I; "it's natur," says I, "and if natur can't blow off one way, it will another. Besides, Tom," says I, "it jest spiles your gals; they get sickly, and down in the mouth; and sometimes they gets ugly – particular yellow girls do, and it's the devil and all gettin' on 'em broke in. Now," says I, "why can't you kinder coax 'em up, and speak 'em fair? Depend on it, Tom, a little humanity, thrown in along, goes a heap further than all your jawin' and crackin'; and it pays better," says I, "depend on't." But Tom couldn't get the hang on't; and he spiled so many for me, that I had to break off with him, though he was a good-hearted fellow, and as fair a business hand as is goin'.'

'And do you find your ways of managing do the business better than Tom's?' said Mr Shelby.

'Why, yes, sir, I may say so. You see, when I anyways can, I takes a leetle care about the onpleasant parts, like selling young uns and that – get the gals out of the way – out of sight, out of mind, you know, and when it's clean done, and can't be helped, they naturally gets used to it. 'Tan't, you know, as if it was white folks, that's brought up in the way of 'spectin' to keep their children and wives, and all that. Niggers, you know, that's fetched up properly, ha'n't no kind of 'spectations of no kind; so all these things comes easier.'

'I'm afraid mine are not properly brought up, then,' said Mr Shelby.

'S'pose not. You Kentucky folks spile your niggers. You mean well by 'em, but 'tan't no real kindness, arter all. Now, a nigger, you see, what's got to be hacked and tumbled round the world, and sold to Tom, and Dick, and the Lord knows who, 'tan't no kindness to be givin' on him notions and expectations, and bringin' on him up too well, for the rough and tumble comes all the harder on him arter. Now, I venture to say, your niggers would be quite chop-fallen in a place where some of your plantation niggers would be singing and whooping like all possessed. Every man, you know, Mr Shelby, naturally thinks well of his own ways; and I think, I treat niggers just about as well as it's ever worth while to treat 'em.'

'It's a happy thing to be satisfied,' said Mr Shelby, with a slight shrug, and some perceptible feelings of a disagreeable nature.

'Well,' said Haley, after they had both silently picked their nuts for a season, 'what do you say?'

'I'll think the matter over, and talk with my wife,' said Mr Shelby. 'Meantime, Haley, if you want the matter carried on in the quiet way you speak of, you'd best not let your business in this neighbourhood be known. It will get out among my boys, and it will not be a particularly quiet business getting away any of my fellows, if they know it, I'll promise you.'

'Oh, certainly, by all means, mum! of course! But I'll tell you, I'm in a devil of a hurry, and shall want to know, as soon as possible, what I may depend on,' said he, rising and putting on his overcoat.

'Well, call up this evening, between six and seven, and you shall have my answer,' said Mr Shelby, and the trader bowed himself out of the apartment.

'I'd like to have been able to kick the fellow down the steps,' said he to himself; as he saw the door fairly closed, 'with his impudent assurance; but he knows how much he has me at advantage. If anybody had ever said to me that I should sell Tom down south to one of those rascally traders, I should have said, "Is thy servant a dog, that he should do this thing?" And now it must come, for aught I see. And Eliza's child, too! I know that I shall have some fuss with wife about that; and, for that matter, about Tom, too. So much for being in debt – heigho! The fellow sees his advantage, and means to push it.'

Perhaps the mildest form of the system of slavery is to be seen in the State of Kentucky. The general prevalence of agricultural pursuits of a quiet and gradual nature, not requiring those periodic seasons of hurry and pressure that are called for in the business of more southern districts, makes the task of the negro a more healthful and reasonable one; while the master, content with a more gradual style of acquisition, has not those temptations to hardheartedness which always overcome frail human nature when the prospect of sudden and rapid gain is weighed in the balance, with no heavier counterpoise than the interests of the helpless and unprotected.

Whoever visits some estates there, and witnesses the good-humoured indulgence of some masters and mistresses, and the affectionate loyalty of some slaves, might be tempted to dream the oft-fabled poetic legend of a patriarchal institution, and all that;[18] but over and above the scene there broods a portentous shadow – the shadow of *law*. So long as the law considers all these human beings, with beating hearts and living affections, only as so many *things* belonging to a master – so long as the failure, or misfortune or imprudence, or death of the kindest owner, may cause them any day to exchange a life of kind protection and indulgence for one of hopeless misery and toil – so long it is impossible to make anything beautiful or desirable in the best-regulated administration of slavery.

Mr Shelby was a fair average kind of man, good-natured and kindly, and disposed to easy indulgence of those around him, and there had never been a lack of anything which might contribute to the physical comfort of the negroes on his estate. He had, however, speculated largely and quite loosely – had involved himself deeply, and his notes to a large amount had come into the hands of Haley; and this small piece of information is the key to the preceding conversation.

Now, it had so happened that, in approaching the door, Eliza had caught enough of the conversation to know that a trader was making offers to her master for somebody.

She would gladly have stopped at the door to listen, as she came out; but her mistress just then calling, she was obliged to hasten away.

Still she thought she heard the trader make an offer for her boy; could she be mistaken? Her heart swelled and throbbed, and she involuntarily strained him so tight that the little fellow looked up into her face in astonishment.

'Eliza, girl, what ails you today?' said her mistress, when Eliza had upset the wash-pitcher, knocked down the work-stand,[19] and finally was abstractedly offering her mistress a long nightgown in place of the silk dress she had ordered her to bring from the wardrobe.

Eliza started. 'Oh, missis!' she said, raising her eyes; then, bursting into tears, she sat down in a chair, and began sobbing.

'Why, Eliza, child! what ails you?' said her mistress.

'Oh, missis, missis,' said Eliza, 'there's been a trader talking with master in the parlour! I heard him.'

'Well, silly child, suppose there has?'

'Oh, missis, *do* you suppose mas'r would sell my Harry?' And the poor creature threw herself into a chair, and sobbed convulsively.

'Sell him! No, you foolish girl! You know your master never deals with those Southern traders, and never means to sell any of his servants as long as they behave well. Why, you silly child, who do you think would want to buy your Harry? Do you think all the world are set on him as you are, you goosie? Come, cheer up, and hook my dress. There now, put my back hair up in that pretty braid you learnt the other day, and don't go listening at doors any more.'

'Well, but, missis, *you* never would give your consent – to – to – '

'Nonsense, child! to be sure, I shouldn't. What do you talk so for? I would as soon have one of my own children sold. But really, Eliza, you are getting altogether too proud of that little fellow. A man can't put his nose into the door, but you think he must be coming to buy him.'

Reassured by her mistress's confident tone, Eliza proceeded nimbly and adroitly with her toilet, laughing at her own fears, as she proceeded.

Mrs Shelby was a woman of a high class, both intellectually and morally. To that natural magnanimity and generosity of mind which one often marks as characteristic of the women of Kentucky, she added high moral and religious sensibility and principle, carried out with great energy and ability into practical results. Her husband, who made no professions to any particular religious character, nevertheless reverenced and respected the consistency of hers, and stood, perhaps, a little in awe of her opinion. Certain it was, that he gave her unlimited scope in all her benevolent efforts for the comfort, instruction, and improvement of her servants, though he never took any decided part in them himself. In fact, if not exactly a believer in the doctrine of the efficiency of the extra good works of saints, he really seemed somehow or other to fancy that his wife had piety and benevolence enough for two – to indulge a shadowy expectation of getting into heaven through her superabundance of qualities to which he made no particular pretension.

The heaviest load on his mind, after his conversation with the trader, lay in the foreseen necessity of breaking to his wife the arrangement contemplated – meeting the importunities and opposition which he knew he should have reason to encounter.

Mrs Shelby, being entirely ignorant of her husband's embarrassments, and knowing only the general kindliness of his temper, had been quite sincere in the entire incredulity with which she had met Eliza's suspicions. In fact, she dismissed the matter from her mind, without a second thought, and, being occupied in preparations for an evening visit, it passed out of her thoughts entirely.

CHAPTER II

The Mother

ELIZA HAD BEEN brought up by her mistress, from girlhood, as a petted and indulged favourite.

The traveller in the South must often have remarked that peculiar air of refinement, that softness of voice and manner, which seems in many cases to be a particular gift to the quadroon and mulatto women. These natural graces in the quadroon are often united with beauty of the most dazzling kind, and in almost every case with a personal appearance prepossessing and agreeable. Eliza, such as we have described her, is not a fancy sketch, but taken from remembrance, as we saw her, years ago, in Kentucky. Safe under the protecting care of her mistress, Eliza had reached maturity without those temptations which make beauty so fatal an inheritance to a slave. She had been married to a bright and talented young mulatto man, who was a slave on a neighbouring estate, and bore the name of George Harris.

This young man had been hired out by his master to work in a bagging factory,[20] where his adroitness and ingenuity caused him to be considered the first hand in the place. He had invented a machine for the cleaning of the hemp, which, considering the education and circumstances of the inventor, displayed quite as much mechanical genius as Whitney's cotton-gin.[21]

He was possessed of a handsome person and pleasing manners, and was a general favourite in the factory. Nevertheless, as this young man was in the eye of the law not a man, but a thing, all these superior qualifications were subject to the control of a vulgar, narrow-minded, tyrannical master. This same gentleman, having heard of the fame of George's invention, took a ride over to the factory, to see what this intelligent chattel had been about. He was received with great enthusiasm by the employer, who congratulated him on possessing so valuable a slave.

He was waited upon over the factory, shown the machinery by George, who, in high spirits, talked so fluently, held himself so erect, looked so handsome and manly, that his master began to feel an uneasy consciousness of inferiority. What business had his slave to be marching round the country, inventing machines, and holding up his head among gentlemen? He'd soon put a stop to it. He'd take him back, and put him to hoeing and digging, and 'see if he'd step about so smart'. Accordingly, the manufacturer and all hands concerned were astounded when he suddenly demanded George's wages, and announced his intention of taking him home.

'But, Mr Harris,' remonstrated the manufacturer, 'isn't this rather sudden?'

'What if it is? Isn't the man *mine*?'

'We would be willing, sir, to increase the rate of compensation.'

'No object at all, sir. I don't need to hire any of my hands out, unless I've a mind to.'

'But, sir, he seems peculiarly adapted to this business.'

'Dare say he may be; never was much adapted to anything that I set him about, I'll be bound.'

'But only think of his inventing this machine,' interposed one of the workmen, rather unluckily.

'Oh, yes! – a machine for saving work, is it? He'd invent that, I'll be bound; let a nigger alone for that, any time. They are all labour-saving machines themselves, every one of 'em. No, he shall tramp!'

George had stood like one transfixed, at hearing his doom thus suddenly pronounced by a power that he knew was irresistible. He folded his arms, tightly pressed in his lips, but a whole volcano of bitter feelings burned in his bosom, and sent streams of fire through his veins. He breathed short, and his large dark eyes flashed like live coals; and he might have broken out into some dangerous ebullition, had not the kindly manufacturer touched him on the arm, and said, in a low tone – 'Give way, George; go with him for the present. We'll try to help you yet.'

The tyrant observed the whisper, and conjectured its import, though he could not hear what was said; and he inwardly strengthened himself in his determination to keep the power he possessed over his victim.

George was taken home, and put to the meanest drudgery of the farm. He had been able to repress every disrespectful word; but the flashing eye, the gloomy and troubled brow, were part of a natural language that could not be repressed – indubitable signs, which showed too plainly that the man could not become a thing.

It was during the happy period of his employment in the factory that George had seen and married his wife. During that period – being much trusted and favoured by his employer – he had free liberty to come and go at discretion. The marriage was highly approved of by Mrs Shelby, who, with a little womanly complacency in match-making, felt pleased to unite her handsome favourite with one of her own class who seemed in every way suited to her; and so they were married in her mistress's great parlour, and her mistress herself adorned the bride's beautiful hair with orange-blossoms, and threw over it the bridal veil, which certainly could scarce have rested on a fairer head; and there was no lack of white gloves, and cake and wine – of admiring guests to praise the bride's beauty, and her mistress's indulgence and liberality. For a year or two Eliza saw her husband frequently, and there was nothing to interrupt their happiness, except the loss of two infant children, to whom she was passionately attached, and whom she mourned with a grief so intense as to call for gentle remonstrance from her mistress, who sought, with maternal anxiety, to direct her naturally passionate feelings within the bounds of reason and religion.

After the birth of little Harry, however, she had gradually become tranquillised and settled; and every bleeding tie and throbbing nerve, once more entwined with that little life, seemed to become sound and healthful, and Eliza was a happy woman up to the time that her husband was rudely torn from his kind employer, and brought under the iron sway of his legal owner.

The manufacturer, true to his word, visited Mr Harris a week or two after George had been taken away, when, as he hoped, the heat of the occasion had passed away, and tried every possible inducement to lead him to restore him to his former employment.

'You needn't trouble yourself to talk any longer,' said he, doggedly: 'I know my own business, sir.'

'I did not presume to interfere with it, sir. I only thought that you might think it for your interest to let your man to us on the terms proposed.'

'Oh, I understand the matter well enough. I saw your winking and whispering, the day I took him out of the factory; but you don't come it over me that way. It's a free country, sir; the man's *mine*, and I do what I please with him – that's it!'

And so fell George's last hope; nothing before him but a life of toil and drudgery, rendered more bitter by every little smarting vexation and indignity which tyrannical ingenuity could devise.

A very humane jurist once said, 'The worst use you can put a man to is to hang him.' No! there is another use that a man can be put to that is WORSE!

CHAPTER III

The Husband and Father

MRS SHELBY HAD GONE on her visit, and Eliza stood in the veranda, rather dejectedly looking after the retreating carriage, when a hand was laid on her shoulder. She turned, and a bright smile lighted up her fine eyes.

'George, is it you? How you frightened me! Well; I am so glad you's come! Missis is gone to spend the afternoon; so come into my little room and we'll have the time all to ourselves.'

Saying this, she drew him into a neat little apartment opening on the veranda, where she generally sat at her sewing, within call of her mistress.

'How glad I am! – why don't you smile? and look at Harry – how he grows!' The boy stood shyly regarding his father through his curls, holding close to the skirts of his mother's dress. 'Isn't he beautiful?' said Eliza, lifting his long curls and kissing him.

'I wish he'd never been born!' said George, bitterly. 'I wish I'd never been born myself!'

Surprised and frightened, Eliza sat down, leaned her head on her husband's shoulder, and burst into tears.

'There now, Eliza, it's too bad for me to make you feel so, poor girl!' said he, fondly – 'it's too bad. Oh, how I wish you never had seen me – you might have been happy!'

'George! George! how can you talk so? What dreadful thing has happened or is going to happen? I am sure we've been very happy till lately.'

'So we have, dear,' said George. Then drawing his child on his knee, he gazed intently on his glorious dark eyes, and passed his hands through his long curls

'Just like you, Eliza; and you are the handsomest woman I ever saw, and the best one I ever wish to see; but, oh, I wish I'd never seen you, nor you me!'

'Oh, George, how can you!'

'Yes, Eliza, it's all misery, misery, misery! My life is bitter as wormwood; the very life is burning out of me. I'm a poor, miserable, forlorn drudge; I shall only drag you down with me, that's all. What's the use of our trying to do anything, trying to know anything, trying to be anything? What's the use of living? I wish I was dead!'

'Oh, now, dear George, that is really wicked! I know how you feel about losing your place in the factory, and you have a hard master; but pray be patient, and perhaps something – '

'Patient!' said he, interrupting her; 'haven't I been patient? Did I say a word when he came and took me away, for no earthly reason, from the place where everybody was kind to me? I'd paid him truly every cent of my earnings; and they all say I worked well.'

'Well, it *is* dreadful,' said Eliza; 'but, after all, he is your master, you know.'

'My master! and who made him my master? That's what I think of – what right has he to me? I'm a man as much as he is; I am a better man than he is. I know more about business than he does; I am a better manager than he is; I can read better than he can; I can write a better hand; and I've learned it all myself, and no thanks to him – I've learned it in spite of him; and now what right has he to make a dray-horse[22] of me? – to take me from things I can do, and do better than he can, and put me to work that any horse can do? He tries to do it; he says he'll bring me down and humble me, and he puts me to just the hardest, meanest and dirtiest work, on purpose!'

'Oh, George – George – you frighten me! Why, I never heard you talk so: I'm afraid you'll do something dreadful. I don't wonder at your feelings at all; but oh, do be careful – do, do – for my sake – for Harry's!'

'I have been careful, and I have been patient, but it's growing worse and worse – flesh and blood can't bear it any longer. Every chance he can get to insult and torment me, he takes. I thought I could do my work well, and keep on quiet, and have some time to read and learn out of work hours; but the more he sees I can do, the more he loads on. He says that though I don't say anything, he sees I've got the devil in me, and he means to bring it out; and one of these days it will come out in a way that he won't like, or I'm mistaken!'

'Oh, dear! what shall we do?' said Eliza, mournfully.

'It was only yesterday,' said George, 'as I was busy loading stones into a cart, that young Mas'r Tom stood there, slashing his whip so near the horse, that the creature was frightened. I asked him to stop, as pleasant as I could, he just kept right on. I begged him again, and then he turned on me, and began striking me. I held his hand, and then he screamed and kicked and ran to his father, and told him that I was fighting him. He came in a rage, and said he'd teach me who was my master; and he tied me to a tree, and cut switches for young master, and told him that he might whip me till he was tired; and he did do it! If I don't make him remember it, some time!'

And the brow of the young man grew dark, and his eyes burned with an expression that made his young wife tremble. 'Who made this man my master – that's what I want to know!' he said.

'Well,' said Eliza, mournfully, 'I always thought that I must obey my master and mistress, or I couldn't be a Christian.'

'There is some sense in it, in your case; they have brought you up like a child – fed you, clothed you, indulged you, and taught you, so that you have a good education – that is some reason why they should claim you. But I have been kicked, and cuffed, and sworn at, and at the best only let alone; and what do I owe? I've paid for all my keeping a hundred times over. I *won't* bear it – no, I *won't*!' he said, clenching his hand with a fierce frown.

Eliza trembled, and was silent. She had never seen her husband in this mood before; and her gentle system of ethics seemed to bend like a reed in the surges of such passions.

'You know poor little Carlo, that you gave me,' added George: 'the creature has been about all the comfort that I've had. He has slept with me nights, and followed me around days, and kind o' looked at me as if he understood how I felt. Well, the other day I was just feeding him with a few old scraps I picked up by the kitchen-door, and mas'r came along, and said I was feeding him up at his expense, and that he couldn't afford to have every nigger keeping his dog, and ordered me to tie a stone to his neck, and throw him in the pond.'

'Oh, George you didn't do it!'

'Do it! – not I; but he did. Mas'r and Tom pelted the poor drowning creature with stones. Poor thing! he looked at me so mournful, as if he wondered why I didn't save him. I had to take a flogging because I wouldn't do it myself. I don't care; mas'r will find out that I'm one that whipping won't tame. My day will come yet, if he don't look out.'

'What are you going to do? Oh, George, don't do anything wicked; if you only trust in God, and try to do right, he'll deliver you.'

'I an't a Christian like you, Eliza; my heart's full of bitterness; I can't trust in God. Why does He let things be so?'

'Oh, George, we must have faith! Mistress says that when all things go wrong to us, we must believe that God is doing the very best.'

'That's easy to say for people that are sitting on their sofas, and riding in their carriages; but let 'em be where I am, I guess it would come some harder. I wish I could be good; but my heart burns, and can't be reconciled, anyhow. You couldn't, in my place, you can't now, if I tell you all I've got to say. You don't know the whole yet.'

'What can be coming now?'

'Well, lately mas'r has been saying that he was a fool to let me marry off the place; that he hates Mr Shelby and all his tribe, because they are proud, and hold their heads up above him, and that I've got proud notions from you; and he says he won't let me come here any more, and that I shall take a wife and settle down on his place. At first he only scolded and grumbled these things; but yesterday he told me that I should take Mina for a wife, and settle down in a cabin with her, or he would sell me down river.'23

'Why – but you were married to *me*, by the minister, as much as if you'd been a white man!' said Eliza, simply.

'Don't you know a slave can't be married? There is no law in this country for that; I can't hold you for my wife, if he chooses to part us. That's why I wish I'd never seen you – why I wish I'd never been born; it would have been better for us both – it would have been better for this poor child if he had never been born. All this may happen to him yet!'

'Oh, but master is so kind!'

'Yes, but who knows? he may die and then he may be sold to nobody knows who. What pleasure is it that he is handsome, and smart, and bright? I tell you, Eliza, that a sword will pierce through your soul for every good and pleasant thing your child is or has – it will make him worth too much for you to keep!'

The words smote heavily on Eliza's heart; the vision of the trader came before her eyes, and, as if someone had struck her a deadly blow, she turned pale and gasped for breath. She looked nervously out on the veranda, where the boy, tired of the grave conversation, had retired, and where he was riding triumphantly up and down on Mr Shelby's walking-stick. She would have spoken to tell her husband her fears, but checked herself.

'No, no, he has enough to bear, poor fellow!' she thought. 'No, I won't tell him; besides, it an't true; missis never deceives us.'

'So, Eliza, my girl,' said the husband, mournfully, 'bear up, now; and goodbye; for I'm going.'

'Going, George! – going where?'

'To Canada,' said he, straightening himself up; 'and when I'm there, I'll buy you – that's all the hope that's left us. You have a kind master that won't refuse to sell you. I'll buy you and the boy – God helping me, I will!'

'Oh, dreadful! – if you should be taken?'

'I won't be taken, Eliza – I'll *die* first! I'll be free, or I'll die!'[24]

'You won't kill yourself!'

'No need of that; they will kill me fast enough; they never will get me down the river alive!'

'Oh, George, for my sake, do be careful! Don't do anything wicked; don't lay hands on yourself, or anybody else! You are tempted too much – too much; but don't – go you must – but go carefully, prudently; pray God to help you.'

'Well, then, Eliza, hear my plan. Mas'r took it into his head to send me right by here, with a note to Mr Symmes, that lives a mile past. I believe he expected I should come here to tell you what I have. It would please him, if he thought it would aggravate "Shelby's folks", as he calls 'em. I'm going home quite resigned, you understand, as if all was over. I've got some preparations made, and there are those that will help me; and, in the course of a week or so, I shall be among the missing, someday. Pray for me, Eliza; perhaps the good Lord will hear *you*.'

'Oh, pray yourself, George, and go trusting in Him; then you won't do anything wicked '

'Well, now, *goodbye*,' said George, holding Eliza's hands, and gazing into her eyes, without moving. They stood silent; then there were last words, and sobs, and bitter weeping – such parting as those may make whose hope to meet again is as the spider's web; and the husband and wife were parted.

CHAPTER IV

An Evening in Uncle Tom's Cabin

THE CABIN OF UNCLE TOM was a small log building, close adjoining to 'the house', as the negro *par excellence* designates his master's dwelling. In front it had a neat garden-patch, where, every summer, strawberries, raspberries, and a variety of fruits and vegetables, flourished under careful tending. The whole front of it was covered by a large scarlet bignonia and a native multiflora rose, which, entwisting and interlacing, left scarce a vestige of the rough logs to be seen. Here, also, in summer, various brilliant annuals, such as marigolds, petunias, four-o'clocks,[25] found an indulgent corner in which to unfold their splendours, and were the delight and pride of Aunt[26] Chloe's heart.

Let us enter the dwelling. The evening meal at the house is over, and Aunt Chloe, who presided over its preparation as head cook, has left to inferior officers in the kitchen the business of clearing away and washing dishes, and come out into her own snug territories, to 'get her ole man's supper'; therefore, doubt not that it is her you see by the fire, presiding with anxious interest over certain frizzling items in a stewpan, and anon with grave consideration lifting the cover of a bake-kettle, from whence steam forth indubitable intimations of 'something good'. A round, black, shining face is hers, so glossy as to suggest the idea that she might have been washed over with white of eggs, like one of her own tea-rusks. Her whole plump countenance beams with satisfaction and contentment from under her well-starched checked turban, bearing on it, however, if we must confess it, a little of that tinge of self-consciousness which becomes the first cook of the neighbourhood, as Aunt Chloe was universally held and acknowledged to be.

A cook she certainly was, in the very bone and centre of her soul. Not a chicken, or turkey, or duck in the barnyard, but looked grave when they saw her approaching, and seemed evidently to be reflecting on their latter end; and certain it was that she was always meditating on trussing, stuffing, and roasting, to a degree that was calculated to inspire terror in any reflecting fowl living. Her corn-cake,[27] in all its varieties of hoe-cake, dodgers, muffins, and other species too numerous to mention, was a sublime mystery to all less practised compounders; and she would shake her fat sides with honest pride and merriment as she would narrate the fruitless efforts that one and another of her compeers had made to attain to her elevation.

The arrival of company at the house, the arranging of dinners and suppers 'in style', awoke all the energies of her soul; and no sight was more welcome to her than a pile of travelling trunks launched on the veranda, for then she foresaw fresh efforts and fresh triumphs.

Just at present, however, Aunt Chloe is looking into the bake-pan; in which congenial operation we shall leave her till we finish our picture of the cottage.

In one corner of it stood a bed, covered neatly with a snowy spread; and by the side of it was a piece of carpeting, of some considerable size. On this piece of carpeting Aunt Chloe took her stand, as being decidedly in the upper walks of life; and it and the bed by which it lay, and the whole corner, in fact, were treated with distinguished consideration, and made, so far as possible, sacred from the marauding inroads and desecrations of little folks. In fact, that corner was the *drawing-room* of the establishment. In the other corner was a bed of much humbler pretensions, and evidently designed for *use*. The wall over the fireplace was adorned with some very brilliant scriptural prints, and a portrait of General Washington,[28] drawn and coloured in a manner which would certainly have astonished that hero, if ever he had happened to meet with its like.

On a rough bench in the corner, a couple of woolly-headed boys, with glistening black eyes and fat shining cheeks, were busy in superintending the first walking operations of the baby, which, as is usually the case, consisted in getting up on its feet, balancing a moment and then tumbling down – each successive failure being violently cheered as something decidedly clever.

A table, somewhat rheumatic in its limbs, was drawn out in front of the fire, and covered with a cloth, displaying cups and saucers of a decidedly brilliant pattern, with other symptoms of an approaching meal. At this table was seated Uncle Tom, Mr Shelby's best hand, who, as he is to be the hero of our story, we must daguerreotype[29] for our readers. He was a large, broad-chested, powerfully-made man, of a full glossy black, and a face whose truly African features were characterised by an expression of grave and steady good sense, united with much kindliness and benevolence. There was something about his whole air self-respecting and dignified, yet united with a confiding and humble simplicity.

He was very busily intent at this moment on a slate lying before him, on which he was carefully and slowly endeavouring to accomplish a copy of some letters; in which operation he was overlooked by young Mas'r George, a smart, bright boy of thirteen, who appeared fully to realise the dignity of his position as instructor.

'Not that way, Uncle Tom – not that way,' said he, briskly, as Uncle Tom laboriously brought up the tail of his *g* the wrong side out: 'that makes a *q*, you see.'

'La sakes, now, does it?' said Uncle Tom, looking with a respectful, admiring air, as his young teacher flourishingly scrawled *q*'s and *g*'s innumerable for his edification; and then, taking the pencil in his big, heavy fingers, he patiently recommenced.

'How easy white folks al'ays does things!' said Aunt Chloe, pausing while she was greasing a griddle with a scrap of bacon on her fork, and regarding young Master George with pride. 'The way he can write, now! and read, too! and then to come out here evenings and read his lessons to us – it's mighty interestin'!'

'But, Aunt Chloe, I'm getting mighty hungry,' said George. 'Isn't that cake in the skillet almost done?'

'Mose done, Mas'r George,' said Aunt Chloe, lifting the lid and peeping in, 'browning beautiful – a real lovely brown. Ah! let me alone for dat! Missis let Sally try to make some cake t'other day, jest to *larn* her, she said. "Oh, go way, misses," says I; "it really hurts my feelin's, now, to see good vittles spiled dat ar way! Cake ris all to one side – no shape at all, no more than my shoe – go way!" '

And with this final expression of contempt for Sally's greenness, Aunt Chloe whipped the cover off the bake-kettle, and disclosed to view a neatly-baked pound-cake, of which no city confectioner need to have been ashamed. This being evidently the central point of the entertainment, Aunt Chloe began now to bustle about earnestly in the supper department.

'Here you, Mose and Pete, get out de way, you niggers! Get away, Polly, honey; mammy'll give her baby somefin by and by. Now, Mas'r George, you jest take off dem books, and set down now with my old man, and I'll take up de sausages, and have de first griddle full of cakes on your plates in less dan no time.'

'They wanted me to come to supper in the house,' said George; 'but I knew what was what too well for that, Aunt Chloe.'

'So you did – so you did, honey,' said Aunt Chloe, heaping the smoking batter-cakes on his plate; 'you know'd your old aunty'd keep the best for you. Oh, let you alone for dat – go way!'

And, with that, Aunty gave George a nudge with her finger, designed to be immensely facetious, and turned again to her griddle with great briskness.

'Now for the cake,' said Mas'r George, when the activity of the griddle department had somewhat subsided; and, with that the youngster flourished a large knife over the article in question.

'La bless you, Mas'r George!' said Aunt Chloe, with earnestness, catching his arm, 'you wouldn't be for cuttin' it wid dat ar great heavy knife! Smash all down – spile all de pretty rise of it! Here, I've got a thin old knife, I keeps sharp a purpose. Dar now, see – comes apart light as a feather! Now eat away – you won't get anything to beat dat ar.'

'Tom Lincon says,' said George, speaking with his mouth full, 'that their Jinny is a better cook than you.'

'Dem Lincons an't much count, no way!' said Aunt Chloe, contemptuously; 'I mean, set alongside *our* folks. They's 'spectable folks enough in a kinder plain way; but, as to gettin' up anything in style, they don't begin to have a notion on't. Set Mas'r Lincon, now, alongside Mas'r Shelby. Good Lor! and Missis Lincon – can she kinder sweep it into a room like my missis – so kinder splendid, yer know? Oh, go way! don't tell me nothin' of dem Lincons!' and Aunt Chloe tossed her head as one who hoped she did know something of the world.

'Well, though, I've heard you say,' said George, 'that Jinny was a pretty fair cook.'

'So I did,' said Aunt Chloe – 'I may say dat. Good, plain, common cookin', Jinny'll do; make a good pone o' bread[30] – bile her taters *far* – her corn-cakes isn't extra, not extra now, Jinny's corn-cakes isn't, but then they's far. But, Lor, come to de higher branches, and what *can* she do? Why, she makes pies – sartin she does; but what kinder crust? Can she make your real flecky paste,[31] as melts in your mouth and lies all up like a puff? Now, I went over thar when Miss Mary was gwine to be married, and Jinny she jest showed me de weddin' pies. Jinny and I is good friends, ye know. I never said nothin'; but go long, Mas'r George! Why, I shouldn't sleep a wink for a week, if I had a batch of pies like dem ar. Why, dey wa'n't no 'count 't all.'

'I suppose Jinny thought they were ever so nice,' said George.

'Thought so! – didn't she? Thar she was, showing 'em, as innocent! Ye see, it's jest here, Jinny *don't know*. Lor, the family an't nothin'! She can't be 'spected to know! 'Ta'nt no fault o' hern. Ah, Mas'r George, you doesn't know half your privileges in yer family and bringin' up!' Here Aunt Chloe sighed, and rolled up her eyes with emotion.

'I'm sure, Aunt Chloe, I understand all my pie-and-pudding privileges,' said George. 'Ask Tom Lincon if I don't crow over him every time I meet him.'

Aunt Chloe sat back in her chair, and indulged in a hearty guffaw of laughter, at this witticism of young Mas'r's, laughing till the tears rolled down her black, shining cheeks, and varying the exercise with playfully slapping and poking Mas'r Georgey, and telling him to go way, and that he was a case – that he was fit to kill her, and that he sartin would kill her one of these days; and, between each of these sanguinary predictions, going off into a laugh, each longer and stronger than the other, till George really began to think that he was a very dangerously witty fellow, and that it became him to be careful how he talked 'as funny as he could'.

'And so ye told Tom, did ye? O Lor! what young uns will be up ter! Ye crowed over Tom? O Lor, Mas'r George, if ye wouldn't make a hornbug[32] laugh!'

'Yes,' said George, 'I says to him, "Tom, you ought to see some of Aunt Chloe's pies; they're the right sort," says I.'

'Pity, now, Tom couldn't,' said Aunt Chloe, on whose benevolent heart the idea of Tom's benighted condition seemed to make a strong impression. 'Ye oughter just ask him here to dinner, some o' these times, Mas'r George,' she added; 'it would look quite pretty of ye. Ye know, Mas'r George, ye oughtenter feel 'bove nobody, on 'count yer privileges, 'cause all our privileges is gi'n to us; we ought al'ays to 'member that,' said Aunt Chloe, looking quite serious.

'Well, I mean to ask Tom here, some day next week,' said George; 'and you do your prettiest, Aunt Chloe, and we'll make him stare. Won't we make him eat so he won't get over it for a fortnight?'

'Yes, yes – sartin,' said Aunt Chloe, delighted; 'you'll see. Lor! to think of some of our dinners! Yer mind dat ar great chicken-pie I made when we guv de dinner to General Knox? I and missis, we come pretty near quarrelling about dat ar crust. What does get into ladies sometimes, I don't know; but sometimes, when a body has de heaviest kind o' 'sponsibility on 'em, as ye may say, and is all kinder "*seris*" and taken up, dey takes dat ar time to be hangin' round and kinder interferin'! Now, missis, she wanted me to do dis way, and she wanted me to do dat way; and finally I got kinder sarcy, and says I, "Now, missis, do jest look at dem beautiful white hands o' yourn, with long fingers, and all a sparkling with rings, like my white lilies when de dew's on 'em; and look at my great black stumpin' hands. Now, don't ye think dat de Lord must have meant *me* to make de pie-crust, and you to stay in de parlour?" Dar! I was jest so sarcy, Mas'r George.'

'And what did mother say?' said George.

'Say? – why, she kinder larfed in her eyes – dem great handsome eyes o' hern; and, says she, "Well, Aunt Chloe, I think you are about in the right on't," says she; and she went off in de parlour. She oughter cracked me over de head for bein' so sarcy; but dar's whar 'tis – I can't do nothin' with ladies in de kitchen!'

'Well, you made out well with that dinner – I remember everybody said so,' said George.

'Didn't I? And wa'n't I behind de dinin'-room door dat bery day? and didn't I see de Gineral pass his plate three times for some more dat bery pie? and, says he, "You must have an uncommon cook, Mrs Shelby." Lor! I was fit to split myself.

'And de Gineral, he knows what cookin' is,' said Aunt Chloe, drawing herself up with an air. 'Bery nice man, de Gineral! He comes of one of de bery *fustest* families in Old Virginny![33] He knows what's what, now, as well as I do – de Gineral. Ye see, there's *pints* in all pies, Mas'r George; but tan't everybody knows what they is, or orter be. But de Gineral, he knows; I knew by his 'marks he made. Yes, he knows what de pints is!'

By this time Master George had arrived at that pass to which even a boy can come (under uncommon circumstances), when he really could not eat another morsel, and, therefore, he was at leisure to notice the pile of woolly heads and glistening eyes which were regarding their operations hungrily from the opposite corner.

'Here you, Mose, Pete,' he said, breaking off liberal bits, and throwing it at them; 'you want some, don't you? Come, Aunt Chloe, bake them some cakes.'

And George and Tom moved to a comfortable seat in the chimney-corner, while Aunt Chloe, after baking a goodly pile of cakes, took her baby on her lap, and began alternately filling its mouth and her own, and distributing to Mose and Pete, who seemed rather to prefer eating theirs as they rolled about on the floor under the table, tickling each other, and occasionally pulling the baby's toes.

'Oh, go long will ye?' said the mother, giving now and then a kick, in a kind of general way, under the table, when the movement became too obstreperous. 'Can't ye be decent when white folks comes to see ye? Stop dat ar, now, will ye? Better mind yerselves, or I'll take ye down a buttonhole lower, when Mas'r George is gone!'

What meaning was couched under this terrible threat, it is difficult to say; but certain it is that its awful indistinctness seemed to produce very little impression on the young sinners addressed.

'La, now!' said Uncle Tom, 'they are so full of tickle all the while, they can't behave theirselves.'

Here the boys emerged from under the table, and, with hands and faces well plastered with molasses, began a vigorous kissing of the baby.

'Get along wid ye!' said the mother, pushing away their woolly heads. 'Ye'll all stick together, and never get clar, if ye do dat fashion. Go long to de spring and wash yerselves!' she said, seconding her exhortations by a slap, which resounded very formidably, but which seemed only to knock out so much more laugh from the young ones, as they tumbled precipitately over each other out-of-doors, where they fairly screamed with merriment.

'Did ye ever see such aggravating young uns?' said Aunt Chloe, rather complacently, as, producing an old towel, kept for such emergencies, she poured a little water out of the cracked teapot on it, and began rubbing off the molasses from the baby's face and hands; and having polished her till she shone, she set her down in Tom's lap, while she busied herself in clearing away supper. The baby employed the intervals in pulling Tom's nose, scratching his face, and burying her fat hands in his woolly hair, which last operation seemed to afford her special content.

'Ain't she a peart young un?' said Tom, holding her from him to take a full-length view; then, getting up, he set her on his broad shoulder, and began capering and dancing with her, while Mas'r George snapped at her with his pocket-handkerchief, and Mose and Pete now returned again, roared after her like bears, till Aunt Chloe declared that they 'fairly took her head off' with their noise. As, according to her own statement, this surgical operation was a matter of daily occurrence in the cabin, the declaration no whit abated the merriment, till everyone had roared, and tumbled, and danced themselves down to a state of composure.

'Well, now, I hopes you're done,' said Aunt Chloe, who had been busy in pulling out a rude box of a trundle-bed; 'and now, you Mose, and you Pete, get into thar; for we's goin' to have the meetin'.'

'Oh, mother, we don't wanter. We wants to sit up to meetin' – meetin's is so curis. We likes 'em.'

'La, Aunt Chloe, shove it under, and let 'em sit up,' said Mas'r George, decisively, giving a push to the rude machine.

Aunt Chloe, having thus saved appearances, seemed highly delighted to push the thing under, saying, as she did so, 'Well, mebbe, 'twill do 'em some good.'

The house now resolved itself into a committee of the whole, to consider the accommodations and arrangements for the meeting.

'What we's to do for cheers, now, *I* declare I don't know,' said Aunt Chloe. As the meeting had been held at Uncle Tom's weekly, for an indefinite length of time, without any more 'cheers', there seemed some encouragement to hope that a way would be discovered at present.

'Old Uncle Peter sung both de legs out of dat oldest cheer, last week,' suggested Mose.

'You go long! I'll boun' you pulled 'em out; some o' your shines,' said Aunt Chloe.

'Well, it'll stand, if it only keeps jam up agin de wall!' said Mose.

'Den Uncle Peter mustn't sit in it, 'cause he al'ays hitches when he gets a singing. He hitched pretty nigh across de room, t'other night,' said Pete.

'Good Lor! get him in it, then,' said Mose, 'and den he'd begin, "Come, saints and sinners, hear me tell,"[34] and den down he'd go.' And Mose imitated precisely the nasal tones of the old man, tumbling on the floor, to illustrate the supposed catastrophe.

'Come, now, be decent, can't ye?' said Aunt Chloe; 'an't yer ashamed?'

Mas'r George, however, joined the offender in the laugh, and declared decidedly that Mose was a 'buster'. So the maternal admonition seemed rather to fail of effect.

'Well, ole man,' said Aunt Chloe, 'you'll have to tote in them ar bar'ls.'

'Mother's bar'ls is like dat ar widder's Mas'r George was reading 'bout in de good book – dey never fails,' said Mose, aside to Pete.

'I'm sure one on 'em caved in last week,' said Pete, 'and let 'em all down in the middle of de singin'; dat ar was failin', warn't it?'

During this aside between Mose and Pete, two empty casks had been rolled into the cabin, and being secured from rolling by stones on each side, boards were laid across them; which arrangement, together with the turning down of certain tubs and pails, and the disposing of the rickety chairs, at last completed the preparation.

'Mas'r George is such a beautiful reader, now, I know he'll stay to read for us,' said Aunt Chloe; ' 'pears like 'twill be so much more interestin'.'

George very readily consented, for your boy is always ready for anything that makes him of importance.

The room was soon filled with a motley assemblage, from the old grey-headed patriarch of eighty to the young girl and lad of fifteen. A little harmless gossip ensued on various themes, such as where old Aunt Sally got her new headkerchief, and how 'missis was a-going to give Lizzy that spotted muslin gown, when she'd got her new berage[35] made up'; and how Mas'r Shelby was thinking of buying a new sorrel colt, that was going to prove an addition to the glories of the place. A few of the worshippers belonged to families hard by, who had got permission to attend, and who brought in various choice scraps of information, about the sayings and doings at the house and on the place, which circulated as freely as the same sort of small change does in higher circles.

After awhile the singing commenced, to the evident delight of all present. Not even all the disadvantage of nasal intonation could prevent the effect of the naturally fine voices, in airs at once wild and spirited. The words were sometimes the well-known and common hymns sung in the churches about, and sometimes of a wilder, more indefinite character, picked up at camp-meetings.

The chorus of one of them, which ran as follows, was sung with great energy and unction –

Die on the field of battle,
Die on the field of battle,
Glory in my soul.[36]

Another special favourite had oft repeated the words –

Oh, I'm going to glory – won't you come along with me?
Don't you see the angels beck'ning, and calling me away?
Don't you see the golden city and the everlasting day?[37]

There were others, which made incessant mention of 'Jordan's banks', and 'Canaan's fields', and the 'New Jerusalem';[38] for the negro mind, impassioned and imaginative, always attaches itself to hymns and expressions of a vivid and pictorial nature; and, as they sang, some laughed, and some cried, and some clapped hands, or shook hands rejoicingly with each other, as if they had fairly gained the other side of the river.

Various exhortations or relations of experience followed, and intermingled with the singing. One old grey-headed woman, long past work, but much revered as a sort of chronicle of the past, rose, and leaning on her staff, said –

'Well, chil'en! Well, I'm mighty glad to hear ye all and see ye all once more, 'cause I don't know when I'll be gone to glory; but I've done got ready, chil'en; 'pears like I'd got my little bundle all tied up, and my bonnet on, jest a waitin' for the stage to come along and take me home; sometimes, in the night, I think I hear the wheels a rattlin', and I'm lookin' out all the time; now, you jest be ready too, for I tell ye all, chil'en,' she said, striking her staff hard on the door, 'dat ar *glory* is a mighty thing! It's a mighty thing, chil'en – you don'no nothing about it – it's *wonderful*.' And the old creature sat down, with streaming tears, as wholly overcome, while the whole circle struck up –

'Oh, Canaan, bright Canaan,
I'm bound for the land of Canaan.'[39]

Mas'r George, by request, read the last chapters of Revelation,[40] often interrupted by such exclamations as 'The *sakes* now!' 'Only hear that!' 'Jest think on't!' 'Is all that a comin' sure enough?'

George, who was a bright boy, and well trained in religious things by his mother, finding himself an object of general admiration, threw in expositions of his own from time to time, with a commendable seriousness and gravity, for which he was admired by the young and blessed by the old; and it was agreed, on all hands, that a 'minister couldn't lay it off better than he did'; that ' 'twas reely 'mazin'!'

Uncle Tom was a sort of patriarch in religious matters, in the neighbourhood. Having, naturally, an organisation in which the *morale*[41] was strongly predominant, together with a greater breadth and cultivation of mind than obtained among his companions, he was looked up to with great respect, as a sort of minister among them; and the simple, hearty, sincere style of his exhortations, might have edified even better educated persons. But it was in prayer that he especially excelled. Nothing could exceed the touching simplicity, the childlike earnestness, of his prayer, enriched with the language of Scripture, which seemed so entirely to have wrought itself into his being, as to have become a part of himself, and to drop from his lips unconsciously; in the language of a pious old negro, he 'prayed right up'. And so much did his prayer always work on the devotional feelings of his audiences, that there seemed often a danger that it would be lost altogether in the abundance of the responses which broke out everywhere around him.

While this scene was passing in the cabin of the man, one quite otherwise passed in the halls of the master.

The trader and Mr Shelby were seated together in the dining-room afore-named, at a table covered with papers and writing utensils.

Mr Shelby was busy in counting some bundles of bills, which, as they were counted, he pushed over to the trader, who counted them likewise.

'All fair,' said the trader; 'and now for signing these yer.'

Mr Shelby hastily drew the bills of sale towards him, and signed them like a man that hurries over some disagreeable business, and then pushed them over with the money. Haley produced, from a well-worn valise, a parchment, which, after looking over it a moment, he handed to Mr Shelby, who took it with a gesture of suppressed eagerness.

'Wal, now the thing's *done*!' said the trader, getting up.

'It's *done*!'[42] said Mr Shelby, in a musing tone; and, fetching a long breath, he repeated, '*It's done!*'

'Yer don't seem to feel much pleased with it, 'pears to me,' said the trader.

'Haley,' said Mr Shelby, 'I hope you'll remember that you promised, on your honour, you wouldn't sell Tom, without knowing what sort of hands he's going into.'

'Why, you've just done it, sir,' said the trader.

'Circumstances, you well know, *obliged* me,' said Shelby, haughtily.

'Wal, you know, they may 'blige *me*, too,' said the trader. 'Howsomever, I'll do the very best I can in gettin' Tom a good berth; as to my treating on him bad, you needn't be a grain afeard. If there's anything that I thank the Lord for, it is that I'm never noways cruel.'

After the expositions which the trader had previously given of his humane principles, Mr Shelby did not feel particularly reassured by these declarations; but as they were the best comfort the case admitted of, he allowed the trader to depart in silence, and betook himself to a solitary cigar.

CHAPTER V

Showing the Feelings of Living Property on Changing Owners

MR AND MRS SHELBY had retired to their apartment for the night. He was lounging in a large easy-chair, looking over some letters that had come in the afternoon mail, and she was standing before her mirror, brushing out the complicated braids and curls in which Eliza had arranged her hair; for, noticing her pale cheeks and haggard eyes, she had excused her attendance that night, and ordered her to bed. The employment, naturally enough, suggested her conversation with the girl in the morning; and, turning to her husband, she said carelessly –

'By the by, Arthur, who was that low-bred fellow that you lugged in to our dinner-table today?'

'Haley is his name,' said Shelby, turning himself rather uneasily in his chair, and continuing with his eyes fixed on a letter.

'Haley! Who is he, and what may be his business here, pray?'

'Well, he's a man that I transacted some business with last time I was at Natchez,' said Mr Shelby.

'And he presumed on it to make himself quite at home, and call and dine here, eh?'

'Why, I invited him; I had some accounts with him,' said Shelby.

'Is he a negro-trader?' said Mrs Shelby, noticing a certain embarrassment in her husband's manner.

'Why, my dear, what put that into your head?' said Shelby, looking up.

'Nothing – only Eliza came in here, after dinner, in a great worry, crying and taking on, and said you were talking with a trader, and that she heard him make an offer for her boy – the ridiculous little goose!'

'She did, eh?' said Mr Shelby, returning to his paper, which he seemed for a few moments quite intent upon, not perceiving that he was holding it bottom upwards.

'It will have to come out,' said he, mentally; 'as well now as ever.'

'I told Eliza,' said Mrs Shelby, as she continued brushing her hair, 'that she was a little fool for her pains, and that you never had anything to do with that sort of persons. Of course, I knew you never meant to sell any of our people – least of all, to such a fellow.'

'Well, Emily,' said her husband, 'so I have always felt and said; but the fact is, my business lies so that I cannot get on without. I shall have to sell some of my hands.'

'To that creature? Impossible! Mr Shelby, you cannot be serious.'

'I'm sorry to say that I am,' said Mr Shelby. 'I've agreed to sell Tom.'

'What! our Tom? – that good, faithful creature! – been your faithful servant from a boy! Oh, Mr Shelby! – and you have promised him his freedom, too – you and I have spoken to him a hundred times of it. Well, I can believe anything now; I can believe *now* that you could sell little Harry, poor Eliza's only child!' said Mrs Shelby, in a tone between grief and indignation.

'Well, since you must know all, it is so. I have agreed to sell Tom and Harry both; and I don't know why I am to be rated as if I were a monster for doing what everyone does every day.'

'But why, of all others, choose these?' said Mrs Shelby. 'Why sell them of all on the place, if you must sell at all?'

'Because they will bring the highest sum of any – that's why. I could choose another, if you say so. The fellow made me a high bid on Eliza, if that would suit you any better,' said Mr Shelby.

'The wretch!' said Mrs Shelby, vehemently.

'Well, I didn't listen to it, a moment – out of regard to your feelings, I wouldn't; so give me some credit.'

'My dear,' said Mrs Shelby, recollecting herself, 'forgive me. I have been hasty. I was surprised, and entirely unprepared for this; but surely you will allow me to intercede for these poor creatures. Tom is a noble-hearted, faithful fellow, if he is black. I do believe, Mr Shelby, that if he were put to it, he would lay down his life for you.'

'I know it, I dare say; but what's the use of all this? I can't help myself.'

'Why not make a pecuniary sacrifice? I'm willing to bear my part of the inconvenience. Oh Mr Shelby, I have tried – tried most faithfully, as a Christian woman should – to do my duty to these poor, simple, dependent creatures. I have cared for them, instructed them, watched over them, and known all their little cares and joys, for years; and how can I ever hold up my head again among them, if, for the sake of a little paltry gain, we sell such a faithful, excellent, confiding creature as poor Tom, and tear from him in a moment all we have taught him to love and value? I have taught them the duties of the family, of parent and child, and husband and wife; and how can I bear to have this open acknowledgement that we care for no tie, no duty, no relation, however sacred, compared with money? I have talked with Eliza about her boy – her duty to him as a Christian mother, to watch over him, pray for him, and bring him up in a Christian way; and now what can I say, if you tear him away, and sell him, soul and body, to a profane, unprincipled man, just to save a little money? I have told her that one soul is worth more than all the money in the world; and how will she believe me when she sees us turn round and sell her child? – sell him, perhaps, to certain ruin of body and soul!'

'I'm sorry you feel so about it, Emily – indeed I am,' said Mr Shelby; 'and I respect your feelings, too, though I don't pretend to share them to their full extent; but I tell you now, solemnly, it's of no use – I can't help myself. I didn't mean to tell you this, Emily; but, in plain words, there is no choice between selling these two and selling everything. Either they must go, or *all* must. Haley has come into possession of a mortgage, which, if I don't clear off with him directly, will take everything before it. I've raked, and scraped, and borrowed, and all but begged, and the price of these two was needed to make up the balance, and I had to give them up. Haley fancied the child; he agreed to settle the matter that way, and no other. I was in his power, and *had* to do it. If you feel so to have them sold, would it be any better to have *all* sold?'

Mrs Shelby stood like one stricken. Finally, turning to her toilet, she rested her face in her hands, and gave a sort of groan.

'This is God's curse on slavery! – a bitter, bitter, most accursed thing! – a curse to the master, and a curse to the slave! I was a fool to think I could make anything good out of such a deadly evil. It is a sin to hold a slave under laws like ours; I always felt it was – I always thought so when I was a girl – I thought so still more after I joined the church; but I thought I could gild it over. I thought by kindness, and care, and instruction, I could make the condition of mine better than freedom. Fool that I was!'

'Why, wife, you are getting to be an Abolitionist,[43] quite.'

'Abolitionist! If they knew all I know about slavery they *might* talk! We don't need them to tell us; you know I never thought that slavery was right – never felt willing to own slaves.'

'Well, therein you differ from many wise and pious men,' said Mr Shelby. 'You remember Mr B.'s sermon, the other Sunday?'

'I don't want to hear such sermons; I never wish to hear Mr B. in our church again. Ministers can't help the evil, perhaps – can't cure it, any more than we can – but defend it! It always went against my common sense. And I think you didn't think much of that sermon, either.'

'Well,' said Shelby, 'I must say these ministers sometimes carry matters further than we poor sinners would exactly dare to do. We men of the world must wink pretty hard at various things, and get used to a deal that isn't the exact thing. But we don't quite fancy when women and ministers come out broad and square, and go beyond us in matters of either modesty or morals, that's a fact. But now, my dear, I trust you see the necessity of the thing, and you see that I have done the very best that circumstances would allow.'

'Oh, yes, yes!' said Mrs Shelby, hurriedly and abstractedly fingering her gold watch. 'I haven't any jewellery of any amount,' she added, thoughtfully; 'but would not this watch do something? – it was an expensive one when it was bought. If I could only at least save Eliza's child, I would sacrifice anything I have.'

'I'm sorry, very sorry, Emily,' said Mr Shelby, 'I'm sorry this takes hold of you so; but it will do no good. The fact is, Emily, the thing's done; the bills of sale are already signed and in Haley's hands; and you must be thankful it is no worse. That man has had it in his power to ruin us all, and now he is fairly off. If you knew the man as I do, you'd think that we had had a narrow escape.'

'Is he so hard, then?'

'Why, not a cruel man, exactly, but a man of leather – a man alive to nothing but trade and profit; cool, and unhesitating, and unrelenting as death and the grave. He'd sell his own mother at a good percentage – not wishing the old woman any harm either.'

'And this wretch owns that good, faithful Tom, and Eliza's child!'

'Well, my dear, the fact is that this goes rather hard with me – it's a thing I hate to think of: Haley wants to drive matters, and take possession tomorrow. I'm going to get out my horse bright and early, and be off. I can't see Tom, that's a fact; and you had better arrange a drive somewhere, and carry Eliza off. Let the thing be done when she is out of sight.'

'No, no,' said Mrs Shelby; 'I'll be in no sense accomplice or help in this cruel business. I'll go and see poor old Tom, God help him, in his distress! They shall see, at any rate, that their mistress can feel for and with them. As to Eliza, I dare not think about it. The Lord forgive us! What have we done, that this cruel necessity should come on us?'

There was one listener to this conversation whom Mr and Mrs Shelby little suspected.

Communicating with their apartment was a large closet, opening by a door into the outer passage. When Mrs Shelby had dismissed Eliza for the night, her feverish and excited mind had suggested the idea of this closet; and she had hidden herself there, and, with her ear pressed close against the crack of the door, had lost not a word of the conversation.

When the voices died into silence, she rose and crept stealthily away. Pale, shivering, with rigid features and compressed lips, she looked an entirely altered being from the soft and timid creature she had been hitherto. She moved cautiously along the entry, paused one moment at her mistress's door, and raised her hands in mute appeal to Heaven, and then turned and glided into her own room. It was a quiet, neat apartment, on the same floor with her mistress's. There was the pleasant, sunny window, where she had often sat singing at her sewing; there a little case of books, and various little fancy articles ranged by them, the gifts of Christmas holidays; there was her simple wardrobe in the closet and in the drawers; there was, in short, her home, and, on the whole, a happy one it had been to her. But there, on the bed, lay her slumbering boy, his long curls falling negligently around his unconscious face, his rosy mouth half open, his little fat hands thrown out over the bedclothes, and a smile spread like a sunbeam over his whole face.

'Poor boy! poor fellow!' said Eliza; 'they have sold you! but your mother will save you yet!'

No tear dropped over that pillow. In such straits as these the heart has no tears to give, it drops only blood, bleeding itself away in silence. She took a piece of paper and pencil, and wrote, hastily – 'Oh, missis! dear missis! don't think me ungrateful – don't think hard of me, anyway – I heard all you and master said tonight, I am going to try to save my boy – you will not blame me! God bless and reward you for all your kindness!'

Hastily folding and directing this, she went to a drawer and made up a little package of clothing for her boy, which she tied with a handkerchief firmly round her waist; and so fond is a mother's remembrance, that, even in the terrors of that hour, she did not forget to put in the little package one or two of his favourite toys, reserving a gaily-painted parrot to amuse him when she should be called on to awaken him. It was some trouble to arouse the little sleeper; but, after some effort, he sat up, and was playing with his bird, while his mother was putting on her bonnet and shawl.

'Where are you going, mother?' said he, as she drew near the bed with his little coat and cap.

His mother drew near, and looked so earnestly into his eyes, that he at once divined that something unusual was the matter.

'Hush, Harry,' she said; 'musn't speak so loud, or they will hear us. A wicked man was coming to take little Harry away from his mother, and carry him 'way off in the dark; but mother won't let him – she's going to put on her little boy's cap and coat, and run off with him, so the ugly man can't catch him.'

Saying these words, she had tied and buttoned on the child's simple outfit, and, taking him in her arms, she whispered to him to be very still; and, opening a door in her room which led into the outer veranda, she glided noiselessly out.

It was a sparkling, frosty, starlight night, and the mother wrapped the shawl close round her child, as, perfectly quiet with vague terror, he clung round her neck.

Old Bruno, a great Newfoundland, who slept at the end of the porch, rose, with a low growl, as she came near. She gently spoke his name, and the animal, an old pet and playmate of hers, instantly wagging his tail, prepared to follow her, though apparently revolving much in his simple dog's head what such an indiscreet midnight promenade might mean. Some dim ideas of imprudence or impropriety in the measure seemed to embarrass him considerably; for he often stopped, as Eliza glided forward, and looked wistfully, first at her and then at the house, and then, as if reassured by reflection, he pattered along after her again. A few minutes brought them to the window of Uncle Tom's cottage, and Eliza, stopping, tapped lightly on the window-pane.

The prayer-meeting at Uncle Tom's had, in the order of hymn-singing, been protracted to a very late hour; and, as Uncle Tom had indulged himself in a few lengthy solos afterwards, the consequence was, that, although it was now between twelve and one o'clock, he and his worthy helpmeet were not yet asleep.

'Good Lord! what's that?' said Aunt Chloe, starting up, and hastily drawing the curtain. 'My sakes alive, if it an't Lizzy! Get on your clothes, ole man, quick! There's old Bruno, too, a-pawin' round – what on airth! I'm gwine to open the door.'

And suiting the action to the word, the door flew open, and the light of the tallow candle, which Tom had hastily lighted, fell on the haggard face and dark wild eyes of the fugitive.

'Lord bless you! I'm skeered to look at ye, Lizzy! Are ye tuck sick, or what's come over ye?'

'I'm running away Uncle Tom and Aunt Chloe – carrying off my child. Master's sold him!'

'Sold him?' echoed both, lifting up their hands in dismay.

'Yes, sold him!' said Eliza, firmly; 'I crept into the closet by mistress's door tonight, and I heard master tell missis that he had sold my Harry, and you, Uncle Tom, both, to a trader; and that he was going off this morning on his horse, and that the man was to take possession today.'

Tom had stood, during this speech with his hands raised, and his eyes dilated, like a man in a dream. Slowly and gradually, as its meaning came over him, he collapsed, rather than seated himself, on his old chair, and sunk his head down upon his knees.

'The good Lord have pity on us!' said Aunt Chloe. 'Oh, it don't seem as if it was true! What has he done that mas'r should sell *him*?'

'He hasn't done anything – it isn't for that. Master don't want to sell; and missis – she's always good – I heard her plead and beg for us; but he told her 'twas no use – that he was in this man's debt, and that this man had got the power over him – and that if he didn't pay him off clear, it would end in his having to sell the place and all the people, and move off. Yes, I heard him say there was no choice between selling these two and selling all, the man was driving him so hard. Master said he was sorry; but oh, missis! you ought to have heard her talk! If she an't a Christian and an angel, there never was one. I'm a wicked girl to leave her so; but then I can't help it. She said herself one soul was worth more than the world; and this boy has a soul, and if I let him be carried off, who knows what'll become of it? It must be right; but if it an't right, the Lord forgive me, for I can't help doing it!'

'Well, ole man!' said Aunt Chloe, 'why don't you go, too? Will you wait to be toted down the river, where they kill niggers with hard work and starving? I'd a heap rather die than go there, any day! There's time for ye; be off with Lizzy – you've got a pass to come and go anytime. Come, bustle up, and I'll get your things together.'

Tom slowly raised his head, and looked sorrowfully but quietly around, and said –

'No, no I an't going. Let Eliza go – it's her right. I wouldn't be the one to say no. 'Tan't in *natur* for her to stay; but you heard what she said. If I must be sold, or all the people on the place, and everything go to rack, why, let me be sold. I s'pose I can b'ar it as well as any on 'em,' he added, while something like a sob and a sigh shook his broad, rough chest convulsively. 'Mas'r always found me on the spot – he always will. I never have broke trust, nor used my pass noways contrary to my word, and I never will. It's better for me alone to go than to break up the place and sell all. Mas'r an't to blame, Chloe; and he'll take care of you and the poor –'

Here he turned to the rough trundle-bed full of little woolly heads, and broke fairly down. He leaned over the back of the chair, and covered his face with his large hands. Sobs, heavy, hoarse and loud, shook the chair, and great tears fell through his fingers on the floor – just such tears, sir, as you dropped into the coffin where lay your first-born son; such tears, woman, as you shed when you heard the cries of your dying babe: for, sir, he was a man, and you are but another man; and, woman, though dressed in silk and jewels, you are but a woman, and, in life's great straits and mighty griefs, ye feel but one sorrow!

'And now,' said Eliza, as she stood in the door, 'I saw my husband only this afternoon, and I little knew then what was to come. They have pushed him to the very last standing place, and he told me today that he was going to run away. Do try, if you can, to get word to him. Tell him how I went and why I went; and tell him I'm going to try and find Canada. You must give my love to him, and tell him, if I never see him again,' she turned away, and stood with her back to them for a moment, and then added, in a husky voice, 'tell him to be as good as he can, and try and meet me in the kingdom of heaven.'

'Call Bruno in there,' she added. 'Shut the door on him, poor beast! He mustn't go with me!'

A few last words and tears, a few simple adieus and blessings, and, clasping her wondering and affrighted child in her arms, she glided noiselessly away.

CHAPTER VI

Discovery

MR AND MRS SHELBY, after their protracted discussion of the night before, did not readily sink to repose, and, in consequence slept somewhat later than usual the ensuing morning.

'I wonder what keeps Eliza,' said Mrs Shelby, after giving her bell repeated pulls, to no purpose.

Mr Shelby was standing before his dressing-glass, sharpening his razor; and just then the door opened, and a coloured boy entered with his shaving-water.

'Andy,' said his mistress, 'step to Eliza's door, and tell her I have rung for her three times. Poor thing!' she added, to herself, with a sigh.

Andy soon returned, with eyes very wide in astonishment.

'Lor, missis! Lizzy's drawers is all open, and her things all lying every which way; and I believe she's just done clared out!'

The truth flashed upon Mr Shelby and his wife at the same moment. He exclaimed –

'Then she suspected it, and she's off!'

'The Lord be thanked!' said Mrs Shelby. 'I trust she is.'

'Wife, you talk like a fool! Really, it will be something pretty awkward for me if she is. Haley saw that I hesitated about selling this child, and he'll think I connived at it to get him out of the way. It touches my honour!' And Mr Shelby left the room hastily.

There was great running and ejaculating, and opening and shutting of doors, and appearance of faces in all shades of colour in different places for about a quarter of an hour. One person only, who might have shed some light on the matter, was entirely silent, and that was the head cook, Aunt Chloe. Silently, and with a heavy cloud settled down over her once joyous face, she proceeded making out her breakfast biscuits, as if she heard and saw nothing of the excitement around her.

Very soon about a dozen young imps were roosting, like so many crows, on the veranda railings, each one determined to be the first one to apprize the strange mas'r of his ill luck.

'He'll be rael mad, I'll be bound,' said Andy.

'*Won't* he swar!' said little black Jake.

'Yes, for he *does* swar,' said woolly-headed Mandy. 'I hearn him yesterday, at dinner. I hearn all about it then, 'cause I got into the closet where missis keeps the great jugs, and I hearn every word.' And Mandy, who had never in her life thought of the meaning of a word she had heard, more than a black cat, now took airs of superior wisdom, and strutted about, forgetting to state that, though actually coiled up among the jugs at the time specified, she had been fast asleep all the time.

When, at last Haley appeared, booted and spurred, he was saluted with the bad tidings on every hand. The young imps on the veranda were not disappointed in their hope of hearing him 'swar', which he did with a fluency and fervency which delighted them all amazingly, as they ducked and dodged hither and thither to be out of the reach of his riding-whip; and all whooping off together, they tumbled, in a pile of immeasurable giggle, on the withered turf under the veranda, where they kicked up their heels and shouted to their full satisfaction.

'If I had the little devils!' muttered Haley, between his teeth.

'But you ha'n't got 'em, though!' said Andy, with a triumphant flourish, and making a string of indescribable mouths at the unfortunate trader's back, when he was fairly beyond hearing.

'I say now, Shelby, this yer's a most extro'rnary business!' said Haley, as he abruptly entered the parlour. 'It seems that gal's off, with her young un.'

'Mr Haley, Mrs Shelby is present,' said Mr Shelby.

'I beg pardon, ma'am,' said Haley, bowing slightly, with a still lowering brow; 'but still I say, as I said before, this yer's a sing'lar report. Is it true, sir?'

'Sir,' said Mr Shelby, 'if you wish to communicate with me, you must observe something of the decorum of a gentleman. Andy, take Mr Haley's hat and riding-whip. Take a seat, sir. Yes, sir; I regret to say that the young woman, excited by overhearing, or having reported to her, something of this business, has taken her child in the night, and made off.'

'I did expect fair dealing in this matter, I confess,' said Haley.

'Well, sir,' said Mr Shelby, turning sharply round upon him, 'what am I to understand by that remark? If any man calls my honour in question, I have but one answer for him.'[44]

The trader cowered at this, and in a somewhat lower tone said that 'it was plaguy hard on a fellow, that had made a fair bargain, to be gulled that way'.

'Mr Haley,' said Mr Shelby, 'if I did not think you had some cause for disappointment, I should not have borne from you the rude and unceremonious style of your entrance into my parlour this morning. I say thus much, however, since appearances call for it, that I shall allow of no insinuations cast upon me, as if I were at all partner to any unfairness in this matter. Moreover, I shall feel bound to give you every assistance, in the use of horses, servants, &c., in the recovery of your property. So, in short, Haley,' said he, suddenly dropping from the tone of dignified coolness to his ordinary one of easy frankness, 'the best way for you is to keep good-natured and eat some breakfast; and we will then see what is to be done.'

Mrs Shelby now rose, and said her engagements would prevent her being at the breakfast-table that morning; and, deputing a very respectable mulatto woman to attend to the gentlemen's coffee at the sideboard, she left the room.

'Old lady don't like your humble servant, over and above,' said Haley, with an uneasy effort to be very familiar.

'I am not accustomed to hear my wife spoken of with such freedom,' said Mr Shelby, dryly.

'Beg pardon; of course, only a joke, you know,' said Haley, forcing a laugh.

'Some jokes are less agreeable than others,' rejoined Shelby.

'Devilish free, now I've signed those papers, cuss him!' muttered Haley to himself; 'quite grand, since yesterday!'

Never did fall of any prime minister at court occasion wider surges of sensation than the report of Tom's fate among his compeers on the place. It was the topic in every mouth, everywhere; and nothing was done in the house or in the field, but to discuss its probable results. Eliza's flight – an unprecedented event on the place – was also a great accessory in stimulating the general excitement.

Black Sam, as he was commonly called, from his being about three shades blacker than any other son of ebony on the place, was revolving the matter profoundly in all its phases and bearings, with a comprehensiveness of vision and a strict look-out to his own personal well-being, that would have done credit to any white patriot in Washington.

'It's an ill wind dat blows nowhar – dat ar a fact,'[45] said Sam, sententiously, giving an additional hoist to his pantaloons, and adroitly substituting a long nail in place of a missing suspender-button, with which effort of mechanical genius he seemed highly delighted.

'Yes, it's an ill wind blows nowhar,' he repeated. 'Now, dar, Tom's down – wal, course der's room for some nigger to be up; and why not dis nigger? – dat's de idee. Tom, a ridin' round de country – boots blacked – pass in his pocket – all grand as Cuffee;[46] who but he? Now, why shouldn't Sam? – dat's what I want to know.'

'Halloo, Sam – Oh, Sam! Mas'r wants you to cotch Bill and Jerry,' said Andy, cutting short Sam's soliloquy.

'High! what's afoot now, young un?'

'Why, you don't know, I s'pose, that Lizzy's cut stick,[47] and clared out, with her young un?'

'You teach your granny!' said Sam, with infinite contempt; 'knowed it a heap sight sooner than you did. This nigger an't so green, now!'

'Well, anyhow, mas'r wants Bill and Jerry geared right up; and you and I's to go with Mas'r Haley, to look arter her.'

'Good, now! dat's de time o' day!' said Sam. 'It's Sam dat's called for in dese yer times. He's de nigger. See if I don't cotch her, now; mas'r'll see what Sam can do!'

'Ah! but, Sam,' said Andy, 'you'd better think twice; for missis don't want her cotched, and she'll be in yer wool.'

'High!' said Sam, opening his eyes. 'How you know dat?'

'Heard her say so, my own self, dis blessed mornin', when I bring in mas'r's shaving-water. She sent me to see why Lizzy didn't come to dress her; and when I telled her she was off, she jest ris up, and ses she, "The Lord be praised!" And mas'r he seemed real mad, and ses he, "Wife, you talk like a fool!" But Lor! she'll bring him to! I knows well enough how that'll be – it's allers best to stand missis' side the fence, now, I tell yer.'

Black Sam upon this scratched his woolly pate, which, if it did not contain very profound wisdom, still contained a great deal of a particular species much in demand among politicians of all complexions and countries, and vulgarly denominated 'knowing which side the bread is buttered'; so, stopping with grave consideration, he again gave a hitch to his pantaloons, which was his regularly organised method of assisting his mental perplexities.

'Der an't no sayin' – never – 'bout no kind o' thing in *dis* yer world,' he said, at last.

Sam spoke like a philosopher, emphasising *this* – as if he had had a large experience in different sorts of worlds, and therefore had come to his conclusions advisedly.

'Now, sartin I'd a said that missis would a scoured the varsal world after Lizzy,' added Sam, thoughtfully.

'So she would,' said Andy; 'but can't ye see through a ladder, ye black nigger? Missis don't want dis yer Mas'r Haley to get Lizzy's boy; dat's de go!'

'High!' said Sam, with an indescribable intonation known only to those who have heard it among the negroes.

'And I'll tell you more 'n all,' said Andy; 'I 'spects you'd better be making tracks for dem hosses – mighty sudden, too – for I hearn missis 'quirin' arter yer, so you've stood foolin' long enough.'

Sam, upon this, began to bestir himself in real earnest, and after a while appeared, bearing down gloriously towards the house, with Bill and Jerry in a full canter, and adroitly throwing himself off before they had any idea of stopping, he brought them up alongside of the horse-post like a tornado. Haley's horse, which was a skittish young colt, winced and bounced, and pulled hard at his halter.

'Ho, ho!' said Sam, 'skeery, are ye?' and his black visage lighted up with a curious, mischievous gleam. 'I'll fix ye now!' said he.

There was a large beech tree overshadowing the place, and the small, sharp, triangular beech-nuts lay scattered thickly on the ground. With one of these in his fingers, Sam approached the colt, stroked and patted, and seemed apparently busy in soothing his agitation. On pretence of adjusting the saddle, he adroitly slipped under it the sharp little nut, in such a manner that the least weight brought upon the saddle would annoy the nervous sensibilities of the animal, without leaving any perceptible graze or wound.

'Dar!' he said, rolling his eyes with an approving grin; 'me fix 'em!'

At this moment Mrs Shelby appeared on the balcony, beckoning to him. Sam approached with as good a determination to pay court as did ever suitor after a vacant place at St James's or Washington.[48]

'Why have you been loitering so, Sam? I sent Andy to tell you to hurry.'

'Lord bless you, misses!' said Sam, 'horses won't be cotched all in a minnit; they'd done clared out way down to the south pasture, and the Lord knows whar!'

'Sam, how often must I tell you not to say "Lord bless you," and "the Lord knows," and such things? It's wicked.'

'O Lord bless my soul! I done forgot, misses! I won't say nothing of de sort no more.'

'Why, Sam, you just *have* said it again.'

'Did I? O, Lord! I mean – I didn't go fur to say it.'

'You must be *careful*, Sam.'

'Just let me get my breath, missis, and I'll start fair. I'll be berry careful.'

'Well, Sam, you are to go with Mr Haley, to show him the road, and help him. Be careful of the horses, Sam; you know Jerry was a little lame last week; *don't ride them too fast.*'

Mrs Shelby spoke the last words with a low voice, and strong emphasis.

'Let dis child alone for dat!' said Sam, rolling up his eyes with a volume of meaning. 'Lord knows! High! Didn't say dat!' said he, suddenly catching his breath, with a ludicrous flourish of apprehension, which made his mistress laugh, spite of herself. 'Yes, misses, I'll look out fur de hosses!'

'Now, Andy,' said Sam, returning to his stand under the beech trees, 'you see I wouldn't be 't all surprised if dat ar gen'lman's crittur should gib a fling, by and by, when he comes to be a gettin' up. You know, Andy, critturs *will* do such things;' and therewith Sam poked Andy in the side, in a highly suggestive manner.

'High!' said Andy, with an air of instant appreciation.

'Yes, you see, Andy, misses wants to make time – dat ar's clar to der most or'nary 'bserver. I jis make a little for her. Now, you see, get all dese yer hosses loose, caperin' permiscus round dis yer lot and down to de wood dar, and I 'spect mas'r won't be off in a hurry.'

Andy grinned.

'Yer see,' said Sam, 'yer see, Andy, if any such thing should happen as that Mas'r Haley's horse *should* begin to act contrary, and cut up, you and I jist lets go of our'n to help him, and *we'll help him* – oh yes!' And Sam and Andy laid their heads back on their shoulders, and broke into a low, immoderate laugh, snapping their fingers and flourishing their heels with exquisite delight.

At this instant, Haley appeared on the veranda. Somewhat mollified by certain cups of very good coffee, he came out smiling and talking, in tolerably restored humour. Sam and Andy, clawing for certain fragmentary palm-leaves, which they were in the habit of considering as hats, flew to the horse-posts, to be ready to 'help mas'r'.

Sam's palm-leaf had been ingeniously disentangled from all pretensions to braid, as respects its brim: and the slivers starting apart, and standing upright, gave it a blazing air of freedom and defiance, quite equal to that of any Fiji chief; while the whole brim of Andy's being departed bodily, he rapped the crown on his head with a dexterous thump, and looked about well pleased, as if to say, 'Who says I haven't got a hat?'

'Well, boys,' said Haley, 'look alive now; we must lose no time.'

'Not a bit of him, mas'r!' said Sam, putting Haley's rein in his hand, and holding his stirrup, while Andy was untying the other two horses.

The instant Haley touched the saddle, the mettlesome creature bounded from the earth with a sudden spring, that threw his master sprawling, some feet off, on the soft, dry turf. Sam, with frantic ejaculations, made a dive at the reins, but only succeeded in brushing the blazing palm-leaf afore-named into the horse's eyes, which by no means tended to allay the confusion of his nerves. So, with great vehemence, he overturned Sam, and, giving two or three contemptuous snorts, flourished his heels vigorously in the air, and was soon prancing away towards the lower end of the lawn, followed by Bill and Jerry, whom Andy had not failed to let loose, according to contract, speeding them off with various direful ejaculations. And now ensued a miscellaneous scene of confusion. Sam and Andy ran and shouted – dogs barked here and there – and Mike, Mose, Mandy, Fanny, and all the smaller specimens on the place, both male and female, raced, clapped hands, whooped, and shouted, with outrageous officiousness and untiring zeal.

Haley's horse, which was a white one, and very fleet and spirited, appeared to enter into the spirit of the scene with great gusto; and having for his coursing ground a lawn of nearly half a mile in extent, gently sloping down on every side into indefinite woodland, he appeared to take infinite delight in seeing how near he could allow his pursuers to approach him, and then, when within a hand's breadth, whisk off with a start and a snort, like a mischievous beast as he was, and career far down into some alley of the wood-lot. Nothing was further from Sam's mind than to have any one of the troop taken until such season as should seem to him most befitting – and the exertions that he made were certainly most heroic. Like the sword of Coeur De Lion,[49] which always blazed in the front and thickest of the battle, Sam's palm-leaf was to be seen everywhere when there was the least danger that a horse could be caught; there he would bear down full tilt, shouting, 'Now for it! cotch him! cotch him!' in a way that would set everything to indiscriminate rout in a moment.

Haley ran up and down, and cursed and swore and stamped miscellaneously. Mr Shelby in vain tried to shout directions from the balcony, and Mrs Shelby from her chamber window alternately laughed and wondered – not without some inkling of what lay at the bottom of all this confusion.

At last, about twelve o'clock, Sam appeared triumphant, mounted on Jerry, with Haley's horse by his side, reeking with sweat, but with flashing eyes and dilated nostrils, showing that the spirit of freedom had not yet entirely subsided.

'He's cotched!' he exclaimed, triumphantly. 'If it hadn't been for me, they might a bust theirselves, all on 'em; but I cotched him!'

'You!' growled Haley, in no amiable mood. 'If it hadn't been for you, this never would have happened.'

'Lord bless us, mas'r,' said Sam, in a tone of the deepest concern, 'and me that has been racin' and chasin' till the sweat jest pours off me!'

'Well, well!' said Haley, 'you've lost me near three hours, with your cursed nonsense. Now let's be off, and have no more fooling.'

'Why, mas'r,' said Sam, in a deprecating tone, 'I believe you mean to kill us all clar, horses and all. Here we are all just ready to drop down, and the critters all in a reek of sweat. Why, mas'r won't think of startin' on now till arter dinner. Mas'r's hoss wants rubben down; see how he splashed hisself; and Jerry limps too; don't think missis would be willin' to have us start dis yer way, no how. Lord bless you, mas'r, we can ketch up, if we do stop. Lizzy never was no great things of a walker.'

Mrs Shelby, who, greatly to her amusement, had overheard this conversation from the veranda, now resolved to do her part. She came forward, and, courteously expressing her concern for Haley's accident, pressed him to stay to dinner, saying that the cook should bring it on the table immediately.

Thus, all things considered, Haley, with rather an equivocal grace, proceeded to the parlour, while Sam, rolling his eyes after him with unutterable meaning, proceeded gravely with the horses to the stable-yard.

'Did yer see him, Andy? – *did* yer see him?' said Sam, when he had got fairly beyond the shelter of the barn, and fastened the horse to a post. 'O Lor, if it warn't as good as a meetin' now to see him a dancin' and kickin' and swarin' at us. Didn't I hear him? Swar away, old fellow (says I to myself); will yer have yer hoss now, or wait till you cotch him? (says I). Lor, Andy, I think I can see him now.' And Sam and Andy leaned up against the barn, and laughed to their hearts' content.

'Yer oughter seen how mad he looked, when I brought the hoss up. Lord, he'd a killed me, if he durs' to; and there I was a standin' as innercent and as humble.'

'Lor, I seed you,' said Andy; 'an't you an old hoss, Sam?'

'Rather 'spects I am,' said Sam; 'did yer see misses upstars at the winder? I seed her laughin'.'

'I'm sure, I was racin' so, I didn't see nothing,' said Andy.

'Well, yer see,' said Sam, proceeding gravely to wash down Haley's pony. 'I'se 'quired what yer may call a habit o' *bobservation*, Andy. It's a very 'portant habit, Andy; and I 'commend yer to be cultivatin' it, now yer young. Hist up that hind foot, Andy. Yer see, Andy it's *bobservation* makes all de difference in niggers. Didn't I see which way the wind blew dis yer mornin'? Didn't I see what misses wanted, though she never let on? Dat ar's bobservation, Andy. I 'spects it's what you may call a faculty. Faculties is different in different peoples, but cultivation of 'em goes a great way.'

'I guess if I hadn't helped your bobservation dis mornin' yer wouldn't have seen your way so smart,' said Andy.

'Andy,' said Sam, 'you's a promisin' child, der an't no manner o' doubt. I thinks lots of yer, Andy; and I don't feel noways ashamed to take idees from you. We oughtenter overlook nobody, Andy, 'cause the smartest on us gets tripped up sometimes. And so, Andy, let's go up to the house now. I'll be boun' missis'll give us an uncommon good bite dis yer time.'

CHAPTER VII

The Mother's Struggle

IT IS IMPOSSIBLE to conceive of a human creature more wholly desolate and forlorn than Eliza when she turned her footsteps from Uncle Tom's cabin.

Her husband's suffering and dangers, and the danger of her child, all blended in her mind, with a confused and stunning sense of the risk she was running, in leaving the only home she had ever known, and cutting loose from the protection of a friend she ever loved and revered. Then there was the parting from every familiar object – the place where she had grown up, the trees under which she had played, the groves where she had walked many an evening in happier days, by the side of her young husband – everything, as it lay in the clear, frosty starlight, seemed to speak reproachfully to her, and ask her whither could she go from a home like that?

But stronger than all was maternal love, wrought into a paroxysm of frenzy by the near approach of a fearful danger. Her boy was old enough to have walked by her side, and, in an indifferent case, she would only have led him by the hand; but now the bare thought of putting him out of her arms made her shudder, and she strained him to her bosom with a convulsive grasp, as she went rapidly forward.

The frosty ground creaked beneath her feet, and she trembled at the sound; every quaking leaf and fluttering shadow sent the blood backward to her heart, and quickened her footsteps. She wondered within herself at the strength that seemed to be come upon her; for she felt the weight of her boy as if it had been a feather, and every flutter of fear seemed to increase the supernatural power that bore her on, while from her pale lips burst forth, in frequent ejaculations, the prayer to a Friend above, 'Lord, help; Lord, save me!'

If it were *your* Harry, mother, or your Willie, that was going to be torn from you by a brutal trader, tomorrow morning – if you had seen the man, and heard that the papers were signed and delivered, and you had only from twelve o'clock till morning to make good your escape – how fast could *you* walk? How many miles could you make in those few brief hours, with the darling at your bosom – the little sleepy head on your shoulder – the small, soft arms trustingly holding on to your neck?

For the child slept. At first, the novelty and alarm kept him waking; but his mother so hurriedly repressed every breath or sound, and so assured him that if he were only still she would certainly save him, that he clung quietly round her neck, only asking, as he found himself sinking to sleep:

'Mother, I don't need to keep awake, do I?'

'No, my darling; sleep, if you want to.'

'But, mother, if I do get asleep, you won't let him get me?'

'No! so may God help me!' said his mother, with a paler cheek, and a brighter light in her large dark eyes.

'You're *sure*, an't you, mother?'

'Yes, *sure*!' said the mother, in a voice that startled herself; for it seemed to her to come from a spirit within, that was no part of her; and the boy dropped his little weary head on her shoulder, and was soon asleep. How the touch of those warm arms, the gentle breathings that came in her neck, seemed to add fire and spirit to her movements! It seemed to her as if strength poured into her in electric streams, from every gentle touch and movement of the sleeping, confiding child. Sublime is the dominion of the mind over the body, that, for a time, can make flesh and nerve impregnable, and string the sinews like steel, so that the weak become so mighty.

The boundaries of the farm, the grove, the wood-lot, passed by her dizzily, as she walked on; and still she went, leaving one familiar object after another, slacking not, pausing not, till reddening daylight found her many a long mile from all traces of any familiar objects upon the open highway.

She had often been, with her mistress, to visit some connections, in the little village of T—, not far from the Ohio river, and knew the road well. To go thither, to escape across the Ohio river, were the first hurried outlines of her plan of escape; beyond that she could only hope in God.

When horses and vehicles began to move along the highway, with that alert perception peculiar to a state of excitement, and which seems to be a sort of inspiration, she became aware that her headlong pace and distracted air might bring on her remark and suspicion. She therefore put the boy on the ground, and, adjusting her dress and bonnet, she walked on at as rapid a pace as she thought consistent with the preservation of appearances. In her little bundle she had provided a store of cakes and apples, which she used as expedients for quickening the speed of the child, rolling the apple some yards before them, when the boy would run with all his might after it; and this ruse, often repeated, carried them over many a half-mile.

After a while, they came to a thick patch of woodland, through which murmured a clear brook. As the child complained of hunger and thirst, she climbed over the fence with him; and sitting down behind a large rock which concealed them from the road, she gave him a breakfast out of her little package. The boy wondered and grieved that she could not eat; and when, putting his arms round her neck, he tried to wedge some of his cake into her mouth, it seemed to her that the rising in her throat would choke her.

'No, no, Harry darling! mother can't eat till you are safe! We must go on – on – till we come to the river!' And she hurried again into the road, and again constrained herself to walk regularly and composedly forward.

She was many miles past any neighbourhood where she was personally known. If she should chance to meet any who knew her, she reflected that the well-known kindness of the family would be of itself a blind to suspicion, as making it an unlikely supposition that she could be a fugitive. As she was also so white as not to be known as of coloured lineage without a critical survey, and her child was white also, it was much easier for her to pass on unsuspected.

On this presumption, she stopped at noon at a neat farmhouse, to rest herself, and buy some dinner for her child and self; for, as the danger decreased with the distance, the supernatural tension of the nervous system lessened, and she found herself both weary and hungry.

The good woman, kindly and gossiping, seemed rather pleased than otherwise with having somebody come in to talk with; and accepted without examination, Eliza's statement, that she 'was going on a little piece, to spend a week with her friends' – all which she hoped in her heart might prove strictly true.

An hour before sunset, she entered the village of T—, by the Ohio river, weary and footsore, but still strong in heart. Her first glance was at the river, which lay like Jordan between her and the Canaan of liberty on the other side.

It was now early spring, and the river was swollen and turbulent; great cakes of floating ice were swinging heavily to and fro in the turbid waters. Owing to the peculiar form of the shore on the Kentucky side, the land bending far out into the water, the ice had been lodged and detained in great quantities, and the narrow channel which swept round the bend was full of ice, piled one cake over another, thus forming a temporary barrier to the descending ice, which lodged, and formed a great undulating raft, filling up the whole river, and extending almost to the Kentucky shore.

Eliza stood for a moment, contemplating this unfavourable aspect of things, which she saw at once must prevent the usual ferry-boat from running, and then turned into a small public house on the bank, to make a few enquiries.

The hostess, who was busy in various fizzing and stewing operations, over the fire, preparatory to the evening meal, stopped, with a fork in her hand, as Eliza's sweet and plaintive voice arrested her.

'What is it?' she said.

'Isn't there any ferry or boat, that takes people over to B—y, now?' she said.

'No, indeed!' said the woman; 'the boats has stopped running.'

Eliza's look of dismay and disappointment struck the woman, and she said, enquiringly –

'Maybe you're wanting to get over? – anybody sick? Ye seem mighty anxious?'

'I've got a child that's very dangerous,' said Eliza. 'I never heard of it till last night, and I've walked quite a piece today, in hopes to get to the ferry.'

'Well, now, that's onlucky,' said the woman, whose motherly sympathies were much aroused; 'I'm re'lly consarned for ye. Solomon!' she called from the window, towards a small back building. A man in leather apron and very dirty hands, appeared at the door.

'I say, Sol,' said the woman, 'is that ar man going to tote them bar'ls over tonight?'

'He said he should try, if 'twas any way prudent,' said the man.

'There's a man a piece down here that's going over with some truck this evening, if he durs' to; he'll be in here to supper tonight, so you'd better set down and wait. That's a sweet little fellow,' added the woman, offering him a cake.

But the child, wholly exhausted, cried with weariness.

'Poor fellow! he isn't used to walking, and I've hurried him on so,' said Eliza.

'Well, take him into this room,' said the woman, opening into a small bedroom, where stood a comfortable bed. Eliza laid the weary boy upon it, and held his hands in hers till he was fast asleep. For her there was no rest. As a fire in her bones, the thought of the pursuer urged her on; and she gazed with longing eyes on the sullen, surging waters that lay between her and liberty.

Here we must take our leave of her for the present, to follow the course of her pursuers.

Though Mrs Shelby had promised that the dinner should be hurried on table, yet it was soon seen, as the thing has often been seen before, that it required more than one to make a bargain. So, although the order was fairly given out in Haley's hearing, and carried to Aunt Chloe by at least half a dozen juvenile messengers, that dignitary only gave certain very gruff snorts, and tosses of her head, and went on with every operation in an unusually leisurely and circumstantial manner.

For some singular reason, an impression seemed to reign among the servants generally that missis would not be particularly disobliged by delay; and it was wonderful what a number of counter-accidents occurred constantly to retard the course of things. One luckless wight contrived to upset the gravy; and then gravy had to be got up *de novo*[50] with due care and formality, Aunt Chloe watching and stirring with dogged precision, answering shortly to all suggestions of haste, that she 'warn't a going to have raw gravy on the table, to help nobody's catchings'. One tumbled down with the water, and had to go to the spring for more; and another precipitated the butter into the path of events; and there was, from time to time, giggling news brought into the kitchen that 'Mas'r Haley was mighty oneasy, and that he couldn't sit in his cheer noways, but was a walkin' and stalkin' to the winders and through the porch.'

'Sarves him right!' said Aunt Chloe, indignantly. 'He'll get wus nor oneasy, one of these days, if he don't mend his ways. *His* Master'll be sending for him, and then see how he'll look!'

'He'll go to torment, and no mistake,' said little Jake.

'He deserves it!' said Aunt Chloe, grimly; 'he's broke a many, many, many hearts, I tell ye all!' she said, stopping, with a fork uplifted in her hands; 'it's like what Mas'r George reads in Ravelations – souls a callin' under the altar![51] and a callin' on the Lord for vengeance on sich! – and by and by the Lord He'll hear 'em – so He will!'

Aunt Chloe, who was much revered in the kitchen, was listened to with open mouth; and, the dinner being now fairly sent in, the whole kitchen was at leisure to gossip with her, and to listen to her remarks.

'Sich'll be burnt up forever, and no mistake; won't ther?' said Andy.

'I'd be glad to see it, I'll be boun',' said little Jake.

'Chil'en!' said a voice, that made them all start. It was Uncle Tom, who had come in and stood listening to the conversation at the door.

'Chil'en!' he said, 'I'm afeard you don't know what ye're sayin'. Forever is a *dre'ful* word, chil'en; it's awful to think on 't. You oughtenter wish that ar to any human crittur.'

'We wouldn't to anybody but the soul-drivers,' said Andy; 'nobody can help wishing it to them, they's so awful wicked.'

'Don't natur herself kinder cry out on em?' said Aunt Chloe. 'Don't dey tear der sucking baby right off his mother's breast, and sell him? And der little children as is crying and holding on by her clothes, don't dey pull 'em off and sells 'em? Don't dey tear wife and husband apart?' said Aunt Chloe, beginning to cry, 'when it's jest takin' the very life on 'em? – and all the while does they feel one bit? don't dey drink, and smoke, and take it oncommon easy? Lor, if the devil don't get them, what's he good for?' And Aunt Chloe covered her face with her checked apron, and began to sob in good earnest.

'Pray for them that 'spitefully use you, the good book says,' says Tom.

'Pray for 'em!' said Aunt Chloe; 'Lor, it's too tough! I can't pray for 'em.'

'It's natur, Chloe, and natur's strong,' said Tom, 'but the Lord's grace is stronger. Besides, you oughter think what an awful state a poor crittur's soul's in that'll do them ar things – you oughter thank God that you an't *like* him, Chloe. I'm sure I'd rather be sold ten thousand times over, than to have all that ar poor crittur's got to answer for.'

'So'd I, a heap,' said Jake. 'Lor, *shouldn't* we cotch it, Andy?'

Andy shrugged his shoulders, and gave an acquiescent whistle.

'I'm glad mas'r didn't go off this morning, as he looked to,' said Tom; 'that ar hurt me more than sellin', it did. Mebbe it might have been natural for him, but 'twould have come desp't hard on me, as has known him from a baby; but I've seen mas'r, and I begin to feel sort o' reconciled to the Lord's will now. Mas'r couldn't help hisself; he did right, but I'm feared things will be kinder goin' to rack when I'm gone. Mas'r can't be 'spected to be a pryin' round everywhar, as I've done, a keepin' up all the ends. The boys all means well, but they's powerful car'less. That ar troubles me.'

The bell here rang, and Tom was summoned to the parlour.

'Tom,' said his master, kindly, 'I want you to notice that I give this gentleman bonds to forfeit a thousand dollars if you are not on the spot when he wants you; he's going today to look after his other business and you can have the day to yourself. Go anywhere you like boy.'

'Thank you, mas'r,' said Tom.

'And mind yerself,' said the trader, 'and don't come it over your master with any o' yer nigger tricks; for I'll take every cent out of him, if you an't thar. If he'd hear to me, he wouldn't trust any on ye – slippery as eels!'

'Mas'r,' said Tom – and he stood very straight – 'I was jist eight years old when ole missis put you into my arms, and you wasn't a year old. "Thar," says she, "Tom, that's to be *your* young mas'r; take good care on him," says she. And now I jist ask you, mas'r, have I ever broke word to you, or gone contrary to you, 'specially since I was a Christian?'

Mr Shelby was fairly overcome, and the tears rose to his eyes.

'My good boy,' said he, 'the Lord knows you say but the truth; and if I was able to help it, all the world shouldn't buy you.'

'And sure as I am a Christian woman,' said Mrs Shelby, 'you shall be redeemed as soon as I can any way bring together means. Sir,' she said to Haley, 'take good account of who you sell him to, and let me know.'

'Lor, yes, for that matter,' said the trader, 'I may bring him up in a year, not much the wuss for wear, and trade him back.'

'I'll trade with you then, and make it for your advantage,' said Mrs Shelby.

'Of course,' said the trader, 'all's equal with me; li'ves trade 'em up as down, so I does a good business. All I want is a livin', you know, ma'am; that's all any on us wants, I s'pose.'

Mr and Mrs Shelby both felt annoyed and degraded by the familiar impudence of the trader, and yet both saw the absolute necessity of putting a constraint on their feelings. The more hopelessly sordid and insensible he appeared, the greater became Mrs Shelby's dread of his succeeding in recapturing Eliza and her child, and of course the greater her motive for detaining him by every female artifice. She, therefore graciously smiled, assented, chatted familiarly, and did all she could to make time pass imperceptibly.

At two o'clock Sam and Andy brought the horses up to the posts, apparently greatly refreshed and invigorated by the scamper of the morning.

Sam was there new oiled from dinner, with an abundance of zealous and ready officiousness. As Haley approached, he was boasting, in flourishing style, to Andy, of the evident and eminent success of the operation, now that he had 'farly come to it'.

'Your master, I s'pose, don't keep no dogs,' said Haley, thoughtfully, as he prepared to mount.

'Heaps on 'em,' said Sam, triumphantly; 'thar's Bruno – he's a roarer! and, besides that, 'bout every nigger of us keeps a pup of some natur' or uther.'

'Poh!' said Haley – and he said something else, too, with regard to the said dogs, at which Sam muttered –

'I don't see no use cussin' on 'em, noway.'

'But your master don't keep no dogs (I pretty much know he don't) for trackin' out niggers.'

Sam knew exactly what he meant, but he kept on a look of earnest and desperate simplicity.

'Our dogs all smells round considerable sharp. I 'spect they's the kind, though they han't never had no practice. They's *far* dogs, though, at most anything, if you'd get 'em started. Here, Bruno,' he called, whistling to the lumbering Newfoundland, who came pitching tumultuously toward them.

'You go hang!' said Haley, getting up. 'Come, tumble up, now.'

Sam tumbled up accordingly, dexterously contriving to tickle Andy as he did so, which occasioned Andy to split out into a laugh, greatly to Haley's indignation, who made a cut at him with his riding-whip.

'I's 'stonished at yer, Andy,' said Sam, with awful gravity. 'This yer's a seris business, Andy. Yer mustn't be a makin' game. This yer an't no way to help mas'r.'

'I shall take the straight road to the river,' said Haley, decidedly, after they had come to the boundaries of the estate. 'I know the way of all of 'em – they makes tracks for the underground.'

'Sartin,' said Sam, 'dat's de idee. Mas'r Haley hits de thing right in de middle. Now, der's two roads to de river – de dirt road and der pike – which mas'r mean to take?'

Andy looked up innocently at Sam, surprised at hearing this new geographical fact, but instantly confirmed what he said by a vehement reiteration.

' 'Cause,' said Sam, 'I'd rather be 'clined to 'magine that Lizzy'd take de dirt road, bein' it's the least travelled.'

Haley, notwithstanding that he was a very old bird, and naturally inclined to be suspicious of chaff, was rather brought up by this view of the case.

'If yer warn't both on yer such cussed liars, now!' said he, contemplatively, as he pondered a moment.

The pensive, reflective tone in which this was spoken appeared to amuse Andy prodigiously, and he drew a little behind, and shook so as apparently to run a great risk of falling off his horse, while Sam's face was immovably composed into the most doleful gravity.

'Course,' said Sam, 'mas'r can do as he'd ruther; go de straight road, if mas'r thinks best – it's all one to us. Now, when I study 'pon it, I think de straight road de best *deridedly*.'

'She would naturally go a lonesome way,' said Haley, thinking aloud, and not minding Sam's remark.

'Dar an't no sayin',' said Sam; 'gals is pecular. They never does nothin' ye thinks they will; mose gen'lly the contrar. Gals is nat'lly made contrar; and so, if you thinks they've gone one road, it is sartin you'd better go t'other, and then you'll be sure to find 'em. Now, my private 'pinion is, Lizzy took der dirt road; so I think we'd better take de straight one.'

This profound generic view of the female sex did not seem to dispose Haley particularly to the straight road; and he announced decidedly that he should go the other, and asked Sam when they should come to it.

'A little piece ahead,' said Sam, giving a wink to Andy with the eye which was on Andy's side of the head; and he added gravely, 'but I've studded on de matter, and I'm quite clar we ought not to go dat ar way. I nebber been over it no way. It's despit lonesome, and we might lose our way – whar we'd come to, de Lord only knows.'

'Nevertheless,' said Haley, 'I shall go that way.'

'Now I think on't, I think I hearn 'em tell that dat ar road was all fenced up and down by der creek, and thar; an't it, Andy?'

Andy wasn't certain; he'd only 'hearn tell' about that road, but never been over it. In short, he was strictly non-committal.

Haley, accustomed to strike the balance of probabilities between lies of greater or lesser magnitude, thought that it lay in favour of the dirt road aforesaid. The mention of the thing he thought he perceived was involuntary on Sam's part at first; and his confused attempts to dissuade him he set down to a desperate lying on second thoughts, as being unwilling to implicate Eliza.

When, therefore, Sam indicated the road, Haley plunged briskly into it, followed by Sam and Andy.

Now the road, in fact, was an old one, that had formerly been a thoroughfare to the river, but abandoned for many years after the laying of the new pike. It was open for about an hour's ride, and after that it was cut across by various farms and fences. Sam knew this fact perfectly well; indeed, the road had been so long closed up that Andy had never heard of it. He therefore rode along with an air of dutiful submission, only groaning and vociferating occasionally that ' 'twas desp't rough, and bad for Jerry's foot'.

'Now, I jest give yer warning,' said Haley, 'I know yer; yer won't get me to turn off this yer road, with all yer fussin' – so you shet up!'

'Mas'r will go his own way!' said Sam, with rueful submission, at the same time winking most portentously to Andy, whose delight was now very near the explosive point.

Sam was in wonderful spirits; professed to keep a very brisk look-out – at one time exclaiming that he saw 'a gal's bonnet' on the top of some distant eminence, or calling to Andy 'if that thar wasn't Lizzy down in the hollow' – always making these exclamations in some rough or craggy part of the road, where the sudden quickening of speed was a special inconvenience to all parties concerned, and thus keeping Haley in a state of constant commotion.

After riding about an hour in this way, the whole party made a precipitate and tumultuous descent into a barnyard belonging to a large farming establishment. Not a soul was in sight, all the hands being employed in the fields; but, as the barn stood conspicuously and plainly square across the road, it was evident that their journey in that direction had reached a decided finale.

'Wa'n't dat ar what I telled mas'r?' said Sam, with an air of injured innocence. 'How does strange gentleman 'spect to know more about a country dan de natives born and raised?'

'You rascal!' said Haley, 'you knew all about this.'

'Didn't I tell yer I know'd, and yer wouldn't believe me? I telled mas'r 'twas all shet up, and fenced up, and I didn't 'spect we could get through – Andy heard me.'

It was all too true to be disputed, and the unlucky man had to pocket his wrath with the best grace he was able, and all three faced to the right about, and took up their line of march for the highway.

In consequence of all the various delays, it was about three quarters of an hour after Eliza had laid her child to sleep in the village tavern that the party came riding into the same place. Eliza was standing by the window, looking out in another direction, when Sam's quick eye caught a glimpse of her. Haley and Andy were two yards behind. At this crisis, Sam contrived to have his hat blown off, and uttered a loud and characteristic ejaculation, which startled her at once: she drew suddenly back; the whole train swept by the window, round to the front door.

A thousand lives seemed to be concentrated in that one moment to Eliza. Her room opened by a side-door to the river. She caught her child, and sprang down the steps towards it. The trader caught a full glimpse of her, just as she was disappearing down the bank; and throwing himself from his horse, and calling loudly on Sam and Andy, he was after her like a hound after a deer. In that dizzy moment, her feet to her scarce seemed to touch the ground, and a moment brought her to the water's edge. Right on behind they came; and, nerved with strength such as God gives only to the desperate, with one wild cry and flying leap she vaulted sheer over the turbid current by the shore, on to the raft of ice beyond. It was a desperate leap – impossible to anything but madness and despair; and Haley, Sam, and Andy, instinctively cried out, and lifted up their hands, as she did it.

The huge green fragment of ice on which she alighted pitched and creaked as her weight came on it, but she stayed there not a moment. With wild cries and desperate energy she leaped to another and still another cake; stumbling – leaping – slipping – springing upwards again! Her shoes are gone – her stockings cut from her feet while blood marked every step; but she saw nothing, felt nothing, till dimly, as in a dream, she saw the Ohio side, and a man helping her up the bank.

'Yer a brave gal, now, whoever ye ar!' said the man, with an oath.

Eliza recognised the voice and face of a man who owned a farm not far from her old home.

'Oh, Mr Symmes! – save me – do save me – do hide me!' said Eliza.

'Why, what's this?' said the man. 'Why, if 'tan't Shelby's gal!'

'My child! – this boy – he'd sold him! There is his mas'r,' said she, pointing to the Kentucky shore. 'Oh, Mr Symmes, you've got a little boy!'

'So I have,' said the man, as he roughly, but kindly, drew her up the steep bank. 'Besides, you're a right brave gal. I like grit wherever I see it.'

When they had gained the top of the bank, the man paused.

'I'd be glad to do something for ye,' said he; 'but then there's nowhar I could take ye. The best I can do is to tell ye to go *thar*,' said he, pointing to a large white house which stood by itself, off the main street of the village. 'Go thar; they're kind folks. Thar's no kind o' danger, but they'll help you – they're up to all that sort o' thing.'

'The Lord bless you!' said Eliza, earnestly.

'No 'casion, no 'casion in the world,' said the man. 'What I've done's of no 'count.'

'And, oh, surely sir, you won't tell anyone!'

'Go to thunder, gal! What do you take a feller for? In course not,' said the man. 'Come, now, go along like a likely, sensible gal, as you are. You've arnt your liberty, and you shall have it, for all me.'

The woman folded her child to her bosom, and walked firmly and swiftly away. The man stood and looked after her.

'Shelby, now, mebbe won't think this yer the most neighbourly thing in the world; but what's a fellow to do? If he catches one of my gals in the same fix, he's welcome to pay back. Somehow I never could see no kind o' critter a strivin' and pantin', and tryin' to clar theirselves, with the dogs arter 'em, and go agin 'em. Besides, I don't see no kind of 'casion for me to be hunter and catcher for other folks, neither.'

So spoke this poor, heathenish Kentuckian, who had not been instructed in his constitutional relations,[52] and consequently, was betrayed into acting in a sort of Christianised manner, which, if he had been better situated and more enlightened, he would not have been left to do.

Haley had stood a perfectly amazed spectator of the scene, till Eliza had disappeared up the bank, when he turned a blank, enquiring look on Sam and Andy.

'That ar was a tolerable fair stroke of business,' said Sam.

'The gal's got seven devils in her, I believe!' said Haley. 'How like a wildcat she jumped!'

'Wal, now,' said Sam, scratching his head, 'I hope mas'r'll 'scuse us tryin' dat ar road. Don't think I feel spry enough for dat ar, no way!' and Sam gave a hoarse chuckle.

'*You* laugh!' said the trader, with a growl.

'Lord bless you, mas'r, I couldn't help it, now,' said Sam, giving way to the long pent-up delight of his soul. 'She looked so curis, a-leapin' and springin', ice a-crackin', and only to hear her – plump! ker chunk! ker splash! Spring! Lord! how she goes it!' And Sam and Andy laughed till the tears rolled down their cheeks.

'I'll make ye laugh t' other side yer mouths!' said the trader, laying about their heads with his riding-whip.

Both ducked, and ran shouting up the bank, and were on their horses before he was up.

'Good-evening, mas'r!' said Sam, with much gravity. 'I berry much 'spect missis be anxious 'bout Jerry. Mas'r Haley won't want us no longer. Missis wouldn't hear of our ridin' the critters over Lizzy's bridge tonight;' and, with a facetious poke into Andy's ribs, he started off, followed by the latter, at full speed, their shouts of laughter coming faintly on the wind.

CHAPTER VIII

Eliza's Escape

ELIZA MADE HER DESPERATE RETREAT across the river just in the dusk of twilight. The grey mist of evening, rising slowly from the river, enveloped her as she disappeared up the bank, and the swollen current and floundering masses of ice presented a hopeless barrier between her and her pursuer. Haley, therefore, slowly and discontentedly returned to the little tavern, to ponder further what was to be done. The woman opened to him the door of a little parlour, covered with a rag carpet, where stood a table with a very shining black oil-cloth, sundry lank, high-backed wood chairs, with some plaster images in resplendent colours on the mantel-shelf, above a very dimly-smoking grate; a long hard-wood settle extended its uneasy length by the chimney, and here Haley sat him down to meditate on the instability of human hopes and happiness in general.

'What did I want with the little cuss, now,' he said to himself, 'that I should have got myself treed like a 'coon, as I am, this yer way?' And Haley relieved himself by repeating over a not very select litany of imprecations on himself, which, though there was the best possible reason to consider them as true, we shall, as a matter of taste, omit.

He was startled by the loud and dissonant voice of a man who was apparently dismounting at the door. He hurried to the window.

'By the land! if this yer an't the nearest, now, to what I've heard folks call Providence,' said Haley. 'I do b'lieve that ar's Tom Loker.'

Haley hastened out. Standing by the bar, in the corner of the room, was a brawny, muscular man, full six feet in height, and broad in proportion. He was dressed in a coat of buffalo-skin, made with the hair outward, which gave him a shaggy and fierce appearance, perfectly in keeping with the whole air of his physiognomy. In the head and face, every organ and lineament expressive of brutal and unhesitating violence was in a state of the highest possible development. Indeed, could our readers fancy a bulldog come unto man's estate, and walking about in a hat and coat, they would have no unapt idea of the general style and effect of his physique. He was accompanied by a travelling companion, in many respects an exact contrast to himself. He was short and slender, lithe and cat-like in his motions, and had a peering, mousing expression about his keen black eyes, with which every feature of his face seemed sharpened into sympathy; his thin, long nose, ran out as if it was eager to bore into the nature of things in general; his sleek, thin black hair, was stuck eagerly forward, and all his motions and evolutions expressed a dry, cautious acuteness. The great big man poured out a big tumbler half full of raw spirits, and gulped it down without a word. The little man stood tiptoe, and putting his head first to one side and then to the other, and snuffing considerately in the directions of the various bottles, ordered at last a mint julep, in a thin and quivering voice, and with an air of great circumspection. When poured out, he took it and looked at it with a sharp, complacent air, like a man who thinks he has done about the right thing, and hit the nail on the head, and proceeded to dispose of it in short and well-advised sips.

'Wal, now, who'd a thought this yer luck 'ad come to me? Why, Loker, how are ye?' said Haley, coming forward, and extending his hand to the big man.

'The devil!' was the civil reply. 'What brought you here, Haley?'

The mousing man, who bore the name of Marks, instantly stopped his sipping, and, poking his head forward, looked shrewdly on the new acquaintance, as a cat sometimes looks at a moving dry leaf, or some other possible object of pursuit.

'I say, Tom, this yer's the luckiest thing in the world. I'm in a devil of a hobble, and you must help me out.'

'Ugh? aw! like enough!' grunted his complaisant acquaintance. 'A body may be pretty sure of that, when *you're* glad to see 'em; something to be made off of 'em. What's the blow now?'

'You've got a friend here?' said Haley, looking doubtfully at Marks; 'partner, perhaps?'

'Yes, I have. Here, Marks! here's that ar feller that I was in with in Natchez.'

'Shall be pleased with his acquaintance,' said Marks, thrusting out a long thin hand, like a raven's claw. 'Mr Haley, I believe?'

'The same, sir,' said Haley. 'And now, gentlemen, seein' as we've met so happily, I think I'll stand up to a small matter of a treat in this here parlour. So, now, old 'coon,' said he to the man at the bar, 'get us hot water, and sugar, and cigars, and plenty of the *real stuff*, and we'll have a blow-out.'

Behold, then, the candles lighted, the fire stimulated to the burning-point in the grate, and our three worthies seated round a table, well spread with all the accessories to good-fellowship enumerated before.

Haley began a pathetic recital of his peculiar troubles. Loker shut up his mouth, and listened to him with gruff and surly attention. Marks, who was anxiously and with much fidgeting, compounding a tumbler of punch to his own peculiar taste, occasionally looked up from his employment, and, poking his sharp nose and chin almost into Haley's face, gave the most earnest heed to the whole narrative. The conclusion of it appeared to amuse him extremely, for he shook his shoulders and sides in silence, and perked up his thin lips with an air of great internal enjoyment.

'So, then, ye'r fairly sewed up, an't ye?' he said; 'he! he! he! It's neatly done, too.'

'This yer young-un business makes lots of trouble in the trade,' said Haley, dolefully.

'If we could get a breed of gals that didn't care, now, for their young uns,' said Marks; 'tell ye, I think 'twould be 'bout the greatest mod'rn improvement I knows on;' and Marks patronised his joke by a quiet introductory sniggle.

'Jest so,' said Haley; 'I never couldn't see into it. Young uns is heaps of trouble to 'em – one would think, now, they'd be glad to get clar on 'em; but they arn't. And the more trouble a young un is, and the more good for nothing, as a gen'l thing, the tighter they sticks to 'em.'

'Wal, Mr Haley,' said Marks, 'jest pass the hot water. Yes, sir; you say jest what I feel and all'us have. Now, I bought a gal once when I was in the trade, a tight, likely wench she was, too, and quite considerable smart – and she had a young un that was mis'able sickly; it had a crooked back, or something or other; and I jest gin't away to a man that thought he'd take his chance raisin' on't, being it didn't cost nothin' – never thought, yer know, of the gal's takin' on about it – but, Lord, yer oughter see how she went on! Why, re'lly, she did seem to me to valley the child more 'cause 'twas sickly and cross, and plagued her; and she warn't making b'lieve, neither – cried about it, she did, and lopped round, as if she'd lost every friend she had. It re'lly was droll to think on't. Lord, there an't no end to women's notions.'

'Wal, jest so with me,' said Haley. 'Last summer, down on Red River, I got a gal traded off on me with a likely lookin' child enough, and his eyes looked as bright as yourn; but, come to look, I found him stone-blind. Fact – he was stone-blind. Wal, ye see, I thought there warn't no harm in my jest passing him along, and not sayin' nothin'; and I'd got him nicely swapped off for a keg of whiskey; but come to get him away from the gal, she was jest like a tiger. So 'twas before we started, and I hadn't got my gang chained up, so, what should she do but ups on a cotton-bale, like a cat, ketches a knife from one of the deck hands, and, I tell ye, she made all fly for a minnit, till she saw 'twan't no use; and she jest turns round, and pitches head-first, young un and all, into the river – went down plump, and never ris.'

'Bah!' said Tom Loker, who had listened to these stories with ill-repressed disgust. 'Shif'less, both on ye! *My* gals don't cut up no such shines,[53] I tell ye!'

'Indeed! how do you help it?' said Marks, briskly.

'Help it? why, I buys a gal, and if she's got a young un to be sold, I jest walks up and puts my fist to her face, and says, "Look here, now; if you give me one word out of your head, I'll smash yer face in. I won't hear one word – not the beginning of a word." I says to 'em, "This yer young un's mine and not yourn, and you've no kind o' business with it. I'm going to sell it, first chance; mind, you don't cut up none o' yer shines about it, or I'll make ye wish ye'd never been born." I tell ye, they sees it an't no play, when I gets hold. I makes 'em as whist[54] as fishes; and if one on 'em begins and gives a yelp, why – ' and Mr Loker brought down his fist with a thump that fully explained the hiatus.

'That ar's what ye may call *emphasis*,' said Marks, poking Haley in the side, and going into another small giggle. 'An't Tom peculiar? he! he! he! I say, Tom, I s'pect you make 'em *understand*, for all niggers' heads is woolly. They don't never have no doubt o' your meaning, Tom. If you an't the devil, Tom, you's his twin brother; I'll say that for ye!'

Tom received the compliment with becoming modesty, and began to look as affable as was consistent, as John Bunyan says, with his doggish nature.[55]

Haley, who had been imbibing very freely of the staple of the evening, began to feel a sensible elevation and enlargement of his moral faculties – a phenomenon not unusual with gentlemen of a serious and reflective turn, under similar circumstances.

'Wal, now, Tom,' he said, 'ye re'lly is too bad, as I al'ays have told ye. Ye know, Tom, you and I used to talk over these yer matters down in Natchez, and I used to prove to ye that we made full as much, and was as well off for this yer world, by treatin' on 'em well, besides keepin' a better chance for comin' in the kingdom at last, when wust comes to wust, and thar an't nothing else left to get, ye know.'

'Boh!' said Tom, '*don't* I know? – don't make me too sick with any o'yer stuff – my stomach is a leetle riled, now;' and Tom drank half a glass of raw brandy.

'I say,' said Haley, and leaning back in his chair and gesturing impressively, 'I'll say this, now, I al'ays meant to drive my trade so as to make money on't, *fust and foremost*, as much as any man; but then, trade an't everything, and money an't everything, 'cause we's all got souls. I don't care, now, who hears me say it – and I think a cussed sight on it, so I may as well come out with it. I b'lieve in religion, and one of these days, when I've got matters tight and snug, I calculates to tend to my soul and them ar matters: and so what's the use of doin' any more wickedness than's re'lly necessary? – it don't seem to me it's 't all prudent.'

'Tend to yer soul!' repeated Tom, contemptuously; 'take a bright look-out to find a soul in you – save yourself any care on that score. If the devil sifts you through a hair sieve, he won't find one.'

'Why, Tom you're cross,' said Haley; 'why can't ye take it pleasant, now, when a feller's talking for your good?'

'Stop that ar jaw o' yourn, there,' said Tom, gruffly. 'I can stand most any talk o' yourn but your pious talk – that kills me right up. After all, what's the odds between me and you? 'Tan't that you care one bit more, or have a bit more feelin' – it's clean, sheer, dog meanness, wanting to cheat the devil and save your own skin; don't I see through it? And your "gettin' religion", as you call it, arter all, is too 'spisin' mean for any crittur; run up a bill with the devil all your life, and then sneak out when pay time comes! Boh!'

'Come, come, gentlemen, I say; this isn't business,' said Marks. 'There's different ways, you know, of looking at all subjects. Mr Haley is a very nice man, no doubt, and has his own conscience; and, Tom, you have your ways, and very good ones, too, Tom; but quarrelling, you know, won't answer no kind of purpose. Let's go to business. Now, Mr Haley, what is it? You want us to undertake to catch this yer gal?'

'The gal's no matter of mine – she's Shelby's; it's only the boy. I was a fool for buying the monkey!'

'You're generally a fool!' said Tom, gruffly.

'Come, now, Loker, none of your huffs,' said Marks, licking his lips; 'you see, Mr Haley's a puttin' us in a way of a good job, I reckon; just hold still – these yer arrangements is my forte. This yer gal, Mr Haley, how is she? What is she?'

'Wal! white and handsome – well brought up. I'd a gin Shelby eight hundred or a thousand, and then made well on her.'

'White and handsome – well brought up!' said Marks, his sharp eyes, nose, and mouth, all alive with enterprise. 'Look here, now, Loker, a beautiful opening. We'll do a business here on our own account; we does the catchin': the boy, of course, goes to Mr Haley – we takes the gal to Orleans to speculate on. An't it beautiful?'

Tom, whose great, heavy mouth had stood ajar during this communication, now suddenly snapped together, as a big dog closes on a piece of meat, and seemed to be digesting the idea at his leisure.

'Ye see,' said Marks to Haley, stirring his punch as he did so, 'ye see, we has justices convenient at all p'ints along shore that does up any little jobs in our line quite reasonable.[56] Tom, he does the knockin' down and that ar; and I come in all dressed up – shining boots – everything first chop, when the swearins to be done. You oughter see me now,' said Marks, in a glow of professional pride, 'how I can tone it off. One day, I'm Mr Twickem, from New Orleans; 'nother day, I'm just come from my plantation on Pearl River, where I works seven hundred niggers; then, again, I come out a distant relation of Henry Clay, or some old cock in Kentuck. Talents is different, you know. Now, Tom's a roarer when there's any thumping or fighting to be done; but at lying, he an't good, Tom an't – ye see it don't come natural to him; but Lord if thar's a feller in the country that can swear to anything and everything, and put in all the circumstances and flourishes with a longer face, and carry't through better'n I can, why, I'd like to see him, that's all! I b'lieve, my heart, I could get along, and snake through, even if justices were more particular than they is. Sometimes I rather wish they was more particular; 'twould be a heap more relishin' if they was – more fun, yer know.'

Tom Loker, who, as we have made it appear, was a man of slow thoughts and movements, here interrupted Marks by bringing his heavy fist down on the table, so as to make all ring again. '*It'll do!*' he said.

'Lord bless ye, Tom, ye needn't break all the glasses,' said Marks; 'save your fist for time o' need.'

'But, gentlemen, an't I to come in for a share of the profits?' said Haley.

'An't it enough we catch the boy for ye?' said Loker. 'What do ye want?'

'Wal,' said Haley, 'if I gives you the job, it's worth something – say ten per cent on the profits, expenses paid.'

'Now,' said Loker, with a tremendous oath, and striking the table with his heavy fist, 'don't I know *you*, Dan Haley? Don't you think to come it over me! Suppose Marks and I have taken up the catchin' trade, jest to 'commodate gentlemen like you, and get nothin' for ourselves? Not by a long chalk! We'll have the gal out and out, and you keep quiet, or, ye see, we'll have both – what's to hinder? Han't you show'd us the game? It's as free to us as you, I hope. If you or Shelby wants to chase us, look where the partridges was last year; if you find them or us you're quite welcome.'

'Oh, wal, certainly, jest let it go at that,' said Haley, alarmed: 'you catch the boy for the job; you allers did trade *far* with me, Tom, and was up to yer word.'

'Ye know that,' said Tom; 'I don't pretend none of your snivelling ways, but I won't lie in my 'counts with the devil himself. What I ses I'll do, I will do; you know *that*, Dan Haley.'

'Jes so, jes so; I said so, Tom,' said Haley; 'and if you'd only promise to have the boy for me in a week, at any point you'll name, that's all I want.'

'But it an't all I want, by a long jump,' said Tom. 'Ye don't think I did business with you, down in Natchez, for nothing, Haley; I've learned to hold an eel when I catch him. You've got to fork over fifty dollars, flat down, or this child don't start a peg. I know yer.'

'Why, when you have a job in hand that may bring a clean profit of somewhere about a thousand or sixteen hundred? Why, Tom, you're onreasonable,' said Haley.

'Yes, and hasn't we business booked for five weeks to come – all we can do? And suppose we leaves all, and goes to bushwhacking round arter yer young un, and finally doesn't catch the gal – and gals allers is the devil *to* catch – what's then? Would you pay us a cent – would you? I think I see you a doin' it – ugh! No, no; flap down your fifty. If we get the job, and it pays, I'll hand it back; if we don't, it's for our trouble – that's *far*, an't it, Marks?'

'Certainly, certainly,' said Marks, with a conciliatory tone. 'It's only a retaining fee, you see – he! he! he! – we lawyers, you know. Wal, we must all keep good-natured, keep easy, yer know. Tom'll have the boy for yer anywhere ye'll name; won't ye, Tom?'

'If I find the young un, I'll bring him on to Cincinnati, and leave him at Granny Belcher's, on the landing,' said Loker.

Marks had got from his pocket a greasy pocket-book, and taking a long paper from thence, he sat down, and fixing his keen black eyes on it, began mumbling over its contents: ' "Barnes – Shelby County[57] – boy Jim, three hundred dollars for him, dead or alive. Edwards – Dick and Lucy – man and wife, six hundred dollars; wench Polly and two children – six hundred for her or her head" – I'm jest a running over our business, to see if we can take up this yer handily. Loker,' he said, after a pause, 'we must set Adams and Springer on the track of these yer; they've been booked some time.'

'They'll charge too much,' said Tom.

'I'll manage that ar; they's young in the business, and must 'spect to work cheap,' said Marks, as he continued to read. 'Ther's three on 'em easy cases, 'cause all you've got to do is to shoot 'em, or swar they is shot; they couldn't, of course, charge much for that. Them other cases,' he said, folding the paper, 'will bear puttin' off a spell. So now let's come to the particulars. Now, Mr Haley, you saw this yer gal when she landed?'

'To be sure – plain as I see you.'

'And a man helpin' on her up the bank?' said Loker.

'To be sure I did.'

'Most likely,' said Marks, 'she's took in somewhere; but where's a question. Tom, what do you say?'

'We must cross the river tonight, no mistake,' said Tom.

'But there's no boat about,' said Marks. 'The ice is running awfully, Tom; an't it dangerous?'

'Don'no nothing 'bout that, only it's got to be done,' said Tom, decidedly.

'Dear me,' said Marks, fidgeting, 'it'll be – I say,' he said, walking to the window, 'it's dark as a wolf's mouth, and Tom –'

'The long and short is, you're scared, Marks; but I can't help that, you've got to go. Suppose you want to lie by a day or two, till the gal's been carried on the underground line up to Sandusky[58] or so, before you –'

'Oh, no; I an't a grain afraid,' said Marks, 'only –'

'Only what?' said Tom.

'Well, about the boat. Yer see there an't any boat.'

'I heard the woman say there was one coming along this evening, and that a man was going to cross over in it. Neck or nothing, we must go with him,' said Tom.

'I s'pose you've got good dogs,' said Haley.

'First rate,' said Marks. 'But what's the use? you han't got nothin' o' hers to smell on.'

'Yes, I have,' said Haley, triumphantly. 'Here's her shawl she left on the bed in her hurry; she left her bonnet, too.'

'That ar's lucky,' said Loker; 'fork over.'

'Though the dogs might damage the gal, if they come on her unawares,' said Haley.

'That ar's a consideration,' said Marks. 'Our dogs tore a feller half to pieces, once, down in Mobile,[59] 'fore we could get 'em off.'

'Well, ye see, for this sort that's to be sold for their looks, that ar won't answer, ye see,' said Haley.

'I do see,' said Marks. 'Besides, if she's got took in, 'tan't no go, neither. Dogs is no 'count in these yer up states where these critters gets carried; of course, ye can't get on their track. They only does down in plantations, where niggers, when they runs, has to do their own running, and don't get no help.'

'Well,' said Loker, who had just stepped out to the bar to make some enquiries, 'they say the man's come with the boat; so Marks – '

That worthy cast a rueful look at the comfortable quarters he was leaving, but slowly rose to obey. After exchanging a few words of further arrangement, Haley, with visible reluctance, handed over the fifty dollars to Tom, and the worthy trio separated for the night.

If any of our refined and Christian readers object to the society into which this scene introduces them, let us beg them to begin and conquer their prejudices in time. The catching business we beg to remind them, is rising to the dignity of a lawful and patriotic profession. If all the broad land between the Mississippi and the Pacific becomes one great market for bodies and souls, and human property retains the locomotive tendencies of this nineteenth century, the trader and catcher may yet be among our aristocracy.

While this scene was going on at the tavern, Sam and Andy, in a state of high felicitation, pursued their way home.

Sam was in the highest possible feather, and expressed his exultation by all sorts of supernatural howls and ejaculations, by divers odd motions, and contortions of his whole system. Sometimes he would sit backward, with his face to the horse's tail and sides, and then, with a whoop and a summerset,[60] come right side up in his place again, and drawing on a grave face, begin to lecture Andy in high-sounding tones for laughing and playing the fool. Anon, slapping his sides with his arms, he would burst forth in peals of laughter, that made the old woods ring as they passed. With all these evolutions, he contrived to keep the horses up to the top of their speed, until, between ten and eleven, their heels resounded on the gravel at the end of the balcony. Mrs Shelby flew to the railings.

'Is that you, Sam? Where are they?'

'Mas'r Haley's a restin' at the tavern; he's dreful fatigued, missis.'

'And Eliza, Sam?'

'Wal, she's clar 'cross Jordan. As a body may say, in the land o' Canaan.'

'Why, Sam, what *do* you mean?' said Mrs Shelby, breathless and almost faint, as the possible meaning of these words came over her.

'Wal, missis, de Lord He persarves His own. Lizzy's done gone over the river into 'Hio, as 'markably as if the Lord took her over in a charrit of fire and two hosses.'

Sam's vein of piety was always uncommonly fervent in his mistress's presence, and he made great capital of scriptural figures and images.

'Come up here, Sam,' said Mr Shelby, who had followed on to the veranda, 'and tell your mistress what she wants. Come, come, Emily,' said he, passing his arm round her, 'you are cold and all in a shiver; you allow yourself to feel too much.'

'Feel too much! Am not I a woman – a mother? Are we not both responsible to God for this poor girl? My God, lay not this sin to our charge!'

'What sin, Emily? You see yourself that we have only done what we are obliged to.'

'There's an awful feeling of guilt about it, though,' said Mrs Shelby. 'I can't reason it away.'

'Here, Andy, you nigger, be alive!' called Sam, under the veranda; 'take these yer hosses to de barn; don't ye hear mas'r a callin'?' and Sam soon appeared, palm-leaf in hand, at the parlour door.

'Now, Sam tell us distinctly how the matter was,' said Mr Shelby. 'Where is Eliza, if you know?'

'Wal, mas'r, I saw her with my own eyes a crossin' on the floatin' ice. She crossed most 'markably: it wasn't no less nor a miracle; and I saw a man help her up the 'Hio side, and then she was lost in the dusk.'

'Sam, I think this rather apocryphal – this miracle. Crossing on floating ice isn't so easily done,' said Mr Shelby.

'Easy! couldn't nobody a done it, without de Lord. Why, now,' said Sam, ' 'twas jist dis yer way. Mas'r Haley, and me, and Andy, we comes up to de little tavern by the river, and I rides a leetle ahead – (I's so zealous to be a cotchin' Lizzy, that I couldn't hold in, noway) – and when I comes by the tavern winder, sure enough there she was, right in plain sight, and dey diggin' on behind. Wal I looses off my hat, and sings out nuff to raise the dead. Course Lizzy she hars, and she dodges back, when Mas'r Haley he goes past the door; and then, I tell ye, she clared out de side door; she went down de river bank; Mas'r Haley he seed her, and yelled out, and him and me, and Andy, we took arter. Down she come to the river, and thar was the current running ten feet wide by the shore, and over t'other side ice a sawin' and a jigglin' up and down, kinder as 'twere a great island. We come right behind her, and I thought my soul he'd got her sure enough – when she gin sich a screech as I never hearn, and thar she was, clar over t'other side the current, on the ice, and then on she went, a screeching and a jumpin' – the ice went crack! c'wallop! chunk! and she a boundin' like a buck! Lord, the spring that ar gal's got in her an't common, I'm o' 'pinion.'

Mrs Shelby sat perfectly silent, pale with excitement, while Sam told his story.

'God be praised, she isn't dead!' she said; 'but where is the poor child now?'

'De Lord will provide,' said Sam, rolling up his eyes piously. 'As I've been a sayin', dis yer's a providence and no mistake, as missis has allers been a instructin' on us. Thar's allers instruments ris up to do de Lord's will. Now, if it hadn't been for me today, she'd a been took a dozen times. Warn't it I started off de hosses, dis yer mornin', and kept 'em chasin' till nigh dinner time? And didn't I car Mas'r Haley nigh five miles out of de road, dis evening? or else he'd a come up with Lizzy as easy as a dog arter a 'coon. These yer's all providences.'

'They are a kind of providences that you'll have to be pretty sparing of, Master Sam. I allow no such practices with gentlemen on my place,' said Mr Shelby, with as much sternness as he could command under the circumstances.

Now, there is no more use in making believe be angry with a negro than with a child; both instinctively see the true state of the case, through all attempts to affect the contrary; and Sam was in no wise disheartened by this rebuke, though he assumed an air of doleful gravity, and stood with the corners of his mouth lowered in most penitential style.

'Mas'r's quite right – quite; it was ugly on me – there's no disputin' that ar; and of course mas'r and missis wouldn't encourage no such works. I'm sensible of dat ar; but a poor nigger like me's 'mazin' tempted to act ugly sometimes, when fellers will cut up such shines as dat ar Mas'r Haley; he an't no gen'l'man no way; anybody's been raised as I've been can't help a seein' dat ar.'

'Well, Sam,' said Mrs Shelby, 'as you appear to have a proper sense of your errors, you may go now and tell Aunt Chloe she may get you some of that cold ham that was left of dinner today. You and Andy must be hungry.'

'Missis is a heap too good for us,' said Sam, making his bow with alacrity, and departing.

It will be perceived, as has been before intimated, that Master Sam had a native talent that might, undoubtedly, have raised him to eminence in political life – a talent of making capital out of everything that turned up, to be invested for his own especial praise and glory; and having done up his piety and humility, as he trusted, to the satisfaction of the parlour, he clapped his palm-leaf on his head, with a sort of rakish, free-and-easy air, and proceeded to the dominions of Aunt Chloe, with the intention of flourishing largely in the kitchen.

'I'll speechify these yer niggers,' said Sam to himself, 'now I've got a chance. Lord, I'll reel it off to make 'em stare!'

It must be observed that one of Sam's special delights had been to ride in attendance on his master to all kinds of political gatherings, where, roosted on some rail fence, or perched aloft in some tree, he would sit watching the orators, with the greatest apparent gusto, and then, descending among the various brethren of his own colour, assembled on the same errand, he would edify and delight them with the most ludicrous burlesques and imitations, all delivered with the most imperturbable earnestness and solemnity; and though the auditors immediately about him were generally of his own colour, it not unfrequently happened that they were fringed pretty deeply with those of a fairer complexion, who listened, laughing and winking, to Sam's great self-congratulation. In fact, Sam considered oratory as his vocation, and never let slip an opportunity of magnifying his office.

Now, between Sam and Aunt Chloe there had existed, from ancient times, a sort of chronic feud, or rather a decided coolness; but, as Sam was meditating something in the provision department as the necessary and obvious foundation of his operations, he determined, on the present occasion, to be eminently conciliatory; for he well knew that although 'missis' orders' would undoubtedly be followed to the letter, yet he should gain a considerable deal by enlisting the spirit also. He therefore, appeared before Aunt Chloe with a touchingly subdued, resigned expression, like one who has suffered immeasurable hardships in behalf of a persecuted fellow-creature – enlarged upon the fact that missis had directed him to come to Aunt Chloe for whatever might be wanting to make up the balance in his solids and fluids – and thus unequivocally acknowledged her right and supremacy in the cooking department, and all thereto pertaining.

The thing took accordingly. No poor, simple, virtuous body was ever cajoled by the attentions of an electioneering politician with more ease than Aunt Chloe was won over by Master Sam's suavities; and if he had been the prodigal son himself,[61] he could not have been overwhelmed with more maternal bountifulness; and he soon found himself seated, happy and glorious, over a large tin pan, containing a sort of *olla podrida*[62] of all that had appeared on the table for two or three days past. Savoury morsels of ham, golden blocks of corn-cake, fragments of pie of every conceivable mathematical figure, chicken wings, gizzards, and drumsticks, all appeared in picturesque confusion; and Sam, as monarch of all he surveyed, sat with his palm-leaf cocked rejoicingly to one side, and patronising Andy at his right hand.

The kitchen was full of all his compeers, who had hurried and crowded in, from the various cabins, to hear the termination of the day's exploits. Now was Sam's hour of glory. The story of the day was rehearsed, with all kinds of ornament and varnishing which might be necessary to heighten its effect; for Sam, like some of our fashionable dilettanti, never allowed a story to lose any of its gilding by passing through his hands. Roars of laughter attended the narration, and were taken up and prolonged by all the small fry, who were lying, in any quantity, about on the floor, or perched in every corner. In the height of the uproar and laughter, Sam, however, preserved an immovable gravity, only from time to time rolling his eyes up, and giving his auditors divers inexpressibly droll glances, without departing from the sententious elevation of his oratory.

'Yer see, fellow-countrymen,' said Sam, elevating a turkey's leg, with energy, 'yer see, now, what dis yer chile's up ter, for 'fendin' yer all – yes, all on yer. For him as tries to get one o' our people is as good as tryin' to get all; yer see the principle's de same – dat ar's clar. And anyone o' these yer drivers that comes smelling round arter any o' our people, why, he's got *me* in his way; *I'm* the feller he's got to set in with – I'm the feller for yer all to come to, brethren – I'll stand up for yer rights – I'll 'fend 'em to the last breath!'

'Why, but Sam, yer telled me, only this mornin', that you'd help this yer mas'r to cotch Lizzy; seems to me yer talk don't hang together,' said Andy.

'I tell you now, Andy,' said Sam, with awful superiority, 'don't yer be a-talkin' 'bout what yer don't know nothin' on; boys like you, Andy, means well, but they can't be 'spected to collusitate the great principles of action.'

Andy looked rebuked, particularly by the hard word 'collusitate', which most of the youngerly members of the company seemed to consider as a settler in the case, while Sam proceeded –

'Dat ar was *conscience*, Andy; when I thought of gwine arter Lizzy, I raily 'spected mas'r was sot dat way. When I found missis was sot the contrar, dat ar was conscience *more yet* – 'cause fellers allers gets more by stickin' to missis' side – so you see I's persistent either way, and sticks up to conscience, and holds on to principles. Yes, *principles*,' said

Sam, giving an enthusiastic toss to a chicken's neck – 'what's principles good for, if we isn't persistent, I wanter know? Thar, Andy, you may have dat ar bone, 'tan't picked quite clean.'

Sam's audience hanging on his words with open mouth, he could not but proceed –

'Dis yer matter 'bout persistence, feller-niggers,' said Sam, with the air of one entering into an abstruse subject, 'dis yer 'sistency's a thing what an't seed into very clar, by most anybody. Now, yer see, when a feller stands up for a thing one day and night, de contrar de next, folks ses (and nat'rally enough they ses), why he an't persistent – hand me dat ar bit o' corn-cake, Andy. But let's look inter it. I hope the gen'lemen and der fair sex will 'scuse my usin' an or'nary sort o' 'parison. Here! I'm a tryin' to get top o' der hay. Wal, I puts up my larder dis yer side; 'tan't no go; den, 'cause I don't try dere no more, but puts my larder right de contrar side, an't I persistent? I'm persistent in wanting to get up which ar side my larder is; don't you see, all on yer?'

'It's the only thing ye ever was persistent in, Lord knows!' muttered Aunt Chloe, who was getting rather restive; the merriment of the evening being to her somewhat after the Scripture comparison – like 'vinegar upon nitre'.[63]

'Yes, indeed!' said Sam, rising, full of supper and glory, for a closing effort. 'Yes, my feller-citizens and ladies of de other sex in general, I has principles – I'm proud to 'oon 'em – they's perquisite to dese yer times, and ter *all* times. I has principles, and I sticks to 'em like forty – jest anything that I thinks is principle, I goes in to't; I wouldn't mind if dey burnt me 'live – I'd walk right up to de stake, I would, and say, Here I comes to shed my last blood fur my principles, fur my country, fur der gen'l interests of s'ciety.'

'Well,' said Aunt Chloe, 'one o' yer principles will have to be to get to bed sometime tonight, and not be a-keepin' everybody up till mornin'; now, every one of you young uns that don't want to he cracked had better be scase, mighty sudden.'

'Niggers! all on yer,' said Sam, waving his palm-leaf with benignity, 'I give yer my blessin'; go to bed now, and be good boys.'

And, with this pathetic benediction, the assembly dispersed.

CHAPTER IX

In Which it Appears that a Senator is but a Man

THE LIGHT OF THE CHEERFUL FIRE shone on the rug and carpet of a cosy parlour, and glittered on the sides of the teacups and well-brightened teapot, as Senator Bird was drawing off his boots, preparatory to inserting his feet in a pair of new handsome slippers, which his wife had been working for him while away on his senatorial tour. Mrs Bird, looking the very picture of delight, was superintending the arrangements of the table, ever and anon mingling admonitory remarks to a number of frolicsome juveniles, who were effervescing in all those modes of untold gambol and mischief that have astonished mothers ever since the flood.

'Tom, let the door-knob alone – there's a man! Mary! Mary! don't pull the cat's tail – poor pussy! Jim, you mustn't climb on that table – no, no! – You don't know, my dear, what a surprise it is to us all, to see you here tonight,' said she, at last, when she found a space to say something to her husband.

'Yes, yes, I thought I'd just make a run down, spend the night, and have a little comfort at home. I'm tired to death, and my head aches!'

Mrs Bird cast a glance at a camphor-bottle,[64] which stood in the half-open closet, and appeared to meditate an approach to it, but her husband interposed –

'No, no, Mary, no doctoring! a cup of your good hot tea, and some of our good home living, is what I want. It's a tiresome business this legislating!'

And the senator smiled, as if he rather liked the idea of considering himself a sacrifice to his country.

'Well,' said his wife, after the business of the tea-table was getting rather slack, 'and what have they been doing in the Senate?'

Now, it was a very unusual thing for gentle little Mrs Bird ever to trouble her head with what was going on in the house of the State, very wisely considering that she had enough to do to mind her own. Mr Bird, therefore, opened his eyes in surprise, and said –

'Not very much of importance.'

'Well; but is it true that they have been passing a law forbidding people to give meat and drink to those poor coloured folks that come along? I heard they were talking of some such law, but I didn't think any Christian legislature would pass it!'

'Why, Mary, you are getting to be a politician all at once.'

'No, nonsense! I wouldn't give a fig for all your politics, generally, but I think this is something downright cruel and unchristian. I hope, my dear, no such law has been passed.'

'There has been a law passed forbidding people to help off the slaves that come over from Kentucky, my dear; so much of that thing has been done by these reckless Abolitionists, that our brethren in Kentucky are very strongly excited, and it seems necessary, and no more than Christian and kind, that something should be done by our State to quiet the excitement.'

'And what is the law? It don't forbid us to shelter these poor creatures a night, does it? and to give 'em something comfortable to eat, and a few old clothes, and send them quietly about their business?'

'Why, yes, my dear; that would be aiding and abetting, you know.'

Mrs Bird was a timid, blushing little woman, of about four feet in height, and with mild blue eyes, and a peach-blow complexion, and the gentlest, sweetest voice in the world; as for courage, a moderate-sized cock-turkey had been known to put her to rout at the very first gobble, and a stout house-dog of moderate capacity would bring her into subjection merely by a show of his teeth. Her husband and children were her entire world, and in these she ruled more by entreaty and persuasion than by command or argument. There was only one thing that was capable of arousing her, and that provocation came in on the side of her unusually gentle and sympathetic nature; anything in the shape of cruelty would throw her into a passion, which was the more alarming and inexplicable in proportion to the general softness of her nature. Generally the most indulgent and easy to be entreated of all mothers, still her boys had a very reverent remembrance of a most vehement chastisement she once bestowed on them because she found them leagued with several graceless boys of the neighbourhood stoning a defenceless kitten.

'I'll tell you what,' Master Bill used to say, 'I was scared that time. Mother came at me so that I thought she was crazy, and I was whipped and tumbled off to bed, without any supper, before I could get over wondering what had come about; and, after that, I heard mother crying outside the door, which made me feel worse than all the rest. I'll tell you what,' he'd say, 'we boys never stoned another kitten!'

On the present occasion, Mrs Bird rose quickly, with very red cheeks, which quite improved her general appearance, and walked up to her husband, with quite a resolute air, and said, in a determined tone, 'Now, John, I want to know if you think such a law as that is right and Christian?'

'You won't shoot me, now, Mary, if I say I do!'

'I never could have thought it of you, John! You didn't vote for it?'

'Even so, my fair politician.'

'You ought to be ashamed, John! Poor, homeless, houseless creatures! It's a shameful, wicked, abominable law, and I'll break it, for one, the first time I get a chance; and I hope I *shall* have a chance, I do! Things have got to a pretty pass, if a woman can't give a warm supper and a bed to poor, starving creatures, just because they are slaves, and have been abused and oppressed all their lives, poor things!'

'But, Mary, just listen to me. Your feelings are all quite right, dear, and interesting, and I love you for them; but, then, dear, we mustn't suffer our feelings to run away with our judgement. You must consider it's not a matter of private feeling; there are great public interests involved, there is such a state of public agitation rising, that we must put aside our private feelings.'

'Now, John, I don't know anything about politics, but I can read my Bible; and there I see that I must feed the hungry, clothe the naked, and comfort the desolate; and that Bible I mean to follow.'

'But in cases where your doing so would involve a great public evil – '

'Obeying God never brings on public evils. I know it can't. It's always safest, all round, to *do as He* bids us.'

'Now, listen to me, Mary, and I can state to you a very clear argument, to show – '

'Oh, nonsense, John! you can talk all night, but you wouldn't do it. I put it to you, John, would *you* now turn away a poor, shivering, hungry creature from your door, because he was a runaway? *Would* you, now?'

Now, if the truth must be told, our senator had the misfortune to be a man who had a particularly humane and accessible nature, and turning away anybody that was in trouble never had been his forte; and what was worse for him in this particular pinch of the argument was, that his wife knew it, and, of course, was making an assault on rather an indefensible point. So he had recourse to the usual means of gaining time for such cases made and provided; he said 'ahem', and coughed several times, took out his pocket-handkerchief, and began to wipe his glasses. Mrs Bird, seeing the defenceless condition of the enemy's territory, had no more conscience than to push her advantage.

'I should like to see you doing that, John – I really should! Turning a woman out-of-doors in a snow-storm, for instance; or, maybe you'd take her up and put her in gaol, wouldn't you? You would make a great hand at that!'

'Of course, it would be a very painful duty – ' began Mr Bird, in a moderate tone.

'Duty, John! don't use that word! You know it isn't a duty – it can't be a duty! If folks want to keep their slaves from running away, let 'em treat 'em well – that's my doctrine. If I had slaves (as I hope I never shall have), I'd risk their wanting to run away from me, or you either, John. I tell you folks don't run away when they are happy; and when they do run, poor creatures! they suffer enough with cold, and hunger and fear, without everybody's turning against them; and, law or no law, I never will, so help me God!'

'Mary! Mary, my dear, let me reason with you.'

'I hate reasoning, John – especially reasoning on such subjects. There's a way you political folks have of coming round and round a plain right thing; and you don't believe in it yourselves, when it comes to practice. I know *you* well enough, John. You don't believe it's right any more than I do; and you wouldn't do it any sooner than I.'

At this critical juncture old Cudjoe, the black man-of-all-work, put his head in at the door, and wished 'Missis would come into the kitchen;' and our senator, tolerably relieved, looked after his little wife with a whimsical mixture of amusement and vexation, and, seating himself in the armchair, began to read the papers.

After a moment his wife's voice was heard at the door, in a quick, earnest tone, 'John! John! I do wish you'd come here a moment.'

He laid down his paper, and went into the kitchen, and started, quite amazed at the sight that presented itself. A young and slender woman, with garments torn and frozen, with one shoe gone, and the stocking torn away from the cut and bleeding foot, was laid back in a deadly swoon upon two chairs. There was the impress of the despised race on her face, yet none could help feeling its mournful and pathetic beauty, while its stony sharpness, its cold, fixed, deathly aspect, struck a solemn chill over him. He drew his breath short, and stood in silence. His wife, and their only coloured domestic, old Aunt Dinah, were busily engaged in restorative measures; while old Cudjoe had got the boy on his knee, and was busy pulling off his shoes and stockings, and chafing his little cold feet.

'Sure, now, if she an't a sight to behold!' said old Dinah, compassionately; ' 'Pears like 'twas the heat that made her faint. She was tol'able peart when she cum in, and asked if she couldn't warm herself here a spell; and I was just a askin' her where she cum from, and she fainted right down. Never done much hard work, guess, by the looks of her hands.'

'Poor creature!' said Mrs Bird, compassionately, as the woman slowly unclosed her large dark eyes, and looked vacantly at her. Suddenly an expression of agony crossed her face, and she sprang up, saying, 'Oh, my Harry! Have they got him?'

The boy, at this, jumped from Cudjoe's knee, and, running to her side, put up his arms. 'Oh, he's here! he's here!' she exclaimed.

'Oh, ma'am!' said she, wildly, to Mrs Bird, 'do protect us! don't let them get him!'

'Nobody shall hurt you here, poor woman,' said Mrs Bird, encouragingly. 'You are safe; don't be afraid.'

'God bless you!' said the woman, covering her face and sobbing; while the little boy, seeing her crying, tried to get into her lap.

With many gentle and womanly offices, which none knew better how to render than Mrs Bird, the poor woman was in time rendered more calm. A temporary bed was provided for her on the settle, near the fire; and, after a short time, she fell into a heavy slumber with the child, who seemed no less weary, soundly sleeping on her arm; for the mother resisted, with nervous anxiety, the kindest attempts to take him from her; and even in sleep her arm encircled him with an unrelaxing clasp, as if she could not even then be beguiled of her vigilant hold.

Mr and Mrs Bird had gone back to the parlour, where, strange as it may appear, no reference was made on either side to the preceding conversation; but Mrs Bird busied herself with her knitting-work, and Mr Bird pretended to be reading the paper.

'I wonder who and what she is!' said Mr Bird, at last, as he laid it down.

'When she wakes up and feels a little rested, we will see,' said Mrs Bird.

'I say, wife!' said Mr Bird, after musing in silence over his newspaper.

'Well, dear!'

'She couldn't wear one of your gowns, could she, by any letting down, or such matter? She seems to be rather larger than you are.'

A quite perceptible smile glimmered on Mrs Bird's face, as she answered, 'We'll see.'

Another pause, and Mr Bird again broke out –

'I say, wife!'

'Well! What now?'

'Why, there's that old bombazine[65] cloak that you keep on purpose to put over me when I take my afternoon's nap; you might as well give her that – she needs clothes.'

At this instant Dinah looked in to say that the woman was awake and wanted to see missis.

Mr and Mrs Bird went into the kitchen, followed by the two eldest boys, the smaller fry having, by this time been safely disposed of in bed.

The woman was now sitting up on the settle by the fire. She was looking steadily into the blaze, with a calm, heartbroken expression, very different from her former agitated wildness.

'Did you want me?' said Mrs Bird, in gentle tones. 'I hope you feel better now, poor woman!'

A long-drawn, shivering sigh was the only answer; but she lifted her dark eyes, and fixed them on her with such a forlorn and imploring expression that the tears came into the little woman's eyes.

'You needn't be afraid of anything; we are friends here, poor woman! Tell me where you came from and what you want,' said she.

'I came from Kentucky,' said the woman.

'When?' said Mr Bird, taking up the interrogatory.

'Tonight.'

'How did you come?'

'I crossed on the ice.'

'Crossed on the ice!' said everyone present.

'Yes,' said the woman, slowly, 'I did. God helping me, I crossed on the ice; for they were behind me – right behind – and there was no other way!'

'Law, missis,' said Cudjoe, 'the ice is all in broken-up blocks a-swinging and a-tettering up and down in the water!'

'I know it was – I know it!' said she, wildly; 'but I did it! I wouldn't have thought I could – I didn't think I should get over, but I didn't care! I could but die, if I didn't. The Lord helped me; nobody knows how much the Lord can help 'em, till they try,' said the woman, with a flashing eye.

'Were you a slave?' said Mr Bird.

'Yes, sir; I belonged to a man in Kentucky.'

'Was he unkind to you?'

'No, sir; he was a good master.'

'And was your mistress unkind to you?'

'No, sir – no! my mistress was always good to me.'

'What could induce you to leave a good home, then, and run away, and go through such dangers?'

The woman looked up at Mrs Bird, with a keen, scrutinising glance, and it did not escape her that she was dressed in deep mourning.

'Ma'am,' she said, suddenly, 'have you ever lost a child?'

The question was unexpected, and it was a thrust on a new wound; for it was only a month since a darling child of the family had been laid in the grave.

Mr Bird turned around and walked to the window, and Mrs Bird burst into tears; but recovering her voice, she said –

'Why do you ask that? I have lost a little one.'

'Then you will feel for me. I have lost two, one after another – left 'em buried there when I came away; and I had only this one left. I never slept a night without him; he was all I had. He was my comfort and pride, day and night; and, ma'am, they were going to take him away from me – to *sell* him – sell him down south, ma'am, to go all alone – a baby that had never been away from his mother in his life! I couldn't stand it, ma'am. I knew I never should be good for anything if they did; and when I knew the papers were signed, and he was sold, I took him and came off in the night; and they chased me – the man that bought him and some of mas'r's folks – and they were coming down right behind me, and I heard 'em. I jumped right on to the ice, and how I got across I don't know; but, first I knew, a man was helping me up the bank.'

The woman did not sob nor weep. She had gone to a place where tears are dry; but everyone around her was, in some way characteristic of themselves, showing signs of hearty sympathy.

The two little boys, after a desperate rummaging in their pockets in search of those pocket-handkerchiefs which mothers know are never to be found there, had thrown themselves disconsolately into the skirts of their mother's gown, where they were sobbing, and wiping their eyes and noses, to their hearts' content; Mrs Bird had her face fairly hidden in her pocket-handkerchief; and old Dinah, with tears streaming down her black, honest face, was ejaculating, 'Lord have mercy on us!' with all the fervour of a camp-meeting; while old Cudjoe, rubbing his eyes very hard with his cuffs, and making a most uncommon variety of wry faces, occasionally responded in the same key, with great fervour. Our senator was a statesman, and of course could not be expected to cry, like other mortals; and so he turned his back to the company, and looked out of the window, and seemed particularly busy in clearing his throat and wiping his spectacle-glasses, occasionally blowing his nose in a manner that was calculated to excite suspicion, had anyone been in a state to observe critically.

'How came you to tell me you had a kind master?' he suddenly exclaimed, gulping down very resolutely some kind of rising in his throat, and turning suddenly round upon the woman.

'Because he *was* a kind master – I'll say that of him, anyway; and my mistress was kind: but they couldn't help themselves. They were owing money; and there was some way, I can't tell how, that a man had a hold on them, and they were obliged to give him his will. I listened, and heard him telling mistress that, and she begging and pleading for me, and he told her he couldn't help himself, and that the papers were all drawn; and then it was I took him and left my home, and came away. I knew 'twas no use of my trying to live, if they did it; for 't 'pears like this child is all I have.'

'Have you no husband?'

'Yes, but he belongs to another man. His master is real hard to him, and won't let him come to see me, hardly ever; and he's grown harder and harder upon us, and he threatens to sell him down south. It's like I'll never see *him* again!'

The quiet tone in which the woman pronounced these words might have led a superficial observer to think that she was entirely apathetic; but there was a calm, settled depth of anguish in her large, dark eye, that spoke of something far otherwise.

'And where do you mean to go, my poor woman?' said Mrs Bird.

'To Canada, if I only knew where that was. Is it very far off, is Canada?' said she, looking up, with a simple, confiding air, to Mrs Bird's face.

'Poor thing!' said Mrs Bird, involuntarily.

'Is 't a very great way off?' said the woman, earnestly.

'Much further than you think, poor child!' said Mrs Bird; 'but we will try to think what can be done for you. Here, Dinah, make her up a bed in your own room, close by the kitchen, and I'll think what to do for her in the morning! Meanwhile, never fear, poor woman. Put your trust in God; He will protect you.'

Mrs Bird and her husband re-entered the parlour. She sat down in her little rocking-chair before the fire, swaying thoughtfully to and fro. Mr Bird strode up and down the room, grumbling to himself. 'Pish! pshaw! confounded awkward business!' At length, striding up to his wife, he said –

'I say, wife, she'll have to get away from here, this very night. That fellow will be down on the scent bright and early tomorrow morning. If 'twas only the woman, she could lie quiet till it was over; but that little chap can't be kept still by a troop of horse and foot, I'll warrant me; he'll bring it all out, popping his head out of some window or door. A pretty kettle of fish it would be for me, too, to be caught with them both here just now! No! they'll have to be got off tonight.'

'Tonight! How is it possible? Where to?'

'Well, I know pretty well where to,' said the senator, beginning to put on his boots, with a reflective air; and, stopping when his leg was half in, he embraced his knee with both hands, and seemed to go off in deep meditation.

'It's a confounded awkward, ugly business,' said he at last, beginning to tug at his boot-straps again, 'and that's a fact!' After one boot was fairly on, the senator sat with the other in his hand, profoundly studying the figure of the carpet. 'It will have to be done, though, for aught I see – hang it all!' And he drew the other boot anxiously on, and looked out of the window.

Now, little Mrs Bird was a discreet woman – a woman who never in her life said, 'I told you so!' and, on the present occasion, though pretty well aware of the shape her husband's meditations were taking, she very prudently forbore to meddle with them, only sat very quietly in her chair, and looked quite ready to hear her liege lord's intentions, when he should think proper to utter them.

'You see,' he said, 'there's my old client, Van Trompe,[66] has come over from Kentucky, and set all his slaves free; and he has bought a place seven miles up the creek here, back in the woods, where nobody goes, unless they go on purpose; and it's a place that isn't found in a hurry. There she'd be safe enough: but the plague of the thing is, nobody could drive a carriage there tonight, but *me*.'

'Why not? Cudjoe is an excellent driver.'

'Ay, ay, but here it is. The creek has to be crossed twice; and the second crossing is quite dangerous unless one knows it as I do. I have crossed it a hundred times on horseback, and know exactly the turns to take. And so, you see, there's no help for it. Cudjoe must put in the horses, as quietly as may be, about twelve o'clock, and I'll take her over; and then, to give colour to the matter, he must carry me on to the next tavern, to take the stage for Columbus[67] that comes by about three or four, and so it will look as if I had had the carriage only for that. I shall get into business bright and early in the morning. But I'm thinking I shall feel rather cheap there, after all that's been said and done; but, hang it, I can't help it!'

'Your heart is better than your head, in this case, John,' said the wife, laying her little white hand on his. 'Could I ever have loved you, had I not known you better than you know yourself?' And the little woman looked so handsome with the tears sparkling in her eyes, that the senator thought he must be a decidedly clever fellow, to get such a pretty creature into such a passionate admiration of him; and so, what could he do but walk off soberly to see about the carriage? At the door, however, he stopped a moment, and then coming back, he said, with some hesitation –

'Mary, I don't know how you'd feel about it, but there's that drawer full of things – of – of – poor little Henry's.' So saying, he turned quickly on his heel, and shut the door after him.

His wife opened the little bedroom door adjoining her room, and, taking the candle, set it down on the top of a bureau there; then from a small recess she took a key, and put it thoughtfully in the lock of a drawer, and made a sudden pause, while two boys, who, boy-like, had followed close on her heels, stood looking, with silent, significant glances, at their mother. And, O mother that reads this, has there never been in your house a drawer, or a closet, the opening of which has been to you like the opening again of a little grave? Ah! happy mother that you are, if it has not been so.[68]

Mrs Bird slowly opened the drawer. There were little coats of many a form and pattern, piles of aprons, and rows of small stockings; and even a pair of little shoes, worn and rubbed at the toes, were peeping from the folds of a paper. There was a toy-horse and wagon, a top, a ball – memorials gathered with many a tear and many a heartbreak! She sat down by the drawer, and, leaning her head on her hands over it, wept till the tears fell through her fingers into the drawer; then suddenly raising her head, she began, with nervous haste, selecting the plainest and most substantial articles, and gathering them into a bundle.

'Mamma,' said one of the boys, gently touching her arm, 'are you going to give away *those* things?'

'My dear boys,' she said, softly and earnestly, 'if our dear, loving little Henry looks down from heaven, he would be glad to have us do this. I could not find it in my heart to give them away to any common person – to anybody that was happy; but I give them to a mother more heartbroken and sorrowful than I am; and I hope God will send His blessings with them!'

There are in this world blessed souls, whose sorrows all spring up into joys for others; whose earthly hopes, laid in the grave with many tears, are the seed from which spring healing flowers and balm for the desolate and the distressed. Among such was the delicate woman who sits there by the lamp, dropping slow tears, while she prepares the memorials of her own lost one for the outcast wanderer.

After a while, Mrs Bird opened a wardrobe, and, taking from thence a plain, serviceable dress or two, she sat down busily to her work-table, and, with needle, scissors, and thimble at hand, quietly commenced the 'letting down' process which her husband had recommended, and continued busily at it till the old clock in the corner struck twelve, and she heard the low rattling of wheels at the door.

'Mary,' said her husband, coming in with his overcoat in his hand, 'you must wake her up now; we must be off.'

Mrs Bird hastily deposited the various articles she had collected in a small plain trunk, and locking it, desired her husband to see it in the carriage, and then proceeded to call the woman. Soon arrayed in a cloak, bonnet, and shawl, that had belonged to her benefactress, she appeared at the door with her child in her arms. Mr Bird hurried her into the carriage, and Mrs Bird pressed on after her to the carriage steps. Eliza leaned out of the carriage, and put out her hand, a hand as soft and beautiful as was given in return. She fixed her large, dark eyes, full of earnest meaning, on Mrs Bird's face, and seemed going to speak. Her lips moved, she tried once or twice, but there was no sound, and pointing upward, with a look never to be forgotten, she fell back in the seat, and covered her face. The door was shut, and the carriage drove on.

What a situation, now, for a patriotic senator, that had been all the week before spurring up the legislature of his native state to pass more stringent resolutions against escaping fugitives, their harbourers and abettors!

Our good senator in his native state had not been exceeded by any of his brethren at Washington, in the sort of eloquence which has won for them immortal renown! How sublimely he had sat with his hands in his pockets, and scouted all sentimental weakness of those who would put the welfare of a few miserable fugitives before great state interests!

He was as bold as a lion about it, and 'mightily convinced' not only himself, but everybody that heard him; but then his idea of a fugitive was only an idea of the letters that spell the word; or, at the most, the image of a little newspaper picture[69] of a man with a stick and bundle, with 'Ran away from the subscriber' under it. The magic of the real presence of distress, the imploring human eye, the frail, trembling human hand, the despairing appeal of helpless agony, these he had never tried. He had never thought that a fugitive might be a hapless mother, a defenceless child, like that one which was now wearing his lost boy's little well-known cap; and so, as our poor senator was not stone or steel, as he was a man, and a downright noble-hearted one, too, he was, as everybody must see, in a sad case for his patriotism. And you need not exult over him, good brother of the Southern States; for we have some inklings that many of you, under similar circumstances, would not do much better. We have reason to know, in Kentucky, as in Mississippi, are noble and generous hearts, to whom never was tale of suffering told in vain. Ah, good brother! is it fair for you to expect of us services which your own brave, honourable heart, would not allow you to render, were you in our place?

Be that as it may, if our good senator was a political sinner, he was in a fair way to expiate it by his night's penance. There had been a long continuous period of rainy weather, and the soft rich earth of Ohio, as everyone knows, is admirably suited to the manufacture of mud, and the road was an Ohio railroad of the good old times.

'And pray, what sort of a road may that be?' says some eastern traveller, who has been accustomed to connect no ideas with a railroad but those of smoothness or speed.

Know then, innocent eastern friend, that in benighted regions of the west, where the mud is of unfathomable and sublime depth, roads are made of round rough logs, arranged transversely side by side, and coated over in their pristine freshness with earth, turf, and whatsoever may come to hand, and then the rejoicing native calleth it a road, and straightway essayeth to ride thereupon. In process of time, the rains wash off all the turf and grass aforesaid, move the logs hither and thither, in picturesque positions, up, down and crosswise, with divers chasms and ruts of black mud intervening.

Over such a road as this our senator went stumbling along, making moral reflections as continuously as under the circumstances could be expected, the carriage proceeding along much as follows: bump! bump! bump! slush! down in the mud! – the senator, woman, and child, reversing their positions so suddenly as to come, without any very accurate adjustment, against the windows of the downhill side. Carriage sticks fast, while Cudjoe on the outside is heard making a great muster among the horses. After various ineffectual pullings and twitchings, just as the senator is losing all patience, the carriage suddenly rights itself with a bounce, two front wheels go down into another abyss, and senator, woman, and child, all tumble promiscuously on to the front seat; senator's hat is jammed over his eyes and nose quite unceremoniously, and he considers himself fairly extinguished; child cries, and Cudjoe on the outside delivers animated addresses to the horses, who are kicking, and floundering, and straining, under repeated cracks of the whip. Carriage springs up with another bounce – down go the hind wheels – senator, woman, and child, fly over on to the back seat, his elbows encountering her bonnet, and both her feet being jammed into his hat, which flies off in the concussion. After a few moments the 'slough' is passed, and the horses stop, panting; the senator finds his hat, the woman straightens her bonnet and hushes her child, and they brace themselves firmly for what is yet to come.

For a while only the continuous bump! bump! intermingled, just by way of variety, with divers side plunges and compound shakes, and they begin to flatter themselves that they are not so badly off after all. At last, with a square plunge, which puts all on to their feet and then down into their seats with incredible quickness, the carriage stops, and, after much outside commotion, Cudjoe appears at the door.

'Please, sir, it's powerful bad spot, this yer. I don't know how we's to get clar out. I'm a thinkin' we'll have to be a gettin' rails.'

The senator despairingly steps out, picking gingerly for some firm foothold. Down goes one foot an immeasurable depth, he tries to pull it up, loses his balance, and tumbles over into the mud, and is fished out in a very despairing condition by Cudjoe.

But we forbear, out of sympathy to our readers' bones. Western travellers, who have beguiled the midnight hour in the interesting process of pulling down rail fences to ply their carriages out of mud holes, will have a respectful and mournful sympathy with our unfortunate hero. We beg them to drop a silent tear and pass on.

It was full late in the night when the carriage emerged, dripping and bespattered, out of the creek, and stood at the door of a large farmhouse. It took no inconsiderable perseverance to arouse the inmates; but at last the respectable proprietor appeared, and undid the door. He was a great, tall, bristling Orson of a fellow,[70] full six feet and some inches in his stockings, and arrayed in a red flannel hunting-shirt. A very heavy *mat* of sandy hair, in a decidedly tousled condition, and a beard of some days' growth, gave the worthy man an appearance, to say the least, not particularly prepossessing. He stood for a few minutes holding the candle aloft, and blinking on our travellers with a dismal and mystified expression that was truly ludicrous. It cost some effort of our senator to induce him to comprehend the case fully; and while he is doing his best at that, we shall give him a little introduction to our readers.

Honest old John Van Trompe was once quite a considerable landholder and slave-owner in the State of Kentucky. Having 'nothing of the bear about him but the skin', and being gifted by nature with a great, honest, just heart, quite equal to his gigantic frame, he had been for some years witnessing with repressed uneasiness the workings of a system equally bad for oppressor and oppressed. At last, one day, John's great heart had swelled altogether too big to wear his bonds any longer; so he just took his pocket-book out of his desk, and went over into Ohio, and bought a quarter of a township of good, rich land, made out free papers for all his people, men, women, and children, packed them up in wagons, and sent them off to settle down; and then honest John turned his face up the creek, and sat quietly down on a snug, retired farm, to enjoy his conscience and his reflections.

'Are you the man that will shelter a poor woman and child from slave-catchers?' said the senator, explicitly.

'I rather think I am,' said honest John, with some considerable emphasis.

'I thought so,' said the senator.

'If there's anybody comes,' said the good man, stretching his tall, muscular form upward, 'why here I'm ready for him; and I've got seven sons, each six foot high, and they'll be ready for 'em. Give our respects to 'em,' said John; 'tell 'em it's no matter how soon they call, make no kinder difference to us,' said John, running his fingers through the shock of hair that thatched his head, and bursting out into a great laugh.

Weary, jaded, and spiritless, Eliza dragged herself up to the door, with her child lying, in a heavy sleep, on her arm. The rough man held the candle to her face, and uttering a kind of compassionate grunt, opened the door of a small bedroom adjoining to the large kitchen where they were standing, and motioned her to go in. He took down a candle, and lighting it, set it upon the table, and then addressed himself to Eliza.

'Now, I say, gal, you needn't be a bit afeard, let who will come here. I'm up to all that sort o' thing,' said he, pointing to two or three goodly rifles over the mantelpiece; 'and most people that know me know that 'twouldn't be healthy to try to get anybody out o' my house when I'm agin it. So *now* you jist go to sleep now, as quiet as if yer mother was a rockin' ye,' said he, as he shut the door.

'Why, this is an uncommon handsome un,' he said to the senator. 'Ah, well; handsome uns has the greatest cause to run sometimes, if they has any kind o' feeling, such as decent women should. I know all about that.'

The senator, in a few words, briefly explained Eliza's history.

'O! ou! aw! now, I want to know?' said the good man, pitifully; 'sho! now, sho! That's natur now, poor crittur! hunted down now like a deer – hunted down, jest for havin' natural feelin's, and doin' what no kind o' mother could help a doin'! I tell ye what, these yer things make me come the nighest to swearin', now, o' most anything,' said honest John, as he wiped his eyes with the back of a great freckled, yellow hand. 'I tell yer what, stranger, it was years and years before I'd jine the church, 'cause the ministers round in our parts used to preach that the Bible went in for these ere cuttings up; and I couldn't be up to 'em with their Greek and Hebrew, and so I took up agin 'em, Bible and all. I never jined the church till I found a minister that was up to 'em all in Greek and all that, and he said right the contrary; and then I took right hold, and jined the church – I did now, fact,' said John, who had been all this time uncorking some very frisky bottled cider, which at this juncture he presented.

'Ye'd better jest put up here, now, till daylight,' said he, heartily, 'and I'll call up the old woman, and have a bed got ready for you in no time.'

'Thank you, my good friend,' said the senator, 'I must be along, to take the night stage for Columbus.'

'Ah, well, then, if you must, I'll go a piece with you, and show you a cross road that will take you there better than the road you came on. That road's mighty bad.'

John equipped himself, and, with a lantern in hand, was soon seen guiding the senator's carriage towards a road that ran down in a hollow, at the back of his dwelling. When they parted, the senator put into his hand a ten-dollar bill.

'It's for her,' he said briefly.

'Ay, ay,' said John, with equal conciseness.

They shook hands and parted.

CHAPTER X

The Property is Carried Off

THE FEBRUARY MORNING looked grey and drizzling through the window of Uncle Tom's cabin. It looked on downcast faces, the images of mournful hearts. The little table stood out before the fire, covered with an ironing-cloth; a coarse but clean shirt or two, fresh from the iron, hung on the back of a chair by the fire, and Aunt Chloe had another spread out before her on the table. Carefully she rubbed and ironed every fold and every hem, with the most scrupulous exactness, every now and then raising her hand to her face to wipe off the tears that were coursing down her cheeks.

Tom sat by, with his Testament[71] open on his knee, and his head leaning upon his hand; but neither spoke. It was yet early, and the children lay all asleep together in their little rude trundle-bed.

Tom, who had to the full the gentle, domestic heart, which, woe for them! has been a peculiar characteristic of his unhappy race, got up and walked silently to look at his children.

'It's the last time,' he said.

Aunt Chloe did not answer, only rubbed away over and over on the coarse shirt, already as smooth as hands could make it; and finally setting her iron suddenly down with a despairing plunge, she sat down to the table, and 'lifted up her voice and wept'.[72]

'S'pose we must be resigned; but, O Lord! how ken I? If I know'd anything whar you's goin', or how they'd sarve you! Missis says she'll try and 'deem ye, in a year or two; but Lor! nobody never comes up that goes down thar! They kills 'em! I've hearn 'em tell how dey works 'em up on dem ar plantations.'

'There'll be the same God there, Chloe, that there is here.'

'Well,' said Aunt Chloe, 's'pose dere will; but de Lord lets dreful things happen, sometimes. I don't seem to get no comfort dat way.'

'I'm in the Lord's hands,' said Tom; 'nothin' can go no furder than He lets it; and thar's *one* thing I can thank Him for. It's *me* that's sold and going down, and not you nur the chil'en. Here you're safe; what comes will come only on me; and the Lord, He'll help me – I know He will.'

Ah, brave, manly heart, smothering thine own sorrow to comfort thy beloved ones! Tom spoke with a thick utterance, and with a bitter choking in his throat – but he spoke brave and strong.

'Let's think on our marcies!' he added tremulously, as if he was quite sure he needed to think on them very hard indeed.

'Marcies!' said Aunt Chloe; 'don't see no marcy in 't! 'tan't right! 'tan't right it should be so! Mas'r never ought ter left it so that ye *could* be took for his debts. Ye've arnt him all he gets for ye, twice over. He owed ye yer freedom, and ought ter gin't to yer years ago. Mebbe he can't help himself now, but I feel it's wrong. Nothing can't beat that ar out o' me. Sich a faithful crittur as ye've been, and allers so't his business 'fore yer own every way, and reckoned on him more than yer own wife and chil'en! Them as sells heart's love and heart's blood to get out thar scrapes, de Lord'll be up to 'em!'

'Chloe! now, if ye love me, ye won't talk so, when perhaps it's jest the last time we'll ever have together! And I'll tell ye, Chloe, it goes agin me to hear one word agin mas'r. Wan't he put in my arms a baby? – it's natur I should think a heap of him. And he couldn't be 'spected to think so much of poor Tom. Mas'rs is used to havin' all these yer things done for 'em, and nat'lly they don't think so much on't. They can't be 'spected to, no way. Set him 'longside of other mas'rs – who's had the treatment and the livin' I have had? And he never would have let this yer come on me if he could have seed it aforehand. I know he wouldn't.'

'Wal, anyway thar's wrong about it *somewhar*,' said Aunt Chloe, in whom a stubborn sense of justice was a predominant trait. 'I can't jest make out whar 'tis, but thar's wrong somewhar, I'm *clar* o' that.'

'Yer ought ter look up to the Lord above; He's above all – thar don't a sparrow fall without Him.'

'It don't seem to comfort me, but I 'spect it orter,' said Aunt Chloe. 'But dar's no use talkin': I'll jes wet up de corn-cake, and get ye one good breakfast, 'cause nobody knows when you'll get another.'

In order to appreciate the sufferings of the negroes sold South, it must be remembered that all the instinctive affections of that race are peculiarly strong. Their local attachments are very abiding. They are not naturally daring and enterprising, but home-loving and affection-ate. Add to this all the terrors with which ignorance invests the unknown, and add to this, again, that selling to the South is set before the negro from childhood as the last severity of punishment. The threat that terrifies more than whipping or torture of any kind is the threat of being sent down river. We have ourselves heard this feeling expressed by them, and seen the unaffected horror with which they will sit in their gossiping hours, and tell frightful stories of that 'down river', which to them is

> That undiscovered country, from whose bourne
> No traveller returns.[73]

A missionary among the fugitives in Canada told us that many of the fugitives confessed themselves to have escaped from comparatively kind masters, and that they were induced to brave the perils of escape, in almost every case, by the desperate horror with which they regarded being sold South – a doom which was hanging either over themselves or their husbands, their wives or children. This nerves the African, naturally patient, timid, and unenterprising, with heroic courage, and leads him to suffer hunger, cold, pain, the perils of the wilderness, and the more dread penalties of recapture.

The simple morning meal now smoked on the table, for Mrs Shelby had excused Aunt Chloe's attendance at the great house that morning. The poor soul had expended all her little energies on this farewell feast – had killed and dressed her choicest chicken, and prepared her corn-cake with scrupulous exactness, just to her husband's taste, and brought out certain mysterious jars on the mantelpiece, some preserves that were never produced except on extreme occasions.

'Lor, Pete,' said Mose, triumphantly, 'han't we got a buster of a breakfast!' at the same time catching at a fragment of the chicken.

Aunt Chloe gave him a sudden box on the ear. 'Thar now! crowing over the last breakfast yer poor daddy's gwine to have to home!'

'O Chloe!' said Tom, gently.

'Wal, I can't help it,' said Aunt Chloe, hiding her face in her apron. 'I's so tossed about, it makes me act ugly.'

The boys stood quite still, looking first at their father and then at their mother, while the baby, climbing up her clothes, began an imperious, commanding cry.

'Thar!' said Aunt Chloe, wiping her eyes and taking up the baby; 'now I's done, I hope – now do eat somethin'. This yer's my nicest chicken. Thar, boys, ye shall have some, poor critturs! Yer mammy's been cross to yer.'

The boys needed no second invitation, and went in with great zeal for the eatables; and it was well they did so, as otherwise there would have been very little performed to any purpose by the party.

'Now,' said Aunt Chloe, bustling about after breakfast, 'I must put up yer clothes. Jest like as not he'll take 'em all away. I know thar ways – mean as dirt, they is! Wal, now, yer flannels for rheumatis is in this corner; so be careful, 'cause there won't nobody make ye no more. Then here's yer old shirts, and these yer is new ones. I toed off these yer stockings last night, and put de ball[74] in 'em to mend with. But Lor! who'll ever mend for ye?' and Aunt Chloe, again overcome, laid her head on the box side, and sobbed. 'To think on't! no crittur to do for ye, sick or well! I don't railly think I ought ter be good now!'

The boys having eaten everything there was on the breakfast-table, began now to take some thought of the case; and, seeing their mother crying, and their father looking very sad, began to whimper and put their hands to their eyes. Uncle Tom had the baby on his knee, and was letting her enjoy herself to the utmost extent, scratching his face and pulling his hair, and occasionally breaking out into clamorous explosions of delight, evidently arising out of her own internal reflections.

'Ay, crow away, poor crittur!' said Aunt Chloe; 'ye'll have to come to it, too! Ye'll live to see yer husband sold; or mebbe be sold yerself; and these yer boys, they's to be sold, I s'pose, too, jest like as not, when dey gets good for somethin'; an't no use in niggers havin' nothin'!'

Here one of the boys cried out, 'Thar's missis a-comin' in!'

'She can't do no good; what's she coming for?' said Aunt Chloe.

Mrs Shelby entered. Aunt Chloe set a chair for her in a manner decidedly gruff and crusty. She did not seem to notice either the action or the manner. She looked pale and anxious.

'Tom,' she said, 'I come to – ' and stopping suddenly, and regarding the silent group, she sat down in the chair, and, covering her face with her handkerchief, began to sob.

'Lor, now, missis, don't – don't!' said Aunt Chloe, bursting out in her turn; and for a few moments they all wept in company. And in those tears they all shed together, the high and the lowly, melted away all the heart-burnings and anger of the oppressed. O, ye who visit the distressed, do ye know that everything your money can buy, given with a cold, averted face, is not worth one honest tear shed in real sympathy?

'My good fellow,' said Mrs Shelby, 'I can't give you anything to do you any good. If I give you money it will only be taken from you. But I tell you solemnly, and before God, that I will keep trace of you, and bring you back as soon as I can command the money; and, till then, trust in God!'

Here the boys called out that Mas'r Haley was coming, and then an unceremonious kick pushed open the door. Haley stood there in very ill-humour, having ridden hard the night before, and being not at all pacified by his ill-success in recapturing his prey.

'Come,' said he, 'ye nigger, ye'r ready? Servant, ma'am!' said he, taking off his hat, as he saw Mrs Shelby.

Aunt Chloe shut and corded the box, and, getting up, looked gruffly on the trader, her tears seeming suddenly turned to sparks of fire.

Tom rose up meekly to follow his new master, and raised up his heavy box on his shoulder. His wife took the baby in her arms to go with him to the wagon, and the children, still crying, trailed on behind.

Mrs Shelby, walking up to the trader, detained him for a few moments, talking with him in an earnest manner; and while she was thus talking, the whole family party proceeded to a wagon that stood ready harnessed at the door. A crowd of all the old and young hands on the place stood gathered around it, to bid farewell to their old associate. Tom had been looked up to, both as a head servant and a Christian teacher, by all the place, and there was much honest sympathy and grief about him, particularly among the women.

'Why, Chloe, you bar it better 'n we do!' said one of the women, who had been weeping freely, noticing the gloomy calmness with which Aunt Chloe stood by the wagon.

'I's done *my* tears!' she said, looking grimly at the trader, who was coming up. 'I does not feel to cry 'fore dat ar old limb, nohow!'[75]

'Get in!' said Haley to Tom, as he strode through the crowd of servants, who looked at him with lowering brows.

Tom got in, and Haley, drawing out from under the wagon-seat a heavy pair of shackles, made them fast around each ankle.

A smothered groan of indignation ran through the whole circle, and Mrs Shelby spoke from the veranda –

'Mr Haley, I assure you that precaution is entirely unnecessary.'

'Don't know, ma'am; I've lost one five hundred dollars from his yer place, and I can't afford to run no more risks.'

'What else could she 'spect on him?' said Aunt Chloe, indignantly; while the two boys, who now seemed to comprehend at once their father's destiny, clung to her gown, sobbing and groaning vehemently.

'I'm sorry,' said Tom, 'that Mas'r George happened to be away.'

George had gone to spend two or three days with a companion on a neighbouring estate, and having departed early in the morning, before Tom's misfortune had been made public, had left without hearing of it.

'Give my love to Mas'r George,' he said, earnestly.

Haley whipped up the horse, and, with a steady, mournful look, fixed to the last on the old place, Tom was whirled away.

Mr Shelby at this time was not at home. He had sold Tom under the spur of a driving necessity, to get out of the power of a man whom he dreaded, and his first feeling, after the consummation of the bargain, had been that of relief. But his wife's expostulations awoke his half-slumbering regrets; and Tom's manly disinterestedness increased the unpleasantness of his feelings. It was in vain that he said to himself that he had a *right* to do it, that everybody did it, and that some did it without even the excuse of necessity; he could not satisfy his own feelings; and that he might not witness the unpleasant scenes of the consummation, he had gone on a short business tour up the country, hoping that all would be over before he returned.[76]

Tom and Haley rattled on along the dusty road, whirling past every old familiar spot, until the bounds of the estate were fairly passed, and they found themselves out on the open pike. After they had ridden about a mile, Haley suddenly drew up at the door of a blacksmith's shop, when, taking out with him a pair of handcuffs, he stepped into the shop to have a little alteration in them.

'These yer's a little too small for his build,' said Haley, showing the fetters, and pointing out to Tom.

'Lor! now, if thar an't Shelby's Tom! He han't sold him, now?' said the smith.

'Yes, he has,' said Haley.

'Now, ye don't! Well, reely,' said the smith, 'who'd a thought it! Why, ye needn't go to fetterin' him up this yer way. He's the faithfullest, best crittur – '

'Yes, yes,' said Haley; 'but your good fellers are just the critturs to want ter run off. Them stupid ones, as doesn't care whar they go, and shiftless, drunken ones, as don't care for nothin', they'll stick by, and like as not be rather pleased to be toted round; but these yer prime fellers they hates it like sin. No way but to fetter 'em; got legs – they'll use 'em, no mistake.'

'Well,' said the smith, feeling among his tools, 'them plantations down thar, stranger, an't jest the place a Kentuck nigger wants to go to; they dies thar tol'able fast, don't they?'

'Wal, yes, tol'able fast, ther dying is; what with the 'climating and one thing and another, they dies so as to keep the market up pretty brisk,' said Haley.

'Wal, now, a feller can't help thinkin' it's a mighty pity to have a nice, quiet, likely feller, as good un as Tom is, go down to be fairly ground up on one of them ar sugar plantations.'

'Wal, he's got a far chance. I promised to do well by him. I'll get him in house-servant in some good old family, and then, if he stands the fever and 'climating, he'll have a berth good as any nigger ought ter ask for.'

'He leaves his wife and chil'en up here, s'pose?'

'Yes; but he'll get another thar. Lord, thar's women enough everywhar,' said Haley.

Tom was sitting very mournfully on the outside of the shop while this conversation was going on. Suddenly he heard the quick, short click of a horse's hoof behind him; and, before he could fairly awake from his surprise, young Master George sprang into the wagon, threw his arms tumultuously round his neck, and was sobbing and scolding with energy.

'I declare, it's real mean! I don't care what they say, any of 'em! It's a nasty, mean shame! If I was a man they shouldn't do it – they should not, *so*!' said George, with a kind of subdued howl.

'Oh! Mas'r George! this does me good!' said Tom. 'I couldn't bar to go off without seein' ye! It does me real good, ye can't tell!' Here Tom made some movement of his feet, and George's eye fell on the fetters.

'What a shame!' he exclaimed, lifting his hands. 'I'll knock that old fellow down – I will!'

'No, you won't, Mas'r George; and you must not talk so loud. It won't help me any to anger him.'

'Well, I won't, then, for your sake; but only to think of it – isn't it a shame? They never sent for me, nor sent me any word, and if it hadn't been for Tom Lincon, I shouldn't have heard it. I tell you, I blew 'em up well, all of 'em, at home!'

'That ar wasn't right, I'm 'feard, Mas'r George.'

'Can't help it! I say it's a shame! Look here, Uncle Tom,' said he, turning his back to the shop, and speaking in a mysterious tone, '*I've brought you my dollar!*'[77]

'Oh! I couldn't think o' takin' on't, Mas'r George, no ways in the world!' said Tom, quite moved.

'But you *shall* take it!' said George; 'look here; I told Aunt Chloe I'd do it, and she advised me just to make a hole in it, and put a string through, so you could hang it round your neck, and keep it out of sight; else this mean scamp would take it away. I tell ye, Tom, I want to blow him up! it would do me good!'

'No, don't, Mas'r George, for it won't do *me* any good.'

'Well, I won't, for your sake,' said George, busily tying his dollar round Tom's neck; 'but there, now, button your coat tight over it, and keep it, and remember, every time you see it, that I'll come down after you, and bring you back. Aunt Chloe and I have been talking about it. I told her not to fear; I'll see to it, and I'll tease father's life out, if he don't do it.'

'Oh, Mas'r George, ye mustn't talk so 'bout yer father!'

'Lor, Uncle Tom, I don't mean anything bad.'

'And now, Mas'r George,' said Tom, 'ye must be a good boy; 'member how many hearts is sot on ye. Al'ays keep close to yer mother. Don't be gettin' into any of them foolish ways boys has, of getting too big to mind their mothers. Tell ye what, Mas'r George, the Lord gives good many things twice over; but he don't give ye a mother but once. Ye'll never see sich another woman, Mas'r George, if ye live to be a hundred years old. So now, you hold on to her, and grow up, and be a comfort to her, thar's my own good boy – you will now, won't ye?'

'Yes, I will, Uncle Tom,' said George, seriously.

'And be careful of yer speaking, Mas'r George. Young boys, when they comes to your age, is wilful, sometimes – it's natur they should be. But real gentlemen, such as I hopes you'll be, never lets fall no words that isn't 'spectful to thar parents. Ye an't 'fended, Mas'r George?'

'No, indeed, Uncle Tom; you always did give me good advice.'

'I's older, ye know,' said Tom, stroking the boy's fine, curly head with his large, strong hand, but speaking in a voice as tender as a woman's, 'and I sees all that's bound up in you. Oh, Mas'r George, you has everything – larnin', privileges, readin', writin' – and you'll grow up to be a great, learned, good man, and all the people on the place and your mother and father'll be so proud on ye! Be a good mas'r, like yer father; and be a Christian, like yer mother. 'Member yer Creator in the days o' yer youth,[78] Mas'r George.'

'I'll be *real* good, Uncle Tom, I tell you,' said George. 'I'm going to be a *first-rater*, and don't you be discouraged. I'll have you back to the place yet. As I told Aunt Chloe this morning, I'll build your house all over, and you shall have a room for a parlour with a carpet on it, when I'm a man. Oh, you'll have good times yet!'

Haley now came to the door with the handcuffs in his hands.

'Look here, now, mister,' said George, with an air of great superiority, as he got out, 'I shall let father and mother know how you treat Uncle Tom!'

'You're welcome,' said the trader.

'I should think you'd be ashamed to spend all your life buying men and women, and chaining them, like cattle! I should think you'd feel mean!' said George.

'So long as your grand folks wants to buy men and women, I'm as good as they is,' said Haley; ' 'tan't any meaner sellin' on 'em, than 'tis buyin'!'

'I'll never do either when I'm a man,' said George; 'I'm ashamed this day, that I'm a Kentuckian. I always was proud of it before;' and George sat very straight on his horse, and looked round with an air as if he expected the state would be impressed with his opinion.

'Well, goodbye, Uncle Tom; keep a stiff upper lip,' said George

'Goodbye, Mas'r George,' said Tom, looking fondly and admiringly at him. 'God Almighty bless you! Ah! Kentucky han't got many like you!' he said, in the fullness of his heart, as the frank, boyish face was lost to his view. Away he went, and Tom looked, till the clatter of his horse's heels died away, the last sound or sight of his home. But over his heart there seemed to be a warm spot, where those young hands had placed that precious dollar. Tom put up his hand, and held it close to his heart.

'Now I tell ye what, Tom,' said Haley, as he came up to the wagon, and threw in the handcuffs, 'I mean to start far with ye, as I gen'ally do with my niggers; and I'll tell ye now, to begin with, you treat me far, and I'll treat you far; I an't never hard on my niggers. Calculates to do the best for 'em I can. Now, ye see, you'd better jest settle down comfortable, and not be tryin' no tricks; because nigger's tricks of all sorts I'm up to, and it's no use. If niggers is quiet, and don't try to get off, they has good times with me; and if they don't, why, it's thar fault, and not mine.'

Tom assured Haley that he had no present intentions of running off. In fact, the exhortation seemed rather a superfluous one to a man with a great pair of iron fetters on his feet. But Mr Haley had got in the habit of commencing his relations with his stock with little exhortations of this nature, calculated, as he deemed, to inspire cheerfulness and confidence, and prevent the necessity of any unpleasant scenes.

And here, for the present, we take our leave of Tom, to pursue the fortunes of other characters in our story.

CHAPTER XI

In Which Property Gets into an Improper State of Mind

IT WAS LATE in a drizzly afternoon that a traveller alighted at the door of a small country hotel, in the village of N—, in Kentucky. In the bar-room he found assembled quite a miscellaneous company, whom stress of weather had driven to harbour, and the place presented the usual scenery of such reunions. Great, tall, raw-boned Kentuckians, attired in hunting-shirts, and trailing their loose joints over a vast extent of territory, with the easy lounge peculiar to the race – rifles stacked away in the corner, shot-pouches, game-bags, hunting-dogs, and little negroes, all rolled together in the corners, were the characteristic features in the picture. At each end of the fireplace sat a long-legged gentleman, with his chair tipped back, his hat on his head, and the heels of his muddy boots reposing sublimely on the mantelpiece – a position, we will inform our readers, decidedly favourable to the turn of reflection incident to Western taverns, where travellers exhibit a decided preference for this particular mode of elevating their understandings.

Mine host, who stood behind the bar, like most of his countrymen, was great of stature, good-natured, and loose-jointed, with an enormous shock of hair on his head, and a great tall hat on the top of that.

In fact, everybody in the room bore on his head this characteristic emblem of man's sovereignty; whether it were felt hat, palm-leaf, greasy beaver, or fine new chapeau,[79] there it reposed with true republican independence. In truth, it appeared to be the characteristic mark of every individual. Some wore them tipped rakishly to one side – these were your men of humour, jolly, free-and-easy dogs; some had them jammed independently down over their noses – these were your hard characters, thorough men, who, when they wore their hats, *wanted* to wear them, and to wear them just as they had a mind to; there were those who had them set far over back – wide-awake men, who wanted a clear prospect; while careless men, who did not know or care, how their hats sat, had them shaking about in all directions. The various hats, in fact, were quite a Shakespearean study.

Divers negroes, in very free-and-easy pantaloons, and with no redundancy in the shirt line, were scuttling about, hither and thither, without bringing to pass any very particular results, except expressing a generic willingness to turn over everything in creation, generally for the benefit of mas'r and his guests. Add to this picture a jolly, crackling, rollicking fire, going rejoicingly up a great wide chimney – the outer door and every window being set wide open, and the calico window-curtain flopping and snapping in a good stiff breeze of damp raw air – and you have an idea of the jollities of a Kentucky tavern.

Your Kentuckian of the present day is a good illustration of the doctrine of transmitted instincts and peculiarities. His fathers were mighty hunters – men who lived in the woods, and slept under the free, open heavens, with the stars to hold their candles; and their descendant to this day always acts as if the house were his camp – wears his hat at all hours, tumbles himself about, and puts his heels on the tops of chairs or mantelpieces, just as his father rolled on the greensward, and put his upon trees and logs – keeps all the windows and doors open, winter and summer, that he may get enough air for his great lungs – calls everybody 'stranger' with nonchalant *bonhomie*,[80] and is altogether the frankest, easiest, most jovial creature living.

Into such an assembly of the free-and-easy our traveller entered. He was a short, thick-set man, carefully dressed, with a round, good-natured countenance, and something rather fussy and particular in his appearance. He was very careful of his valise and umbrella, bringing them in with his own hands, and resisting, pertinaciously, all offers from the various servants to relieve him of them. He looked round the bar-room with rather an anxious air, and, retreating with his valuables to the warmest corner, disposed them under his chair, sat down, and looked rather apprehensively up at the worthy whose heels illustrated the end of the mantelpiece, who was spitting from right to left with a courage and energy rather alarming to gentlemen of weak nerves and particular habits.

'I say, stranger, how are ye?' said the aforesaid gentleman, firing an honorary salute of tobacco-juice in the direction of the new arrival.

'Well, I reckon,' was the reply of the other, as he dodged, with some alarm, the threatening honour.

'Any news?' said the respondent, taking out a strip of tobacco and a large hunting-knife from his pocket.

'Not that I know of,' said the man.

'Chaw?' said the first speaker, handing the old gentleman a bit of his tobacco with a decidedly brotherly air.

'No, thank ye; it don't agree with me,' said the little man, edging off.

'Don't, eh?' said the other, easily, and stowing away the morsel in his own mouth, in order to keep up the supply of tobacco-juice for the general benefit of society.

The old gentleman uniformly gave a little start whenever his long-sided brother fired in his direction; and this being observed by his companion, he very good-naturedly turned his artillery to another quarter, and proceeded to storm one of the fire-irons with a degree of military talent fully sufficient to take a city.

'What's that?' said the old gentleman, observing some of the company formed in a group around a large handbill.

'Nigger advertised!' said one of the company, briefly.

Mr Wilson – for that was the old gentleman's name – rose up, and after carefully adjusting his valise and umbrella, proceeded deliberately to take out his spectacles and fix them on his nose; and, this operation being performed, read as follows:

> 'Ran away from the subscriber, my mulatto boy, George. Said George, six feet in height, a very light mulatto, brown curly hair; is very intelligent, speaks handsomely, can read and write; will probably try to pass for a white man; is deeply scarred on his back and shoulders; has been branded in his right hand with the letter H. I will give four hundred dollars for him alive, and the same sum for satisfactory proof that he has been killed.'

The old gentleman read this advertisement from end to end, in a low voice, as if he were studying it.

The long-legged veteran, who had been besieging the fire-irons, as before related, now took down his cumbrous length, and rearing aloft his tall form, walked up to the advertisement, and very deliberately spat a full discharge of tobacco-juice on it.

'There's my mind upon that!' said he, briefly, and sat down again.

'Why, now, stranger, what's that for?' said mine host.

'I'd do it all the same to the writer of that ar paper, if he was here,' said the long man, coolly resuming his old employment of cutting tobacco. 'Any man that owns a boy like that, and can't find any better way o' treating on him, *deserves* to lose him. Such papers as these is a shame to Kentucky; that's my mind right out, if anybody wants to know!'

'Well, now, that's a fact,' said mine host, as he made an entry in his book.

'I've got a gang of boys, sir,' said the long man, resuming his attack on the fire-irons, 'and I jest tells 'em – "Boys," says I – "*run* now! dig! put! jest when ye want to! I never shall come to look after you!" That's the way I keep mine. Let 'em know they are free to run any time, and it jest breaks up their wanting to. More 'n all, I've got free papers[81] for 'em all recorded, in case I gets keeled up any o' these times, and they knows it; and I tell ye, stranger, there an't a fellow in our parts gets more out of his niggers than I do. Why, my boys have been to Cincinnati, with five hundred dollars' worth of colts, and brought me back the money, all straight, time and agin. It stands to reason they should. Treat 'em like dogs, and you'll have dogs' works and dogs' actions. Treat 'em like men, and you'll have men's works.' And the honest drover, in his warmth, endorsed this moral sentiment by firing a perfect *feu de joie*[82] at the fireplace.

'I think you're altogether right, friend,' said Mr Wilson; 'and this boy described here *is* a fine fellow – no mistake about that. He worked for me some half-dozen years in my bagging factory, and he was my best hand, sir. He is an ingenious fellow, too; he invented a machine for the cleaning of hemp – a really valuable affair; it's gone into use in several factories. His master holds the patent of it.'

'I'll warrant ye,' said the drover, 'holds it and makes money out of it, and then turns round and brands the boy in his right hand. If I had a fair chance, I'd mark him, I reckon, so that he'd carry it *one* while.'

'These yer knowin' boys is allers aggravatin' and sarcy,' said a coarse-looking fellow, from the other side of the room; 'that's why they gets cut up and marked so. If they behaved themselves, they wouldn't.'

'That is to say, the Lord made 'em men, and it's a hard squeeze getting 'em down into beasts,' said the drover, dryly.

'Bright niggers isn't no kind of 'vantage to their masters,' continued the other, well entrenched in a coarse, unconscious obtuseness, from the contempt of his opponent. 'What's the use o' talents and them things, if you can't get the use on 'em yourself? Why, all the use they make on't is to get round you. I've had one or two of these fellers, and I jest sold 'em down river. I knew I'd got to lose 'em, first or last, if I didn't.'

'Better send orders up to the Lord to make you a set, and leave out their souls entirely,' said the drover.

Here the conversation was interrupted by the approach of a small one-horse buggy to the inn. It had a genteel appearance, and a well-dressed, gentlemanly man, sat on the seat, with a coloured servant driving.

The whole party examined the newcomer with the interest with which a set of loafers in a rainy day usually examine every newcomer. He was very tall, with a dark, Spanish complexion, fine, expressive black eyes, and close-curling hair, also of a glossy blackness. His well-formed aquiline nose, straight thin lips, and the admirable contour of his finely-formed limbs, impressed the whole company instantly with the idea of something uncommon. He walked easily in among the company, and with a nod indicated to his waiter where to place his trunk, bowed to the company, and, with his hat in his hand, walked up leisurely to the bar, and gave in his name as Henry Butler, Oaklands, Shelby County. Turning, with an indifferent air, he sauntered up to the advertisement, and read it over.

'Jim,' he said to his man, 'seems to me we met a boy something like this, up at Bernan's, didn't we?'

'Yes, mas'r!' said Jim, 'only I an't sure about the hand.'

'Well, I didn't look, of course,' said the stranger, with a careless yawn. Then, walking up to the landlord, he desired him to furnish him with a private apartment, as he had some writing to do immediately.

The landlord was all obsequious, and a relay of about seven negroes, old and young, male and female, little and big, were soon whizzing about, like a covey of partridges, bustling, hurrying, treading on each other's toes, and tumbling over each other, in their zeal to get mas'r's room ready, while he seated himself easily on a chair in the middle of the room, and entered into conversation with the man who sat next to him.

The manufacturer, Mr Wilson, from the time of the entrance of the stranger, had regarded him with an air of disturbed and uneasy curiosity. He seemed to himself to have met and been acquainted with him somewhere, but he could not recollect. Every few moments, when the man spoke, or moved, or smiled, he would start and fix his eyes on him, and then suddenly withdraw them, as the bright, dark eyes met his with such unconcerned coolness. At last, a sudden recollection seemed to flash upon him, for he stared at the stranger with such an air of blank amazement and alarm, that he walked up to him.

'Mr Wilson, I think,' said he, in a tone of recognition, and extending his hand. 'I beg your pardon, I didn't recollect you before. I see you remember me – Mr Butler, of Oaklands, Shelby County.'

'Ye–yes–yes, sir,' said Mr Wilson, like one speaking in a dream.

Just then a negro boy entered, and announced that mas'r's room was ready.

'Jim, see to the trunks,' said the gentleman, negligently; then addressing himself to Mr Wilson, he added – 'I should like to have a few moments' conversation with you on business, in my room, if you please.'

Mr Wilson followed him, as one who walks in his sleep; and they proceeded to a large upper chamber, where a new-made fire was crackling, and various servants flying about, putting finishing touches to the arrangements.

When all was done, and the servants departed, the young man deliberately locked the door, and putting the key in his pocket, faced about, and folding his arms on his bosom, looked Mr Wilson full in the face.

'George!' said Mr Wilson.

'Yes, George,' said the young man.

'I couldn't have thought it!'

'I am pretty well disguised, I fancy,' said the young man, with a smile. 'A little walnut bark has made my yellow skin a genteel brown, and I've dyed my hair black; so you see I don't answer to the advertisement at all.'

'Oh, George! but this is a dangerous game you are playing. I could not have advised you to it.'

'I can do it on my own responsibility,' said George, with the same proud smile.

We remark, *en passant*,[83] that George was, by his father's side, of white descent. His mother was one of those unfortunates of her race, marked out by personal beauty to be the slave of the passions of her possessor, and the mother of children who may never know a father. From one of the proudest families in Kentucky he had inherited a set of fine European features, and a high indomitable spirit. From his mother he had received only a slight mulatto tinge, amply compensated by its accompanying rich dark eye. A slight change in the tint of the skin and the colour of his hair had metamorphosed him into the Spanish-looking fellow he then appeared; and as gracefulness of movement and gentlemanly manners had always been perfectly natural to him, he found no difficulty in playing the bold part he had adopted – that of a gentleman travelling with his domestic.

Mr Wilson, a good-natured but extremely fidgety and cautious old gentleman, ambled up and down the room, appearing, as John Bunyan hath it, 'much tumbled up and down in his mind',[84] and divided between his wish to help George, and a certain confused notion of maintaining law and order: so, as he shambled about, he delivered himself as follows –

'Well, George, I s'pose you're running away – leaving your lawful master, George – (I don't wonder at it) – at the same time I am sorry,

George – yes, decidedly – I think I must say that, George – it's my duty to tell you so.'

'Why are you sorry, sir?' said George, calmly.

'Why to see you, as it were, setting yourself in opposition to the laws of your country.'

'*My* country!' said George, with a strong and bitter emphasis; 'what country have I, but the grave? – and I wish to God that I was laid there!'

'Why, George, no – no – it won't do; this way of talking is wicked – unscriptural. George, you've got a hard master – in fact, he is – well he conducts himself reprehensibly – I can't pretend to defend him. But you know how the angel commanded Hagar to return to her mistress, and submit herself under her hand; and the apostle sent back Onesimus[85] to his master.'

'Don't quote Bible at me that way, Mr Wilson,' said George, with a flashing eye, 'don't! for my wife is a Christian, and I mean to be, if ever I get to where I can; but to quote Bible to a fellow in my circumstances is enough to make him give it up altogether. I appeal to God Almighty; I'm willing to go with the case to Him, and ask Him if I do wrong to seek my freedom.'

'These feelings are quite natural, George,' said the good-natured man, blowing his nose. 'Yes they're natural, but it is my duty not to encourage 'em in you. Yes, my boy, I'm sorry for you, now; it's a bad case – very bad; but the apostle says, "Let everyone abide in the condition in which he is called."[86] We must all submit to the indications of Providence, George – don't you see?'

George stood with his head drawn back, his arms folded tightly over his broad breast, and a bitter smile curling his lips.

'I wonder, Mr Wilson, if the Indians should come and take you a prisoner away from your wife and children, and want to keep you all your life hoeing corn for them, if you'd think it your duty to abide in the condition in which you were called! I rather think that you'd think the first stray horse you could find an indication of Providence – shouldn't you?'

The little old gentleman stared with both eyes at this illustration of the case; but though not much of a reasoner, he had the sense in which some logicians on this particular subject do not excel – that of saying nothing where nothing could be said. So, as he stood carefully stroking his umbrella, and folding and patting down all the creases in it, he proceeded on with his exhortations in a general way.

'You see, George, you know, now, I always have stood your friend;

and whatever I've said, I've said for your good. Now, here, it seems to me, you're running an awful risk. You can't hope to carry it out. If you're taken, it will be worse with you than ever; they'll only abuse you, and half-kill you, and sell you down river.'

'Mr Wilson, I know all this,' said George. 'I *do* run a risk, but – ' he threw open his overcoat, and showed two pistols and a bowie-knife. 'There!' he said, 'I'm ready for 'em! Down south I never *will* go. No! if it comes to that, I can earn myself at least six feet of free soil – the first and last I shall ever own in Kentucky!'

'Why, George, this state of mind is awful! it's getting really desperate, George! I'm concerned. Going to break the laws of your country!'

'My country again! Mr Wilson, *you* have a country; but what country have *I*, or anyone like me, born of slave mothers? What laws are there for us? We don't make them – we don't consent to them – we have nothing to do with them; all they do for us is to crush us, and keep us down. Haven't I heard your Fourth-of-July speeches? Don't you tell us all, once a year, that governments derive their just power from the consent of the governed?[87] Can't a fellow *think* that hears such things? Can't he put this and that together, and see what it comes to?'

Mr Wilson's mind was one of those that may not inaptly be represented by a bale of cotton – downy, soft, benevolently fuzzy, and confused. He really pitied George with all his heart, and had a sort of dim and cloudy perception of the style of feeling that agitated him; but he deemed it his duty to go on talking *good* to him, with infinite pertinacity.

'George, this is bad. I must tell you, you know, as a friend, you'd better not be meddling with such notions; they are bad, George, very bad, for boys in your condition – very;' and Mr Wilson sat down to a table, and began nervously chewing the handle of his umbrella.

'See here, now, Mr Wilson,' said George, coming up and sitting himself determinately down in front of him; 'look at me, now. Don't I sit before you, every way, just as much a man as you are? Look at my face – look at my hands – look at my body,' and the young man drew himself up proudly. 'Why am I *not* a man, as much as anybody? Well, Mr Wilson, hear what I can tell you. I had a father – one of your Kentucky gentlemen – who didn't think enough of me to keep me from being sold with his dogs and horses, to satisfy the estate, when he died. I saw my mother put up at sheriff's sale,[88] with her seven children. They were sold before her eyes, one by one, all to different masters; and I was the youngest. She came and kneeled down before old mas'r, and begged him to buy her with me, that she might have at least one child with her; and he kicked her away with his heavy boot. I saw him do it; and the last that I heard was her moans and screams, when I was tied to his horse's neck, to be carried off to his place.'

'Well, then?'

'My master traded with one of the men, and bought my oldest sister. She was a pious, good girl – a member of the Baptist church – and as handsome as my poor mother had been. She was well brought up, and had good manners. At first, I was glad she was bought, for I had one friend near me. I was soon sorry for it. Sir, I have stood at the door and heard her whipped, when it seemed as if every blow cut into my naked heart, and I couldn't do anything to help her; and she was whipped, sir, for wanting to live a decent Christian life, such as your laws give no slave-girl a right to live; and at last I saw her chained with a trader's gang, to be sent to market in Orleans – sent there for nothing else but that – and that's the last I know of her. Well, I grew up – long years and years – no father, no mother, no sister, not a living soul that cared for me more than a dog: nothing but whipping, scolding, starving. Why, sir, I've been so hungry that I have been glad to take the bones they threw to their dogs; and yet, when I was a little fellow, and laid awake whole nights and cried, it wasn't the hunger, it wasn't the whipping, I cried for. No, sir; it was for *my mother* and *my sisters* – it was because I hadn't a friend to love me on earth. I never knew what peace or comfort was. I never had a kind word spoken to me till I came to work in your factory. Mr Wilson, you treated me well; you encouraged me to do well, and to learn to read and write, and to try to make something of myself; and God knows how grateful I am for it. Then, sir, I found my wife; you've seen her – you know how beautiful she is. When I found she loved me, when I married her, I scarcely could believe I was alive, I was so happy; and, sir, she is as good as she is beautiful. But now what? Why, now comes my master, takes me right away from my work, and my friends, and all I like, and grinds me down into the very dirt! And why? Because, he says, I forgot who I was; he says, to teach me that I am only a nigger! After all, and last of all, he comes between me and my wife, and says I shall give her up, and live with another woman. And all this your laws give him power to do, in spite of God or man. Mr Wilson, look at it! There isn't *one* of all these things, that have broken the hearts of my mother and my sister, and my wife and myself, but your laws allow, and give every man power to do, in Kentucky, and none can say to him nay! Do you call these the laws of *my* country? Sir, I haven't any country, any more than I have any father. But I'm going to have one. I don't want anything of *your* country, except to be let alone – to go peaceably out of it; and when I get to Canada, where the laws will own me and protect me, *that* shall be my country, and its laws I will obey. But if any man tries to stop me, let him take care, for I am desperate. I'll fight for my liberty to the last breath I breathe. You say your fathers did it; if it was right for them, it is right for me.'

This speech, delivered partly while sitting at the table, and partly walking up and down the room – delivered with tears, and flashing eyes, and despairing gestures – was altogether too much for the good-natured old body to whom it was addressed, who had pulled out a great yellow silk pocket-handkerchief, and was mopping up his face with great energy.

'Blast 'em all!' he suddenly broke out. 'Haven't I always said so – the infernal old cusses? I hope I an't swearing now. Well! go ahead, George, go ahead; but be careful, my boy; don't shoot anybody, George, unless – well – you'd *better* not shoot, I reckon; at least, I wouldn't *hit* anybody, you know. Where is your wife, George?' he added, as he nervously rose, and began walking the room.

'Gone, sir – gone, with her child in her arms, the Lord only knows where. Gone after the north star; and when we ever meet, or whether we meet at all in this world, no creature can tell.'

'Is it possible! astonishing! from such a kind family?'

'Kind families get in debt, and the laws of *our* country allow them to sell the child out of its mother's bosom to pay its master's debts,' said George, bitterly.

'Well, well,' said the honest old man, fumbling in his pocket. 'I s'pose, perhaps, I an't following my judgement – hang it, I *won't* follow my judgement!' he added, suddenly; 'so here, George,' and, taking out a roll of bills from his pocket-book, he offered them to George.

'No, my kind, good sir!' said George, 'you've done a great deal for me, and this might get you into trouble. I have money enough, I hope, to take me as far as I need it.'

'No; but you must, George. Money is a great help everywhere; can't have too much, if you get it honestly. Take it – *do* take it, *now* – do, my boy!'

'On condition, sir, that I may repay it at some future time, I will,' said George, taking up the money.

'And now, George, how long are you going to travel in this way? – not long, or far, I hope. It's well carried on, but too bold. And this black fellow, who is he?'

'A true fellow, who went to Canada more than a year ago. He heard after he got there, that his master was so angry at him for going off that he had whipped his poor old mother; and he has come all the way back to comfort her, and get a chance to get her away.'

'Has he got her?'

'Not yet; he has been hanging about the place, and found no chance yet. Meanwhile, he is going with me as far as Ohio, to put me among friends that helped him, and then he will come back after her.'

'Dangerous, very dangerous!' said the old man.

George drew himself up, and smiled disdainfully.

The old gentleman eyed him from head to foot, with a sort of innocent wonder.

'George, something has brought you out wonderfully. You hold up your head, and speak and move like another man,' said Mr Wilson.

'Because I'm a *free man*!' said George, proudly. 'Yes, sir; I've said "mas'r" for the last time to any man. *I'm free!*'

'Take care! You are not sure – you may be taken.'

'All men are free and equal *in the grave*, if it comes to that, Mr Wilson,' said George.

'I'm perfectly dumbfoundered with your boldness!' said Mr Wilson, 'to come right here to the nearest tavern!'

'Mr Wilson, it is *so* bold, and this tavern is *so* near, that they will never think of it; they will look for me on ahead, and you yourself wouldn't know me. Jim's master don't live in this county; he isn't known in these parts. Besides, he is given up; nobody is looking after him, and nobody will take me up from the advertisement, I think.'

'But the mark in your hand?'

George drew off his glove, and showed a newly-healed scar in his hand.

'That is a parting proof of Mr Harris' regard,' he said, scornfully. 'A fortnight ago, he took it into his head to give it to me, because he said he believed I should try to get away one of these days. Looks interesting, doesn't it?' he said, drawing his glove on again.

'I declare my very blood runs cold when I think of it – your condition and your risks!' said Mr Wilson.

'Mine has run cold a good many years, Mr Wilson; at present, it's about up to the boiling point,' said George.

'Well, my good sir,' continued George, after a few moments' silence, 'I saw you knew me; I thought I'd just have this talk with you, lest your surprised looks should bring me out. I leave early tomorrow morning, before daylight; by tomorrow night I hope to sleep safe in Ohio. I shall travel by daylight, stop at the best hotels, go to the dinner-tables with the lords of the land. So, goodbye, sir; if you hear that I'm taken, you may know that I'm dead!'

George stood up like a rock, and put out his hand with the air of a prince. The friendly little old man shook it heartily, and after a little shower of caution, he took his umbrella, and fumbled his way out of the room.

George stood thoughtfully looking at the door as the old man closed it. A thought seemed to flash across his mind. He hastily stepped to it, and opening it, said –

'Mr Wilson, one word more.'

The old gentleman entered again, and George, as before, locked the door, and then stood for a few moments looking on the floor, irresolutely. At last, raising his head with a sudden effort –

'Mr Wilson, you have shown yourself a Christian in your treatment of me – I want to ask one last deed of Christian kindness of you.'

'Well, George.'

'Well, sir, what you said was true. I *am* running a dreadful risk. There isn't, on earth, a living soul to care if I die,' he added, drawing his breath hard, and speaking with a great effort. 'I shall be kicked out and buried like a dog, and nobody'll think of it a day after – *only my poor wife*! Poor soul! she'll mourn and grieve; and if you'd only contrive, Mr Wilson, to send this little pin to her. She gave it to me for a Christmas present, poor child! Give it to her, and tell her I loved her to the last. Will you? *Will* you?' he added earnestly.

'Yes, certainly poor fellow!' said the old gentleman, taking the pin, with watery eyes, and a melancholy quiver in his voice.

'Tell her one thing,' said George; 'it's my last wish, if she *can* get to Canada, to go there. No matter how kind her mistress is – no matter how much she loves her home; beg her not to go back – for slavery always ends in misery. Tell her to bring up our boy a free man, and then he won't suffer as I have. Tell her this, Mr Wilson, will you?'

'Yes, George, I'll tell her; but I trust you won't die. Take heart, you're a brave fellow. Trust in the Lord, George. I wish in my heart you were safe through, though – that's what I do.'

'*Is* there a God to trust in?' said George, in such a tone of bitter despair as arrested the old gentleman's words. 'Oh, I've seen things all my life that have made me feel that there can't be a God. Yet, Christians don't know how these things look to us. There's a God for you, but is there any for us?'

'Oh, now, don't – don't, my boy!' said the old man, almost sobbing as he spoke; 'don't feel so! There is – there is; clouds and darkness are around about Him, but righteousness and judgement are the habitation of His throne.[89] There's a *God*, George – believe it; trust in Him, and I'm sure He'll help you. Everything will be set right – if not in this life, in another.'

The real piety and benevolence of the simple old man invested him with a temporary dignity and authority, as he spoke. George stopped his distracted walk up and down the room, stood thoughtfully a moment, and then said, quietly –

'Thank you for saying that, my good friend; I'll *think of that*.'

CHAPTER XII

Select Incident of Lawful Trade

In Ramah there was a voice heard – weeping, and lamentation, and great mourning: Rachel weeping for her children, and would not be comforted.[90]

MR HALEY AND TOM jogged onward in their wagon, each, for a time, absorbed in his own reflections. Now, the reflections of two men sitting side by side are a curious thing – seated on the same seat having the same eyes, ears, hands and organs of all sorts, and having pass before their eyes the same objects: it is wonderful what a variety we shall find in these same reflections!

As, for example, Mr Haley; he thought first of Tom's length, and breadth, and height, and what he would sell for, if he was kept fat and in good case till he got him into market. He thought of how he should make out his gang; he thought of the respective market value of certain supposititious men and women and children who were to compose it, and other kindred topics of the business; then he thought of himself, and how humane he was, that whereas other men chained their 'niggers' hand and foot both, he only put fetters on the feet, and left Tom the use of his hands, as long as he behaved well; and he sighed to think how ungrateful human nature was, so that there was even room to doubt whether Tom appreciated his mercies. He had been taken in so by 'niggers' whom he had favoured; but still he was astonished to consider how good-natured he yet remained!

As to Tom, he was thinking over some words of an unfashionable old book, which kept running through his head, again and again, as follows: 'We have here no continuing city, but we seek one to come; wherefore God himself is not ashamed to be called our God; for He hath prepared for us a city.'[91] These words of an ancient volume, got up principally by 'ignorant and unlearned men', have, through all time, kept up somehow a strange sort of power over the minds of poor, simple fellows, like Tom. They stir up the soul from its depths, and rouse, as with trumpet call, courage, energy, and enthusiasm, where before was only the blackness of despair.[92]

Mr Haley, pulled out of his pocket sundry newspapers, and began looking over their advertisements with absorbed interest. He was not a remarkably fluent reader, and was in the habit of reading in a sort of recitative, half-aloud, by way of calling in his ears to verify the deductions of his eyes. In this tone he slowly recited the following paragraph –

'EXECUTORS' SALE – NEGROES! – Agreeably to order of Court, will be sold, on Tuesday, February 20, before the courthouse door, in the town of Washington, Kentucky, the following negroes – Hagar, aged 60; John, aged 30; Ben, aged 21; Saul, aged 25; Albert, aged 14. Sold for the benefit of the creditors and heirs of the estate of Jesse Blutchford, Esq.

SAMUEL MORRIS
THOMAS FLINT } *Executors*[93]

'This yer I must look at,' said he to Tom, for want of somebody else to talk to. 'Ye see, I'm going to get up a prime gang to take down with ye, Tom; it'll make it sociable and pleasant like – good company will, ye know. We must drive right to Washington first and foremost, and then I'll clap you into jail while I does the business.'

Tom received this agreeable intelligence quite meekly; simply wondering, in his own heart, how many of these doomed men had wives and children, and whether they would feel as he did about leaving them. It is to be confessed, too, that the naïve, off-hand information that he was to be thrown into jail by no means produced an agreeable impression on a poor fellow who had always prided himself on a strictly honest and upright course of life. Yes, Tom, we must confess it, was rather proud of his honesty, poor fellow – not having very much else to be proud of; if he had belonged to some of the higher walks of society, he, perhaps, would never have been reduced to such straits. However, the day wore on, and the evening saw Haley and Tom comfortably accommodated in Washington – the one in a tavern, and the other in a jail.

About eleven o'clock the next day, a mixed throng was gathered around the courthouse steps – smoking, chewing, spitting, swearing, and conversing, according to their respective tastes and turns, waiting for the auction to commence. The men and women to be sold sat in a group apart, talking in a low tone to each other. The woman who had been advertised by the name of Hagar was a regular African in feature and figure. She might have been sixty, but was older than that by hard work and disease, was partially blind, and somewhat crippled with rheumatism. By her side stood her only remaining son, Albert, a bright-looking little fellow of fourteen years. The boy was the only survivor of a large family, who had been successively sold away from her to a Southern market. The mother held on to him with both her shaking hands, and eyed with intense trepidation everyone who walked up to examine him.

'Don't be fear'd, Aunt Hagar,' said the oldest of the men, 'I spoke to Mas'r Thomas 'bout it, and he thought he might manage to sell you in a lot both together.'

'Dey needn't call me worn out yet,' said she, lifting her shaking hands. 'I can cook yet, and scrub, and scour – I'm wuth a buying, if I do come cheap; tell em dat ar – you *tell* 'em,' she added, earnestly.

Haley here forced his way into the group, walked up to the old man, pulled his mouth open and looked in, felt of his teeth, made him stand and straighten himself, bend his back, and perform various evolutions to show his muscles; and then passed on to the next, and put him through the same trial. Walking up last to the boy, he felt of his arms, straightened his hands, and looked at his fingers, and made him jump, to show his agility.

'He an't gwine to be sold widout me!' said the old woman with passionate eagerness; 'he and I goes in a lot together; I's rail-strong yet, mas'r, and can do heaps o' work – heaps on it, mas'r.'

'On plantation?' said Haley, with a contemptuous glance. 'Likely story!' and, as if satisfied with his examination, he walked out and looked, and stood with his hands in his pocket, his cigar in his mouth, and his hat cocked on one side, ready for action.

'What think of 'em?' said a man who had been following Haley's examination, as if to make up his own mind from it.

'Wal,' said Haley, spitting, 'I shall put in, I think, for the youngerly ones and the boy.'

'They want to sell the boy and the old woman together,' said the man.

'Find it a tight pull; why, she's an old rack o' bones – not worth her salt.'

'You wouldn't then?' said the man.

'Anybody'd be a fool 'twould. She's half blind, crooked with rheumatis, and foolish to boot.'

'Some buys up these yer old critturs, and ses there's a sight more wear in 'em than a body'd think,' said the man, reflectively.

'No go, 'tall,' said Haley; 'wouldn't take her for a present – fact: I've *seen*, now.'

'Wal, 'tis kinder pity, now, not to buy her with her son – her heart seems so sot on him; s'pose they fling her in cheap.'

'Them that's got money to spend that ar way, it's all well enough. I shall bid off on that ar boy for a plantation-hand; wouldn't be bothered with her, no way – not if they'd give her to me,' said Haley.

'She'll take on desp't,' said the man.

'Nat'lly, she will,' said the trader, coolly.

The conversation was here interrupted by a busy hum in the audience; and the auctioneer, a short, bustling, important fellow, elbowed his way into the crowd. The old woman drew in her breath, and caught instinctively at her son.

'Keep close to yer mammy, Albert – close – dey'll put us up togedder,' she said.

'Oh, mammy, I'm feard they won't,' said the boy.

'Dey must, child; I can't live, no ways, if they don't,' said the old creature vehemently.

The stentorian tones of the auctioneer, calling out to clear the way, now announced that the sale was about to commence. A place was cleared, and the bidding began. The different men on the list were soon knocked off at prices which showed a pretty brisk demand in the market; two of them fell to Haley.

'Come, now, young un,' said the auctioneer, giving the boy a touch with his hammer, 'be up and show your springs, now.'

'Put us two up togedder, togedder – do please, mas'r,' said the old woman, holding fast to her boy.

'Be off,' said the man, gruffly, pushing her hands away; 'you come last. Now, darkey, spring;' and, with the word, he pushed the boy toward the block, while a deep, heavy groan rose behind him. The boy paused, and looked back; but there was no time to stay, and dashing the tears from his large, bright eyes, he was up in a moment.

His fine figure, alert limbs, and bright face, raised an instant competition, and half a dozen bids simultaneously met the ear of the auctioneer. Anxious, half-frightened, he looked from side to side, as he heard the clatter of contending bids, now here, now there – till the hammer fell. Haley had got him. He was pushed from the block towards his new master, but stopped one moment, and looked back, when his poor old mother, trembling in every limb, held out her shaking hands toward him.

'Buy me, too, mas'r, for de dear Lord's sake! – buy me – I shall die if you don't!'

'You'll die if I do, that's the kink of it,' said Haley. 'No!' And he turned on his heel.

The bidding for the poor old creature was summary. The man who had addressed Haley, and who seemed not destitute of compassion, bought her for a trifle, and the spectators began to disperse.

The poor victims of the sale, who had been brought up in one place together for years, gathered round the despairing old mother, whose agony was pitiful to see.

'Couldn't dey leave me one? Mas'r allers said I should have one – he did,' she repeated over and over, in heartbroken tones.

'Trust in the Lord, Aunt Hagar,' said the oldest of the men, sorrowfully.

'What good will it do?' said she, sobbing passionately.

'Mother, mother! Don't! don't!' said the boy. 'They say you's got a good master.'

'I don't care – I don't care. Oh, Albert! Oh, my boy! you's my last baby. Lord, how ken I?'

'Come, take her off, can't some of ye?' said Haley, dryly. 'Don't do no good for her to go on that ar way.'

The old men of the company, partly by persuasion and partly by force, loosed the poor creature's last despairing hold, and, as they led her off to her new master's wagon, strove to comfort her.

'Now!' said Haley, pushing his three purchases together, and producing a bundle of handcuffs, which he proceeded to put on their wrists; then fastening each handcuff to a long chain, he drove them before him to the jail.

A few days saw Haley, with his possessions, safely deposited on one of the Ohio boats. It was the commencement of his gang, to be augmented as the boat moved on, by various other merchandise of the same kind, which he, or his agent, had stored for him in various points along shore.

The *La Belle Rivière*,[94] as brave and beautiful a boat as ever walked the waters of her namesake river, was floating gayly down the stream, under a brilliant sky, the stripes and stars of free America waving and fluttering overhead; the guards crowded with well-dressed ladies and gentlemen, walking and enjoying the delightful day. All was full of life, buoyant, and rejoicing! all but Haley's gang, who were stored, with other freight, on the lower deck, and who, somehow, did not seem to appreciate their various privileges, as they sat in a knot, talking to each other in low tones

'Boys,' said Haley, coming up, briskly, 'I hope you keep up good heart, and are cheerful. Now, no sulks, ye see; keep stiff upper lip, boys; do well by me, and I'll do well by you.'

The boys addressed responded the invariable 'Yes, mas'r', for ages the watchword of poor Africa; but it's to be owned they did not look particularly cheerful. They had their various little prejudices in favour of wives, mothers, sisters and children, seen for the last time, and though 'they that wasted them required of them mirth',[95] it was not instantly forthcoming.

'I've got a wife,' spoke out the article enumerated as 'John, aged thirty', and he laid his chained hand on Tom's knee, 'and she don't know a word about this, poor girl!'

'Where does she live?' said Tom.

'In a tavern a piece down here,' said John; 'I wish, now, I *could* see her once more in this world,' he added.

Poor John! It *was* rather natural; and the tears that fell, as he spoke, came as naturally as if he had been a white man. Tom drew a long breath from a sore heart, and tried, in his poor way, to comfort him.

And overhead, in the cabin, sat fathers and mothers, husbands and wives; and merry, dancing children moved round among them, like so many little butterflies, and everything was going on quite easy and comfortable.

'Oh, mamma,' said a boy, who had just come up from below, 'there's a negro trader on board, and he's brought four or five slaves down there.'

'Poor creatures!' said the mother, in a tone between grief and indignation.

'What's that?' said another lady.

'Some poor slaves below,' said the mother.

'And they've got chains on,' said the boy.

'What a shame to our country that such sights are to be seen!' said another lady.

'Oh, there's a great deal to be said on both sides of the subject,' said a genteel woman, who sat at her stateroom door, sewing, while her little girl and boy were playing round her. 'I've been South, and I must say I think the negroes are better off than they would be to be free.'

'In some respects, some of them are well off, I grant,' said the lady to whose remark she had answered. 'The most dreadful part of slavery, to my mind, is its outrages on the feelings and affections – the separating of families, for example.'

'That *is* a bad thing, certainly,' said the other lady, holding up a baby's dress she had just completed, and looking intently on its trimmings; 'but then, I fancy, it don't occur often.'

'Oh, it does,' said the first lady, eagerly; 'I've lived many years in Kentucky and Virginia both, and I've seen enough to make anyone's heart sick. Suppose, ma'am, your two children there, should be taken from you, and sold?'

'We can't reason from our feelings to those of this class of persons,' said the other lady, sorting out some worsteds on her lap.

'Indeed, ma'am, you can know nothing of them, if you say so,' answered the first lady, warmly. 'I was born and brought up among them. I know they *do* feel, just as keenly – even more so, perhaps – as we do.'

The lady said, 'Indeed!' yawned, and looked out the cabin window, and finally repeated, for a finale, the remark with which she had begun – 'After all, I think they are better off than they would be to be free.'

'It's undoubtedly the intention of Providence that the African race should be servants – kept in a low condition,' said a grave-looking gentleman in black, a clergyman, seated by the cabin-door. ' "Cursed be Canaan; a servant of servants shall he be," the Scripture says.'[96]

'I say, stranger, is that ar what that text means?' said a tall man, standing by.

'Undoubtedly. It pleased Providence, for some inscrutable reason, to doom the race to bondage ages ago; and we must not set up our opinion against that.'

'Well, then, we'll all go ahead and buy up niggers,' said the man, 'if that's the way of Providence: won't we squire?' said he, turning to Haley, who had been standing, with his hands in his pockets, by the stove, and intently listening to the conversation.

'Yes,' continued the tall man; 'we must all be resigned to the decrees of Providence. Niggers must be sold, and trucked round, and kept under; it's what they's made for. 'Pears like this yer view's quite refreshing, an't it, stranger?' said he to Haley.

'I never thought on't,' said Haley. 'I couldn't have said as much, myself: I ha'nt no larning. I took up the trade just to make a living; if 'tan't right, I calculated to 'pent on't in time, *ye* know.'

'And now you'll save yerself the trouble, won't ye?' said the tall man. 'See what 'tis, now, to know Scripture. If ye'd only studied yer Bible, like this yer good man, ye might have know'd it before, and saved ye a heap o' trouble. Ye could jist have said, "Cussed be" – what's his name? – and 'twould all have come right.' And the stranger, who was no other than the honest drover whom we introduced to our readers in the Kentucky tavern, sat down, and began smoking, with a curious smile on his long, dry face.

A tall, slender young man, with a face expressive of great feeling and intelligence, here broke in, and repeated the words, ' "All things whatsoever ye would that men should do unto you, do ye even so unto them." [97] I suppose,' he added, '*that* is Scripture, as much as, "Cursed be Canaan." '

'Wal, it seems quite *as* plain a text, stranger,' said John, the drover, 'to poor fellows like us, now;' and John smoked on like a volcano.

The young man paused, looked as if he was going to say more, when suddenly the boat stopped, and the company made the usual steamboat rush to see where they were landing.

'Both them ar chaps parsons?' said John to one of the men, as they were going out.

The man nodded.

As the boat stopped, a black woman came running wildly up the plank, darted into the crowd, flew up to where the slave-gang sat, and threw her arms round that unfortunate piece of merchandise before enumerated 'John, aged thirty', and with sobs and tears bemoaned him as her husband.

But what needs tell the story, told too oft – every day told – of heartstrings rent and broken – the weak broken and torn for the profit and convenience of the strong! It needs not to be told; every day is telling it – telling it, too, in the ear of One who is not deaf, though He be long silent.

The young man who had spoken for the cause of humanity and God before, stood with folded arms, looking on this scene. He turned, and Haley was standing at his side. 'My friend,' he said, speaking with thick utterance, 'how can you, how dare you, carry on a trade like this? Look at those poor creatures! Here I am, rejoicing in my heart that I am going home to my wife and child! and the same bell which is a signal to carry me onward towards them will part this poor man and his wife for ever. Depend upon it, God will bring you into judgement for this.' [98]

The trader turned away in silence.

'I say, now,' said the drover, touching his elbow, 'there's differences in parsons, an't there? "Cussed be Canaan" don't seem to go down with this 'un, does it?'

Haley gave an uneasy growl.

'And that ar an't the worst on't,' said John; 'mabbe it won't go down with the Lord, neither, when ye come to settle with Him, one o' these days, as all on us must, I reckon.'

Haley walked reflectively to the other end of the boat.

'If I make pretty handsomely on one or two next gangs,' he thought, 'I reckon I'll stop off this yer; it's really getting dangerous.' And he took out his pocket-book, and began adding over his accounts, a process which many gentlemen besides Mr Haley have found a specific[99] for an uneasy conscience.

The boat swept proudly away from the shore, and all went on merrily, as before. Men talked, and loafed, and read, and smoked. Women sewed, and children played, and the boat passed on her way.

One day, when she lay to for a while at a small town in Kentucky, Haley went up into the place on a little matter of business.

Tom, whose fetters did not prevent his taking a moderate circuit, had drawn near the side of the boat, and stood listlessly gazing over the railings. After a time, he saw the trader returning, with an alert step, in company with a coloured woman, bearing in her arms a young child. She was dressed quite respectably, and a coloured man followed her, bringing along a small trunk. The woman came cheerfully onward, talking, as she came, with the man who bore her trunk, and so passed up the plank into the boat. The bell rang, the steamer whizzed, the engine groaned and coughed, and away swept the boat down the river.

The woman walked forward among the boxes and bales of the lower deck, and sitting down, busied herself with chirruping to her baby.

Haley made a turn or two about the boat, and then, coming up, seated himself near her, and began saying something to her in an indifferent undertone.

Tom soon noticed a heavy cloud passing over the woman's brow, and that she answered rapidly, and with great vehemence,

'I don't believe it; I won't believe it!' he heard her say. 'You're jist a foolin' with me.'

'If you won't believe it, look here!' said the man, drawing out a paper; 'this yer's the bill of sale, and there's your master's name to it; and I paid down good solid cash for it, too, I can tell you – so now!'

'I don't believe mas'r would cheat me so; it can't be true!' said the woman, with increasing agitation.

'You can ask any of these men here that can read writing. Here!' he said, to a man that was passing by, 'jist read this yer, won't you! This yer gal won't believe me, when I tell her what 'tis.'

'Why, it's a bill of sale, signed by John Fosdick,' said the man, 'making over to you the girl Lucy and her child. It's all straight enough, for aught I see.'

The woman's passionate exclamations collected a crowd around her, and the trader briefly explained to them the cause of the agitation.

'He told me that I was going down to Louisville,[100] to hire out as cook to the same tavern where my husband works; that's what mas'r told me, his own self, and I can't believe he'd lie to me,' said the woman.

'But he has sold you, my poor woman, there's no doubt about it,' said a good-natured looking man, who had been examining the papers; 'he has done it, and no mistake.'

'Then it's no account talking,' said the woman, suddenly growing quite calm; and, clasping her child tighter in her arms, she sat down on her box, turned her back round, and gazed listlessly into the river.

'Going to take it easy, after all!' said the trader. 'Gal's got grit, I see.'

The woman looked calm, as the boat went on; and a beautiful, soft, summer breeze passed, like a compassionate spirit, over her head – the gentle breeze, that never enquires whether the brow is dusky or fair that it fans. And she saw sunshine sparkling on the water, in golden ripples, and heard gay voices, full of ease and pleasure, talking around her everywhere; but her heart lay as if a great stone had fallen on it. Her baby raised himself up against her, and stroked her cheeks with his little hands; and, springing up and down, crowing and chatting, seemed determined to arouse her. She strained him suddenly and tightly in her arms, and slowly one tear after another fell on his wondering, unconscious face; and gradually she seemed, and little by little, to grow calmer, and busied herself with tending and nursing him.

The child, a boy of ten months, was uncommonly large and strong of his age, and very vigorous in his limbs. Never, for a moment, still, he kept his mother constantly busy in holding him, and guarding his springing activity.

'That's a fine chap!' said a man, suddenly stopping opposite to him, with his hands in his pockets. 'How old is he?'

'Ten months and a half,' said the mother.

The man whistled to the boy, and offered him part of a stick of candy, which he eagerly grabbed at, and very soon had it in a baby's general depository; to wit, his mouth.

'Rum fellow!' said the man. 'Knows what's what!' and he whistled and walked on. When he had got to the other side of the boat, he came across Haley, who was smoking on top of a pile of boxes.

The stranger produced a match and lighted a cigar, saying, as he did so –

'Decentish kind o' wench you've got round there, stranger.'

'Why, I reckon she *is* tol'able fair,' said Haley, blowing the smoke out of his mouth.

'Taking her down south?' said the man.

Haley nodded, and smoked on.

'Plantation hand?' said the man.

'Wal,' said Haley, 'I'm filling out an order for a plantation, and I think I shall put her in. They told me she was a good cook; and they can use her for that, or set her at the cotton-picking. She's got the right fingers for that; I looked at 'em. Sell well, either way;' and Haley resumed his cigar.

'They won't want the young'un on a plantation,' said the man.

'I shall sell him, first chance I find,' said Haley, lighting another cigar.

'S'pose you'd be selling him tol'able cheap,' said the stranger, mounting the pile of boxes, and sitting down comfortably.

'Don't know 'bout that,' said Haley; 'he's a pretty smart young'un – straight, fat, strong; flesh as hard as a brick!'

'Very true; but then there's all the bother and expense of raisin'.'

'Nonsense!' said Haley; 'they is raised as easy as any kind of critter there is going; they an't a bit more trouble than pups. This yer chap will be running all round in a month.'

'I've got a good place for raisin', and I thought of takin' in a little more stock,' said the man. 'One cook lost a young 'un last week – got drownded in a wash-tub, while she was a hangin' out clothes; and I reckon it would be well enough to set her to raisin' this yer.'

Haley and the stranger smoked a while in silence, neither seeming willing to broach the test question of the interview. At last the man resumed –

'You wouldn't think of wantin' more than ten dollars for that ar chap, seeing you *must* get him off yer hands, anyhow?'

Haley shook his head and spat impressively.

'That won't do, no ways,' he said, and began his smoking again.

'Well, stranger, what will you take?'

'Well, now,' said Haley, 'I *could* raise that ar chap myself, or get him raised; he's oncommon likely and healthy, and he'd fetch a hundred dollars six months hence; and, in a year or two, he'd bring two hundred, if I had him in the right spot; so I shan't take a cent less nor fifty for him now.'

'Oh, stranger! that's rediculous, altogether,' said the man.

'Fact!' said Haley, with a decisive nod of his head.

'I'll give thirty for him,' said the stranger, 'but not a cent more.'

'Now, I'll tell ye what I will do,' said Haley, spitting again, with renewed decision. 'I'll split the difference, and say forty-five; and that's the most I will do.'

'Well, agreed!' said the man, after an interval.

'Done!' said Haley. 'Where do you land?'

'At Louisville,' said the man.

'Louisville,' said Haley. 'Very fair, we get there about dusk. Chap will be asleep – all fair – get him off quietly, and no screaming – happens beautiful – I like to do everything quietly – I hates all kind of agitation and fluster.' And so, after a transfer of certain bills had passed from the man's pocket-book to the trader's, he resumed his cigar.

It was a bright, tranquil evening when the boat stopped at the wharf at Louisville. The woman had been sitting with her baby in her arms, now wrapped in a heavy sleep. When she heard the name of the place called out, she hastily laid the child down in a little cradle formed by the hollow among the boxes, first carefully spreading under it her cloak; and then she sprang to the side of the boat, in hopes that, among the various hotel-waiters who thronged the wharf, she might see her husband. In this hope, she pressed forward to the front rails, and, stretching far over them, strained her eyes intently on the moving heads on the shore, and the crowd pressed in between her and the child.

'Now's your time,' said Haley, taking the sleeping child up, and handing him to the stranger. 'Don't wake him up, and set him to crying, now; it would make a devil of a fuss with the gal.' The man took the bundle carefully, and was soon lost in the crowd that went up the wharf.

When the boat, creaking, and groaning, and puffing, had loosed from the wharf, and was beginning slowly to strain herself along, the woman returned to her old seat. The trader was sitting there – the child was gone!

'Why, why – where?' she began, in bewildered surprise.

'Lucy,' said the trader, 'your child's gone; you may as well know it first as last. You see, I know'd you couldn't take him down south; and I got a chance to sell him to a first-rate family, that'll raise him better than you can.'

The trader had arrived at that stage of Christian and political perfection which has been recommended by some preachers and politicians of the North, lately, in which he had completely overcome every humane weakness and prejudice. His heart was exactly where yours, sir, and mine could be brought, with proper effort and cultivation. The wild look of anguish and utter despair that the woman cast on him might have disturbed one less practised; but he was used to it. He had seen that same look hundreds of times. You can get used to such things, too, my friend; and it is the great object of recent efforts to make our whole Northern community used to them, for the glory of the Union. So the trader only regarded the mortal anguish which he saw working in those dark features, those clenched hands, and suffocating breathings, as necessary incidents of the trade, and merely calculated whether she was going to scream, and get up a commotion on the boat; for, like other supporters of our peculiar institutions, he decidedly disliked agitation.

But the woman did not scream. The shot had passed too straight and direct through the heart for cry or tear.

Dizzily she sat down. Her slack hands fell lifeless by her side. Her eyes looked straight forward, but she saw nothing. All the noise and hum of the boat, the groaning of the machinery, mingled dreamily to her bewildered ear; and the poor, dumb-stricken heart had neither cry nor tear to show for its utter misery. She was quite calm.

The trader, who, considering his advantages, was almost as humane as some of our politicians, seemed to feel called on to administer such consolation as the case admitted of.

'I know this yer comes kinder hard, at first, Lucy,' said he; 'but such a smart, sensible gal as you are, won't give way to it. You see it's *necessary*, and can't be helped!'

'Oh, don't, mas'r, don't!' said the woman, with a voice like one that is smothering.

'You're a smart wench, Lucy,' he persisted; 'I mean to do well by ye, and get ye a nice place down river; and you'll soon get another husband, such a likely gal as you – '

'Oh, mas'r, if you *only* won't talk to me now,' said the woman, in a voice of such quick and living anguish, that the trader felt that there was something at present in the case beyond his style of operation. He got up, and the woman turned away, and buried her head in her cloak.

The trader walked up and down for a time, and occasionally stopped and looked at her.

'Takes it hard, rather,' he soliloquised, 'but quiet, tho'. Let her sweat a while – she'll come right, by and by!'

Tom had watched the whole transaction from first to last, and had a perfect understanding of its results. To him, it looked like something unutterably horrible and cruel, because, poor, ignorant black soul! he had not learned to generalise, and to take enlarged views. If he had only been instructed by certain ministers of Christianity, he might have thought better of it, and seen in it an everyday incident of a lawful trade; a trade which is the vital support of an institution which an American divine* tells us, has '*no evils but such as are inseparable from any other relations in social and domestic life*'.[101] But Tom, as we see, being a poor, ignorant fellow, whose reading had been confined entirely to the New Testament, could not comfort and solace himself with views like these. His very soul bled within him for what seemed to him the *wrongs* of the poor suffering thing that lay like a crushed reed on the boxes; the feeling, living, bleeding, yet immortal *thing*, which American state law coolly classes with the bundles, and bales, and boxes, among which she is lying.

Tom drew near, and tried to say something; but she only groaned. Honestly, and with tears running down his own cheeks, he spoke of a heart of love in the skies, of a pitying Jesus, and an eternal home; but the ear was deaf with anguish, and the palsied heart could not feel.

Night came on – night calm, unmoved, and glorious, shining down with her innumerable and solemn angel eyes, twinkling, beautiful, but silent. There was no speech nor language, no pitying voice or helping hand, from that distant sky. One after another the voices of business or pleasure died away; all on the boat were sleeping, and the ripples at the prow were plainly heard. Tom stretched himself out on a box, and there, as he lay, he heard, ever and anon, a smothered sob or cry from the prostrate creature. 'Oh, what shall I do? Oh, Lord! Oh, good Lord, do help me!' and so, ever and anon, until the murmur died away in silence.

At midnight, Tom waked, with a sudden start. Something black passed quickly by him to the side of the boat, and he heard a splash in the water. No one else saw or heard anything. He raised his head – the woman's place was vacant! He got up, and sought about him in vain. The poor bleeding heart was still, at last, and the river rippled and dimpled just as brightly as if it had not closed above it.

Patience! patience! ye whose hearts swell indignant at wrongs like these. Not one throb of anguish, not one tear of the oppressed, is forgotten by the Man of Sorrows,[102] the Lord of Glory. In his patient, generous bosom he bears the anguish of a world. Bear thou, like him, in patience, and labour in love; for sure as he is God, 'the year of his redeemed *shall* come'.[103]

The trader waked up bright and early, and came out to see to his live stock. It was now his turn to look about in perplexity.

'Where alive is that gal?' he said to Tom.

Tom, who had learned the wisdom of keeping counsel, did not feel called on to state his observations and suspicions, but said he did not know.

'She surely couldn't have got off in the night at any of the landings, for I was awake, and on the look-out whenever the boat stopped. I never trust these yer things to other folks.'

This speech was addressed to Tom quite confidentially, as if it was something that would be specially interesting to him. Tom made no answer.

The trader searched the boat from stem to stern, among boxes, bales and barrels, around the machinery, by the chimneys, in vain.

'Now, I say, Tom, be fair about this yer,' he said, when, after a fruitless search, he came where Tom was standing. 'You know something about it, now. Don't tell me – I know you do. I saw the gal stretched out here about ten o'clock, and agin at twelve, and agin between one and two; and then at four she was gone, and you was a sleeping right there all the time. Now, you know something – you can't help it.'

'Well, mas'r,' said Tom, 'towards morning something brushed by me, and I kinder half woke; and then I hearn a great splash, and then I clare woke up, and the gal was gone. That's all I know on't.'

The trader was not shocked nor amazed; because, as we said before, he was used to a great many things that you are not used to. Even the awful presence of Death struck no solemn chill upon him. He had seen Death many times – met him in the way of trade, and got acquainted with him – and he only thought of him as a hard customer, that embarrassed his property operations very unfairly; and so he only swore that the gal was a baggage, and that he was devilish unlucky, and that, if things went on in this way, he should not make a cent on the trip. In short, he seemed to consider himself an ill-used man, decidedly; but there was no help for it, as the woman had escaped into a State which *never will* give up a fugitive – not even at the demand of the whole glorious Union. The trader, therefore, sat discontentedly down, with his little account-book, and put down the missing body and soul under the head of *losses*!

'He's a shocking creature, isn't he, this trader? – so unfeeling! It's dreadful, really!'

'Oh, but nobody thinks anything of these traders! They are universally despised – never received into any decent society.'

But who, sir, makes the trader? Who is most to blame? The enlightened, cultivated, intelligent man, who supports the system of which the trader is the inevitable result, or the poor trader himself? You make the public sentiment that calls for his trade, that debauches and depraves him, till he feels no shame in it; and in what are you better than he?

Are you educated and he ignorant, you high and he low, you refined and he coarse, you talented and he simple?

In the day of a future judgement these very considerations may make it more tolerable for him than for you.

In concluding these little incidents of lawful trade, we must beg the world not to think that American legislators are entirely destitute of humanity, as might, perhaps, be unfairly inferred from the great efforts made in our national body to protect and perpetuate this species of traffic.

Who does not know how our great men are outdoing themselves in declaiming against the *foreign* slave-trade. There are a perfect host of Clarksons and Wilberforces[104] risen up among us on that subject, most edifying to hear and behold. Trading negroes from Africa, dear reader, is so horrid! It is not to be thought of! But trading them from Kentucky – that's quite another thing!

CHAPTER XIII

The Quaker Settlement[105]

A QUIET SCENE now rises before us. A large, roomy, neatly-painted kitchen, its yellow floor glossy and smooth, and without a particle of dust; a neat, well-blacked cooking-stove; rows of shining tin, suggestive of unmentionable good things to the appetite; glossy green wood chairs, old and firm; a small flag-bottomed rocking-chair, with a patch-work cushion in it, neatly contrived out of small pieces of different coloured woollen goods, and a larger sized one, motherly and old, whose wide arms breathed hospitable invitation, seconded by the solicitations of its feather cushions – a real, comfortable, persuasive old chair, and worth, in the way of honest, homely enjoyment, a dozen of your plush or brochetelle[106] drawing-room gentry; and in the chair, gently swaying back and forward, her eyes bent on some fine sewing, sat our old friend Eliza. Yes, there she is, paler and thinner than in her Kentucky home, with a world of quiet sorrow lying under the shadow of her long eyelashes, and marking the outline of her gentle mouth! It was plain to see how old and firm the girlish heart was grown under the discipline of heavy sorrow; and when, anon, her large dark eye was raised to follow the gambols of her little Harry, who was sporting, like some tropical butterfly, hither and thither over the floor, she showed a depth of firmness and steady resolve that was never there in her earlier and happier days.

By her side sat a woman with a bright tin pan in her lap, into which she was carefully sorting some dried peaches. She might be fifty-five or sixty; but hers was one of those faces that time seems to touch only to brighten and adorn. The snowy lisse crape[107] cap, made after the strait Quaker pattern, the plain white muslin handkerchief, lying in placid folds across her bosom, the drab shawl and dress, showed at once the community to which she belonged. Her face was round and rosy, with a healthful downy softness, suggestive of a ripe peach. Her hair, partially silvered by age, was parted smoothly back from a high placid forehead, on which time had written no inscription except, 'Peace on earth, goodwill to men'; and beneath shone a large pair of clear, honest, loving, brown eyes: you only needed to look straight into them, to feel that you saw to the bottom of a heart as good and true as ever throbbed in woman's bosom. So much has been said and sung of beautiful young girls, why don't somebody wake up to the beauty of old women? If any want to get up an inspiration under this head, we refer them to our good friend Rachel Halliday, just as she sits there in her little rocking-chair. It had a turn for quacking and squeaking – that chair had – either from having taken cold in early life, or from some asthmatic affection, or perhaps from nervous derangement; but, as she gently swung backward and forward, the chair kept up a kind of subdued 'creechy crawchy', that would have been intolerable in any other chair. But old Simeon Halliday often declared it was as good as any music to him; and the children all avowed that they wouldn't miss of hearing mother's chair for anything in the world. For why? for twenty years or more, nothing but loving words, and gentle moralities, and motherly loving-kindness, had come from that chair – headaches and heart-aches innumerable had been cured there – difficulties spiritual and temporal solved there – all by one good, loving woman. God bless her!

'And so thee still thinks of going to Canada, Eliza?' she said, as she was quietly looking over her peaches.

'Yes, ma'am,' said Eliza, firmly. 'I must go onward. I dare not stop.'

'And what'll thee do, when thee gets there? Thee must think about that, my daughter.'

'My daughter,' came naturally from the lips of Rachel Halliday; for hers was just the face and form that made 'mother' seem the most natural word in the world.

Eliza's hands trembled, and some tears fell on her fine work; but she answered firmly –

'I shall do – anything I can find. I hope I can find something.'

'Thee knows thee can stay here, as long as thee pleases,' said Rachel.

'Oh, thank you,' said Eliza, 'but' – she pointed to Harry – 'I can't sleep nights; I can't rest. Last night I dreamed I saw that man coming into the yard,' she said, shuddering.

'Poor child!' said Rachel, wiping her eyes; 'but thee mustn't feel so. The Lord hath ordered it so that never hath a fugitive been stolen from our village. I trust thine will not be the first.'

The door here opened, and a little, short, round, pin-cushiony woman, stood at the door, with a cheery, blooming face, like a ripe apple. She was dressed, like Rachel, in sober grey, with the muslin folded neatly across her round, plump little chest.

'Ruth Stedman,' said Rachel, coming joyfully forward; 'how is thee, Ruth?' she said, heartily taking both her hands.

'Nicely,' said Ruth, taking off her little drab bonnet, and dusting it with her handkerchief, displaying, as she did so, a round little head, on which the Quaker cap sat with a sort of jaunty air, despite all the stroking and patting of the small fat hands, which were busily applied to arranging it. Certain stray locks of decidedly curly hair, too, had escaped here and there, and had to be coaxed and cajoled into their place again; and then the newcomer, who might have been five-and-twenty, turned from the small looking-glass, before which she had been making these arrangements, and looked well pleased – as most people who looked at her might have been; for she was decidedly a wholesome, whole-hearted, chirruping little woman, as ever gladdened man's heart withal.

'Ruth, this friend is Eliza Harris; and this is the little boy I told thee of.'

'I am glad to see thee, Eliza – very,' said Ruth, shaking hands, as if Eliza were an old friend she had long been expecting: 'and this is thy dear boy – I brought a cake for him,' she said, holding out a little heart to the boy, who came up, gazing through his curls, and accepted it shyly.

'Where's thy baby, Ruth?' said Rachel.

'Oh, he's coming; but thy Mary caught him as I came in, and ran off with him to the barn, to show him to the children.'

At this moment, the door opened, and Mary, an honest, rosy-looking girl, with large brown eyes, like her mother's, came in with the baby.

'Ah! ha!' said Rachel, coming up, and taking the great, white, fat fellow in her arms; 'how good he looks, and how he does grow!'

'To be sure, he does,' said little bustling Ruth, as she took the child, and began taking off a little blue silk hood, and various layers and wrappers of outer garments; and having given a twitch here, and a pull there, and variously adjusted and arranged him, and kissed him heartily, she set him on the floor to collect his thoughts. Baby seemed quite used to this mode of proceeding, for he put his thumb in his mouth (as if it were quite a thing of course), and seemed soon absorbed in his own reflections, while the mother seated herself, and taking out a long stocking of mixed blue and white yarn, began to knit with briskness.

'Mary, thee'd better fill the kettle, hadn't thee?' gently suggested the mother.

Mary took the kettle to the well, and soon reappearing, placed it over the stove, where it was soon purring and steaming, a sort of censer of hospitality and good cheer. The peaches, moreover, in obedience to a few gentle whispers from Rachel, were soon deposited, by the same hand, in a stew-pan over the fire.

Rachel now took down a snowy moulding-board, and, tying on an apron, proceeded quietly to making up some biscuits, first saying to Mary, 'Mary, hadn't thee better tell John to get a chicken ready?' and Mary disappeared accordingly.

'And how is Abigail Peters?' said Rachel, as she went on with her biscuits.

'Oh, she's better,' said Ruth; 'I was in, this morning; made the bed, tidied up the house. Leah Hills went in this afternoon, and baked bread and pies enough to last some days; and I engaged to go back to get her up, this evening.'

'I will go in tomorrow, and do any cleaning there may be, and look over the mending,' said Rachel.

'Ah! that is well,' said Ruth. 'I've heard,' she added, 'that Hannah Stanwood is sick. John was up there, last night – I must go there tomorrow.'

'John can come in here to his meals, if thee needs to stay all day,' suggested Rachel.

'Thank thee, Rachel; we'll see, tomorrow. But here comes Simeon.'

Simeon Halliday, a tall, straight, muscular man, in drab coat and pantaloons, and broad-brimmed hat, now entered.

'How is thee, Ruth?' he said, warmly, as he spread his broad open hand for her little fat palm; 'and how is John?'

'Oh! John is well, and all the rest of our folks,' said Ruth, cheerily.

'Any news, father?' said Rachel, as she was putting her biscuits into the oven.

'Peter Stebbins told me that they should be along tonight, with *friends*,' said Simeon, significantly, as he was washing his hands at a neat sink, in a little back porch.

'Indeed!' said Rachel, looking thoughtfully, and glancing at Eliza.

'Did thee say thy name was Harris?' said Simeon to Eliza, as he re-entered.

Rachel glanced quickly at her husband, as Eliza tremulously answered – 'yes'; her fears, ever uppermost, suggesting that possibly there might be advertisements out for her.

'Mother!' said Simeon, standing in the porch, and calling Rachel out.

'What does thee want, father?' said Rachel, rubbing her floury hands, as she went into the porch.

'This child's husband is in the settlement, and will be here tonight,' said Simeon.

'Now, thee doesn't say that, father?' said Rachel, all her face radiant with joy.

'It's really true. Peter was down yesterday, with the wagon, to the other stand, and there he found an old woman and two men; and one said his name was George Harris; and, from what he told of his history, I am certain who he is. He is a bright, likely fellow too.'

'Shall we tell her now?' said Simeon.

'Let's tell Ruth,' said Rachel. 'Here, Ruth! – come here!'

Ruth laid down her knitting-work, and was in the back porch in a moment.

'Ruth, what does thee think?' said Rachel. 'Father says Eliza's husband is in the last company, and will be here tonight.'

A burst of joy from the little Quakeress interrupted the speech. She gave such a bound from the floor, as she clapped her little hands, that two stray curls fell from under her Quaker cap, and lay brightly on her white neckerchief.

'Hush thee, dear!' said Rachel, gently; 'hush, Ruth! Tell us, shall we tell her now?'

'Now! to be sure, this very minute. Why, now, suppose 'twas my John, how should I feel? Do tell her right off.'

'Thee uses thyself only to learn how to love thy neighbour, Ruth,' said Simeon, looking with a beaming face, on Ruth.

'To be sure. Isn't it what we are made for? If I didn't love John and the baby, I should not know how to feel for her. Come, now, do tell her – do!' and she laid her hands persuasively on Rachel's arm. 'Take her into thy bedroom, there, and let me fry the chicken while thee does it.'

Rachel came out into the kitchen, where Eliza was sewing, and opening the door of a small bedroom, said gently, 'Come in here with me, my daughter; I have news to tell thee.'

The blood flushed in Eliza's pale face; she rose, trembling with nervous anxiety, and looked towards her boy.

'No, no,' said little Ruth, darting up, and seizing her hands. 'Never thee fear; it's good news, Eliza – go in, go in!' And she gently pushed her to the door, which closed after her; and then, turning round, she caught little Harry in her arms, and began kissing him.

'Thee'll see thy father, little one. Does thee know it? Thy father is coming,' she said, over and over again, as the boy looked wonderingly at her.

Meanwhile, within the door, another scene was going on. Rachel Halliday drew Eliza toward her, and said, 'The Lord hath had mercy on thee, daughter; thy husband hath escaped from the house of bondage.'

The blood flushed to Eliza's cheek in a sudden glow, and went back to her heart with as sudden a rush. She sat down pale and faint.

'Have courage, child,' said Rachel, laying her hand on her head. 'He is among friends, who will bring him here tonight.'

'Tonight!' Eliza repeated. 'Tonight!' The words lost all meaning to her; her head was dreamy and confused; all was mist for a moment.

When she awoke, she found herself snugly tucked up on the bed, with a blanket over her, and little Ruth rubbing her hands with camphor. She opened her eyes in a state of dreamy, delicious languor, such as one has who has long been bearing a heavy load, and now feels it gone, and would rest. The tension of the nerves, which had never ceased a moment since the first hour of her flight, had given way, and a strange feeling of security and rest came over her; and, as she lay, with her large, dark eyes open, she followed, as in a quiet dream, the motions of those about her. She saw the door open into the other room; saw the supper table, with its snowy cloth; heard the dreamy murmur of the singing tea-kettle; saw Ruth tripping backward and forward, with plates of cake and saucers of preserves, and ever and anon stopping to put a cake into Harry's hand, or pat his head, or twine his long curls round her snowy fingers. She saw the ample, motherly form of Rachel, as she ever and anon came to the bedside, and smoothed and arranged something about the bedclothes, and gave a tuck here and there, by way of expressing her goodwill; and was conscious of a kind of sunshine beaming down upon her from her large, clear, brown eyes. She saw Ruth's husband come in – saw her fly up to him, and commence whispering very earnestly, ever and anon, with impressive gesture, pointing her little finger toward the room. She saw her, with the baby in her arms, sitting down to tea; she saw them all at table, and little Harry in a high chair, under the shadow of Rachel's ample wing; there were low murmurs of talk, gentle tinkling of tea-spoons and musical clatter of cups and saucers, and all mingled in a delightful dream of rest; and Eliza slept as she had not slept before, since the fearful midnight hour when she had taken her child and fled through the frosty starlight.

She dreamed of a beautiful country – a land, it seemed to her, of rest – green shores, pleasant islands, and beautifully glittering water;[108] and there, in a house which kind voices told her was a home, she saw her boy playing, a free and happy child. She heard her husband's footsteps; she felt him coming nearer; his arms were around her, his tears falling on her face, and she awoke! It was no dream. The daylight had long faded; her child lay calmly sleeping by her side; a candle was burning dimly on the stand, and her husband was sobbing by her pillow.

The next morning was a cheerful one at the Quaker house. 'Mother' was up betimes, and surrounded by busy girls and boys, whom we had scarce time to introduce to our readers yesterday, and who all moved obediently to Rachel's gentle 'Thee had better', or more gentle 'Hadn't thee better?' in the work of getting breakfast; for a breakfast in the luxurious valleys of Indiana is a thing complicated and multiform, and, like picking up the rose-leaves and trimming the bushes in Paradise, asking other hands than those of the original mother. While, therefore, John ran to the spring for fresh water, and Simeon the second sifted meal for corn-cakes, and Mary ground coffee, Rachel moved gently and quietly about, making biscuits, cutting up chicken, and diffusing a sort of sunny radiance over the whole proceeding generally. If there was any danger of friction or collision from the ill-regulated zeal of so many young operators, her gentle 'Come! come!' or 'I wouldn't, now', was quite sufficient to allay the difficulty. Bards have written of the cestus[109] of Venus, that turned the heads of all the world in successive generations. We had rather, for our part, have the cestus of Rachel

Halliday, that kept heads from being turned, and made everything go on harmoniously. We think it is more suited to our modern days, decidedly.

While all other preparations were going on, Simeon the elder stood in his shirt-sleeves before a little looking-glass in the corner, engaged in the anti-patriarchal operation of shaving. Everything went on so sociably, so quietly, so harmoniously, in the great kitchen – it seemed so pleasant to everyone to do just what they were doing, there was such an atmosphere of mutual confidence and good fellowship everywhere – even the knives and forks had a social clatter as they went on to the table; and the chicken and ham had a cheerful and joyous fizzle in the pan, as if they rather enjoyed being cooked than otherwise; and when George and Eliza and little Harry came out, they met such a hearty, rejoicing welcome, no wonder it seemed to them like a dream.

At last, they were all seated at breakfast, while Mary stood at the stove, baking griddle-cakes, which, as they gained the true, exact, golden-brown tint of perfection, were transferred quite handily to the table.

Rachel never looked so truly and benignly happy as at the head of her table. There was so much motherliness and full-heartedness even in the way she passed a plate of cakes or poured a cup of coffee, that it seemed to put a spirit into the food and drink she offered.

It was the first time that ever George had sat down on equal terms at any white man's table; and he sat down, at first, with some constraint and awkwardness; but they all exhaled and went off like fog, in the genial morning rays of this simple, overflowing kindness.

This, indeed, was a home – *home* – a word that George had never yet known a meaning for; and a belief in God, and trust in His providence, began to encircle his heart, as, with a golden cloud of protection and confidence, dark, misanthropic, pining, atheistic doubts, and fierce despair, melted away before the light of a living Gospel, breathed in living faces, preached by a thousand unconscious acts of love and goodwill, which, like the cup of cold water given in the name of a disciple, shall never lose their reward.

'Father, what if thee should get found out again?' said Simeon second, as he buttered his cake.

'I should pay my fine,' said Simeon, quietly.

'But what if they put thee in prison?'

'Couldn't thee and mother manage the farm?' said Simeon, smiling.

'Mother can do almost everything,' said the boy. 'But isn't it a shame to make such laws?'

'Thee mustn't speak evil of thy rulers, Simeon,' said his father, gravely. 'The Lord only gives us our worldly goods that we may do justice and mercy; if our rulers require a price of us for it, we must deliver it up.'

'Well, I hate those old slave-holders!' said the boy, who felt as unchristian as became any modern reformer.

'I am surprised at thee, son,' said Simeon; 'thy mother never taught thee so. I would do even the same for the slave-holder as for the slave, if the Lord brought him to my door in affliction.'

Simeon second blushed scarlet; but his mother only smiled, and said, 'Simeon is my good boy; he will grow older, by and by, and then he will be like his father.'

'I hope, my good sir, that you are not exposed to any difficulty on our account?' said George anxiously.

'Fear nothing, George, for therefore are we sent into the world. If we would not meet trouble for a good cause, we were not worthy of our name.'

'But, for *me*,' said George, 'I could not bear it.'

'Fear not, then, friend George; it is not for thee, but for God and man, we do it,' said Simeon. 'And now thou must lie by quietly this day, and tonight, at ten o'clock, Phineas Fletcher will carry thee onward to the next stand – thee and the rest of thy company. The pursuers are hard after thee; we must not delay.'

'If that is the case, why wait till evening?' said George.

'Thou art safe here by daylight, for everyone in the settlement is a Friend, and all are watching. Moreover, it is safer to travel by night.'

CHAPTER XIV

Evangeline

A young star! which shone
O'er life – too sweet an image for such glass!
A lovely being, scarcely formed or moulded;
A rose with all its sweetest leaves yet folded.[110]

THE MISSISSIPPI! How, as by an enchanted wand, have its scenes been changed, since Chateaubriand[111] wrote his prose-poetic description of it, as a river of mighty, unbroken solitudes, rolling amid undreamed wonders of vegetable and animal existence.

But, as in an hour, this river of dreams and wild romance has emerged to a reality scarcely less visionary and splendid. What other river of the world bears on its bosom to the ocean the wealth and enterprise of such another country? – a country whose products embrace all between the tropics and the poles! Those turbid waters, hurrying, foaming, tearing along, an apt resemblance of that headlong tide of business which is poured along its wave by a race more vehement and energetic than any the old world ever saw. Ah! would that they did not also bear along a more fearful freight, the tears of the oppressed, the sighs of the helpless, the bitter prayers of poor, ignorant hearts to an unknown God – unknown, unseen, and silent, but who will yet 'come out of his place to save all the poor of the earth!'[112]

The slanting light of the setting sun quivers on the sea-like expanse of the river; the shivery canes, and the tall, dark cypress, hung with wreaths of dark, funereal moss, glow in the golden ray, as the heavily-laden steamboat marches onward.

Piled with cotton-bales, from many a plantation, up over deck and sides, till she seems in the distance a square, massive block of grey, she moves heavily onward to the nearing mart. We must look some time among its crowded decks before we shall find again our humble friend Tom. High on the upper deck, in a little nook among the everywhere predominant cotton-bales, at last we may find him.

Partly from confidence inspired by Mr Shelby's representations, and partly from the remarkably inoffensive and quiet character of the man,

Tom had insensibly won his way far into the confidence even of such a man as Haley.

At first he had watched him narrowly through the day, and never allowed him to sleep at night unfettered; but the uncomplaining patience and apparent contentment of Tom's manner led him gradually to discontinue these restraints, and for some time Tom had enjoyed a sort of parole of honour, being permitted to come and go freely where he pleased on the boat.

Ever quiet and obliging, and more than ready to lend a hand in every emergency which occurred among the workmen below, he had won the good opinion of all the hands, and spent many hours in helping them with as hearty a goodwill as ever he worked on a Kentucky farm.

When there seemed to be nothing for him to do, he would climb to a nook among the cotton-bales of the upper deck, and busy himself in studying over his Bible – and it is there we see him now.

For a hundred or more miles above New Orleans, the river is higher than the surrounding country, and rolls its tremendous volume between massive levees twenty feet in height. The traveller from the deck of the steamer, as from some floating castle top, overlooks the whole country for miles and miles around. Tom, therefore, had spread out full before him, in plantation after plantation, a map of the life to which he was approaching.

He saw the distant slaves at their toil; he saw afar their villages of huts, gleaming out in long rows on many a plantation, distant from the stately mansions and pleasure-grounds[113] of the master; and as the moving picture passed on, his poor, foolish heart would be turning backward to the Kentucky farm, with its old shadowy beeches – to the master's house, with its wide, cool halls, and, near by the little cabin, overgrown with the multiflora and bignonia. There he seemed to see familiar faces of comrades, who had grown up with him from infancy; he saw his busy wife, bustling in her preparations for his evening meals; he heard the merry laugh of his boys at their play, and the chirrup of the baby at his knee, and then, with a start, all faded, and he saw again the cane-brakes and cypresses of gliding plantations, and heard again the creaking and groaning of the machinery, all telling him too plainly that all that phase of life had gone by forever.

In such a case you write to your wife, and send messages to your children; but Tom could not write – the mail for him had no existence, and the gulf of separation was unbridged by even a friendly word or signal.

Is it strange, then, that some tears fall on the pages of his Bible, as he lays it on the cotton-bale, and, with patient finger, threading his slow way from word to word, traces out its promises? Having learned late in life, Tom was but a slow reader, and passed on laboriously from verse to verse. Fortunate for him was it that the book he was intent on was one which slow reading cannot injure – nay, one whose words, like ingots of gold, seem often to need to be weighed separately, that the mind may take in their priceless value. Let us follow him a moment, as, pointing to each word, and pronouncing each half aloud, he reads –

'Let – not – your – heart – be – troubled. In – my Father's – house – are – many – mansions. I – go – to – prepare – a – place – for – you.'[114]

Cicero,[115] when he buried his darling and only daughter, had a heart as full of honest grief as poor Tom's – perhaps no fuller, for both were only men; but Cicero could pause over no such sublime words of hope, and look to no such future reunion; and if he *had* seen them, ten to one he would not have believed – he must fill his head first with a thousand questions of authenticity of manuscript, and correctness of translation. But to poor Tom, there it lay, just what he needed, so evidently true and divine that the possibility of a question never entered his simple head. It must be true; for, if not true, how could he live?

As for Tom's Bible, though it had no annotations and helps in margin from learned commentators, still it had been embellished with certain way-marks and guide-boards of Tom's own invention, and which helped him more than the most learned expositions could have done. It had been his custom to get the Bible read to him by his master's children, in particular by young Master George; and, as they read, he would designate, by bold strong marks and dashes, with pen and ink, the passages which more particularly gratified his ear or affected his heart. His Bible was thus marked through, from one end to the other, with a variety of styles and designations; so he could in a moment seize upon his favourite passages, without the labour of spelling out what lay between them; and while it lay there before him, every passage breathing of some old home scene, and recalling some past enjoyment, his Bible seemed to him all of this life that remained, as well as the promise of a future one.

Among the passengers on the boat was a young gentleman of fortune and family, resident in New Orleans, who bore the name of St Clare. He had with him a daughter between five and six years of age, together with a lady who seemed to claim relationship to both, and to have the little one especially under her charge.

Tom had often caught glimpses of this little girl, for she was one of those busy, tripping creatures, that can be no more contained in one place than a sunbeam or a summer breeze, nor was she one that, once seen, could be easily forgotten.

Her form was the perfection of childish beauty, without its usual chubbiness and squareness of outline. There was about it an undulating and aerial grace, such as one might dream of for some mythic and allegorical being. Her face was remarkable less for its perfect beauty of feature than for a singular and dreamy earnestness of expression, which made the ideal start when they looked at her, and by which the dullest and most literal were impressed, without exactly knowing why. The shape of her head and the turn of her neck and bust was peculiarly noble; and the long, golden-brown hair that floated like a cloud around it, the deep, spiritual gravity of her violet blue eyes, shaded by heavy fringes of golden brown – all marked her out from other children, and made everyone turn and look after her, as she glided hither and thither on the boat. Nevertheless, the little one was not what you would have called either a grave child or a sad one. On the contrary, an airy and innocent playfulness seemed to flicker like the shadow of summer leaves over her childish face, and around her buoyant figure. She was always in motion, always with a half smile on her rosy mouth, flying hither and thither, with an undulating and cloud-like tread, singing to herself as she moved as in a happy dream. Her father and female guardian were incessantly busy in pursuit of her, but, when caught, she melted from them again like a summer cloud; and as no word of chiding or reproof ever fell on her ear for whatever she chose to do, she pursued her own way all over the boat. Always dressed in white, she seemed to move like a shadow through all sorts of places, without contracting spot or stain; and there was not a corner or nook, above or below, where those fairy footsteps had not glided, and that visionary golden head, with its deep blue eyes, fleeted along.

The fireman, as he looked up from his sweaty toil, sometimes found those eyes looking wonderingly into the raging depths of the furnace, and fearfully and pityingly at him, as if she thought him in some dreadful danger. Anon the steersman at the wheel paused and smiled, as the picture-like head gleamed through the window of the round house, and in a moment was gone again. A thousand times a day rough voices blessed her, and smiles of unwonted softness stole over hard faces, as she passed; and when she tripped fearlessly over dangerous places, rough, sooty hands were stretched involuntarily out to save her, and smooth her path.

Tom, who had the soft, impressible nature of his kindly race, ever yearning toward the simple and childlike, watched the little creature with daily increasing interest. To him she seemed something almost divine; and whenever her golden head and deep blue eyes peered out upon him from behind some dusky cotton-bale, or looked down upon him over some ridge of packages, he half believed that he saw one of the angels stepped out of his New Testament.

Often and often she walked mournfully round the place where Haley's gang of men and women sat in their chains. She would glide in among them, and look at them with an air of perplexed and sorrowful earnestness; and sometimes she would lift their chains with her slender hands, and then sigh woefully, as she glided away. Several times she appeared suddenly among them, with her hands full of candy, nuts, and oranges, which she would distribute joyfully to them, and then be gone again.

Tom watched the little lady a great deal, before he ventured on any overtures towards acquaintanceship. He knew an abundance of simple acts to propitiate and invite the approaches of the little people, and he resolved to play his part right skilfully. He could cut cunning little baskets out of cherry-stones, could make grotesque faces on hickory-nuts, or odd-jumping figures out of elder-pith, and he was a very Pan[116] in the manufacture of whistles of all sizes and sorts. His pockets were full of miscellaneous articles of attraction, which he had hoarded in days of old for his master's children, and which he now produced, with commendable prudence and economy, one by one, as overtures for acquaintance and friendship.

The little one was shy, for all her busy interest in everything going on, and it was not easy to tame her. For a while, she would perch like a canary-bird on some box or package near Tom, while busy in the little arts aforesaid, and take from him, with a kind of grave bashfulness, the little articles he offered. But at last they got on quite confidential terms.

'What's little missy's name?' said Tom, at last, when he thought matters were ripe to push such an enquiry.

'Evangeline St Clare,' said the little one, 'though papa and everybody else call me Eva. Now, what's your name?'

'My name's Tom; the little chil'en used to call me Uncle Tom, way back thar in Kentuck.'

'Then I mean to call you Uncle Tom, because, you see, I like you,' said Eva. 'So, Uncle Tom, where are you going?'

'I don't know, Miss Eva.'

'Don't know?' said Eva.

'No. I am going to be sold to somebody. I don't know who.'

'My papa can buy you,' said Eva, quickly; 'and if he buys you, you will have good times. I mean to ask him to, this very day.'

'Thank you, my little lady,' said Tom.

The boat here stopped at a small landing to take in wood, and Eva, hearing her father's voice, bounded nimbly away. Tom rose up, and went forward to offer his service in wooding, and soon was busy among the hands.

Eva and her father were standing together by the railings to see the boat start from the landing-place, the wheel had made two or three revolutions in the water, when, by some sudden movement, the little one suddenly lost her balance, and fell sheer over the side of the boat into the water. Her father, scarce knowing what he did, was plunging in after her, but was held back by some behind him, who saw that more efficient aid had followed his child.

Tom was standing just under her on the lower deck, as she fell. He saw her strike the water, and sink, and was after her in a moment. A broad-chested, strong-armed fellow, it was nothing for him to keep afloat in the water, till, in a moment or two, the child rose to the surface, and he caught her in his arms, and, swimming with her to the boat-side, handed her up, all dripping, to the grasp of hundreds of hands, which, as if they had all belonged to one man, were stretched eagerly out to receive her. A few moments more, and her father bore her, dripping and senseless, to the ladies' cabin, where, as is usual in cases of the kind, there ensued a very well-meaning and kind-hearted strife among the female occupants generally, as to who should do the most things to make a disturbance, and to hinder her recovery in every way possible.

It was a sultry, close day, the next day, as the steamer drew near to New Orleans. A general bustle of expectation and preparation was spread through the boat; in the cabin, one and another were gathering their things together, and arranging them, preparatory to going ashore. The steward and chambermaid, and all, were busily engaged in cleaning, furbishing, and arranging the splendid boat, preparatory to a grand *entrée*.

On the lower deck sat our friend Tom, with his arms folded, and anxiously, from time to time, turning his eyes towards a group on the other side of the boat.

There stood the fair Evangeline, a little paler than the day before, but otherwise exhibiting no traces of the accident which had befallen her. A graceful, elegantly-formed young man stood by her, carelessly leaning one elbow on a bale of cotton, while a large pocket-book lay open before him. It was quite evident, at a glance, that the gentleman was Eva's father. There was the same noble cast of head, the same large blue eyes, the same golden-brown hair; yet the expression was wholly different. In the large, clear blue eyes, though in form and colour exactly similar, there was wanting that misty, dreamy depth of expression; all was clear, bold, and bright, but with a light wholly of this world: the beautifully-cut mouth had a proud and somewhat sarcastic expression, while an air of free-and-easy superiority sat not ungracefully in every turn and movement of his fine form. He was listening, with a good-humoured, negligent air, half comic, half contemptuous, to Haley, who was very volubly expatiating on the quality of the article for which they were bargaining.

'All the moral and Christian virtues bound in black morocco,[117] complete!' he said, when Haley had finished. 'Well, now, my good fellow, what's the damage, as they say in Kentucky; in short, what's to be paid out for this business? How much are you going to cheat me, now? out with it!'

'Wal,' said Haley, 'if I should say thirteen hundred dollars for that ar fellow, I shouldn't but just save myself – I shouldn't, now, raily.'

'Poor fellow!' said the young man, fixing his keen, mocking blue eye on him; 'but I suppose you'd let me have him for that, out of a particular regard for me.'

'Well, the young lady here seems to be sot on him, and nat'lly enough.'

'Oh, certainly, there's a call on your benevolence, my friend. Now, as a matter of Christian charity, how cheap could you afford to let him go, to oblige a young lady that's particular sot on him?'

'Wal, now, just think on't,' said the trader; 'just look at them limbs – broad-chested, strong as a horse. Look at his head; them high forrads al'ays shows calculatin' niggers, that'll do any kind o' thing. I've marked that ar. Now, a nigger of that ar heft and build is worth considerable, just, as you may say, for his body, supposin' he's stupid; but come to put in his calculatin' faculties, and them which I can show he has oncommon, why, of course, it makes him come higher. Why, that ar fellow managed his master's whole farm. He has a strornary talent for business.'

'Bad, bad, very bad; knows altogether too much!' said the young man, with the same mocking smile playing about his mouth. 'Never will do, in the world. Your smart fellows are always running off, stealing horses, and raising the devil generally. I think you'll have to take off a couple of hundred for his smartness.'

'Wal, there might be something in that ar, if it warnt for his character; but I can show recommends from his master and others, to prove he is one of your real pious – the most humble, prayin', pious crittur ye ever did see. Why, he's been called a preacher in them parts he came from.'

'And I might use him for a family chaplain, possibly,' added the young man, dryly. 'That's quite an idea. Religion is a remarkably scarce article at our house.'

'You're joking, now.'

'How do you know I am? Didn't you just warrant him for a preacher? Has he been examined by any synod or council? Come, hand over your papers.'

If the trader had not been sure, by a certain good-humoured twinkle in the large blue eye, that all this banter was sure, in the long run, to turn out a cash concern, he might have been somewhat out of patience; as it was, he laid down a greasy pocket-book on the cotton-bales, and began anxiously studying over certain papers in it, the young man standing by the while, looking down on him with an air of careless, easy drollery.

'Papa, do buy him! it's no matter what you pay,' whispered Eva softly, getting up on a package, and putting her arm around her father's neck. 'You have money enough, I know. I want him.'

'What for, pussy? Are you going to use him for a rattle-box, or a rocking-horse, or what?'

'I want to make him happy.'

'An original reason, certainly.'

Here the trader handed up a certificate, signed by Mr Shelby, which the young man took with the tips of his long fingers, and glanced over carelessly.

'A gentlemanly hand,' he said, 'and well spelt, too. Well, now, but I'm not sure, after all, about this religion,' said he, the old wicked expression returning to his eye; 'the country is almost ruined with pious white people: such pious politicians as we have just before elections – such pious goings on in all departments of church and state, that a fellow does not know who'll cheat him next. I don't know, either, about religion's being up in the market, just now. I have not looked in the papers lately, to see how it sells. How many hundred dollars, now, do you put on for this religion?'

'You like to be a jokin', now,' said the trader; 'but, then, there's *sense* under all that ar. I know there's differences in religion. Some kinds is mis'rable: there's your meetin pious; there's your singin', roarin' pious; them ar an't no account, in black or white: but these rayly is; and I've seen it in niggers as often as any, your rail softly, quiet, stiddy, honest, pious, that the hull world couldn't tempt 'em to do nothing that they thinks is wrong; and ye see in this letter what Tom's old master says about him.'

'Now,' said the young man, stooping gravely over his book of bills, 'if you can assure me that I really can buy *this* kind of pious, and that it will be set down to my account in the book up above, as something belonging to me, I wouldn't care if I did go a little extra for it. How d'ye say?'

'Wal, raily, I can't do that,' said the trader 'I'm a thinkin that every man'll have to hang on his own hook, in them ar quarters.'

'Rather hard on a fellow that pays extra on religion, and can't trade with it in the state where he wants it most, an't it, now?' said the young man, who had been making out a roll of bills while he was speaking. 'There, count your money, old boy!' he added, as he handed the roll to the trader.

'All right,' said Haley, his face beaming with delight; and pulling out an old inkhorn, he proceeded to fill out a bill of sale, which, in a few moments, he handed to the young man.

'I wonder, now if I was divided up and inventoried,' said the latter, as he ran over the paper, 'how much I might bring. Say so much for the shape of my head, so much for a high forehead, so much for arms, and hands, and legs, and then so much for education, learning, talent, honesty, religion! Bless me! there would be small charge on that last, I'm thinking. But come, Eva,' he said; and taking the hand of his daughter, he stepped across the boat, and carelessly putting the tip of his finger under Tom's chin, said, good-humouredly, 'Look up, Tom, and see how you like your new master.'

Tom looked up. It was not in nature to look into that gay, young, handsome face, without a feeling of pleasure; and Tom felt the tears start in his eyes as he said, heartily, 'God bless you, mas'r!'

'Well, I hope he will. What's your name? Tom? Quite as likely to do it for your asking as mine, from all accounts. Can you drive horses, Tom?'

'I've been al'ays used to horses,' said Tom. 'Mas'r Shelby raised heaps on 'em.'

'Well, I think I shall put you in coachy, on condition that you won't be drunk more than once a week, unless in cases of emergency, Tom.'

Tom looked surprised, and rather hurt, and said, 'I never drink, mas'r.'

'I've heard that story before, Tom; but then we'll see. It will be a special accommodation to all concerned, if you don't. Never mind, my boy,' he added, good-humouredly, seeing Tom still looked grave; 'I don't doubt you mean to do well.'

'I sartin do, mas'r,' said Tom.

'And you shall have good times,' said Eva. 'Papa is very good to everybody, only he always will laugh at them.'

'Papa is much obliged to you for his recommendation,' said St Clare laughing, as he turned on his heel, and walked away.

CHAPTER XV

Of Tom's New Master, and Various Other Matters

SINCE THE THREAD of our humble hero's life has now become interwoven with that of higher ones, it is necessary to give some brief introduction to them.

Augustine St Clare was the son of a wealthy planter of Louisiana. The family had its origin in Canada. Of two brothers, very similar in temperament and character, one had settled on a flourishing farm in Vermont, and the other became an opulent planter in Louisiana. The mother of Augustine was a Huguenot[118] French lady, whose family had emigrated to Louisiana during the days of its early settlement. Augustine and another brother were the only children of their parents. Having inherited from his mother an exceeding delicacy of constitution, he was, at the instance of physicians, during many years of his boyhood, sent to the care of his uncle in Vermont, in order that his constitution might be strengthened by the cold of a more bracing climate.

In childhood, he was remarkable for an extreme and marked sensitiveness of character, more akin to the softness of woman than the ordinary hardness of his own sex. Time, however, overgrew this softness with the rough bark of manhood, and but few knew how living and fresh it still lay at the core. His talents were of the very first order, although his mind showed a preference always for the ideal and the aesthetic; and there was about him that repugnance to the actual business of life which is the common result of this balance of the faculties. Soon after the completion of his college course, his whole nature was kindled into one intense and passionate effervescence of romantic passion. His hour came – the hour that comes only once; his star rose in the horizon – that star that rises so often in vain, to be remembered only as a thing of dreams; and it rose for him in vain. To drop the figure, he saw and won the love of a high minded and beautiful woman, in one of the Northern States, and they were affianced. He returned south to make arrangements for their marriage, when, most unexpectedly, his letters were returned to him by mail, with a short note from her guardian, stating to him that ere this reached him the lady would be the wife of another. Stung to madness, he vainly hoped, as many another has done, to fling the whole thing from his heart by one desperate effort. Too proud to supplicate or seek explanation, he threw himself at once into a whirl of fashionable society, and in a fortnight from the time of the fatal letter was the accepted lover of the reigning belle of the season; and as soon as arrangements could be made, he became the husband of a fine figure, a pair of bright dark eyes, and a hundred thousand dollars; and, of course, everybody thought him a happy fellow.

The married couple were enjoying their honeymoon, and entertaining a brilliant circle of friends in their splendid villa, near Lake Pontchartrain,[119] when, one day a letter was brought to him in *that* well-remembered writing. It was handed to him while he was in full tide of gay and successful conversation, in a whole room-full of company. He turned deadly pale when he saw the writing, but still preserved his composure, and finished the playful warfare of badinage which he was at the moment carrying on with a lady opposite; and, a short time after, was missed from the circle. In his room, alone, he opened and read the letter, now worse than idle and useless to be read. It was from her, giving a long account of a persecution to which she had been exposed by her guardian's family, to lead her to unite herself with their son; and she related how, for a long time, his letters had ceased to arrive; how she had written time and again, till she became weary and doubtful; how her health had failed under her anxieties, and how, at last, she had discovered the whole fraud which had been practised on them both. The letter ended with expressions of hope and thankfulness, and professions of undying affection, which were more bitter than death to the unhappy young man. He wrote to her immediately –

'I have received yours – but too late. I believed all I heard. I was desperate. *I am married*, and all is over. Only forget – it is all that remains for either of us.'

And thus ended the whole romance and ideal of life for Augustine St Clare; but the *real* remained – the *real*, like the flat, bare, oozy tide-mud, when the blue sparkling wave, with all its company of gliding boats and white-winged ships, its music of oars and chiming waters, has gone down, and there it lies, flat, slimy, bare – exceedingly real.

Of course, in a novel, people's hearts break, and they die, and that is the end of it; and in a story this is very convenient. But in real life we do not die when all that makes life bright dies to us. There is a most busy and important round of eating, drinking, dressing, walking, visiting, buying, selling, talking, reading, and all that makes up what is commonly called *living*, yet to be gone through; and this yet remained to Augustine. Had his wife been a whole woman, she might yet have done something – as woman can – to mend the broken threads of life, and weave again into a tissue of brightness. But Marie St Clare could not even see that they had been broken. As before stated, she consisted of a fine figure, a pair of splendid eyes, and a hundred thousand dollars; and none of these items were precisely the ones to minister to a mind diseased.[120]

When Augustine, pale as death, was found lying on the sofa, and pleaded sudden sick-headache as the cause of his distress, she recommended to him to smell of hartshorn;[121] and when the paleness and headache came on week after week, she only said that she never thought Mr St Clare was sickly; but it seems he was very liable to sick-headaches, and that it was a very unfortunate thing for her, because he didn't enjoy going into company with her, and it seemed odd to go so much alone, when they were just married. Augustine was glad in his heart that he had married so undiscerning a woman; but as the glosses and civilities of the honeymoon wore away, he discovered that a beautiful young woman, who has lived all her life to be caressed and waited on, might prove quite a hard mistress in domestic life. Marie never had possessed much capability of affection, or much sensibility, and the little that she had had been merged into a most intense and unconscious selfishness; a selfishness the more hopeless from its quiet obtuseness, its utter ignorance of any claims but her own. From her infancy she had been surrounded with servants, who lived only to study her caprices; the idea that they had either feelings or rights had never dawned upon her, even in distant perspective. Her father, whose only child she had been, had never denied her anything that lay within the compass of human possibility; and when she entered life, beautiful, accomplished, and an heiress, she had, of course, all the eligibles and non-eligibles of the other sex sighing at her feet, and she had no doubt that Augustine was a most fortunate man in having obtained her. It is a great mistake to suppose that a woman with no heart will be an easy creditor in the exchange of affection. There is not on earth a more merciless exactor of love from others than a thoroughly selfish woman; and the more unlovely she grows, the more jealously and scrupulously she exacts love, to the uttermost farthing. When, therefore, St Clare began to drop off those gallantries and small attentions which flowed at first through the habitude of courtship, he found his sultana no way ready to resign her slave; there were abundance of tears, poutings, and small tempests, there were discontents, pinings, upbraidings. St Clare was good-natured and self-indulgent, and sought to buy off with presents and flatteries; and when Marie became mother to a beautiful daughter, he really felt awakened, for a time, to something like tenderness.

St Clare's mother had been a woman of uncommon elevation and purity of character, and he gave to this child his mother's name, fondly fancying that she would prove a reproduction of her image. The thing had been remarked with petulant jealousy by his wife, and she regarded her husband's absorbing devotion to the child with suspicion and dislike; all that was given to her seemed so much taken from herself. From the time of the birth of this child her health gradually sank. A life of constant inaction, bodily and mental – the friction of ceaseless *ennui* and discontent, united to the ordinary weakness which attended the period of maternity – in course of a few years changed the blooming young belle into a yellow, faded, sickly woman, whose time was divided among a variety of fanciful diseases, and who considered herself, in every sense, the most ill-used and suffering person in existence.

There was no end of her various complaints; but her principal forte appeared to lie in sick-headache, which sometimes would confine her to her room three days out of six. As, of course, all family arrangements fell into the hands of servants, St Clare found his *ménage* anything but comfortable. His only daughter was exceedingly delicate, and he feared that, with no one to look after her and attend to her, her health and life might yet fall a sacrifice to her mother's inefficiency. He had taken her with him on a tour to Vermont, and had persuaded his cousin, Miss Ophelia St Clare, to return with him to his Southern residence; and they are now returning on this boat, where we have introduced them to our readers.

And now, while the distant domes and spires of New Orleans rise to our view, there is yet time for an introduction to Miss Ophelia.

Whoever has travelled in the New England States will remember, in some cool village, the large farmhouse,[122] with its clean-swept grassy yard, shaded by the dense and massive foliage of the sugar maple; and remember the air of order and stillness, of perpetuity and unchanging repose, that seemed to breathe over the whole place. Nothing lost, or out of order; not a picket loose in the fence, not a particle of litter in the turfy yard, with its clumps of lilac-bushes growing up under the windows. Within, he will remember wide, clean rooms, where nothing ever seems to be doing or going to be done, where everything is once and for ever rigidly in place, and where all household arrangements move with the punctual exactness of the old clock in the corner. In the family 'keeping-room', as it is termed, he will remember the staid, respectable old bookcase, with its glass doors, where Rollin's History, Milton's *Paradise Lost*, Bunyan's *Pilgrim's Progress*, and *Scott's Family Bible*,[123] stand side by side in decorous order, with multitudes of other books, equally solemn and respectable. There are no servants in the house, but the lady in the snowy cap, with the spectacles, who sits sewing every afternoon among her daughters, as if nothing ever had been done, or were to be done – she and her girls, in some long-forgotten fore-part of the day, '*did up the work*', and for the rest of the time, probably at all hours when you would see them, it is '*done up*'. The old kitchen floor never seems stained or spotted; the tables, the chairs, and the various cooking utensils, never seem deranged or disordered: though three and sometimes four meals a day are got there, though the family washing and ironing is there performed, and though pounds of butter and cheese are in some silent and mysterious manner there brought into existence.

On such a farm, in such a house and family, Miss Ophelia had spent a quiet existence of some forty-five years, when her cousin invited her to visit his Southern mansion. The eldest of a large family, she was still considered by her father and mother as one of 'the children', and the proposal that she should go to Orleans was a most momentous one to the family circle. The old grey-headed father took down *Morse's Atlas* out of the bookcase, and looked out the exact latitude and longitude; and read Flint's *Travels in the South and West*,[124] to make up his own mind as to the nature of the country.

The good mother enquired, anxiously, 'if Orleans wasn't an awful wicked place'; saying, 'that it seemed to her most equal to going to the Sandwich Islands,[125] or anywhere among the heathen'.

It was known at the minister's, and at the doctor's, and at Miss Peabody's milliner's shop, that Ophelia St Clare was 'talking about going away down to Orleans with her cousin'; and of course the whole village could do no less than help this very important process of *talking about* the matter. The minister, who inclined strongly to Abolitionist views, was quite doubtful whether such a step might not tend some-what to encourage the Southerners in holding on to their slaves; while the doctor, who was a staunch colonisationist,[126] inclined to the opinion that Miss Ophelia ought to go, to show the Orleans people that we don't think hardly of them, after all. He was of opinion, in fact, that Southern people needed encouraging. When, however, the fact that she had resolved to go was fully before the public mind, she was solemnly invited out to tea by all her friends and neighbours for the space of a fortnight, and her prospects and plans duly canvassed and enquired into. Miss Moseley, who came into the house to help to do the dressmaking, acquired daily accessions of importance from the developments with regard to Miss Ophelia's wardrobe which she had been enabled to make. It was credibly ascertained that Squire Sinclare, as his name was commonly contracted in the neighbourhood, had counted out fifty dollars, and given them to Miss Ophelia, and told her to buy any clothes she thought best; and that two new silk dresses, and a bonnet, had been sent for from Boston. As to the propriety of this extraordinary outlay, the public mind was divided; some affirming that it was well enough, all things considered, for once in one's life, and others stoutly affirming that the money had better have been sent to the missionaries; but all parties agreed that there had been no such parasol seen in those parts as had been sent on from New York and that she had one silk dress that might fairly be trusted to stand alone, whatever might be said of its mistress. There were credible rumours, also, of a hem-stitched pocket-handkerchief; and report even went so far as to state that Miss Ophelia had one pocket-handkerchief with lace all around it – it was even added that it was worked in the corners; but this latter point was never satisfactorily ascertained, and remains, in fact, unsettled to this day.

Miss Ophelia, as you now behold her, stands before you, in a very shining brown linen travelling-dress, tall, square-formed, and angular. Her face was thin, and rather sharp in its outlines; the lips compressed, like those of a person who is in the habit of making up her mind definitely on all subjects; while the keen, dark eyes, had a peculiarly searching, advised movement, and travelled over everything, as if they were looking for something to take care of.

All her movements were sharp, decided, and energetic; and, though she was never much of a talker, her words were remarkably direct and to the purpose, when she did speak.

In her habits, she was a living impersonation of order, method, and exactness. In punctuality, she was as inevitable as a clock, and as inexorable as a railroad-engine; and she held in most decided contempt and abomination anything of a contrary character.

The great sin of sins in her eyes – the sum of all evils – was expressed by one very common and important word in her vocabulary – 'shiftlessness'. Her finale and ultimatum of contempt consisted in a very emphatic pronunciation of the word 'shiftless'; and by this she characterised all modes of procedure which had not a direct and inevitable relation to accomplishment of some purpose then definitely had in mind. People who did nothing, or who did not know exactly what they were going to do, or who did not take the most direct way to accomplish what they set their hands to, were objects of her entire contempt; a contempt shown less frequently by anything she said than by a kind of stony grimness, as if she scorned to say anything about the matter.

As to mental cultivation, she had a clear, strong, active mind, was well and thoroughly read in history and the older English classics, and thought with great strength within certain narrow limits. Her theological tenets were all made up, labelled in most positive and distinct forms, and put by, like the bundles in her patch trunk; there were just so many of them, and there were never to be any more. So, also, were her ideas with regard to most matters of practical life – such as housekeeping in all its branches, and the various political relations of her native village. And, underlaying all, deeper than anything else, higher and broader, lay the strongest principle of her being – conscientiousness. Nowhere is conscience so dominant and all-absorbing as with New-England women. It is the granite formation, which lies deepest, and rises out, even to the tops of the highest mountains.

Miss Ophelia was the absolute bond-slave of the '*ought*'. Once make her certain that the 'path of duty', as she commonly phrased it, lay in any given direction, and fire and water could not keep her from it. She would walk straight down into a well, or up to a loaded cannon's mouth, if she were only quite sure that there the path lay. Her standard of right was so high, so all-embracing, so minute, and making so few concessions to human frailty, that though she strove with heroic ardour to reach it, she never actually did so, and of course was burdened with a constant and often harassing sense of deficiency. This gave a severe and somewhat gloomy cast to her religious character.

But, how in the world can Miss Ophelia get along with Augustine St Clare – gay, easy, unpunctual, unpractical, sceptical – in short, walking with impudent and nonchalant freedom over every one of her most cherished habits and opinions?

To tell the truth, then, Miss Ophelia loved him. When a boy, it had been hers to teach him his catechism, mend his clothes, comb his hair, and bring him up generally in the way he should go; and her heart having a warm side to it, Augustine had, as he usually did with most people, monopolised a large share of it for himself, and therefore it was that he succeeded very easily in persuading her that the 'path of duty' lay in the direction of New Orleans, and that she must go with him to take care of Eva, and keep everything from going to wreck and ruin during the frequent illnesses of his wife. The idea of a house without anybody to take care of it went to her heart; then she loved the lovely little girl, as few could help doing; and though she regarded Augustine as very much of a heathen, yet she loved him, laughed at his jokes, and forbore with his failings, to an extent which those who knew him thought perfectly incredible. But what more or other is to be known of Miss Ophelia our reader must discover by a personal acquaintance.

There she is, sitting now in her stateroom, surrounded by a mixed multitude of little and big carpet-bags, boxes, baskets, each containing some separate responsibility which she is tying, binding up, packing, or fastening, with a face of great earnestness.

'Now, Eva, have you kept count of your things? Of course you haven't – children never do: there's the spotted carpet-bag and the little blue band-box with your best bonnet – that's two; then the India rubber satchel is three; and my tape and needle box is four; and my band-box, five; and my collar-box, six; and that little hair trunk, seven. What have you done with your sunshade? Give it to me, and let me put a paper round it, and tie it to my umbrella with my shade: there, now.'

'Why, aunty, we are only going up home – what is the use?'

'To keep it nice, child; people must take care of their things if they ever mean to have anything. And now, Eva, is your thimble put up?'

'Really, aunty, I don't know.'

'Well, never mind; I'll look your box over. – Thimble, wax, two spoons, scissors, knife, tape-needle;[127] all right – put it in here. What did you ever do, child, when you were coming on with only your papa? I should have thought you'd a lost everything you had.'

'Well, aunty, I did lose a great many; and then, when we stopped anywhere, papa would buy some more of whatever it was.'

'Mercy on us, child, what a way!'

'It was a very easy way, aunty,' said Eva.

'It's a dreadful shiftless one,' said aunty.

'Why, aunty, what'll you do now?' said Eva. 'That trunk is too full to be shut down.'

'It *must* shut down,' said aunty, with the air of a general, as she squeezed the things in, and sprang upon the lid; still a little gap remained about the mouth of the trunk.

'Get up here, Eva!' said Miss Ophelia, courageously; 'what has been done can be done again. This trunk has *got to be* shut and locked there are no two ways about it.'

And the trunk, intimidated, doubtless, by this resolute statement, gave in. The hasp snapped sharply in its hole, and Miss Ophelia turned the key, and pocketed it in triumph.

'Now we're ready. Where's your papa? I think it time this baggage was set out. Do look out, Eva, and see if you see your papa.'

'Oh, yes, he's down the other end of the gentlemen's cabin, eating an orange.'

'He can't know how near we are coming,' said aunty; 'hadn't you better run and speak to him?'

'Papa never is in a hurry about anything,' said Eva, 'and we haven't come to the landing. Do step on the guards, aunty. Look! there's our house, up that street!'

The boat now began, with heavy groans, like some vast, tired monster, to prepare to push up among the multiplied steamers at the levee. Eva joyously pointed out the various spires, domes, and way-marks, by which she recognised her native city.

'Yes, yes, dear; very fine,' said Miss Ophelia. 'But mercy on us! the boat has stopped! where is your father?'

And now ensued the usual turmoil of landing – waiters running twenty ways at once – men tugging trunks, carpet-bags, boxes – women anxiously calling to their children, and everybody crowding in a dense mass to the plank towards the landing.

Miss Ophelia seated herself resolutely on the lately vanquished trunk, and marshalling all her goods and chattels in fine military order, seemed resolved to defend them to the last.

'Shall I take your trunk, ma'am?' 'Shall I take your baggage?' 'Let me 'tend to your baggage, missis?' 'Shan't I carry out these yer, missis?' rained down upon her unheeded. She sat with grim determination, upright as a darning-needle stuck in a board, holding onto her bundle of umbrella and parasols, and replying with a determination that was enough to strike dismay even into a hackman,[128] wondering to Eva, in each interval, 'what upon earth her papa could be thinking of; he couldn't have fallen over, now – but something must have happened': and just as she had begun to work herself into a real distress, he came up, with his usually careless motion, and giving Eva a quarter of the orange he was eating, said –

'Well, Cousin Vermont, I suppose you are all ready.'

'I've been ready, waiting, nearly an hour,' said Miss Ophelia; 'I began to be really concerned about you.'

'That's a clever fellow, now,' said he. 'Well, the carriage is waiting, and the crowd are now off, so that one can walk out in a decent and

Christian manner, and not be pushed and shoved. Here,' he added to a driver who stood behind him, 'take these things.'

'I'll go and see to his putting them in,' said Miss Ophelia.

'O, pshaw, cousin; what's the use?' said St Clare.

'Well, at any rate, I'll carry this, and this, and this,' said Miss Ophelia, singling out three boxes and a small carpet-bag.

'My dear Miss Vermont, positively you mustn't come the Green Mountains over us[129] that way. You must adopt at least a piece of a Southern principle, and not walk out under all that load. They'll take you for a waiting-maid; give them to this fellow; he'll put them down as if they were eggs, now.'

Miss Ophelia looked despairingly, as her cousin took all her treasures from her, and rejoiced to find herself once more in the carriage with them, in a state of preservation:

'Where's Tom?' said Eva.

'Oh, he's on the outside, Pussy. I'm going to take Tom up to mother for a peace-offering, to make up for that drunken fellow that upset the carriage.'

'Oh, Tom will make a splendid driver, I know,' said Eva; 'he'll never get drunk.'

The carriage stopped in front of an ancient mansion, built in that odd mixture of Spanish and French style, of which there are specimens in some parts of New Orleans. It was built in the Moorish fashion[130] – a square building enclosing a courtyard, into which the carriage drove through an arched gateway. The court, in the inside, had evidently been arranged to gratify a picturesque and voluptuous ideality. Wide galleries ran all around the four sides, whose Moorish arches, slender pillars, and arabesque ornaments, carried the mind back, as in a dream, to the reign of Oriental romance in Spain. In the middle of the court, a fountain threw high its silvery water, falling in a never-ceasing spray into a marble basin, fringed with a deep border of fragrant violets. The water in the fountain, pellucid as crystal, was alive with myriads of gold and silver fishes, twinkling and darting through it like so many living jewels. Around the fountain ran a walk, paved with a mosaic of pebbles, laid in various fanciful patterns; and this, again, was surrounded by turf, smooth as green velvet, while a carriage-drive enclosed the whole. Two large orange trees, now fragrant with blossoms, threw a delicious shade; and, ranged in a circle round upon the turf, were marble vases of arabesque sculpture, containing the choicest flowering plants of the tropics. Huge pomegranate trees, with their glossy leaves and flame-coloured flowers, dark-leaved Arabian jessamines, with their silvery stars, geraniums, luxuriant roses bending beneath their heavy abundance of flowers, golden jessamines, lemon-scented verbenum, all united their bloom and fragrance, while here and there a mystic old aloe,[131] with its strange, massive leaves, sat looking like some hoary old enchanter, sitting in weird grandeur among the more perishable bloom and fragrance around it.

The galleries that surrounded the court were festooned with a curtain of some kind of Moorish stuff, and could be drawn down at pleasure, to exclude the beams of the sun. On the whole, the appearance of the place was luxurious and romantic.

As the carriage drove in, Eva seemed like a bird ready to burst from a cage, with the wild eagerness of her delight.

'Oh, isn't it beautiful, lovely, my own dear, darling home!' she said to Miss Ophelia. 'Isn't it beautiful?'

' 'Tis a pretty place,' said Miss Ophelia, as she alighted; 'though it looks rather old and heathenish to me.'

Tom got down from the carriage, and looked about with an air of calm, still enjoyment. The negro, it must be remembered, is an exotic of the most gorgeous and superb countries of the world, and he has, deep in his heart, a passion for all that is splendid, rich, and fanciful; a passion which, rudely indulged by an untrained taste, draws on them the ridicule of the colder and more correct white race.

St Clare, who was in his heart a poetical voluptuary, smiled as Miss Ophelia made her remark on his premises, and, turning to Tom, who was standing looking round, his beaming black face perfectly radiant with admiration, he said –

'Tom, my boy, this seems to suit you.'

'Yes, mas'r, it looks about the right thing,' said Tom.

All this passed in a moment, while trunks were being hustled off, hackman paid, and while a crowd, of all ages and sizes – men, women, and children, came running through the galleries, both above and below, to see mas'r come in. Foremost among them was a highly-dressed young mulatto man, evidently a very *distingué*[132] personage, attired in the ultra extreme of the mode, and gracefully waving a scented cambric handkerchief in his hand.

This personage had been exerting himself, with great alacrity, in driving all the flock of domestics to the other end of the veranda.

'Back! all of you. I am ashamed of you,' he said, in a tone of authority. 'Would you intrude on master's domestic relations, in the first hour of his return?'

All looked abashed at this elegant speech, delivered with quite an air, and stood huddled together at a respectful distance, except two stout porters, who came up and began conveying away the baggage.

Owing to Mr Adolph's systematic arrangements, when St Clare turned round from paying the hackman, there was nobody in view but Mr Adolph himself, conspicuous in satin vest, gold guard-chain, and white pants, and bowing with inexpressible grace and suavity.

'Ah, Adolph, is it you?' said his master, offering his hand to him: 'how are you, boy?' while Adolph poured forth, with great fluency, an extemporary speech, which he had been preparing, with great care, for a fortnight before.

'Well, well,' said St Clare, passing on, with his usual air of negligent drollery, 'that's very well got up, Adolph. See that the baggage is well bestowed. I'll come to the people in a minute;' and so saying, he led Miss Ophelia to a large parlour that opened on to the veranda.

While this had been passing, Eva had flown like a bird, through the porch and parlour, to a little boudoir opening likewise on the veranda.

A tall, dark-eyed, sallow woman, half rose from a couch on which she was reclining.

'Mamma!' said Eva, in a sort of a rapture, throwing herself on her neck, and embracing her over and over again.

'That'll do – take care, child – don't, you make my head ache!' said the mother, after she had languidly kissed her.

St Clare came in, embraced his wife in true, orthodox, husbandly fashion, and then presented to her his cousin. Marie lifted her large eyes on her cousin with an air of some curiosity, and received her with languid politeness. A crowd of servants now pressed to the entry door, and among them a middle-aged mulatto woman, of very respectable appearance, stood foremost, in a tremor of expectation and joy, at the door.

'Oh, there's Mammy!' said Eva, as she flew across the room; and, throwing herself into her arms, she kissed her repeatedly.

This woman did not tell her that she made her head ache, but, on the contrary, she hugged her, and laughed, and cried, till her sanity was a thing to be doubted of; and when released from her, Eva flew from one to another, shaking hands and kissing, in a way that Miss Ophelia afterwards declared fairly turned her stomach.

'Well!' said Miss Ophelia, 'you Southern children can do something that *I* couldn't.'

'What, now, pray?' said St Clare.

'Well, I want to be kind to everybody, and I wouldn't have anything hurt; but as to kissing – '

'Niggers,' said St Clare, 'that you're not up to; eh?'

'Yes, that's it. How can she?'

St Clare laughed, as he went into the passage. 'Halloa, here, what's to pay out here? Here, you all – Mammy, Jimmy, Polly, Sukey – glad to see mas'r?' he said, as he went shaking hands from one to another. 'Look out for the babies!' he added, as he stumbled over a sooty little urchin, who was crawling upon all-fours. 'If I step upon anybody, let 'em mention it.'

There was an abundance of laughing and blessing mas'r, as St Clare distributed small pieces of change among them.

'Come, now, take yourselves off, like good boys and girls,' he said; and the whole assemblage, dark and light, disappeared through a door into a large veranda, followed by Eva, who carried a large satchel, which she had been filling with apples, nuts, candy, ribbons laces, and toys of every description, during her whole homeward journey.

As St Clare turned to go back, his eye fell upon Tom, who was standing uneasily, shifting from one foot to the other, while Adolph stood negligently leaning against the banisters, examining Tom through an opera-glass, with an air that would have done credit to any dandy living.

'Puh! you puppy,' said his master, striking down the opera-glass; 'is that the way you treat your company? Seems to me, Dolph,' he added, laying his finger on the elegant figured satin vest that Adolph was sporting, 'seems to me that's *my* vest.'

'Oh! Master, this vest all stained with wine; of course, a gentleman in master's standing never wears a vest like this. I understood I was to take it. It does for a poor nigger-fellow, like me.'

And Adolph tossed his head, and passed his fingers through his scented hair, with a grace.

'So, that's it, is it?' said St Clare, carelessly. 'Well, here, I'm going to show this Tom to his mistress, and then you take him to the kitchen; and mind you don't put on any of your airs to him. He's worth two such puppies as you.'

'Master always will have his joke,' said Adolph, laughing. 'I'm delighted to see master in such spirits.'

'Here, Tom,' said St Clare, beckoning.

Tom entered the room. He looked wistfully on the velvet carpets and the before unimagined splendours of mirrors, pictures, statues, and curtains, and, like the Queen of Sheba before Solomon,[133] there was no more spirit in him. He looked afraid even to set his feet down.

'See here, Marie,' said St Clare to his wife, 'I've bought you a coachman, at last, to order. I tell you, he's a regular hearse for blackness and sobriety, and will drive you like a funeral, if you want. Open your eyes, now, and look at him. Now, don't say I never think about you when I'm gone.'

Marie opened her eyes, and fixed them on Tom, without rising.

'I know he'll get drunk,' she said.

'No, he's warranted a pious and sober article.'

'Well, I hope he may turn out well,' said the lady; 'it's more than I expect though.'

'Dolph,' said St Clare, 'show Tom downstairs; and mind yourself,' he added; 'remember what I told you.'

Adolph tripped gracefully forward, and Tom, with lumbering tread, went after.

'He's a perfect behemoth!' said Marie.

'Come, now, Marie,' said St Clare, seating himself on a stool beside her sofa, 'be gracious, and say something pretty to a fellow.'

'You've been gone a fortnight beyond the time,' said the lady, pouting.

'Well, you know I wrote you the reason.'

'Such a short, cold letter!' said the lady.

'Dear me! the mail was just going, and it had to be that or nothing.'

'That's just the way, always,' said the lady; 'always something to make your journeys long, and letters short.'

'See here, now,' he added, drawing an elegant velvet case out of his pocket, and opening it, 'here's a present I got for you in New York.' It was a daguerreotype, clear and soft as an engraving, representing Eva and her father sitting hand in hand.

Marie looked at it with a dissatisfied air.

'What made you sit in such an awkward position?' she said.

'Well, the position may be a matter of opinion; but what do you think of the likeness?'

'If you don't think anything of my opinion in one case, I suppose you wouldn't in another,' said the lady, shutting the daguerreotype.

'Hang the woman!' said St Clare, mentally; but aloud he added, 'Come, now, Marie, what do you think of the likeness? Don't be nonsensical, now.'

'It's very inconsiderate of you, St Clare,' said the lady, 'to insist on my talking and looking at things. You know I've been lying all day with the sick-headache; and there's been such a tumult made ever since you came, I'm half dead.'

'You're subject to the sick-headache, ma'am?' said Miss Ophelia, suddenly rising from the depths of the large armchair, where she had sat quietly, taking an inventory of the furniture, and calculating its expense.

'Yes, I'm a perfect martyr to it,' said the lady.

'Juniper-berry tea is good for sick-headache,' said Miss Ophelia; 'at least, Auguste, Deacon Abraham Perry's wife, used to say so; and she was a great nurse.'

'I'll have the first juniper-berries that get ripe in our garden by the lake brought in for that especial purpose,' said St Clare, gravely pulling the bell as he did so; 'meanwhile, cousin, you must be wanting to retire to your apartment, and refresh yourself a little, after your journey. Dolph,' he added, 'tell Mammy to come here.' The decent mulatto woman whom Eva had caressed so rapturously soon entered; she was dressed neatly, with a high red and yellow turban on her head, the recent gift of Eva, and which the child had been arranging on her head. 'Mammy,' said St Clare, 'I put this lady under your care; she is tired, and wants rest. Take her to her chamber, and be sure she is made comfortable;' and Miss Ophelia disappeared in the rear of Mammy.

CHAPTER XVI

Tom's Mistress and Her Opinions

'AND NOW, MARIE,' said St Clare, 'your golden days are dawning. Here is our practical, businesslike New England cousin, who will take the whole budget of cares off your shoulders, and give you time to refresh yourself, and grow young and handsome. The ceremony of delivering the keys had better come off forthwith.'

This remark was made at the breakfast-table, a few mornings after Miss Ophelia had arrived.

'I'm sure she's welcome,' said Marie, leaning her head languidly on her hand. 'I think she'll find one thing, if she does, and that is, that it's we mistresses that are the slaves, down here.'

'Oh, certainly, she will discover that, and a world of wholesome truths besides, no doubt,' said St Clare.

'Talk about our keeping slaves, as if we did it for our *convenience*,' said Marie. 'I'm sure, if we consulted *that*, we might let them all go at once.'

Evangeline fixed her large, serious eyes on her mother's face, with an earnest and perplexed expression, and said, simply, 'What do you keep them for, mamma?'

'I don't know, I'm sure, except for a plague; they are the plague of my life. I believe that more of my ill health is caused by them than by any one thing; and ours, I know, are the very worst that ever anybody was plagued with.'

'Oh, come, Marie, you've got the blues this morning,' said St Clare. 'You know 'tisn't so. There's Mammy, the best creature living – what could you do without her?'

'Mammy is the best I ever knew,' said Marie; 'and yet Mammy, now, is selfish – dreadfully selfish; it's the fault of the whole race.'

'Selfishness *is* a dreadful fault,' said St Clare, gravely.

'Well, now, there's Mammy,' said Marie, 'I think it's selfish of her to sleep so sound nights; she knows I need little attentions almost every hour, when my worst turns are on, and yet she's so hard to wake. I absolutely am worse, this very morning, for the efforts I had to make to wake her last night.'

'Hasn't she sat up with you a good many nights, lately, mamma?' said Eva.

'How should you know that?' said Marie, sharply; 'she's been complaining, I suppose.'

'She didn't complain; she only told me what bad nights you'd had – so many in succession.'

'Why don't you let Jane or Rosa take her place, a night or two,' said St Clare, 'and let her rest?'

'How can you propose it?' said Marie. 'St Clare, you really are inconsiderate! So nervous as I am, the least breath disturbs me; and a strange hand about me would drive me absolutely frantic. If Mammy felt the interest in me she ought to, she'd wake easier – of course she would. I've heard of people who had such devoted servants, but it never was *my* luck;' and Marie sighed.

Miss Ophelia had listened to this conversation with an air of shrewd, observant gravity; and she still kept her lips tightly compressed, as if determined fully to ascertain her longitude and position, before she committed herself.

'Now, Mammy has a *sort* of goodness,' said Marie; 'she's smooth and respectful, but she's selfish at heart. Now, she never will be done fidgeting and worrying about that husband of hers. You see, when I was married and came to live here, of course I had to bring her with me, and her husband my father couldn't spare. He was a blacksmith, and, of course, very necessary; and I thought and said, at the time, that Mammy and he had better give each other up, as it wasn't likely to be convenient for them ever to live together again. I wish now I'd insisted on it, and married Mammy to somebody else; but I was foolish and indulgent, and didn't want to insist. I told Mammy, at the time, that she mustn't ever expect to see him more than once or twice in her life again, for the air of father's place doesn't agree with my health, and I can't go there; and I advised her to take up with somebody else; but no – she wouldn't. Mammy has a kind of obstinacy about her, in spots, that everybody don't see as I do.'

'Has she children?' said Miss Ophelia.

'Yes; she has two.'

'I suppose she feels the separation from them?'

'Well of course, I couldn't bring them. They were little dirty things – I couldn't have them about; and, besides, they took up too much of her time; but I believe that Mammy has always kept up a sort of sulkiness about this. She won't marry anybody else; and I do believe, now, though she knows how necessary she is to me, and how feeble my health is, she would go back to her husband tomorrow, if she only could. I *do*, indeed,' said Marie; 'they are just so selfish, now, the best of them.'

'It's distressing to reflect upon,' said St Clare, dryly.

Miss Ophelia looked keenly at him, and saw the flush of mortification and repressed vexation, and the sarcastic curl of the lip, as he spoke.

'Now, Mammy has always been a pet with me,' said Marie. 'I wish some of your Northern servants could look at her closets of dresses – silks and muslins, and one real linen cambric, she has hanging there. I've worked sometimes whole afternoons, trimming her caps, and getting her ready to go to a party. As to abuse, she don't know what it is. She never was whipped more than once or twice in her whole life. She has her strong coffee or her tea every day, with white sugar in it. It's abominable, to be sure; but St Clare will have high life below stairs, and they, every one of them live just as they please. The fact is, our servants are over-indulged. I suppose it is partly our fault that they are selfish, and act like spoiled children; but I've talked to St Clare till I am tired.'

'And I, too,' said St Clare, taking up the morning paper.

Eva, the beautiful Eva, had stood listening to her mother, with that expression of deep and mystic earnestness which was peculiar to her. She walked softly round to her mother's chair, and put her arms round her neck.

'Well, Eva, what now?' said Marie.

'Mamma, couldn't I take care of you one night – just one? I know I shouldn't make you nervous, and I shouldn't sleep. I often lie awake nights, thinking – '

'Oh, nonsense, child – nonsense!' said Marie; 'you are such a strange child!'

'But may I, mamma? I think,' she said, timidly, 'that Mammy isn't well. She told me her head ached all the time, lately.'

'Oh, that's just one of Mammy's fidgets! Mammy is just like all the rest of them – makes such a fuss about every little headache or finger-ache; it'll never do to encourage it – never! I'm principled about this matter,' said she, turning to Miss Ophelia; 'you'll find the necessity of it. If you encourage servants in giving way to every little disagreeable feeling, and complaining of every little ailment, you'll have your hands full. I never complain myself – nobody knows what I endure. I feel it a duty to bear it quietly, and I do.'

Miss Ophelia's round eyes expressed an undisguised amazement at this peroration, which struck St Clare as so supremely ludicrous, that he burst into a loud laugh.

'St Clare always laughs when I make the least allusion to my ill health,' said Marie, with the voice of a suffering martyr. 'I only hope the day won't come when he'll remember it!' and Marie put her handkerchief to her eyes.

Of course, there was rather a foolish silence. Finally, St Clare got up, looked at his watch, and said he had an engagement down street. Eva tripped away after him, and Miss Ophelia and Marie remained at the table alone.

'Now, that's just like St Clare!' said the latter, withdrawing her handkerchief with somewhat of a spirited flourish when the criminal to be affected by it was no longer in sight.

'He never realises, never can, never will, what I suffer, and have for years. If I was one of the complaining sort, or ever made any fuss about my ailments, there would be some reason for it. Men do get tired, naturally, of a complaining wife. But I've kept things to myself, and borne, and borne, till St Clare has got in the way of thinking I can bear anything.'

Miss Ophelia did not exactly know what she was expected to answer to this.

While she was thinking what to say, Marie gradually wiped away her tears, and smoothed her plumage in a general sort of way, as a dove might be supposed to make toilet after a shower, and began a housewifely chat with Miss Ophelia, concerning cupboards, closets, linen-presses, store-rooms, and other matters, of which the latter was, by common understanding, to assume the direction – giving her so many cautious directions and charges, that a head less systematic and businesslike than Miss Ophelia's would have been utterly dizzied and confounded.

'And now,' said Marie, 'I believe I've told you everything; so that, when my next sick turn comes on, you'll be able to go forward entirely, without consulting me; only about Eva – she requires watching.'

'She seems to be a good child, very,' said Miss Ophelia; 'I never saw a better child.'

'Eva's peculiar,' said her mother, 'very. There are things about her so singular; she isn't like me, now, a particle;' and Marie sighed, as if this was a truly melancholy consideration.

Miss Ophelia in her own heart said, 'I hope she isn't,' but had prudence enough to keep it down.

'Eva always was disposed to be with servants; and I think that well enough with some children. Now, I always played with father's little negroes – it never did me any harm. But Eva somehow always seems to put herself on an equality with every creature that comes near her. It's a strange thing about the child. I never have been able to break her of it. St Clare, I believe, encourages her in it. The fact is, St Clare indulges every creature under this roof but his own wife.'

Again Miss Ophelia sat in blank silence.

'Now, there's no way with servants,' said Marie, 'but to *put them down*, and keep them down. It was always natural to me, from a child. Eva is enough to spoil a whole house-full. What she will do when she comes to keep house herself, I'm sure I don't know. I hold to being *kind* to servants – I always am; but you must make 'em *know their place*. Eva never does; there's no getting into the child's head the first beginning of an idea what a servant's place is! You heard her offering to take care of me nights, to let Mammy sleep! That's just a specimen of the way the child would be doing all the time, if she was left to herself.'

'Why,' said Miss Ophelia, bluntly, 'I suppose you think your servants are human creatures, and ought to have some rest when they are tired.'

'Certainly, of course. I'm very particular in letting them have everything that comes convenient – anything that doesn't put one at all out of the way, you know. Mammy can make up her sleep, sometime or other; there's no difficulty about that. She's the sleepiest concern that ever I saw; sewing, standing, or sitting, that creature will go to sleep, and sleep anywhere and everywhere. No danger but Mammy gets sleep enough. But this treating servants as if they were exotic flowers, or china vases, is really ridiculous,' said Marie, as she plunged languidly into the depths of a voluminous and pillowy lounge, and drew towards her an elegant cut-glass vinaigrette.[134]

'You see,' she continued, in a faint and lady-like voice, like the last dying breath of an Arabian jessamine, or something equally ethereal, 'you see, Cousin Ophelia, I don't often speak of myself. It isn't my *habit*, 'tisn't agreeable to me. In fact, I haven't strength to do it. But there are points where St Clare and I differ. St Clare never understood me, never appreciated me. I think it lies at the root of all my ill health. St Clare means well, I am bound to believe; but men are constitutionally selfish and inconsiderate to woman. That, at least, is my impression.'

Miss Ophelia, who had not a small share of the genuine New England caution, and a very particular horror of being drawn into family difficulties, now began to foresee something of this kind impending; so, composing her face into a grim neutrality, and drawing out of her pocket about a yard and a quarter of stocking, which she kept as a specific against what Dr Watts asserts to be a personal habit of Satan when people have idle hands,[135] she proceeded to knit most energetically, shutting her lips together in a way that said, as plain as words could, 'You needn't try to make me speak. I don't want anything to do with your affairs' – in fact, she looked about as sympathising as a stone lion. But Marie didn't care for that. She had got somebody to talk to, and she felt it her duty to talk, and that was enough; and reinforcing herself by smelling again at her vinaigrette, she went on.

'You see, I brought my own property and servants into the connection, when I married St Clare, and I am legally entitled to manage them my own way. St Clare had his fortune and his servants, and I'm well enough content he should manage them his way; but St Clare will be interfering. He has wild, extravagant notions about things, particularly about the treatment of servants. He really does act as if he set his servants before me, and before himself, too; for he lets them make him all sorts of trouble, and never lifts a finger. Now, about some things, St Clare is really frightful – he frightens me – good-natured as he looks, in general. Now, he has set down his foot that, come what will, there shall not be a blow struck in this house, except what he or I strike; and he does it in a way that I really dare not cross him. Well, you may see what that leads to; for St Clare wouldn't raise his hand, if every one of them walked over him, and I – you see how cruel it would be to require me to make the exertion. Now, you know these servants are nothing but grown-up children.'

'I don't know anything about it, and I thank the Lord that I don't!' said Miss Ophelia, shortly.

'Well, but you will have to know something, and know it to your cost, if you stay here. You don't know what a provoking, stupid, careless, unreasonable, childish, ungrateful set of wretches they are.'

Marie seemed wonderfully supported, always, when she got upon this topic; and she now opened her eyes, and seemed quite to forget her languor.

'You don't know, and you can't, the daily, hourly trials that beset a housekeeper from them, everywhere and every way. But it's no use to complain to St Clare. He talks the strangest stuff. He says we have made them what they are, and ought to bear with them. He says their faults are all owing to us, and that it would be cruel to make the fault and punish it too. He says we shouldn't do any better, in their place; just as if one could reason from them to us, you know.'

'Don't you believe that the Lord made them of one blood[136] with us?' said Miss Ophelia, shortly.

'No indeed, not I! A pretty story, truly! They are a degraded race.'

'Don't you think they've got immortal souls?' said Miss Ophelia with increasing indignation.

'Oh, well,' said Marie, yawning, 'that, of course – nobody doubts that. But as to putting them on any sort of equality with us, you know, as if we could be compared, why, it's impossible! Now, St Clare really has talked to me as if keeping Mammy from her husband was like keeping me from mine. There's no comparing in this way. Mammy couldn't have the feelings that I should. It's a different thing altogether – of course, it is; and yet St Clare pretends not to see it. And just as if Mammy could love her little dirty babies as I love Eva! Yet St Clare once really and soberly tried to persuade me that it was my duty, with my weak health, and all I suffer, to let Mammy go back, and take somebody else in her place. That was a little too much even for *me* to bear. I don't often show my feelings. I make it a principle to endure everything in silence; it's a wife's hard lot, and I bear it. But I did break out, that time; so that he has never alluded to the subject since. But I know by his looks, and little things that he says, that he thinks so as much as ever; and it's so trying, so provoking!'

Miss Ophelia looked very much as if she was afraid she should say something; but she rattled away with her needles in a way that had volumes of meaning in it, if Marie could only have understood it.

'So, you just see,' she continued, 'what you've got to manage. A household without any rule; where servants have it all their own way, do what they please, and have what they please, except so far as I, with my feeble health, have kept up government. I keep my cowhide[137] about, and sometimes I do lay it on; but the exertion is always too much for me. If St Clare would only have this thing done as others do – '

'And how's that?'

'Why, send them to the calaboose,[138] or some of the other places to be flogged. That's the only way. If I wasn't such a poor, feeble piece, I believe I should manage with twice the energy that St Clare does.'

'And how does St Clare contrive to manage?' said Miss Ophelia. 'You say he never strikes a blow.'

'Well, men have a more commanding way, you know; it is easier for them; besides, if you ever looked full in his eye, it's peculiar – that eye – and if he speaks decidedly, there's a kind of flash. I'm afraid of it, myself; and the servants know they must mind. I couldn't do as much by a regular storm and scolding as St Clare can by one turn of his eye, if once he is in earnest. Oh, there's no trouble about St Clare; that's the reason he's no more feeling for me. But you'll find, when you come to manage, that there's no getting along without severity, they are so bad, so deceitful, so lazy.'

'The old tune,' said St Clare, sauntering in. 'What an awful account these wicked creatures will have to settle, at last, especially for being lazy! You see, cousin,' said he, as he stretched himself at full length on a lounge opposite to Marie, 'it's wholly inexcusable in them, in the light of the example that Marie and I set them, this laziness.'

'Come, now, St Clare, you are too bad!' said Marie.

'Am I, now? Why, I thought I was talking good, quite remarkably for me. I try to enforce your remarks, Marie, always.'

'You know you meant no such thing, St Clare,' said Marie.

'Oh, I must have been mistaken, then. Thank you, my dear, for setting me right.'

'You do really try to be provoking,' said Marie.

'Oh, come, Marie, the day is growing warm, and I have just had a long quarrel with Dolph, which has fatigued me excessively; so, pray be agreeable, now, and let a fellow repose in the light of your smile.'

'What's the matter about Dolph?' said Marie. 'That fellow's impudence has been growing to a point that is perfectly intolerable to me. I only wish I had the undisputed management of him a while. I'd bring him down!'

'What you say, my dear, is marked with your usual acuteness and good sense,' said St Clare. 'As to Dolph, the case is this: that he has so long been engaged in imitating my graces and perfections, that he has, at last, really mistaken himself for his master; and I have been obliged to give him a little insight into his mistake.'

'How?' said Marie.

'Why, I was obliged to let him understand explicitly that I preferred to keep some of my clothes for my own personal wearing; also, I put his magnificence upon an allowance of cologne-water, and actually was so cruel as to restrict him to one dozen of my cambric handkerchiefs. Dolph was particularly huffy about it, and I had to talk to him like a father, to bring him round.'

'Oh! St Clare, when will you learn how to treat your servants? It's abominable, the way you indulge them!' said Marie.

'Why, after all, what's the harm of the poor dog's wanting to be like his master; and if I haven't brought him up any better than to find his chief good in Cologne and cambric handkerchiefs, why shouldn't I give them to him?'

'And why haven't you brought him up better?' said Miss Ophelia, with blunt determination.

'Too much trouble – laziness, cousin, laziness – which ruins more souls than you can shake a stick at. If it weren't for laziness, I should have been a perfect angel, myself. I'm inclined to think that laziness is what your old Dr Botherem, up in Vermont, used to call the "essence of moral evil". It's an awful consideration, certainly.'

'I think you slave-holders have an awful responsibility upon you,' said Miss Ophelia. 'I wouldn't have it, for a thousand worlds. You ought to educate your slaves, and treat them like reasonable creatures, like immortal creatures, that you've got to stand before the bar of God with. That's my mind,' said the good lady, breaking suddenly out with a tide of zeal that had been gaining strength in her mind all the morning.

'Oh! come, come,' said St Clare, getting up quickly; 'what do you know about us?' And he sat down to the piano, and rattled a lively piece of music. St Clare had a decided genius for music. His touch was brilliant and firm, and his fingers flew over the keys with a rapid and bird-like motion, airy, and yet decided. He played piece after piece, like a man who is trying to play himself into a good humour. After pushing the music aside, he rose up, and said, gayly, 'Well, now, cousin, you've given us a good talk, and done your duty; on the whole, I think the better of you for it. I make no manner of doubt that you threw a very diamond of truth at me, though you see it hit me so directly in the face that it wasn't exactly appreciated, at first.'

'For my part, I don't see any use in such sort of talk,' said Marie. 'I'm sure, if anybody does more for servants than we do, I'd like to know who; and it don't do 'em a bit good – not a particle, they get worse and worse. As to talking to them, or anything like that; I'm sure I have talked till I was tired and hoarse, telling them their duty, and all that; and I'm sure they can go to church when they like, though they don't understand a word of the sermon, more than so many pigs, so it isn't of any great use for them to go, as I see; but they do go, and so they have every chance; but, as I said before, they are a degraded race, and always will be, and there isn't any help for them; you can't make anything of them, if you try. You see, Cousin Ophelia, I've tried, and you haven't; I was born and bred among them, and I know.'

Miss Ophelia thought she had said enough, and therefore sat silent. St Clare whistled a tune.

'St Clare, I wish you wouldn't whistle,' said Marie; 'it makes my head worse.'

'I won't,' said St Clare. 'Is there anything else you wouldn't wish me to do?'

'I wish you *would* have some kind of sympathy for my trials; you never have any feeling for me.'

'My dear accusing angel!' said St Clare.

'It's provoking to be talked to in that way.'

'Then, how will you be talked to? I'll talk to order – any way you'll mention, only to give satisfaction.'

A gay laugh from the court rang through the silken curtains of the veranda. St Clare stepped out, and lifting up the curtain, laughed too.

'What is it?' said Miss Ophelia, coming to the railing.

There sat Tom, on a little mossy seat in the court, every one of his buttonholes stuck full of cape jessamines, and Eva, gayly laughing, was hanging a wreath of roses round his neck; and then she sat down on his knee, like a chip-sparrow, still laughing.

'Oh, Tom, you look so funny!'

Tom had a sober, benevolent smile, and seemed, in his quiet way, to be enjoying the fun quite as much as his little mistress. He lifted his eyes, when he saw his master, with a half-deprecating, apologetic air.

'How can you let her?' said Miss Ophelia.

'Why not?' said St Clare.

'Why, I don't know, it seems so dreadful!'

'You would think no harm in a child's caressing a large dog, even if he was black; but a creature that can think, and reason, and feel, and is immortal, you shudder at; confess it, cousin. I know the feeling among some of you Northerners well enough. Not that there is a particle of virtue in our not having it; but custom with us does what Christianity ought to do – obliterates the feeling of personal prejudice. I have often noticed, in my travels north, how much stronger this was with you than with us. You loathe them as you would a snake or a toad, yet you are indignant at their wrongs. You would not have them abused; but you don't want to have anything to do with them yourselves. You would send them to Africa, out of your sight and smell, and then send a missionary or two to do up all the self-denial of elevating them compendiously. Isn't that it?'

'Well, cousin,' said Miss Ophelia, thoughtfully, 'there may be some truth in this.'

'What would the poor and lowly do, without children?' said St Clare, leaning on the railing, and watching Eva, as she tripped off, leading Tom with her. 'Your little child is your only true democrat. Tom, now, is a hero to Eva; his stories are wonders in her eyes, his songs and Methodist hymns are better than an opera, and the traps and little bits of trash in his pocket a mine of jewels, and he the most wonderful Tom that ever wore a black skin. This is one of the roses of Eden that the Lord has dropped down expressly for the poor and lowly, who get few enough of any other kind.'

'It's strange, cousin,' said Miss Ophelia; 'one might almost think you were a *professor*, to hear you talk.'

'A professor?' said St Clare.

'Yes; a professor of religion.'

'Not at all; not a professor, as your town-folks have it; and, what is worse, I'm afraid, not a *practiser*, either.'

'What makes you talk so, then?'

'Nothing is easier than talking,' said St Clare. 'I believe Shakespeare makes somebody say, "I could sooner show twenty what were good to be done, than be one of the twenty to follow my own teaching."[139] Nothing like division of labour. My forte lies in talking, and yours, cousin, lies in doing.'

In Tom's external situation, at this time, there was, as the world says, nothing to complain of. Little Eva's fancy for him – the instinctive gratitude and loveliness of a noble nature – had led her to petition her father that he might be her especial attendant, whenever she needed the escort of a servant, in her walks or rides; and Tom had general orders to let everything else go, and attend to Miss Eva whenever she wanted him – orders which our readers may fancy were far from disagreeable to him. He was kept well dressed, for St Clare was fastidiously particular on this point. His stable services were merely a sinecure, and consisted simply in a daily care and inspection, and directing an under-servant in his duties; for Marie St Clare declared that she could not have any smell of the horses about him when he came near her, and that he must positively not be put to any service that would make him unpleasant to her, as her nervous system was entirely inadequate to any trial of that nature; one snuff of anything disagreeable being, according to her account, quite sufficient to close the scene, and put an end to all her earthly trials at once. Tom, therefore, in his well-brushed broadcloth suit, smooth beaver, glossy boots, faultless wristbands and collar, with his grave, good-natured black face, looked respectable enough to be a Bishop of Carthage,[140] as men of his colour were, in other ages.

Then, too, he was in a beautiful place, a consideration to which his sensitive race are never indifferent; and he did enjoy with a quiet joy the birds, the flowers, the fountains, the perfume, and light and beauty of the court, the silken hangings, and pictures, and lustres, and statuettes, and gilding, that made the parlours within a kind of Aladdin's palace[141] to him.

If ever Africa shall show an elevated and cultivated race – and come it must, sometime, her turn to figure in the great drama of human improvement – life will awake there with a gorgeousness and splendour of which our cold western tribes faintly have conceived. In that far-off mystic land of gold, and gems, and spices, and waving palms, and wondrous flowers and miraculous fertility, will awake new forms of art, new styles of splendour; and the negro race, no longer despised and trodden down, will, perhaps, show forth some of the latest and most magnificent revelations of human life. Certainly they will, in their gentleness, their lowly docility of heart, their aptitude to repose on a superior mind and rest on a higher power, their childlike simplicity of affection, and facility of forgiveness. In all these they will exhibit the highest form of the peculiarly *Christian life*, and, perhaps, as God chasteneth whom he loveth, he hath chosen poor Africa in the furnace of affliction, to make her the highest and noblest in that kingdom which he will set up, when every other kingdom has been tried, and failed; for the first shall be last, and the last first.[142]

Was this what Marie St Clare was thinking of, as she stood, gorgeously dressed, on the veranda, on Sunday morning, clasping a diamond bracelet on her slender wrist? Most likely it was. Or, if it wasn't that, it was something else, for Marie patronised good things, and she was going now, in full force – diamonds, silk, and lace, and jewels, and all – to a fashionable church, to be very religious. Marie always made a point to be very pious on Sundays. There she stood, so slender, so elegant, so airy and undulating in all her motions, her lace scarf enveloping her like a mist. She looked a graceful creature, and she felt very good and very elegant indeed. Miss Ophelia stood at her side, a perfect contrast. It was not that she had not as handsome a silk dress and shawl, and as fine a pocket-handkerchief; but stiffness and squareness, and bolt-uprightness, enveloped her with as indefinite yet appreciable a presence as did grace her elegant neighbour; not the grace of God, however – that is quite another thing!

'Where's Eva?' said Marie.

'The child stopped on the stairs, to say something to Mammy.'

And what was Eva saying to Mammy on the stairs? Listen, reader, and you will hear, though Marie does not.

'Dear Mammy, I know your head is aching dreadfully.'

'Lord bless you, Miss Eva! my head allers aches lately. You don't need to worry.'

'Well, I'm glad you're going out; and here – ' and the little girl threw her arms around her.– 'Mammy, you shall take my vinaigrette.'

'What! your beautiful gold thing, thar, with them diamonds! Lor, miss, 'twouldn't be proper, noways.'

'Why not? You need it, and I don't. Mamma always uses it for headache, and it'll make you feel better. No, you shall take it, to please me, now.'

'Do hear the darling talk,' said Mammy, as Eva thrust it into her bosom, and, kissing her, ran downstairs to her mother.

'What were you stopping for?'

'I was just stopping to give Mammy my vinaigrette, to take to church with her.'

'Eva!' said Marie, stamping impatiently, 'your gold vinaigrette to *Mammy*! When will you learn what's *proper*? Go right and take it back, this moment!'

Eva looked downcast and aggrieved, and turned slowly.

'I say, Marie, let the child alone; she shall do as she pleases,' said St Clare.

'St Clare, how will she ever get along in the world?' said Marie.

'The Lord knows,' said St Clare; 'but she'll get along in heaven better than you or I.'

'O papa, don't,' said Eva, softly touching his elbow; 'it troubles mother.'

'Well, cousin are you ready to go to meeting?' said Miss Ophelia, turning square about on St Clare.

'I'm not going, thank you.'

'I do wish St Clare ever would go to church,' said Marie; 'but he hasn't a particle of religion about him. It really isn't respectable.'

'I know it,' said St Clare. 'You ladies go to church to learn how to get along in the world, I suppose, and your piety sheds respectability on us. If I did go at all, I would go where Mammy goes; there's something to keep a fellow awake there, at least.'

'What! those shouting Methodists? Horrible!' said Marie.

'Anything but the dead sea of your respectable churches, Marie. Positively, it's too much to ask of a man. Eva, do you like to go? Come, stay at home and play with me.'

'Thank you, papa; but I'd rather go to church.'

'Isn't it dreadful tiresome?' said St Clare.

'I think it is tiresome, some,' said Eva; 'and I am sleepy, too, but I try to keep awake.'

'What do you go for, then?'

'Why, you know, papa,' she said, in a whisper, 'cousin told me that God wants to have us; and he gives us everything, you know; and it isn't much to do it, if he wants us to. It isn't so very tiresome, after all.'

'You sweet, little obliging soul!' said St Clare, kissing her; 'go along, that's a good girl, and pray for me.'

'Certainly, I always do,' said the child, as she sprang after her mother into the carriage.

St Clare stood on the steps and kissed his hand to her, as the carriage drove away; large tears were in his eyes.

'O Evangeline! rightly named,'[143] he said; 'hath not God made thee an evangel to me?'

So he felt a moment; and then he smoked a cigar, and read the *Picayune*, and forgot his little gospel. Was he much unlike other folks?

'You see, Evangeline,' said her mother, 'it's always right and proper to be kind to servants, but it isn't proper to treat them *just* as we would our relations, or people in our own class of life. Now, if Mammy was sick, you wouldn't want to put her in your own bed.'

'I should feel just like it, mamma,' said Eva, 'because then it would be handier to take care of her, and because, you know, my bed is better than hers.'

Marie was in utter despair at the entire want of moral perception evinced in this reply.

'What can I do to make this child understand me?' she said.

'Nothing,' said Miss Ophelia, significantly.

Eva looked sorry and disconcerted for a moment; but children, luckily, do not keep to one impression long, and in a few moments she was merrily laughing at various things which she saw from the coach-windows, as it rattled along.

'Well, ladies,' said St Clare, as they were comfortably seated at the dinner-table, 'and what was the bill of fare at church today?'

'Oh, Dr G— preached a splendid sermon,' said Marie. 'It was just such a sermon as you ought to hear; it expressed all my views exactly.'

'It must have been very improving,' said St Clare. 'The subject must have been an extensive one.'

'Well, I mean all my views about society, and such things,' said Marie. 'The text was, "He hath made everything beautiful in its season";[144] and he showed how all the orders and distinctions in society came from God; and that it was so appropriate, you know, and beautiful, that some should be high and some low, and that some were born to rule and some to serve, and all that, you know; and he applied it so well to all this ridiculous fuss that is made about slavery, and he proved distinctly that the Bible was on our side, and supported all our institutions so convincingly, I only wish you'd heard him.'

'Oh I didn't need it,' said St Clare. 'I can learn what does me as much good as that from the *Picayune*,[145] any time, and smoke a cigar besides; which I can't do, you know, in a church.'

'Why,' said Miss Ophelia, 'don't you believe in these views?'

'Who – I? You know I'm such a graceless dog that these religious aspects of such subjects don't edify me much. If I was to say anything on this slavery matter, I would say out, fair and square, "We're in for it; we've got 'em, and mean to keep 'em – it's for our convenience and our interest"; for that's the long and short of it, that's just the whole of what all this sanctified stuff amounts to, after all; and, I think that will be intelligible to everybody, everywhere.'

'I do think, Augustine, you are so irreverent!' said Marie. 'I think it's shocking to hear you talk.'

'Shocking! it's the truth. This religious talk on such matters, why don't they carry it a little further, and show the beauty, in its season, of a fellow's taking a glass too much, and sitting a little too late over his cards, and various providential arrangements of that sort, which are pretty frequent among us young men; we'd like to hear that those are right and godly, too.'

'Well,' said Miss Ophelia, 'do you think slavery right or wrong?'

'I'm not going to have any of your horrid New England directness, cousin,' said St Clare, gayly. 'If I answer that question, I know you'll be at me with half a dozen others, each one harder than the last; and I'm not a going to define my position. I am one of the sort that lives by throwing stones at other people's glass houses; but I never mean to put up one for them to stone.'

'That's just the way he's always talking,' said Marie; 'you can't get any satisfaction out of him. I believe it's just because he don't like religion, that he's always running out in this way he's been doing.'

'Religion!' said St Clare, in a tone that made both ladies look at him. 'Religion! Is what you hear at church religion? Is that which can bend and turn, and descend and ascend, to fit every crooked phase of selfish, worldly society, religion? Is that religion which is less scrupulous, less generous, less just, less considerate for man than even my own ungodly, worldly, blinded nature? No! When I look for a religion, I must look for something above me, and not something beneath.'

'Then you don't believe that the Bible justifies slavery,' said Miss Ophelia.

'The Bible was my *mother's* book,' said St Clare. 'By it she lived and died, and I would be very sorry to think it did. I'd as soon desire to have it proved that my mother could drink brandy, chew tobacco, and swear, by way of satisfying me that I did right in doing the same. It wouldn't make me at all more satisfied with these things in myself, and it would take from me the comfort of respecting her; and it really is a comfort, in this world, to have anything one can respect. In short, you see,' said he, suddenly resuming his gay tone, 'all I want is that different things be kept in different boxes. The whole framework of society, both in Europe and America, is made up of various things which will not stand the scrutiny of any very ideal standard of morality. It's pretty generally understood that men don't aspire after the absolute right, but only to do about as well as the rest of the world. Now, when anyone speaks up, like a man, and says slavery is necessary to us, we can't get along without it, we should be beggared if we give it up, and, of course, we mean to hold on to it – this is strong, clear, well-defined language; it has the respectability of truth to it; and, if we may judge by their practice, the majority of the world will bear us out in it. But when he begins to put on a long face, and snuffle, and quote Scripture, I incline to think he isn't much better than he should be.'

'You are very uncharitable,' said Marie.

'Well,' said St Clare, 'suppose that something should bring down the price of cotton once and for ever, and make the whole slave property a drug in the market, don't you think we should soon have another version of the Scripture doctrine? What a flood of light would pour into the church, all at once, and how immediately it would be discovered that everything in the Bible and reason went the other way!'

'Well, at any rate,' said Marie, as she reclined herself on a lounge, 'I'm thankful I'm born where slavery exists; and I believe it's right – indeed, I feel it must be; and, at any rate, I'm sure I couldn't get along without it.'

'I say, what do you think, pussy?' said her father to Eva, who came in at this moment, with a flower in her hand.

'What about, papa?'

'Why, which do you like the best; to live as they do at your uncle's, up in Vermont, or to have a house full of servants, as we do?'

'Oh, of course, our way is the pleasantest,' said Eva.

'Why so?' said St Clare, stroking her head.

'Why, it makes so many more round you to love, you know,' said Eva, looking up earnestly.

'Now, that's just like Eva,' said Marie; 'just one of her odd speeches.'

'Is it an odd speech, papa?' said Eva, whisperingly, as she got upon his knee.

'Rather, as this world goes, pussy,' said St Clare. 'But where has my little Eva been, all dinner-time?'

'Oh, I've been up in Tom's room, hearing him sing, and Aunt Dinah gave me my dinner.'

'Hearing Tom sing, eh?'

'Oh, yes! he sings such beautiful things about the New Jerusalem, and bright angels, and the land of Canaan.'

'I dare say; it's better than the opera, isn't it?'

'Yes; and he's going to teach them to me.'

'Singing lessons, eh? – you *are* coming on.'

'Yes, he sings for me, and I read to him in my Bible; and he explains what it means, you know.'

'On my word,' said Marie, laughing, 'that is the latest joke of the season.'

'Tom isn't a bad hand, now, at explaining Scripture, I'll dare swear,' said St Clare. 'Tom has a natural genius for religion. I wanted the horses out early, this morning, and I stole up to Tom's cubiculum[146] there, over the stables, and there I heard him holding a meeting by himself; and, in fact, I haven't heard anything quite so savoury as Tom's prayer, this some time. He put in for me, with a zeal that was quite apostolic.'

'Perhaps he guessed you were listening. I've heard of that trick before.'

'If he did, he wasn't very polite; for he gave the Lord his opinion of me, pretty freely. Tom seemed to think there was decidedly room for improvement in me, and seemed very earnest that I should be converted.'

'I hope you'll lay it to heart,' said Miss Ophelia.

'I suppose you are much of the same opinion,' said St Clare. 'Well, we shall see – shan't we, Eva?'

CHAPTER XVII

The Free Man's Defence

THERE WAS A GENTLE BUSTLE at the Quaker house, as the afternoon drew to a close. Rachel Halliday moved quietly to and fro, collecting from her household stores such needments as could be arranged in the smallest compass, for the wanderers who were to go forth that night. The afternoon shadows stretched eastward, and the round red sun stood thoughtfully on the horizon, and his beams shone yellow and calm into the little bedroom where George and his wife were sitting. He was sitting with his child on his knee, and his wife's hand in his. Both looked thoughtful and serious, and traces of tears were on their cheeks.

'Yes, Eliza,' said George, 'I know all you say is true. You are a good child – a great deal better than I am; and I will try to do as you say. I'll try to act worthy of a free man. I'll try to feel like a Christian. God Almighty knows that I've meant to do well – tried hard to do well – when everything has been against me; and now I'll forget all the past, and put away every hard and bitter feeling, and read my Bible, and learn to be a good man.'

'And when we get to Canada,' said Eliza, 'I can help you. I can do dressmaking very well; and I understand fine washing and ironing; and between us we can find something to live on.'

'Yes, Eliza, so long as we have each other and our boy. Oh, Eliza, if these people only knew what a blessing it is for a man to feel that his wife and child belong to *him*! I've often wondered to see men that could call their wives and children *their own*, fretting and worrying about anything else. Why, I feel rich and strong, though we have nothing but our bare hands. I feel as if I could scarcely ask God for any more. Yes, though I've worked hard every day, till I am twenty-five years old, and have not a cent of money, nor a roof to cover me, nor a spot of land to call my own, yet, if they will only let me alone now, I will be satisfied – thankful; I will work, and send back the money for you and my boy. As to my old master, he has been paid five times over for all he ever spent for me. I don't owe him anything.'

'But yet we are not quite out of danger,' said Eliza; 'we are not yet in Canada.'

'True,' said George, 'but it seems as if I smelt the free air, and it makes me strong.'

At this moment, voices were heard in the outer apartment, in earnest conversation, and very soon a rap was heard on the door. Eliza started and opened it.

Simeon Halliday was there, and with him a Quaker brother, whom he introduced as Phineas Fletcher. Phineas was tall and lathy, red-haired, with an expression of great acuteness and shrewdness in his face. He had not the placid, quiet, unworldly air of Simeon Halliday; on the contrary, a particularly wide-awake and *au-fait*[147] appearance, like a man who rather prides himself on knowing what he is about, and keeping a bright look-out ahead; peculiarities which sorted rather oddly with his broad brim and formal phraseology.

'Our friend Phineas hath discovered something of importance to the interests of thee and thy party, George,' said Simeon; 'it were well for thee to hear it.'

'That I have,' said Phineas, 'and it shows the use of a man's always sleeping with one ear open, in certain places, as I've always said. Last night I stopped at a little lone tavern, back on the road. Thee remembers the place, Simeon, where we sold some apples, last year, to that fat woman, with the great earrings. Well, I was tired with hard driving; and, after my supper, I stretched myself down on a pile of bags in the corner, and pulled a buffalo[148] over me, to wait till my bed was ready; and what does I do, but get fast asleep.'

'With one ear open, Phineas?' said Simeon, quietly.

'No! I slept, ears and all, for an hour or two, for I was pretty well tired; but when I came to myself a little, I found that there were some men in the room, sitting round a table, drinking and talking; and I thought, before I made much muster, I'd just see what they were up to, especially as I heard them say something about the Quakers. "So," says one, "they are up in the Quaker settlement, no doubt," says he. Then I listened with both ears, and I found that they were talking about this very party. So I lay and heard them lay off all their plans. This young man, they said, was to be sent back to Kentucky, to his master who was going to make an example of him, to keep all niggers from running away; and his wife two of them were going to run down to New Orleans to sell, on their own account, and they calculated to get sixteen or eighteen hundred dollars for her; and the child, they said, was going to a trader, who had bought him; and then there was the boy Jim, and his mother, they were to go back to their masters in Kentucky. They said that there were two constables, in a town a little piece ahead, who would go in with 'em to get 'em taken up, and the young woman was to be taken before a judge; and one of the fellows, who is small and smooth-spoken, was to swear to her for his property, and get her delivered over to him to take south. They've got a right notion of the track we are going tonight; and they'll be down after us, six or eight strong. So, now, what's to be done?'

The group that stood in various attitudes, after this communication, were worthy of a painter. Rachel Halliday, who had taken her hands out of a batch of biscuit, to hear the news, stood with them upraised and floury, and with a face of the deepest concern. Simeon looked profoundly thoughtful; Eliza had thrown her arms around her husband, and was looking up to him. George stood with clenched hands and glowing eyes, and looking as any other man might look, whose wife was to be sold at auction, and son sent to a trader, all under the shelter of a Christian nation's laws.

'What *shall* we do, George?' said Eliza, faintly.

'I know what *I* shall do,' said George, as he stepped into the little room, and began examining his pistols.

'Ay, ay,' said Phineas, nodding his head to Simeon; 'thou seest, Simeon, how it will work.'

'I see,' said Simeon, sighing; 'I pray it come not to that.'

'I don't want to involve anyone with or for me,' said George. 'If you will lend me your vehicle and direct me, I will drive alone to the next stand. Jim is a giant in strength, and brave as death and despair, and so am I.'

'Ah, well, friend,' said Phineas, 'but thee'll need a driver, for all that. Thee's quite welcome to do all the fighting, thee knows; but I know a thing or two about the road that thee doesn't.'

'But I don't want to involve you,' said George.

'Involve?' said Phineas, with a curious and keen expression of face.

'When thee does involve me, please to let me know.'

'Phineas is a wise and skilful man,' said Simeon. 'Thee does well, George, to abide by his judgement; and,' he added, laying his hand kindly on George's shoulder, and pointing to the pistols, 'be not over hasty with these – young blood is hot.'

'I will attack no man,' said George. 'All I ask of this country is to be let alone, and I will go out peaceably; but' – he paused, and his brow darkened and his face worked – 'I've had a sister sold in that New Orleans market. I know what they are sold for; and am I gong to stand by and see them take my wife and sell her, when God has given me a pair of strong arms to defend her? No; God help me! I'll fight to the last breath, before they shall take my wife and son. Can you blame me?'

'Mortal man cannot blame thee, George. Flesh and blood could not do otherwise,' said Simeon. 'Woe unto the world because of offences, but woe unto them through whom the offence cometh.'[149]

'Would not even you, sir, do the same, in my place?'

'I pray that I be not tried,' said Simeon; 'the flesh is weak.'

'I think my flesh would be pretty tolerable strong, in such a case,' said Phineas, stretching out a pair of arms like the sails of a windmill. 'I an't sure, friend George, that I shouldn't hold a fellow for thee if thee had any accounts to settle with him.'

'If man should ever resist evil,' said Simeon, 'then George should feel free to do it now: but the leaders of our people taught a more excellent way; for the wrath of man worketh not the righteousness of God; but it goes sorely against the corrupt will of man, and none can receive it save they to whom it is given. Let us pray the Lord that we be not tempted.'

'And so *I* do, ' said Phineas; 'but if we are tempted too much – why, let them look out, that's all.'

'It's quite plain thee wasn't born a Friend,' said Simeon, smiling. 'The old nature hath its way in thee pretty strong as yet.'

To tell the truth, Phineas had been a hearty, two-fisted backwoodsman, a vigorous hunter, and a dead shot at a buck; but having wooed a pretty Quakeress, had been moved by the power of her charms to join the society in his neighbourhood; and though he was an honest, sober, and efficient member, and nothing particular could be alleged against him, yet the more spiritual among them could not but discern an exceeding lack of savour in his developments.

'Friend Phineas will ever have ways of his own,' said Rachel Halliday, smiling; 'but we all think that his heart is in the right place, after all.'

'Well,' said George, 'isn't it best that we hasten our flight?'

'I got up at four o'clock, and came on with all speed, full two or three hours ahead of them, if they start at the time they planned. It isn't safe to start till dark, at any rate; for there are some evil persons in the villages ahead, that might be disposed to meddle with us, if they saw our wagon, and that would delay us more than the waiting; but in two hours I think we may venture. I will go over to Michael Cross, and engage him to come behind on his swift nag, and keep a bright look-out on the road, and warn us if any company of men come on. Michael keeps a horse that can soon get ahead of most other horses; and he could shoot ahead and let us know, if there were any danger. I am going out now to warn Jim and the old woman to be in readiness, and to see about the horse. We have a pretty fair start, and stand a good chance to get to the stand before they can come up with us. So, have good courage, friend George; this isn't the first ugly scrape that I've been in with thy people,' said Phineas, as he closed the door.

'Phineas is pretty shrewd,' said Simeon. 'He will do the best that can be done for thee, George.'

'All I am sorry for,' said George, 'is the risk to you.'

'Thee'll much oblige us, friend George, to say no more about that. What we do we are conscience bound to do; we can do no other way. And now, mother,' said he, turning to Rachel, 'hurry thy preparations for these friends, for we must not send them away fasting.'

And while Rachel and her children were busy making corn-cake, and cooking ham and chicken, and hurrying on the *et ceteras* of the evening meal, George and his wife sat in their little room, with their arms folded about each other, in such talk as husband and wife have when they know that a few hours may part them forever.

'Eliza,' said George, 'people that have friends, and houses, and lands, and money, and all those things, *can't* love as we do, who have nothing but each other. Till I knew you, Eliza, no creature ever had loved me, but my poor, heartbroken mother and sister. I saw poor Emily that morning the trader carried her off. She came to the corner where I was lying asleep, and said, "Poor George, your last friend is going. What will become of you, poor boy?" And I got up and threw my arms round her, and cried and sobbed and she cried too; and those were the last kind words I got for ten long years; and my heart all withered up, and felt as dry as ashes, till I met you. And your loving me – why, it was almost like raising one from the dead! I've been a new man ever since! And now, Eliza, I'll give my last drop of blood, but they *shall not* take you from me. Whoever gets you must walk over my dead body.'

'O Lord, have mercy!' said Eliza, sobbing. 'If he will only let us get out of this country together, that is all we ask.'

'Is God on their side?' said George, speaking less to his wife than pouring out his own bitter thoughts. 'Does he see all they do? Why does he let such things happen? And they tell us that the Bible is on their side; certainly all the power is. They are rich, and healthy, and happy; they are members of churches, expecting to go to heaven; and they get along so easy in the world, and have it all their own way; and poor, honest, faithful Christians – Christians as good or better than they – are lying in the very dust under their feet. They buy 'em and sell 'em, and make trade of their heart's blood, and groans and tears – and God *lets* them.'

'Friend George,' said Simeon, from the kitchen, 'listen to this Psalm; it may do thee good.'

George drew his seat near the door, and Eliza, wiping her tears, came forward also to listen, while Simeon read as follows: 'But as for me, my feet were almost gone; my steps had well-nigh slipped. For I was envious of the foolish, when I saw the prosperity of the wicked. They are not in trouble like other men, neither are they plagued like other men. Therefore pride compasseth them as a chain; violence covereth them as a garment. Their eyes stand out with fatness; they have more than heart could wish. They are corrupt, and speak wickedly concerning oppression; they speak loftily. Therefore his people return, and the waters of a full cup are wrung out to them, and they say, How doth God know? and is there knowledge in the Most High?' 'Is not that the way thee feels, George?'

'It is so, indeed,' said George, 'as well as I could have written it myself.'

'Then, hear,' said Simeon: ' "When I thought to know this, it was too painful for me until I went unto the sanctuary of God. Then understood I their end. Surely thou didst set them in slippery places, thou castedst them down to destruction. As a dream when one awaketh, so, O Lord, when thou awakest, thou shalt despise their image. Nevertheless, I am continually with thee; thou hast holden me by my right hand. Thou shalt guide me by thy counsel, and afterwards receive me to glory. It is good for me to draw near unto God. I have put my trust in the Lord God." '[150]

The words of holy trust, breathed by the friendly old man, stole like sacred music over the harassed and chafed spirit of George; and after he ceased, he sat with a gentle and subdued expression on his fine features.

'If this world were all, George,' said Simeon, 'thee might, indeed, ask, Where is the Lord? But it is often those who have least of all in this life whom He chooseth for the kingdom. Put thy trust in Him, and, no matter what befalls thee here, He will make all right hereafter.'

If these words had been spoken by some easy, self-indulgent exhorter, from whose mouth they might have come merely as pious and rhetorical flourish, proper to be used to people in distress, perhaps they might not have had much effect; but, coming from one who daily and calmly risked fine and imprisonment for the cause of God and man, they had a weight that could not but be felt, and both the poor, desolate fugitives found calmness and strength breathing into them from it.

And now Rachel took Eliza's hand kindly, and led the way to the supper table. As they were sitting down, a light tap sounded at the door, and Ruth entered.

'I just ran in,' she said, 'with these little stockings for the boy – three pair, nice, warm woollen ones. It will be so cold, thee knows in Canada. Does thee keep up good courage, Eliza?' she added, tripping round to Eliza's side of the table, and shaking her warmly by the hand, and slipping a seed-cake into Harry's hand. 'I brought a little parcel of these for him,' she said, tugging at her pocket to get out the package. 'Children, thee knows, will always be eating.'

'Oh, thank you; you are too kind,' said Eliza.

'Come, Ruth, sit down to supper,' said Rachel.

'I couldn't, anyway. I left John with the baby, and some biscuits in the oven; and I can't stay a moment, else John will burn up all the biscuits, and give the baby all the sugar in the bowl. That's the way he does,' said the little Quakeress, laughing. 'So, goodbye, Eliza; goodbye, George; the Lord grant thee a safe journey;' and, with a few tripping steps, Ruth was out of the apartment.

A little while after supper a large covered-wagon drew up before the door; the night was clear starlight, and Phineas jumped briskly down from his seat to arrange his passengers. George walked out of the door, with his child on one arm and his wife on the other. His step was firm, his face settled and resolute. Rachel and Simeon came out after them.

'You get out a moment,' said Phineas to those inside, 'and let me fix the back of the wagon, there, for the womenfolks and the boy.'

'Here are the two buffaloes,' said Rachel. 'Make the seats as comfortable as may be; it's hard riding all night.'

Jim came out first, and carefully assisted out his old mother, who clung to his arm, and looked anxiously about, as if she expected the pursuer every moment.

'Jim, are your pistols all in order?' said George, in a low, firm voice.

'Yes, indeed,' said Jim.

'And you've no doubt what you shall do if they come?'

'I rather think I haven't,' said Jim, throwing open his broad chest, and taking a deep breath. 'Do you think I'll let them get mother again?'

During this brief colloquy Eliza had been taking her leave of her kind friend, Rachel, and was handed into the carriage by Simeon, and, creeping into the back part with her boy, sat down among the buffalo-skins. The old woman was next handed in and seated, and George and Jim placed on a rough board seat front of them, and Phineas mounted in front.

'Farewell, my friends,' said Simeon, from without.

'God bless you!' answered all from within.

And the wagon drove off, rattling and jolting over the frozen road.

There was no opportunity for conversation, on account of the roughness of the way and the noise of the wheels. The vehicle therefore rambled on, through long, dark stretches of woodland, over wide dreary plains, up hills, and down valleys, and on, on, on they jogged, hour after hour. The child soon fell asleep, and lay heavily in his mother's lap. The poor, frightened old woman at last forgot her fears; and, even Eliza, as the night waned, found all her anxieties insufficient to keep her eyes from closing. Phineas seemed, on the whole, the briskest of the company, and beguiled his long drive with whistling certain very un-Quaker-like songs, as he went on.

But about three o'clock George's ear caught the hasty and decided click of a horse's hoof coming behind them at some distance, and jogged Phineas by the elbow. Phineas pulled up his horses, and listened.

'That must be Michael,' he said; 'I think I know the sound of his gallop;' and he rose up and stretched his head anxiously back over the road.

A man riding in hot haste was now dimly descried at the top of a distant hill.

'There he is, I do believe!' said Phineas. George and Jim both sprang out of the wagon, before they knew what they were doing. All stood intensely silent, with their faces turned towards the expected messenger. On he came. Now he went down into a valley, where they could not see him; but they heard the sharp, hasty tramp, rising nearer and nearer; at last they saw him emerge on the top of an eminence, within hail.

'Yes, that's Michael!' said Phineas; and, raising his voice, 'Halloa, there, Michael!'

'Phineas! is that thee?'

'Yes; what news? – they coming?'

'Right on behind, eight or ten of them, hot with brandy, swearing and foaming like so many wolves.'

And, just as he spoke, a breeze brought the faint sound of galloping horsemen towards them.

'In with you – quick, boys, *in*!' said Phineas. 'If you must fight, wait till I get you a piece ahead.' And, with the word, both jumped in, and Phineas lashed the horses to a run, the horseman keeping close beside them. The wagon rattled, jumped, almost flew, over the frozen ground; but plainer, and still plainer, came the noise of pursuing horsemen behind. The women heard it, and, looking anxiously out, saw, far in the rear, on the brow of a distant hill, a party of men looming up against the red-streaked sky of early dawn. Another hill, and their pursuers had evidently caught sight of their wagon, whose white, cloth-covered top, made it conspicuous at some distance, and a loud yell of brutal triumph came forward on the wind. Eliza sickened, and strained her child closer to her bosom; the old woman prayed and groaned, and George and Jim clenched their pistols with the grasp of despair. The pursuers gained on them fast; the carriage made a sudden turn, and brought them near a ledge of a steep overhanging rock, that rose in an isolated ridge or clump in a large lot, which was, all around it, quite clear and smooth. This isolated pile, or range of rocks, rose up black and heavy against the brightening sky, and seemed to promise shelter and concealment. It was a place well known to Phineas, who had been familiar with the spot in his hunting days; and it was to gain this point he had been racing his horses.

'Now for it!' said he, suddenly checking his horses, and springing from his seat to the ground. 'Out with you, in a twinkling, everyone, and up into these rocks with me. Michael, thee tie thy horse to the wagon, and drive ahead to Amariah's, and get him and his boys to come back and talk to these fellows.'

In a twinkling they were all out of the carriage.

'There,' said Phineas, catching up Harry, 'you, each of you, see to the women; and run, *now*, if you ever *did* run!'

There needed no exhortation. Quicker than we can say it, the whole party were over the fence, making with all speed for the rocks, while Michael, throwing himself from his horse, and fastening the bridle to the wagon, began driving it rapidly away.

'Come ahead,' said Phineas, as they reached the rocks, and saw, in the mingled starlight and dawn, the traces of a rude but plainly marked footpath leading up among them; 'this is one of our old hunting-dens. Come up!'

Phineas went before, springing up the rocks like a goat, with the boy in his arms. Jim came second, bearing his trembling old mother over his shoulder, and George and Eliza brought up the rear. The party of horsemen came up to the fence, and, with mingled shouts and oaths, were dismounting, to prepare to follow them. A few moments' scrambling brought them to the top of the ledge; the path then passed between a narrow defile, where only one could walk at a time, till suddenly they came to a rift or chasm more than a yard in breadth, and beyond which lay a pile of rocks, separate from the rest of the ledge, standing full thirty feet high, with its sides steep and perpendicular as those of a castle. Phineas easily leaped the chasm, and sat down the boy on a smooth, flat platform of crisp white moss, that covered the top of the rock.

'Over with you!' he called; 'spring, now, once, for your lives!' said he, as one after another sprang across. Several fragments of loose stone formed a kind of breastwork, which sheltered their position from the observation of those below.

'Well, here we all are,' said Phineas, peeping over the stone breastwork to watch the assailants, who were coming tumultuously up under the rocks. 'Let 'em get us, if they can. Whoever comes here has to walk single file between those two rocks, in fair range of your pistols, boys, d'ye see?'

'I do see,' said George; 'and now, as this matter is ours, let us take all the risk, and do all the fighting.'

'Thee's quite welcome to do the fighting, George,' said Phineas, chewing some checkerberry-leaves[151] as he spoke; 'but I may have the fun of looking on, I suppose. But see, these fellows are kinder debating down there, and looking up, like hens when they are going to fly up on to the roost. Hadn't thee better give 'em a word of advice, before they come up, just to tell 'em handsomely they'll be shot if they do?'

The party beneath, now more apparent in the light of the dawn, consisted of our old acquaintances, Tom Loker and Marks, with two constables, and a posse consisting of such rowdies at the last tavern as could be engaged by a little brandy to go and help the fun of trapping a set of niggers.

'Well, Tom, yer coons are farly treed,' said one.

Yes, I see 'em go up right here,' said Tom; 'and here's a path. I'm for going right up. They can't jump down in a hurry, and it won't take long to ferret 'em out.'

'But, Tom, they might fire at us from behind the rocks,' said Marks. 'That would be ugly, you know.'

'Ugh!' said Tom, with a sneer. 'Always for saving your skin, Marks! No danger! niggers are too plaguy scared!'

'I don't know why I *shouldn't* save my skin,' said Marks. 'It's the best I've got; and niggers *do* fight like the devil, sometimes.'

At this moment, George appeared on the top of a rock above them, and, speaking in a calm, clear voice, said, 'Gentlemen, who are you, down there, and what do you want?'

'We want a party of runaway niggers,' said Tom Loker. 'One George Harris, and Eliza Harris, and their son, and Jim Selden, and an old woman. We've got the officers, here, and a warrant to take 'em; and we're going to have 'em, too. D'ye hear? An't you George Harris, that belongs to Mr Harris, of Shelby county, Kentucky?'

'I am George Harris. A Mr Harris, of Kentucky, did call me his property. But now I'm a free man, standing on God's free soil; and my wife and my child I claim as mine. Jim and his mother are here. We have arms to defend ourselves, and we mean to do it. You can come up, if you like; but the first one of you that comes within the range of our bullets is a dead man, and the next, and the next; and so on till the last.'

'Oh, come! come!' said a short, puffy man, stepping forward, and blowing his nose as he did so. 'Young man, this an't no kind of talk at all for you. You see, we're officers of justice. We've got the law on our side, and the power, and so forth; so you'd better give up peaceably, you see; for you'll certainly have to give up at last.'

'I know very well that you've got the law on your side, and the power,' said George, bitterly. 'You mean to take my wife to sell in New Orleans, and put my boy like a calf in a trader's pen, and send Jim's old mother to the brute that whipped and abused her before, because he couldn't abuse her son. You want to send Jim and me back to be whipped and tortured, and ground down under the heels of them that you call masters; and your laws *will* bear you out in it – more shame for you and them! But you haven't got us. We don't own your laws; we don't own your country; we stand here as free, under God's sky, as you are; and, by the great God that made us, we'll fight for our liberty till we die.'[152]

George stood out in fair sight, on the top of the rock, as he made his declaration of independence; the glow of dawn gave a flush to his swarthy cheek, and bitter indignation and despair gave fire to his dark eye; and, as if appealing from man to the justice of God, he raised his hand to heaven as he spoke.

If it had been only a Hungarian youth, now bravely defending in some mountain fastness the retreat of fugitives escaping from Austria into America, this would have been sublime heroism; but as it was a youth of African descent, defending the retreat of fugitives through America into Canada, of course we are too well instructed and patriotic to see any heroism in it; and if any of our readers do, they must do it on their own private responsibility. When despairing Hungarian fugitives make their way, against all the search-warrants and authorities of their lawful government, to America, press and political cabinet ring with applause and welcome.[153] When despairing African fugitives do the same thing, it is – what *is* it?

Be it as it may, it is certain that the attitude, eye, voice, manner of the speaker, for a moment struck the party below to silence. There is something in boldness and determination that for a time hushes even the rudest nature. Marks was the only one who remained wholly untouched. He was deliberately cocking his pistol, and, in the momentary silence that followed George's speech, he fired at him.

'Ye see ye get jist as much for him dead as alive in Kentucky,' he said coolly, as he wiped his pistol on his coat-sleeve.

George sprang backward – Eliza uttered a shriek – the ball had passed close to his hair, had nearly grazed the cheek of his wife, and struck in the tree above.

'It's nothing, Eliza,' said George, quickly.

'Thee'd better keep out of sight, with thy speechifying,' said Phineas; 'they're mean scamps.'

'Now, Jim,' said George, 'look that your pistols are all right, and watch that pass with me. The first man that shows himself I fire at; you take the second, and so on. It won't do, you know, to waste two shots on one.'

'But what if you don't hit?'

'I *shall* hit,' said George, coolly.

'Good! now, there's stuff in that fellow,' muttered Phineas, between his teeth.

The party below, after Marks had fired, stood, for a moment, rather undecided.

'I think you must have hit some on 'em,' said one of the men. 'I heard a squeal!'

'I'm going right up for one,' said Tom. 'I never was afraid of niggers, and I an't going to be now. Who goes after?' he said, springing up the rocks.

George heard the words distinctly. He drew up his pistol, examined it, pointed it towards that point in the defile where the first man would appear.

One of the most courageous of the party followed Tom, and, the way being thus made, the whole party began pushing up the rock – the hindermost pushing the front ones faster than they would have gone of themselves. On they came, and in a moment the burly form of Tom appeared in sight, almost at the verge of the chasm.

George fired – the shot entered his side; but, though wounded, he would not retreat, but, with a yell like that of a mad bull, he was leaping right across the chasm into the party.

'Friend,' said Phineas, suddenly stepping to the front, and meeting him with a push from his long arms, 'thee isn't wanted here.'

Down he fell into the chasm, crackling down among trees, bushes, logs, loose stones, till he lay, bruised and groaning, thirty feet below. The fall might have killed him, had it not been broken and moderated by his clothes catching in the branches of a large tree; but he came down with some force, however – more than was at all agreeable or convenient.

'Lord, help us, they are perfect devils!' said Marks, heading the retreat down the rocks with much more of a will than he had joined the ascent, while all the party came tumbling precipitately after him – the fat constable, in particular, blowing and puffing in a very energetic manner.

'I say, fellers,' said Marks, 'you jist go round and pick up Tom there, while I run and get on to my horse, to go back for help – that's you;' and, without minding the hootings and jeers of his company, Marks was as good as his word, and was soon seen galloping away.

'Was ever such a sneaking varmint?' said one of the men. 'To come on his business, and he clear out and leave us this yer way!'

'Well, we must pick up that feller,' said another. 'Cuss me if I much care whether he is dead or alive.'

The men, led by the groans of Tom, scrambled and crackled through stumps, logs and bushes, to where that hero lay groaning and swearing, with alternate vehemence.

'Ye keep it a-going pretty loud, Tom,' said one. 'Ye much hurt?'

'Don't know. Get me up, can't ye? Blast that infernal Quaker! If it had not been for him, I'd a pitched some on 'em down here, to see how they liked it.'

With much labour and groaning, the fallen hero was assisted to rise; and, with one holding him up under each shoulder, they got him as far as the horses.

'If you could only get me a mile back to that ar tavern – Give me a handkerchief or something, to stuff into this place, and stop this infernal bleeding.'

George looked over the rocks, and saw them trying to lift the burly form of Tom into the saddle. After two or three ineffectual attempts, he reeled, and fell heavily to the ground.

'Oh, I hope he isn't killed!' said Eliza, who, with all the party, stood watching the proceeding.

'Why not?' said Phineas. 'Serves him right.'

'Because after death comes the judgement,' said Eliza.

'Yes,' said the old woman, who had been groaning and praying, in her Methodist fashion, during all the encounter, 'it's an awful case for the poor crittur's soul.'

'On my word, they're leaving him, I do believe,' said Phineas.

It was true; for after some appearance of irresolution and consultation, the whole party got on their horses and rode away. When they were quite out of sight, Phineas began to bestir himself.

'Well, we must go down and walk a piece,' he said. 'I told Michael to go forward and bring help, and be along back here with the wagon; but we shall have to walk a piece along the road, I reckon, to meet them. The Lord grant he be along soon! It's early in the day; there won't be much travel afoot yet a while; we an't much more than two miles from our stopping-place. If the road hadn't been so rough last night, we could have outrun 'em entirely.'

As the party neared the fence, they discovered in the distance, along the road, their own wagon coming back, accompanied by some men on horseback.

'Well, now, there's Michael, and Stephen, and Amariah,' exclaimed Phineas, joyfully. 'Now we *are* made, as safe as if we'd got there.'

'Well, do stop, then,' said Eliza, 'and do something for that poor man; he's groaning dreadfully.'

'It would be no more than Christian,' said George; 'let's take him up and carry him on.'

'And doctor him up among the Quakers!' said Phineas; 'pretty well, that! Well, I don't care if we do. Here, let's have a look at him!' and Phineas, who, in the course of his hunting and backwoods life, had acquired some rude experience of surgery, kneeled down by the wounded man, and began a careful examination of his condition.

'Marks,' said Tom, feebly, 'is that you, Marks?'

'No, I reckon 'tan't, friend,' said Phineas. 'Much Marks cares for thee, if his own skin's safe. He's off, long ago.'

'I believe I'm done for,' said Tom. 'The cussed sneaking dog, to leave me to die alone! My poor old mother always told me 'twould be so.'

'La sakes! jist hear the poor crittur. He's got a mammy, now,' said the old negress. 'I can't help kinder pityin' on him.'

'Softly, softly; don't thee snap and snarl, friend,' said Phineas, as Tom winced and pushed his hand away. 'Thee has no chance, unless I stop the bleeding.' And Phineas busied himself with making some off-hand surgical arrangements with his own pocket-handkerchief and such as could be mustered in the company.

'You pushed me down there,' said Tom, faintly.

'Well, if I hadn't, thee would have pushed us down, thee sees,' said Phineas, as he stooped to apply his bandage. 'There, there – let me fix this bandage. We mean well to thee; we bear no malice. Thee shall be taken to a house where they'll nurse thee first-rate – as well as thy own mother could.'

Tom groaned, and shut his eyes. In men of his class, vigour and resolution are entirely a physical matter, and ooze out with the flowing of the blood; and the gigantic fellow really looked piteous in his helplessness.

The other party now came up. The seats were taken out of the wagon. The buffalo-skins, doubled in fours, were spread all along one side, and four men, with great difficulty, lifted the heavy form of Tom into it. Before he was gotten in, he fainted entirely. The old negress, in the abundance of her compassion, sat down on the bottom, and took his head in her lap. Eliza, Harry, and Jim, bestowed themselves, as well as they could, in the remaining space, and the whole party set forward.

'What do you think of him?' said George, who sat by Phineas, in front.

'Well, it's only a pretty deep flesh-wound; but, then, tumbling and scratching down that place didn't help him much. It has bled pretty freely – pretty much dreaned him out, courage and all; but he'll get over it, and maybe learn a thing or two by it.'

'I'm glad to hear you say so,' said George. 'It would always be a heavy thought to me if I'd caused his death, even in a just cause.'

'Yes,' said Phineas, 'killing is an ugly operation, any way they'll fix it, man or beast. I've been a great hunter, in my day, and I tell thee I've seen a buck that was shot down, and a dying, look that way on a feller with his eye that it reely most made a feller feel wicked for killing on him; and human creatures is a more serious consideration yet, bein', as thy wife says, that the judgement comes to 'em after death. So I don't know as our people's notions on these matters is too strict; and, considerin' how I was raised, I fell in with them pretty considerably.'

'What shall you do with this poor fellow?' said George.

'Oh, carry him along to Amariah's. There's old Grandmam Stephens there – Dorcas, they call her – she's most an amazin' nurse. She takes to nursing real natural, and an't never better suited than when she gets a sick body to tend. We may reckon on turning him over to her for a fortnight or so.'

A ride of about an hour more brought the party to a neat farmhouse, where the weary travellers were received to an abundant breakfast. Tom Loker was soon carefully deposited in a much cleaner and softer bed than he had ever been in the habit of occupying. His wound was carefully dressed and bandaged, and he lay languidly opening and shutting his eyes on the white window-curtains and gently-gliding figures of his sickroom, like a weary child. And here, for the present, we shall take our leave of one party.

CHAPTER XVIII

Miss Ophelia's Experiences and Opinions

OUR FRIEND TOM, in his own simple musings, often compared his more fortunate lot, in the bondage into which he was cast, with that of Joseph in Egypt;[154] and, in fact, as time went on, and he developed more and more under the eye of his master, the strength of the parallel increased.

St Clare was indolent and careless of money. Hitherto the providing and marketing had been principally done by Adolph, who was, to the full, as careless and extravagant as his master; and, between them both, they had carried on the dispersing process with great alacrity. Accustomed, for many years, to regard his master's property as his own care, Tom saw, with an uneasiness he could scarcely repress, the wasteful expenditure of the establishment; and, in the quiet indirect way which his class often acquire, would sometimes make his own suggestions.

St Clare at first employed him occasionally; but, struck with his soundness of mind and good business capacity, he confided in him more and more, till gradually all the marketing and providing for the family were entrusted to him.

'No, no, Adolph,' he said, one day, as Adolph was deprecating the passing of power out of his hands; 'let Tom alone. You only understand what you want – Tom understands cost and come to; and there may be some end to money, by and by, if we don't let somebody do that.'

Trusted to an unlimited extent by a careless master, who handed him a bill without looking at it, and pocketed the change without counting it, Tom had every facility and temptation to dishonesty; and nothing but an impregnable simplicity of nature, strengthened by Christian faith, could have kept him from it. But to that nature, the very unbounded trust reposed in him was bond and seal for the most scrupulous accuracy.

With Adolph the case had been different. Thoughtless and self-indulgent, and unrestrained by a master who found it easier to indulge than to regulate, he had fallen into an absolute confusion as to *meum* and *tuum*[155] with regard to himself and his master, which sometimes troubled even St Clare. His own good sense taught him that such a training of his servants was unjust and dangerous. A sort of chronic remorse went with him everywhere, although not strong enough to make any decided change in his course; and this very remorse reacted again into indulgence. He passed lightly over the most serious faults, because he told himself that, if he had done his part, his dependants had not fallen into them.

Tom regarded his gay, airy, handsome young master with an odd mixture of fealty, reverence, and fatherly solicitude. That he never read the Bible; never went to church; that he jested and made free with any and everything that came in the way of his wit; that he spent his Sunday evenings at the opera or theatre; that he went to wine parties and clubs, and suppers, oftener than was at all expedient – were all things that Tom could see as plainly as anybody, and on which he based a conviction that 'mas'r wasn't a Christian'; a conviction, however, which he would have been very slow to express to anyone else, but on which he founded many prayers, in his own simple fashion, when he was by himself in his little dormitory. Not that Tom had not his own way of speaking his mind occasionally, with something of the tact often observable in his class; as, for example, the very day after the Sabbath we have described, St Clare was invited out to a convivial party of choice spirits, and was helped home, between one and two o'clock at night, in a condition when the physical had decidedly attained the upper hand of the intellectual. Tom and Adolph assisted to get him composed for the night, the latter in high spirits, evidently regarding the matter as a good joke, and laughing heartily at the rusticity of Tom's horror, who really was simple enough to lie awake most of the rest of the night, praying for his young master.

'Well, Tom, what are you waiting for?' said St Clare, the next day, as he sat in his library, in dressing-gown and slippers. St Clare had just been entrusting Tom with some money, and various commissions. 'Isn't all right there, Tom?' he added, as Tom still stood waiting.

'I'm 'fraid not, mas'r,' said Tom, with a grave face.

St Clare laid down his paper, and set down his coffee-cup, and looked at Tom.

'Why, Tom, what's the case? You look as solemn as a coffin.'

'I feel very bad, mas'r. I al'ays have thought that mas'r would be good to everybody.'

'Well, Tom, haven't I been? Come, now, what do you want? There's something you haven't got, I suppose, and this is the preface.'

'Mas'r al'ays been good to me. I haven't nothing to complain of, on that head. But there is one that mas'r isn't good to.'

'Why, Tom, what's got into you? Speak out; what do you mean?'

'Last night, between one and two, I thought so. I studied upon the matter then. Mas'r isn't good to *himself*.'

Tom said this with his back to his master, and his hand on the door-knob. St Clare felt his face flush crimson, but he laughed.

'Oh, that's all, is it?' he said, gayly.

'All!' said Tom, turning suddenly round and falling on his knees. 'Oh, my dear young mas'r! I'm 'fraid it will be *loss of all – all* – body and soul. The good Book says, "it biteth like a serpent and stingeth like an adder!"[156] my dear mas'r!'

Tom's voice choked, and the tears ran down his cheeks.

'You poor, silly fool!' said St Clare, with tears in his own eyes. 'Get up, Tom: I'm not worth crying over.'

But Tom wouldn't rise, and looked imploring.

'Well, I won't go to any more of their cursed nonsense, Tom,' said St Clare; 'on my honour, I won't. I don't know why I haven't stopped long ago. I've always despised *it*, and myself for it, so now, Tom, wipe up your eyes, and go about your errands. Come, come,' he added, 'no blessings. I'm not so wonderfully good, now,' he said, as he gently pushed Tom to the door. 'There, I'll pledge my honour to you, Tom, you don't see me so again,' he said; and Tom went off, wiping his eyes, with great satisfaction.

'I'll keep my faith with him, too,' said St Clare, as he closed the door. And St Clare did so; for gross sensualism, in any form, was not the peculiar temptation of his nature.

But, all this time, who shall detail the tribulations manifold of our friend Miss Ophelia, who had begun the labours of a Southern housekeeper?

There is all the difference in the world in the servants of Southern establishments, according to the character and capacity of the mistresses who have brought them up.

South as well as North, there are women who have an extraordinary talent for command, and tact in educating. Such are enabled, with apparent ease, and without severity, to subject to their will, and bring into harmonious and systematic order, the various members of their small estate, to regulate their peculiarities, and so balance and compensate the deficiencies of one by the excess of another as to produce a harmonious and orderly system.

Such a housekeeper was Mrs Shelby, whom we have already described; and such our readers may remember to have met with. If they are not common at the South, it is because they are not common in the world. They are to be found there as often as anywhere; and, when existing, find in that peculiar state of society a brilliant opportunity to exhibit their domestic talent.

Such a housekeeper Marie St Clare was not, nor her mother before her. Indolent and childish, unsystematic and improvident, it was not to be expected that servants trained under her care should not be so likewise; and she had very justly described to Miss Ophelia the state of confusion she would find in the family, though she had not ascribed it to the proper cause.

The first morning of her regency, Miss Ophelia was up at four o'clock; and having attended to all the adjustments of her own chamber, as she had done ever since she came there, to the great amazement of the chambermaid, she prepared for a vigorous onslaught on the cupboards and closets of the establishment of which she had the keys.

The store-room, the linen-presses, the china-closet, the kitchen and cellar, that day, all went under an awful review. Hidden things of darkness were brought to light to an extent that alarmed all the principalities and powers of kitchen and chamber, and caused many wonderings and murmurings about 'dese yer Northern ladies' from the domestic cabinet.

Old Dinah, the head cook, and principal of all rule and authority in the kitchen department, was filled with wrath at what she considered an invasion of privilege. No feudal baron in Magna Charta[157] times could have more thoroughly resented some incursion of the Crown.

Dinah was a character in her own way, and it would be injustice to her memory not to give the reader a little idea of her. She was a native and essential cook, as much as Aunt Chloe – cooking being an indigenous talent of the African race; but Chloe was a trained and methodical one, who moved in an orderly domestic harness, while Dinah was a self-taught genius, and, like geniuses in general, was positive, opinionated and erratic, to the last degree.

Like a certain class of modern philosophers, Dinah perfectly scorned logic and reason in every shape, and always took refuge in intuitive certainty; and here she was perfectly impregnable. No possible amount of talent, or authority, or explanation, could ever make her believe that any other way was better than her own, or that the course she had pursued in the smallest matter could be in the least modified. This had been a conceded point with her old mistress, Marie's mother; and 'Miss Marie', as Dinah always called her young mistress, even after her marriage, found it easier to submit than contend; and so Dinah had ruled supreme. This was the easier, in that she was perfect mistress of that diplomatic art which unites the utmost subservience of manner with the utmost inflexibility as to measure.

Dinah was mistress of the whole art and mystery of excuse-making, in all its branches. Indeed, it was an axiom with her that the cook can do no wrong; and a cook in a Southern kitchen finds abundance of heads and shoulders on which to lay off every sin and frailty, so as to maintain her own immaculateness entire. If any part of the dinner was a failure, there were fifty indisputably good reasons for it; and it was the fault undeniably of fifty other people, whom Dinah berated with unsparing zeal.

But it was very seldom that there was any failure in Dinah's last results. Though her mode of doing everything was peculiarly meandering and circuitous, and without any sort of calculation as to time and place – though her kitchen generally looked as if it had been arranged by a hurricane blowing through it, and she had about as many places for each cooking utensil as there were days in the year, yet, if one would have patience to wait her own good time, up would come her dinner in perfect order, and in a style of preparation with which an epicure could find no fault.

It was now the season of incipient preparation for dinner. Dinah, who required large intervals of reflection and repose, and was studious of ease in all her arrangements, was seated on the kitchen floor, smoking a short stumpy pipe, to which she was much addicted, and which she always kindled up, as a sort of censer, whenever she felt the need of an inspiration in her arrangements. It was Dinah's mode of invoking the domestic Muses.[158]

Seated around her were various members of that rising race with which a Southern household abounds, engaged in shelling peas, peeling potatoes, picking pin-feathers out of fowls, and other preparatory arrangements, Dinah every once in a while interrupting her meditations to give a poke, or a rap on the head, to some of the young operators, with the pudding-stick that lay by her side. In fact, Dinah ruled over the woolly heads of the younger members with a rod of iron, and seemed to consider them born for no earthly purpose but to 'save her steps', as she phrased it. It was the spirit of the system under which she had grown up, and she carried it out to its full extent.

Miss Ophelia, after passing on her reformatory tour through all the other parts of the establishment, now entered the kitchen. Dinah had heard, from various sources, what was going on, and resolved to stand on defensive and conservative ground, mentally determined to oppose and ignore every new measure, without any actual and observable contest.

The kitchen was a large brick-floored apartment, with a great old-fashioned fireplace stretching along one side of it, an arrangement which St Clare had vainly tried to persuade Dinah to exchange for the convenience of a modern cook-stove. Not she. No Puseyite,[159] or Conservative of any school, was ever more inflexibly attached to time-honoured inconveniencies than Dinah.

When St Clare had first returned from the North, impressed with the system and order of his uncle's kitchen arrangements, he had largely provided his own with an array of cupboards, drawers, and various apparatus, to induce systematic regulation, under the sanguine illusion that it would be of any possible assistance to Dinah in her arrangements. He might as well have provided them for a squirrel or a magpie. The more drawers and closets there were, the more hiding-holes could Dinah make for the accommodation of old rags, hair-combs, old shoes, ribbons, cast-off artificial flowers, and other articles of *vertù*,[160] wherein her soul delighted.

When Miss Ophelia entered the kitchen, Dinah did not rise, but smoked on in sublime tranquillity, regarding her movements obliquely out of the corner of her eye, but apparently intent only on the operations around her.

Miss Ophelia commenced opening a set of drawers.

'What is this drawer for, Dinah?' she said.

'It's handy for most anything, missis,' said Dinah. So it appeared to be. From the variety it contained, Miss Ophelia pulled out first a fine damask tablecloth stained with blood, having evidently been used to envelope some raw meat.

'What's this, Dinah? You don't wrap up meat in your mistress's best tablecloths?'

'O Lor, missis, no; the towels was all a missin' – so I jest did it. I laid out to wash that ar – that's why I put it thar.'

'Shiftless!' said Miss Ophelia to herself, proceeding to tumble over the drawer, where she found a nutmeg-grater and two or three nutmegs, a Methodist hymn-book, a couple of soiled Madras[161] handkerchiefs, some yarn and knitting-work, a paper of tobacco and a pipe, a few crackers, one or two gilded china-saucers with some pomade in them, one or two thin old shoes, a piece of flannel carefully pinned up enclosing some small white onions, several damask table-napkins, some coarse crash[162] towels, some twine and darning-needles, and several broken papers, from which sundry sweet herbs were sifting into the drawer.

'Where do you keep your nutmegs, Dinah?' said Miss Ophelia, with the air of one who prayed for patience.

'Most anywhar, missis; there's some in that cracked teacup, up there, and there's some over in that ar cupboard.'

'Here are some in the grater,' said Miss Ophelia, holding them up.

'Laws, yes, I put 'em there this morning, I likes to keep my things handy,' said Dinah. 'You, Jake! what are you stopping for! You'll cotch it! Be still, thar!' she added, with a dive of her stick at the criminal.

'What's this?' said Miss Ophelia, holding up the saucer of pomade.

'Laws, it's my har *grease*; I put it thar to have it handy.'

'Do you use your mistress's best saucers for that?'

'Law! it was 'cause I was driv, and in sich a hurry; I was gwine to change it this very day.'

'Here are two damask table-napkins.'

'Them table-napkins I put thar, to get 'em washed out, someday.'

'Don't you have some place here on purpose for things to be washed?'

'Well, Mas'r St Clare got dat ar chest, he said, for dat; but I likes to mix up biscuit and hev my things on it some days, and then it an't handy a liftin' up the lid.'

'Why don't you mix your biscuits on the pastry-table, there?'

'Law, missis, it gets sot so full of dishes, and one thing and another, der an't no room, noways – '

'But you should wash your dishes, and clear them away.'

'Wash my dishes!' said Dinah, in a high key, as her wrath began to rise over her habitual respect of manner. 'What does ladies know 'bout work, I want to know? When'd mas'r ever get his dinner if I was to spend all my time a-washin' and a-puttin' up dishes? Miss Marie never told me so, nohow.'

'Well, here are these onions.'

'Laws, yes!' said Dinah; 'that *is* whar I put 'em, now. I couldn't 'member. Them's particular onions I was a savin' for dis yer very stew. I'd forgot they was in dat ar old flannel.'

Miss Ophelia lifted out the sifting papers of sweet herbs.

'I wish missis wouldn't touch dem ar. I likes to keep my things where I knows whar to go to 'em,' said Dinah, rather decidedly.

'But you don't want these holes in the papers.'

'Them's handy for siftin' on't out,' said Dinah.

'But you see it spills all over the drawer.'

'Laws, yes! if missis will go a-tumblin' things all up so, it will. Missis has spilt lots dat ar way,' said Dinah, coming uneasily to the drawers. 'If missis only will go up stars till my clarin'-up time comes, I'll have everything right; but I can't do nothin' when ladies is round a henderin'. You, Sam, don't you gib the baby dat ar sugar-bowl! I'll crack ye over, if ye don't mind!'

'I'm going through the kitchen, and going to put everything in order, *once*, Dinah; and then I'll expect you to keep it so.'

'Lor, now! Miss Phelia, dat ar an't no way for ladies to do. I never did see ladies doin' no sich; my old missis nor Miss Marie never did, and I don't see no kinder need on't;' and Dinah stalked indignantly about, while Miss Ophelia piled and sorted dishes, emptied dozens of scattering bowls of sugar into one receptacle, sorted napkins, tablecloths, and towels for washing; washing, wiping, and arranging with her own hands, and with a speed and alacrity which perfectly amazed Dinah.

'Lor now! if dat ar de way dem Northern ladies do, dey an't ladies, nohow,' she said to some of her satellites, when at a safe hearing distance. 'I has things as straight as anybody, when my clarin'-up time comes; but I don't want ladies round, a henderin', and getting my things all where I can't find 'em.'

To do Dinah justice, she had, at irregular periods, paroxysms of reformation and arrangement, which she called 'clarin'-up times', when she would begin with great zeal, and turn every drawer and closet wrong side outward, on to the floor or tables, and make the ordinary confusion sevenfold more confounded. Then she would light her pipe, and leisurely go over her arrangements, looking things over, and discoursing upon them; making all the young fry scour most vigorously on the tin things, and keeping up for several hours a most energetic state of confusion, which she would explain to the satisfaction of all enquirers by the remark that she was a 'clarin' up'. 'She couldn't hev things a-gwine on so as they had been, and she was gwine to make these yer young ones keep better order;' for Dinah herself somehow indulged the illusion that she, herself, was the soul of order, and it was only the *young uns*, and the everybody else in the house, that were the cause of anything that fell short of perfection in this respect. When all the tins were scoured, and the tables scrubbed snowy white, and everything that could offend tucked out of sight in holes and corners, Dinah would dress herself up in a smart dress, clean apron, and high, brilliant Madras turban, and tell all marauding 'young uns' to keep out of the kitchen, for she was gwine to have things kept nice. Indeed, these periodic seasons were often an inconvenience to the whole household; for Dinah would contract such an immoderate attachment to her scoured tin, as to insist upon it that it shouldn't be used again for any possible purpose, at least till the ardour of the 'clarin'-up' period abated.

Miss Ophelia, in a few days, thoroughly reformed every department of the house to a systematic pattern; but her labours in all departments that depended on the co-operation of servants were like those of Sisyphus or the Danaides.[163] In despair, she one day appealed to St Clare.

'There is no such thing as getting anything like system in this family!'

'To be sure there isn't,' said St Clare.

'Such shiftless management, such waste, such confusion, I never saw!'

'I dare say you didn't.'

'You would not take it so coolly, if you were housekeeper.'

'My dear cousin, you may as well understand, once for all, that we masters are divided into two classes, oppressors and oppressed. We who are good-natured and hate severity make up our minds to a good deal of inconvenience. If we *will keep* a shambling, loose, untaught set in the community, for our convenience, why, we must take the consequence. Some rare cases I have seen of persons who, by a peculiar tact, can produce order and system without severity; but I'm not one of them, and so I made up my mind, long ago, to let things go just as they do. I will not have the poor devils thrashed and cut to pieces, and they know it; and, of course, they know the staff is in their own hands.'

'But to have no time, no place, no order – all going on in this shiftless way!'

'My dear Vermont, your natives up by the North Pole set an extravagant value on time! What on earth is the use of time to a fellow who has twice as much of it as he knows what to do with? As to order and system, where there is nothing to be done but lounge on the sofa and read, an hour sooner or later in breakfast or dinner isn't of much account. Now, there's Dinah gets you a capital dinner – soup, ragout, roast fowl, dessert, ice-creams and all – and she creates it all out of Chaos and old Night down there in that kitchen. I think it really sublime, the way she manages. But, heaven bless us! if we are to go down there, and view all the smoking and squatting about, the hurryscurryation of the prepatory process, we should never eat more! My good cousin, absolve yourself from that! It's more than a Catholic penance, and does no more good. You'll only lose your temper, and utterly confound Dinah. Let her go her own way.'

'But, Augustine, you don't know how I found things.'

'Don't I? Don't I know that the rolling-pin is under her bed, and the nutmeg-grater in her pocket with her tobacco, that there are sixty-five different sugar-bowls, one in every hole in the house – that she washes dishes with a dinner-napkin one day, and with a fragment of an old petticoat the next? But the upshot is, she gets up glorious dinners, makes superb coffee; and you must judge her as warriors and statesmen are judged, by *her success*.'

'But the waste, the expense!'

'Oh, well! Lock everything you can, and keep the key. Give out by driblets, and never enquire for odds and ends – it isn't best.'

'That troubles me, Augustine. I can't help feeling as if these servants were not *strictly honest*. Are you sure they can be relied on?'

Augustine laughed immoderately at the grave and anxious face with which Miss Ophelia propounded the question.

'Oh, cousin, that's too good. *Honest*! – as if that's a thing to be expected! Honest! – why, of course, they ar'n't. Why should they be? What upon earth is to make them so?'

'Why don't you instruct?'

'Instruct! Oh, fiddlestick! What instructing do you think I should do? I look like it! As to Marie, she has spirit enough, to be sure, to kill off a whole plantation, if I'd let her manage; but she wouldn't get the cheatery out of them.'

'Are there no honest ones?'

'Well, now and then one, whom Nature makes so impracticably simple, truthful and faithful, that the worst possible influence can't destroy it. But, you see, from the mother's breast the coloured child feels and sees that there are none but underhand ways open to it. It can get along no other way with its parents, its mistress, its young master and missie playfellows. Cunning and deception become necessary, inevitable habits. It isn't fair to expect anything else of him. He ought not to be punished for it. As to honesty, the slave is kept in that dependent, semi-childish state, that there is no making him realise the rights of property, or feel that his master's goods are not his own, if he can get them. For my part I don't see how they *can* be honest. Such a fellow as Tom here is, is a moral miracle!'

'And what becomes of their souls?' said Miss Ophelia.

'That isn't my affair, as I know of,' said St Clare; 'I am only dealing in facts of the present life. The fact is, that the whole race are pretty generally understood to be turned over to the devil, for our benefit, in this world, however it may turn out in another!'

'This is perfectly horrible!' said Miss Ophelia; 'you ought to be ashamed of yourselves!'

'I don't know as I am. We are in pretty good company, for all that,' said St Clare, 'as people in the broad road generally are. Look at the high and the low, all the world over, and it's the same story; the lower class used up, body, soul and spirit, for the good of the upper.[164] It is so in England; it is so everywhere; and yet all Christendom stands aghast, with virtuous indignation, because we do the thing in a little different shape from what they do it.'

'It isn't so in Vermont.'

'Ah, well, in New England, and in the free States, you have the better of us, I grant. But there's the bell; so, cousin, let us for a while lay aside our sectional prejudices, and come out to dinner.'

As Miss Ophelia was in the kitchen in the latter part of the afternoon, some of the sable children called out, 'La, sakes! thar's Prue a-coming, grunting along like she allers does.'

A tall, bony coloured woman now entered the kitchen, bearing on her head a basket of rusks and hot rolls.

'Ho, Prue! you've come,' said Dinah.

Prue had a peculiar scowling expression of countenance, and a sullen, grumbling voice. She set down her basket, squatted herself down, and resting her elbows on her knees, said –

'O Lord! I wish I's dead!'

'Why do you wish you were dead?' said Miss Ophelia.

'I'd be out of my misery,' said the woman, gruffly, without taking her eyes from the floor.

'What need you getting drunk, then, and cutting up, Prue?' said a spruce quadroon chambermaid, dangling, as she spoke, a pair of coral eardrops.

The woman looked at her with a sour, surly glance.

'Maybe you'll come to it, one of these yer days. I'd be glad to see you, I would; then you'll be glad of a drop, like me, to forget your misery.'

'Come, Prue,' said Dinah, 'let's look at your rusks. Here's missis will pay for them.'

Miss Ophelia took out a couple of dozen.

'Thar's some tickets in that ar old cracked jug on the top shelf,' said Dinah. 'You, Jake, climb up and get it down.'

'Tickets – what are they for?' said Miss Ophelia.

'We buys tickets of her mas'r, and she gives us bread for 'em.'

'And they counts my money and tickets, when I gets home, to see if I's got the change; and if I han't, they half kills me.'

'And serves you right,' said Jane, the pert chambermaid, 'if you will take their money to get drunk on. That's what she does, missis.'

'And that's what I *will* do – I can't live no other ways, drink and forget my misery.'

'You are very wicked and very foolish,' said Miss Ophelia, 'to steal your master's money to make yourself a brute with.'

'It's mighty likely, missis; but I will do it, yes, I will. O Lord! I wish I's dead, I do, I wish I's dead, and out of my misery!' and slowly and stiffly the old creature rose, and got her basket on her head again; but before she went out, she looked at the quadroon girl, who still stood playing with her eardrops.

'Ye think ye're mighty fine with them ar, a frolickin' and a tossin' your head, and a lookin' down on everybody. Well, never mind – you may live to be a poor, old, cut-up crittur, like me. Hope to the Lord ye will, I do; then see if ye won't drink – drink – drink – yerself into torment; and sarve ye right, too – ugh!' and, with a malignant howl, the woman left the room.

'Disgusting old beast!' said Adolph, who was getting his master's shaving-water. 'If I was her master, I'd cut her up worse than she is.'

'Ye couldn't do that ar, no ways,' said Dinah. 'Her back's a far sight now – she can't never get a dress together over it.'

'I think such low creatures ought not to be allowed to go round to genteel families,' said Miss Jane. 'What do you think, Mr St Clare?' she said, coquettishly tossing her head at Adolph.

It must be observed that, among other appropriations from his master's stock, Adolph was in the habit of adopting his name and address; and that the style under which he moved, among the coloured circle's of new Orleans, was that of *Mr St Clare*.

'I'm certainly of your opinion, Miss Benoir,' said Adolph.

Benoir was the name of Marie St Clare's family, and Jane was one of her servants.

'Pray, Miss Benoir, may I be allowed to ask if those drops are for the ball tomorrow night? They are certainly bewitching!'

'I wonder, now, Mr St Clare, what the impudence of you men will come to!' said Jane, tossing her pretty head till the eardrops twinkled again. 'I shan't dance with you for a whole evening, if you go to asking me any more questions.'

'Oh, you couldn't be so cruel, now! I was just dying to know whether you would appear in your pink tarletane,'[165] said Adolph.

'What is it?' said Rosa, a bright, piquant little quadroon, who came skipping downstairs at this moment.

'Why, Mr St Clare's so impudent!'

'On my honour,' said Adolph, 'I'll leave it to Miss Rosa, now.'

'I know he's always a saucy creature,' said Rosa, poising herself on one of her little feet, and looking maliciously at Adolph. 'He's always getting me so angry with him.'

'Oh, ladies, ladies, you will certainly break my heart, between you,' said Adolph. 'I shall be found dead in my bed, some morning, and you'll have it to answer for.'

'Do hear the horrid creature talk!' said both ladies, laughing immoderately.

'Come, clar out, you! I can't have you cluttering up the kitchen,' said Dinah; 'in my way, foolin' round here.'

'Aunt Dinah's glum, because she can't go to the ball,' said Rosa.

'Don't want none o' your light-coloured balls,' said Dinah; 'cuttin' round, makin' believe you's white folks. Arter all, you's niggers, much as I am.'

'Aunt Dinah greases her wool stiff, every day, to make it lie straight,' said Jane.

'And it will be wool, after all,' said Rosa, maliciously shaking down her long silky curls

'Well, in the Lord's sight, an't wool as good as har, any time?' said Dinah. 'I'd like to have missis say which is worth the most – a couple such as you, or one like me. Get out wid ye, ye trumpery – I won't have ye round!'

Here the conversation was interrupted in a twofold manner. St Clare's voice was heard at the head of the stairs, asking Adolph if he meant to stay all night with his shaving-water; and Miss Ophelia, coming out of the dining-room, said –

'Jane and Rosa, what are you wasting your time for, here? Go in and attend to your muslins.'

Our friend Tom, who had been in the kitchen during the conversation with the old rusk-woman, had followed her out into the street. He saw her go on, giving every once in a while a suppressed groan. At last she set her basket down on a doorstep, and began arranging the old, faded shawl which covered her shoulders.

'I'll carry your basket a piece,' said Tom, compassionately.

'Why should ye?' said the woman. 'I don't want no help.'

'You seem to be sick, or in trouble, or somethin',' said Tom.

'I an't sick,' said the woman, shortly.

'I wish,' said Tom, looking at her earnestly, 'I wish I could persuade you to leave off drinking. Don't you know it will be the ruin of ye, body and soul?'

'I knows I'm gwine to torment,' said the woman, sullenly. 'Ye don't need to tell me that ar. I's ugly – I's wicked – I's gwine straight to torment. O, Lord! I wish I's thar!'

Tom shuddered at these frightful words, spoken with a sullen, impassioned earnestness.

'O Lord have mercy on ye! poor crittur. Han't ye never heard of Jesus Christ?'

'Jesus Christ! – who's He?'

'Why, He's *the Lord*,' said Tom.

'I think I've hearn tell o' the Lord, and the judgement and torment. I've heard o' that.'

'But didn't anybody ever tell you of the Lord Jesus, that loved us poor sinners, and died for us?'

'Don't know nothin' 'bout that,' said the woman; 'nobody han't never loved me, since my old man died.'

'Where was you raised?' said Tom.

'Up in Kentuck. A man kept me to breed chil'en for market, and sold 'em as fast as they got big enough; last of all, he sold me to a speculator, and my mas'r got me o' him.'

'What set you into this bad way of drinkin'?'

'To get shet o' my misery. I had one child after I come here; and I thought then I'd have one to raise, 'cause mas'r wasn't a speculator. It was the peartest little thing! and missis she seemed to think a heap on't, at first; it never cried – it was likely and fat. But missis tuck sick, and I tended her; and I tuck the fever, and my milk all left me, and the child it pined to skin and bone, and missis wouldn't buy milk for it. She wouldn't hear to me, when I telled her I hadn't milk. She said she knowed I could feed it on what other folks eat; and the child kinder pined and cried, and cried, and cried, day and night, and got all gone to skin and bones, and missis got sot agin it, and she said 'twan't nothin' but crossness. She wished it was dead, she said; and she wouldn't let me have it o' nights, 'cause, she said, it kept me awake, and made me good for nothing. She made me sleep in her room; and I had to put it away off in a little kind o' garret, and thar it cried itself to death, one night. It did; and I tuck to drinkin', to keep its crying out of my ears! I did – and I will drink! I will, if I do go to torment for it! Mas'r says I shall go to torment, and I tell him I've got thar now!'

'O ye poor crittur!' said Tom, 'han't nobody never telled ye how the Lord Jesus loved ye, and died for ye? Han't they telled ye that He'll help ye, and ye can go to heaven, and have rest, at last?'

'I looks like gwine to heaven,' said the woman; 'an't thar where white folks is gwine? S'pose they'd have me thar? I'd rather go to torment, and get away from mas'r and missis. I had *so*,' she said, as, with her usual groan, she got her basket on her head, and walked sullenly away.

Tom turned, and walked sorrowfully back to the house. In the court he met little Eva – a crown of tuberoses on her head, and her eyes radiant with delight.

'Oh, Tom! here you are. I'm glad I've found you. Papa says you may get out the ponies, and take me in my little new carriage,' she said, catching his hand. 'But what's the matter, Tom? – you look sober.'

'I feel bad, Miss Eva,' said Tom, sorrowfully. 'But I'll get the horses for you.'

'But do tell me, Tom, what is the matter. I saw you talking to cross old Prue.'

Tom, in simple, earnest phrase, told Eva the woman's history. She did not exclaim, or wonder, or weep, as other children do. Her cheeks grew pale, and a deep, earnest shadow passed over her eyes. She laid both hands on her bosom, and sighed heavily.[166]

CHAPTER XIX

Miss Ophelia's Experiences
and Opinions, continued

'TOM, YOU NEEDN'T get me the horses. I don't want to go,' she said.

'Why not, Miss Eva?'

'These things sink into my heart, Tom,' said Eva; 'they sink into my heart,' she repeated, earnestly. 'I don't want to go;' and she turned from Tom, and went into the house.

A few days after, another woman came, in old Prue's place, to bring the rusks; Miss Ophelia was in the kitchen.

'Lor!' said Dinah, 'what's got Prue?'

'Prue isn't coming any more,' said the woman, mysteriously.

'Why not?' said Dinah. 'She an't dead, is she?'

'We doesn't exactly know. She's down cellar,' said the woman, glancing at Miss Ophelia.

After Miss Ophelia had taken the rusks, Dinah followed the woman to the door.

'What *has* got Prue, anyhow?' she said.

The woman seemed desirous, yet reluctant to speak, and answered in a low, mysterious tone.

'Well, you mustn't tell nobody. Prue, she got drunk agin – and they had her down cellar – and thar they left her all day; and I hearn 'em saying that the *flies had got to her* – and *she's dead*!'

Dinah held up her hands, and, turning, saw close by her side the spirit-like form of Evangeline, her large, mystic eyes dilated with horror and every drop of blood driven from her lips and cheeks.

'Lor bless us! Miss Eva's gwine to faint away! What got us all, to let her har such talk? Her pa'll be rail mad.'

'I shan't faint, Dinah,' said the child, firmly; 'and why shouldn't I hear it? It an't so much for me to hear it, as for poor Prue to suffer it.'

'*Lor sakes!* it isn't for sweet, delicate young ladies, like you – these yer stories isn't; it's enough to kill 'em!'

Eva sighed again, and walked upstairs with a slow and melancholy step.

Miss Ophelia anxiously enquired the woman's story. Dinah gave a very garrulous version of it, to which Tom added the particulars which he had drawn from her that morning.

'An abominable business – perfectly horrible!' she exclaimed, as she entered the room where St Clare lay, reading his paper.

'Pray, what iniquity has turned up now?' said he.

'What now? why, those folks have whipped Prue to death!' said Miss Ophelia, going on, with great strength of detail, into the story, and enlarging on its most shocking particulars.

'I thought it would come to that, sometime,' said St Clare, going on with his paper.

'Thought so! – an't you going to *do* anything about it?' said Miss Ophelia. 'Haven't you got any *selectmen*,[167] or anybody, to interfere and look after such matters?'

'It's commonly supposed that the *property* interest is a sufficient guard in these cases. If people choose to ruin their own possessions, I don't know what's to be done. It seems the poor creature was a thief and a drunkard; and so there won't be much hope to get up sympathy for her.'

'It is perfectly outrageous – it is horrid, Augustine! It will certainly bring down vengeance upon you.'

'My dear cousin, I didn't do it, and I can't help it; I would, if I could. If low-minded, brutal people will act like themselves, what am I to do? They have absolute control; they are irresponsible despots. There would be no use in interfering; there is no law that amounts to anything practically for such a case. The best we can do is to shut our eyes and ears, and let it alone. It's the only resource left us.'

'How can you shut your eyes and ears? How can you let such things alone?'

'My dear child, what do you expect? Here is a whole class – debased, uneducated, indolent, provoking – put, without any sort of terms or conditions, entirely into the hands of such people as the majority in our world are; people who have neither consideration nor self-control, who haven't even an enlightened regard to their own interest – for that's the case with the largest half of mankind.[168] Of course, in a community so organised, what can a man of honourable and humane feelings do, but shut his eyes all he can, and harden his heart? I can't buy every poor wretch I see. I can't turn knight-errant, and undertake to redress every individual case of wrong in such a city as this. The most I can do is to try and keep out of the way of it.'

St Clare's fine countenance was for a moment overcast; he looked annoyed, but suddenly calling up a gay smile, he said –

'Come, cousin, don't stand there looking like one of the Fates;[169] you've only seen a peep through the curtain – a specimen of what is going on the world over, in some shape or other. If we are to be prying and spying into all the dismals of life, we should have no heart to anything. 'Tis like looking too close into the details of Dinah's kitchen;' and St Clare lay back on the sofa, and busied himself with his paper.

Miss Ophelia sat down, and pulled out her knitting-work, and sat there, grim with indignation. She knit, and knit; but while she mused the fire burned. At last she broke out –

'I tell you, Augustine, I can't get over things so, if you can. It's a perfect abomination for you to defend such a system – that's my mind!'

'What now?' said St Clare, looking up. 'At it again, eh?'

'I say it's perfectly abominable for you to defend such a system!' said Miss Ophelia, with increasing warmth.

'*I* defend it, my dear lady? Who ever said I did defend it?' said St Clare.

'Of course, you defend it – you all do – all you Southerners. What do you have slaves for, if you don't?'

'Are you such a sweet innocent as to suppose nobody in this world ever does what they don't think is right? Don't you, or didn't you ever, do anything that you did not think quite right?'

'If I do, I repent of it, I hope,' said Miss Ophelia, rattling her needles with energy.

'So do I,' said St Clare, peeling his orange; 'I'm repenting of it all the time.'

'What do you keep on doing it for?'

'Didn't you ever keep on doing wrong, after you'd repented, my good cousin?'

'Well, only when I've been very much tempted,' said Miss Ophelia.

'Well, I'm very much tempted,' said St Clare; 'that's just my difficulty.'

'But I always resolve I won't, and I try to break off.'

'Well, I have been resolving I won't, off and on, these ten years,' said St Clare; 'but I haven't, somehow, got clear. Have you got clear of all your sins, cousin?'

'Cousin Augustine,' said Miss Ophelia, seriously, and laying down her knitting-work, 'I suppose I deserve that you should reprove my shortcomings. I know all you say is true enough; nobody else feels them more than I do; but it does seem to me, after all, there is some difference between me and you. It seems to me I would cut off my right hand sooner than keep on, from day to day, doing what I thought was wrong. But then my conduct is so inconsistent with my profession, I don't wonder you reprove me.'

'Oh, now, cousin,' said Augustine, sitting down on the floor, and laying his head back in her lap, 'don't take on so awfully serious! You know what a good-for-nothing, saucy boy I always was. I love to poke you up – that's all – just to see you get earnest. I do think you are desperately, distressingly good; it tires me to death to think of it.'

'But this is a serious subject, my boy, Auguste,' said Miss Ophelia, laying her hand on his forehead.

'Dismally so,' said he; 'and I – well, I never want to talk seriously in hot weather. What with mosquitoes and all, a fellow can't get himself up to any very sublime moral flights; and I believe,' said St Clare, suddenly rousing himself up, 'there's a theory, now! I understand now why northern nations are always more virtuous than southern ones – I see into that whole subject.'

'Oh, Auguste, you are a sad rattlebrain!'

'Am I? Well, so I am, I suppose; but for once I will be serious, now; but you must hand me that basket of oranges – you see, you'll have to "stay me with flagons and comfort me with apples"[170] if I'm going to make this effort. Now,' said Augustine, drawing the basket up, 'I'll begin: When, in the course of human events,[171] it becomes necessary for a fellow to hold two or three dozen of his fellow worms in captivity, a decent regard to the opinions of society requires – '

'I don't see that you are growing more serious,' said Miss Ophelia.

'Wait – I am coming on – you'll hear. The short of the matter is, cousin,' said he, his handsome face suddenly settling into an earnest and serious expression, 'on this abstract question of slavery there can, as I think, be but one opinion. Planters, who have money to make by it – clergymen, who have planters to please – politicians who want to rule by it – may warp and bend language and ethics to a degree that shall astonish the world at their ingenuity; they can press nature and the Bible, and nobody knows what else, into the service; but, after all, neither they nor the world believe in it one particle the more. It comes from the devil, that's the short of it; and, to my mind, it's a pretty respectable specimen of what he can do in his own line.'

Miss Ophelia stopped her knitting, and looked surprised; and St Clare, apparently enjoying her astonishment, went on.

'You seem to wonder; but if you will get me fairly at it, I'll make a clean breast of it. This cursed business, accursed of God and man, what is it? Strip it of all its ornament, run it down to the root and nucleus of the whole, and what is it? Why, because my brother Quashy[172] is ignorant and weak, and I am intelligent and strong – because I know how, and can do it – therefore, I may steal all he has, keep it, and give him only such and so much as suits my fancy. Whatever is too hard, too dirty, too disagreeable, for me, I may set Quashy to doing. Because I don't like work, Quashy shall work. Because the sun burns me, Quashy shall stay in the sun. Quashy shall earn the money, and I will spend it. Quashy shall lie down in every puddle, that I may walk over dryshod. Quashy shall do my will, and not his, all the days of his mortal life, and have such chance of getting to heaven at last as I find convenient. This I take to be about what slavery *is*. I defy anybody on earth to read our slave-code, as it stands in our law-books, and make anything else of it. Talk of the *abuses* of slavery! Humbug! The *thing itself* is the essence of all abuse! And the only reason why the land don't sink under it, like Sodom and Gomorrah,[173] is because it is *used* in a way infinitely better than it is. For pity's sake, for shame's sake, because we are men born of women, and not savage beasts, many of us do not, and dare not – we would *scorn* to use the full power which our savage laws put into our hands. And he who goes the furthest, and does the worst, only uses within limits the power that the law gives him.'

St Clare had started up, and, as his manner was when excited, was walking, with hurried steps, up and down the floor. His fine face, classic as that of a Greek statue, seemed actually to burn with the fervour of his feelings. His large blue eyes flashed, and he gestured with an unconscious eagerness. Miss Ophelia had never seen him in this mood before, and she sat perfectly silent.

'I declare to you,' said he, suddenly stopping before his cousin – 'it's no sort of use to talk or to feel on this subject – but I declare to you, there have been times when I have thought, if the whole country would sink, and hide all this injustice and misery from the light, I would willingly sink with it. When I have been travelling up and down on our boats, or about on my collecting tours, and reflected that every brutal, disgusting, mean, low-lived fellow I met, was allowed by our laws to become absolute despot of as many men, women and children, as he could cheat, steal, or gamble money enough to buy – when I have seen such men in actual ownership of helpless children, of young girls and women – I have been ready to curse my country, to curse the human race!'

'Augustine! Augustine!' said Miss Ophelia, 'I'm sure you've said enough. I never, in my life, heard anything like this, even at the North.'

'At the North!' said St Clare, with a sudden change of expression, and resuming something of his habitual careless tone. 'Pooh! your Northern folks are cold-blooded; you are cool in everything! You can't begin to curse up hill and down, as we can, when we get fairly at it.'

'Well, but the question is,' said Miss Ophelia.

'Oh, yes, to be sure, the *question is* – and a deuce of a question it is! – How came *you* in this state of sin and misery? Well, I shall answer in the good old words you used to teach me, Sundays. I came so by ordinary generation. My servants were my father's, and, what is more, my mother's; and now they are mine, they and their increase, which bids fair to be a pretty considerable item. My father, you know, came first from New England; and he was just such another man as your father – a regular old Roman; upright, energetic, noble-minded, with an iron will. Your father settled down in New England, to rule over rocks and stones, and to force an existence out of Nature; and mine settled in Louisiana, to rule over men and women, and force existence out of them. My mother,' said St Clare, getting up and walking to a picture at the end of the room, and gazing upward with a face fervent with veneration, '*she* was *divine*! Don't look at me so! – you know what I mean! She probably was of mortal birth; but, as far as ever I could observe, there was no trace of any human weakness or error about her; and everybody that lives to remember her, whether bond or free, servant, acquaintance, relation, all say the same. Why, cousin, that mother has been all that has stood between me and utter unbelief for years. She was a direct embodiment and personification of the New Testament – a living fact, to be accounted for, and to be accounted for in no other way than by its truth. O mother! mother!' said St Clare, clasping his hands, in a sort of transport; and then suddenly checking himself, he came back, and seating himself on an ottoman, he went on.

'My brother and I were twins; and they say, you know, that twins ought to resemble each other; but we were in all points a contrast. He had black, fiery eyes, coal-black hair, a strong, fine Roman profile, and a rich brown complexion. I had blue eyes, golden hair, a Greek outline, and fair complexion. He was active and observing, I dreamy and inactive. He was generous to his friends and equals, but proud, dominant, overbearing, to inferiors, and utterly unmerciful to whatever set itself up against him. Truthful we both were; he from pride and courage, I from a sort of abstract ideality. We loved each other about as boys generally do, off and on, and in general; he was my father's pet, and I my mother's.

'There was a morbid sensitiveness and acuteness of feeling in me on all possible subjects, of which he and my father had no kind of understanding, and with which they could have no possible sympathy. But mother did; and so, when I had quarrelled with Alfred, and father looked sternly on me, I used to go off to mother's room, and sit by her. I remember just how she used to look, with her pale cheeks, her deep, soft, serious eyes, her white dress – she always wore white – and I used to think of her whenever I read in Revelations about the saints that were arrayed in fine linen, clean and white.[174] She had a great deal of genius of one sort and another, particularly in music; and she used to sit at her organ, playing fine old majestic music of the Catholic church, and singing with a voice more like an angel than a mortal woman; and I would lay my head down on her lap, and cry, and dream, and feel – oh, immeasurably! – things that I had no language to say!

'In those days, this matter of slavery had never been canvassed as it has now; nobody dreamed of any harm in it.[175]

'My father was a born aristocrat. I think, in some pre-existent state, he must have been in the higher circles of spirits, and brought all his old court pride along with him; for it was ingrain, bred in the bone, though he was originally of poor and not in any way of noble family. My brother was begotten in his image.

'Now, an aristocrat, you know, the world over, has no human sympathies, beyond a certain line in society. In England the line is in one place, in Burma in another, and in America in another; but the aristocrat of all these countries never goes over it. What would be hardship and distress and injustice in his own class, is a cool matter of course in another one. My father's dividing line was that of colour. *Among his equals*, never was a man more just and generous; but he considered the negro, through all possible gradations of colour, as an intermediate link between man and animals, and graded all his ideas of justice or generosity on this hypothesis. I suppose, to be sure, if anybody had asked him, plump and fair, whether they had human immortal souls, he might have hemmed and hawed, and said yes. But my father was not a man much troubled with spiritualism; religious sentiment he had none, beyond a veneration for God, as decidedly the head of the upper classes.

'Well, my father worked some five hundred negroes; he was an inflexible, driving, punctilious businessman; everything was to move by system – to be sustained with unfailing accuracy and precision. Now, if you take into account that all this was to be worked out by a set of lazy, twaddling, shiftless labourers, who had grown up, all their lives, in the absence of every possible motive to learn how to do anything but "shirk", as you Vermonters say, and you'll see that there might naturally be on his plantation a great many things that looked horrible and distressing to a sensitive child like me.

'Besides all, he had an overseer – a great, tall, slab-sided, two-fisted renegade son of Vermont (begging your pardon), who had gone through a regular apprenticeship in hardness and brutality, and taken his degree to be admitted to practice. My mother never could endure him, nor I; but he obtained an entire ascendency over my father; and this man was the absolute despot of the estate.

'I was a little fellow then, but I had the same love that I have now for all kinds of human things – a kind of passion for the study of humanity, come in what shape it would. I was found in the cabins and among the field-hands a great deal, and, of course, was a great favourite; and all sorts of complaints and grievances were breathed in my ear; and I told them to mother, and we, between us, formed a sort of committee for a redress of grievances. We hindered and repressed a great deal of cruelty, and congratulated ourselves on doing a vast deal of good, till, as often happens, my zeal overacted. Stubbs complained to my father that he couldn't manage the hands, and must resign his position. Father was a fond, indulgent husband, but a man that never flinched from anything that he thought necessary; and so he put down his foot, like a rock, between us and the field-hands. He told my mother, in language perfectly respectful and deferential, but quite explicit, that over the house-servants she should be entire mistress, but that with the field-hands he could allow no interference. He revered and respected her above all living beings; but he would have said it all the same to the Virgin Mary herself, if she had come in the way of his system.

'I used sometimes to hear my mother reasoning cases with him – endeavouring to excite his sympathies. He would listen to the most pathetic appeals with the most discouraging politeness and equanimity. "It all resolves itself into this," he would say; "must I part with Stubbs, or keep him? Stubbs is the soul of punctuality, honesty, and efficiency, a thorough business hand, and as humane as the general run. We can't have perfection; and if I keep him, I must sustain his administration as a *whole*, even if there are, now and then, things that are exceptionable. All government includes some necessary hardness. General rules will bear hard on particular cases." This last maxim my father seemed to consider a settler in most alleged cases of cruelty. After he had said *that*, he commonly drew up his feet on the sofa, like a man that has disposed of a business, and betook himself to a nap or the newspaper, as the case might be.

'The fact is, my father showed the exact sort of talent for a statesman. He could have divided Poland as easily as an orange, or trod on Ireland[176] as quietly and systematically as any man living. At last my mother gave up, in despair. It never will be known, till the last account, what noble and sensitive natures like hers have felt, cast, utterly helpless, into what seems to them an abyss of injustice and cruelty, and which seems so to nobody about them. It has been an age of long sorrow of such natures, in such a hell-begotten sort of world as ours. What remained for her, but to train her children in her own views and sentiments? Well, after all you say about training, children will grow up substantially what they *are* by nature, and only that. From the cradle, Alfred was an aristocrat; and as he grew up, instinctively, all his sympathies and all his reasonings were in that line, and all mother's exhortations went to the winds. As to me, they sank deep into me. She never contradicted, in form, anything that my father said, or seemed directly to differ from him; but she impressed, burnt into my very soul, with all the force of her deep, earnest nature, an idea of the dignity and worth of the meanest human soul. I have looked in her face with solemn awe, when she would point up to the stars in the evening, and say to me, "See there, Auguste! the poorest, meanest soul on our place will be living, when all these stars are gone forever – will live as long as God lives!"

'She had some fine old paintings; one, in particular, of Jesus healing a blind man.[177] They were very fine, and used to impress me strongly. "See there, Auguste," she would say; "the blind man was a beggar, poor and loathsome; therefore, he would not heal him *afar off*! He called him to him, and put *his hands on him*! Remember this, my boy." If I had lived to grow up under her care, she might have stimulated me to I know not what of enthusiasm. I might have been a saint, reformer, martyr – but, alas! alas! I went from her when I was only thirteen, and I never saw her again!'

St Clare rested his head on his hands, and did not speak for some minutes. After a while, he looked up, and went on –

'What poor, mean trash this whole business of human virtue is! A mere matter, for the most part, of latitude and longitude, and geographical position, acting with natural temperament. The greater part is nothing but an accident! Your father, for example, settles in Vermont, in a town where all are, in fact, free and equal; becomes a regular church member and deacon, and in due time joins an Abolitionist society, and thinks us all little better than heathens. Yet he is, for all the world, in constitution and habit, a duplicate of my father. I can see it leaking out in fifty different ways – just that same strong, overbearing, dominant spirit. You know very well how impossible it is to persuade some of the folks in your village that Squire Sinclair does not feel above them. The fact is, though he has fallen on democratic times, and embraced a democratic theory, he is to the heart an aristocrat, as much as my father, who ruled over five or six hundred slaves.'

Miss Ophelia felt rather disposed to cavil at this picture, and was laying down her knitting to begin, but St Clare stopped her.

'Now, I know every word you are going to say. I do not say they *were* alike, in fact. One fell into a condition where everything acted against the natural tendency, and the other where everything acted for it; and so one turned out a pretty wilful, stout, overbearing old democrat, and the other a wilful, stout old despot. If both had owned plantations in Louisiana, they would have been as like as two old bullets cast in the same mould.'

'What an undutiful boy you are!' said Miss Ophelia.

'I don't mean them any disrespect,' said St Clare. 'You know irreverence is not my forte. But, to go back to my history –

'When father died, he left the whole property to us twin boys, to be divided as we should agree. There does not breathe on God's earth a nobler-souled, more generous fellow, than Alfred, in all that concerns his equals; and we got on admirably with this property question, without a single unbrotherly word or feeling. We undertook to work the plantation together; and Alfred, whose outward life and capabilities had double the strength of mine, became an enthusiastic planter, and a wonderfully successful one.

'But two years trial satisfied me that I could not be a partner in that matter. To have a great gang of seven hundred, whom I could not know personally, or feel any individual interest in, bought and driven, housed, fed, worked like so many horned cattle, strained up to military precision – the question of how little of life's commonest enjoyments would keep them in working order being a constantly recurring problem, the *necessity* of drivers and overseers, the ever-necessary whip, first, last, and only argument – the whole thing was insufferably disgusting and loathsome to me; and when I thought of my mother's estimate of one poor human soul, it became even frightful.

'It's all nonsense to talk to me about slaves *enjoying* all this! To this day, I have no patience with the unutterable trash that some of your patronising Northerners have made up, as in their zeal to apologise for our sins. We all know better. Tell me that any man living wants to work all his days, from day-dawn till dark, under the constant eye of a master, without the power of putting forth one irresponsible volition, on the same dreary, monotonous, unchanging toil, and all for two pairs of pantaloons and a pair of shoes a year, with enough food and shelter to keep him in working order! Any man who thinks that human beings can, as a general thing, be made about as comfortable that way as any other, I wish he might try it. I'd buy the dog, and work him, with a clear conscience!'

'I always have supposed,' said Miss Ophelia, 'that you, all of you, approved of these things, and thought them *right*, according to Scripture.'

'Humbug! We are not quite reduced to that yet. Alfred, who is as determined a despot as ever walked, does not pretend to this kind of defence; no, he stands, high and haughty, on that good old respectable ground, *the right of the strongest*; and he says, and I think quite sensibly, that the American planter is "only doing, in another form, what the English aristocracy and capitalists are doing by the lower classes";[178] that is, I take it, *appropriating* them, body and bone, soul and spirit, to their use and convenience. He defends both – and I think, at least, *consistently*. He says that there can be no high civilisation without enslavement of the masses, either nominal or real. There must, he says, be a lower class, given up to physical toil and confined to an animal nature; and a higher one thereby acquires leisure and wealth for a more expanded intelligence and improvement, and becomes the directing soul of the lower. So he reasons, because, as I said, he is born an aristocrat; so I don't believe, because I was born a democrat.'

'How in the world can the two things be compared?' said Miss Ophelia. 'The English labourer is not sold, traded, parted from his family, whipped.'

'He is as much at the will of his employer as if he were sold to him. The slave-owner can whip his refractory slave to death – the capitalist can starve him to death. As to family security, it is hard to say which is the worst – to have one's children sold, or see them starve to death at home.'

'But it's no kind of apology for slavery, to prove that it isn't worse than some other bad thing.'

'I didn't give it for one – nay, I'll say, besides, that ours is the more bold and palpable infringement of human rights; actually buying a man up, like a horse – looking at his teeth, cracking his joints, and trying his paces, and then paying down for him – having speculators, breeders, traders, and brokers in human bodies and souls – sets the thing before the eyes of the civilised world in a more tangible form, though the thing done be, after all in its nature, the same; that is, appropriating one set of human beings to the use and improvement of another, without any regard to their own.'

'I never thought of the matter in this light,' said Miss Ophelia.

'Well, I've travelled in England some, and I've looked over a good many documents as to the state of their lower classes; and I really think there is no denying Alfred, when he says that his slaves are better off than a large class of the population of England. You see, you must not infer, from what I have told you, that Alfred is what is called a hard master; for he isn't. He is despotic, and unmerciful to insubordination; he would shoot a fellow down with as little remorse as he would shoot a buck, if he opposed him. But, in general, he takes a sort of pride in having his slaves comfortably fed and accommodated.

'When I was with him, I insisted that he should do something for their instruction; and, to please me, he did get a chaplain, and used to have them catechised Sunday, though, I believe, in his heart, that he thought it would do about as much good to set a chaplain over his dogs and horses. And the fact is, that a mind stupefied and animalised by every bad influence from the hour of birth, spending the whole of every weekday in unreflecting toil, cannot be done much with by a few hours on Sunday. The teachers of Sunday-schools among the manufacturing population of England, and among plantation-hands in our country, could perhaps testify to the same result, *there and here*. Yet some striking exceptions there are among us, from the fact that the negro is naturally more impressible to religious sentiment than the white.'

'Well,' said Miss Ophelia, 'how came you to give up your plantation life?'

'Well, we jogged on together some time, till Alfred saw plainly that I was no planter. He thought it absurd, after he had reformed, and altered, and improved everywhere, to suit my notions, that I still remained unsatisfied. The fact was, it was, after all the THING that I hated – the using these men and women, the perpetuation of all this ignorance, brutality and vice – just to make money for me!

'Besides, I was always interfering in the details. Being myself one of the laziest of mortals, I had altogether too much fellow-feeling for the lazy; and when poor, shiftless dogs put stones at the bottom of their cotton-baskets to make them weigh heavier, or filled their sacks with dirt, with cotton at the top, it seemed so exactly like what I should do if I were they, I couldn't and wouldn't have them flogged for it. Well, of course, there was an end of plantation discipline; and Alf and I came to about the same point that I and my respected father did, years before. So he told me that I was a womanish sentimentalist, and would never do for business life; and advised me to take the bank-stock and the New Orleans family mansion, and go to writing poetry, and let him manage the plantation. So we parted, and I came here.'

'But why didn't you free your slaves?'

'Well, I wasn't up to that. To hold them as tools for money-making, I could not; have them to help spend money, you know, didn't look quite so ugly to me. Some of them were old house-servants, to whom I was much attached; and the younger ones were children to the old. All were well satisfied to be as they were.' He paused, and walked reflectively up and down the room.

'There was,' said St Clare, 'a time in my life when I had plans and hopes of doing something in this world, more than to float and drift. I had vague, indistinct yearnings to be a sort of emancipator – to free my native land from this spot and stain. All young men have had such fever-fits, I suppose, sometime – but then – '

'Why didn't you?' said Miss Ophelia; 'you ought not to put your hand to the plough, and look back.'

'Oh, well, things didn't go with me as I expected, and I got the despair of living that Solomon did. I suppose it was a necessary incident to wisdom in us both; but, somehow or other, instead of being actor and regenerator in society, I became a piece of driftwood, and have been floating and eddying about, ever since. Alfred scolds me, every time we meet; and he has the better of me, I grant; for he really does something. His life is a logical result of his opinions, and mine is a contemptible *non sequitur*.'[179]

'My dear cousin, can you be satisfied with such a way of spending your probation?'

'Satisfied! Was I not just telling you I despised it? But, then, to come back to this point – we were on this liberation business. I don't think my feelings about slavery are peculiar. I find many men who, in their hearts, think of it just as I do. The land groans under it; and bad as it is for the slave, it is worse, if anything, for the master. It takes no spectacles to see that a great class of vicious, improvident, degraded people, among us, are an evil to us, as well as to themselves. The capitalist and aristocrat of England cannot feel that as we do, because they do not mingle with the class they degrade as we do. They are in our houses; they are the associates of our children, and they form their minds faster than we can; for they are a race that children always will cling to and assimilate with. If Eva, now, was not more angel than ordinary, she would be ruined. We might as well allow the smallpox to run among them, and think our children would not take it, as to let them be uninstructed and vicious, and think our children will not be affected by that. Yet our laws positively and utterly forbid any efficient general educational system, and they do it wisely, too; for, just begin and thoroughly educate one generation, and the whole thing would be blown sky high. If we did not give them liberty, they would take it.'

'And what do you think will be the end of this?' said Miss Ophelia.

'I don't know. One thing is certain – that there is a mustering among the masses, the world over; and there is a *dies irae*[180] coming on, sooner or later. The same thing is working in Europe, in England, and in this country. My mother used to tell me of a millennium that was coming, when Christ should reign,[181] and all men should be free and happy. And she taught me, when I was a boy, to pray, "Thy kingdom come." Sometimes I think all this sighing, and groaning, and stirring among the dry bones foretells what she used to tell me was coming. But who may abide the day of His appearing?'

'Augustine, sometimes I think you are not far from the kingdom,' said Miss Ophelia, laying down her knitting, and looking anxiously at her cousin.

'Thank you for your good opinion; but it's up and down with me – up to heaven's gate in theory, down in earth's dust in practice. But there's the tea-bell – do let's go – and don't say, now, I haven't had one downright serious talk, for once in my life.'

At table, Marie alluded to the incident of Prue. 'I suppose you'll think, cousin,' she said, 'that we are all barbarians.'

'I think that's a barbarous thing,' said Miss Ophelia, 'but I don't think you are all barbarians.'

'Well, now,' said Marie, 'I know it's impossible to get along with some of these creatures. They are so bad they ought not to live. I don't feel a particle of sympathy for such cases. If they'd only behave themselves, it would not happen.'

'But, mamma,' said Eva, 'the poor creature was unhappy; that's what made her drink.'

'Oh, fiddlestick! as if that were any excuse! I'm unhappy, very often. I presume,' she said, pensively, 'that I've had greater trials than ever she had. It's just because they are so bad. There's some of them that you cannot break in by any kind of severity. I remember father had a man that was so lazy he would run away just to get rid of work, and lie round in the swamps, stealing and doing all sorts of horrid things. That man was caught and whipped, time and again, and it never did him any good; and the last time he crawled off, though he couldn't but just go, and died in the swamp. There was no sort of reason for it, for father's hands were always treated kindly.'

'I broke a fellow in, once,' said St Clare, 'that all the overseers and masters had tried their hands on in vain.'

'You!' said Marie; 'well, I'd be glad to know when *you* ever did anything of the sort.'

'Well, he was a powerful, gigantic fellow – a native-born African; and he appeared to have the rude instinct of freedom in him to an uncommon degree. He was a regular African lion. They called him Scipio.[182] Nobody could do anything with him; and he was sold round from overseer to overseer, till at last Alfred bought him, because he thought he could manage him. Well, one day he knocked down the overseer, and was fairly off into the swamps. I was on a visit to Alf's plantation, for it was after we had dissolved partnership. Alfred was greatly exasperated; but I told him that it was his own fault, and laid him any wager that I could break the man; and finally it was agreed that, if I caught him, I should have him to experiment on. So they mustered out a party of some six or seven, with guns and dogs, for the hunt. People, you know, can get up just as much enthusiasm in hunting a man as a deer, if it is only customary; in fact, I got a little excited myself, though I had only put in as a sort of mediator, in case he was caught.

'Well, the dogs bayed and howled, and we rode and scampered, and finally we started him. He ran and bounded like a buck, and kept us well in the rear for some time; but at last he got caught in an impenetrable thicket of cane; then he turned to bay, and I tell you he fought the dogs right gallantly. He dashed them to right and left, and actually killed three of them with only his naked fists, when a shot from a gun brought him down, and he fell, wounded and bleeding, almost at my feet. The poor fellow looked up at me with manhood and despair both in his eye. I kept back the dogs and the party, as they came pressing up, and claimed him as my prisoner. It was all I could do to keep them from shooting him, in the flush of success; but I persisted in my bargain, and Alfred sold him to me. Well, I took him in hand, and in one fortnight I had him tamed down as submissive and tractable as heart could desire.'

'What in the world did you do to him?' said Marie.

'Well, it was quite a simple process. I took him to my own room, had a good bed made for him, dressed his wounds, and tended him myself, until he got fairly on his feet again. And, in process of time, I had free papers made out for him, and told him he might go where he liked.'

'And did he go?' said Miss Ophelia.

'No. The foolish fellow tore the paper in two, and absolutely refused to leave me. I never had a braver, better fellow – trusty and true as steel. He embraced Christianity afterwards, and became as gentle as a child. He used to oversee my place on the lake, and did it capitally, too. I lost him the first cholera season. In fact, he laid down his life for me. For I was sick, almost to death; and when, through the panic, everybody else fled, Scipio worked for me like a giant, and actually brought me back into life again. But, poor fellow! he was taken, right after, and there was no saving him. I never felt anybody's loss more.'

Eva had come gradually nearer and nearer to her father, as he told the story – her small lips apart, her eyes wide and earnest with absorbing interest.

As he finished, she suddenly threw her arms around his neck, burst into tears, and sobbed convulsively.

'Eva, dear child! what is the matter?' said St Clare, as the child's small frame trembled and shook with the violence of her feelings. 'This child,' he added, 'ought not to hear any of this kind of thing, she's nervous.'

'No, papa, I'm not nervous,' said Eva, controlling herself, suddenly, with a strength of resolution singular in such a child. 'I'm not nervous, but these things *sink into my heart*.'

'What do you mean, Eva?'

'I can't tell you, papa. I think a great many thoughts. Perhaps someday I shall tell you.'

'Well, think away, dear – only don't cry and worry your papa,' said St Clare. 'Look here – see what a beautiful peach I have got for you!'

Eva took it, and smiled, though there was still a nervous twitching about the corners of her mouth.

'Come, look at the goldfish,' said St Clare, taking her hand and stepping on to the veranda. A few moments, and merry laughs were heard through the silken curtains, as Eva and St Clare were pelting each other with roses, and chasing each other among the alleys of the court.

There is danger that our humble friend Tom be neglected amid the adventures of the higher born; but, if our readers will accompany us up to a little loft over the stable they may, perhaps, learn a little of his affairs. It was a decent room, containing a bed, a chair, and a small, rough stand, where lay Tom's Bible and hymn-book; and where he sits, at present, with his slate before him, intent on something that seems to cost him a great deal of anxious thought.

The fact was, that Tom's home-yearnings had become so strong, that he had begged a sheet of writing-paper of Eva, and, mustering up all his small stock of literary attainment acquired by Mas'r George's instructions, he conceived the bold idea of writing a letter; and he was busy now, on his slate, getting out his first draft. Tom was in a good deal of trouble, for the forms of some of the letters he had forgotten entirely; and of what he did remember, he did not know exactly which to use. And while he was working, and breathing very hard, in his earnestness, Eva alighted like a bird, on the round of his chair behind him, and peeped over his shoulder.

'Oh, Uncle Tom! what funny things you *are* making, there!'

'I'm trying to write to my poor old woman, Miss Eva, and my little chil'en,' said Tom, drawing the back of his hand over his eyes; 'but, somehow, I'm feard I shan't make it out.'

'I wish I could help you, Tom! I've learnt to write some. Last year I could make all the letters, but I'm afraid I've forgotten.'

So Eva put her little golden head close to his, and the two commenced a grave and anxious discussion, each one equally earnest, and about equally ignorant; and, with a deal of consulting and advising over every word, the composition began, as they both felt very sanguine, to look quite like writing.

'Yes, Uncle Tom, it really begins to look beautiful,' said Eva, gazing delightedly on it. 'How pleased your wife'll be, and the poor little children! Oh, it's a shame you ever had to go away from them! I mean to ask papa to let you go back, sometime.'

'Missis said that she would send down money for me, as soon as they could get it together,' said Tom. 'I'm 'spectin' she will. Young Mas'r George, he said he'd come for me; and he gave me this yer dollar as a sign;' and Tom drew from under his clothes the precious dollar.

'Oh, he'll certainly come, then!' said Eva. 'I'm so glad!'

'And I wanted to send a letter, you know, to let 'em know whar I was, and tell poor Chloe that I was well off, 'cause she felt so drefful, poor soul!'

'I say, Tom!' said St Clare's voice, coming in the door at this moment.

Tom and Eva both started.

'What's here?' said St Clare, coming up and looking at the slate.

'Oh, it's Tom's letter. I'm helping him to write it,' said Eva; 'isn't it nice?'

'I wouldn't discourage either of you,' said St Clare, 'but I rather think, Tom, you'd better get me to write your letter for you. I'll do it, when I come home from my ride.'

'It's very important he should write,' said Eva, 'because his mistress is going to send down money to redeem him, you know, papa; he told me they told him so.'

St Clare thought, in his heart, that this was probably only one of those things which good-natured owners say to their servants, to alleviate their horror of being sold, without any intention of fulfilling the expectation thus excited. But he did not make any audible comment upon it – only ordered Tom to get the horses out for a ride.

Tom's letter was written in due form for him that evening, and safely lodged in the post-office.

Miss Ophelia still persevered in her labours in the housekeeping line. It was universally agreed, among all the household, from Dinah down to the youngest urchin, that Miss Ophelia was decidedly 'curis' – a term by which a Southern servant implies that his or her betters don't exactly suit them.

The higher circle in the family – to wit, Adolph, Jane and Rosa – agreed that she was no lady; ladies never kept working about as she did; that she had no *air* at all; and they were surprised that she should be any relation of the St Clares. Even Marie declared that it was absolutely fatiguing to see Cousin Ophelia always so busy. And, in fact, Miss Ophelia's industry was so incessant as to lay some foundation for the complaint. She sewed and stitched away, from daylight till dark, with the energy of one who is pressed on by some immediate urgency; and then, when the light faded, and the work was folded away, with one turn out came the ever-ready knitting-work, and there she was again, going on as briskly as ever. It really was a labour to see her.

CHAPTER XX

Topsy

ONE MORNING, while Miss Ophelia was busy in some of her domestic cares, St Clare's voice was heard, calling her at the foot of the stairs.

'Come down here, cousin; I've something to show you.'

'What is it?' said Miss Ophelia, coming down, with her sewing in her hand.

'I've made a purchase for your department – see here,' said St Clare; and, with the word, he pulled along a little negro girl, about eight or nine years of age.

She was one of the blackest of her race; and her round, shining eyes, glittering as glass beads, moved with quick and restless glances over everything in the room. Her mouth, half open with astonishment at the wonders of the new mas'r's parlour, displayed a white and brilliant set of teeth. Her woolly hair was braided in sundry little tails, which stuck out in every direction. The expression of her face was an odd mixture of shrewdness and cunning, over which was oddly drawn, like a kind of veil, an expression of the most doleful gravity and solemnity. She was dressed in a single filthy, ragged garment, made of bagging; and stood with her hands demurely folded before her. Altogether, there was something odd and goblin-like about her appearance – something, as Miss Ophelia afterwards said, 'so heathenish', as to inspire that good lady with utter dismay; and, turning to St Clare, she said –

'Augustine, what in the world have you brought that thing here for?'

'For you to educate, to be sure, and train in the way she should go.[183] I thought she was rather a funny specimen in the Jim Crow line. Here, Topsy,' he added, giving a whistle, as a man would to call the attention of a dog, 'give us a song, now, and show us some of your dancing.'

The black, glassy eyes glittered with a kind of wicked drollery, and the thing struck up, in a clear shrill voice, an odd negro melody, to which she kept time with her hands and feet, spinning round, clapping her hands, knocking her knees together, in a wild, fantastic sort of time, and producing in her throat all those odd guttural sounds which distinguish the native music of her race; and finally, turning a summerset or two, and giving a prolonged closing note, as odd and unearthly as that of a steam-whistle, she came suddenly down on the carpet, and stood with her hands folded, and a most sanctimonious expression of meekness and solemnity over her face, only broken by the cunning glances which she shot askance from the corners of her eyes.

Miss Ophelia stood silent, perfectly paralysed with amazement.

St Clare, like a mischievous fellow as he was, appeared to enjoy her astonishment; and, addressing the child again, said –

'Topsy, this is your new mistress. I'm going to give you up to her; see now that you behave yourself.'

'Yes, mas'r,' said Topsy, with sanctimonious gravity, her wicked eyes twinkling as she spoke.

'You're going to be good, Topsy, you understand,' said St Clare.

'Oh, yes, mas'r,' said Topsy, with another twinkle, her hands still devoutly folded.

'Now, Augustine, what upon earth is this for?' said Miss Ophelia. 'Your house is so full of these little plagues, now, that a body can't set down their foot without treading on 'em. I get up in the morning, and find one asleep behind the door, and see one black head poking out from under the table, one lying on the doormat, and they are mopping and mowing and grinning between all the railings, and tumbling over the kitchen floor! What on earth did you want to bring this one for?'

'For you to educate – didn't I tell you? You're always preaching about educating. I thought I would make you a present of a fresh-caught specimen, and let you try your hand on her, and bring her up in the way she should go.'

'*I* don't want her, I am sure; I have more to do with 'em now than I want to.'

'That's you Christians, all over! You'll get up a society, and get some poor missionary to spend all his days among just such heathen. But let me see one of you that would take one into your house with you, and take the labour of their conversion on yourselves! No; when it comes to that, they are dirty and disagreeable, and it's too much care, and so on.'

'Augustine, you know I didn't think of it in that light,' said Miss Ophelia, evidently softening. 'Well, it might be a real missionary work,' said she, looking rather more favourably on the child.

St Clare had touched the right string. Miss Ophelia's conscientiousness was ever on the alert. 'But,' she added, 'I really didn't see the need of buying this one – there are enough now, in your house, to take all my time and skill.'

'Well, then, cousin,' said St Clare, drawing her aside, 'I ought to beg your pardon for my good-for-nothing speeches. You are so good, after all, that there's no sense in them. Why, the fact is, this concern belonged to a couple of drunken creatures that keep a low restaurant, that I have to pass by every day, and I was tired of hearing her screaming, and them beating and swearing at her. She looked bright and funny, too, as if something might be made of her; so I bought her, and I'll give her to you. Try, now, and give her a good orthodox New England bringing up, and see what it'll make of her. You know I haven't any gift that way; but I'd like you to try.'

'Well, I'll do what I can,' said Miss Ophelia; and she approached her new subject very much as a person might be supposed to approach a black spider, supposing them to have benevolent designs toward it.

'She's dreadfully dirty, and half naked,' she said.

'Well, take her downstairs, and make some of them clean and clothe her up.'

Miss Ophelia carried her to the kitchen regions.

'Don't see what Mas'r St Clare wants of 'nother nigger!' said Dinah, surveying the new arrival with no friendly air. 'Won't have her round under *my* feet, *I* know!'

'Pah!' said Rosa and Jane, with supreme disgust; 'let her keep out of our way! What in the world mas'r wanted another of these low niggers for, I can't see!'

'You go long! No more nigger dan you be, Miss Rosa,' said Dinah, who felt this last remark a reflection on herself. 'You seem to tink yourself white folks. You an't nerry one, black *nor* white. I'd like to be one or turrer.'

Miss Ophelia saw that there was nobody in the camp that would undertake to oversee the cleansing and dressing of the new arrival; and so she was forced to do it herself, with some very ungracious and reluctant assistance from Jane.

It is not for ears polite to hear the particulars of the first toilet of a neglected, abused child. In fact, in this world, multitudes must live and die in a state that it would be too great a shock to the nerves of their fellow-mortals even to hear described. Miss Ophelia had a good, strong, practical deal of resolution; and she went through all the disgusting details with heroic thoroughness, though, it must be confessed, with no very gracious air – for endurance was the utmost to which her principles could bring her. When she saw, on the back and shoulders of the child, great welts and calloused spots, ineffaceable marks of the system under which she had grown up thus far, her heart became pitiful within her.

'See there!' said Jane, pointing to the marks, 'don't that show she's a limb?[184] We'll have fine works with her, I reckon. I hate these nigger young uns! so disgustin'! I wonder that mas'r would buy her!'

The 'young un' alluded to heard all these comments with the subdued and doleful air which seemed habitual to her, only scanning with a keen and furtive glance of her flickering eyes, the ornaments which Jane wore in her ears. When arrayed at last in a suit of decent and whole clothing, her hair cropped short to her head, Miss Ophelia, with some satisfaction, said she looked more Christian-like than she did, and in her own mind began to mature some plans for her instruction.

Sitting down before her, she began to question her.

'How old are you, Topsy?'

'Dun 'no, missis,' said the image, with a grin that showed all her teeth.

'Don't know how old you are? Didn't anybody ever tell you? Who was your mother?'

'Never had none!' said the child, with another grin.

'Never had any mother? What do you mean? Where were you born?'

'Never was born!' persisted Topsy, with another grin, that looked so goblin-like, that, if Miss Ophelia had been at all nervous, she might have fancied that she had got hold of some sooty gnome from the land of Diablerie;[185] but Miss Ophelia was not nervous, but plain and businesslike, and she said, with some sternness –

'You mustn't answer me in that way, child; I'm not playing with you. Tell me where you were born, and who your father and mother were.'

'Never was born,' reiterated the creature, more emphatically; 'never had no father, nor mother, nor nothin'. I was raised by a speculator, with lots of others. Old Aunt Sue used to take car on us.'

The child was evidently sincere; and Jane, breaking into a short laugh, said –

'Laws, missis, there's heaps of 'em. Speculators buys 'em up cheap, when they's little, and gets 'em raised for market.'

'How long have you lived with your master and mistress?'

'Dun 'no, missis.'

'Is it a year, or more, or less?'

'Dun 'no, missis.'

'Laws, missis, those low negroes – they can't tell; they don't know anything about time,' said Jane; 'they don't know what a year is; they don't know their own ages.'

'Have you ever heard anything about God, Topsy?'

The child looked bewildered, but grinned as usual.

'Do you know who made you?'

'Nobody, as I knows on,' said the child, with a short laugh.

The idea appeared to amuse her considerably; for her eyes twinkled, and she added –

'I 'spect I grow'd. Don't think nobody never made me.'

'Do you know how to sew?' said Miss Ophelia, who thought she would turn her enquiries to something more tangible.

'No, missis.'

'What can you do? – what did you do for your master and mistress?'

'Fetch water, and wash dishes, and rub knives, and wait on folks.'

'Were they good to you?'

' 'Spect they was,' said the child, scanning Miss Ophelia cunningly.

Miss Ophelia rose from this encouraging colloquy; St Clare was leaning over the back of her chair.

'You find virgin soil there, cousin; put in your own ideas – you won't find many to pull up.'

Miss Ophelia's ideas of education, like all her other ideas, were very set and definite; and of the kind that prevailed in New England a century ago, and which are still preserved in some very retired and unsophisticated parts, where there are no railroads. As nearly as could be expressed, they could be comprised in very few words: to teach them to mind when they were spoken to; to teach them the catechism, sewing, and reading; and to whip them if they told lies. And though, of course, in the flood of light that is now poured on education,[186] these are left far away in the rear, yet it is an undisputed fact that our grandmothers raised some tolerably fair men and women under this regime, as many of us can remember and testify. At all events, Miss Ophelia knew of nothing else to do; and, therefore, applied her mind to her heathen with the best diligence she could command.

The child was announced and considered in the family as Miss Ophelia's girl; and, as she was looked upon with no gracious eye in the kitchen, Miss Ophelia resolved to confine her sphere of operation and instruction chiefly to her own chamber. With a self-sacrifice which some of our readers will appreciate, she resolved, instead of comfortably making her own bed, sweeping and dusting her own chamber – which she had hitherto done, in utter scorn of all offers of help from the chambermaid of the establishment – to condemn herself to the martyrdom of instructing Topsy to perform these operations. Ah, woe the day! Did any of our readers ever do the same, they will appreciate the amount of her self-sacrifice.

Miss Ophelia began with Topsy by taking her into her chamber the first morning, and solemnly commencing a course of instruction in the art and mystery of bed-making.

Behold, then, Topsy, washed and shorn of all the little braided tails wherein her heart had delighted, arrayed in a clean gown, with wellstarched apron, standing reverently before Miss Ophelia with an expression of solemnity well befitting a funeral.

'Now, Topsy, I'm going to show you just how my bed is to be made. I am very particular about my bed. You must learn exactly how to do it.'

'Yes, ma'am,' says Topsy, with a deep sigh, and a face of woeful earnestness.

'Now, Topsy, look here; this is the hem of the sheet – this is the right side of the sheet, and this is the wrong; will you remember?'

'Yes, ma'am,' says Topsy, with another sigh.

'Well, now the under sheet you must bring over the bolster – so – and tuck it clear down under the mattress nice and smooth, so, do you see?'

'Yes, ma'am,' said Topsy, with profound attention.

'But the upper sheet,' said Miss Ophelia, 'must be brought down in this way, and tucked under firm and smooth at the foot – so – the narrow hem at the foot.'

'Yes, ma'am,' said Topsy, as before; but we will add, what Miss Ophelia did not see, that, during the time when the good lady's back was turned, in the zeal of her manipulations, the young disciple had contrived to snatch a pair of gloves and a ribbon, which she had adroitly slipped into her sleeves, and stood with her hands dutifully folded, as before.

'Now, Topsy, let's see *you* do this,' said Miss Ophelia, pulling off the clothes, and seating herself.

Topsy, with great gravity and adroitness, went through the exercise completely to Miss Ophelia's satisfaction; smoothing the sheets, patting out every wrinkle, and exhibiting, through the whole process, a gravity and seriousness with which her instructress was greatly edified. By an unlucky slip, however, a fluttering fragment of the ribbon hung out of one of her sleeves, just as she was finishing, and caught Miss Ophelia's attention. Instantly she pounced upon it. 'What's this? You naughty, wicked child – you've been stealing this!'

The ribbon was pulled out of Topsy's own sleeve, yet was she not in the least disconcerted; she only looked at it with an air of the most surprised and unconscious innocence.

'Laws! why, that ar's Miss Feely's ribbon, an't it? How could it a got caught in my sleeve?'

'Topsy, you naughty girl, don't you tell me a lie, you stole that ribbon!'

'Missis, I declar for't, I didn't; never seed it till dis yer blessed minnit.'

'Topsy,' said Miss Ophelia, 'don't you know it's wicked to tell lies?'

'I never tells no lies, Miss Feely,' said Topsy, with virtuous gravity; 'it's jist the truth I've been a tellin' now, and an't nothin' else.'

'Topsy, I shall have to whip you, if you tell lies so.'

'Laws, missis, if you's to whip all day, couldn't say no other way,' said Topsy, beginning to blubber. 'I never seed dat ar, it must a got caught in my sleeve. Miss Feely must have left it on the bed, and it got caught in the clothes, and so got in my sleeve.'

Miss Ophelia was so indignant at the barefaced lie, that she caught the child and shook her.

'Don't you tell me that again!'

The shake brought the gloves on to the floor, from the other sleeve.

'There, you!' said Miss Ophelia, 'will you tell me now, you didn't steal the ribbon?'

Topsy now confessed to the gloves, but still persisted in denying the ribbon.

'Now, Topsy,' said Miss Ophelia, 'if you'll confess all about it, I won't whip you this time.' Thus adjured, Topsy confessed to the ribbon and gloves, with woeful protestations of penitence.

'Well, now, tell me. I know you must have taken other things since you have been in the house, for I let you run about all day yesterday. Now, tell me if you took anything, and I shan't whip you.'

'Laws, missis! I took Miss Eva's red thing she wars on her neck.'

'You did, you naughty child! Well, what else?'

'I took Rosa's yer-rings – them red ones.'

'Go bring them to me this minute, both of 'em.'

'Laws, missis! I can't, they's burnt up!'

'Burnt up! what a story! Go get 'em, or I'll whip you.'

Topsy, with loud protestations, and tears, and groans, declared that she *could* not. 'They's burnt up – they was.'

'What did you burn 'em up for?' said Miss Ophelia.

' 'Cause I's wicked, I is. I's mighty wicked, anyhow. I can't help it.'

Just at this moment, Eva came innocently into the room, with the identical coral necklace on her neck.

'Why, Eva, where did you get your necklace?' said Miss Ophelia.

'Get it? Why, I've had it on all day,' said Eva.

'Did you have it on yesterday?'

'Yes; and what is funny, Aunty, I had it on all night. I forgot to take it off when I went to bed.'

Miss Ophelia looked perfectly bewildered; the more so, as Rosa at that instant, came into the room, with a basket of newly-ironed linen poised on her head, and the coral eardrops shaking in her ears!

'I'm sure I can't tell anything what to do with such a child!' she said, in despair. 'What in the world did you tell me you took those things for, Topsy?'

'Why, missis said I must 'fess; and I couldn't think of nothin' else to 'fess,' said Topsy, rubbing her eyes.

'But, of course, I didn't want you to confess things you didn't do,' said Miss Ophelia; 'that's telling a lie, just as much as the other.'

'Laws, now, is it?' said Topsy, with an air of innocent wonder.

'La, there an't any such thing as truth in that limb,' said Rosa, looking indignantly at Topsy. 'If I was Mas'r St Clare, I'd whip her till the blood run, I would! I'd let her catch it!'

'No, no, Rosa,' said Eva, with an air of command, which the child could assume at times; 'you mustn't talk so, Rosa. I can't bear to hear it.'

'La sakes! Miss Eva, you's so good, you don't know nothing how to get along with niggers. There's no way but to cut 'em well up, I tell ye.'

'Rosa!' said Eva, 'hush! Don't you say another word of that sort.' And the eye of the child flashed, and her cheek deepened its colour.

Rosa was cowed in a moment.

'Miss Eva has got the St Clare blood in her, that's plain. She can speak, for all the world, just like her papa,' she said, as she passed out of the room.

Eva stood looking at Topsy.

There stood the two children, representatives of the two extremes of society. The fair, high-bred child, with her golden head, her deep eyes, her spiritual, noble brow, and prince-like movements; and her black, keen, subtle, cringing, yet acute neighbour. They stood, the representatives of their races. The Saxon, born of ages of cultivation, command, education, physical and moral eminence; the Afric, born of ages of oppression, submission, ignorance, toil, and vice!

Something, perhaps, of such thoughts struggled through Eva's mind. But a child's thoughts are rather dim, undefined instincts; and in Eva's noble nature many such were yearning and working, for which she had no power of utterance. When Miss Ophelia expatiated on Topsy's naughty, wicked conduct, the child looked perplexed and sorrowful, but said, sweetly –

'Poor Topsy, why need you steal? You're going to be taken good care of now. I'm sure I'd rather give you anything of mine, than have you steal it.'

It was the first word of kindness the child had ever heard in her life; and the sweet tone and manner struck strangely on the wild, rude heart, and a sparkle of something like a tear shone in the keen, round, glittering eye; but it was followed by the short laugh and habitual grin. No! the ear that has never heard anything but abuse is strangely incredulous of anything so heavenly as kindness; and Topsy only thought Eva's speech something funny and inexplicable – she did not believe it.

But what was to be done with Topsy? Miss Ophelia found the case a puzzler; her rules for bringing up didn't seem to apply. She thought she would take time to think of it; and, by the way of gaining time, and in hopes of some indefinite moral virtues supposed to be inherent in dark closets, Miss Ophelia shut Topsy up in one till she had arranged her ideas further on the subject.

'I don't see,' said Miss Ophelia to St Clare, 'how I'm going to manage that child, without whipping her.'

'Well, whip her, then, to your heart's content; I'll give you full power to do what you like.'

'Children always have to be whipped,' said Miss Ophelia; 'I never heard of bringing them up without.'

'Oh, well, certainly,' said St Clare; 'do as you think best. Only I'll make one suggestion: I've seen this child whipped with a poker and knocked down with the shovel or tongs, whichever came handiest; seeing that she is used to that style of operation, I think your whippings will have to be pretty energetic, to make much impression.'

'What is to be done with her, then?' said Miss Ophelia.

'You have started a serious question,' said St Clare; 'I wish you'd answer it. What is to be done with a human being that can be governed only by the lash? – *that* fails – it's a very common state of things down here!'

'I'm sure I don't know; I never saw such a child as this.'

'Such children are very common among us, and such men and women, too. How are they to be governed?' said St Clare.

'I'm sure it's more than I can say,' said Miss Ophelia.

'Or I either,' said St Clare. 'The horrid cruelties and outrages that once and a while find their way into the papers – such cases as Prue's, for example – what do they come from? In many cases, it is a gradual hardening process on both sides – the owner growing more and more cruel, and the servant more and more callous. Whipping and abuse are like laudanum;[187] you have to double the dose as the sensibilities decline. I saw this very early when I became an owner; and I resolved never to begin, because I did not know when I should stop; and I resolved, at least, to protect my own moral nature. The consequence is, that my servants act like spoiled children; but I think that better than for us both to be brutalised together. You have talked a great deal about our responsibilities in educating, cousin. I really wanted you to try with one child who is a specimen of thousands among us.'

'It is your system makes such children,' said Miss Ophelia.

'I know it; but they are *made* – they exist – and what is to be done with them?'

'Well, I can't say I thank you for the experiment. But, then, as it appears to be a duty, I shall persevere and try, and do the best I can,' said Miss Ophelia; and Miss Ophelia, after this, did labour, with a commendable degree of zeal and energy, on her new subject. She instituted regular hours and employments for her, and undertook to teach her to read and to sew.

In the former art the child was quick enough. She learned her letters as if by magic, and was very soon able to read plain reading; but the sewing was a more difficult matter. The creature was as lithe as a cat and as active as a monkey, and the confinement of sewing was her abomination; so she broke her needles, threw them slyly out of windows, or down in chinks of the walls; she tangled, broke, or dirtied her thread, or, with a sly movement, would throw a spool away altogether. Her motions were almost as quick as those of a practised conjurer, and her command of her face quite as great; and though Miss Ophelia could not help feeling that so many accidents could not possibly happen in succession, yet she could not, without a watchfulness which would leave her no time for anything else, detect her.

Topsy was soon a noted character in the establishment. Her talent for every species of drollery, grimace, and mimicry – for dancing, tumbling, climbing, singing, whistling, imitating every sound that hit her fancy – seemed inexhaustible. In her play-hours, she invariably had every child in the establishment at her heels, open-mouthed with admiration and wonder – not excepting Miss Eva, who appeared to be fascinated by her wild diablerie, as a dove is sometimes charmed by a glittering serpent. Miss Ophelia was uneasy that Eva should fancy Topsy's society so much, and implored St Clare to forbid it.

'Poh! let the child alone,' said St Clare. 'Topsy will do her good.'

'But so depraved a child – are you not afraid she will teach her some mischief?'

'She can't teach her mischief; she might teach it to some children, but evil rolls off Eva's mind like dew off a cabbage-leaf, not a drop sinks in.'

'Don't be too sure,' said Miss Ophelia. 'I know I'd never let a child of mine play with Topsy.'

'Well, your children needn't,' said St Clare, 'but mine may; if Eva could have been spoiled, it would have been done years ago.'

Topsy was at first despised and contemned by the upper servants. They soon found reason to alter their opinion. It was very soon discovered that whoever cast an indignity on Topsy was sure to meet with some inconvenient accident shortly after – either a pair of earrings or some cherished trinket would be missing, or an article of dress would be suddenly found utterly ruined, or the person would stumble accidentally into a pail of hot water, or a libation of dirty slop would unaccountably deluge them from above when in full gala dress; and on all these occasions, when investigation was made, there was nobody found to stand sponsor for the indignity. Topsy was cited, and had up before all the domestic judicatories, time and again; but always sustained her examinations with most edifying innocence and gravity of appearance. Nobody in the world ever doubted who did the things; but not a scrap of any direct evidence could be found to establish the suppositions, and Miss Ophelia was too just to feel at liberty to proceed to any lengths without it.

The mischiefs done were always so nicely timed, also, as further to shelter the aggressor. Thus, the times for revenge on Rosa and Jane, the two chambermaids, were always chosen in those seasons when (as not unfrequently happened) they were in disgrace with their mistress, when any complaint from them would of course meet with no sympathy. In short, Topsy soon made the household understand the propriety of letting her alone; and she was let alone, accordingly.

Topsy was smart and energetic in all manual operations, learning everything that was taught her with surprising quickness. With a few lessons, she had learned to do the proprieties of Miss Ophelia's chamber in a way with which even that particular lady could find no fault. Mortal hands could not lay spread smoother, adjust pillows more accurately, sweep and dust and arrange more perfectly than Topsy, when she chose – but she didn't very often choose. If Miss Ophelia, after three or four days of careful and patient supervision, was so sanguine as to suppose that Topsy had at last fallen into her way, could do without overlooking, and so go off and busy herself about something else, Topsy would hold a perfect carnival of confusion, for some one or two hours. Instead of making the bed, she would amuse herself with pulling off the pillow-cases, butting her woolly head among the pillows, till it would sometimes be grotesquely ornamented with feathers sticking out in various directions; she would climb the posts, and hang head downward from the tops; flourish the sheets and spreads all over the apartment; dress the bolster up in Miss Ophelia's night-clothes, and enact various scenic performances with that – singing and whistling, and making grimaces at herself in the looking-glass; in short, as Miss Ophelia phrased it, 'raising Cain'[188] generally.

On one occasion, Miss Ophelia found Topsy with her very best scarlet India Canton crape shawl[189] wound round her head for turban, going on with her rehearsals before the glass in great style – Miss Ophelia having, with carelessness most unheard-of in her, left the key for once in her drawer.

'Topsy!' she would say, when at the end of all patience, 'what does make you act so?'

'Dun 'no, missis – I 'spects 'cause I's so wicked!'

'I don't know anything what I shall do with you, Topsy.'

'Law, missis, you must whip me; my old missis allers whipped me. I an't used to workin' unless I gets whipped.'

'Why, Topsy. I don't want to whip you. You can do well, if you've a mind to; what is the reason you won't?'

'Laws, missis, I's used to whippin'; I 'spects it's good for me.'

Miss Ophelia tried the recipe, and Topsy invariably made a terrible commotion, screaming, groaning and imploring, though half an hour afterwards, when roosted on some projection of the balcony, and surrounded by a flock of admiring 'young uns', she would express the utmost contempt of the whole affair.

'Law, Miss Feely whip! – wouldn't kill a skeeter, her whippin's. Oughter see how old mas'r made the flesh fly; old mas'r know'd how!'

Topsy always made great capital of her own sins and enormities, evidently considering them as something peculiarly distinguishing.

'Law, you niggers,' she would say to some of her auditors, 'does you know you's all sinners? Well, you is, everybody is. White folks is sinners too – Miss Feely says so; but I 'spects niggers is the biggest ones; but lor! ye an't any on ye up to me. I's so awful wicked there can't nobody do nothin' with me. I used to keep old missis a swarin' at me half de time. I 'spects I's the wickedest critter in the world;' and Topsy would cut a summerset, and come up brisk and shining on to a higher perch, and evidently plume herself on the distinction.

Miss Ophelia busied herself very earnestly on Sundays, teaching Topsy the catechism. Topsy had an uncommon verbal memory, and committed with a fluency that greatly encouraged her instructress.

'What good do you expect it is going to do her?' said St Clare.

'Why, it always has done children good. It's what children always have to learn, you know,' said Miss Ophelia.

'Understand it or not,' said St Clare.

'Oh, children never understand it at the time; but, after they are grown up it'll come to them.'

'Mine hasn't come to me yet,' said St Clare, 'though I'll bear testimony that you put it into me pretty thoroughly when I was a boy.'

'Ah, you were always good at learning, Augustine. I used to have great hopes of you,' said Miss Ophelia.

'Well, haven't you now?' said St Clare.

'I wish you were as good as you were when you were a boy, Augustine.'

'So do I, that's a fact, cousin,' said St Clare. 'Well, go ahead and catechise Topsy; maybe you'll make out something yet.'

Topsy, who had stood like a black statue during this discussion, with hands decently folded, now, at a signal from Miss Ophelia, went on –

'Our first parents, being left to the freedom of their own will, fell from the state wherein they were created.'[190]

Topsy's eyes twinkled, and she looked enquiringly.

'What is it, Topsy?' said Miss Ophelia.

'Please, missis, was dat ar state Kintuck?'

'What state, Topsy?'

'Dat state dey fell out of. I used to hear mas'r tell how we came down from Kentuck.'

St Clare laughed.

'You'll have to give her a meaning, or she'll make one,' said he. 'There seems to be a theory of emigration suggested there.'

'Oh, Augustine, be still,' said Miss Ophelia; 'how can I do anything if you'll be laughing?'

'Well I won't disturb the exercises again, on my honour;' and St Clare took his paper into the parlour, and sat down till Topsy had finished her recitations. They were all very well, only that now and then she would oddly transpose some important words, and persist in the mistake, in spite of every effort to the contrary; and St Clare after all his promises of goodness, took a wicked pleasure in these mistakes, calling Topsy to him whenever he had a mind to amuse himself, and getting her to repeat the offending passages, in spite of Miss Ophelia's remonstrances.

'How do you think I can do anything with the child, if you will go on so, Augustine?' she would say.

'Well, It is too bad, I won't again; but I do like to hear the droll little image stumble over those big words!'

'But you confirm her in the wrong way.'

'What's the odds? One word is as good as another to her.'

'You wanted me to bring her up right; and you ought to remember she is a reasonable creature, and be careful of your influence over her.'

'Oh, dismal! so I ought; but, as Topsy herself says, I's so wicked!'

In very much this way Topsy's training proceeded, for a year or two – Miss Ophelia worrying herself, from day to day, with her, as a kind of chronic plague, to whose inflictions she became, in time, as accustomed as persons sometimes do to the neuralgia or sick headache.

St Clare took the same kind of amusement in the child that a man might in the tricks of a parrot or a pointer. Topsy, whenever her sins brought her into disgrace in other quarters, always took refuge behind his chair; and St Clare, in one way or other, would make peace for her. From him she got many a stray picayune, which she laid out in nuts and candies, and distributed, with careless generosity, to all the children in the family; for Topsy, to do her justice, was good-natured and liberal, And only spiteful in self-defiance. She is fairly introduced into our *corps de ballet*,[191] and will figure from time to time, in her turn, with other performers.

CHAPTER XXI

Kentuck

OUR READERS may not be unwilling to glance back, for a brief interval, at Uncle Tom's cabin, on the Kentucky farm, and see what has been transpiring among those whom he had left behind.

It was late in the summer afternoon, and the doors and windows of the large parlour all stood open, to invite any stray breeze that might feel in a good humour to enter. Mr Shelby sat in a large hall opening into the room, and running through the whole length of the house to a balcony on either end. Leisurely tipped back in one chair, with his heels in another, he was enjoying his after-dinner cigar. Mrs Shelby sat in the door, busy about some fine sewing; she seemed like one who had something on her mind, which she was seeking an opportunity to introduce.

'Do you know,' she said, 'that Chloe has had a letter from Tom?'

'Ah! has she? Tom's got some friend there, it seems. How is the old boy?'

'He has been bought by a very fine family, I should think,' said Mrs Shelby, 'is kindly treated, and has not much to do.'

'Ah! well, I'm glad of it – very glad,' said Mr Shelby, heartily. 'Tom, I suppose, will get reconciled to a Southern residence – hardly want to come up here again.'

'On the contrary, he enquires very anxiously,' said Mrs Shelby, 'when the money for his redemption is to be raised.'

'I'm sure *I* don't know,' said Mr Shelby. 'Once get business running wrong, there does seem to be no end to it. It's like jumping from one bog to another, all through a swamp; borrow of one to pay another, and then borrow of another to pay one – and these confounded notes falling due before a man has time to smoke a cigar and turn round – dunning letters and dunning messages – all scamper and hurry-scurry.'

'It does seem to me, my dear, that something might be done to straighten matters. Suppose we sell off all the horses, and sell one of your farms, and pay up square?'

'Oh! ridiculous, Emily! You are the finest woman in Kentucky, but still you haven't sense to know that you don't understand business; women never do, and never can.'

'But, at least,' said Mrs Shelby, 'could not you give me some little insight into yours? – a list of all your debts, at least, and of all that is owed to you, and let me try and see if I can't help you to economise.'

'Oh, bother! don't plague me, Emily! – I can't tell exactly. I know somewhere about what things are likely to be; but there's no trimming and squaring my affairs, as Chloe trims crust off her pies. You don't know anything about business, I tell you.'

And Mr Shelby, not knowing any other way of enforcing his ideas, raised his voice; a mode of arguing very convenient and convincing, when a gentleman is discussing matters of business with his wife.

Mrs Shelby ceased talking, with something of a sigh. The fact was, that though her husband had stated she was a woman, she had a clean energetic, practical mind, and a force of character every way superior to that of her husband; so that it would not have been so very absurd a supposition to have allowed her capable of managing, as Mr Shelby supposed. Her heart was set on performing her promise to Tom and Aunt Chloe, and she sighed as discouragements thickened around her.

'Don't you think we might in some way contrive to raise that money? Poor Aunt Chloe! her heart is so set on it!'

'I'm sorry, if it is. I think I was premature in promising. I'm not sure, now, but it's the best way to tell Chloe, and let her make up her mind to it. Tom'll have another wife in a year or two, and she had better take up with somebody else.'

'Mr Shelby, I have taught my people that their marriages are as sacred as ours. I never could think of giving Chloe such advice.'

'It's a pity, wife, that you have burdened them with a morality above their condition and prospects. I always thought so.'

'It's only the morality of the Bible, Mr Shelby.'

'Well, well, Emily, I don't pretend to interfere with your religious notions; only they seem extremely unfitted for people in that condition.'

'They are, indeed,' said Mrs Shelby, 'and that is why, from my soul, I hate the whole thing. I tell you, my dear, *I* cannot absolve myself from the promises I make to these helpless creatures. If I can get the money no other way, I will take music-scholars; I could get enough, I know, and earn the money myself.'

'You wouldn't degrade yourself that way, Emily? I never could consent to it.'

'Degrade! would it degrade me as much as to break my faith with the helpless? No, indeed!'

'Well, you are always heroic and transcendental,' said Mr Shelby, 'but I think you had better think before you undertake such a piece of Quixotism.'[192]

Here the conversation was interrupted by the appearance of Aunt Chloe, at the end of the veranda.

'If you please, missis – ' said she.

'Well, Chloe, what is it?' said her mistress, rising, and going to the end of the balcony.

'If missis would come and look at dis yer lot o' poetry.'

Chloe had a particular fancy for calling poultry poetry, an application of language in which she always persisted, notwithstanding frequent corrections and advisings from the young members of the family.

'La sakes!' she would say, 'I can't see; one jis good as turrer – poetry suthin' good, anyhow;' and so poetry Chloe continued to call it.

Mrs Shelby smiled as she saw a prostrate lot of chickens and ducks, over which Chloe stood, with a very grave face of consideration.

'I'm a thinkin' whether missis would be a havin a chicken pie o' dese yer.'

'Really, Aunt Chloe, I don't much care; serve them any way you like.'

Chloe stood handling them over abstractedly; it was quite evident that the chickens were not what she was thinking of. At last, with the short laugh with which her tribe often introduced a doubtful proposal, she said –

'Laws me, missis! what should mas'r and missis be a troublin' theirselves 'bout de money, and not a usin what's right in der hands?' and Chloe laughed again.

'I don't understand you, Chloe,' said Mrs Shelby, nothing doubting, from her knowledge of Chloe's manner, that she had heard every word of the conversation that had passed between her and her husband.

'Why, laws me, missis!' said Chloe, laughing again, 'other folks hires out der niggers and makes money on 'em! Don't keep sich a tribe eatin' 'em out of house and home.'

'Well, Chloe, who do you propose that we should hire out?'

'Laws! I an't a proposin' nothin'; only Sam he said der was one of dese yer *perfectioners*, dey calls 'em, in Louisville, said he wanted a good hand at cake and pastry; and said he'd give four dollars a week to one, he did.'

'Well, Chloe.'

'Well, laws, I's a thinkin, missis, it's time Sally was put along to be doin' something. Sally's been under my care, now, dis some time, and she does most as well as me, considerin'; and if missis would only let me go, I would help fetch up de money. I an't afraid to put my cake, nor pies nother, 'long side no *perfectioner's*.'

'Confectioner's, Chloe.'

'Law sakes, missis! 'tan't no odds; words is so curis, can't never get 'em right!'

'But, Chloe, do you want to leave your children?'

'Laws, missis! de boys is big enough to do day's works; dey does well enough; and Sally, she'll take de baby – she's such a peart young un, she won't take no lookin' arter.'

'Louisville is a good way off.'

'Law sakes! who's afeard? it's down river, somer near my old man, perhaps?' said Chloe, speaking the last in the tone of a question, and looking at Mrs Shelby.

'No, Chloe; it's many a hundred miles off,' said Mrs Shelby.

Chloe's countenance fell.

'Never mind; your going there shall bring you nearer, Chloe. Yes, you may go; and your wages shall every cent of them be laid aside for your husband's redemption.'

As when a bright sunbeam turns a dark cloud to silver, so Chloe's dark face brightened immediately; it really shone.

'Laws! if missis isn't too good! I was thinking of dat ar very thing; 'cause I shouldn't need no clothes, nor shoes, nor nothin'. I could save every cent. How many weeks is der in a yer, missis?'

'Fifty-two,' said Mrs Shelby.

'Laws! now, dere is? and four dollars for each on 'em. Why, how much'd dat ar be?'

'Two hundred and eight dollars,' said Mrs Shelby.

'Why–e!' said Chloe, with an accent of surprise and delight; 'and how long would it take me to work it out, missis?'

'Some four or five years, Chloe; but, then, you needn't do it all, I shall add something to it.'

'I wouldn't hear to missis' givin lessons nor nothin'. Mas'r's quite right in dat ar; 'twouldn't do no ways. I hope none our family ever be brought to dat ar, while I's got hands.'

'Don't fear, Chloe; I'll take care of the honour of the family,' said Mrs Shelby, smiling. 'But when do you expect to go?'

'Well, I warn't expectin' nothin'; only Sam, he's a gwine to de river with some colts, and he said I could go long with him; so I jes put my things together. If missis was willin', I'd go with Sam tomorrow mornin', if missis would write my pass, and write me a commendation.'

'Well, Chloe, I'll attend to it, if Mr Shelby has no objections. I must speak to him.'

Mrs Shelby went upstairs, and Aunt Chloe, delighted, went out to her cabin, to make her preparation.

'Law sakes, Mas'r George! ye didn't know I's a gwine to Louisville tomorrow!' she said to George, as, entering her cabin, he found her busy in sorting over her baby's clothes. 'I thought I'd jis look over Sis's things, and get 'em straightened up. But I'm gwine, Mas'r George – gwine to have four dollars a week; and missis is gwine to lay it all up, to buy back my old man agin!'

'Whew!' said George, 'here's a stroke of business, to be sure! How are you going?'

'Tomorrow, wid Sam. And now, Mas'r George, I knows you'll jis sit down and write to my old man, and tell him all about it – won't ye?'

'To be sure,' said George; 'Uncle Tom'll be right glad to hear from us. I'll go right in the house, for paper and ink; and then, you know, Aunt Chloe, I can tell about the new colts and all.'

'Sartin, sartin, Mas'r George; you go 'long, and I'll get ye up a bit o' chicken, or some sich; ye won't have many more suppers wid yer poor old aunty.'

CHAPTER XXII

'The Grass Withereth – the Flower Fadeth'[193]

LIFE PASSES with us all, a day at a time; so it passed with our friend
Tom, till two years were gone. Though parted from all his soul held
dear, and though often yearning for what lay beyond, still was he never
positively and consciously miserable; for, so well is the harp of human
feeling strung, that nothing but a crash that breaks every string can
wholly mar its harmony; and, on looking back to seasons which in
review appear to us as those of deprivation and trial we can remember
that each hour, as it glided, brought its diversions and alleviations, so
that, though not happy wholly, we were not, either, wholly miserable.

Tom read in his only literary cabinet, of one who had 'learned, in
whatsoever state he was, therewith to be content'.[194] It seemed to him
good and reasonable doctrine, and accorded well with the settled and
thoughtful habit which he had acquired from the reading of that same
book.

His letter homeward, as we related in the last chapter, was in due
time answered by Master George, in a good, round, schoolboy hand,
that Tom said might be read 'most acrost the room'. It contained
various refreshing items of home intelligence, with which our reader is
fully acquainted; stated how Aunt Chloe had been hired out to a
confectioner in Louisville, where her skill in the pastry line was gaining
wonderful sums of money, all of which, Tom was informed, was to be
laid up to go to make up the sum of his redemption money; Mose and
Pete were thriving, and the baby was trotting all about the house,
under the care of Sally and the family generally.

Tom's cabin was shut up for the present; but George expatiated
brilliantly on ornaments and additions to be made to it when Tom
came back.

The rest of this letter gave a list of George's school studies, each one
headed by a flourishing capital; and also told the names of four new
colts that had appeared on the premises since Tom left; and stated, in
the same connection, that father and mother were well. The style of
the letter was decidedly concise and terse; but Tom thought it the most

wonderful specimen of composition that had appeared in modern times. He was never tired of looking at it, and even held a council with Eva on the expediency of getting it framed, to hang up in his room. Nothing but the difficulty of arranging it so that both sides of the page would show at once, stood in the way of this undertaking.

The friendship between Tom and Eva had grown with the child's growth. It would be hard to say what place she held in the soft, impressible heart of her faithful attendant. He loved her as something frail and earthly, yet almost worshipped her as something heavenly and divine. He gazed on her as the Italian sailor gazes on his image of the child Jesus – with a mixture of reverence and tenderness; and to humour her graceful fancies, and meet those thousand simple wants which invest childhood like a many-coloured rainbow, was Tom's chief delight. In the market, at morning, his eyes were always on the flower-stalls for rare bouquets for her, and the choicest peach or orange was slipped into his pocket to give to her when he came back; and the sight that pleased him most was her sunny head looking out the gate for his distant approach, and her childish question, 'Well, Uncle Tom, what have you got for me today?'

Nor was Eva less zealous in kind offices, in return. Though a child, she was a beautiful reader; a fine, musical ear, a quick poetic fancy, and an instinctive sympathy with what is grand and noble, made her such a reader of the Bible as Tom had never before heard. At first she read to please her humble friend; but soon her own earnest nature threw out its tendrils, and wound itself around the majestic book; and Eva loved it, because it woke in her strange yearnings, and strong, dim emotions, such as impassioned, imaginative children love to feel.

The parts that pleased her most were the Revelations and the Prophecies[195] – parts whose dim and wondrous imagery, and fervent language impressed her the more, that she questioned vainly of their meaning; and she and her simple friend, the old child and the young one, felt just alike about it. All that they knew was that they spoke of a glory to be revealed – a wondrous something yet to come, wherein their soul rejoiced, yet knew not why; and though it be not so in the physical, yet in moral science that which cannot be understood is not always profitless. For the soul awakes, a trembling stranger, between two dim eternities – the eternal past, the eternal future. The light shines only on a small space around her; therefore, she needs must yearn towards the unknown; and the voices and shadowy movings which come to her from out the cloudy pillar of inspiration have each one echoes and answers in her own expecting nature. Its mystic imageries are so many talismans and gems inscribed with unknown hieroglyphics: she folds them in her bosom, and expects to read them when she passes beyond the veil.

At this time in our story, the whole St Clare establishment is, for the time being, removed to their villa on Lake Pontchartrain. The heats of summer had driven all who were able to leave the sultry and unhealthy city to seek the shores of the lake, and its cool sea-breezes.

St Clare's villa was an East Indian cottage, surrounded by light verandas of bamboo-work, and opening on all sides into gardens and pleasure-grounds. The common sitting-room opened on to a large garden, fragrant with every picturesque plant and flower of the tropics, where winding paths ran down to the very shores of the lake whose silvery sheet of water lay there, rising and falling in the sunbeams – a picture never for an hour the same, yet every hour more beautiful.

It is now one of those intensely golden sunsets which kindles the whole horizon into one blaze of glory, and makes the water another sky. The lake lay in rosy or golden streaks, save where white-winged vessels glided hither and thither, like so many spirits, and little golden stars twinkled through the glow, and looked down at themselves as they trembled in the water.

Tom and Eva were seated on a little mossy seat, in an arbour at the foot of the garden. It was Sunday evening, and Eva's Bible lay open on her knee. She read, 'And I saw a sea of glass, mingled with fire.'[196]

'Tom,' said Eva, suddenly stopping, and pointing to the lake, 'there 'tis.'

'What, Miss Eva?'

'Don't you see – there?' said the child, pointing to the glassy water, which, as it rose and fell, reflected the golden glow of the sky. 'There's a "sea of glass, mingled with fire".'

'True enough, Miss Eva,' said Tom; and Tom sang –

> 'Oh, had I the wings of the morning,
>   I'd fly away to Canaan's shore;
> Bright angels should convey me home,
>   To the New Jerusalem.'[197]

'Where do you suppose new Jerusalem is, Uncle Tom?' said Eva.

'Oh, up in the clouds, Miss Eva.'

'Then I think I see it,' said Eva. 'Look in those clouds! they look like great gates of pearl;[198] and you can see beyond them – far, far off – it's all gold. Tom, sing about "spirits bright".'

Tom sang the words of a well-known Methodist hymn –

> 'I see a band of spirits bright,
>   That taste the glories there;
> They all are robed in spotless white,
>   And conquering palms they bear.'[199]

'Uncle Tom, I've seen *them*,' said Eva.

Tom had no doubt of it all; it did not surprise him in the least. If Eva had told him she had been to heaven, he would have thought it entirely probable.

'They come to me sometimes in my sleep, those spirits;' and Eva's eyes grew dreamy, and she hummed, in a low voice –

> 'They all are robed in spotless white,
>   And conquering palms they bear.

'Uncle Tom,' said Eva, 'I am going there.'

'Where, Miss Eva?'

The child rose, and pointed her little hand to the sky; the glow of evening lit her golden hair and flushed cheek with a kind of unearthly radiance, and her eyes were bent earnestly on the skies.

'I'm going *there*!' she said, 'to the spirits bright, Tom; *I'm going, before long*.'

The faithful old heart felt a sudden thrust; and Tom thought how often he had noticed, within six months, that Eva's little hands had grown thinner, and her skin more transparent, and her breath shorter; and how, when she ran or played in the garden, as she once could for hours, she became soon so tired and languid. He had heard Miss Ophelia speak often enough of a cough, that all her medicaments could not cure; and even now that fervent cheek and little hand were burning with hectic fever; and yet the thought that Eva's words suggested had never come to him till now.

Has there ever been a child like Eva?[200] Yes, there have been; but their names are always on gravestones, and their sweet smiles, their heavenly eyes, their singular words and ways, are among the buried treasures of yearning hearts. In how many families do you hear the legend that all the goodness and graces of the living are nothing to the peculiar charms of one who *is not*! It is as if heaven had an especial band of angels, whose office it was to sojourn for a season here, and endear to them the wayward human heart, that they might bear it upward with them in their homeward flight. When you see that deep, spiritual light in the eye – when the little soul reveals itself in words sweeter and wiser than the ordinary words of children – hope not to retain that child; for the seal of Heaven is on it, and the light of immortality looks out from its eyes.

Even so, beloved Eva! fair star of thy dwelling! Thou art passing away; but they that love thee dearest know it not.

The colloquy between Tom and Eva was interrupted by a hasty call from Miss Ophelia.

'Eva – Eva! – why, child, the dew is falling; you mustn't be out there!' Eva and Tom hastened in.

Miss Ophelia was old, and skilled in the tactics of nursing. She was from New England, and knew well the first guileful footsteps of that soft, insidious disease[201] which sweeps away so many of the fairest and loveliest and, before one fibre of life seems broken, seals them irrevocably for death.

She had noted the slight, dry cough, the daily brightening cheek; nor could the lustre of the eye, and the airy buoyancy born of fever, deceive her.

She tried to communicate her fears to St Clare; but he threw back her suggestions with a restless petulance, unlike his usual careless good-humour.

'Don't be croaking, cousin – I hate it!' he would say; 'don't you see that the child is only growing? Children always lose strength when they grow fast.'

'But she has that cough!'

'Oh, nonsense of that cough – it is not anything. She has taken a little cold, perhaps.'

'Well, that was just the way Eliza Jane was taken, and Ellen and Maria Sanders.'

'Oh, stop these hobgoblin nurse legends! You old hands have got so wise that a child cannot cough, or sneeze, but you see desperation and ruin at hand. Only take care of the child, keep her from the night air, and don't let her play too hard, and she'll do well enough.'

So St Clare said; but he grew nervous and restless. He watched Eva feverishly day by day, as might be told by the frequency with which he repeated over that 'the child was quite well' – that there wasn't anything in that cough – it was only some little stomach affection, such as children often had. But he kept by her more than before, took her oftener to ride with him, brought home every few days some receipt or strengthening mixture – 'not,' he said, 'that the child *needed* it, but then it would not do her any harm'.

If it must be told, the thing that struck a deeper pang to his heart than anything else was the daily increasing maturity of the child's mind and feelings. While still retaining all a child's fanciful graces, yet she often dropped, unconsciously, words of such a reach of thought, and strange unworldly wisdom, that they seemed to be an inspiration. At such times, St Clare would feel a sudden thrill, and clasp her in his arms, as if that fond clasp could save her; and his heart rose up with wild determination to keep her, never to let her go.

The child's whole heart and soul seemed absorbed in works of love and kindness. Impulsively generous she had always been; but there was a touching and womanly thoughtfulness about her now, that everyone noticed. She still loved to play with Topsy, and the various coloured children; but she now seemed rather a spectator than an actor of their plays, and she would sit for half an hour at a time laughing at the odd tricks of Topsy – and then a shadow would seem to pass across her face, her eyes grew misty, and her thoughts were afar.

'Mamma,' she said, suddenly, to her mother, one day, 'why don't we teach our servants to read?'

'What a question, child! People never do.'

'Why don't they?' said Eva.

'Because it is no use for them to read. It don't help them to work any better, and they are not made for anything else.'

'But they ought to read the Bible, mamma, to learn God's will.'

'Oh, they can get that read to them all *they* need.'

'It seems to me, mamma, the Bible is for everyone to read themselves. They need it a great many times when there is nobody to read it.'

'Eva, you are an odd child,' said her mother.

'Miss Ophelia has taught Topsy to read,' continued Eva.

'Yes, and you see how much good it does. Topsy is the worst creature I ever saw!'

'Here's poor Mammy!' said Eva. 'She does love the Bible so much, and wishes so she could read! And what will she do when I can't read to her?'

Marie was busy, turning over the contents of a drawer, as she answered –

'Well, of course, by and by, Eva, you will have other things to think of, besides reading the Bible round to servants. Not but that is very proper; I've done it myself, when I had health. But when you come to be dressing and going into company, you won't have time. See here!' she added, 'these jewels I'm going to give you when you come out. I wore them to my first ball. I can tell you, Eva, I made a sensation.'

Eva took the jewel-case, and lifted from it a diamond necklace. Her large, thoughtful eyes rested on them, but it was plain her thoughts were elsewhere.

'How sober you look, child!' said Marie.

'Are these worth a great deal of money, mamma?'

'To be sure, they are. Father sent to France for them They are worth a small fortune.'

'I wish I had them,' said Eva, 'to do what I pleased with!'

'What would you do with them?'

'I'd sell them, and buy a place in the free States, and take all our people there, and hire teachers, to teach them to read and write.'

Eva was cut short by her mother's laughing.

'Set up a boarding-school! Wouldn't you teach them to play on the piano, and paint on velvet?'

'I'd teach them to read their own Bible, and write their own letters, and read letters that are written to them,' said Eva, steadily. 'I know, mamma, it does come very hard on them that they can't do these things. Tom feels it – Mammy does – many do. I think it's wrong.'

'Come, come, Eva; you are only a child! You don't know anything about these things,' said Marie; 'besides, your talking makes my head ache.'

Marie always had a headache on hand for any conversation that did not exactly suit her. Eva stole away; but after that, she assiduously gave Mammy reading lessons.

CHAPTER XXIII

Henrique

ABOUT THIS TIME, St Clare's brother Alfred, with his eldest son, a boy of twelve, spent a day or two with the family at the lake.

No sight could be more singular and beautiful than that of these twin brothers. Nature, instead of instituting resemblances between them, had made them opposites on every point; yet a mysterious tie seemed to unite them in a closer friendship than ordinary.

They used to saunter, arm in arm, up and down the alleys and walks of the garden – Augustine, with his blue eyes and golden hair, his ethereally flexible form and vivacious features; and Alfred, dark-eyed, with haughty Roman profile, firmly-knit limbs, and decided bearing. They were always abusing each other's opinions and practices, and yet never a whit the less absorbed in each other's society; in fact, the very contrariety seemed to unite them.

Henrique, the eldest son of Alfred, was a noble, dark-eyed, princely boy, full of vivacity and spirit; and, from the first moment of introduction, seemed to be perfectly fascinated by the *spirituelle* graces of his cousin Evangeline.

Eva had a little pet pony, of a snowy whiteness. It was easy as a cradle, and as gentle as its little mistress; and this pony was now brought up to the back veranda by Tom, while a little mulatto boy of about thirteen led along a small black Arabian, which had just been imported, at a great expense, for Henrique.

Henrique had a boy's pride in his new possession; and, as he advanced and took the reins out of the hands of his little groom, he looked carefully over him, and his brow darkened.

'What's this, Dodo, you little lazy dog! you haven't rubbed my horse down this morning.'

'Yes, mas'r,' said Dodo, submissively; 'he got that dust on his own self.'

'You rascal, shut your mouth!' said Henrique, violently raising his riding-whip. 'How dare you speak?'

The boy was a handsome, bright-eyed mulatto, of just Henrique's size, and his curling hair hung round a high, bold forehead. He had white blood in his veins, as could be seen by the quick flush in his cheek, and the sparkle of his eye, as he eagerly tried to speak.

'Mas'r Henrique – !' he began.

Henrique struck him across the face with his riding-whip, and, seizing one of his arms, forced him on to his knees, and beat him till he was out of breath.

'There, you impudent dog! Now will you learn not to answer back when I speak to you? Take the horse back, and clean him properly. I'll teach you your place!'

'Young mas'r,' said Tom, 'I 'specs what he was gwine to say was, that the horse would roll when he was bringing him up from the stable; he's so full of spirits – that's the way he got that dirt on him; I looked to his cleaning.'

'You hold your tongue till you're asked to speak!' said Henrique, turning on his heel, and walking up the steps to speak to Eva, who stood in her riding-dress.

'Dear cousin, I'm sorry this stupid fellow has kept you waiting,' he said. 'Let's sit down here, on this seat, till they come. What's the matter, cousin? – you look sober.'

'How could you be so cruel and wicked to poor Dodo?' said Eva.

'Cruel – wicked!' said the boy, with unaffected surprise. 'What do you mean, dear Eva?'

'I don't want you to call me dear Eva, when you do so,' said Eva.

'Dear cousin, you don't know Dodo; it's the only way to manage him, he's so full of lies and excuses. The only way is to put him down at once – not let him open his mouth; that's the way papa manages.'

'But Uncle Tom said it was an accident, and he never tells what isn't true.'

'He's an uncommon old nigger, then!' said Henrique. 'Dodo will lie as fast as he can speak.'

'You frighten him into deceiving, if you treat him so.'

'Why, Eva, you've really taken such a fancy to Dodo, that I shall be jealous.'

'But you beat him, and he didn't deserve it.'

'Oh, well it may go for some time when he does, and don't get it. A few cuts never come amiss with Dodo – he's a regular spirit, I can tell you; but I won't beat him again before you, if it troubles you.'

Eva was not satisfied, but found it in vain to try to make her handsome cousin understand her feelings.

Dodo soon appeared, with the horses.

'Well, Dodo, you've done pretty well, this time,' said his young master, with a more gracious air. 'Come, now, and hold Miss Eva's horse, while I put her on to the saddle.'

Dodo came and stood by Eva's pony. His face was troubled; his eyes looked as if he had been crying.

Henrique, who valued himself on his gentlemanly adroitness in all matters of gallantry, soon had his fair cousin in the saddle, and, gathering the reins, placed them in her hands.

But Eva bent to the other side of the horse, where Dodo was standing, and said, as he relinquished the reins, 'That's a good boy, Dodo – thank you!'

Dodo looked up in amazement into the sweet young face; the blood rushed to his cheeks, and the tears to his eyes.

'Here, Dodo,' said his master, imperiously.

Dodo sprang and held the horse, while his master mounted.

'There's a picayune for you to buy candy with, Dodo,' said Henrique; 'go get some.'

And Henrique cantered down the walk after Eva. Dodo stood

looking after the two children. One had given him money; and one had given him what he wanted far more – a kind word, kindly spoken. Dodo had been only a few months away from his mother. His master had bought him at a slave warehouse, for his handsome face, to be a match to the handsome pony; and he was now getting his breaking in, at the hands of his young master.

The scene of the beating had been witnessed by the two brothers St Clare, from another part of the garden.

Augustine's cheek flushed; but he only observed, with his usual sarcastic carelessness, 'I suppose that's what we may call republican education, Alfred?'

'Henrique is a devil of a fellow, when his blood's up,' said Alfred, carelessly.

'I suppose you consider this an instructive practice for him,' said Augustine, dryly.

'I couldn't help it if I didn't. Henrique is a regular little tempest – his mother and I have given him up, long ago. But, then, that Dodo is a perfect sprite – no amount of whipping can hurt him.'

'And this by way of teaching Henrique the first verse of a republican's catechism, "All men are born free and equal"!'[202]

'Poh!' said Alfred; 'one of Tom Jefferson's pieces of French sentiment and humbug. It's perfectly ridiculous to have that going the rounds among us, to this day.'

'I think it is,' said St Clare, significantly.

'Because,' said Alfred, 'we can see plainly enough that all men are *not* born free, nor born equal; they are born anything else. For my part, I think half this republican talk sheer humbug. It is the educated, the intelligent, the wealthy, the refined, who ought to have equal rights, and not the *canaille*.'[203]

'If you can keep the *canaille* of that opinion,' said Augustine. 'They took *their* turn once, in France.'

'Of course, they must be *kept down*, consistently, steadily, as I *should*,' said Alfred, setting his foot hard down, as if he were standing on somebody.

'It makes a terrible slip when they get up,' said Augustine, 'in St Domingo,[204] for instance.'

'Poh!' said Alfred, 'we'll take care of that, in this country. We must set our face against all this educating, elevating talk that is getting about now; the lower class must not be educated.'

'That is past praying for,' said Augustine; 'educated they will be, and we have only to say how. Our system is educating them in barbarism and brutality. We are breaking all humanising ties, and making them brute beasts; and, if they get the upper hand, such we shall find them.'

'They never shall get the upper hand!' said Alfred.

'That's right,' said St Clare; 'put on the steam, fasten down the escape-valve, and sit on it, and see where you'll land.'

'Well,' said Alfred. 'we *will* see. I'm not afraid to sit on the escape-valve, as long as the boilers are strong, and the machinery works well.'

'The nobles in Louis XVI's time thought just so; and Austria and Pius IX[205] think so now; and, some pleasant morning, you may all be caught up to meet each other in the air, *when the boilers burst.*'

'*Dies declarabit,*'[206] said Alfred, laughing.

'I tell you,' said Augustine, 'if there is anything that is revealed with the strength of a divine law in our times, it is that the masses are to rise, and the under class become the upper one.'

'That's one of your red republican humbugs, Augustine! Why didn't you ever take to the stump? You'd make a famous stump orator! Well, I hope I shall be dead before this millennium of your greasy masses comes on.'

'Greasy or not greasy, they will govern *you*, when their time comes,' said Augustine; 'and they will be just such rulers as you make them. The French noblesse chose to have the people "*sans culottes*",[207] and they had "*sans culotte*" governors to their hearts' content. The people of Haiti – '

'Oh, come, Augustine! as if we hadn't had enough of that abominable, contemptible Haiti! The Haitians were not Anglo-Saxons; if they had been, there would have been another story. The Anglo-Saxon is the dominant race of the world, and *is to be so.*'

'Well, there is a pretty fair infusion of Anglo-Saxon blood among our slaves now,' said Augustine. 'There are plenty among them who have only enough of the African to give a sort of tropical warmth and fervour to our calculating firmness and foresight. If ever the San Domingo hour comes, Anglo-Saxon blood will lead on the day.[208] Sons of white fathers, with all our haughty feelings burning in their veins, will not always be bought and sold and traded. They will rise, and raise with them their mother's race.'

'Stuff! – nonsense!'

'Well,' said Augustine, 'there goes an old saying to this effect, "As it was in the days of Noah, so shall it be; they ate, they drank, they planted, they builded, and knew not till the flood came and took them." '[209]

'On the whole, Augustine, I think your talents might do for a circuit rider,'[210] said Alfred, laughing. 'Never you fear for us! possession is our nine points. We've got the power. This subject race,' said he, stamping firmly, 'is down, and shall *stay* down! We have energy enough to manage our own powder.'

'Sons trained like your Henrique will be grand guardians of your powder-magazines,' said Augustine; 'so cool and self-possessed! The proverb says, "They that cannot govern themselves cannot govern others." '[211]

'There is a trouble there,' said Alfred, thoughtfully; 'there's no doubt that our system is a difficult one to train children under. It gives too free scope to the passions, altogether, which, in our climate, are hot enough. I find trouble with Henrique. The boy is generous and warm-hearted, but a perfect fire-cracker when excited. I believe I shall send him north for his education, where obedience is more fashionable, and where he will associate more with equals, and less with dependants.'

'Since training children is the staple work of the human race,' said Augustine, 'I should think it something of a consideration that our system does not work well there.'

'It does not for some things,' said Alfred; 'for others, again, it does. It makes boys manly and courageous; and the very vices of an abject race tend to strengthen in them the opposite virtues. I think Henrique, now, has a keener sense of the beauty of truth, from seeing lying and deception the universal badge of slavery.'

'A Christian-like view of the subject, certainly!' said Augustine.

'It's true, Christian-like or not; and is about as Christian-like as most other things in the world,' said Alfred.

'That may be,' said St Clare.

'Well, there's no use in talking, Augustine. I believe we've been round and round this old track five hundred times, more or less. What do you say to a game of backgammon?'

The two brothers ran up the veranda steps, and were soon seated at a light bamboo stand, with the backgammon-board between them. As they were setting their men, Alfred said –

'I tell you, Augustine, if I thought as you do, I should do something.'

'I dare say you would – you are one of the doing sort, but what?'

'Why, elevate your own servants, for a specimen,' said Alfred, with a half-scornful smile.

'You might as well set Mount Etna[212] on them flat, and tell them to stand up under it, as tell me to elevate my servants under all the superincumbent mass of society upon them. One man can do nothing, against the whole action of a community. Education, to do anything, must be a state education; or there must be enough agreed in it to make a current.'

'You take the first throw,' said Alfred; and the brothers were soon lost in the game, and heard no more till the scraping of horses' feet was heard under the veranda.

'There come the children,' said Augustine, rising 'Look here, Alf! Did you ever see anything so beautiful?' And, in truth, it *was* a beautiful sight. Henrique, with his bold brow, and dark, glossy curls, and glowing cheek, was laughing gayly, as he bent towards his fair cousin, as they came on. She was dressed in a blue riding-dress, with a cap of the same colour. Exercise had given a brilliant hue to her cheeks, and heightened the effect of her singularly transparent skin and golden hair.

'Good heavens! what perfectly dazzling beauty!' said Alfred. 'I tell you, Auguste, won't she make some hearts ache, one of these days?'

'She will, too truly – God knows I'm afraid so!' said St Clare, in a tone of sudden bitterness, as he hurried down to take her off her horse.

'Eva, darling! you're not much tired?' he said, as he clasped her in his arms.

'No papa,' said the child; but her short, hard breathing alarmed her father.

'How could you ride so fast, dear? you know it's bad for you.'

'I felt so well, papa, and liked it so much, I forgot.'

St Clare carried her in his arms into the parlour, and laid her on the sofa.

'Henrique you must be careful of Eva,' said he; 'you mustn't ride fast with her.'

'I'll take her under my care,' said Henrique, seating himself by the sofa, and taking Eva's hand.

Eva soon found herself much better. Her father and uncle resumed their game, and the children were left together.

'Do you know, Eva, I'm so sorry papa is only going to stay two days here, and then I shan't see you again for ever so long! If I stayed with you, I'd try to be good, and not be cross to Dodo, and so on. I don't mean to treat Dodo ill; but, you know, I've got such a quick temper. I'm not really bad to him, though. I give him a picayune, now and then; and you see he dresses well. I think, on the whole, Dodo's pretty well off.'

'Would you think you were well off, if there were not one creature in the world near you to love you?'

'I? Well, of course not.'

'And you have taken Dodo away from all the friends he ever had, and now he has not a creature to love him; nobody can be good that way.'

'Well, I can't help it, as I know of. I can't get his mother, and I can't love him myself, nor anybody else, as I know of.'

'Why can't you?' said Eva.

'*Love* Dodo! Why, Eva, you wouldn't have me! I may *like* him well enough; but you don't *love* your servants.'

'I do, indeed.'

'How odd!'

'Don't the Bible say we must love everybody?'[213]

'Oh, the Bible! To be sure, it says a great many such things; but, then, nobody ever thinks of doing them – you know, Eva, nobody does.'

Eva did not speak; her eyes were fixed and thoughtful, for a few moments.

'At any rate,' she said, 'dear cousin, do love poor Dodo, and be kind to him, for my sake!'

'I could love anything, for your sake, dear cousin; for I really think you are the loveliest creature that I ever saw!' And Henrique spoke with an earnestness that flushed his handsome face. Eva received it with perfect simplicity, without even a change of feature; merely saying, 'I'm glad you feel so, dear Henrique! I hope you will remember.'

The dinner-bell put an end to the interview.

CHAPTER XXIV

Foreshadowings

TWO DAYS AFTER THIS, Alfred St Clare and Augustine parted; and Eva, who had been stimulated, by the society of her young cousin, to exertions beyond her strength, began to fail rapidly. St Clare was at last willing to call in medical advice, a thing from which he had always shrunk, because it was the admission of an unwelcome truth. But for a day or two, Eva was so unwell as to be confined to the house; and the doctor was called.

Marie St Clare had taken no notice of the child's gradually decaying health and strength, because she was completely absorbed in studying out two or three new forms of disease to which she believed she herself was a victim. It was the first principle of Marie's belief that nobody ever was or could be so great a sufferer as *herself*; and therefore she always repelled quite indignantly any suggestion that anyone around her could be sick. She was always sure in such a case, that it was nothing but laziness or want of energy; and that if they had had the suffering *she* had they would soon know the difference.

Miss Ophelia had several times tried to awaken her maternal fears about Eva; but to no avail.

'I don't see as anything ails the child,' she would say; 'she runs about and plays.'

'But she has a cough.'

'Cough! you don't need to tell me about a cough. I've always been subject to a cough, all my days. When I was of Eva's age, they thought I was in a consumption. Night after night, Mammy used to sit up with me. Oh, Eva's cough is not anything.'

'But she gets weak, and is short-breathed.'

'Law! I've had that, years and years; it's only a nervous affection.'

'But she sweats so, nights!'

'Well, I have these ten years. Very often, night after night, my clothes will be wringing wet. There won't be a dry thread in my night-clothes, and the sheets will be so that Mammy has to hang them up to dry! Eva doesn't sweat anything like that!'

Miss Ophelia shut her mouth for a season. But, now that Eva was fairly and visibly prostrated, and a doctor called, Marie all on a sudden, took a new turn.

She knew it, she said, she always felt it, that she was destined to be the most miserable of mothers. Here she was, with her wretched health, and her only darling child going down to the grave before her eyes! And Marie routed up Mammy at nights, and rumpussed and scolded with more energy than ever all day, on the strength of this new misery.

'My dear Marie, don't talk so!' said St Clare. 'You ought not to give up the case so, at once.'

'You have not a mother's feelings, St Clare! You never could understand me! – you don't now.'

'But don't talk so, as if it were a gone case!'

'I can't take it as indifferently as you can, St Clare. If *you* don't feel when your only child is in this alarming state, *I* do. It's a blow too much for me, with all I was bearing before.'

'It's true,' said St Clare, 'that Eva is very delicate – that I always knew; and that she has grown so rapidly as to exhaust her strength; and that her situation is critical. But just now she is only prostrated by the heat of the weather, and by the excitement of her cousin's visit, and the exertions she made. The physician says there is room for hope.'

'Well, of course, if you can look on the bright side, pray do; it's a mercy if people haven't sensitive feelings, in this world. I am sure I wish I didn't feel as I do – it only makes me completely wretched! I wish I *could* be as easy as the rest of you!'

And the 'rest of them' had good reason to breathe the same prayer, for Marie paraded her new misery as the reason and apology for all sorts of inflictions on everyone about her. Every word that was spoken by anybody, everything that was done or was not done everywhere, was only a new proof that she was surrounded by hard-hearted, insensible beings, who were unmindful of her peculiar sorrows. Poor Eva heard some of these speeches; and nearly cried her little eyes out in pity for her mamma, and in sorrow that she should make her so much distress.

In a week or two there was a great improvement of symptoms – one of those deceitful lulls, by which her inexorable disease so often beguiles the anxious heart, even on the verge of the grave. Eva's step was again in the garden – in the balconies; she played and laughed again, and her father, in a transport, declared that they should soon have her as hearty as anybody. Miss Ophelia and the physician alone felt no encouragement from this illusive truce. There was one other heart, too, that felt the same certainty, and that was the little heart of Eva. What is it that sometimes speaks in the soul so calmly, so clearly, that its earthly time is short? Is it the secret instinct of decaying nature, or the soul's impulsive throb, as immortality draws on? Be it what it may, it rested in the heart of Eva, a calm, sweet, prophetic certainty that Heaven was near; calm as the light of sunset, sweet as the bright stillness of autumn: there her little heart reposed, only troubled by sorrow for those who loved her so dearly.

For the child, though nursed so tenderly, and though life was unfolding before her with every brightness that love and wealth could give, had no regret for herself in dying.

In that Book which she and her simple old friend had read so much together, she had seen and taken to her young heart the image of One who loved the little child; and, as she gazed and mused, he had ceased to be an image and a picture of the distant past, and come to be a living, all-surrounding reality. His love enfolded her childish heart with more than mortal tenderness; and it was to Him, she said, she was going, and to His home.

But her heart yearned with sad tenderness for all that she was to leave behind – her father most; for Eva, though she never distinctly thought so, had an instinctive perception that she was more in his heart than any other. She loved her mother because she was so loving a creature, and all the selfishness that she had seen in her only saddened and perplexed her; for she had a child's implicit trust that her mother could not do wrong. There was something about her that Eva never could make out; and she always smoothed it over with thinking that, after all, it was mamma, and she loved her very dearly indeed.

She felt, too, for those fond, faithful servants, to whom she was as daylight and sunshine. Children do not usually generalise; but Eva was an uncommonly mature child, and the things that she had witnessed of the evils of the system under which they were living had fallen, one by one, into the depths of her thoughtful, pondering heart. She had vague longings to do something for them – to bless and save not only them, but all in their condition – longings that contrasted sadly with the feebleness of her little frame.

'Uncle Tom,' she said, one day, when she was reading to her friend, 'I can understand why Jesus *wanted* to die for us.'

'Why, Miss Eva?'

'Because I've felt so, too.'

'What is it, Miss Eva? – I don't understand.'

'I can't tell you; but, when I saw those poor creatures on the boat, you know, when you came up and I, some had lost their mothers, and some their husbands, and some mothers cried for their little children; and when I heard about poor Prue – oh, wasn't that dreadful! – and a great many other times I've felt that I would be glad to die, if my dying could stop all this misery. I *would die* for them, Tom, if I could,' said the child earnestly, laying her little thin hand on his.

Tom looked at the child with awe: and when she, hearing her father's voice, glided away, he wiped his eyes many times as he looked after her.

'It's jest no use tryin' to keep Miss Eva here,' he said to Mammy, whom he met a moment after. 'She's got the Lord's mark in her forehead.'

'Ah, yes, yes,' said Mammy, raising her hands, 'I've allers said so. She wasn't never like a child that's to live – there was allers something deep in her eyes, I've told missis so, many the time; it's a comin' true – we all sees it – dear, little, blessed lamb!'

Eva came tripping up the veranda steps to her father. It was late in the afternoon, and the rays of the sun formed a kind of glory behind her, as she came forward in her white dress, with her golden hair and glowing cheeks, her eyes unnaturally bright with the slow fever that burned in her veins.

St Clare had called her to show a statuette that he had been buying for her; but her appearance, as she came on, impressed him suddenly and painfully. There is a kind of beauty so intense, yet so fragile, that we cannot bear to look at it. Her father folded her suddenly in his arms, and almost forgot what he was going to tell her.

'Eva, dear, you are better nowadays, are you not?'

'Papa,' said Eva, with sudden firmness, 'I've had things I wanted to say to you a great while. I want to say them now, before I get weaker.'

St Clare trembled as Eva seated herself in his lap. She laid her head on his bosom and said –

'It's all no use, papa, to keep it to myself any longer. The time is coming that I am going to leave you. I am going, and never to come back!' and Eva sobbed.

'Oh, now, my dear little Eva!' said St Clare, trembling as he spoke, but speaking cheerfully, 'you've got nervous and low-spirited; you mustn't indulge such gloomy thoughts. See here, I've bought a statuette for you!'

'No, papa,' said Eva, putting it gently away, 'don't deceive yourself! I am *not* any better – I know it perfectly well; and I am going before long. I am not nervous – I am not low-spirited. If it were not for you, papa, and my friends, I should be perfectly happy. I want to go – I long to go!'

'Why, dear child, what has made your poor little heart so sad? You have had everything to make you happy, that could be given you?'

'I had rather be in heaven; though, only for my friends' sake I would be willing to live. There are a great many things here that make me sad, that seem dreadful to me. I had rather be there; but I don't want to leave you – it almost breaks my heart!'

'What makes you sad, and seems dreadful, Eva?'

'Oh, things that are done, and done all the time. I feel sad for our poor people; they love me dearly, and they are all good and kind to me. I wish, papa, they were all *free*.'

'Why, Eva, child, don't you think they are well enough off now?'

'Oh, but, papa, if anything should happen to you, what would become of them? There are very few men like you, papa. Uncle Alfred isn't like you, and mamma isn't; and then think of poor old Prue's owners! What horrid things people do, and can do!' And Eva shuddered.

'My dear child, you are too sensitive. I'm sorry I ever let you hear such stories.'

'Oh, that's what troubles me, papa. You want me to live so happy, and never to have any pain, never suffer anything, not even hear a sad story, when other poor creatures have nothing but pain and sorrow all their lives; it seems selfish. I ought to know such things – I ought to feel about them! Such things always sank into my heart; they went down deep; I've thought and thought about them. Papa, isn't there any way to have all slaves made free?'

'That's a difficult question, dearest. There's no doubt that this way is a very bad one; a great many people think so; I do myself: I heartily wish that there were not a slave in the land, but then I don't know what is to be done about it!'

'Papa, you are such a good man, and so noble, and kind, and you always have a way of saying things that is so pleasant, couldn't you go all round and try to persuade people to do right about this? When I am dead, papa, then you will think of me, and do it for my sake. I would do it, if I could.'

'When you are dead, Eva,' said St Clare, passionately. 'Oh, child, don't talk to me so! You are all I have on earth.'

'Poor old Prue's child was all that she had; and yet she had to hear it crying, and she couldn't help it! Papa, these poor creatures love their children as much as you do me. Oh, do something for them! There's poor Mammy loves her children; I've seen her crying when she talked about them. And Tom loves his children; and it's dreadful, papa, that such things are happening, all the time!'

'There, there, darling,' said St Clare, soothingly; 'only don't distress yourself, and don't talk of dying, and I will do anything you wish.'

'And promise me, dear father, that Tom shall have his freedom as soon as – ' She stopped, and said in a hesitating tone – 'I am gone!'

'Yes, dear, I will do anything in the world – anything you could ask me to.'

'Dear papa,' said the child, laying her burning cheek against his, 'how I wish we could go together!'

'Where, dearest?' said St Clare.

'To our Saviour's home; it's so sweet and peaceful there – it is all so loving there!' The child spoke unconsciously, as of a place where she had often been. 'Don't you want to go, papa?' she said.

St Clare drew her closer to him, but was silent.

'You will come to me,' said the child, speaking in a voice of calm certainty which she often used unconsciously.

'I shall come after you. I shall not forget you.'

The shadows of the solemn evening closed round them deeper and deeper, as St Clare sat silently holding the little frail form to his bosom.

He saw no more the deep eyes, but the voice came over him as a spirit voice; and, as in a sort of judgement vision, his whole past life rose in a moment before his eyes – his mother's prayers and hymns – his own early yearnings and aspirings for good; and, between them and this hour, years of worldliness and scepticism, and what man calls respectable living. We can think *much*, very much, in a moment. St Clare saw and felt many things, but spoke nothing; and, as it grew darker, he took his child to her bedroom; and when she was prepared for rest, he sent away the attendants, and rocked her in his arms, and sang to her till she was asleep.

CHAPTER XXV

The Little Evangelist

IT WAS SUNDAY AFTERNOON. St Clare was stretched on a bamboo lounge in the veranda, solacing himself with a cigar. Marie lay reclined on a sofa, opposite the window opening on the veranda, closely secluded, under an awning of transparent gauze, from the outrages of the mosquitoes, and languidly holding in her hand an elegantly bound prayer-book. She was holding it because it was Sunday, and she imagined she had been reading it – though, in fact, she had been only taking a succession of short naps, with it open in her hand.

Miss Ophelia, who, after some rummaging, had hunted up a small Methodist meeting within riding distance, had gone out, with Tom as driver, to attend it; and Eva had accompanied them.

'I say, Augustine,' said Marie after dozing a while, 'I must send to the city after my old Dr Posey; I'm sure I've got the complaint of the heart.'

'Well; why need you send for him? This doctor that attends Eva seems skilful.'

'I would not trust him in a critical case,' said Marie; 'and I think I may say mine is becoming so! I've been thinking of it these two or three nights past; I have such distressing pains, and such strange feelings.'

'Oh, Marie, you are blue; I don't believe it's heart complaint.'

'I dare say *you* don't,' said Marie; 'I was prepared to expect *that*. You can be alarmed enough, if Eva coughs or has the least thing the matter with her; but you never think of me.'

'If it's particularly agreeable to you to have heart disease, why, I'll try and maintain you have it,' said St Clare; 'I didn't know it was.'

'Well, I only hope you won't be sorry for this, when it's too late!' said Marie; 'but, believe it or not, my distress about Eva, and the exertions I have made with that dear child, have developed what I have long suspected.'

What the *exertions* were which Marie referred to, it would have been difficult to state. St Clare quietly made this commentary to himself, and went on smoking, like a hard-hearted wretch of a man as he was, till a carriage drove up before the veranda, and Eva and Miss Ophelia alighted.

Miss Ophelia marched straight to her own chamber, to put away her bonnet and shawl, as was always her manner, before she spoke a word on any subject; while Eva came at St Clare's call, and was sitting on his knee, giving him an account of the services they had heard.

They soon heard loud exclamations from Miss Ophelia's room (which, like the one in which they were sitting, opened on to the veranda), and violent reproof addressed to somebody.

'What new witchcraft has Tops been brewing?' asked St Clare. 'That commotion is of her raising, I'll be bound!'

And, in a moment after, Miss Ophelia, in high indignation, came dragging the culprit along.

'Come out here, now!' she said. 'I *will* tell your master!'

'What's the case now?' asked Augustine.

'The case is that I cannot be plagued with this child, any longer! It's past all bearing; flesh and blood cannot endure it! Here, I locked her up, and gave her a hymn to study; and what does she do, but spy out where I put my key, and has gone to my bureau, and got a bonnet-trimming, and cut it all to pieces, to make dolls' jackets! I never saw anything like it in my life!'

'I told you, cousin,' said Marie, 'that you'd find out that these creatures can't be brought up without severity. If I had *my* way, now.' she said, looking reproachfully at St Clare, 'I'd send that child out, and have her thoroughly whipped; I'd have her whipped till she couldn't stand!'

'I don't doubt it,' said St Clare. 'Tell me of the lovely rule of woman! I never saw above a dozen women that wouldn't half kill a horse, or a servant, either, if they had their own way with them, let alone a man.'

'There is no use in this shilly-shally way of yours, St Clare!' said Marie. 'Cousin is a woman of sense, and she sees it now as plain as I do.'

Miss Ophelia had just the capability of indignation that belongs to the thorough-paced housekeeper, and this had been pretty actively roused by the artifice and wastefulness of the child; in fact, many of my lady readers must own that they should have felt just so in her circumstances; but Marie's words went beyond her, and she felt less heat.

'I wouldn't have the child treated so, for the world,' she said; 'but, I am sure, Augustine, I don't know what to do. I've taught and taught; I've talked till I'm tired; I've whipped her; I've punished her in every way I can think of, and still she's just what she was at first.'

'Come here, Tops, you monkey!' said St Clare, calling the child up to him.

Topsy came up; her round, hard eyes glittering and blinking with a mixture of apprehensiveness and their usual odd drollery.

'What makes you behave so?' said St Clare, who could not help being amused with the child's expression.

' 'Spects it's my wicked heart,' said Topsy, demurely; 'Miss Feely says so.'

'Don't you see how much Miss Ophelia has done for you? She says she has done everything she can think of.'

'Lor, yes, mas'r! old missis used to say so, too. She whipped me a heap harder, and used to pull my har, and knock my head agin the door; but it didn't do me no good! I 'spects, if they's to pull every spear o' har out o' my head, it wouldn't do no good, neither – I's so wicked! Laws! I's nothin but a nigger, no ways!'

'Well, I shall have to give her up,' said Miss Ophelia; 'I can't have that trouble any longer.'

'Well, I'd just like to ask one question,' said St Clare.

'What is it?'

'Why, if your Gospel is not strong enough to save one heathen child, that you can have at home here, all to yourself, what's the use of sending one or two poor missionaries off with it among thousands of just such? I suppose this child is about a fair sample of what thousands of your heathen are.'

Miss Ophelia did not make an immediate answer; and Eva, who had stood a silent spectator of the scene thus far, made a silent sign to Topsy to follow her. There was a little glass-room at the corner of the veranda, which St Clare used as a sort of reading-room; and Eva and

Topsy disappeared into this place.

'What's Eva going about, now?' said St Clare; 'I mean to see.'

And, advancing on tiptoe, he lifted up a curtain that covered the glass-door, and looked in. In a moment, laying his finger on his lips, he made a silent gesture to Miss Ophelia to come and look. There sat the two children on the floor, with their side faces towards them – Topsy, with her usual air of careless drollery and unconcern; but, opposite to her, Eva, her whole face fervent with feeling, and tears in her large eyes.

'What does make you so bad, Topsy? Why won't you try and be good? Don't you love *anybody*, Topsy?'

'Dun 'no nothing 'bout love; I loves candy and sich, that's all,' said Topsy.

'But you love your father and mother?'

'Never had none, ye know. I telled ye that, Miss Eva.'

'Oh, I know,' said Eva, sadly; 'but hadn't you any brother, or sister, or aunt, or – '

'No, none on 'em – never had nothing nor nobody.'

'But, Topsy, if you'd only try to be good, you might – '

'Couldn't never be nothin' but a nigger, if I was ever so good,' said Topsy. 'If I could be skinned, and come white, I'd try then.'

'But people can love you, if you are black, Topsy. Miss Ophelia would love you, if you were good.'

Topsy gave the short, blunt laugh that was her common mode of expressing incredulity.

'Don't you think so?' said Eva.

'No; she can't bar me, 'cause I'm a nigger! – she'd's soon have a toad touch her! There can't nobody love niggers, and niggers can't do nothin'. *I* don't care,' said Topsy, beginning to whistle.

'O Topsy, poor child, *I* love you!' said Eva, with a sudden burst of feeling, and laying her little thin, white hand on Topsy's shoulder; 'I love you, because you haven't had any father, or mother, or friends – because you've been a poor, abused child! I love you, and I want you to be good. I am very unwell, Topsy, and I think I shan't live a great while; and it really grieves me to have you be so naughty. I wish you would try to be good, for my sake; it's only a little while I shall be with you.'

The round, keen eyes of the black child were overcast with tears; large, bright drops rolled heavily down, one by one, and fell on the little white hand. Yes in that moment, a ray of real belief, a ray of heavenly love, had penetrated the darkness of her heathen soul! She laid her head down between her knees, and wept and sobbed; while the beautiful child, bending over her, looked like the picture of some bright angel stooping to reclaim a sinner.

'Poor Topsy!' said Eva, 'don't you know that Jesus loves all alike? He is just as willing to love you as me. He loves you just as I do, only more, because he is better. He will help you to be good; and you can go to Heaven at last, and be an angel for ever, just as much as if you were white. Only think of it, Topsy, *you* can be one of those spirits bright, Uncle Tom sings about.'

'O dear Miss Eva, dear Miss Eva!' said the child; 'I will try! I will try! I never did care nothin' about it before.'

St Clare, at this instant, dropped the curtain. 'It puts me in mind of mother,' he said to Miss Ophelia. 'It is true what she told me; if we want to give sight to the blind, we must be willing to do as Christ did – call them to us, and *put our hands on them.*'

'I've always had a prejudice against negroes,' said Miss Ophelia, 'and it's a fact, I never could bear to have that child touch me; but I didn't think she knew it.'

'Trust any child to find that out,' said St Clare; 'there's no keeping it from them. But I believe that all the trying in the world to benefit a child, and all the substantial favours you can do them, will never excite one emotion of gratitude, while that feeling of repugnance remains in the heart; it's a queer kind of a fact, but so it is.'

'I don't know how I can help it,' said Miss Ophelia; 'they *are* disagreeable to me – this child in particular. How can I help feeling so?'

'Eva does, it seems.'

'Well, she's so loving! After all, though, she's no more than Christlike,' said Miss Ophelia; 'I wish I were like her. She might teach me a lesson.'

'It wouldn't be the first time a little child had been used to instruct an old disciple, if it *were* so,' said St Clare.

CHAPTER XXVI

Death

Weep not for those whom the veil of the tomb,
In life's early morning, hath hid from our eyes.[214]

EVA'S BEDROOM was a spacious apartment, which, like all the other rooms in the house, opened on to the broad veranda. The room communicated, on one side, with her father and mother's apartment; on the other, with that appropriated to Miss Ophelia. St Clare had gratified his own eye and taste in furnishing this room in a style that had a peculiar keeping with the character of her for whom it was intended. The windows were hung with curtains of rose-coloured and white muslin, the floor was spread with a matting which had been ordered in Paris, to a pattern of his own device, having round it a border of rosebuds and leaves, and a centre-piece with full-blown roses. The bedstead, chairs and lounges were of bamboo, wrought in peculiarly graceful and fanciful patterns. Over the head of the bed was an alabaster bracket, on which a beautiful sculptured angel stood, with drooping wings, holding out a crown of myrtle-leaves. From this depended, over the bed, light curtains of rose-coloured gauze, striped with silver, supplying that protection from mosquitoes which is an indispensable addition to all sleeping accommodation in that climate. The graceful bamboo lounges were amply supplied with cushions of rose-coloured damask, while over them, depending from the hands of sculptured figures, were gauze curtains similar to those of the bed. A light, fanciful bamboo table stood in the middle of the room, where a Parian vase,[215] wrought in the shape of a white lily, with its buds, stood, ever filled with flowers. On this table lay Eva's books and little trinkets, with an elegantly wrought alabaster writing-stand, which her father had supplied to her when he saw her trying to improve herself in writing. There was a fireplace in the room, and on the marble mantle above stood a beautifully wrought statuette of Jesus receiving little children, and on either side marble vases, for which it was Tom's pride and delight to offer bouquets every morning. Two or three exquisite paintings of children, in various attitudes, embellished the wall. In short, the eye could turn nowhere without meeting images of childhood, of beauty, and of peace. Those little eyes never opened, in the morning light, without falling on something which suggested to the heart soothing and beautiful thoughts.

The deceitful strength which had buoyed Eva up for a little while was fast passing away; seldom and more seldom her light footstep was heard in the veranda, and oftener and oftener she was found reclined on a little lounge by the open window, her large, deep eyes fixed on the rising and falling waters of the lake.

It was towards the middle of the afternoon, as she was so reclining – her Bible half open, her little transparent fingers lying listlessly between the leaves – when suddenly she heard her mother's voice, in sharp tones, in the veranda.

'What now, you baggage! – what new piece of mischief? You've been picking the flowers, eh?' and Eva heard the sound of a smart slap.

'Law, missis! they's for Miss Eva,' she heard a voice say, which she knew belonged to Topsy.

'Miss Eva! A pretty excuse! you suppose she wants *your* flowers, you good-for-nothing nigger! Get along off with you!'

In a moment, Eva was off from her lounge, and in the veranda.

'Oh, don't, mother! I should like the flowers; do give them to me; I want them!'

'Why, Eva, your room is full now.'

'I can't have too many,' said Eva. 'Topsy, do bring them here.'

Topsy, who had stood sullenly, holding down her head, now came up and offered her flowers. She did it with a look of hesitation and bashfulness, quite unlike the eldritch[216] boldness and brightness which was usual with her.

'It's a beautiful bouquet!' said Eva, looking at it.

It was rather a singular one – a brilliant scarlet geranium, and one single white japonica, with its glossy leaves. It was tied up with an evident eye to the contrast of colour, and the arrangement of every leaf had carefully been studied.

Topsy looked pleased, as Eva said, 'Topsy, you arrange flowers very prettily. Here,' she said, 'is a vase I haven't any flowers for. I wish you'd arrange something every day for it.'

'Well, that's odd!' said Marie. 'What in the world do you want that for?'

'Never mind, mamma; you'd as lief as not Topsy should do it – had you not?'

'Of course, anything you please, dear! Topsy, you hear your young mistress; see that you mind.'

Topsy made a short curtsey, and looked down; and, as she turned away, Eva saw a tear roll down her dark cheek.

'You see, mamma, I knew poor Topsy wanted to do something for me,' said Eva to her mother.

'Oh, nonsense! it's only because she likes to do mischief. She knows she mustn't pick flowers – so she does it; that's all there is to it. But, if you fancy to have her pluck them, so be it.'

'Mamma, I think Topsy is different from what she used to be; she's trying to be a good girl.'

'She'll have to try a good while before *she* gets to be good,' said Marie, with a careless laugh.

'Well, you know, mamma, poor Topsy! everything has always been against her.'

'Not since she's been here, I'm sure. If she hasn't been talked to, and preached to, and every earthly thing done that anybody could do; and she's just so ugly, and always will be; you can't make anything of the creature!'

'But, mamma, it's so different to be brought up as I've been, with so many friends, so many things to make me good and happy; and to be brought up as she's been, all the time, till she came here!'

'Most likely,' said Marie, yawning. 'Dear me, how hot it is!'

'Mamma, you believe, don't you, that Topsy could become an angel, as well as any of us, if she were a Christian?'

'Topsy! what a ridiculous idea! Nobody but you would ever think of it. I suppose she could, though.'

'But, mamma, isn't God her father, as much as ours? Isn't Jesus her Saviour?'

'Well, that may be. I suppose God made everybody,' said Marie. 'Where is my smelling-bottle?'

'It's such a pity – oh! *such* a pity!' said Eva, looking out on the distant lake, and speaking half to herself.

'What's a pity?' said Marie.

'Why, that anyone, who could be a bright angel, and live with angels, should go all down, down, down, and nobody help them! Oh, dear!'

'Well, we can't help it; it's no use worrying, Eva! I don't know what's to be done; we ought to be thankful for our own advantages.'

'I hardly can be,' said Eva, 'I'm so sorry to think of poor folks that haven't any.'

'That's odd enough,' said Marie; 'I'm sure my religion makes me thankful for my advantages.'

'Mamma,' said Eva, 'I want to have some of my hair cut off – a good deal of it.'

'What for?' said Marie.

'Mamma, I want to give some away to my friends, while I am able to give it to them myself. Won't you ask aunty to come and cut it for me?'

Marie raised her voice, and called Miss Ophelia, from the other room.

The child half rose from her pillow as she came in, and, shaking down her long golden-brown curls, said, rather playfully, 'Come, aunty, shear the sheep!'

'What's that?' said St Clare, who just then entered with some fruit he had been out to get for her.

'Papa, I just want aunty to cut off some of my hair; there's too much of it, and it makes my head hot. Besides, I want to give some of it away.'

Miss Ophelia came, with her scissors.

'Take care, don't spoil the looks of it!' said her father; 'cut underneath, where it won't show. Eva's curls are my pride.'

'Oh, papa!' said Eva, sadly.

'Yes, and I want them kept handsome against the time I take you up to your uncle's plantation, to see Cousin Henrique,' said St Clare, in a gay tone.

'I shall never go there, papa; I am going to a better country. Oh, do believe me! Don't you see, papa, that I get weaker, every day?'

'Why do you insist that I shall believe such a cruel thing, Eva?' said her father.

'Only because it is *true*, papa: and, if you will believe it now, perhaps you will get to feel about it as I do.'

St Clare closed his lips, and stood gloomily eyeing the long beautiful curls, which, as they were separated from the child's head, were laid, one by one, in her lap. She raised them up, looked earnestly at them, twined them around her thin fingers, and looked from time to time anxiously at her father.

'It's just what I've been foreboding!' said Marie; 'it's just what has been preying on my health from day to day, bringing me downward to the grave, though nobody regards it. I have seen this long. St Clare, you will see, after a while, that I was right.'

'Which will afford you great consolation, no doubt!' said St Clare, in a dry, bitter tone.

Marie lay back on a lounge, and covered her face with her cambric handkerchief.

Eva's clear blue eye looked earnestly from one to the other. It was the calm, comprehending gaze of a soul half loosed from its earthly bonds; it was evident she saw, felt, and appreciated the difference between the two.

She beckoned with her hand to her father. He came, and sat down by her.

'Papa, my strength fades away every day, and I know I must go. There are some things I want to say and do, that I ought to do; and you are so unwilling to have me speak a word on this subject. But it must come; there's no putting it off. Do be willing I should speak now!'

'My child, I *am* willing!' said St Clare, covering his eyes with one hand, and holding up Eva's hand with the other.

'Then, I want to see all our people together. I have some things I *must* say to them,' said Eva.

'*Well*,' said St Clare, in a tone of dry endurance.

Miss Ophelia despatched a messenger, and soon the whole of the servants were convened in the room.

Eva lay back on her pillows; her hair hanging loosely about her face, her crimson cheeks contrasting painfully with the intense whiteness of her complexion and the thin contour of her limbs and features, and her large, soul-like eyes fixed earnestly on everyone.

The servants were struck with a sudden emotion. The spiritual face, the long locks of hair cut off and lying by her, her father's averted face, and Marie's sobs, struck at once upon the feelings of a sensitive and impressible race; and, as they came in, they looked one on another, sighed, and shook their heads. There was a deep silence, like that of a funeral.

Eva raised herself, and looked long and earnestly round at everyone. All looked sad and apprehensive. Many of the women hid their faces in their aprons.

'I sent for you all, my dear friends,' said Eva, 'because I love you. I love you all; and I have something to say to you, which I want you always to remember . . . I am going to leave you. In a few more weeks, you will see me no more – '

Here the child was interrupted by bursts of groans, sobs, and lamentations, which broke from all present, and in which her slender voice was lost entirely. She waited a moment, and then, speaking in a tone that checked the sobs of all, she said –

'If you love me, you must not interrupt me so. Listen to what I say. I want to speak to you about your souls . . . Many of you, I am afraid, are very careless. You are thinking only about this world. I want you to remember that there is a beautiful world, where Jesus is. I am going there, and you can go there; it is for you, as much as me. But, if you want to go there, you must not live idle, careless, thoughtless lives; you must be Christians. You must remember that each one of you can become angels, and be angels for ever . . . If you want to be Christians, Jesus will help you. You must pray to him; you must read – '

The child checked herself, looked piteously at them, and said sorrowfully –

'Oh, dear! you *can't* read. Poor souls!' and she hid her face in the pillow and sobbed, while many a smothered sob from those she was addressing, who were kneeling on the floor, aroused her.

'Never mind,' she said, raising her face and smiling brightly through her tears, 'I have prayed for you; and I know Jesus will help you, even if you can't read. Try all to do the best you can; pray every day; ask Him to help you, and get the Bible read to you whenever you can; and I think I shall see you all in heaven.'

'Amen,' was the murmured response from the lips of Tom and Mammy, and some of the elder ones, who belonged to the Methodist church. The younger and more thoughtless ones, for the time completely overcome, were sobbing, with their heads bowed upon their knees.

'I know,' said Eva, 'you all love me.'

'Yes; oh, yes! indeed we do. Lord bless her!' was the involuntary answer of all.

'Yes, I know you do! There isn't one of you that hasn't always been very kind to me; and I want to give you something that, when you look at, you shall always remember me. I'm going to give all of you a curl of my hair; and, when you look at it, think that I loved you and am gone to heaven, and that I want to see you all there.'

It is impossible to describe the scene, as, with tears and sobs, they gathered round the little creature, and took from her hands what seemed to them a last mark of her love. They fell on their knees; they sobbed, and prayed, and kissed the hem of her garment; and the elder ones poured forth words of endearment, mingled in prayers and blessings, after the manner of their susceptible race.

As each one took their gift, Miss Ophelia, who was apprehensive for the effect of all this excitement on her little patient, signed to each one to pass out of the apartment.

At last, all were gone but Tom and Mammy.

'Here, Uncle Tom,' said Eva, 'is a beautiful one for you. Oh, I am so happy, Uncle Tom, to think I shall see you in heaven, for I'm sure I shall; and Mammy – dear, good, kind Mammy!' she said, fondly throwing her arms round her old nurse, 'I know you'll be there, too.'

'Oh, Miss Eva, don't see how I can live without ye, no how!' said the faithful creature. ' 'Pears like it's just taking everything off the place to oncet!' and Mammy gave way to a passion of grief.

Miss Ophelia pushed her and Tom gently from the apartment, and thought they were all gone; but, as she turned, Topsy was standing there.

'Where did you start up from?' she said, suddenly.

'I was here,' said Topsy, wiping the tears from her eyes. 'Oh, Miss Eva, I've been a bad girl; but won't you give *me* one, too?'

'Yes, poor Topsy! to be sure, I will. There – every time you look at that, think that I love you, and wanted you to be a good girl!'

'Oh, Miss Eva, I *is* tryin!' said Topsy, earnestly; 'but, Lor, it's so hard to be good! 'Pears like I an't used to it, no ways!'

'Jesus knows it, Topsy; he is sorry for you; he will help you.'

Topsy, with her eyes hid in her apron, was silently passed from the apartment by Miss Ophelia; but, as she went, she hid the precious curl in her bosom.

All being gone, Miss Ophelia shut the door. That worthy lady had wiped away many tears of her own, during the scene; but concern for the consequence of such an excitement to her young charge was uppermost in her mind.

St Clare had been sitting, during the whole time, with his hand shading his eyes, in the same attitude. When they were all gone, he sat so still.

'Papa!' said Eva, gently, laying her hand on his.

He gave a sudden start and shiver; but made no answer.

'Dear papa!' said Eva.

'I *cannot*,' said St Clare, rising, 'I *cannot* have it so! The Almighty hath dealt *very bitterly* with me!' and St Clare pronounced these words with a bitter emphasis indeed.

'Augustine! has not God a right to do what he will with his own?' said Miss Ophelia.

'Perhaps so; but that doesn't make it any easier to bear,' said he, with a dry, hard, tearless manner, as he turned away.

'Papa, you break my heart!' said Eva, rising and throwing herself into his arms; 'you must not feel so!' and the child sobbed and wept with a violence which alarmed them all, and turned her father's thoughts at once to another channel.

'There, Eva – there, dearest! Hush! hush! I was wrong; I was wicked. I will feel any way, do any way – only don't distress yourself; don't sob so. I will be resigned; I was wicked to speak as I did.'

Eva soon lay like a wearied dove in her father's arms; and he, bending over her, soothed her by every tender word he could think of.

Marie rose and threw herself out of the apartment into her own, where she fell into violent hysterics.

'You didn't give me a curl, Eva,' said her father, smiling sadly.

'They are all yours, papa,' said she, smiling – 'yours and mamma's; and you must give dear aunty as many as she wants. I only gave them to our poor people myself, because you know, papa, they might be forgotten when I am gone, and because I hoped it might help them remember . . . You are a Christian, are you not, papa?' said Eva, doubtfully.

'Why do you ask me?'

'I don't know. You are so good, I don't see how you can help it.'

'What is being a Christian, Eva?'

'Loving Christ most of all,' said Eva.

'Do you, Eva?'

'Certainly I do.'

'You never saw Him,' said St Clare.

'That makes no difference,' said Eva. 'I believe in Him, and in a few days I shall *see* Him;' and the young face grew fervent, radiant with joy.

St Clare said no more. It was a feeling which he had seen before in his mother; but no chord within vibrated to it.

Eva, after this declined rapidly; there was no more any doubt of the event; the fondest hope could not be blinded. Her beautiful room was avowedly a sickroom; and Miss Ophelia day and night performed the duties of a nurse – and never did her friends appreciate her value more than in that capacity. With so well-trained a hand and eye, such perfect adroitness and practice in every art which could promote neatness and comfort, and keep out of sight every disagreeable incident of sickness – with such a perfect sense of time, such a clear, untroubled head, such exact accuracy in remembering every prescription and direction of the doctors – she was everything to the household. They who had shrugged their shoulders at her little peculiarities and setnesses, so unlike the careless freedom of Southern manners, acknowledged that now she was the exact person that was wanted.

Uncle Tom was much in Eva's room. The child suffered much from nervous restlessness, and it was a relief to her to be carried; and it was Tom's greatest delight to carry her little frail form in his arms, resting on a pillow, now up and down her room, now out into the veranda; and when the fresh sea-breezes blew from the lake, and the child felt freshest in the morning, he would sometimes walk with her under the orange trees in the garden, or, sitting down in some of their old seats, sing to her their favourite old hymns.

Her father often did the same thing; but his frame was slighter, and when he was weary, Eva would say to him –

'Oh, papa, let Tom take me. Poor fellow! it pleases him; and you know it's all he can do now, and he wants to do something!'

'So do I, Eva!' said her father.

'Well, papa, you can do everything, and are everything to me. You read to me – you sit up nights – and Tom has only this one thing, and his singing; and I know, too, he does it easier than you can. He carries me so strong!'

The desire to do something was not confined to Tom. Every servant in the establishment showed the same feeling, and in their way did what they could.

Poor Mammy's heart yearned towards her darling; but she found no opportunity, night or day, as Marie declared that the state of her mind was such, it was impossible for her to rest; and, of course, it was against her principles to let anyone else rest. Twenty times in a night, Mammy would be roused to rub her feet, to bathe her head, to find her pocket-handkerchief, to see what the noise was in Eva's room, to let down a curtain because it was too light, or to put it up because it was too dark; and, in the daytime, when she longed to have some share in the nursing of her pet, Marie seemed unusually ingenious in keeping her busy anywhere and everywhere all over the house, or about her own person; so that stolen interviews and momentary glimpses were all she could obtain.

'I feel it my duty to be particularly careful of myself, now,' she would say, 'feeble as I am, and with the whole care and nursing of that dear child upon me.'

'Indeed, my dear,' said St Clare, 'I thought our cousin relieved you of that.'

'You talk like a man, St Clare – just as if a mother *could* be relieved of the care of a child in that state; but, then, it's all alike – no one ever knows what I feel! I can't throw things off, as you do.'

St Clare smiled. You must excuse him, he couldn't help it – for St Clare could smile yet. For so bright and placid was the farewell voyage of the little spirit – by such sweet and fragrant breezes was the small bark borne towards the heavenly shores – that it was impossible to realise that it was death that was approaching The child felt no pain – only a tranquil, soft weakness, daily and almost insensibly increasing; and she was so beautiful, so loving, so trustful, so happy, that one could not resist the soothing influence of that air of innocence and peace which seemed to breathe around her. St Clare found a strange calm coming over him. It was not hope – that was impossible; it was not resignation; it was only a calm resting in the present, which seemed so beautiful that he wished to think of no future. It was like that hush of spirit which we feel amid the bright, mild woods of autumn, when the bright hectic flush is on the trees, and the last lingering flowers by the brook; and we joy in it all the more, because we know that soon it will all pass away.

The friend who knew most of Eva's own imaginings and foreshadowings was her faithful bearer, Tom. To him she said what she would not disturb her father by saying. To him she imparted those mysterious intimations which the soul feels, as the cords begin to unbind, ere it leaves its clay for ever.

Tom, at last, would not sleep in his room, but lay all night in the outer veranda, ready to rouse at every call.

'Uncle Tom, what alive have you taken to sleeping anywhere and everywhere, like a dog, for?' said Miss Ophelia. 'I thought you was one of the orderly sort, that liked to lie in bed in a Christian way.'

'I do, Miss Feely,' said Tom, mysteriously. 'I do, but now – '

'Well, what now?'

'We mustn't speak loud; Mas'r St Clare won't hear on't; but Miss Feely, you know there must be somebody watchin' for the bridegroom.'

'What do you mean, Tom?'

'You know it says in Scripture, "At midnight there was a great cry made, Behold, the bridegroom cometh." [217] That's what I'm 'spectin now, every night, Miss Feely – and I couldn't sleep out o' hearin, no ways.'

'Why, Uncle Tom, what makes you think so?'

'Miss Eva, she talks to me. The Lord, he sends his messenger in the soul. I must be thar, Miss Feely; for when that ar blessed child goes into the kingdom, they'll open the door so wide, we'll all get a look in at the glory, Miss Feely.'

'Uncle Tom, did Miss Eva say she felt more unwell than usual tonight?'

'No; but she told me, this morning, she was coming nearer – thar's them that tells it to the child, Miss Feely. It's the angels.

"It's the trumpet sound afore the break o' day", '[218] said Tom, quoting from a favourite hymn.

This dialogue passed between Miss Ophelia and Tom, between ten and eleven, one evening, after her arrangements had all been made for the night, when, on going to bolt her outer door, she found Tom stretched along by it, in the outer veranda.

She was not nervous or impressible; but the solemn, heartfelt manner struck her. Eva had been unusually bright and cheerful that afternoon, and had sat raised in her bed, and looked over all her little trinkets and precious things, and designated the friends to whom she would have them given; and her manner was more animated, and her voice more natural, than they had known it for weeks. Her father had been in, in the evening, and had said that Eva appeared more like her former self than ever she had done since her sickness; and when he kissed her for the night, he said to Miss Ophelia, 'Cousin, we may keep her with us, after all; she is certainly better;' and he had retired with a lighter heart in his bosom than he had had there for weeks.

But at midnight – strange, mystic hour! – when the veil between the frail present and the eternal future grows thin – then came the messenger!

There was a sound in that chamber, first of one who stepped quickly. It was Miss Ophelia, who had resolved to sit up all night with her little charge, and who, at the turn of the night, had discerned what experienced nurses significantly call 'a change'. The outer door was quickly opened, and Tom, who was watching outside, was on the alert in a moment.

'Go for the doctor, Tom! lose not a moment,' said Miss Ophelia; and, stepping across the room, she rapped at St Clare's door.

'Cousin,' she said, 'I wish you would come.'

Those words fell on his heart like clods upon a coffin. Why did they? He was up and in the room in an instant, and bending over Eva, who still slept.

What was it he saw that made his heart stand still? Why was no word spoken between the two? Thou canst say, who hast seen that same expression on the face dearest to thee; that look indescribable, hopeless, unmistakable, that says to thee that thy beloved is no longer thine.

On the face of the child, however, there was no ghastly imprint – only a high and almost sublime expression – the overshadowing presence of spiritual natures, the dawning of immortal life in that childish soul.

They stood there so still, gazing upon her, that even the ticking of the watch seemed too loud. In a few moments Tom returned with the doctor. He entered, gave one look, and stood silent as the rest.

'When did this change take place?' said he, in a low whisper, to Miss Ophelia.

'About the turn of the night,' was the reply.

Marie, roused by the entrance of the doctor, appeared, hurriedly from the next room.

'Augustine! Cousin! – Oh! – what – ?' she hurriedly began.

'Hush!' said St Clare, hoarsely; '*she is dying!*'

Mammy heard the words, and flew to awaken the servants. The house was soon roused – lights were seen, footsteps heard, anxious faces thronged the veranda, and looked tearfully through the glass doors; but St Clare heard and said nothing, he saw only that look on the face of the little sleeper.

'Oh, if she would only wake, and speak once more!' he said; and, stooping over her, he spoke in her ear – 'Eva, darling!'

The large blue eyes unclosed – a smile passed over her face; she tried to raise her head, and to speak.

'Do you know me, Eva?'

'Dear papa,' said the child, with a last effort, throwing her arms about his neck. In a moment they dropped again; and, as St Clare raised his head, he saw a spasm of mortal agony pass over the face – she struggled for breath, and threw up her little hands.

'O God, this is dreadful!' he said, turning away in agony, and wringing Tom's hand, scarce conscious what he was doing. 'Oh, Tom, my boy, it is killing me!'

Tom had his master's hands between his own; and, with tears streaming down his dark cheeks, looked up for help where he had always been used to look.

'Pray that this may be cut short!' said St Clare, 'this wrings my heart.'

'Oh, bless the Lord! it's over – it's over, dear master!' said Tom; 'look at her.'

The child lay panting on her pillows, as one exhausted – the large clear eyes rolled up and fixed. Ah, what said those eyes, that spoke so much of heaven? Earth was passed, and earthly pain; but so solemn, so mysterious, was the triumphant brightness of that face, that it checked even the sobs of sorrow. They pressed around her, in breathless stillness.

'Eva,' said St Clare, gently.

She did not hear.

'Oh, Eva, tell us what you see! What is it?' said her father.

A bright, a glorious smile passed over her face, and she said, brokenly – 'Oh! love – joy – peace!' gave one sigh, and passed from death unto life!

'Farewell, beloved child! the bright, eternal doors have closed after thee; we shall see thy sweet face no more. Oh, woe for them who watched thy entrance into heaven, when they shall wake and find only the cold grey sky of daily life, and thou gone for ever!'[219]

CHAPTER XXVII

'This is the Last of Earth'[220]

JOHN Q. ADAMS

THE STATUETTES AND PICTURES in Eva's room were shrouded in white napkins, and only hushed breathings and muffled footfalls were heard there, and the light stole in solemnly through windows partially darkened by closed blinds.

The bed was draped in white; and there, beneath the drooping angel-figure, lay a little sleeping form – sleeping never to awake!

There she lay, robed in one of the simple white dresses she had been wont to wear when living; the rose-coloured light through the curtains cast over the icy coldness of death a warm glow. The heavy eyelashes drooped softly on the pure cheek; the head was turned a little to one side, as if in natural sleep, but there was diffused over every lineament of the face that high celestial expression, that mingling of rapture and repose, which showed it was no earthly or temporary sleep, but the long, sacred rest which 'He giveth to his beloved'.[221]

There is no death to such as thou, dear Eva! neither darkness nor shadow of death; only such a bright fading as when the morning star fades in the golden dawn. Thine is the victory without the battle, the crown without the conflict.

So did St Clare think, as, with folded arms, he stood there gazing. Ah! who shall say what he did think? for, from the hour that voices had said, in the dying chamber, 'she is gone', it had been all a dreary mist, a heavy 'dimness of anguish'.[222] He had heard voices around him; he had had questions asked, and answered them; they had asked him when he would have the funeral, and where they should lay her; and he had answered impatiently, that he cared not.

Adolph and Rosa had arranged the chamber; volatile, fickle and childish, as they generally were, they were soft-hearted and full of feeling; and while Miss Ophelia presided over the general details of order and neatness, it was their hands that added those soft poetic touches to the arrangements, that took from the death-room the grim and ghastly air which too often marks a New England funeral.

There were still flowers on the shelves – all white, delicate, and fragrant, with graceful, drooping leaves. Eva's little table, covered with white, bore on it her favourite vase, with a single white moss rosebud in it. The folds of the drapery, the fall of the curtains, had been arranged and re-arranged, by Adolph and Rosa, with that nicety of eye which characterises their race. Even now, while St Clare stood there thinking, little Rosa tripped softly into the chamber with a basket of white flowers. She stepped back when she saw St Clare, and stopped respectfully; but, seeing that he did not observe her, she came forward to place them around the dead. St Clare saw her as in a dream, while she placed in the small hands a fair cape jessamine, and, with admirable taste, disposed other flowers around the couch.

The door opened again, and Topsy, her eyes swelled with crying, appeared, holding something under her apron. Rosa made a quick, forbidding gesture; but she took a step into the room.

'You must go out,' said Rosa, in a sharp positive whisper; '*you* haven't any business here!'

'Oh, do let me! I brought a flower – such a pretty one!' said Topsy, holding up a half-blown tea rosebud. 'Do let me put just one there.'

'Get along!' said Rosa, more decidedly.

'Let her stay!' said St Clare, suddenly stamping his foot. 'She shall come.'

Rosa suddenly retreated, and Topsy came forward and laid her offering at the feet of the corpse; then suddenly, with a wild and bitter cry, she threw herself on the floor alongside the bed, and wept and moaned aloud.

Miss Ophelia hastened into the room, and tried to raise and silence her; but in vain.

'Oh, Miss Eva! Oh, Miss Eva! I wish I's dead, too – I do!'

There was a piercing wildness in the cry; the blood flushed into St Clare's white, marble-like face, and the first tears he had shed since Eva died stood in his eyes.

'Get up, child,' said Miss Ophelia, in a softened voice; 'don't cry so.

Miss Eva is gone to heaven; she is an angel.'

'But I can't see her!' said Topsy. 'I never shall see her!' and she sobbed again.

They all stood a moment in silence.

'*She* said she *loved* me,' said Topsy – 'she did! Oh, dear! oh, dear! there an't *nobody* left now – there an't!'

'That's true enough,' said St Clare; 'but do,' he said to Miss Ophelia, 'see if you can't comfort the poor creature.'

'I jist wish I hadn't never been born,' said Topsy. 'I didn't want to be born, no ways; and I don't see no use on't.'

Miss Ophelia raised her gently, but firmly, and took her from the room; but, as she did so, some tears fell from her eyes.

'Topsy, you poor child,' she said, as she led her into her room, 'don't give up! *I* can love you, though I am not like that dear little child. I hope I've learnt something of the love of Christ from her. I can love you; I do, and I'll try to help you to grow up a good Christian girl.'

Miss Ophelia's voice was more than her words, and more than that were the honest tears that fell down her face. From that hour she acquired an influence over the mind of the destitute child that she never lost.

'Oh, my Eva, whose little hour on earth did so much of good,' thought St Clare, 'what account have I to give for my long years?'

There were, for a while, soft whisperings and footfalls in the chamber, as one after another stole in, to look at the dead; and then came the little coffin; and then there was a funeral, and carriages drove to the door, and strangers came and were seated; and there were white scarfs and ribbons, and crape bands, and mourners dressed in black crape; and there were words read from the Bible, and prayers offered; and St Clare lived, and walked, and moved, as one who has shed every tear. To the last he saw only one thing, that golden head in the coffin; but then he saw the cloth spread over it, the lid of the coffin closed; and he walked, when he was put beside the others, down to a little place at the bottom of the garden, and there, by the mossy seat where she and Tom had talked, and sung, and read so often, was the little grave. St Clare stood beside it – looked vacantly down; he saw them lower the little coffin; he heard, dimly, the solemn words. 'I am the Resurrection and the Life; he that believeth in me, though he were dead, yet shall he live;'[223] and, as the earth was cast in and filled up the little grave, he could not realise that it was his Eva that they were hiding from his sight.

Nor was it – not Eva, but only the frail seed of that bright, immortal form with which she shall yet come forth, in the day of the Lord Jesus!

And then all were gone, and the mourners went back to the place which should know her no more; and Marie's room was darkened, and she lay on the bed, sobbing and moaning in uncontrollable grief, and calling every moment for the attentions of all her servants. Of course, they had no time to cry – why should they? the grief was *her* grief, and she was fully convinced that nobody on earth did, could, or would feel it as she did.

'St Clare did not shed a tear,' she said; 'he didn't sympathise with her; it was perfectly wonderful to think how hard-hearted and unfeeling he was, when he must know how she suffered.'

So much are people the slave of their eye and ear, that many of the servants really thought that missis was the principal sufferer in the case, especially as Marie began to have hysterical spasms, and sent for the doctor, and at last declared herself dying; and, in the running and scampering, and bringing up hot bottles, and heating of flannels, and chafing, and fussing, that ensued, there was quite a diversion.

Tom, however, had a feeling at his own heart that drew him to his master. He followed him wherever he walked, wistfully and sadly, and when he saw him sitting, so pale and quiet, in Eva's room, holding before his eyes her little open Bible, though seeing no letter or word of what was in it, there was more sorrow to Tom in that still, fixed, tearless eye, than in all Marie's moans and lamentations.

In a few days the St Clare family were back again in the city; Augustine, with the restlessness of grief, longing for another scene, to change the current of his thoughts. So they left the house and garden, with its little grave, and came back to New Orleans; and St Clare walked the streets busily, and strove to fill up the chasm in his heart with hurry and bustle, and change of place; and people who saw him in the street, or met him at the café, knew of his loss only by the weed[224] on his hat; for there he was, smiling and talking, and reading the newspaper, and speculating on politics, and attending to business matters; and who could see that all this smiling outside was but a hollowed shell over a heart that was a dark and silent sepulchre?

'Mr St Clare is a singular man,' said Marie to Miss Ophelia, in a complaining tone. 'I used to think, if there was anything in the world he did love, it was our dear little Eva; but he seems to be forgetting her very easily. I cannot ever get him to talk about her. I really did think he would show more feeling!'

'Still waters run deepest, they used to tell me,' said Miss Ophelia, oracularly.

'Oh, I don't believe in such things; it's all talk. If people have feeling, they will show it – they can't help it; but, then, it's a great misfortune to have feeling. I'd rather have been made like St Clare. My feelings prey upon me so!'

'Sure, missis, Mas'r St Clare is gettin' thin as a shader. They say, he don't never eat nothin',' said Mammy. 'I know he don't forget Miss Eva; I know there couldn't nobody – dear, little, blessed cretur!' she added, wiping her eyes.

'Well, at all events, he has no consideration for me,' said Marie; 'he hasn't spoken one word of sympathy, and he must know how much more a mother feels than any man can.'

'The heart knoweth its own bitterness,'[225] said Miss Ophelia, gravely.

'That's just what I think. I know just what I feel – nobody else seems to. Eva used to, but she is gone!' and Marie lay back on her lounge, and began to sob disconsolately.

Marie was one of those unfortunately constituted mortals, in whose eyes whatever is lost and gone assumes a value which it never had in possession. Whatever she had, she seemed to survey only to pick flaws in it; but, once fairly away, there was no end to her valuation of it.

While this conversation was taking place in the parlour, another was going on in St Clare's library.

Tom, who was always uneasily following his master about, had seen him go to his library, some hours before; and, after vainly waiting for him to come out, determined, at last, to make an errand in. He entered softly. St Clare lay on his lounge, at the further end of the room. He was lying on his face, with Eva's Bible open before him, at a little distance. Tom walked up, and stood by the sofa. He hesitated; and, while he was hesitating, St Clare suddenly raised himself up. The honest face, so full of grief, and with such an imploring expression of affection and sympathy, struck his master. He laid his hand on Tom's, and bowed down his forehead on it.

'Oh, Tom, my boy, the whole world is as empty as an eggshell.'

'I know it, mas'r, I know it,' said Tom. 'But, oh, if mas'r could only look up – up where our dear Miss Eva is – up to the dear Lord Jesus!'

'Ah, Tom! I do look up; but the trouble is, I don't see anything, when I do. I wish I could.'

Tom sighed heavily.

'It seems to be given to children, and poor, honest fellows like you, to see what we can't,' said St Clare. 'How comes it?'

'Thou hast "hid from the wise and prudent, and revealed unto babes",' murmured Tom; ' "even so, Father, for so it seemed good in thy sight".'[226]

'Tom, I don't believe – I can't believe, I've got the habit of doubting,' said St Clare. 'I want to believe this Bible – and I can't.'

'Dear mas'r, pray to the good Lord – "Lord, I believe; help thou my unbelief." '227

'Who knows anything about anything?' said St Clare, his eyes wandering dreamily, and speaking to himself. 'Was all that beautiful love and faith only one of the ever-shifting phases of human feeling, having nothing real to rest on, passing away with the little breath? And is there no more Eva – no heaven – no Christ – nothing?'

'O dear mas'r, there is! I know it; I'm sure of it,' said Tom, falling on his knees. 'Do, do, dear mas'r, believe it!'

'How do you know there's any Christ, Tom? You never saw the Lord.'

'Felt him in my soul, mas'r – feel him now! Oh, mas'r, when I was sold away from my old woman and the children, I was jest a'most broke up. I felt as if there warn't nothin' left; and then the good Lord, he stood by me, and he says, "Fear not, Tom;" and he brings light and joy into a poor feller's soul – makes all peace; and I's so happy, and loves everybody, and feels willin' jest to be the Lord's, and have the Lord's will done, and be put jest where the Lord wants to put me. I know it couldn't come from me, 'cause I's a poor, complainin' cretur; it comes from the Lord; and I know he's willin' to do for mas'r.'

Tom spoke with fast-running tears and choking voice. St Clare leaned his head on his shoulder, and wrung the hard, faithful, black hand.

'Tom, you love me,' he said.

'I's willin' to lay down my life, this blessed day, to see mas'r a Christian.'

'Poor, foolish boy!' said St Clare, half-raising himself. 'I'm not worthy of the love of one good, honest heart, like yours.'

'Oh, mas'r, dere's more than me loves you – the blessed Lord Jesus loves you.'

'How do you know that, Tom?' said St Clare.

'Feels it in my soul. Oh, mas'r! "the love of Christ, that passeth knowledge".'228

'Singular!' said St Clare, turning away, 'that the story of a man that lived and died eighteen hundred years ago can affect people so yet. But he was no man,' he added, suddenly. 'No man ever had such long and living power! Oh, that I could believe what my mother taught me, and pray as I did when I was a boy!'

'If mas'r pleases,' said Tom, 'Miss Eva used to read this so beautifully. I wish mas'r'd be so good as read it. Don't get no readin', hardly, now Miss Eva's gone.'

The chapter was the eleventh of John – the touching account of the raising of Lazarus.[229] St Clare read it aloud, often pausing to wrestle down feelings which were roused by the pathos of the story. Tom knelt before him, with clasped hands, and with an absorbed expression of love, trust, adoration, on his quiet face.

'Tom,' said his master, 'this is all real to you!'

'I can jest fairly *see* it, mas'r,' said Tom.

'I wish I had your eyes, Tom.'

'I wish, to the dear Lord mas'r had!'

'But, Tom, you know that I have a great deal more knowledge than you. What if I should tell you that I don't believe this Bible?'

'Oh, mas'r!' said Tom, holding up his hands, with a deprecating gesture.

'Wouldn't it shake your faith some, Tom?'

'Not a grain,' said Tom.

'Why, Tom, you must know I know the most.'

'Oh, mas'r, haven't you jest read how He hides from the wise and prudent, and reveals unto babes?[230] But mas'r wasn't in earnest, for sartin, now?' said Tom, anxiously.

'No, Tom, I was not. I don't disbelieve, and I think there is reason to believe; and still I don't. It's a troublesome bad habit I've got, Tom.'

'If mas'r would only pray!'

'How do you know I don't, Tom?'

'Does mas'r?'

'I would, Tom, if there was anybody there when I pray; but it's all speaking unto nothing, when I do. But come, Tom, you pray, now, and show me how.'

Tom's heart was full; he poured it out in prayer, like waters that have been long suppressed. One thing was plain enough; Tom thought there was somebody to hear, whether there were or not. In fact, St Clare felt himself borne, on the tide of his faith and feeling, almost to the gates of that heaven he seemed so vividly to conceive. It seemed to bring him nearer to Eva.

'Thank you, my boy,' said St Clare, when Tom rose. 'I like to hear you, Tom; but go, now, and leave me alone; some other time, I'll talk more.'

Tom silently left the room.

CHAPTER XXVIII

Reunion

WEEK AFTER WEEK glided away in the St Clare mansion, and the waves of life settled back to their usual flow, where that little bark had gone down. For how imperiously, how coolly, in disregard of all one's feeling, does the hard, cold, uninteresting course of daily realities move on! Still must we eat, and drink, and sleep, and wake again – still bargain, buy, sell, ask and answer questions – pursue, in short, a thousand shadows, though all interest in them be over; the cold mechanical habit of living remaining, after all vital interest in it has fled.

All the interests and hopes of St Clare's life had unconsciously wound themselves around this child. It was for Eva that he had managed his property; it was for Eva that he had planned the disposal of his time; and to do this and that for Eva – to buy, improve, alter, and arrange, or dispose something for her – had been so long his habit, that now she was gone, there seemed nothing to be thought of, and nothing to be done.

True, there was another life – a life which, once believed in, stands as a solemn, significant figure before the otherwise unmeaning ciphers of time, changing them to orders of mysterious, untold value. St Clare knew this well; and often, in many a weary hour, he heard that slender, childish voice calling him to the skies, and saw that little hand pointing to him the way of life; but a heavy lethargy of sorrow lay on him – he could not arise. He had one of those natures which could better and more clearly conceive of religious things from its own perceptions and instincts than many a matter-of-fact and practical Christian. The gift to appreciate and the sense to feel the finer shades and relations of moral things, often seems an attribute of those whose whole life shows a careless disregard of them. Hence Moore, Byron, Goethe,[231] often speak words more wisely descriptive of the true religious sentiment than another man whose whole life is governed by it. In such minds, disregard of religion is a more fearful treason – a more deadly sin.

St Clare had never pretended to govern himself by any religious obligation; and a certain fineness of nature gave him such an instinctive view of the extent of the requirements of Christianity, that he shrank, by anticipation, from what he felt would be the exactions of his own conscience, if he once did resolve to assume them. For, so inconsistent is human nature, especially in the ideal, that not to undertake a thing at all seems better than to undertake and come short.

Still St Clare was, in many respects, another man. He read his little Eva's Bible seriously and honestly; he thought more soberly and practically of his relations to his servants – enough to make him extremely dissatisfied with both his past and present course; and one thing he did, soon after his return to New Orleans, and that was to commence the legal steps necessary to Tom's emancipation, which was to be perfected as soon as he could get through the necessary formalities. Meantime, he attached himself to Tom more and more, every day. In all the wide world, there was nothing that seemed to remind him so much of Eva; and he would insist on keeping him constantly about him, and, fastidious and unapproachable as he was with regard to his deeper feelings, he almost thought aloud to Tom. Nor would anyone have wondered at it, who had seen the expression of affection and devotion with which Tom continually followed his young master.

'Well, Tom,' said St Clare, the day after he had commenced the legal formalities for his enfranchisement, 'I'm going to make a free man of you; so, have your trunk packed, and get ready to set out for Kentuck.'

The sudden light of joy that shone in Tom's face as he raised his hands to heaven, his emphatic 'Bless the Lord!' rather discomposed St Clare; he did not like it that Tom should be so ready to leave him.

'You haven't had such very bad times here, that you need be in such a rapture, Tom,' he said, dryly.

'No, no, mas'r! 'tan't that, it's bein' a *free man*! That's what I'm joyin' for.'

'Why, Tom, don't you think, for your own part, you've been better off than to be free?'

'*No, indeed*, Mas'r St Clare,' said Tom, with a flash of energy. 'No, indeed!'

'Why, Tom, you couldn't possibly have earned, by your work, such clothes and such living as I have given you.'

'Knows all that, Mas'r St Clare; mas'r's been too good; but, mas'r, I'd rather have poor clothes, poor house, poor everything, and have 'em *mine*, than have the best, and have 'em any man's else! I had so, mas'r; I think it's natur, mas'r!'

'I suppose so, Tom, and you'll be going off and leaving me, in a month or so,' he added, rather discontentedly. 'Though why you shouldn't, no mortal knows,' he said, in a gayer tone; and, getting up, he began to walk the floor.

'Not while mas'r is in trouble,' said Tom. 'I'll stay with mas'r as long as he wants me – so as I can be any use.'

'Not while I'm in trouble, Tom?' said St Clare, looking sadly out of the window. 'And when will *my* trouble be over?'

'When Mas'r St Clare's a Christian,' said Tom.

'And you really mean to stay by till that day comes?' said St Clare, half smiling, as he turned from the window, and laid his hand on Tom's shoulder. 'Ah, Tom, you soft, silly boy! I won't keep you till that day. Go home to your wife and children, and give my love to all.'

'I's faith to believe that day will come,' said Tom, earnestly, and with tears in his eyes; 'the Lord has a work for mas'r.'

'A work, eh?' said St Clare; 'well, now, Tom, give me your views on what sort of a work it is; let's hear.'

'Why, even a poor fellow like me has a work from the Lord; and Mas'r St Clare, that has larnin, and riches, and friends, how much he might do for the Lord!'

'Tom, you seem to think the Lord needs a great deal done for him,' said St Clare, smiling.

'We does for the Lord when we does for his critturs,' said Tom.

'Good theology, Tom; better than Dr B. preaches, I dare swear,' said St Clare.

The conversation was here interrupted by the announcement of some visitors.

Marie St Clare felt the loss of Eva as deeply as she could feel anything; and, as she was a woman that had a great faculty of making everybody unhappy when she was, her immediate attendants had still stronger reason to regret the loss of their young mistress, whose winning ways and gentle intercessions had so often been a shield to them from the tyrannical and selfish exactions of her mother. Poor old Mammy, in particular, whose heart, severed from all natural domestic ties, had consoled itself with this one beautiful being, was almost heartbroken. She cried day and night, and was, from excess of sorrow, less skilful and alert in her ministrations on her mistress than usual, which drew down a constant storm of invectives on her defenceless head.

Miss Ophelia felt the loss; but, in her good and honest heart, it bore fruit unto everlasting life. She was more softened, more gentle; and though equally assiduous in every duty, it was with a chastened and quiet air, as one who communed with her own heart not in vain. She was more diligent in teaching Topsy – taught her mainly from the Bible – did not any longer shrink from her touch, or manifest an ill-repressed disgust, because she felt none. She viewed her now through the softened medium that Eva's hand had first held before her eyes, and saw in her only an immortal creature, whom God had sent to be led by her to glory and virtue. Topsy did not become at once a saint; but the life and death of Eva did work a marked change in her. The callous indifference was gone; there was now sensibility, hope, desire, and the striving for good – a strife irregular, interrupted, suspended oft, but yet renewed again.

One day, when Topsy had been sent for by Miss Ophelia, she came, hastily thrusting something into her bosom.

'What are you doing there, you limb? You've been stealing something, I'll be bound,' said the imperious little Rosa, who had been sent to call her, seizing her, at the same time, roughly by the arm.

'You go 'long, Miss Rosa!' said Topsy, pulling from her; ' 'tan't none o' your business!'

'None o' your sa'ce!' said Rosa. 'I saw you hiding something – I know yer tricks,' and Rosa seized her arm, and tried to force her hand into her bosom, while Topsy, enraged, kicked and fought valiantly for what she considered her rights. The clamour and confusion of the battle drew Miss Ophelia and St Clare both to the spot.

'She's been stealing!' said Rosa.

'I han't, neither!' vociferated Topsy, sobbing with passion.

'Give me that, whatever it is!' said Miss Ophelia, firmly.

Topsy hesitated; but, on a second order, pulled out of her bosom a little parcel done up in the foot of one of her own old stockings.

Miss Ophelia turned it out. There was a small book, which had been given to Topsy by Eva, containing a single verse of Scripture, arranged for every day in the year, and in a paper the curl of hair that she had given her on that memorable day when she had taken her last farewell.

St Clare was a good deal affected at the sight of it; the little book had been rolled in a long strip of black crape, torn from the funeral weeds.

'What did you wrap *this* round the book for?' said St Clare, holding up the crape.

' 'Cause – 'cause – 'cause 'twas Miss Eva. Oh, don't take 'em away, please!' she said; and, sitting flat down on the floor, and putting her apron over her head, she began to sob vehemently.

It was a curious mixture of the pathetic and the ludicrous – the little old stocking – black crape – text-book – fair, soft curl – and Topsy's utter distress.

St Clare smiled; but there were tears in his eyes, as he said –

'Come, come – don't cry; you shall have them!' and, putting them together, he threw them into her lap, and drew Miss Ophelia with him into the parlour.

'I really think you can make something of that concern,' he said, pointing with his thumb backward over his shoulder. 'Any mind that is capable of a *real sorrow* is capable of good. You must try and do something with her.'

'The child has improved greatly,' said Miss Ophelia. 'I have great hopes of her; but Augustine,' she said, laying her hand on his arm, 'one thing I want to ask; whose is this child to be? – yours or mine?'

'Why, I gave her to *you*,' said Augustine.

'But not legally; I want her to be mine legally,' said Miss Ophelia.

'Whew! cousin,' said Augustine. 'What will the Abolition Society think? They'll have a day of fasting appointed for this backsliding, if you become a slave-holder!'

'Oh, nonsense! I want her mine, that I may have a right to take her to the free States, and give her her liberty, that all I am trying to do be not undone.'

'Oh, cousin, what an awful "doing evil that good may come!"[232] I can't encourage it.'

'I don't want you to joke, but to reason,' said Miss Ophelia. 'There is no use in my trying to make this child a Christian child, unless I save her from all the chances and reverses of slavery; and, if you really are willing I should have her, I want you to give me a deed of gift, or some legal paper.'

'Well, well,' said St Clare, 'I will;' and he sat down, and unfolded a newspaper to read.

'But I want it done now,' said Miss Ophelia.

'What's your hurry?'

'Because now is the only time there ever is to do a thing in,' said Miss Ophelia. 'Come, now, here's paper, pen, and ink; just write a paper.'

St Clare, like most men of his class of mind, cordially hated the present tense of action, generally; and, therefore, he was considerably annoyed by Miss Ophelia's downrightness.

'Why, what's the matter?' said he. 'Can't you take my word? One would think you had taken lessons of the Jews, coming at a fellow so!'

'I want to make sure of it,' said Miss Ophelia. 'You may die, or fail, and then Topsy be hustled off to auction, spite of all I can do.'

'Really, you are quite provident. Well, seeing I'm in the hands of a Yankee, there is nothing for it but to concede;' and St Clare rapidly wrote off a deed of gift, which, as he was well versed in the forms of law, he could easily do, and signed his name to it in sprawling capitals, concluding by a tremendous flourish.

'There, isn't that black and white, now, Miss Vermont?' he said, as he handed it to her.

'Good boy,' said Miss Ophelia, smiling. 'But must it not be witnessed?'

'Oh, bother! – yes. Here,' he said, opening the door into Marie's apartment, 'Marie, cousin wants your autograph; just put your name down here.'

'What's this?' said Marie, as she ran over the paper. 'Ridiculous! I thought cousin was too pious for such horrid things,' she added, as she carelessly wrote her name; 'but, if she has a fancy for that article, I am sure she's welcome.'

'There, now, she's yours, body and soul,' said St Clare, handing the paper.

'No more mine now than she was before,' said Miss Ophelia. 'Nobody but God has a right to give her to me; but I can protect her now.'

'Well, she's yours by a fiction of law, then,' said St Clare, as he turned back into the parlour, and sat down to his paper.

Miss Ophelia, who seldom sat much in Marie's company, followed him into the parlour, having first carefully laid away the paper.

'Augustine,' she said, suddenly, as she sat knitting, 'have you ever made any provision for your servants, in case of your death?'

'No,' said St Clare, as he read on.

'Then all your indulgence to them may prove a great cruelty, by and by.'

St Clare had often thought the same thing himself; but he answered, negligently –

'Well, I mean to make a provision, by and by.'

'When?' said Miss Ophelia.

'Oh, one of these days.'

'What if you should die first?'

'Cousin, what's the matter?' said St Clare, laying down his paper and looking at her. 'Do you think I show symptoms of yellow fever or cholera, that you are making *post mortem* arrangements with such zeal?'

' "In the midst of life we are in death," '[233] said Miss Ophelia.

St Clare rose up, and laying the paper down, carelessly, walked to the door that stood open on the veranda, to put an end to a conversation that was not agreeable to him. Mechanically, he repeated the last word again – '*Death!*' – and, as he leaned against the railings, and watched the sparkling water as it rose and fell in the fountain; and, as in a dim and dizzy haze, saw the flowers and trees and vases of the courts, he repeated again the mystic word so common in every mouth, yet of such fearful power, 'Death!' 'Strange that there should be such a word,' he said, 'and such a thing, and we ever forget it; that one should be living, warm and beautiful, full of hopes, desires and wants, one day, and the next be gone, utterly gone, and for ever!'

It was a warm, golden evening; and, as he walked to the other end of the veranda, he saw Tom busily intent on his Bible, pointing, as he did so, with his finger to each successive word, and whispering them to himself with an earnest air.

'Want me to read to you, Tom?' said St Clare, seating himself carelessly by him.

'If mas'r pleases,' said Tom, gratefully. 'Mas'r makes it so much plainer.'

St Clare took the book and glanced at the place, and began reading one of the passages which Tom had designated by the heavy marks around it. It ran as follows: 'When the Son of man shall come in his glory, and all his holy angels with him, then shall he sit upon the throne of his glory: and before him shall be gathered all nations; and he shall separate them one from another, as a shepherd divideth his sheep from the goats.' St Clare read on in an animated voice, till he came to the last of the verses.

'Then shall the King say unto them on his left hand, Depart from me, ye cursed, into everlasting fire: for I was an hungered, and ye gave me no meat: I was thirsty, and ye gave me no drink: I was a stranger, and ye took me not in: naked, and ye clothed me not: I was sick, and in prison, and ye visited me not. Then shall they answer unto him, Lord, when saw we thee an hungered, or athirst, or a stranger, or naked, or sick, or in prison, and did not minister unto thee? Then shall he say unto them, Inasmuch as ye did it not to one of the least of these my brethren, ye did it not to me.'[234]

St Clare seemed struck with this last passage, for he read it twice – the second time slowly, and as if he were revolving the words in his mind.

'Tom,' he said, 'these folks that get such hard measure seem to have been doing just what I have, living good, easy, respectable lives; and not troubling themselves to enquire how many of their brethren were hungry or athirst, or sick, or in prison.'

Tom did not answer.

St Clare rose up and walked thoughtfully up and down the veranda, seeming to forget everything in his own thoughts; so absorbed was he, that Tom had to remind him twice that the tea-bell had rung, before he could get his attention.

St Clare was absent and thoughtful, all tea-time. After tea, he and Marie and Miss Ophelia took possession of the parlour, almost in silence.

Marie disposed herself on a lounge, under a silken mosquito curtain, and was soon sound asleep. Miss Ophelia silently busied herself with her knitting. St Clare sat down to the piano, and began playing a soft and melancholy movement with the Aeolian[235] accompaniment. He seemed in a deep reverie, and to be soliloquising to himself by music. After a little, he opened one of the drawers, took out an old music-book whose leaves were yellow with age, and began turning it over.

'There,' he said to Miss Ophelia, 'this was one of my mother's books, and here is her handwriting – come and look at it. She copied and arranged this from Mozart's Requiem.' Miss Ophelia came accordingly.

'It was something she used to sing often,' said St Clare. 'I think I can hear her now.'

He struck a few majestic chords, and began singing that grand old Latin piece, the 'Dies Irae'.[236]

Tom, who was listening in the outer veranda, was drawn by the sound to the very door, where he stood earnestly. He did not understand the words, of course; but the music and manner of singing appeared to affect him strongly, especially when St Clare sang the more pathetic parts. Tom would have sympathised more heartily, if he had known the meaning of the beautiful words –

Recordare, Jesu pie,	Think, O Jesus, for what reason
Quod sum causa tuae viae,	Thou endured'st earth's spite
Ne me perdas, illa die.	and treason,
Quaerens me, sedisti lassus,	Nor me lose, in that dread season.
Redemisti crucem passus,	Seeking me, thy worn feet hasted,
Tantus labor non sit cassus.	On the cross thy soul death tasted,
	Let not all these toils be wasted.

St Clare threw a deep and pathetic expression into the words; for the shadowy veil of years seemed drawn away, and he seemed to hear his mother's voice leading his. Voice and instrument seemed both living, and threw out with vivid sympathy those strains which the ethereal Mozart first conceived as his own dying requiem.

When St Clare had done singing, he sat leaning his head upon his hand a few moments, and then began walking up and down the floor.

'What a sublime conception is that of a last judgement!' said he. 'A righting of all the wrongs of ages! – a solving of all moral problems, by an unanswerable wisdom! It is, indeed, a wonderful image.'

'It is a fearful one to us,' said Miss Ophelia.

'It ought to be to me, I suppose,' said St Clare, stopping, thoughtfully. 'I was reading to Tom this afternoon that chapter in Matthew that gives an account of it, and I have been quite struck with it. One should have expected some terrible enormities charged to those who are excluded from Heaven, as the reason; but no – they are condemned for *not* doing positive good, as if that included every possible harm.'

'Perhaps,' said Miss Ophelia, 'it is impossible for a person who does no good not to do harm.'

'And what,' said St Clare, speaking abstractedly, but with deep feeling, 'what shall be said of one whose own heart, whose education, and the wants of society, have called in vain to some noble purpose; who has floated on, a dreamy, neutral, spectator of the struggles, agonies, and wrongs of man, when he should have been a worker?'

'I should say,' said Miss Ophelia, 'that he ought to repent, and begin now.'

'Always practical and to the point!' said St Clare, his face breaking out into a smile. 'You never leave me any time for general reflections, cousin; you always bring me short up against the actual present; you have a kind of eternal *now*, always in your mind.'

'*Now* is all the time I have anything to do with,' said Miss Ophelia.

'Dear little Eva – poor child!' said St Clare, 'she had set her little simple soul on a good work for me.'

It was the first time since Eva's death that he had ever said as many words as these of her, and he spoke now evidently repressing very strong feeling.

'My view of Christianity is such,' he added, 'that I think no man can consistently profess it without throwing the whole weight of his being against this monstrous system of injustice that lies at the foundation of all our society; and, if need be, sacrificing himself in the battle. That is, I mean that *I* could not be a Christian otherwise, though I have certainly had intercourse with a great many enlightened and Christian people who did no such thing; and I confess that the apathy of religious people on this subject, their want of perception of wrongs that filled me with horror, have engendered in me more scepticism than any other thing.'

'If you knew all this,' said Miss Ophelia, 'why didn't you do it?'

'Oh, because I have had only that kind of benevolence which consists in lying on a sofa, and cursing the church and clergy for not being martyrs and confessors. One can see, you know, very easily, how others ought to be martyrs.'

'Well, are you going to do differently now?' said Miss Ophelia.

'God only knows the future,' said St Clare. 'I am braver than I was, because I have lost all; and he who has nothing to lose can afford all risks.'

'And what are you going to do?'

'My duty, I hope, to the poor and lowly, as fast as I find it out,' said St Clare, 'beginning with my own servants, for whom I have yet done nothing; and, perhaps, at some future day, it may appear that I can do something for a whole class; something to save my country from the disgrace of that false position in which she now stands before all civilised nations.'

'Do you suppose it possible that a nation ever will voluntarily emancipate?' said Miss Ophelia.

'I don't know,' said St Clare. 'This is a day of great deeds. Heroism and disinterestedness are rising up, here and there, in the earth. The Hungarian nobles[237] set free millions of serfs, at an immense pecuniary loss; and, perhaps, among us may be found generous spirits, who do not estimate honour and justice by dollars and cents.'

'I hardly think so,' said Miss Ophelia.

'But, suppose we should rise up tomorrow and emancipate, who would educate these millions, and teach them how to use their freedom? They never would rise to do much among us. The fact is, we are too lazy and unpractical ourselves ever to give them much of an idea of that industry and energy which is necessary to form them into men. They will have to go north, where labour is the fashion – the universal custom; and tell me, now, is there enough Christian philanthropy among your Northern States to bear with the process of their education and elevation?[238] You send thousands of dollars to foreign missions; but could you endure to have the heathen sent into your towns and villages, and give your time, and thoughts, and money, to raise them to the Christian standard? That's what I want to know. If we emancipate, are you willing to educate? How many families, in your town, would take in a negro man and woman, teach them, bear with them, and seek to make them Christians? How many merchants would take Adolph, if I wanted to make him a clerk; or mechanics, if I wanted him taught a trade? If I wanted to put Jane and Rosa to a school, how many schools are there in the Northern States that would take them in? how many families that would board them? and yet they are as white as many a woman, North or South. You see, cousin, I want justice done us. We are in a bad position. We are the more *obvious* oppressors of the negro; but the unchristian prejudice of the North is an oppressor almost equally severe.'

'Well, cousin, I know it is so,' said Miss Ophelia. 'I know it was so with me, till I saw that it was my duty to overcome it; but, I trust I have overcome it; and I know there are many good people at the North who in this matter need only to be *taught* what their duty is, to do it. It would certainly be a greater self-denial to receive heathen among us, than to send missionaries to them; but I think we would do it.'

'*You* would, I know,' said St Clare. 'I'd like to see anything you wouldn't do, if you thought it your duty!'

'Well, I'm not uncommonly good,' said Miss Ophelia. 'Others would, if they saw things as I do. I intend to take Topsy home, when I go. I suppose our folks will wonder, at first; but I think they will be brought to see as I do. Besides, I know there are many people at the North who do exactly what you said.'

'Yes, but they are a minority; and, if we should begin to emancipate to any extent, we should soon hear from you.'

Miss Ophelia did not reply. There was a pause of some moments; and St Clare's countenance was overcast by a sad, dreamy expression.

'I don't know what makes me think of my mother so much, tonight,' he said. 'I have a strange kind of feeling, as if she were near me. I keep thinking of things she used to say. Strange, what brings these past things so vividly back to us, sometimes!'

St Clare walked up and down the room for some minutes more, and then said –

'I believe I'll go down street, a few moments, and hear the news, tonight.'

He took his hat, and passed out.

Tom followed him to the passage, out of the court, and asked if he should attend him.

'No, my boy,' said St Clare. 'I shall be back in an hour.'

Tom sat down in the veranda. It was a beautiful moonlight evening, and he sat watching the rising and falling spray of the fountain, and listening to its murmur. Tom thought of his home, and that he should soon be a free man, and able to return to it at will. He thought how he should work to buy his wife and boys. He felt the muscles of his brawny arms with a sort of joy, as he thought they would soon belong to himself, and how much they could do to work out the freedom of his family. Then he thought of his noble young master, and, ever second to that, came the habitual prayer that he had always offered for him; and then his thoughts passed on to the beautiful Eva, whom he now thought of among the angels; and he thought till he almost fancied that that bright face and golden hair were looking upon him, out of the spray of the fountain. And, so musing, he fell asleep, and dreamed he saw her coming bounding towards him, just as she used to come, with a wreath of jessamine in her hair, her cheeks bright, and her eyes radiant with delight; but, as he looked, she seemed to rise from the ground; her cheeks wore a paler hue – her eyes had a deep, divine radiance, a golden halo seemed around her head – and she vanished from his sight; and Tom was awakened by a loud knocking, and a sound of many voices at the gate.

He hastened to undo it; and, with smothered voices and heavy tread, came several men, bringing a body, wrapped in a cloak, and lying on a shutter. The light of the lamp fell full on the face; and Tom gave a wild cry of amazement and despair that rang through all the galleries as the men advanced, with their burden to the open parlour door, where Miss Ophelia still sat knitting.

St Clare had turned into a café, to look over an evening paper. As he was reading, an affray arose between two gentlemen in the room, who were both partially intoxicated. St Clare and one or two others made an effort to separate them, and St Clare received a fatal stab in the side with a bowie-knife, which he was attempting to wrest from one of them.

The house was full of cries and lamentations, shrieks and screams; servants frantically tearing their hair, throwing themselves on the ground, or running distractedly about, lamenting. Tom and Miss Ophelia alone seemed to have any presence of mind; for Marie was in strong hysteric convulsions. At Miss Ophelia's direction, one of the lounges in the parlour was hastily prepared, and the bleeding form laid upon it. St Clare had fainted, through pain and loss of blood; but, as Miss Ophelia applied restoratives, he revived, opened his eyes, looked fixedly on them, looked earnestly around the room, his eyes travelling wistfully over every object, and finally they rested on his mother's picture.

The physician now arrived, and made his examination. It was evident, from the expression of his face, that there was no hope; but he applied himself to dressing the wound, and he and Miss Ophelia and Tom proceeded composedly with this work, amid the lamentations and sobs and cries of the affrighted servants, who had clustered about the doors and windows of the veranda.

'Now,' said the physician, 'we must turn all these creatures out; all depends on his being kept quiet.'

St Clare opened his eyes, and looked fixedly on the distressed beings, whom Miss Ophelia and the doctor were trying to urge from the apartment. 'Poor creatures!' he said, and an expression of bitter self-reproach passed over his face. Adolph absolutely refused to go. Terror had deprived him of all presence of mind; he threw himself along on the floor, and nothing could persuade him to rise. The rest yielded to Miss Ophelia's urgent representations, that their master's safety depended on their stillness and obedience.

St Clare could say but little; he lay with his eyes shut, but it was evident that he wrestled with bitter thoughts. After a while, he laid his hand on Tom's, who was kneeling beside him, and said, 'Tom! poor fellow!'

'What, mas'r?' said Tom, earnestly.

'I am dying!' said St Clare, pressing his hand; 'pray!'

'If you would like a clergyman – ' said the physician.

St Clare hastily shook his head, and said again to Tom, more earnestly, 'Pray!'

And Tom did pray, with all his mind and strength, for the soul that was passing – the soul that seemed looking so steadily and mournfully from those large, melancholy blue eyes. It was literally prayer offered with strong crying and tears.[239]

When Tom ceased to speak, St Clare reached out and took his hand, looking earnestly at him, but saying nothing. He closed his eyes, but still retained his hold; for, in the gates of eternity, the black hand and the white hold each other with an equal clasp. He murmured softly to himself, at broken intervals,

'Recordare, Jesu pie –

Ne me perdas – illa die.
Quaerens me – sedisti lassus.'[240]

It was evident that the words he had been singing that evening were passing through his mind – words of entreaty addressed to Infinite Pity. His lips moved at intervals, as parts of the hymn fell brokenly from them.

'His mind is wandering,' said the doctor.

'No! it is coming HOME at last!' said St Clare, energetically; 'at last! at last!'

The effort of speaking exhausted him. The sinking paleness of death fell on him; but with it there fell, as if shed from the wings of some pitying spirit, a beautiful expression of peace, like that of a wearied child who sleeps.

So he lay for a few moments. They saw that the mighty hand was on him. Just before the spirit parted, he opened his eyes, with a sudden light, as of joy and recognition, and said, '*Mother!*' and then he was gone!

CHAPTER XXIX

The Unprotected

WE HEAR OFTEN of the distress of the negro servants on the loss of a kind master; and with good reason; for no creature on God's earth is left more utterly unprotected and desolate than the slave in these circumstances.

The child who has lost a father has still the protection of friends and of the law; he is something, and can do something – has acknowledged rights and position; the slave has none. The law regards him, in every respect, as devoid of rights as a bale of merchandise. The only possible acknowledgement of any of the longings and wants of a human and immortal creature, which are given to him, comes to him through the sovereign and irresponsible will of his master; and when that master is stricken down, nothing remains.

The number of those men who know how to use wholly irresponsible power humanely and generously is small. Everybody knows this, and the slave knows it best of all; so that he feels that there are ten chances of his finding an abusive and tyrannical master, to one of his finding a considerate and kind one. Therefore is it that the wail over a kind master is loud and long, as well it may be.

When St Clare breathed his last, terror and consternation took hold of all his household. He had been stricken down so in a moment, in the flower and strength of his youth! Every room and gallery of the house resounded with sobs and shrieks of despair.

Marie, whose nervous system had been enervated by a constant course of self-indulgence, had nothing to support the terror of the shock, and, at the time her husband breathed his last, was passing from one fainting fit to another; and he to whom she had been joined in the mysterious tie of marriage passed from her for ever, without the possibility of even a parting word.

Miss Ophelia, with characteristic strength and self-control, had remained with her kinsman to the last – all eye, all ear, all attention; doing everything of the little that could be done, and joining with her whole soul in the tender and impassioned prayers which the poor slave had poured forth for the soul of his dying master.

When they were arranging him for his last rest, they found upon his bosom a small, plain miniature case, opening with a spring. It was the miniature of a noble and beautiful female face; and on the reverse, under a crystal, a lock of dark hair. They laid them back on the lifeless breast – dust to dust – poor mournful relics of early dreams, which once made that cold heart beat so warmly!

Tom's whole soul was filled with thoughts of eternity; and while he ministered around the lifeless clay, he did not once think that the sudden stroke had left him in hopeless slavery. He felt at peace about his master; for in that hour, when he had poured forth his prayer into the bosom of his Father, he had found an answer of quietness and assurance springing up within himself. In the depths of his own affectionate nature, he felt able to perceive something of the fullness of Divine love; for an old oracle hath thus written, 'He that dwelleth in love dwelleth in God, and God in him.'[241] Tom hoped and trusted, and was at peace.

But the funeral passed, with all its pageant of black crape, and prayers, and solemn faces; and back rolled the cool, muddy waves of everyday life; and up came the everlasting hard enquiry of, 'What is to be done next?'

It rose to the mind of Marie, as, dressed in loose morning robes, and surrounded by anxious servants, she sat up in a great easy-chair, and inspected samples of crape and bombazine. It rose to Miss Ophelia, who began to turn her thoughts towards her Northern home. It rose, in silent terrors, to the minds of the servants, who well knew the unfeeling, tyrannical character of the mistress in whose hands they were left. All knew, very well, that the indulgences which had been accorded to them were not from their mistress, but from their master; and that, now he was gone, there would be no screen between them and every tyrannous infliction which a temper soured by affliction might devise.

It was about a fortnight after the funeral, that Miss Ophelia, busied one day in her apartment, heard a gentle tap at the door. She opened it, and there stood Rosa, the pretty young quadroon whom we have before often noticed, her hair in disorder, and her eyes swollen with crying.

'Oh, Miss Feely,' she said, falling on her knees, and catching the skirt of her dress, '*do, do* go to Miss Marie for me! do plead for me! She's goin' to send me out to be whipped – look there!' And she handed to Miss Ophelia a paper.

It was an order, written in Marie's delicate Italian hand, to the master of a whipping-establishment, to give the bearer fifteen lashes.

'What have you been doing?' said Miss Ophelia.

'You know, Miss Feely, I've got such a bad temper; it's very bad of me. I was trying on Miss Marie's dress, and she slapped my face; and I spoke out before I thought, and was saucy; and she said that she'd bring me down, and have me know, once for all, that I wasn't going to be so topping as I had been; and she wrote this, and says I shall carry it. I'd rather she'd kill me, right out.'

Miss Ophelia stood considering, with the paper in her hand.

'You see, Miss Feely,' said Rosa, 'I don't mind the whipping so much, if Miss Marie or you was to do it; but, to be sent to a *man* – and such a horrid man, the shame of it, Miss Feely!'

Miss Ophelia well knew that it was the universal custom to send women and young girls to whipping-houses, to the hands of the lowest of men – men vile enough to make this their profession – there to be subjected to brutal exposure and shameful correction. She had *known* it before; but hitherto she had never realised it, till she saw the slender form of Rosa almost convulsed with distress. All the honest blood of womanhood, the strong New England blood of liberty, flushed to her cheeks, and throbbed bitterly in her indignant heart; but, with habitual prudence and self-control, she mastered herself, and, crushing the paper firmly in her hand, she merely said to Rosa –

'Sit down, child, while I go to your mistress.'

'Shameful! monstrous! outrageous!' she said to herself, as she was crossing the parlour.

She found Marie sitting up in her easy-chair, with Mammy standing by her, combing her hair; Jane sat on the ground before her, busy in chafing her feet.

'How do you find yourself, today?' said Miss Ophelia.

A deep sigh, and a closing of the eyes was the only reply, for a moment, and then Marie answered, 'Oh, I don't know, cousin; I suppose I'm as well as I ever shall be!' And Marie wiped her eyes with a cambric handkerchief, bordered with an inch deep of black.

'I came,' said Miss Ophelia, with a short, dry cough, such as commonly introduces a difficult subject – 'I came to speak with you about poor Rosa.'

Marie's eyes were open wide enough now, and a flush rose to her sallow cheeks, as she answered, sharply –

'Well! what about her?'

'She is very sorry for her fault.'

'She is, is she? She'll be sorrier, before I've done with her! I've endured that child's impudence long enough; and now I'll bring her down – I'll make her lie in the dust!'

'But could not you punish her some other way, some way that would be less shameful?'

'I mean to shame her; that's just what I want. She has all her life presumed on her delicacy, and her good looks, and her ladylike airs, till she forgets who she is; and I'll give her one lesson that will bring her down, I fancy!'

'But, cousin, consider that if you destroy delicacy and a sense of shame in a young girl, you deprave her very fast.'

'Delicacy!' said Marie, with a scornful laugh; 'a fine word for such as she! I'll teach her, with all her airs, that she's no better than the raggedest black wench that walks the streets! She'll take no more airs with me!'

'You will answer to God for such cruelty!' said Miss Ophelia.

'Cruelty! I'd like to know what the cruelty is? I wrote orders for only fifteen lashes, and told him to put them on lightly. I'm sure there's no cruelty there!'

'No cruelty!' said Miss Ophelia. 'I'm sure any girl might rather be killed outright!'

'It might seem so to anybody with your feeling, but all these creatures get used to it; it's the only way they can be kept in order. Once let them feel that they are to take any airs about delicacy, and all that, and they'll run all over you, just as my servants always have. I've begun now to bring them under; and I'll have them all to know that I'll send one out to be whipped, as soon as another, if they don't mind themselves!' said Marie, looking around her decidedly.

Jane hung her head and cowered at this, for she felt as if it was particularly directed to her. Miss Ophelia sat for a moment, as if she had swallowed some explosive mixture, and were ready to burst. Then, recollecting the utter uselessness of contention with such a nature, she shut her lips resolutely, gathered herself up, and walked out of the room.

It was hard to go back and tell Rosa that she could do nothing for her; and, shortly after, one of the manservants came to say that her mistress had ordered him to take Rosa with him to the whipping-house, whither she was hurried, in spite of her tears and entreaties.

A few days after, Tom was standing musing by the balconies, when he was joined by Adolph, who, since the death of his master, had been entirely crestfallen and disconsolate. Adolph knew that he had always been an object of dislike to Marie; but while his master lived he had paid but little attention to it. Now that he was gone, he had moved about in daily dread and trembling, not knowing what might befall him next. Marie had held several consultations with her lawyer; after communicating with St Clare's brother, it was determined to sell the place, and all the servants, except her own personal property, and these she intended to take with her, and go back to her father's plantation.

'Do ye know, Tom, that we've all got to be sold?' said Adolph.

'How did you hear that?' said Tom.

'I hid myself behind the curtains when missis was talking with the lawyer. In a few days we shall all be sent off to auction, Tom.'

'The Lord's will be done!' said Tom, folding his arms and sighing heavily.

'We'll never get another such a master,' said Adolph, apprehensively; 'but I'd rather be sold than take my chance under missis.'

Tom turned away; his heart was full. The hope of liberty, the thought of distant wife and children, rose up before his patient soul, as to the mariner shipwrecked almost in port rises the vision of the church-spire and loving roofs of his native village, seen over the top of some black wave only for one last farewell. He drew his arms tightly over his bosom, and choked back the bitter tears, and tried to pray. The poor old soul had such a singular, unaccountable prejudice in favour of liberty, that it was a hard wrench for him; and the more he said, 'Thy will be done,'[242] the worse he felt.

He sought Miss Ophelia, who, ever since Eva's death, had treated him with marked and respectful kindness.

'Miss Feely,' he said, 'Mas'r St Clare promised me my freedom. He told me that he had begun to take it out for me; and now, perhaps, if Miss Feely would be good enough to speak about it to missis, she would feel like goin' on with it, as it was Mas'r St Clare's wish.'

'I'll speak for you, Tom, and do my best,' said Miss Ophelia; 'but, if it depends on Mrs St Clare, I can't hope much for you; nevertheless, I will try.'

This incident occurred a few days after that of Rosa, while Miss Ophelia was busied in preparations to return north.

Seriously reflecting within herself, she considered that perhaps she had shown too hasty a warmth of language in her former interview with Marie; and she resolved that she would now endeavour to moderate her zeal, and to be as conciliatory as possible. So the good soul gathered herself up, and, taking her knitting, resolved to go into Marie's room, be as agreeable as possible, and negotiate Tom's case with all the diplomatic skill of which she was mistress.

She found Marie reclining at length upon a lounge, supporting herself on one elbow by pillows, while Jane, who had been out shopping, was displaying before her certain samples of thin black stuffs.

'That will do,' said Marie, selecting one; 'only I'm not sure about its being properly mourning.'

'Laws, missis,' said Jane, volubly, 'Mrs General Derbennon wore just this very thing, after the general died, last summer; it makes up lovely!'

'What do you think?' said Marie to Miss Ophelia.

'It's a matter of custom, I suppose,' said Miss Ophelia. 'You can judge about it better than I.'

'The fact is,' said Marie, 'that I haven't a dress in the world that I can wear; and, as I am going to break up the establishment, and go off next week, I must decide upon something.'

'Are you going so soon?'

'Yes. St Clare's brother has written, and he and the lawyer think that the servants and furniture had better be put up at auction, and the place left with our lawyer.'

'There's one thing I wanted to speak with you about,' said Miss Ophelia. 'Augustine promised Tom his liberty, and began the legal forms necessary to it. I hope you will use your influence to have it perfected.'

'Indeed, I shall do no such thing!' said Marie, sharply. 'Tom is one of the most valuable servants on the place – it couldn't be afforded, anyway. Besides, what does he want of liberty? He's a great deal better off as he is.'

'But he does desire it, very earnestly, and his master promised it,' said Miss Ophelia.

'I dare say he does want it,' said Marie; 'they all want it, just because they are a discontented set, always wanting what they haven't got. Now, I'm principled against emancipating, in any case. Keep a negro under the care of a master, and he does well enough and is respectable; but set them free, and they get lazy and won't work, and take to drinking, and go all down to be mean, worthless fellows. I've seen it tried hundreds of times. It's no favour to set them free.'

'But Tom is so steady, industrious, and pious.'

'Oh, you needn't tell me! I've seen a hundred like him. He'll do very well, as long as he's taken care of, that's all.'

'But then, consider,' said Miss Ophelia, 'when you set him up for sale, the chances of his getting a bad master.'

'Oh, that's all humbug!' said Marie. 'It isn't one time in a hundred that a good fellow gets a bad master; most masters are good, for all the talk that is made. I've lived and grown up here, in the South, and I never yet was acquainted with a master that didn't treat his servants well, quite as well as is worth while. I don't feel any fears on that head.'

'Well,' said Miss Ophelia, energetically, 'I know it was one of the last wishes of your husband that Tom should have his liberty; it was one of the promises that he made to dear little Eva on her deathbed, and I should not think you would feel at liberty to disregard it.'

Marie had covered her face with her handkerchief at this appeal, and began sobbing and using her smelling-bottle, with great vehemence.

'Everybody goes against me!' she said. 'Everybody is so inconsiderate! I shouldn't have expected that *you* would bring up all these remembrances of my troubles to me; it's so inconsiderate! But nobody ever does consider – my trials are so peculiar! It's so hard, that when I had only one daughter, she should have been taken! – and when I had a husband that just exactly suited me – and I'm so hard to be suited! – he should be taken! And you seem to have so little feeling for me, and keep bringing it up to me so carelessly – when you know how it overcomes me! I suppose you mean well; but it is very inconsiderate, very!' And Marie sobbed, and gasped for breath, and called Mammy to open the window, and to bring her the camphor-bottle, and to bathe her head, and unhook her dress. And, in the general confusion that ensued, Miss Ophelia made her escape to her apartment.

She saw at once, that it would do no good to say anything more; for Marie had an indefinite capacity for hysteric fits; and after this, whenever her husband's or Eva's wishes with regard to the servants were alluded to, she always found it convenient to set one in operation. Miss Ophelia therefore did the next best thing she could for Tom; she wrote a letter to Mrs Shelby for him, stating his troubles, and urging them to send to his relief.

The next day, Tom and Adolph, and some half a dozen other servants, were marched down to a slave-warehouse to await the convenience of the trader, who was going to make up a lot for auction.

CHAPTER XXX

The Slave Warehouse

A SLAVE-WAREHOUSE! Perhaps some of my readers conjure up horrible visions of such a place. They fancy some foul, obscure den, some horrible Tartarus '*informis, ingens, cui lumen ademptum*'.[243] But no, innocent friend! in these days men have learned the art of sinning expertly and genteelly, so as not to shock the eyes and senses of respectable society. Human property is high in the market; and is therefore well fed, well cleaned, tended and looked after, that it may come to sale sleek, and strong, and shining. A slave-warehouse in New Orleans is a house externally not much unlike many others, kept with neatness; and where every day you may see arranged, under a sort of shed along the outside, rows of men and women, who stand there as a sign of the property sold within.

Then you shall be courteously entreated to call and examine, and shall find an abundance of husbands, wives, brothers, sisters, fathers, mothers, and young children, to be 'sold separately, or in lots to suit the convenience of the purchaser'; and that soul immortal, once bought with blood and anguish by the Son of God, when the earth shook, and the rocks rent, and the graves were opened, can be sold, leased, mortgaged, exchanged for groceries or dry goods, to suit the phases of trade or the fancy of the purchaser.

It was a day or two after the conversation between Marie and Miss Ophelia, that Tom, Adolph, and about half a dozen others of the St Clare estate, were turned over to the loving-kindness of Mr Skeggs, the keeper of a depot on — Street, to await the auction, next day.

Tom had with him quite a sizeable trunk full of clothing, as had most others of them. They were ushered, for the night, into a long room, where many other men, of all ages, sizes, and shades of complexion, were assembled, and from which roars of laughter and unthinking merriment were proceeding.

'Ah, ah! that's right. Go it, boys! – go it!' said Mr Skeggs, the keeper. 'My people are always so merry! Sambo, I see!' he said, speaking approvingly to a burly negro who was performing tricks of low buffoonery, which occasioned the shouts which Tom had heard.

As might be imagined, Tom was in no humour to join these proceedings; and, therefore, setting his trunk as far as possible from the noisy group, he sat down on it and leaned his face against the wall.

The dealers in the human article make scrupulous and systematic efforts to promote noisy mirth among them, as a means of drowning reflection and rendering them insensible to their condition. The whole object of the training to which the negro is put, from the time he is sold in the Northern market till he arrives South, is systematically directed towards making him callous, unthinking, and brutal. The slave-dealer collects his gang in Virginia or Kentucky, and drives them to some convenient, healthy place – often a watering place – to be fattened. Here they are fed full daily; and, because some incline to pine, a fiddle is kept commonly going among them, and they are made to dance daily; and he who refuses to be merry – in whose soul thoughts of wife, or child, or home, are too strong for him to be gay – is marked as sullen and dangerous, and subjected to all the evils which the ill-will of an utterly irresponsible and hardened man can inflict upon him. Briskness, alertness, and cheerfulness of appearance, especially before observers, are constantly enforced upon them, both by the hope of thereby getting a good master, and the fear of all that the driver may bring upon them, if they prove unsaleable.

'What dat ar nigger doin' here?' said Sambo, coming up to Tom, after Mr Skeggs had left the room. Sambo was a full black, of great size, very lively, voluble, and full of trick and grimace.

'What you doin' here?' said Sambo, coming up to Tom, and poking him facetiously in the side. 'Meditatin', eh?'

'I am to be sold at the auction, tomorrow!' said Tom, quietly.

'Sold at auction – haw! haw! boys, an't this yer fun? I wish't I was gwine that ar way! – tell ye, wouldn't I make em laugh? But how is it – dis yer whole lot gwine tomorrow?' said Sambo, laying his hand freely on Adolph's shoulder.

'Please to let me alone!' said Adolph, fiercely, straightening himself up, with extreme disgust.

'Law, now, boys! dis yer's one o' yer white niggers – kind o' cream colour, ye know, scented!' said he, coming up to Adolph and snuffing. 'O, Lor! he'd do for a tobaccer-shop; they could keep him to scent snuff! Lor, he'd keep a whole shop agwine – he would!'

'I say, keep off, can't you?' said Adolph, enraged.

'Lor, now, how touchy we is – we white niggers! Look at us, now!' and Sambo gave a ludicrous imitation of Adolph's manner; 'here's de airs and graces. We's been in a good family, I 'spects.'

'Yes,' said Adolph; 'I had a master that could have bought you all for old truck!'[244]

'Laws, now, only think,' said Sambo, 'the gentlemens that we is!'

'I belonged to the St Clare family,' said Adolph, proudly.

'Lor, you did! Be hanged if they ar'n't lucky to get shet of ye. 'Spects they's gwine to trade ye off with a lot o' cracked teapots and sich like!' said Sambo, with a provoking grin.

Adolph, enraged at this taunt, flew furiously at his adversary, swearing and striking on every side of him. The rest laughed and shouted, and the uproar brought the keeper to the door.

'What now, boys? Order, order!' he said, coming in and flourishing a large whip.

All fled in different directions, except Sambo, who, presuming on the favour which the keeper had to him as a licensed wag, stood his ground, ducking his head with a facetious grin, whenever the master made a dive at him.

'Lor, mas'r, 'tan't us, we's reg'lar stiddy – it's these yer new hands; they's real aggravatin' – kinder pickin' at us, all time!'

The keeper at this turned upon Tom and Adolph, and distributing a few kicks and cuffs without much enquiry, and leaving general orders for all to be good boys and go to sleep, left the apartment.

While this scene was going on in the men's sleeping-room, the reader may be curious to take a peep at the corresponding apartment allotted to the women. Stretched out in various attitudes over the floor, he may see numberless sleeping forms of every shade of complexion, from the purest ebony to white, and of all years, from childhood to old age, lying now asleep. Here is a fine bright girl, of ten years, whose mother was sold out yesterday, and who tonight cried herself to sleep when nobody was looking at her. Here, a worn old negress, whose thin arms and callous fingers tell of hard toil, waiting to be sold tomorrow, as a cast-off article, for what can be got for her; and some forty or fifty others, with heads variously enveloped in blankets or articles of clothing, lie stretched around them. But, in a corner, sitting apart from the rest, are two females of a more interesting appearance than common. One of these is a respectably-dressed mulatto woman between forty and fifty, with soft eyes and a gentle and pleasing physiognomy. She has on her head a high-raised turban, made of a gay red Madras handkerchief, of the first quality, and her dress is neatly fitted, and of good material, showing that she has been provided for with a careful hand. By her side, and nestling closely to her, is a young girl of fifteen – her daughter. She is a quadroon, as may be seen from her fairer complexion, though her likeness to her mother is quite discernible. She has the same soft dark eye, with longer lashes, and her curling hair is of a luxuriant brown. She also is dressed with great neatness, and her white, delicate hands, betray very little acquaintance with servile toil. These two are to be sold tomorrow, in the same lot with the St Clare servants; and the gentleman to whom they belong, and to whom the money for their sale is to be transmitted, is a member of a Christian Church in New York, who will receive the money, and go thereafter to the sacrament of his Lord and theirs, and think no more of it.

These two, whom we shall call Susan and Emmeline, had been the personal attendants of an amiable and pious lady of New Orleans, by whom they had been carefully and piously instructed and trained. They had been taught to read and write, diligently instructed in the truths of religion, and their lot had been as happy a one as in their condition it was possible to be. But the only son of their protectress had the management of her property; and, by carelessness and extravagance, involved it to a large amount, and at last failed. One of the largest creditors was the respectable firm of B. & Co., in New York. B. & Co. wrote to their lawyer in New Orleans, who attached the real estate (these two articles and a lot of plantation hands formed the most valuable part of it), and wrote word to that effect to New York. Brother B. being, as we have said, a Christian man, and a resident in a free State, felt some uneasiness on the subject. He didn't like trading in slaves and souls of men – of course he didn't; but then there were thirty thousand dollars in the case, and that was rather too much money to be lost for a principle; and so, after much considering, and asking advice from those that he knew would advise to suit him, Brother B. wrote to his lawyer to dispose of the business in the way that seemed to him the most suitable, and remit the proceeds.

The day after the letter arrived in New Orleans, Susan and Emmeline were attached, and sent to the depot to await a general auction on the following morning; and as they glimmer faintly upon us in the moonlight which steals through the grated window, we may listen to their conversation. Both are weeping, but each quietly, that the other may not hear.

'Mother, just lay your head on my lap, and see if you can't sleep a little,' says the girl, trying to appear calm.

'I haven't any heart to sleep, Em! I can't; it's the last night we may be together!'

'O, mother, don't say so! perhaps we shall get sold together – who knows?'

'If 'twas anybody's else case, I should say so, too, Em,' said the woman; 'but I'm so 'feard of losin' you that I don't see anything but the danger.'

'Why, mother, the man said we were both likely, and would sell well.'

Susan remembered the man's looks and words. With a deadly sickness at her heart, she remembered how he had looked at Emmeline's hands, and lifted up her curly hair, and pronounced her a first-rate article. Susan had been trained as a Christian, brought up in the daily reading of the Bible, and had the same horror of her child's being sold to a life of shame that any other Christian mother might have; but she had no hope, no protection.

'Mother, I think we might do first rate, if you could get a place as cook, and I as chamber-maid or seamstress, in some family. I dare say we shall. Let's both look as bright and lively as we can, and tell all we can do, and perhaps we shall,' said Emmeline.

'I want you to brush your hair all back straight tomorrow,' said Susan.

'What for, mother? I don't look near so well, that way.'

'Yes, but you'll sell better so.'

'I don't see why!' said the child.

'Respectable families would be more apt to buy you, if they saw you looked plain and decent, as if you wasn't trying to look handsome. I know their ways better'n you do,' said Susan.

'Well, mother, then I will.'

'And, Emmeline, if we shouldn't ever see each other again, after tomorrow – if I'm sold way up on a plantation somewhere, and you somewhere else – always remember how you've been brought up, and all missis has told you; take your Bible with you, and your hymn-book; and if you're faithful to the Lord, he'll be faithful to you.'

So speaks the poor soul, in sore discouragement; for she knows that tomorrow any man, however vile and brutal, however godless and merciless, if he only has money to pay for her, may become owner of her daughter, body and soul; and then, how is the child to be faithful? She thinks of all this as she holds her daughter in her arms, and wishes that she were not handsome and attractive. It seems almost an aggravation to her to remember how purely and piously, how much above the ordinary lot she has been brought up. But she has no resort but to *pray*; and many such prayers to God have gone up from those same trim, neatly-arranged, respectable slave-prisons – prayers which God has not forgotten, as a coming day shall show; for it is written, 'Whoso causeth one of these little ones to offend, it were better for him that a millstone were hanged about his neck, and that he were drowned in the depths of the sea.'[245]

The soft, earnest, quiet moonbeam looks in fixedly, marking the bars of the grated windows on the prostrate, sleeping forms. The mother and daughter are singing together a wild and melancholy dirge, common as a funeral hymn among the slaves –

> 'Oh, where is weeping Mary?
> Oh, where is weeping Mary?
>   Gone to the goodly land.
> She is dead and gone to heaven;
> She is dead and gone to heaven;
>   'Rived in the goodly land.'[246]

These words, sung by voices of a peculiar and melancholy sweetness, in an air which seemed like the sighing of earthly despair after heavenly hope, floated through the dark prison-rooms with a pathetic cadence, as verse after verse was breathed out –

> 'Oh, where are Paul and Silas?
> Oh, where are Paul and Silas?
>   Gone to the goodly land.
> They are dead and gone to heaven;
> They are dead and gone to heaven;
>   'Rived in the goodly land.'

Sing on, poor souls! The night is short, and the morning will part you for ever!

But now it is morning, and everybody is astir; and the worthy Mr Skeggs is busy and bright, for a lot of goods is to be fitted out for auction. There is a brisk look-out on the toilet; injunctions passed around to everyone to put on their best face and be spry; and now all

are arranged in a circle for a last review, before they are marched up to
the Bourse.[247]

Mr Skeggs, with his palmetto on and his cigar in his mouth, walks
around to put farewell touches on his wares.

'How's this?' he said, stepping in front of Susan and Emmeline.
'Where's your curls, gal?'

The girl looked timidly at her mother, who, with the smooth
adroitness common among her class, answers –

'I was telling her last night to put up her hair smooth and neat, and
not havin' it flying about in curls – looks more respectable so!'

'Bother!' said the man, peremptorily, turning to the girl. 'You go
right along, and curl yourself real smart!' He added, giving a crack to a
rattan he held in his hand; 'and be back in quick time, too! You go and
help her,' he added, to the mother. 'Them curls may make a hundred
dollars difference in the sale of her.'

Beneath a splendid dome were men of all nations, moving to and fro
over the marble *pavé*.[248] On every side of the circular area were little
tribunes, or stations, for the use of speakers and auctioneers. Two of
these, on opposite sides of the area, were now occupied by brilliant and
talented gentlemen, enthusiastically forcing up, in English and French
commingled, the bids of connoisseurs in their various wares. A third
one, on the other side, still unoccupied, was surrounded by a group,
waiting the moment of sale to begin. And here we may recognise the St
Clare servants, Tom, Adolph, and others; and there, too, Susan and
Emmeline, awaiting their turn with anxious and dejected faces. Various
spectators, intending to purchase, or not intending, as the case might
be, gathered around the group, handling, examining, and commenting
on their various points and faces with the same freedom that a set of
jockeys discuss the merits of a horse.

'Hallo, Alf! what brings you here?' said a young exquisite, slapping
the shoulder of a sprucely-dressed young man, who was examining
Adolph through an eyeglass.

'Well, I was wanting a valet, and I heard that St Clare's lot was going.
I thought I'd just look at his – '

'Catch me ever buying any of St Clare's people! Spoilt niggers, every
one. Impudent as the devil!' said the other.

'Never fear that!' said the first. 'If I get 'em, I'll soon have their airs
out of them; they'll soon find that they've another kind of master to
deal with than Monsieur St Clare. 'Pon my word, I'll buy that fellow. I
like the shape of him.'

'You'll find it'll take all you've got to keep him. He's deucedly extravagant!'

'Yes, but my lord will find that he *can't* be extravagant with *me*. Just let him be sent to the calaboose a few times, and thoroughly dressed down! I'll tell you if it don't bring him to a sense of his ways! Oh, I'll reform him, up hill and down – you'll see! I buy him, that's flat!'

Tom had been standing wistfully examining the multitude of faces thronging around him, for one whom he would wish to call master; and if you should ever be under the necessity, sir, of selecting, out of two hundred men, one who was to become your absolute owner and disposer, you would, perhaps, realise, just as Tom did, how few there were that you would feel at all comfortable in being made over to. Tom saw abundance of men, great, burly, gruff men; little, chirping, dried men; long-favoured, lank, hard men; and every variety of stubbed-looking, common-place men, who pick up their fellow-men as one picks up chips, putting them into the fire or a basket with equal unconcern, according to their convenience; but he saw no St Clare.

A little before the sale commenced, a short, broad, muscular man, in a checked shirt considerably open at the bosom, and pantaloons much the worse for dirt and wear, elbowed his way through the crowd, like one who is going actively into a business; and, coming up to the group, began to examine them systematically. From the moment that Tom saw him approaching, he felt an immediate and revolting horror at him, that increased as he came near. He was evidently, though short, of gigantic strength. His round, bullet head, large, light-grey eyes, with their shaggy, sandy eyebrows, and stiff, wiry, sun-burned hair, were rather unprepossessing items, it is to be confessed; his large, coarse mouth was distended with tobacco, the juice of which, from time to time, he ejected from him with great decision and explosive force; his hands were immensely large, hairy, sun-burned, freckled, and very dirty, and garnished with long nails, in a very foul condition. This man proceeded to a very free personal examination of the lot. He seized Tom by the jaw, and pulled open his mouth to inspect his teeth; made him strip up his sleeve, to show his muscle; turned him round, made him jump and spring, to show his paces.

'Where was you raised?' he added briefly to these investigations.

'In Kintuck, mas'r,' said Tom, looking about, as if for deliverance.

'What have you done?'

'Had care of mas'r's farm,' said Tom.

'Likely story!' said the other, shortly, as he passed on. He paused a moment before Dolph; then spitting a discharge of tobacco-juice on his well-blacked boots, and giving a contemptuous umph, he walked on. Again he stopped before Susan and Emmeline. He put out his heavy, dirty hand, and drew the girl towards him; passed it over her neck and bust, felt her arms, looked at her teeth, and then pushed her back against her mother, whose patient face showed the suffering she had been going through at every motion of the hideous stranger.

The girl was frightened, and began to cry.

'Stop that, you minx!' said the salesman; 'no whimpering here, the sale is going to begin.' And accordingly the sale began.

Adolph was knocked off, at a good sum, to the young gentleman who had previously stated his intention of buying him; and the other servants of the St Clare lot went to various bidders.

'Now, up with you, boy! d'ye hear?' said the auctioneer to Tom.

Tom stepped upon the block, gave a few anxious looks round; all seemed mingled in a common, indistinct noise – the clatter of the salesman crying off his qualifications in French and English, the quick fire of French and English bids; and almost in a moment came the final thump of the hammer, and the clear ring on the last syllable of the word '*dollars*', as the auctioneer announced his price, and Tom was made over. He had a master!

He was pushed from the block; the short, bullet-headed man, seizing him roughly by the shoulder, pushed him to one side, saying, in a harsh voice, 'Stand there, *you*!'

Tom hardly realised anything; but still the bidding went on – rattling, clattering, now French, now English. Down goes the hammer again – Susan is sold! She goes down from the block, stops, looks wistfully back; her daughter stretches her hands towards her. She looks with agony in the face of the man who has bought her – a respectable middle-aged man, of benevolent countenance.

'O mas'r, please do buy my daughter!'

'I'd like to, but I'm afraid I can't afford it!' said the gentleman, looking, with painful interest, as the young girl mounted the block, and looked around her with a frightened and timid glance.

The blood flushes painfully in her otherwise colourless cheek, her eye has a feverish fire, and her mother groans to see that she looks more beautiful than she ever saw her before. The auctioneer sees his advantage, and expatiates volubly in mingled French and English, and bids rise in rapid succession.

'I'll do anything in reason,' said the benevolent-looking gentleman, pressing in, and joining with the bids. In a few moments they have run beyond his purse. He is silent; the auctioneer grows warmer; but bids gradually drop off. It lies now between an aristocratic old citizen and our bullet-headed acquaintance. The citizen bids for a few turns, contemptuously measuring his opponent; but the bullet-head has the advantage over him, both in obstinacy and concealed length of purse, and the controversy lasts but a moment; the hammer falls – he has got the girl, body and soul, unless God help her!

Her master is Mr Legree, who owns a cotton plantation on the Red River.[249] She is pushed along into the same lot with Tom and two other men, and goes off, weeping as she goes.

The benevolent gentleman is sorry; but, then, the thing happens every day! One sees girls and mothers crying, at these sales *always*! it can't be helped, &c.; and he walks off with his acquisition in another direction.

Two days after, the lawyer of the Christian firm of B. & Co., New York, sent on their money to them. On the reverse of that draft, so obtained, let them write these words of the great Paymaster, to whom they shall make up their account in a future day – '*When he maketh inquisition for blood, he forgetteth not the cry of the humble!*'[250]

CHAPTER XXXI

The Middle Passage[251]

> *Thou art of purer eyes than to behold evil, and canst not look upon iniquity: wherefore lookest thou upon them that deal treacherously, and holdest thy tongue when the wicked devoureth the man that is more righteous than he?*
>
> Habakkuk 1. 13

ON THE LOWER PART of a small, mean boat, on the Red River, Tom sat – chains on his wrists, chains on his feet, and a weight heavier than chains lay on his heart. All had faded from his sky – moon and star; all had passed by him, as the trees and banks were now passing, to return no more. Kentucky home, with wife and children, and indulgent owners; St Clare home, with all its refinements and splendours; the golden head of Eva, with its saint-like eyes; the proud, gay, handsome, seemingly careless, yet ever-kind St Clare; hours of ease and indulgent leisure – all gone! and in place thereof, *what* remains?

It is one of the bitterest apportionments of a lot of slavery, that the negro, sympathetic and assimilative, after acquiring, in a refined family, the tastes and feelings which form the atmosphere of such a place, is not the less liable to become the bond-slave of the coarsest and most brutal – just as a chair or table, which once decorated the superb saloon, comes, at last, battered and defaced, to the bar-room of some filthy tavern, or some low haunt of vulgar debauchery. The great difference is, that the table and chair cannot feel, and the *man* can; for even a legal enactment that he shall be 'taken, reputed, adjudged in law, to be a chattel personal',[252] cannot blot out his soul, with its own private little world of memories, hopes, loves, fears, and desires.

Mr Simon Legree, Tom's master, had purchased slaves at one place and another, in New Orleans, to the number of eight, and driven them, handcuffed, in couples of two and two, down to the good steamer *Pirate*, which lay at the levee, ready for a trip up the Red River.

Having got them fairly on board, and the boat being off, he came round, with that air of efficiency which ever characterised him, to take a review of them. Stopping opposite to Tom, who had been attired for sale in his best broadcloth suit, with well-starched linen and shining boots, he briefly expressed himself as follows –

'Stand up.'

Tom stood up.

'Take off that stock!' and, as Tom, encumbered by his fetters, proceeded to do it, he assisted him, by pulling it, with no gentle hand, from his neck, and putting it in his pocket.

Legree now turned to Tom's trunk, which, previous to this, he had been ransacking, and, taking from it a pair of old pantaloons and a dilapidated coat, which Tom had been wont to put on about his stable-work, he said, liberating Tom's hands from the handcuffs, and pointing to a recess in among the boxes –

'You go there, and put these on.'

Tom obeyed, and in a few moments returned.

'Take off your boots,' said Mr Legree.

Tom did so.

'There,' said the former, throwing him a pair of coarse, stout shoes, such as were common among the slaves, 'put these on.'

In Tom's hurried exchange, he had not forgotten to transfer his cherished Bible to his pocket. It was well he did so; for Mr Legree, having refitted Tom's handcuffs, proceeded deliberately to investigate the contents of his pockets. He drew out a silk handkerchief, and put it into his own pocket. Several little trifles, which Tom had treasured, chiefly because they had amused Eva, he looked upon with a contemptuous grunt, and tossed them over his shoulder into the river.

Tom's Methodist hymn-book, which, in his hurry, he had forgotten, he now held up and turned over.

'Humph! pious, to be sure. So, what's yer name? – you belong to the church, eh?'

'Yes, mas'r,' said Tom, firmly.

'Well, I'll soon have *that* out of you. I have none o' yer bawling, praying, singing niggers on my place; so remember. Now, mind yourself,' he said, with a stamp and a fierce glance of his grey eye, directed at Tom, '*I'm* your church now! You understand – you've got to be as *I* say.'

Something within the silent black man answered *No!* and, as if repeated by an invisible voice, came the words of an old prophetic scroll, as Eva had often read them to him – 'Fear not! for I have redeemed thee. I have called thee by my name. Thou art MINE!'[253]

But Simon Legree heard no voice. That voice is one he never shall hear. He only glared for a moment on the downcast face of Tom, and walked off. He took Tom's trunk, which contained a very neat and abundant wardrobe, to the forecastle, where it was soon surrounded by various hands of the boat. With much laughing, at the expense of niggers who tried to be gentlemen, the articles very readily were sold to one and another, and the empty trunk finally put up at auction. It was a good joke, they all thought, especially to see how Tom looked after his things, as they were going this way and that; and then the auction of the trunk, that was funnier than all, and occasioned abundant witticisms.

This little affair being over, Simon sauntered up again to his property.

'Now, Tom, I've relieved you of any extra baggage, you see. Take mighty good care of them clothes. It'll be long enough 'fore you get more. I go in for making niggers careful; one suit has to do for one year, on my place.'

Simon next walked up to the place where Emmeline was sitting, chained to another woman.

'Well, my dear,' he said, chucking her under the chin, 'keep up your spirits.'

The involuntary look of horror, fright and aversion with which the girl regarded him, did not escape his eye. He frowned fiercely.

'None o' your shines, gal! you's got to keep a pleasant face, when I speak to ye – d'ye hear? And you, you old yellow poco moonshine!'[254] he said, giving a shove to the mulatto woman to whom Emmeline was chained, 'don't you carry that sort of face! You's got to look chipper, I tell ye!'

'I say, all on ye,' he said retreating a pace or two back, 'look at me – look at me – look me right in the eye – *straight*, now!' said he, stamping his foot at every pause.

As by a fascination, every eye was now directed to the glaring greenish-grey eye of Simon.

'Now,' said he, doubling his great, heavy fist into something resembling a blacksmith's hammer, 'd' ye see this fist? Heft it!' he said, bringing it down on Tom's hand. 'Look at these yer bones! Well, I tell ye this yer fist has got as hard as iron *knocking down niggers*. I never see the nigger yet I couldn't bring down with one crack,' said he, bringing his fist down so near to the face of Tom that he winked and drew back. 'I don't keep none o' yer cussed overseers; I does my own overseeing; and I tell you things *is* seen to. You's everyone on ye got to toe the mark, I tell ye; quick – straight – the moment I speak. That's the way to keep in with me. Ye won't find no soft spot in me, nowhere. So, now, mind yerselves; for I don't show no mercy!'

The women involuntarily drew in their breath, and the whole gang sat with downcast, dejected faces. Meanwhile, Simon turned on his heel, and marched up to the bar of the boat for a dram.

'That's the way I begin with my niggers,' he said, to a gentlemanly man who had stood by him during his speech. 'It's my system to begin strong – just let 'em know what to expect.'

'Indeed!' said the stranger, looking upon him with the curiosity of a naturalist studying some out-of-the-way specimen.

'Yes, indeed. I'm none o' yer gentlemen planters, with lily fingers, to slop round and be cheated by some old cuss of an overseer! Just feel of my knuckles, now; look at my fist. Tell ye, sir, the flesh on't has come jest like a stone, practising on niggers – feel on it.'

The stranger applied his finger to the implement in question, and simply said –

' 'Tis hard enough; and, I suppose,' he added, 'practice has made your heart just like it.'

'Why, yes, I may say so,' said Simon, with a hearty laugh. 'I reckon there's as little soft in me as in anyone going. Tell you, nobody comes it over me! Niggers never gets round me, neither with squalling nor soft soap – that's a fact.'

'You have a fine lot there.'

'Real,' said Simon. 'There's that Tom, they told me he was suthin' uncommon. I paid a little high for him, 'tending him for a driver and a managing chap; only get the notions out that he's larnt by bein' treated as niggers never ought to be, he'll do prime! The yellow woman I got took in. I rayther think she's sickly, but I shall put her through for what she's worth. She may last a year or two. I don't go for savin' niggers. Use up, and buy more's my way; makes you less trouble, and I'm quite sure it comes cheaper in the end;' and Simon, sipped his glass.

'And how long do they generally last?' said the stranger.

'Well, dun 'no; 'cordin' as their constitution is. Stout fellers last six or seven years; trashy ones gets worked up in two or three. I used to, when I fust begun, have considerable trouble fussin' with 'em and trying to make 'em hold out – doctorin' on 'em up when they's sick, and givin' on 'em clothes and blankets, and what not, tryin' to keep 'em all sort o' decent and comfortable. Law, 'twasn't no sort o' use; I lost money on 'em, and 'twas heaps o' trouble. Now, you see, I just put 'em straight through, sick or well. When one nigger's dead, I buy another; and I find it comes cheaper and easier, every way.'

The stranger turned away, and seated himself beside a gentleman, who had been listening to the conversation with repressed uneasiness.

'You must not take that fellow to be any specimen of Southern planters,' said he.

'I should hope not,' said the young gentleman, with emphasis.

'He is a mean, low, brutal fellow!' said the other.

'And yet your laws allow him to hold any number of human beings subject to his absolute will, without even a shadow of protection; and, low as he is, you cannot say that there are not many such.'

'Well,' said the other, 'there are also many considerate and humane men among planters.'

'Granted,' said the young man; 'but, in my opinion, it is you considerate, humane men, that are responsible for all the brutality and outrage wrought by these wretches; because if it were not for your sanction and influence, the whole system could not keep foot-hold for an hour. If there were no planters except such as that one,' said he, pointing with his finger to Legree, who stood with his back to them, 'the whole thing would go down like a millstone. It is your respectability and humanity that licenses and protects his brutality.'

'You certainly have a high opinion of my good nature,' said the planter, smiling; 'but I advise you not to talk quite so loud, as there are people on board the boat who might not be quite so tolerant to opinion as I am. You had better wait till I get up to my plantation, and there you may abuse us all, quite at your leisure.'

The young gentleman coloured and smiled, and the two were soon busy in a game of backgammon. Meanwhile, another conversation was going on in the lower part of the boat, between Emmeline and the mulatto woman with whom she was confined. As was natural, they were exchanging with each other some particulars of their history.

'Who did you belong to?' said Emmeline.

'Well, my mas'r was Mr Ellis – lived on Levee Street. P'raps you've seen the house.'

'Was he good to you?' said Emmeline.

'Mostly, till he tuk sick. He's lain sick, off and on, more than six months, and been orful oneasy. 'Pears like he warnt willin' to have nobody rest, day nor night; and got so curous, there couldn't nobody suit him. 'Pears like he just grew crosser every day; kept me up nights till I got farly beat out, and couldn't keep awake no longer; and 'cause I got to sleep, one night, Lors, he talk so orful to me, and he tell me he'd sell me to just the hardest master he could find; and he'd promised me my freedom, too, when he died.'

'Had you any friends?' said Emmeline.

'Yes, my husband, he's a blacksmith. Mas'r gen'ly hired him out. They took me off so quick, I didn't even have time to see him; and I's got four children. Oh, dear me!' said the woman, covering her face with her hands.

It is a natural impulse, in everyone, when they hear a tale of distress, to think of something to say by way of consolation. Emmeline wanted to say something, but she could not think of anything to say. What was there to be said? As by a common consent, they both avoided, with fear and dread, all mention of the horrible man who was now their master.

True, there is religious trust for even the darkest hour. The mulatto woman was a member of the Methodist church, and had an unenlightened but very sincere spirit of piety. Emmeline had been educated much more intelligently – taught to read and write and diligently instructed in the Bible, by the care of a faithful and pious mistress; yet, would it not try the faith of the firmest Christian, to find themselves abandoned apparently of God, in the grasp of ruthless violence? How much more must it shake the faith of Christ's poor little ones, weak in knowledge and tender in years!

The boat moved on – freighted with its weight of sorrow – up the

red, muddy, turbid current, through the abrupt, tortuous w
the Red River; and sad eyes gazed wearily on the steep red-c
as they glided by in dreary sameness. At last the boat stopped
town, and Legree with his party disembarked.

CHAPTER XXXII

Dark Places

The dark places of the earth are full of the habitations of cruelty.[255]

TRAILING WEARILY BEHIND a rude wagon, and over a ruder road,
Tom and his associates faced onward.

In the wagon was seated Simon Legree; and the two women, still
fettered together, were stowed away with some baggage in the back
part of it, and the whole company were seeking Legree's plantation,
which lay a good distance off.

It was a wild, forsaken road, now winding through dreary pine
barrens, where the wind whispered mournfully, and now over log
causeways, through long cypress swamps, the doleful trees rising out of
the slimy, spongy ground, hung with long wreaths of funereal black
moss, while ever and anon the loathsome form of the moccasin snake
might be seen sliding among broken stumps and shattered branches
that lay here and there, rotting in the water.

It is disconsolate enough, this riding, to the stranger, who, with well-
filled pocket and well-appointed horse, threads the lonely way on some
errand of business; but wilder, drearier, to the man enthralled, whom
every weary step bears further from all that man loves and prays for.

So one should have thought, that witnessed the sunken and dejected
expression on those dark faces; the wistful, patient weariness with
which those sad eyes rested on object after object that passed them in
their sad journey.

Simon rode on, however, apparently well pleased, occasionally
pulling away at a flask of spirit, which he kept in his pocket.

'I say, *you*!' he said, as he turned back and caught a glance at the
dispirited faces behind him; 'strike up a song, boys – come!'

The men looked at each other, and the '*come*' was repeated, with a smart crack of the whip which the driver carried in his hands. Tom began a Methodist hymn –

> 'Jerusalem, my happy home,
>   Name ever dear to me!
> When shall my sorrows have an end?
>   Thy joys when shall – '[256]

'Shut up, you black cuss!' roared Legree; 'did ye think I wanted any o' yer infernal old Methodism? I say, tune up, now, something real rowdy – quick!'

One of the other men struck up one of those unmeaning songs common among the slaves –

> 'Mas'r see'd me cotch a coon,
>   High boys, high!
> He laughed to split – d' ye see the moon?
>   Ho! ho! ho! boys, ho!
>   Ho! yo! hi–e! oh!'

The singer appeared to make up the song to his own pleasure, generally hitting on rhyme, without much attempt at reason; and all the party took up the chorus at intervals –

> 'Ho! ho! ho! boys, ho!
> High–e–oh! high–e–oh!'

It was sung very boisterously, and with a forced attempt at merriment; but no wail of despair, no words of impassioned prayer, could have had such a depth of woe in them as the wild notes of the chorus. As if the poor, dumb heart, threatened – prisoned – took refuge in that inarticulate sanctuary of music, and found there a language in which to breathe its prayer to God! There was a prayer in it which Simon could not hear. He only heard the boys singing noisily, and was well pleased; he was making them 'keep up their spirits.'

'Well, my little dear,' said he, turning to Emmeline, and laying his hand on her shoulder, 'we're almost home!'

When Legree scolded and stormed, Emmeline was terrified; but when he laid his hand on her, and spoke as he now did, she felt as if she had rather he would strike her. The expression of his eyes made her soul sick, and her flesh creep. Involuntarily she clung closer to the mulatto woman by her side, as if she were her mother.

'You didn't ever wear earrings,' he said, taking hold of her small ear with his coarse fingers.

'No, mas'r!' said Emmeline, trembling and looking down.

'Well, I'll give you a pair, when we get home, if you're a good girl. You needn't be so frightened; I don't mean to make you work very hard. You'll have fine times with me, and live like a lady – only be a good girl.'

Legree had been drinking to that degree that he was inclining to be very gracious; and it was about this time that the enclosures of the plantation rose to view. The estate had formerly belonged to a gentleman of opulence and taste, who had bestowed some considerable attention to the adornment of his grounds. Having died insolvent, it had been purchased, at a bargain, by Legree, who used it, as he did everything else, merely as an implement for money-making. The place had that ragged, forlorn appearance, which is always produced by the evidence that the care of the former owner has been left to go to utter decay.

What was once a smooth-shaven lawn before the house, dotted here and there with ornamental shrubs, was now covered with frowsy tangled grass, with horse-posts set up, here and there, in it, where the turf was stamped away, and the ground littered with broken pails, cobs of corn, and other slovenly remains. Here and there a mildewed jessamine or honeysuckle hung raggedly from some ornamental support, which had been pushed to one side by being used as a horse-post. What once was a large garden was now all grown over with weeds, through which, here and there, some solitary exotic reared its forsaken head. What had been a conservatory had now no window-sashes, and on the mouldering shelves stood some dry, forsaken flower-pots, with sticks in them, whose dried leaves showed they had once been plants.

The wagon rolled up a weedy gravel walk, under a noble avenue of China trees,[257] whose graceful forms and ever-springing foliage seemed to be the only things there that neglect could not daunt or alter – like noble spirits, so deeply rooted in goodness, as to flourish and grow stronger amid discouragement and decay.

The house had been large and handsome. It was built in a manner common at the South; a wide veranda of two storeys running round every part of the house, into which every outer door opened, the lower tier being supported by brick pillars.

But the place looked desolate and uncomfortable; some windows stopped up with boards, some with shattered panes, and shutters hanging by a single hinge – all telling of coarse neglect and discomfort.

Bits of board, straw, old decayed barrels and boxes, garnished the ground in all directions; and three or four ferocious looking dogs, roused by the sound of the wagon-wheels, came tearing out, and were with difficulty restrained from laying hold of Tom and his companions by the effort of the ragged servants who came after them.

'Ye see what ye'd get!' said Legree, caressing the dogs with grim satisfaction, and turning to Tom and his companions; 'Ye see what ye'd get, if ye try to run off. These yer dogs has been raised to track niggers; and they'd jest as soon chaw one on ye up as eat their supper. So, mind yerself. How now, Sambo!' he said, to a ragged fellow, without any brim to his hat, who was officious in his attentions. 'How have things been going?'

'Fust rate, mas'r.'

'Quimbo,' said Legree to another, who was making zealous demonstrations to attract his attention, 'ye minded what I telled ye?'

'Guess I did, didn't I?'

These two coloured men were the two principal hands on the plantation. Legree had trained them in savageness and brutality as systematically as he had his bulldogs; and, by long practice in hardness and cruelty, brought their whole nature to about the same range of capacities. It is a common remark, and one that is thought to militate strongly against the character of the race, that the negro overseer is always more tyrannical and cruel than the white one. This is simply saying that the negro mind has been more crushed and debased than the white. It is no more true of this race than of every oppressed race, the world over. The slave is always a tyrant, if he can get a chance to be one.

Legree, like some potentates we read of in history, governed his plantation by a sort of resolution of forces. Sambo and Quimbo cordially hated each other; the plantation hands, one and all, cordially hated them; and by playing off one against another he was pretty sure, through one or the other of the three parties, to get informed of whatever was on foot in the place.

Nobody can live entirely without social intercourse; and Legree encouraged his two black satellites to a kind of coarse familiarity with him – a familiarity, however, at any moment liable to get one or the other of them into trouble; for, on the slightest provocation, one of them always stood ready at a nod to be a minister of his vengeance on the other.

As they stood there now by Legree, they seemed an apt illustration of the fact that brutal men are lower even than animals. Their coarse, dark, heavy features; their great eyes, rolling enviously on each other; their barbarous, guttural, half-brute intonation; their dilapidated garments fluttering in the wind – were all in admirable keeping with the vile and unwholesome character of everything about the place.

'Here, you Sambo,' said Legree, 'take these yer boys down to the quarters; and here's a gal I've got for *you*,' said he, as he separated the mulatto woman from Emmeline and pushed her towards him; 'I promised to bring you one, you know.'

The woman gave a sudden start, and, drawing back, said, suddenly –

'Oh, mas'r! I left my old man in New Orleans.'

'What of that, you —! won't you want one here? None o' your words – go 'long!' said Legree, raising his whip.

'Come, mistress,' he said to Emmeline, 'you go in here with me.'

A dark, wild face was seen, for a moment, to glance at the window of the house; and, as Legree opened the door, a female voice said something in a quick imperative tone. Tom, who was looking with anxious interest after Emmeline, as she went in, noticed this, and heard Legree answer angrily, 'You may hold your tongue! I'll do as I please, for all you!'

Tom heard no more; for he was soon following Sambo to the quarters. The quarters was a little sort of street of rude shanties, in a row, in a part of the plantation far off from the house. They had a forlorn, brutal, forsaken air. Tom's heart sank when he saw them. He had been comforting himself with the thought of a cottage, rude, indeed, but one which he might make neat and quiet, and where he might have a shelf for his Bible, and a place to be alone out of his labouring hours. He looked into several; they were mere rude shells, destitute of any species of furniture, except a heap of straw foul with dirt, spread confusedly over the floor, which was merely the bare ground, trodden hard by the tramping of innumerable feet.

'Which of these will be mine?' said he to Sambo, submissively.

'Dun 'no; ken turn in here, I s'pose,' said Sambo; ' 'spects thar's room for another thar; thar's a pretty smart heap o' niggers to each on 'em, now; sure, I dun 'no what I's to do with more.'

It was late in the evening when the weary occupants of the shanties came flocking home – men and women, in soiled and tattered garments, surly and uncomfortable, and in no mood to look pleasantly on newcomers. The small village was alive with no inviting sounds;

hoarse, guttural voices contending at the hand-mills where their morsel of hard corn was yet to be ground into meal, to fit it for the cake that was to constitute their only supper. From the earliest dawn of the day, they had been in the fields, pressed to work under the driving lash of the overseers; for it was now in the very heat and hurry of the season, and no means was left untried to press everyone up to the top of their capabilities. 'True,' says the negligent lounger; 'picking cotton isn't hard work.' Isn't it? And it isn't much inconvenience, either, to have one drop of water fall on your head; yet the worst torture of the Inquisition[258] is produced by drop after drop, drop after drop, falling moment after moment, with monotonous succession, on the same spot; and work in itself not hard becomes so by being pressed, hour after hour, with unvarying, unrelenting sameness, with not even the consciousness of free-will to take from its tediousness. Tom looked in vain among the gang, as they poured along, for companionable faces. He saw only sullen, scowling, embruted men, and feeble, discouraged women, or women that were not women – the strong pushing away the weak – the gross, unrestricted animal selfishness of human beings, of whom nothing good was expected and desired; and who, treated in every way like brutes, had sunk as nearly to their level as it was possible for human beings to do. To a late hour in the night the sound of the grinding was protracted; for the mills were few in number compared with the grinders, and the weary and feeble ones were driven back by the strong, and came on last in their turn.

'Ho yo!' said Sambo, coming to the mulatto woman, and throwing down a bag of corn before her, 'what a cuss yo name?'

'Lucy,' said the woman.

'Wal, Lucy, yo my woman now. Yo grind dis yer corn, and get *my* supper baked, ye har?'

'I an't your woman, and I won't be!' said the woman, with the sharp, sudden courage of despair; 'you go 'long!'

'I'll kick yo, then!' said Sambo, raising his foot threateningly.

'Ye may kill me, if ye choose, the sooner the better! Wish't I was dead!' said she.

'I say, Sambo, you go to spilin' the hands, I'll tell mas'r o' you,' said Quimbo, who was busy at the mill, from which he had viciously driven two or three tired women, who were waiting to grind their corn.

'And I'll tell him ye won't let the women come to the mills, yo old nigger!' said Sambo. 'Yo jes keep to yo own row.'

Tom was hungry with his day's journey, and almost faint for want of food.

'Thar, yo!' said Quimbo, throwing down a coarse bag, which contained a peck of corn; 'thar, nigger, grab – take car on't, yo won't get no more *dis* yer week.'

Tom waited till a late hour to get a place at the mills; and then, moved by the utter weariness of two women, whom he saw trying to grind their corn there, he ground for them, put together the decaying brands of the fire, where many had baked cakes before them, and then went about getting his own supper. It was a new kind of work there – a deed of charity, small as it was; but it woke an answering touch in their hearts – an expression of womanly kindness came over their hard faces. They mixed his cake for him, and tended its baking; and Tom sat down by the light of the fire, and drew out his Bible – for he had need of comfort.

'What's that?' said one of the women.

'A Bible,' said Tom.

'Good Lord! han't seen un since I was in Kentucky.'

'Was you raised in Kentucky?' said Tom, with interest.

'Yes, and well raised, too; never 'spected to come to dis yer!' said the woman, sighing.

'What's dat ar book, anyway?' said the other woman.

'Why, the Bible.'

'Laws a me! what's dat?' said the woman.

'Do tell! you never hearn on't?' said the other woman. 'I used to har missis a readin' on't, sometimes, in Kentucky; but, laws o' me! we don't har nothin' here but crackin' and swarin'.'

'Read a piece, anyways!' said the first woman, curiously, seeing Tom attentively poring over it.

Tom read, 'Come unto ME, all ye that labour and are heavy laden, and I will give you rest.'[259]

'Them's good words, enough,' said the woman; 'who says 'em?'

'The Lord,' said Tom.

'I jest wish I know'd whar to find Him,' said the woman. 'I would go. 'Pears like I never should get rested agin. My flesh is fairly sore, and I tremble all over, every day, and Sambo's allers a jawin' at me, 'cause I doesn't pick faster; and nights it's most midnight 'fore I can get my supper; and then 'pears like I don't turn over and shut my eyes 'fore I hear de horn blow to get up, and at it agin in de mornin'. If I knew whar de Lor was, I'd tell him.'

'He's here, he's everywhere,' said Tom.

'Lor! you an't gwine to make me believe dat ar! I know de Lord an't here,' said the woman; ' 'tan't no use talking, though. I's jest gwine to camp down, and sleep while I ken.'

The women went off to their cabins, and Tom sat alone, by the smouldering fire, that flickered up redly in his face.

The silver, fair-browed moon rose in the purple sky, and looked down, calm and silent, as God looks on the scene of misery and oppression – looked calmly on the lone black man, as he sat with his arms folded, and his Bible on his knee.

'Is God HERE?' Ah, how is it possible for the untaught heart to keep its faith, unswerving, in the face of dire misrule, and palpable, unrebuked injustice? In that simple heart waged a fierce conflict: the crushing sense of wrong, the foreshadowing of a whole life of future misery, the wreck of all past hopes, mournfully tossing in the soul's sight, like dead corpses of wife, and child, and friend, rising from the dark wave, and surging in the face of the half-drowned mariner! Ah, was it easy *here* to believe and hold fast the great password of Christian faith, that 'God is, and is the REWARDER of them that diligently seek Him'?[260]

Tom rose, disconsolate, and stumbled into the cabin that had been allotted to him. The floor was already strewn with weary sleepers, and the foul air of the place almost repelled him; but the heavy night dews were chill, and his limbs weary, and, wrapping about him a tattered blanket, which formed his only bed-clothing, he stretched himself in the straw and fell asleep.

In dreams, a gentle voice came over his ear; he was sitting on the mossy seat in the garden by Lake Pontchartrain, and Eva, with her serious eyes bent downward, was reading to him from the Bible; and he heard her read –

'When thou passest through the waters, I will be with thee; and the rivers, they shall not overflow thee; when thou walkest through the fire, thou shalt not be burned, neither shall the flame kindle upon thee: for I am the Lord thy God, the Holy One of Israel, thy Saviour.'[261]

Gradually the words seemed to melt and fade, as in a divine music; the child raised her deep eyes, and fixed them lovingly on him, and rays of warmth and comfort seemed to go from them to his heart; and, as if wafted on the music, she seemed to rise on shining wings, from which flakes and spangles of gold fell off like stars, and she was gone.

Tom woke. Was it a dream? Let it pass for one. But who shall say that that sweet young spirit, which in life so yearned to comfort and console the distressed, was forbidden of God to assume this ministry after death?

It is a beautiful belief,
That ever round our head
Are hovering, on angel wings,
The spirits of the dead.

CHAPTER XXXIII

Cassy

*And behold, the tears of such as were oppressed, and they
had no comforter; and on the side of their oppressors
there was* power, *but they had no comforter.*

Ecclesiastes iv. 1.

IT TOOK BUT A SHORT TIME to familiarise Tom with all that was to be
hoped or feared in his new way of life. He was an expert and efficient
workman in whatever he undertook; and was, both from habit and
principle, prompt and faithful. Quiet and peaceable in his disposition,
he hoped, by unremitting diligence, to avert from himself at least a
portion of the evils of his condition. He saw enough of abuse and misery
to make him sick and weary; but he determined to toil on with religious
patience, committing himself to Him that judgeth righteously, not
without hope that some way of escape might yet be opened to him.

Legree took silent note of Tom's availability. He rated him as a first-
class hand; and yet he felt a secret dislike to him – the native antipathy
of bad to good. He saw, plainly, that when, as was often the case, his
violence and brutality fell on the helpless, Tom took notice of it; for, so
subtle is the atmosphere of opinion, that it will make itself felt, without
words; and the opinion even of a slave may annoy a master. Tom in
various ways manifested a tenderness of feeling, a commiseration for
his fellow-sufferers, strange and new to them, which was watched with
a jealous eye by Legree. He had purchased Tom with a view of
eventually making him a sort of overseer, with whom he might at times
entrust his affairs in short absences; and, in his view, the first, second,
and third requisite for that place, was *hardness*. Legree made up his
mind, that, as Tom was not hard to his hand, he would harden him

forthwith; and some few weeks after Tom had been on the place, he determined to commence the process.

One morning, when the hands were mustered for the field, Tom noticed with surprise a newcomer among them, whose appearance excited his attention. It was a woman, tall and slenderly formed, with remarkably delicate hands and feet, and dressed in neat and respectable garments. By the appearance of her face, she might have been between thirty-five and forty; and it was a face that, once seen, could never be forgotten – one of those that at a glance seem to convey to us an idea of a wild, painful, and romantic history. Her forehead was high, and her eyebrows marked with beautiful clearness. Her straight, well-formed nose, her finely-cut mouth, and the graceful contour of her head and neck, showed that she must once have been beautiful; but her face was deeply wrinkled with lines of pain, and of proud and bitter endurance. Her complexion was sallow and unhealthy, her cheeks thin, her features sharp, and her whole form emaciated. But her eye was the most remarkable feature – so large, so heavily black, overshadowed by long lashes of equal darkness, and so wildly, mournfully despairing. There was a fierce pride and defiance in every line of her face, in every curve of the flexible lip, in every motion of her body; but in her eye was a deep, settled night of anguish – an expression so hopeless and unchanging as to contrast fearfully with the scorn and pride expressed by her whole demeanour.

Where she came from, or who she was, Tom did not know. The first he did know, she was walking by his side, erect and proud, in the dim grey of the dawn. To the gang, however, she was known; for there was much looking and turning of heads, and a smothered yet apparent exultation among the miserable, ragged, half-starved creatures by whom she was surrounded.

'Got to come to it at last – glad of it!' said one.

'He! he! he!' said another; 'you'll know how good it is, misse!'

'We'll see her work!'

'Wonder if she'll get a cutting up, at night, like the rest of us!'

'I'd be glad to see her down for a flogging, I'll bound!' said another.

The woman took no notice of these taunts, but walked on with the same expression of angry scorn, as if she heard nothing. Tom had always lived among refined and cultivated people, and he felt intuitively, from her air and bearing, that she belonged to that class; but how or why she could be fallen to these degrading circumstances he could not tell. The woman neither looked at him nor spoke to him, though, all the way to the field, she kept close at his side.

Tom was soon busy at his work; but, as the woman was at no great distance from him, he often glanced an eye to her, at her work. He saw at a glance that a native adroitness and handiness made the task to her an easier one than it proved to many. She picked very fast and very clean, and with an air of scorn, as if she despised both the work and the disgrace and humiliation of the circumstances in which she was placed.

In the course of the day, Tom was working near the mulatto woman who had been bought in the same lot with himself. She was evidently in a condition of great suffering, and Tom often heard her praying, as she wavered and trembled, and seemed about to fall down. Tom silently, as he came near to her, transferred several handfuls of cotton from his own sack to hers.

'Oh, don't, don't!' said the woman, looking surprised; 'it'll get you into trouble.'

Just then Sambo came up. He seemed to have a special spite against this woman; and, flourishing his whip, said, in brutal, guttural tones, 'What dis yer, Luce – foolin' a'?' and, with the word, kicking the woman with his heavy cow-hide shoe, he struck Tom across the face with his whip.

Tom silently resumed his task; but the woman, before at the last point of exhaustion, fainted.

'I'll bring her to!' said the driver, with a brutal grin. 'I'll give her something better than camphire!' and, taking a pin from his coat-sleeve, he buried it to the head in her flesh. The woman groaned, and half rose. 'Get up, you beast, and work, will yer, or I'll show yer a trick more!'

The woman seemed stimulated, for a few moments, to an unnatural strength, and worked with desperate eagerness.

'See that you keep to dat ar,' said the man, 'or yer'll wish yer's dead tonight, I reckin!'

'That I do now!' Tom heard her say; and again he heard her say, 'O Lord, how long! O Lord, why don't you help us?'

At the risk of all that he might suffer, Tom came forward again, and put all the cotton in his sack into the woman's.

'Oh, you mustn't! you don'no what they'll do to ye!' said the woman.

'I can bar it!' said Tom, 'better'n you;' and he was at his place again. It passed in a moment.

Suddenly the stranger woman whom we have described, and who had, in the course of her work, come near enough to hear Tom's last words, raised her heavy black eyes, and fixed them for a second on him; then, taking a quantity of cotton from her basket, she placed it in his.

'You know nothing about this place,' she said, 'or you wouldn't have done that. When you've been here a month, you'll be done helping anybody; you'll find it hard enough to take care of your own skin!'

'The Lord forbid, missis!' said Tom, using instinctively to his field companion the respectful form proper to the high-bred with whom he had lived.

'The Lord never visits these parts,' said the woman, bitterly, as she went nimbly forward with her work; and again the scornful smile curled her lips.

But the action of the woman had been seen by the driver, across the field; and, flourishing his whip, he came up to her.

'What! what!' he said to the woman, with an air of triumph, 'you a foolin'? Go along! yer under me now – mind yourself, or yer'll cotch it!'

A glance like sheet-lightning suddenly flashed from those black eyes; and, facing about, with quivering lip and dilated nostrils, she drew herself up, and fixed a glance, blazing with rage and scorn, on the driver.

'Dog!' she said, 'touch *me*, if you dare! I've power enough, yet, to have you torn by the dogs, burnt alive, cut to inches! I've only to say the word!'

'What de devil you here for, den?' said the man, evidently cowed, and sullenly retreating a step or two. 'Didn't mean no harm, Misse Cassy!'

'Keep your distance, then!' said the woman. And, in truth, the man seemed greatly inclined to attend to something at the other end of the field, and started off in quick time.

The woman suddenly turned to her work, and laboured with a despatch that was perfectly astonishing to Tom. She seemed to work by magic. Before the day was through, her basket was filled, crowded down, and piled, and she had several times put largely into Tom's. Long after dusk, the whole weary train, with their baskets on their heads, defiled up to the building appropriated to the storing and weighing of the cotton. Legree was there, busily conversing with the two drivers.

'Dat ar Tom's gwine to make a powerful deal o' trouble; kept a puttin' into Lucy's basket. One o' these yer dat will get all der niggers to feelin' 'bused, if mas'r don't watch him!' said Sambo.

'Hey-dey! The black cuss!' said Legree. 'He'll have to get a breakin' in – won't he, boys?'

Both negroes grinned a horrid grin, at this intimation.

'Ay, ay! let Mas'r Legree alone, for breakin' in! De debil heself couldn't beat mas'r at dat!' said Quimbo.

'Wal, boys, the best way is to give him the flogging to do, till he gets over his notions. Break him in!'

'Lord, mas'r'll have hard work to get dat out o' him!'

'It'll have to come out of him, though!' said Legree, as he rolled his tobacco in his mouth.

'Now, dar's Lucy – de aggravatinest, ugliest wench on de place!' pursued Sambo.

'Take care, Sam; I shall begin to think what's the reason for your spite agin Lucy.'

'Well, mas'r knows she sot herself up agin mas'r, and wouldn't have me, when he tell'd her to.'

'I'd a flogged her into't,' said Legree, spitting, 'only there's such a press o' work, it don't seem wuth a while to upset her jist now. She's slender; but these yer slender gals will bear half killin' to get their own way!'

'Wal, Lucy was real aggravatin' and lazy, sulkin' round; wouldn't do nothin' – and Tom he tuck up for her.'

'He did, eh? Wal, then, Tom shall have the pleasure of flogging her. It'll be a good practice for him, and he won't put it on to the gal like you devils, neither.'

'Ho, ho! haw! haw! haw!' laughed both the sooty wretches; and the diabolical sounds seemed, in truth, a not unapt expression of the fiendish character which Legree gave them.

'Wal, but, mas'r, Tom and Misse Cassy, and dey among 'em, filled Lucy's basket. I ruther guess der weight's in it, mas'r!'

'*I do the weighing*!' said Legree, emphatically.

Both the drivers again laughed their diabolical laugh.

'So!' he added, 'Misse Cassy did her day's work.'

'She picks like de debil and all his angels!'

'She's got 'em all in her, I believe!' said Legree; and, growling a brutal oath, he proceeded to the weighing-room.

Slowly the weary, dispirited creatures wound their way into the room, and, with crouching reluctance, presented their baskets to be weighed.

Legree noted on a slate, on the side of which was pasted a list of names, the amount.

Tom's basket was weighed and approved; and he looked, with an anxious glance for the success of the woman he had befriended.

Tottering with weakness, she came forward, and delivered her basket. It was of full weight, as Legree well perceived; but, affecting anger, he said –

'What, you lazy beast! short again! Stand aside, you'll catch it, pretty soon!'

The woman gave a groan of utter despair, and sat down on a board.

The person who had been called Misse Cassy now came forward, and, with a haughty, negligent air, delivered her basket. As she delivered it, Legree looked in her eyes with a sneering yet enquiring glance.

She fixed her black eyes steadily on him, her lips moved slightly, and she said something in French. What it was, no one knew; but Legree's face became perfectly demoniacal in its expression, as she spoke; he half raised his hand, as if to strike – a gesture which she regarded with fierce disdain, as she turned and walked away.

'And now,' said Legree, 'come here, you Tom. You see, I told ye I didn't buy ye jest for the common work; I mean to promote ye, and make a driver of ye; and tonight ye may jest as well begin to get yer hand in. Now, ye jest take this yer gal and flog her; ye've seen enough on't to know how.'

'I beg mas'r's pardon,' said Tom; 'hopes mas'r won't set me at that. It's what I an't used to – never did – and can't do, no way possible.'

'Ye'll larn a pretty smart chance of things ye never did know, before I've done with ye!' said Legree, taking up a cow-hide, and striking Tom a heavy blow across the cheek, and following up the infliction by a shower of blows.

'There!' he said, as he stopped to rest; 'now will ye tell me ye can't do it?'

'Yes, mas'r,' said Tom, putting up his hand, to wipe the blood that trickled down his face. 'I'm willin' to work, night and day, and work while there's life and breath in me; but this yer thing I can't feel it right to do; and, mas'r, I *never* shall do it – *never*!'

Tom had a remarkably smooth, soft voice, and a habitually respectful manner, that had given Legree an idea that he would be cowardly, and easily subdued. When he spoke these last words, a thrill of amazement went through everyone; the poor woman clasped her hands, and said, 'O Lord!' and everyone involuntarily looked at each other and drew in their breath, as if to prepare for the storm that was about to burst.

Legree looked stupefied and confounded; but at last burst forth –

'What! ye blasted black beast! tell *me* ye don't think it *right* to do what I tell ye! What have any of you cussed cattle to do with thinking what's right? I'll put a stop to it! Why, what do ye think ye are? Maybe ye think ye'r a gentleman, master Tom, to be a telling your master what's right, and what an't! So you pretend it's wrong to flog the gal!'

'I think so, mas'r,' said Tom. 'The poor crittur's sick and feeble; 'twould be downright cruel, and it's what I never will do, nor begin to. Mas'r, if you mean to kill me, kill me; but, as to my raising my hand agin anyone here, I never shall – I'll die first!'

Tom spoke in a mild voice, but with a decision that could not be mistaken. Legree shook with anger; his greenish eyes glared fiercely, and his very whiskers seemed to curl with passion; but, like some ferocious beast, that plays with its victim before he devours it, he kept back his strong impulse to proceed to immediate violence, and broke out into bitter raillery.

'Well, here's a pious dog, at last, let down among us sinners! – a saint, a gentleman, and no less, to talk to us sinners about our sins! Powerful holy critter, he must be! Here, you rascal, you make believe to be so pious – didn't you never hear, out of yer Bible, "Servants, obey yer masters?"[262] An't I yer master? Didn't I pay down twelve hundred dollars, cash, for all there is inside yer old cussed black shell? An't yer mine, now, body and soul?' he said, giving Tom a violent kick with his heavy boot; 'tell me!'

In the very depth of physical suffering, bowed by brutal oppression, this question shot a gleam of joy and triumph through Tom's soul. He suddenly stretched himself up, and, looking earnestly to heaven, while the tears and blood that flowed down his face mingled, he exclaimed –

'No! no! no! my soul an't yours, mas'r! You haven't bought it – ye can't buy it! It's been bought and paid for by One that's able to keep it. No matter, no matter, you can't harm me!'

'I can't!' said Legree, with a sneer; 'we'll see! Here, Sambo! Quimbo! give this dog such a breakin' in as he won't get over this month!'

The two gigantic negroes that now laid hold of Tom, with fiendish exultation in their faces, might have formed no unapt personification of the powers of darkness. The poor woman screamed with apprehension, and all rose, as by a general impulse, while they dragged him unresisting from the place.

CHAPTER XXXIV

The Quadroon's Story

*And behold the tears of such as are oppressed; and on the side of
their oppressors there was power. Wherefore I praised the dead
that are already dead more than the living that are yet alive.*

Ecclesiastes iv. 1, 2

IT WAS LATE at night, and Tom lay groaning and bleeding alone, in an
old forsaken room of the gin-house, among pieces of broken
machinery, piles of damaged cotton, and other rubbish which had there
accumulated.

The night was damp and close, and the thick air swarmed with
myriads of mosquitoes, which increased the restless torture of his
wounds; whilst a burning thirst – a torture beyond all others – filled up
the uttermost measure of physical anguish.

'O good Lord! *Do* look down – give me the victory! – give me the
victory over all!' prayed poor Tom, in his anguish.

A footstep entered the room behind him, and the light of a lantern
flashed on his eyes.

'Who's there? Oh, for the Lord's massy, please give me some water!'

The woman Cassy – for it was she – set down her lantern, and,
pouring water from a bottle, raised his head, and gave him drink.
Another and another cup were drained, with feverish eagerness.

'Drink all ye want,' she said; 'I knew how it would be. It isn't the first
time I've been out in the night, carrying water to such as you.'

'Thank you, missis,' said Tom, when he had done drinking.

'Don't call me missis! I'm a miserable slave like yourself – a lower
one than you can ever be!' said she, bitterly. 'But now,' said she, going
to the door, and dragging in a small palliasse, over which she had
spread linen cloths wet with cold water, 'try, my poor fellow, to roll
yourself on to this.'

Stiff with wounds and bruises, Tom was a long time in accomplishing
this movement; but when done, he felt a sensible relief from the
cooling application to his wounds.

The woman, whom long practice with the victims of brutality had made familiar with many healing arts, went on to make many applications to Tom's wounds, by means of which he was soon somewhat relieved.

'Now,' said the woman, when she had raised his head on a roll of damaged cotton, which served for a pillow, 'there's the best I can do for you.'

Tom thanked her; and the woman, sitting down on the floor, drew up her knees, and embracing them with her arms, looked fixedly before her, with a bitter and painful expression of countenance. Her bonnet fell back, and long wavy streams of black hair fell around her singular and melancholy face.

'It's no use, my poor fellow!' she broke out, at last, 'it's of no use, this you've been trying to do. You were a brave fellow – you had the right on your side; but it's all in vain, and out of the question, for you to struggle. You are in the devil's hands; he is the strongest, and you must give up!'

Give up! and, had not human weakness and physical agony whispered that, before? Tom started; for the bitter woman, with her wild eyes and melancholy voice, seemed to him an embodiment of the temptation with which he had been wrestling.

'O Lord! O Lord!' he groaned, 'how can I give up?'

'There's no use calling on the Lord – he never hears,' said the woman, steadily. 'There isn't any God, I believe; or, if there is, he's taken sides against us. All goes against us, heaven and earth. Everything is pushing us into hell. Why shouldn't we go?'

Tom closed his eyes, and shuddered at the dark, atheistic words.

'You see,' said the woman, '*you* don't know anything about it – I do. I've been on this place five years, body and soul, under this man's foot; and I hate him as I do the devil! Here you are, on a lone plantation, ten miles from any other, in the swamps; not a white person here who could testify if you were burned alive – if you were scalded, cut into inch-pieces, set up for the dogs to tear, or hung up and whipped to death. There's no law here, of God or man, that can do you or any one of us the least good; and, this man! there's no earthly thing that he's too good to do. I could make anyone's hair rise, and their teeth chatter, if I should only tell what I've seen and been knowing to here – and it's no use resisting! Did I *want* to live with him? Wasn't I a woman delicately bred? and he – God in heaven! what was he, and is he? And yet, I've lived with him these five years, and cursed every moment of my life – night and day! And now, he's got a new one – a young thing, only fifteen, and she brought up, she says, piously. Her good mistress taught her to read the Bible; and she's brought her Bible here – to hell with her!' and the woman laughed a wild and doleful laugh, that rang with a strange supernatural sound through the old ruined shed.

Tom folded his hands; all was darkness and horror.

'O Jesus! Lord Jesus! have you quite forgot us poor critturs?' burst forth, at last. 'Help, Lord, I perish!'

The woman sternly continued –

'And what are these miserable low dogs you work with, that you should suffer on their account? Every one of them would turn against you the first time they got a chance. They are all of 'em as low and cruel to each other as they can be; there's no use in your suffering to keep from hurting them.'

'Poor critturs!' said Tom, 'what made 'em cruel? And, if I give out, I shall get used to't, and grow, little by little, just like em! No, no, missis! I've lost everything – wife, and children, and home, and a kind mas'r – and he would have set me free, if he'd only lived a week longer. I've lost everything in *this* world, and it's clean gone, for ever – and now I *can't* lose heaven, too; no, I can't get to be wicked, besides all!'

'But it can't be that the Lord will lay sin to our account,' said the woman; 'he won't charge it to us, when we're forced to it; he'll charge it to them that drove us to it.'

'Yes,' said Tom; 'but that won't keep us from growing wicked. If I get to be as hard-hearted as that ar' Sambo, and as wicked, it won't make much odds to me how I come so; it's the *bein'* so – that ar's what I'm a dreadin'.'

The woman fixed a wild and startled look on Tom, as if a new thought had struck her; and then, heavily groaning, said –

'O God a' mercy! you speak the truth! Oh – Oh – Oh!' And, with groans, she fell on the floor, like one crushed and writhing under the extremity of mental anguish.

There was a silence awhile, in which the breathing of both parties could be heard, when Tom faintly said, 'Oh, please, missis – !'

The woman suddenly rose up, with her face composed to its usual stern, melancholy expression.

'Please, missis, I saw 'em throw my coat in that ar' corner, and in my coat-pocket is my Bible – if missis would please get it for me.'

Cassy went and got it. Tom opened, at once, to a heavily marked passage, much worn, of the last scenes in the life of Him by whose stripes we are healed.

'If missis would only be so good as read that ar' – it's better than water.'

Cassy took the book, with a dry, proud air, and looked over the passage. She then read aloud, in a soft voice, and with a beauty of intonation that was peculiar, that touching account of anguish and of glory. Often, as she read, her voice faltered, and sometimes failed her altogether, when she would stop, with an air of frigid composure, till she had mastered herself. When she came to the touching words, 'Father forgive them, for they know not what they do,'[263] she threw down the book, and, burying her face in the heavy masses of her hair, she sobbed aloud, with a convulsive violence.

Tom was weeping also, and occasionally uttering a smothered ejaculation.

'If we only could keep up to that ar'!' said Tom – 'it seemed to come so natural to him, and we have to fight so hard for 't! O Lord, help us! O blessed Lord Jesus, do help us!'

'Missis,' said Tom, after a while, 'I can see that, somehow, you're quite 'bove me in everything; but there's one thing missis might learn even from poor Tom. Ye said the Lord took sides against us, because he lets us be 'bused and knocked round; but ye see what come on his own Son – the blessed Lord of Glory. Wan't he allays poor? and have we, any on us, yet come so low as he come? The Lord han't forgot us – I'm sartin' o' that ar'. If we suffer with him, we shall also reign, Scripture says; but, if we deny him, he also will deny us. Didn't they all suffer? – the Lord and all his? It tells how they was stoned and sawn asunder, and wandered about in sheepskins and goatskins, and was destitute, afflicted, tormented. Sufferin' an't no reason to make us think the Lord's turned agin us; but jest the contrary, if only we hold on to him, and doesn't give up to sin.'

'But why does he put us where we can't help but sin?' said the woman.

'I think we *can* help it,' said Tom.

'You'll see,' said Cassy. 'What'll you do? Tomorrow they'll be at you again. I know 'em, I've seen all their doings; I can't bear to think of all they'll bring you to – and they'll make you give out, at last!'

'Lord Jesus!' said Tom, 'you *will* take care of my soul? O Lord, do! – don't let me give out!'

'Oh, dear!' said Cassy; 'I've heard all this crying and praying before; and yet they've been broken down, and brought under. There's Emmeline, she's trying to hold on, and you're trying – but what use? You must give up, or be killed by inches.'

'Well, then, I *will* die!' said Tom. 'Spin it out as long as they can, they can't help my dying, sometime! – and, after that, they can't do no more. I'm clar, I'm set! I *know* the Lord'll help me, and bring me through.'

The woman did not answer; she sat with her black eyes intently fixed on the floor.

'Maybe it's the way,' she murmured to herself; 'but those that *have* given up, there's no hope for them! – none! We live in filth and grow loathsome, till we loathe ourselves! And we long to die, and we don't dare to kill ourselves. No hope! no hope! no hope! – this girl now – just as old as I was. You see me now,' she said, speaking to Tom very rapidly; 'see what I am! Well, I was brought up in luxury. The first I remember is playing about, when I was a child, in splendid parlours – when I was kept dressed up like a doll, and company and visitors used to praise me. There was a garden opening from the saloon windows; and there I used to play hide-and-go-seek, under the orange trees, with my brothers and sisters. I went to a convent, and there I learned music, French and embroidery, and what not; and when I was fourteen, I came out to my father's funeral. He died very suddenly, and when the property came to be settled, they found that there was scarcely enough to cover the debts; and when the creditors took an inventory of the property, I was set down in it. My mother was a slave woman, and my father had always meant to set me free; but he had not done it, and so I was set down in the list. I'd always known who I was, but never thought much about it. Nobody ever expects that a strong, healthy man is going to die. My father was a well man only four hours before he died – it was one of the first cholera cases in New Orleans. The day after the funeral my father's wife took her children, and went up to her father's plantation. I thought they treated me strangely, but didn't know why. There was a young lawyer who they left to settle the business; and he came every day, and was about the house, and spoke very politely to me. He brought with him one day a young man, whom I thought the handsomest I had ever seen. I shall never forget that evening; I walked with him in the garden. I was lonesome and full of sorrow, and he was so kind and gentle to me; and he told me that he had seen me before I went to the convent, and that he had loved me a great while, and that he would be my friend and protector. In short, though he didn't tell me he had paid two thousand dollars for me, and I was his property, I became his willingly, for I loved him. Loved!' said the woman, stopping. 'Oh, how I *did* love that man! How I love him now, and always shall, while I breathe! He was so beautiful, so high, so noble! He put me into a beautiful house, with servants, horses, and carriages, and furniture, and dresses. Everything that money could buy he gave me;

but I didn't set any value on all that, I only cared for him. I loved him better than my God and my own soul; and, if I tried, I couldn't do any other way from what he wanted me to.

'I wanted only one thing – I did want him to *marry* me. I thought, if he loved me as he said he did, and if I was what he seemed to think I was, he would be willing to marry me and set me free. But he convinced me that it would be impossible; and he told me that, if we were only faithful to each other, it was marriage before God. If that is true, wasn't I that man's wife? Wasn't I faithful? For seven years, didn't I study every look and motion, and only live and breathe to please him? He had the yellow fever,[264] and for twenty days and nights I watched with him – I alone, and gave him all his medicine, and did everything for him; and then he called me his good angel, and said I'd saved his life. We had two beautiful children. The first was a boy, and we called him Henry. He was the image of his father – he had such beautiful eyes, such a forehead, and his hair hung all in curls around it – and he had all his father's spirit, and his talent, too. Little Elise, he said, looked like me. He used to tell me that I was the most beautiful woman in Louisiana, he was so proud of me and the children. He used to love to have me dress them up, and take them and me about in an open carriage, and hear the remarks that people would make on us; and he used to fill my ears constantly with the fine things that were said in praise of me and the children. Oh, those were happy days! I thought I was as happy as anyone could be; but then there came evil times. He had a cousin come to New Orleans, who was his particular friend – he thought all the world of him; but, from the first time I saw him, I couldn't tell why, I dreaded him, for I felt sure he was going to bring misery on us. He got Henry to going out with him, and often he would not come home nights till two or three o'clock. I did not dare say a word; for Henry was so high-spirited, I was afraid to. He got him to the gaming-houses; and he was one of the sort that, when he once got a-going there, there was no holding back. And then he introduced him to another lady, and I saw soon that his heart was gone from me. He never told me, but I saw it – I knew it, day after day. I felt my heart breaking, but I could not say a word! At this the wretch offered to buy me and the children off Henry, to clear off his gambling debts, which stood in the way of his marrying as he wished – and *he sold us*. He told me one day that he had business in the country, and should be gone two or three weeks. He spoke kinder than usual, and said he should come back; but it didn't deceive me, I knew that the time had come; I was just like one turned into stone; I couldn't speak, nor shed a tear. He kissed me and kissed the children a good many times, and went out. I saw him get on his horse, and I watched him till he was quite out of sight; and then I fell down, and fainted.

'Then *he* came, the cursed wretch! he came to take possession. He told me that he had bought me and my children, and showed me the papers. I cursed him before God, and told him I'd die sooner than live with him.

' "Just as you please," said he; "but, if you don't behave reasonably I'll sell both the children, where you shall never see them again." He told me that he always had meant to have me, from the first time he saw me; and that he had drawn Henry on, and got him in debt, on purpose to make him willing to sell me. That he got him in love with another woman; and that I might know, after all that, that he should not give up for a few airs and tears, and things of that sort.

'I gave up, for my hands were tied. He had my children; whenever I resisted his will anywhere, he would talk about selling them, and he made me as submissive as he desired. Oh, what a life it was! to live with my heart breaking, every day – to keep on, on, on, loving, when it was only misery; and to be bound, body and soul, to one I hated. I used to love to read to Henry, to play to him, to waltz with him, and sing to him; but everything I did for this one was a perfect drag – yet I was afraid to refuse anything. He was very imperious, and harsh to the children. Elise was a timid little thing; but Henry was bold and high-spirited, like his father, and he had never been brought under in the least by anyone. He was always finding fault, and quarrelling with him; and I used to live in daily fear and dread. I tried to make the child respectful – I tried to keep them apart, for I held on to those children like death; but it did no good. *He sold both those children.* He took me to ride, one day, and when I came home, they were nowhere to be found! He told me he had sold them; he showed me the money, the price of their blood. Then it seemed as if all good forsook me. I raved and cursed – cursed God and man; and, for a while, I believe, he really was afraid of me. But he didn't give up so. He told me that my children were sold, but whether I ever saw their faces again depended on him; and that, if I wasn't quiet, they should smart for it. Well, you can do anything with a woman when you've got her children. He made me submit; he made me be peaceable; he flattered me with hopes that perhaps he would buy them back; and so things went on, a week or two. One day I was out walking, and passed by the calaboose; I saw a crowd about the gate, and heard a child's voice – and suddenly my Henry broke away from two or three men who were holding him, and ran, screaming, and caught my dress. They came up to him, swearing dreadfully; and one man, whose face I shall never forget, told him that he wouldn't get away so; that he was going with him into the calaboose, and he'd get a lesson there he'd never forget. I tried to beg and plead – they only laughed; the poor boy screamed and looked into my face, and held on to me, until, in tearing him off, they tore the skirt of my dress half away; and they carried him in screaming "Mother! mother! mother!" There was one man stood there seemed to pity me. I offered him all the money I had, if he'd only interfere. He shook his head, and said that the boy had been impudent and disobedient, ever since he bought him; that he was going to break him in, once for all. I turned and ran; and every step of the way, I thought that I heard him scream. I got into the house; ran all out of breath, to the parlour, where I found Butler. I told him, and begged him to go and interfere. He only laughed, and told me the boy had got his deserts. He'd got to be broken in – the sooner the better; "what did I expect?" he asked.

'It seemed to me something in my head snapped at that moment. I felt dizzy and furious. I remember seeing a great sharp bowie-knife on the table; I remember something about catching it, and flying upon him! and then all grew dark, and I didn't know any more – not for days and days.

'When I came to myself, I was in a nice room; but not mine. An old black woman tended me; and a doctor came to see me, and there was a great deal of care taken of me. After a while, I found that he had gone away, and left me at this house to be sold; and that's why they took such pains with me.

'I didn't mean to get well, and hoped I shouldn't; but, in spite of me, the fever went off, and I grew healthy, and finally got up. Then they made me dress up every day; and gentlemen used to come in and stand and smoke their cigars, and look at me, and ask questions, and debate my price. I was so gloomy and silent that none of them wanted me. They threatened to whip me if I wasn't gayer, and didn't take some pains to make myself agreeable. At length, one day, came a gentleman named Stuart. He seemed to have some feeling for me; he saw that something dreadful was on my heart, and he came to see me alone, a great many times, and finally persuaded me to tell him. He bought me at last, and promised to do all he could to find and buy back my children. He went to the hotel where my Henry was; they told him he had been sold to a planter up on Pearl River;[265] that was the last that I ever heard. Then he found where my daughter was; an old woman was keeping her. He offered an immense sum for her, but they would not

sell her. Butler found out that it was for me he wanted her; and he sent
me word that I should never have her. Captain Stuart was very kind to
me; he had a splendid plantation, and took me to it. In the course of a
year I had a son born. Oh, that child! – how I loved it! How just like my
poor Henry the little thing looked! But I had made up my mind – yes, I
had. I would never again let a child live to grow up! I took the little
fellow in my arms, when he was two weeks old, and kissed him and
cried over him; and then I gave him laudanum, and held him close to
my bosom, while he slept to death. How I mourned and cried over it!
and whoever dreamed that it was anything but a mistake that had made
me give it the laudanum? but it's one of the few things that I'm glad of
now. I am not sorry to this day; he, at least, is out of pain. What better
than death could I give him, poor child! After a while the cholera came,
and Captain Stuart died; everybody died that wanted to live, and I – I,
though I went down to death's door – *I lived*! Then I was sold, and
passed from hand to hand, till I grew faded and wrinkled, and I had a
fever; and then this wretch bought me, and brought me here – and here
I am!'

The woman stopped. She had hurried on through her story, with a
wild, passionate utterance; sometimes seeming to address it to Tom
and sometimes speaking as in a soliloquy. So vehement and overpowering was the force with which she spoke, that, for a season, Tom was
beguiled even from the pain of his wounds; and, raising himself on one
elbow, watched her as she paced restlessly up and down, her long black
hair swaying heavily about her, as she moved.

'You tell me,' she said, after a pause, 'that there is a God – a God that
looks down and sees all these things. Maybe it's so. The sisters in the
convent used to tell me of a day of judgement, when everything is
coming to light; won't there be vengeance then!

'They think it's nothing, what we suffer – nothing what our children
suffer! It's all a small matter; yet I've walked the streets when it seemed
as if I had misery enough in my one heart to sink the city. I've wished
the houses would fall on me, or the stones sink under me. Yes! and, in
the judgement day I will stand up before God, a witness against those
that have ruined me and my children, body and soul!

'When I was a girl, I thought I was religious; I used to love God and
prayer. Now, I'm a lost soul, pursued by devils that torment me day
and night; they keep pushing me on and on – and I'll do it, too, some of
these days!' she said, clenching her hand, while an insane light glanced
in her heavy black eyes. 'I'll send him where he belongs – a short way,
too – one of these nights, if they burn me alive for it!' A wild, long

laugh, rang through the deserted room, and ended in a hysteric sob; she threw herself on the floor, in convulsive sobbings and struggles.

In a few moments, the frenzy fit seemed to pass off; she rose slowly, and seemed to collect herself.

'Can I do anything more for you, my poor fellow?' she said, approaching where Tom lay; 'shall I give you some more water?'

There was a graceful and compassionate sweetness in her voice and manner, as she said this, that formed a strange contrast with the former wildness.

Tom drank the water, and looked earnestly and pitifully into her face.

'O missis, I wish you'd go to him that can give you living waters!'

'Go to him! Where is he? Who is he?' said Cassy.

'Him that you read of to me – the Lord.'

'I used to see the picture of him, over the altar, when I was a girl,' said Cassy, her dark eyes fixing themselves in an expression of mournful reverie; 'but, *he isn't here*! there's nothing here, but sin and long, long, long despair! Oh!' She laid her hand on her breast and drew in her breath, as if to lift a heavy weight.

Tom looked as if he would speak again; but she cut him short with a decided gesture.

'Don't talk, my poor fellow. Try to sleep, if you can.' And, placing water in his reach, and making whatever little arrangements for his comfort she could, Cassy left the shed.

CHAPTER XXXV

The Tokens

*And slight withal may be the things that bring
Back on the heart the weight which it would fling
Aside for ever; it may be a sound,
A flower, the wind, the ocean, which shall wound –
Striking the electric chain wherewith we're darkly bound.*[266]

Childe Harold's Pilgrimage, Canto iv

THE SITTING-ROOM of Legree's establishment was a large, long room, with a wide ample fireplace. It had once been hung with a showy and expensive paper, which now hung mouldering, torn and discoloured, from the damp walls. The place had that peculiar sickening, unwholesome smell, compounded of mingled damp, dirt and decay, which one often notices in close old houses. The wallpaper was defaced, in spots, by slops of beer and wine; or garnished with chalk memoranda; and long sums footed up, as if somebody had been practising arithmetic there. In the fireplace stood a brazier full of burning charcoal; for, though the weather was not cold, the evenings always seemed damp and chilly in that great room; and Legree, moreover, wanted a place to light his cigars, and heat his water for punch. The ruddy glare of the charcoal displayed the confused and unpromising aspect of the room – saddles, bridles, several sorts of harness, riding-whips, overcoats, and various articles of clothing, scattered up and down the room in confused variety; and the dogs of which we have before spoken, had encamped themselves among them, to suit their own taste and convenience.

Legree was just mixing himself a tumbler of punch, pouring his hot water from a cracked and broken-nosed pitcher, grumbling, as he did so –

'Plague on that Sambo, to kick up this yer row between me and the new hands! The fellow won't be fit to work for a week now – right in the press of the season!'

'Yes, just like you,' said a voice behind his chair. It was the woman

Cassy, who had stolen upon his soliloquy.

'Ha! you she-devil! you've come back, have you?'

'Yes, I have,' she said, coolly; 'come to have my own way, too!'

'You lie, you jade! I'll be up to my word. Either behave yourself, or stay down to the quarters, and fare and work with the rest.'

'I'd rather, ten thousand times,' said the woman, 'live in the dirtiest hole at the quarters than be under your hoof!'

'But you *are* under my hoof, for all that,' said he, turning upon her, with a savage grin; 'that's one comfort. So, sit down here on my knee, my dear, and hear to reason,' said he, laying hold on her wrist.

'Simon Legree, take care!' said the woman, with a sharp flash of her eye – a glance so wild and insane in its light as to be almost appalling. 'You're afraid of me, Simon,' she said, deliberately; 'and you've reason to be! But be careful, for I've got the devil in me!'

The last words she whispered in a hissing tone, close to his ear.

'Get out! I believe, to my soul, you have!' said Legree, pushing her from him, and looking uncomfortably at her. 'After all, Cassy,' he said, 'why can't you be friends with me, as you used to?'

'Used to!' said she, bitterly. She stopped short – a world of choking feelings, rising in her heart, kept her silent.

Cassy had always kept over Legree the kind of influence that a strong, impassioned woman can ever keep over the most brutal man; but, of late, she had grown more and more irritable and restless under the hideous yoke of her servitude, and her irritability at times broke out into raving insanity; and this liability made her a sort of object of dread to Legree, who had that superstitious horror of insane persons which is common to coarse and uninstructed minds. When Legree brought Emmeline to the house, all the smouldering embers of womanly feeling flashed up in the worn heart of Cassy, and she took part with the girl; and a fierce quarrel ensued between her and Legree. Legree, in a fury, swore she should be put to field-service, if she would not be peaceable. Cassy, with proud scorn, declared she *would* go to the field. And she worked there one day, as we have described, to show how perfectly she scorned the threat.

Legree was secretly uneasy all day; for Cassy had an influence over him from which he could not free himself. When she presented her basket at the scales, he had hoped for some concession, and addressed her in a sort of half conciliatory, half scornful tone; and she had answered with the bitterest contempt.

The outrageous treatment of poor Tom had roused her still more; and she had followed Legree to the house, with no particular intention but to upbraid him for his brutality.

'I wish, Cassy,' said Legree, 'you'd behave yourself decently.'

'*You* talk about behaving decently! And what have you been doing? You, who haven't even sense enough to keep from spoiling one of your best hands, right in the most pressing season, just for your devilish temper!'

'I was a fool, it's a fact, to let any such brangle[267] come up,' said Legree; 'but, when the boy set up his will, he had to be broke in.'

'I reckon you won't break *him* in!'

'Won't I?' said Legree, rising, passionately. 'I'd like to know if I won't? He'll be the first nigger that ever came it round me! I'll break every bone in his body but he *shall* give up!'

Just then the door opened, and Sambo entered. He came forward bowing, and holding out something in a paper.

'What's that, you dog?' said Legree.

'It's a witch thing, mas'r!'

'A what?'

'Something that niggers gets from witches. Keeps 'em from feelin' when they's flogged. He had it tied round his neck, with a black string.'

Legree, like most godless and cruel men, was superstitious. He took the paper, and opened it uneasily.

There dropped out of it a silver dollar, and a long, shining curl of fair hair – hair which, like a living thing, twined itself round Legree's fingers.

'Damnation!' he screamed, in sudden passion, stamping on the floor, and pulling furiously at the hair, as if it burned him. 'Where did this come from? Take it off! – burn it up! – burn it up!' he screamed, tearing it off, and throwing it into the charcoal. 'What did you bring it to me for?'

Sambo stood with his heavy mouth wide open, and aghast with wonder; and Cassy, who was preparing to leave the apartment, stopped, and looked at him in perfect amazement.

'Don't you bring me any more of your devilish things!' said he, shaking his fist at Sambo, who retreated hastily towards the door; and, picking up the silver dollar, he sent it smashing through the window-pane out into the darkness.

Sambo was glad to make his escape. When he was gone, Legree seemed a little ashamed of his fit of alarm. He sat doggedly down in his chair, and began sullenly sipping his tumbler of punch.

Cassy prepared herself for going out, unobserved by him; and slipped away to minister to poor Tom, as we have already related.

And what was the matter with Legree? and what was there in a simple curl of fair hair to appal that brutal man, familiar with every form of cruelty? To answer this, we must carry the reader backward in his history. Hard and reprobate as the godless man seemed now, there had been a time when he had been rocked on the bosom of a mother – cradled with prayers and pious hymns – his now seared brow bedewed with the waters of holy baptism. In early childhood, a fair-haired woman had led him, at the sound of Sabbath bell, to worship and to pray. Far in New England that mother had trained her only son, with long, unwearied love, and patient prayers. Born of a hard-tempered sire, on whom that gentle woman had wasted a world of unvalued love, Legree had followed in the steps of his father. Boisterous, unruly, and tyrannical, he despised all her counsel, and would none of her reproof; and, at an early age, broke from her, to seek his fortunes at sea. He never came home but once after; and then his mother, with the yearning of a heart that must love something, and has nothing else to love, clung to him, and sought, with passionate prayers and entreaties, to win him from a life of sin, to his soul's eternal good.

That was Legree's day of grace; then good angels called him; then he was almost persuaded, and Mercy held him by the hand. His heart inly relented – there was a conflict – but sin got the victory, and he set all the force of his rough nature against the conviction of his conscience. He drank and swore, was wilder and more brutal than ever. And one night, when his mother, in the last agony of her despair, knelt at his feet, he spurned her from him, threw her senseless on the floor, and, with brutal curses, fled to his ship. The next Legree heard of his mother was when, one night, as he was carousing among drunken companions, a letter was put into his hand. He opened it, and a lock of long, curling hair fell from it, and twined about his fingers. The letter told him his mother was dead, and that, dying, she blest and forgave him.

There is a dread, unhallowed necromancy of evil, that turns things sweetest and holiest to phantoms of horror and affright. That pale, loving mother – her dying prayers, her forgiving love – wrought in that demoniac heart of sin only as a damning sentence, bringing with it a fearful looking for of judgement and fiery indignation. Legree burned the hair, and burned the letter; and when he saw them hissing and crackling in the flame, inly shuddered as he thought of everlasting fires. He tried to drink, and revel, and swear away the memory; but often, in the deep night, whose solemn stillness arraigns the bad soul in forced communion with herself, he had seen that pale mother rising by his bedside, and felt the soft twining of that hair around his fingers till the cold sweat would roll down his face, and he would spring from his bed in horror. Ye who have wondered to hear, in the same evangel, that 'God is love', and that 'God is a consuming fire',[268] see ye not how, to the soul resolved in evil, perfect love is the most fearful torture, the seal and sentence of the direst despair?

'Blast it!' said Legree to himself, as he sipped his liquor; 'where did he get that? If it didn't look just like – whoo! I thought I'd forgot that. Curse me, if I think there's any such thing as forgetting anything, anyhow – hang it! I'm lonesome! I mean to call Em. She hates me – the monkey! I don't care – I'll *make* her come!'

Legree stepped out into a large entry, which went upstairs by what had formerly been a superb winding staircase; but the passage-way was dirty and dreary, encumbered with boxes and unsightly litter. The stairs, uncarpeted, seemed winding up, in the gloom, to nobody knew where! The pale moonlight streamed through a shattered fanlight over the door; the air was unwholesome and chilly, like that of a vault.

Legree stopped at the foot of the stairs, and heard a voice singing. It seemed strange and ghostlike in that dreary old house, perhaps because of the already tremulous state of his nerves. Hark! what is it?

A wild, pathetic voice, chants a hymn common among the slaves:

> 'Oh, there'll be mourning, mourning, mourning,
> Oh, there'll be mourning, at the judgement-seat of Christ!'[269]

'Blast the girl!' said Legree. 'I'll choke her. – Em! Em!' he called, harshly; but only a mocking echo from the walls answered him. The sweet voice still sang on –

> 'Parents and children there shall part!
> Parents and children there shall part!
> Shall part to meet no more!'

And clear and loud swelled through the empty halls the refrain –

> 'Oh, there'll be mourning, mourning, mourning,
> Oh, there'll be mourning, at the judgement-seat of Christ!'

Legree stopped. He would have been ashamed to tell of it, but large drops of sweat stood on his forehead, his heart beat heavy and thick with fear; he even thought he saw something white rising and glimmering in the gloom before him, and shuddered to think what if the form of his dead mother should suddenly appear to him.

'I know one thing,' he said to himself, as he stumbled back in the sitting-room, and sat down; 'I'll let that fellow alone after this! What did I want of his cussed paper? I b'lieve I am bewitched, sure enough! I've been shivering and sweating ever since! Where did he get that hair? It couldn't have been *that*! I burnt *that* up, I know I did! It would be a joke, if hair could rise from the dead!'

Ah, Legree! that golden tress *was* charmed; each hair had in it a spell of terror and remorse for thee, and was used by a mightier power to bind thy cruel hands from inflicting uttermost evil on the helpless!

'I say,' said Legree, stamping and whistling to the dogs, 'wake up, some of you, and keep me company!' but the dogs only opened one eye at him, sleepily, and closed it again.

'I'll have Sambo and Quimbo up here, to sing and dance one of their hell dances, and keep off these horrid notions,' said Legree; and, putting on his hat, he went on to the veranda and blew a horn, with which he commonly summoned his two sable drivers.

Legree was often wont, when in a gracious humour, to get these two worthies into his sitting-room, and, after warming them up with whisky, amuse himself by setting them to singing, dancing or fighting, as the humour took him.

It was between one and two o'clock at night, as Cassy was returning from her ministrations to poor Tom, that she heard the sound of wild shrieking, whooping, halloing, and singing, from the sitting-room, mingled with the barking of dogs and other symptoms of general uproar.

She came up on the veranda steps, and looked in. Legree and both the drivers, in a state of furious intoxication, were singing, whooping, upsetting chairs, and making all manner of ludicrous and horrid grimaces at each other.

She rested her small, slender hand on the window-blind, and looked fixedly at them. There was a world of anguish, scorn, and fierce bitterness in her black eyes, as she did so. 'Would it be a sin to rid the world of such a wretch?' she said to herself.

She turned hurriedly away, and, passing round to a back door, glided upstairs, and tapped at Emmeline's door.

CHAPTER XXXVI

Emmeline and Cassy

CASSY ENTERED the room, and found Emmeline sitting, pale with fear, in the furthest corner of it. As she came in, the girl started up nervously; but, on seeing who it was, rushed forward, and catching her arm, said, 'Oh, Cassy, is it you? I'm so glad you've come! I was afraid it was – Oh, you don't know what a horrid noise there has been downstairs all this evening!'

'I ought to know,' said Cassy, dryly. 'I've heard it often enough.'

'Oh, Cassy! do tell me, couldn't we get away from this place? I don't care where – into the swamp among the snakes, anywhere! *Couldn't* we get *somewhere* away from here?'

'Nowhere, but into our graves,' said Cassy.

'Did you ever try?'

'I've seen enough of trying, and what comes of it,' said Cassy.

'I'd be willing to live in the swamps, and gnaw the bark from trees. I an't afraid of snakes! I'd rather have one near me than him,' said Emmeline, eagerly.

'There have been a good many here of your opinion,' said Cassy. 'But you couldn't stay in the swamps – you'd be tracked by the dogs, and brought back, and then – then – '

'What would he do?' said the girl, looking, with breathless interest, into her face.

'What *wouldn't* he do, you'd better ask,' said Cassy. 'He's learned his trade well, among the pirates in the West Indies. You wouldn't sleep much if I should tell you things I've seen – things that he tells of, sometimes, for good jokes. I've heard screams here that I haven't been able to get out of my head for weeks and weeks. There's a place way out down by the quarters, where you can see a black, blasted tree, and the ground all covered with black ashes. Ask anyone what was done there, and see if they will dare to tell you.'

'Oh, what do you mean?'

'I won't tell you. I hate to think of it. And I tell you, the Lord only knows what we may see tomorrow, if that poor fellow holds out as he's begun.'

'Horrid!' said Emmeline, every drop of blood receding from her cheeks. 'Oh, Cassy, do tell me what I shall do!'

'What I've done. Do the best you can; do what you must, and make it up in hating and cursing.'

'He wanted to make me drink some of his hateful brandy,' said Emmeline; 'and I hate it so –'

'You'd better drink,' said Cassy. 'I hated it, too; and now I can't live without it. One must have something; things don't look so dreadful when you take that.'

'Mother used to tell me never to touch any such thing,' said Emmeline.

'*Mother* told you!' said Cassy, with a thrilling and bitter emphasis on the word mother. 'What use is it for mothers to say anything? You are all to be bought and paid for, and your souls belong to whoever gets you. That's the way it goes. I say, *drink* brandy; drink all you can, and it'll make things come easier.'

'Oh, Cassy! do pity me!'

'Pity you! don't I? Haven't I a daughter? – Lord knows where she is, and whose she is now! Going the way her mother went before her, I suppose, and that her children must go after her! There's no end to the curse forever!'

'I wish I'd never been born!' said Emmeline, wringing her hands.

'That's an old wish with me,' said Cassy. 'I've got used to wishing that. I'd die, if I dared to,' she said, looking out into the darkness with that still, fixed despair, which was the habitual expression of her face when at rest.

'It would be wicked to kill oneself,' said Emmeline.

'I don't know why, no wickeder than things we live and do day after day. But the sisters told me things when I was in the convent that make me afraid to die. If it would only be the end of us, why then –'

Emmeline turned away and hid her face in her hands.

While this conversation was passing in the chamber, Legree, overcome with his carouse, had sunk to sleep in the room below. Legree was not an habitual drunkard. His coarse, strong nature craved, and could endure, a continual stimulation that would have utterly wrecked and crazed a finer one. But a deep underlying spirit of cautiousness prevented his often yielding to appetite in such measure as to lose control of himself.

This night, however, in his feverish efforts to banish from his mind those fearful elements of woe and remorse which woke within him, he had indulged more than common; so that, when he had discharged his sable attendants, he fell heavily on a settle in the room, and was sound asleep.

Oh, how dares the bad soul to enter the shadowy world of sleep? – that land whose dim outlines lie so fearfully near to the mystic scene of retribution! Legree dreamed. In his heavy and feverish sleep a veiled form stood beside him, and laid a cold, soft hand upon him. He thought he knew who it was; and shuddered, with creeping horror, though the face was veiled. Then he thought he felt *that hair* twining round his fingers; and then, that it slid smoothly round his neck, and tightened and tightened, and he could not draw his breath; and then he thought voices *whispered* to him – whispers that chilled him with horror. Then it seemed to him he was on the edge of a frightful abyss, holding on and struggling in mortal fear, while dark hands stretched up, and were pulling him over; and Cassy came behind him, laughing, and pushed him. And then rose up that solemn veiled figure, and drew aside the veil. It was his mother; and she turned away from him, and he fell down, down, down, amid a confused noise of shrieks, and groans, and shouts of demon laughter – and Legree awoke.

Calmly the rosy hue of dawn was stealing into the room. The morning star stood, with its solemn, holy eye of light, looking down on the man of sin, from out the brightening sky. Oh, with what freshness, what solemnity and beauty, is each new day born; as if to say to insensate man, 'Behold! thou hast one more chance! *Strive* for immortal glory!' There is no speech nor language where this voice is not heard; but the bold, bad man, heard it not. He woke with an oath and a curse. What to him was the gold and purple, the daily miracle of morning! What to him the sanctity of that star which the Son of God has hallowed as his own emblem? Brute-like, he saw without perceiving; and, stumbling forward, poured out a tumbler of brandy, and drank half of it.

'I've had a hell of a night!' he said to Cassy, who just then entered from an opposite door.

'You'll get plenty of the same sort by and by,' said she, dryly.

'What do you mean, you minx?'

'You'll find out, one of these days,' returned Cassy in the same tone. 'Now, Simon, I've one piece of advice to give you.'

'The devil you have!'

'My advice is,' said Cassy, steadily, as she began adjusting some things about the room, 'that you let Tom alone.'

'What business is 't of yours?'

'What? To be sure, I don't know what it should be. If you want to pay twelve hundred for a fellow, and use him right up in the press of the season, just to serve your own spite, it's no business of mine. I've done what I could for him.'

'You have? What business have you meddling in my matters?'

'None, to be sure. I've saved you some thousands of dollars, at different times, by taking care of your hands – that's all the thanks I get. If your crop comes shorter into market than any of theirs, you won't lose your bet, I suppose? Tompkins won't lord it over you, I suppose; and you'll pay down your money like a lady, won't you? I think I see you doing it!'

Legree, like many other planters, had but one form of ambition – to have in the heaviest crop of the season; and he had several bets on this very present season pending in the next town. Cassy, therefore, with woman's tact, touched the only string that could be made to vibrate.

'Well, I'll let him off at what he's got,' said Legree; 'but he shall beg my pardon, and promise better fashions.'

'That he won't do,' said Cassy.

'Won't, eh?'

'No, he won't,' said Cassy.

'I'd like to know why, mistress,' said Legree, in the extreme of scorn.

'Because he's done right, and he knows it, and won't say he's done wrong.'

'Who a cuss cares what he knows? The nigger shall say what I please, or –'

'Or, you'll lose your bet on the cotton crop, by keeping him out of the field just at this very press.'

'But he *will* give up, course he will; don't I know what niggers is? He'll beg like a dog, this morning.'

'He won't, Simon; you don't know this kind. You may kill him by inches, you won't get the first word of confession out of him.'

'We'll see. Where is he?' said Legree, going out.

'In the waste-room of the gin-house,' said Cassy.

Legree, though he talked so stoutly to Cassy, still sallied forth from the house with a degree of misgiving which was not common with him. His dreams of the past night, mingled with Cassy's prudential suggestions, considerably affected his mind. He resolved that nobody should be witness of his encounter with Tom; and determined, if he could not subdue him by bullying, to defer his vengeance to be wreaked in a more convenient season.

The solemn light of dawn, the angelic glory of the morning-star, had looked in through the rude window of the shed where Tom was lying; and, as if descending on that star-beam, came the solemn words, 'I am the root and offspring of David, and the bright and morning-star.'[270] The mysterious warnings and intimations of Cassy, so far from discouraging his soul, in the end had roused it as with a heavenly call. He did not know but that the day of his death was dawning in the sky; and his heart throbbed with solemn throes of joy and desire, as he thought that the wondrous *all*, of which he had often pondered, the great white throne, with its ever radiant rainbow; the white-robed multitude, with voices as many waters; the crowns, the palms, the harps – might all break upon his vision before that sun should set again, and therefore, without shuddering or trembling, he heard the voice of his persecutor as he drew near.

'Well, my boy,' said Legree, with a contemptuous kick, 'how do you find yourself? Didn't I tell yer I could larn yer a thing or two? How do yer like it, eh? How did yer whaling agree with yer, Tom? An't quite so crank[271] as ye was last night. Ye couldn't treat a poor sinner now to a bit of a sermon, could yer, eh?'

Tom answered nothing.

'Get up, you beast!' said Legree, kicking him again.

This was a difficult matter for one so bruised and faint; and, as Tom made efforts to do so, Legree laughed brutally.

'What makes ye so spry this morning, Tom? Cotched cold, maybe, last night.'

Tom by this time had gained his feet, and was confronting his master with a steady, unmoved front.

'The devil you can!' said Legree, looking him over. 'I believe you haven't got enough yet. Now, Tom, get right down on yer knees and beg my pardon, for yer shines last night.'

Tom did not move.

'Down, you dog!' said Legree, striking him with his riding-whip.

'Mas'r Legree,' said Tom, 'I can't do it. I did only what I thought was right. I shall do just so again, if ever the time comes. I never will do a cruel thing, come what may.'

'Yes, but ye don't know what may come, Master Tom. Ye think what you've got is something. I tell you 'tan't anything – nothing 'tall. How would ye like to be tied to a tree, and have a slow fire lit up around ye? Wouldn't that be pleasant – eh, Tom?'

'Mas'r,' said Tom, 'I know ye can do dreadful things; but' – he stretched himself upward and clasped his hands – 'but after ye've killed the body, there an't no more ye can do. And oh, there's all *eternity* to come, after that!'

ETERNITY! The word thrilled through the black man's soul with light and power, as he spoke – it thrilled through the sinner's soul, too, like the bite of a scorpion. Legree gnashed on him with his teeth, but rage kept him silent; and Tom, like a man disenthralled, spoke in a clear and cheerful voice.

'Mas'r Legree, as ye bought me, I'll be a true and faithful servant to ye. I'll give ye all the work of my hands, all my time, all my strength; but my soul I won't give up to mortal man. I will hold on to the Lord, and put his commands before all, die or live; you may be sure on't. Mas'r Legree, I an't a grain afeard to die. I'd as soon die as not. Ye may whip me, starve me, burn me – it'll only send me sooner where I want to go.'

'I'll make ye give out, though, 'fore I've done!' said Legree, in a rage.

'I shall have *help*,' said Tom. 'You'll never do it.'

'Who the devil's going to help you?' said Legree, scornfully.

'The Lord Almighty,' said Tom.

'Damn you!' said Legree, as with one blow of his fist he felled Tom to the earth.

A cold soft hand fell on Legree's at this moment. He turned – it was Cassy's; but the cold soft touch recalled his dream of the night before, and, flashing through the chambers of his brain, came all the fearful images of the night-watches, with a portion of the horror that accompanied them.

'Will you be a fool?' said Cassy, in French. 'Let him go! Let me alone to get him fit to be in the field again. Isn't it just as I told you?'

They say the alligator and the rhinoceros, though enclosed in bullet-proof mail, have each a spot where they are vulnerable; and fierce, reckless, unbelieving reprobates, have commonly this point in superstitious dread.

Legree turned away, determined to let the point go for the time.

'Well, have it your own way,' he said, doggedly, to Cassy.

'Hark ye!' he said to Tom; 'I won't deal with ye now, because the business is pressing, and I want all my hands; but I *never* forget. I'll score it against ye, and sometime I'll have my pay out o' yer old black hide – mind ye!'

Legree turned, and went out.

'There you go,' said Cassy, looking darkly after him; 'your reckoning's to come yet! My poor fellow, how are you?'

'The Lord God hath sent his angel, and shut the lion's mouth for this time,'[272] said Tom.

'For this time, to be sure,' said Cassy; 'but now you've got his ill-will upon you, to follow you day in and day out, hanging like a dog on your throat! sucking your blood, bleeding away your life, drop by drop! I know the man.'

CHAPTER XXXVII

Liberty

No matter with what solemnities he may have been devoted upon the altar of slavery, the moment he touches the sacred soil of Britain, the altar and the God sink together in the dust, and he stands redeemed, regenerated, and disenthralled, by the irresistible genius of universal emancipation.

CURRAN[273]

AWHILE WE MUST LEAVE Tom in the hands of his persecutors, while we turn to pursue the fortunes of George and his wife, whom we left in friendly hands, in a farmhouse on the roadside.

Tom Loker we left groaning and touzling[274] in a most immaculately clean Quaker bed, under the motherly supervision of Aunt Dorcas, who found him to the full as tractable a patient as a sick bison.

Imagine a tall, dignified, spiritual woman, whose clear muslin cap shades waves of silvery hair, parted on a broad, clear forehead, which overarches thoughtful grey eyes; a snowy handkerchief of lisse crape is folded neatly across her bosom; her glossy brown silk dress rustles peacefully, as she glides up and down the chamber.

'The devil!' says Tom Loker, giving a great throw to the bedclothes.

'I must request thee, Thomas, not to use such language,' says Aunt Dorcas, as she quietly rearranged the bed.

'Well, I won't, granny, if I can help it,' says Tom; 'but it is enough to make a fellow swear, so cursedly hot!'

Dorcas removed a comforter from the bed, straightened the clothes again, and tucked them in till Tom looked something like a chrysalis, remarking, as she did so –

'I wish, friend, thee would leave off cursing and swearing, and think upon thy ways.'

'What the devil,' said Tom, 'should I think of *them* for? Last thing ever *I* want to think of – hang it all!' And Tom flounced over, untucking and disarranging everything, in a manner frightful to behold.

'That fellow and gal are here, I s'pose,' said he, sullenly, after a pause.

'They are so,' said Dorcas.

'They'd better be off up to the lake,' said Tom; 'the quicker the better.'

'Probably they will do so,' said Aunt Dorcas, knitting peacefully.

'And hark ye,' said Tom; 'we've got correspondents in Sandusky, that watch the boats for us. I don't care if I tell, now. I hope they *will* get away, just to spite Marks – the cursed puppy! – damn him!'

'Thomas!' said Dorcas.

'I tell you, granny, if you bottle a fellow up too tight, he shall split,' said Tom. 'But about the gal – tell 'em to dress her up some way so's to alter her. Her description's out in Sandusky.'

'We will attend to that matter,' said Dorcas, with characteristic composure.

As we at this place take leave of Tom Loker, we may as well say that, having lain three weeks at the Quaker dwelling, sick with a rheumatic fever, which set in, in company with his other afflictions, Tom arose from his bed a somewhat sadder and wiser man; and, in place of slave-catching, betook himself to life in one of the new settlements, where his talents developed themselves more happily in trapping bears, wolves, and other inhabitants of the forest, in which he made himself quite a name in the land. Tom always spoke reverently of the Quakers. 'Nice people,' he would say; 'wanted to convert me, but couldn't come it exactly. But tell ye what, stranger, they do fix up a sick fellow first-rate, no mistake. Make jist the tallest kind o' broth and knicknacks.'

As Tom had informed them that their party would be looked for in Sandusky, it was thought prudent to divide them. Jim, with his old mother, was forwarded separately; and a night or two after, George and Eliza, with their child, were driven privately into Sandusky, and lodged beneath a hospitable roof, preparatory to taking their last passage on the lake.

Their night was now far spent, and the morning star of liberty rose fair before them. Liberty! electric word! What is it? Is there anything more in it than a name, a rhetorical flourish? Why, men and women of America, does your heart's blood thrill at that word, for which your fathers bled, and your braver mothers were willing that their noblest and best should die?

Is there anything in it glorious and dear for a nation, that is not also glorious and dear for a man? What is freedom to a nation, but freedom to the individuals in it? What is freedom to that young man who sits there with his arms folded over his broad chest, the tint of African blood in his cheek, its dark fires in his eye – what is freedom to George Harris? To your fathers, freedom was the right of a nation to be a nation. To him, it is the right of a man to be a man and not a brute; the right to call the wife of his bosom his wife, and to protect her from lawless violence; the right to protect and educate his child; the right to have a home of his own, a religion of his own, a character of his own, unsubject to the will of another. All these thoughts were rolling and seething in George's breast, as he was pensively leaning his head on his hand, watching his wife, as she was adapting to her slender and pretty form the articles of man's attire, in which it was deemed safest she should make her escape.

'Now for it,' said she, as she stood before the glass, and shook down her silky abundance of black curly hair. 'I say, George, it's almost a pity, isn't it,' she said, as she held up some of it playfully. 'Pity it's all got to come off?'

George smiled sadly, and made no answer.

Eliza turned to the glass, and the scissors glittered as one long lock after another was detached from her head.

'There now, that'll do,' she said, taking up a hairbrush; 'now for a few fancy touches.'

'There, an't I a pretty young fellow?' she said, turning around to her husband, laughing and blushing at the same time.

'You always will be pretty, do what you will,' said George.

'What does make you so sober?' said Eliza, kneeling on one knee and laying her hand on his. 'We are only within twenty-four hours of Canada, they say. Only a day and a night on the lake, and then – oh, then!'

'Oh, Eliza!' said George, drawing her towards him; 'that is it! Now my fate is all narrowing down to a point. To come so near, to be almost in sight, and then lose all. I should never live under it, Eliza.'

'Don't fear,' said his wife, hopefully. 'The good Lord would not have brought us so far if he didn't mean to carry us through. I seem to feel him with us, George.'

'You are a blessed woman, Eliza!' said George, clasping her with a convulsive grasp. 'But – oh, tell me! can this great mercy be for us? Will these years and years of misery come to an end? – shall we be free?'

'I am sure of it, George,' said Eliza, looking upward, while tears of hope and enthusiasm shone on her long, dark lashes. 'I feel it in me, that God is going to bring us out of bondage, this very day.'

'I will believe you, Eliza,' said George, rising suddenly up. 'I will believe, come, let's be off. Well, indeed,' said he, holding her off at arm's length, and looking admiringly at her, 'you *are* a pretty little fellow. That crop of little, short curls, is quite becoming. Put on your cap. So – a little to one side. I never saw you look quite so pretty. But it's almost time for the carriage; I wonder if Mrs Smyth has got Harry rigged?'

The door opened, and a respectable middle-aged woman entered, leading little Harry, dressed in girl's clothes.

'What a pretty girl he makes,' said Eliza, turning him round. 'We call him Harriet, you see; don't the name come nicely?'

The child stood gravely regarding his mother in her new and strange attire, observing a profound silence, and occasionally drawing deep sighs, and peeping at her from under his dark curls.

'Does Harry know mamma?' said Eliza, stretching her hands toward him.

The child clung shyly to the woman.

'Come, Eliza, why do you try to coax him, when you know that he has got to be kept away from you?'

'I know it's foolish,' said Eliza; 'yet, I can't bear to have him turn away from me. But come – where's my cloak? Here – how is it men put on cloaks, George?'

'You must wear it so,' said her husband, throwing it over his shoulders.

'So, then,' said Eliza, imitating the motion; 'and I must stamp, and take long steps, and try to look saucy.'

'Don't exert yourself,' said George. 'There is, now and then, a modest young man; and I think it would be easier for you to act that character.'

'And these gloves! mercy upon us!' said Eliza; 'why, my hands are lost in them.'

'I advise you to keep them on pretty strictly,' said George. 'Your little slender paw might bring us all out. Now, Mrs Smyth, you are to go under our charge, and be our aunty – you mind.'

'I've heard,' said Mrs Smyth, 'that there have been men down, warning all the packet-captains against a man and woman, with a little boy.'

'They have!' said George. 'Well, if we see any such people we can tell them.'

A hack now drove to the door, and the friendly family who had received the fugitives crowded around them with farewell greetings.

The disguises the party had assumed were in accordance with the hints of Tom Loker. Mrs Smyth, a respectable woman from the settlement in Canada, whither they were fleeing, being fortunately about crossing the lake to return thither, had consented to appear as the aunt of little Harry; and, in order to attach him to her, he had been allowed to remain, the two last days, under her sole charge; and an extra amount of petting, joined to an indefinite amount of seed-cakes and candy, had cemented a very close attachment on the part of the young gentleman.

The hack drove to the wharf. The two young men, as they appeared, walked up the plank into the boat, Eliza gallantly giving her arm to Mrs Smyth, and George attending to their baggage.

George was standing at the captain's office, settling for his party, when he overheard two men talking by his side.

'I've watched everyone that came on board,' said one, 'and I know they're not on this boat.'

The voice was that of the clerk of the boat. The speaker whom he addressed was our sometime friend Marks, who, with that valuable perseverance which characterised him, had come on to Sandusky, seeking whom he might devour.

'You would scarcely know the woman from a white one,' said Marks. 'The man is a very light mulatto. He has a brand in one of his hands.'

The hand with which George was taking the tickets and change trembled a little; but he turned coolly around, fixed an unconcerned glance on the face of the speaker, and walked leisurely toward another part of the boat, where Eliza stood waiting for him.

Mrs Smyth, with little Harry, sought the seclusion of the ladies' cabin, where the dark beauty of the supposed little girl drew many flattering comments from the passengers.

George had the satisfaction, as the bell rang out its farewell peal, to see Marks walk down the plank to the shore; and drew a long sigh of relief when the boat had put a returnless distance between them.

It was a superb day. The blue waves of Lake Erie danced rippling and sparkling in the sunlight. A fresh breeze blew from the shore, and the lordly boat ploughed her way right gallantly onward.

Oh, what an untold world there is in one human heart! Who thought, as George walked calmly up and down the deck of the steamer, with his shy companion at his side, of all that was burning in his bosom? The mighty good that seemed approaching seemed too good, too fair, even to be a reality; and he felt a jealous dread every moment of the day that something would rise to snatch it from him.

But the boat swept on – hours fleeted, and, at last, clear and full rose the blessed English shore – shores charmed by a mighty spell – with one touch to dissolve every incantation of slavery, no matter in what language pronounced, or by what national power confirmed.

George and his wife stood arm in arm, as the boat neared the small town of Amherstberg, in Canada. His breath grew thick and short; a mist gathered before his eyes; he silently pressed the little hand that lay trembling on his arm. The bell rang – the boat stopped. Scarcely seeing what he did, he looked out his baggage, and gathered his little party. The little company were landed on the shore. They stood still till the boat had cleared; and then, with tears and embracings, the husband[275] and wife, with their wondering child in their arms, knelt down and lifted up their hearts to God!

> 'Twas something like the burst from death to life;
>   From the grave's cerements to the robes of heaven;
> From sin's dominion, and from passion's strife,
>   To the pure freedom of a soul forgiven;
>   Where all the bonds of death and hell are riven,
> And mortal puts on immortality,
> When Mercy's hand hath turned the golden key,
> And Mercy's voice hath said, 'Rejoice, thy soul is free!'

The little party were soon guided by Mrs Smyth to the hospitable abode of a good missionary, whom Christian charity has placed here as a shepherd to the outcast and wandering, who are constantly finding an asylum on this shore.

Who can speak the blessedness of that first day of freedom? Is not the *sense* of liberty a higher and a finer one than any of the five? To move, speak and breathe, go out and come in unwatched and free from danger! Who can speak the blessings of that rest which comes down on the free man's pillow, under laws which ensure to him the rights that God has given to man? How fair and precious to that mother was that sleeping child's face, endeared by the memory of a thousand dangers! How impossible was it to sleep, in the exuberant possession of such blessedness! And yet, these two had not one acre of ground, not a roof that they could call their own; they had spent their all, to the last dollar. They had nothing more than the birds of the air, or the flowers of the field – yet they could not sleep for joy. 'O ye who take freedom from man, with what words shall ye answer it to God?'

CHAPTER XXXVIII

The Victory

Thanks be unto God, who giveth us the victory.[276]

HAVE NOT MANY OF US, in the weary way of life, felt, in some hours, how far easier it were to die than to live?

The martyr, when faced even by a death of bodily anguish and horror, finds in the very terror of his doom a strong stimulant and tonic. There is a vivid excitement, a thrill and fervour, which may carry through any crisis of suffering that is the birth-hour of eternal glory and rest.

But to live, to wear on day after day of mean, bitter, low, harassing servitude, every nerve dampened and depressed, every power of feeling gradually smothered – this long and wasting heart-martyrdom, this slow, daily bleeding away of the inward life, drop by drop, hour after hour – this is the true searching test of what there may be in man or woman.

When Tom stood face to face with his persecutor, and heard his threats, and thought in his very soul that his hour was come, his heart swelled bravely in him, and he thought he could bear torture and fire, bear anything, with the vision of Jesus and heaven just a step beyond; but when he was gone, and the present excitement passed off, came back the pain of his bruised and weary limbs, came back the sense of his utterly degraded, hopeless, forlorn estate; and the day passed wearily enough.

Long before his wounds were healed, Legree insisted that he should be put to the regular fieldwork; and then came day after day of pain and weariness, aggravated by every kind of injustice and indignity that the ill-will of a mean and malicious mind could devise. Whoever, in *our* circumstances, has made trial of pain, even with all the alleviations which for us usually attend it, must know the irritation that comes with it. Tom no longer wondered at the habitual surliness of his associates; nay, he found the placid, sunny temper which had been the habitude of his life broken in on and sorely strained by the inroads of the same thing. He had flattered himself on leisure to read his Bible; but there was no such thing as leisure there. In the height of the season, Legree did not hesitate to press all his hands through, Sundays and weekdays alike. Why shouldn't he? He made more cotton by it, and gained his wager; and if it wore out a few more hands, he could buy better ones. At first, Tom used to read a verse or two of his Bible by the flicker of the fire, after he had returned from his daily toil; but, after the cruel treatment he received, he used to come home so exhausted, that his head swam and his eyes failed when he tried to read, and he was fain to stretch himself down with the others in utter exhaustion.

Is it strange that the religious peace and trust which had upborne him hitherto should give way to tossings of soul and despondent darkness. The gloomiest problem of this mysterious life was constantly before his eyes: souls crushed and ruined, evil triumphant, and God silent. It was weeks and months that Tom wrestled, in his own soul, in darkness and sorrow. He thought of Miss Ophelia's letter to his Kentucky friends, and would pray earnestly that God would send him deliverance; and then he would watch, day after day, in the vague hope of seeing somebody sent to redeem him; and, when nobody came, he would crush back to his soul bitter thoughts – that it was vain to serve God, that God had forgotten him. He sometimes saw Cassy; and sometimes, when summoned to the house, caught a glimpse of the dejected form of Emmeline, but held very little communion with either; in fact, there was no time for him to commune with anybody.

One evening, he was sitting in utter dejection and prostration by a few decaying brands, where his coarse supper was baking. He put a few bits of brushwood on the fire, and strove to raise the light, and then drew his worn Bible from his pocket. There were all the marked passages, which had thrilled his soul so often – words of patriarchs and seers, poets and sages, who from early time had spoken courage to man – voices from the great cloud of witnesses who ever surround us in the race of life. Had the word lost its power, or could the failing eye and weary sense no longer answer to the touch of that mighty inspiration? Heavily sighing, he put it in his pocket. A coarse laugh roused him; he looked up – Legree was standing opposite to him.

'Well, old boy,' he said, 'you find your religion don't work, it seems! I thought I should get that through your wool at last!'

The cruel taunt was more than hunger, and cold and nakedness. Tom was silent.

'You were a fool,' said Legree; 'for I meant to do well by you when I bought you. You might have been better off than Sambo, or Quimbo either, and had easy times; and, instead of getting cut up and thrashed every day or two, ye might have had liberty to lord it round, and cut up the other niggers; and ye might have had, now and then, a good warming of whiskey-punch. Come, don't you think you'd better be reasonable? Heave that ar' old pack of trash in the fire and join my church!'

'The Lord forbid!' said Tom, fervently.

'You see the Lord an't going to help you; if he had been, he wouldn't have let *me* get you! This yer religion is all a mess of lying trumpery, Tom. I know all about it. Ye'd better hold to me; I'm somebody, and can do something!'

'No, mas'r,' said Tom; 'I'll hold on. The Lord may help me, or not help: but I'll hold to him, and believe him to the last!'

'The more fool you!' said Legree, spitting scornfully at him and spurning him with his foot. 'Never mind, I'll chase you down yet, and bring you under, you'll see!' and Legree turned away.

When a heavy weight presses the soul to the lowest level at which endurance is possible, there is an instant and desperate effort of every physical and moral nerve to throw off the weight; and hence the heaviest anguish often precedes a return tide of joy and courage. So was it now with Tom. The atheistic taunts of his cruel master sank his before dejected soul to the lowest ebb; and, though the hand of faith still held to the eternal rock, it was with a numb, despairing grasp. Tom sat, like one stunned at the fire. Suddenly everything around him seemed to fade, and a vision rose before him of one crowned with thorns, buffeted and bleeding. Tom gazed in awe and wonder at the majestic patience of the face; the deep pathetic eyes thrilled him to his inmost heart; his soul woke as, with floods of emotion, he stretched out his hands and fell upon his knees; when gradually the vision changed, the sharp thorns became rays of glory, and in splendour inconceivable, he saw that same face bending compassionately towards him, and a voice said, 'He that overcometh shall sit down with me on my throne, even as I also overcame, and am set down with my Father on his throne.'

How long Tom lay there, he knew not. When he came to himself, the fire was gone out, his clothes were wet with the chill and drenching dews; but the dread soul-crisis was past, and, in the joy that filled him, he no longer felt hunger, cold, degradation, disappointment, wretchedness. From his deepest soul, he that hour loosed and parted from every hope in the life that now is, and offered his own will an unquestioning sacrifice to the Infinite. Tom looked up to the silent, ever-living stars, types of the angelic hosts who ever look down on man; and the solitude of the night rang with the triumphant words of a hymn, which he had sung often in happier days, but never with such feeling as now –

> The earth shall be dissolved like snow,
>   The sun shall cease to shine;
> But God, who called me here below,
>   Shall be forever mine.
>
> And when this mortal life shall fail,
>   And flesh and sense shall cease,
> I shall possess within the veil
>   A life of joy and peace.
>
> When we've been there ten thousand years,
>   Bright shining like the sun,
> We've no less days to sing God's praise
>   Than when we first begun.[277]

Those who have been familiar with the religious histories of the slave-population, know that relations like that we have narrated are very common among them. We have heard some from their own lips of a very touching and affecting character. The psychologist tells us of a state in which the affections and images of the mind become so dominant and overpowering, that they press into their service the outward senses, and make them give tangible shape to the inward imagining. Who shall measure what an all-pervading Spirit may do with these capabilities of our mortality, or the ways in which He may encourage the desponding souls of the desolate? If the poor forgotten slave believes that Jesus hath appeared and spoken to him, who shall contradict him? Did He not say that his mission in all ages, was to bind up the broken-hearted, and set at liberty them that are bruised?

When the dim grey of dawn woke the slumberers to go forth to the field, there was among those tattered and shivering wretches one who walked with an exultant tread; for firmer than the ground he trod on was his strong faith in Almighty, eternal Love. Ah, Legree! try all your forces now! Utmost agony, woe, degradation, want, and loss of all things, shall only hasten on the process by which he shall be made a king and a priest unto God!

From this time, an inviolable sphere of peace encompassed the lowly heart of the oppressed one – an ever-present Saviour hallowed it as a temple. Past now the bleeding of earthly regrets – past its fluctuations of hope, and fear, and desire – the human will, bent, and bleeding, and struggling long, was now entirely merged in the divine. So short now seemed the remaining voyage of life – so near, so vivid, seemed eternal blessedness – that life's uttermost woes fell from him unharming.

All noticed the change in his appearance. Cheerfulness and alertness seemed to return to him, and a quietness which no insult or injury could ruffle seemed to possess him.

'What the devil's got into Tom?' Legree said to Sambo. 'A while ago he was all down in the mouth, and now he's peart as a cricket.'

'Dun 'no, mas'r; gwine to run off, mebbe.'

'Like to see him try that,' said Legree, with a savage grin, 'wouldn't we, Sambo?'

'Guess we would! haw! ho!' said the sooty gnome, laughing obsequiously. 'Lord, de fun! To see him stickin' in de mud, chasin' and tearin' through de bushes, dogs a-holdin' on to him! Lord, I laughed fit to split, dat ar' time we cotched Molly. I thought they'd a had her all stripped up afore I could get 'em off. She car's de marks o' dat ar' spree yet.'

'I reckon she will, to her grave,' said Legree. 'But now, Sambo, you look sharp! If the nigger's got anything of this sort going, trip him up.'

'Mas'r, let me 'lone for dat,' said Sambo. 'I'll tree de coon. Ho! ho! ho!'

This was spoken as Legree was getting on to his horse, to go to the neighbouring town. That night, as he was returning, he thought he would turn his horse and ride round the quarters, and see if all was safe.

It was a superb moonlight night, and the shadows of the graceful china trees lay minutely pencilled on the turf below, and there was that transparent stillness in the air which it seems almost unholy to disturb. Legree was at a little distance from the quarters when he heard the voice of someone singing. It was not a usual sound there, and he paused to listen. A musical tenor voice sang,

> 'When I can read my title clear
> To mansions in the skies,
> I'll bid farewell to every fear,
> And wipe my weeping eyes.

Should earth against my soul engage,
    And hellish darts be hurled,
Then I can smile at Satan's rage,
    And face a frowning world.

Let cares like a wild deluge come,
    And storms of sorrow fall,
May I but safely reach my home,
    My God, my Heaven, my all!'[278]

'So ho!' said Legree to himself, 'he thinks so, does he? How I hate these cursed Methodist hymns! Here, you nigger,' said he, coming suddenly out upon Tom, and raising his riding-whip, 'how dare you be gettin' up this yer row, when you ought to be in bed? Shut yer old black gash, and get along in with you!'

'Yes, mas'r,' said Tom, with ready cheerfulness, as he rose to go in.

Legree was provoked beyond measure by Tom's evident happiness; and, riding up to him, belaboured him over his head and shoulders.

'There, you dog,' he said, 'see if you'll feel so comfortable after that!'

But the blows fell now only on the outer man, and not, as before, on the heart. Tom stood perfectly submissive; and yet Legree could not hide from himself that his power over his bond-thrall was somehow gone. And, as Tom disappeared in his cabin, and he wheeled his horse suddenly round, there passed through his mind one of those vivid flashes that often send the lightning of conscience across the dark and wicked soul. He understood full well that it was God who was standing between him and his victim, and he blasphemed Him. That submissive and silent man, whom taunts, nor threats, nor stripes, nor cruelties could disturb, roused a voice within him, such as of old his Master roused in the demoniac soul, saying, 'What have we to do with thee, thou Jesus of Nazareth? Art thou come to torment us before the time?'[279]

Tom's whole soul overflowed with compassion and sympathy for the poor wretches by whom he was surrounded. To him it seemed as if his life-sorrows were now over, and as if, out of that strange treasury of peace and joy with which he had been endowed from above, he longed to pour out something for the relief of their woes. It is true, opportunities were scanty; but on the way to the fields, and back again, and during the hours of labour, chances fell in his way of extending a helping-hand to the weary, the disheartened and discouraged. The poor, worn-down, brutalised creatures, at first, could scarce comprehend this; but when it was continued week after week, and month after month, it began to awaken long silent chords in their benumbed hearts. Gradually and imperceptibly the strange, silent, patient man, who was ready to bear everyone's burden, and sought help from none – who stood aside for all, and came last, and took least, yet was foremost to share his little all with any who needed – the man who, in cold nights, would give up his tattered blanket to add to the comfort of some woman who shivered with sickness, and who filled the baskets of the weaker ones in the field, at the terrible risk of coming short in his own measure – and who, though pursued with unrelenting cruelty by their common tyrant, never joined in uttering a word of reviling or cursing – this man at last began to have a strange power over them; and when the more pressing season was past, and they were allowed again their Sundays for their own use, many would gather together to hear from him of Jesus. They would gladly have met to hear, and pray, and sing, in some place, together; but Legree would not permit it, and more than once broke up such attempts with oaths and brutal execrations, so that the blessed news had to circulate from individual to individual. Yet who can speak the simple joy with which some of those poor outcasts, to whom life was a joyless journey to a dark unknown, heard of a compassionate Redeemer and a heavenly home? It is the statement of missionaries, that, of all races of the earth, none have received the Gospel with such eager docility as the African. The principle of reliance and unquestioning faith, which is its foundation is more a native element in this race than any other; and it has often been found among them, that a stray seed of truth, borne on some breeze of accident into hearts the most ignorant, has sprung up into fruit, whose abundance has shamed that of higher and more skilful culture.

The poor mulatto woman, whose simple faith had been well-nigh crushed and overwhelmed by the avalanche of cruelty and wrong which had fallen upon her, felt her soul raised up by the hymns and passages of Holy Writ which this lowly missionary breathed into her ear in intervals, as they were going to and returning from work; and even the half-crazed and wandering mind of Cassy was soothed and calmed by his simple and unobtrusive influences.

Stung to madness and despair by the crushing agonies of a life, Cassy had often resolved in her soul an hour of retribution, when her hand should avenge on her oppressor all the injustice and cruelty to which she had been witness, or which *she* had in her own person suffered.

One night, after all in Tom's cabin were sunk in sleep, he was suddenly aroused by seeing her face at the hole between the logs, that served for a window. She made a silent gesture for him to come out.

Tom came out the door. It was between one and two o'clock at night – broad, calm, still moonlight. Tom remarked, as the light of the moon fell upon Cassy's large, black eyes, that there was a wild and peculiar glare in them, unlike their wonted fixed despair.

'Come here, Father Tom,' she said, laying her small hand on his wrist, and drawing him forward with a force as if the hand were of steel; 'come here – I've news for you.'

'What, Misse Cassy?' said Tom, anxiously.

'Tom, wouldn't you like your liberty?'

'I shall have it, misse, in God's time,' said Tom.

'Ay, but you may have it tonight,' said Cassy, with a flash of sudden energy. 'Come on.'

Tom hesitated.

'Come!' said she, in a whisper, fixing her black eyes on him. 'Come along! He's asleep – sound. I put enough into his brandy to keep him so. I wish I'd had more, I shouldn't have wanted you. But come, the back door is unlocked; there's an axe there, I put it there – his room door is open; I'll show you the way. I'd a done it myself, only my arms are so weak. Come along!'

'Not for ten thousand worlds, misse!' said Tom firmly, stopping and holding her back, as she was pressing forward.

'But think of all these poor creatures,' said Cassy. 'We might set them all free, and go somewhere in the swamps and find an island, and live by ourselves; I've heard of its being done. Any life is better than this.'

'No!' said Tom firmly. 'No! good never comes of wickedness. I'd sooner chop my right hand off!'

'Then *I* shall do it,' said Cassy, turning.

'Oh, Misse Cassy!' said Tom, throwing himself before her, 'for the dear Lord's sake that died for ye, don't sell your precious soul to the devil that way! Nothing but evil will come of it. The Lord hasn't called us to wrath. We must suffer, and wait his time.'

'Wait!' said Cassy. 'Haven't I waited? – waited till my head is dizzy and my heart sick? What has he made me suffer? What has he made hundreds of poor creatures suffer? Isn't he wringing the life-blood out of you? I'm called on! they call me! His time's come, and I'll have his heart's blood!'

'No, no, no!' said Tom, holding her small hands, which were clenched with spasmodic violence. 'No, ye poor, lost soul, that ye mustn't do. The dear, blessed Lord never shed no blood but his own, and that he poured out for us when we was enemies. Lord, help us to follow his steps and love our enemies.'[280]

'Love!' said Cassy, with a fierce glare; 'love *such* enemies! It isn't in flesh and blood.'

'No, misse, it isn't,' said Tom, looking up; 'but *He* gives it to us, and that's the *victory*. When we can love and pray over all and through all, the battle's past and the victory's come – glory be to God!' And, with streaming eyes and choking voice, the black man looked up to heaven.

And this, O Africa! – latest called of nations, called to the crown of thorns, the scourge, the bloody sweat, the cross of agony – this is to be *thy* victory; by this shalt thou reign with Christ when his kingdom shall come on earth.

The deep fervour of Tom's feelings, the softness of his voice, his tears, fell like dew on the wild, unsettled spirit of the poor woman. A softness gathered over the lurid fires of her eye; she looked down, and Tom could feel the relaxing muscles of her hands, as she said –

'Didn't I tell you that evil spirits followed me? O Father Tom, I can't pray! I wish I could. I never have prayed since my children were sold! What you say must be right – I know it must; but when I try to pray, I can only hate and curse. I can't pray!'

'Poor soul!' said Tom, compassionately. 'Satan desires to have ye, and sift ye as wheat. I pray the Lord for ye. Oh! Misse Cassy, turn to the dear Lord Jesus. He came to bind up the broken-hearted, and comfort all that mourn.'

Cassy stood silent, while large, heavy tears dropped from her downcast eyes.

'Misse Cassy,' said Tom, in a hesitating tone, after surveying her a moment in silence, 'if ye only could get away from here – if the thing was possible – I'd 'vise ye and Emmeline to do it; that is, if ye could go without blood-guiltiness – not otherwise.'

'Would you try it with us, Father Tom?'

'No,' said Tom; 'time was when I would; but the Lord's given me a work among these yer poor souls, and I'll stay with 'em and bear my cross with 'em till the end. It's different with you; it's a snare to you – it's more'n you can stand; and you'd better go, if you can.'

'I know no way but through the grave,' said Cassy. 'There's no beast or bird but can find a home somewhere; even the snakes and the alligators have their places to lie down and be quiet; but there's no place for us. Down in the darkest swamps, their dogs will hunt us out, and find us. Everybody and everything is against us; even the very beasts side against us; and where shall we go?'

Tom stood silent; at length he said –

'Him that saved Daniel in the den of lions – that saved the children in the fiery furnace – Him that walked on the sea, and bade the winds be still – He's alive yet; and I've faith to believe He can deliver you. Try it, and I'll pray with all my might for you.'

By what strange law of mind is it that an idea long overlooked, and trodden under foot as a useless stone, suddenly sparkles out in new light, as a discovered diamond?

Cassy had often revolved, for hours, all possible or probable schemes of escape, and dismissed them all as hopeless and impracticable; but at this moment there flashed through her mind a plan, so simple and feasible in all its details, as to awaken an instant hope.

'Father Tom, I'll try it!' she said, suddenly.

'Amen!' said Tom. 'The Lord help ye!'

CHAPTER XXXIX

The Stratagem

The way of the wicked is as darkness;
he knoweth not at what he stumbleth.

Proverbs iv. 19

THE GARRET OF THE HOUSE that Legree occupied, like most other garrets, was a great, desolate space, dusty, hung with cobwebs, and littered with cast-off lumber. The opulent family that had inhabited the house in the days of its splendour had imported a great deal of splendid furniture, some of which they had taken away with them, while some remained standing desolate in mouldering, unoccupied rooms, or stored away in this place. One or two immense packing-boxes, in which this furniture was brought, stood against the sides of the garret. There was a small window there, which let in through its dingy, dusty panes, a scanty, uncertain light on the tall, high-backed chairs and dusty tables, that had once seen better days. Altogether, it was a weird and ghostly place; but, ghostly as it was, it wanted not in legends among the superstitious negroes to increase its terrors. Some few years before, a negro woman who had incurred Legree's displeasure, was confined there for several weeks. What passed there, we do not say; the negroes used to whisper darkly to each other; but it was known that the body of the unfortunate creature was one day taken down from there, and buried; and, after that, it was said that oaths and cursings, and the sound of violent blows, used to ring through that old garret, and mingled with wailings and groans of despair. Once, when Legree chanced to overhear something of this kind, he flew into a violent passion, and swore that the next one that told stories about that garret should have an opportunity of knowing what was there, for he would chain them up there for a week. This hint was enough to repress talking, though, of course, it did not disturb the credit of the story in the least.

Gradually the staircase that led to the garret, and even the passage-way to the staircase, were avoided by everyone in the house, from everyone fearing to speak of it, and the legend was gradually falling into desuetude. It had suddenly occurred to Cassy to make use of the superstitious excitability which was so great in Legree for the purpose of her liberation, and that of her fellow-sufferer.

The sleeping-room of Cassy was directly under the garret. One day, without consulting Legree, she suddenly took it upon her, with some considerable ostentation, to change all the furniture and appurtenances of the room to one at some considerable distance. The under-servants, who were called on to effect this movement, were running and bustling about with great zeal and confusion, when Legree returned from a ride.

'Hallo! you Cass!' said Legree, 'what's in the wind now?'

'Nothing; only I choose to have another room,' said Cassy, doggedly.

'And what for, pray?' said Legree.

'I choose to,' said Cassy.

'The devil you do! And what for?'

'I'd like to get some sleep, now and then.'

'Sleep! well, what hinders your sleeping?'

'I could tell, I suppose, if you want to hear,' said Cassy, dryly.

'Speak out, you minx!' said Legree.

'Oh! nothing. I suppose it wouldn't disturb *you*! Only groans, and people scuffling, and rolling round on the garret floor, half the night, from twelve to morning!'

'People up in the garret!' said Legree, uneasily, but forcing a laugh; 'who are they, Cassy?'

Cassy raised her sharp, black eyes, and looked in the face of Legree, with an expression that went through his bones as she said, 'To be sure, Simon, who are they? I'd like to have *you* tell me. You don't know, I suppose!'

With an oath, Legree struck at her with his riding-whip; but she glided to one side, and passed through the door, and looking back, said, 'If you'll sleep in that room, you'll know all about it. Perhaps you'd better try it!' and then immediately she shut and locked the door.

Legree blustered and swore, and threatened to break down the door; but apparently thought better of it, and walked uneasily into the sitting-room. Cassy perceived that her shaft had struck home; and, from that hour, with the most exquisite address, she never ceased to continue the train of influences she had begun.

In a knot-hole of the garret she had inserted the neck of an old bottle, in such a manner that when there was the least wind, most doleful and lugubrious wailing sounds proceeded from it, which, in a high wind, increased to a perfect shriek, such as to credulous and superstitious ears might easily seem to be that of horror and despair.

These sounds were from time to time heard by the servants, and revived in full force the memory of the old ghost legend. A superstitious creeping horror seemed to fill the house; and though no one dared to breathe it to Legree, he found himself encompassed by it as by an atmosphere.

No one is so thoroughly superstitious as the godless man. The Christian is composed by the belief of a wise, all-ruling Father, whose presence fills the void unknown with light and order; but to the man who has dethroned God, the spirit-land is, indeed, in the words of the Hebrew poet, 'a land of darkness and the shadow of death',[281] without any order, where the light is as darkness. Life and death to him are haunted grounds, filled with goblin forms of vague and shadowy dread.

Legree had had the slumbering moral element in him roused by his encounters with Tom – roused, only to be resisted by the determinate force of evil; but still there was a thrill and commotion of the dark, inner world, produced by every word, or prayer, or hymn, that reacted in superstitious dread.

The influence of Cassy over him was of a strange and singular kind. He was her owner, her tyrant and tormentor. She was, as he knew, wholly, and without any possibility of help or redress, in his hands; and yet so it is, that the most brutal man cannot live in constant association with a strong female influence, and not be greatly controlled by it. When he first bought her, she was, as she had said, a woman delicately bred; and then he crushed her, without scruple, beneath the foot of his brutality. But, as time, and debasing influences and despair, hardened womanhood within her and woke the fires of fiercer passions, she had become in a measure his mistress, and he alternately tyrannised over and dreaded her.

This influence had become more harassing and decided, since partial insanity had given a strange, weird, unsettled cast to all her words and language.

A night or two after this, Legree was sitting in the old sitting-room, by the side of a flickering wood fire, that threw uncertain glances round the room. It was a stormy, windy night, such as raises whole squadrons of nondescript noises in rickety old houses. Windows were rattling, shutters flapping, the wind carousing, rumbling, and tumbling down the chimney, and, every once in a while, puffing out smoke and ashes, as if a legion of spirits were coming after them. Legree had been casting up accounts and reading newspapers for some hours, while Cassy sat in the corner, sullenly looking into the fire. Legree laid down his paper, and seeing an old book lying on the table, which he had noticed Cassy reading, the first part of the evening, took it up, and began to turn it over. It was one of those collections of stories of bloody murders, ghostly legends, and supernatural visitations, which, coarsely got up and illustrated, have a strange fascination for one who once begins to read them.

Legree poohed and pished, but read, turning page after page, till, finally, after reading some way, he threw down the book, with an oath.

'You don't believe in ghosts, do you, Cass?' said he, taking the tongs and settling the fire. 'I thought you'd more sense than to let noises scare *you*.'

'No matter what I believe,' said Cassy, sullenly.

'Fellows used to try to frighten me with their yarns at sea,' said Legree. 'Never come it round me that way. I'm too tough for any such trash, tell ye.'

Cassy sat looking intensely at him in the shadow of the corner. There was that strange light in her eyes that always impressed Legree with uneasiness.

'Them noises was nothing but rats and the wind,' said Legree. 'Rats will make a devil of a noise. I used to hear 'em sometimes down in the hold of the ship; and wind – Lord's sake! ye can make anything out o' wind.'

Cassy knew Legree was uneasy under her eyes, and therefore she made no answer, but sat fixing them on him with that strange, unearthly expression, as before.

'Come, speak out, woman – don't you think so?' said Legree.

'Can rats walk downstairs, and come walking through the entry, and open a door when you've locked it and set a chair against it?' said

Cassy; 'and come walk, walk, walking right up to your bed, and put out their hand, so?'

Cassy kept her glittering eyes fixed on Legree as she spoke, and he stared at her like a man in the nightmare, till, when she finished by laying her hand, icy cold, on his, he sprang back, with an oath.

'Woman! what do you mean? Nobody did!'

'Oh, no – of course not – did I say they did?' said Cassy, with a smile of chilling derision.

'But – did – have you really seen? – Come, Cass, what is it, now – speak out!'

'You may sleep there yourself,' said Cassy, 'if you want to know.'

'Did it come from the garret, Cassy?'

'*It* – what?' said Cassy.

'Why, what you told of.'

'I didn't tell you anything,' said Cassy, with dogged sullenness.

Legree walked up and down the room, uneasily.

'I'll have this yer thing examined. I'll look into it this very night. I'll take my pistols – '

'Do,' said Cassy; 'sleep in that room. I'd like to see you doing it. Fire your pistols – do!'

Legree stamped his foot, and swore violently.

'Don't swear,' said Cassy; 'nobody knows who may be hearing you. Hark! What was that?'

'What?' said Legree, starting.

A heavy old Dutch clock, that stood in the corner of the room, began, and slowly struck twelve.

For some reason or other Legree neither spoke nor moved; a vague horror fell on him; while Cassy, with a keen, sneering glitter in her eyes, stood looking at him, counting the strokes.

'Twelve o'clock; well, *now* we'll see,' said she, turning, and opening the door into the passage-way, and standing as if listening.

'Hark! What's that?' said she, raising her finger.

'It's only the wind,' said Legree. 'Don't you hear how cursedly it blows?'

'Simon, come here,' said Cassy, in a whisper, laying her hand on his, and leading him to the foot of the stairs; 'do you know what *that* is? Hark!'

A wild shriek came pealing down the stairway. It came from the garret. Legree's knees knocked together; his face grew white with fear.

'Hadn't you better get your pistols?' said Cassy, with a sneer that froze Legree's blood. 'It's time this thing was looked into, you know.

I'd like to have you go up now; *they're at it.*'

'I won't go!' said Legree, with an oath.

'Why not? There an't any such thing as ghosts, you know! Come!' and Cassy flitted up the winding stairway, laughing, and looking back after him. 'Come on.'

'I believe you *are* the devil!' said Legree. 'Come back, you hag! – come back, Cass! You shan't go!'

But Cassy laughed wildly, and fled on. He heard her open the entry doors that led to the garret. A wild gust of wind swept down extinguishing the candle he held in his hand, and with it the fearful, unearthly screams; they seemed to be shrieked in his very ear.

Legree fled frantically into the parlour, whither, in a few moments, he was followed by Cassy, pale, calm, cold as an avenging spirit, and with that same fearful light in her eye.

'I hope you are satisfied,' said she.

'Blast you, Cass!' said Legree.

'What for?' said Cassy. 'I only went up and shut the doors. *What's the matter with that garret,* Simon, do you suppose?' said she.

'None of your business!' said Legree.

'Oh, it an't? Well,' said Cassy, 'at any rate, I'm glad *I* don't sleep under it.'

Anticipating the rising of the wind, that very evening, Cassy had been up and opened the garret window. Of course, the moment the doors were opened, the wind had drafted down, and extinguished the light.

This may serve as a specimen of the game that Cassy played with Legree, until he would sooner have put his head into a lion's mouth than to have explored that garret. Meanwhile, in the night, when everybody else was asleep, Cassy slowly and carefully accumulated there a stock of provisions sufficient to afford subsistence for some time; she transferred, article by article, a greater part of her own and Emmeline's wardrobe. All things being arranged, they only waited a fitting opportunity to put their plan in execution.

By cajoling Legree, and taking advantage of a good-natured interval, Cassy had got him to take her with him to the neighbouring town, which was situated directly on the Red River. With a memory sharpened to almost preternatural clearness, she remarked every turn in the road, and formed a mental estimate of the time to be occupied in traversing it.

At the time when all was matured for action, our readers may, perhaps like to look behind the scenes, and see the final *coup d'état.*[282]

It was now near evening. Legree had been absent, on a ride to a neighbouring farm. For many days Cassy had been unusually gracious and accommodating in her humours; and Legree and she had been, apparently, on the best of terms. At present, we may behold her and Emmeline in the room of the latter, busy in sorting and arranging two small bundles.

'There, these will be large enough,' said Cassy. 'Now put on your bonnet, and let's start: it's just about the right time.'

'Why, they can see us yet,' said Emmeline.

'I mean they shall,' said Cassy, coolly. 'Don't you know that they must have their chase after us, at any rate? The way of the thing is to be just this: We will steal out of the back door, and run down by the quarters. Sambo or Quimbo will be sure to see us. They will give chase, and we will get into the swamp; then, they can't follow us any further till they go up and give the alarm, and turn out the dogs, and so on; and, while they are blundering round, and tumbling over each other, as they always do, you and I will just slip along to the creek that runs back of the house, and wade along in it till we get opposite the back door. That will put the dogs all at fault; for scent won't lie in the water. Everyone will run out of the house to look after us, and then we'll whip in at the back door, and up into the garret, where I've got a nice bed made up in one of the great boxes. We must stay in that garret a good while; for, I tell you, he will raise heaven and earth after us. He'll muster some of those old overseers on the other plantations, and have a great hunt? and they'll go over every inch of ground in that swamp. He makes it his boast that nobody ever got away from him. So let him hunt at his leisure.'

'Cassy, how well you have planned it!' said Emmeline. 'Who ever would have thought of it but you?'

There was neither pleasure nor exultation in Cassy's eyes – only a despairing firmness.

'Come,' she said, reaching her hand to Emmeline.

The two fugitives glided noiselessly from the house, and flitted, through the gathering shadows of evening, along by the quarters. The crescent moon, set like a silver signet in the western sky, delayed a little the approach of night. As Cassy expected, when quite near the verge of the swamps that encircled the plantation, they heard a voice calling to them to stop. It was not Sambo, however, but Legree, who was pursuing them with violent execrations. At the sound, the feebler spirit of Emmeline gave way; and, laying hold of Cassy's arm, she said, 'Oh, Cassy, I'm going to faint!'

'If you do, I'll kill you!' said Cassy, drawing a small, glittering stiletto, and flashing it before the eyes of the girl.

The diversion accomplished the purpose. Emmeline did not faint, and succeeded in plunging, with Cassy into a part of the labyrinth of swamp, so deep and dark that it was perfectly hopeless for Legree to think of following them without assistance.

'Well,' said he, chuckling brutally; 'at any rate, they've got themselves into a trap now – the baggages! They're safe enough. They shall sweat for it!'

'Hallo, there! Sambo! Quimbo! All hands!' called Legree, coming to the quarters when the men and women were just returning from work. 'There's two runaways in the swamps. I'll give five dollars to any nigger as catches 'em. Turn out the dogs! Turn out Tiger, and Fury, and the rest!'

The sensation produced by this news was immediate. Many of the men sprang forward officiously to offer their services, either from the hope of the reward, or from that cringing subserviency which is one of the most baleful effects of slavery. Some ran one way, and some another. Some were for getting flambeaux[283] of pine-knots. Some were uncoupling the dogs, whose hoarse, savage bay, added not a little to the animation of the scene.

'Mas'r, shall we shoot 'em, if we can't cotch 'em?' said Sambo, to whom his master brought out a rifle.

'You may fire on Cass, if you like; it's time she was gone to the devil, where she belongs; but the gal, not,' said Legree. 'And now, boys, be spry and smart. Five dollars for him that gets 'em; and a glass of spirits to every one of you, anyhow.'

The whole band, with the glare of blazing torches, and whoop, and shout, and savage yell, of man and beast, proceeded down to the swamp, followed at some distance by every servant in the house. The establishment was, of a consequence, wholly deserted when Cassy and Emmeline glided into it the back way. The whooping and shouts of their pursuers were still filling the air; and, looking from the sitting-room windows, Cassy and Emmeline could see the troop, with their flambeaux, just dispersing themselves along the edge of the swamp.

'See there!' said Emmeline, pointing to Cassy; 'the hunt is begun! Look how those lights dance about! Hark! the dogs! Don't you hear? If we were only *there*, our chance wouldn't be worth a picayune. Oh, for pity's sake, do let's hide ourselves. Quick!'

'There's no occasion for hurry,' said Cassy, coolly; 'they are all out after the hunt – that's the amusement of the evening! We'll go upstairs, by and by. Meanwhile,' said she, deliberately taking a key from the pocket of a coat that Legree had thrown down in his hurry, 'meanwhile I shall take something to pay our passage.

She unlocked the desk, took from it a roll of bills, which she counted over rapidly.

'Oh, don't let's do that!' said Emmeline.

'Don't!' said Cassy; 'why not? Would you have us starve in the swamps, or have that that will pay our way to the free states? Money will do anything, girl.' And as she spoke she put the money in her bosom.

'It would be stealing,' said Emmeline, in a distressed whisper.

'Stealing!' said Cassy, with a scornful laugh. 'They who steal body and soul needn't talk to us. Every one of these bills is stolen – stolen from poor, starving, sweating creatures, who must go to the devil at last, for his profit. Let *him* talk about stealing! But come, we may as well go up to the garret; I've got a stock of candles there, and some books to pass away the time. You may be pretty sure they won't come *there* to enquire after us. If they do, I'll play ghost for them.'

When Emmeline reached the garret, she found an immense box, in which some heavy pieces of furniture had once been brought, turned on its side, so that the opening faced the wall, or rather the eaves. Cassy lit a small lamp, and, creeping round under the eaves, they established themselves in it. It was spread with a couple of small mattresses and some pillows; a box near by was plentifully stored with candles, provisions, and all the clothing necessary to their journey, which Cassy had arranged into bundles of an astonishingly small compass.

'There,' said Cassy, as she fixed the lamp into a small hook, which she had driven into the side of the box for that purpose; 'this is to be our home for the present. How do you like it?'

'Are you sure they won't come and search the garret?'

'I'd like to see Simon Legree doing that,' said Cassy. 'No, indeed; he will be too glad to keep away. As to the servants, they would any of them stand and be shot sooner than show their faces here.'

Somewhat reassured, Emmeline settled herself back on her pillow.

'What did you mean, Cassy, by saying you would kill me?' she said, simply.

'I meant to stop your fainting,' said Cassy, 'and I did it. And now I tell you, Emmeline, you must make up your mind *not* to faint, let what will come; there's no sort of need of it. If I had not stopped you, that wretch might have had his hands on you now.'

Emmeline shuddered.

The two remained some time in silence. Cassy busied herself with a French book; Emmeline, overcome with the exhaustion, fell into a doze, and slept some time. She was awakened by loud shouts and outcries, the tramp of horses' feet, and the baying of dogs. She started up, with a faint shriek.

'Only the hunt coming back,' said Cassy, coolly; 'never fear. Look out of this knot-hole. Don't you see 'em all down there? Simon has to give it up for this night. Look, how muddy his horse is, flouncing about in the swamp; the dogs, too, look rather crestfallen. Ah, my good sir! you'll have to try the race again and again – the game isn't there.'

'O, don't speak a word!' said Emmeline; 'what if they should hear you?'

'If they do hear anything, it will make them very particular to keep away,' said Cassy. 'No danger; we may make any noise we please, and it will only add to the effect.'

At length the stillness of midnight settled down over the house. Legree, cursing his ill luck, and vowing dire vengeance on the morrow, went to bed.

CHAPTER XL

The Martyr

Deem not the just by Heaven forgot
  Though life its common gifts deny –
Though, with a crushed and bleeding heart,
  And spurned of man, he goes to die!
For God hath marked each sorrowing day,
  And numbered every bitter tear;
And heaven's long years of bliss shall pay
  For all his children suffer here.[284]

BRYANT

THE LONGEST WAY must have its close – the gloomiest night will wear on to a morning. An eternal, inexorable lapse of moments is ever hurrying the day of the evil to an eternal night, and the night of the just to an eternal day. We have walked with our humble friend thus far in the valley of slavery; first through flowery fields of ease and indulgence, then through heartbreaking separations from all that man holds dear. Again, we have waited with him in a sunny island, where generous hands concealed his chains with flowers; and, lastly, we have followed him when the last ray of earthly hope went out in night, and seen how, in the blackness of earthly darkness, the firmament of the unseen has blazed with stars of new and significant lustre.

The morning-star now stands over the tops of the mountains, and gales and breezes, not of earth, show that the gates of day are unclosing.

The escape of Cassy and Emmeline irritated the before surly temper of Legree to the last degree; and his fury, as was to be expected, fell upon the defenceless head of Tom. When he hurriedly announced the tidings among his hands, there was a sudden light in Tom's eye, a sudden upraising of his hands, that did not escape him. He saw that he did not join the muster of the pursuers. He thought of forcing him to do it; but, having had, of old, experience of his inflexibility when commanded to take part in any deed of inhumanity, he would not, in his hurry, stop to enter into any conflict with him.

Tom, therefore remained behind, with a few who had learned of him to pray, and offered up prayers for the escape of the fugitives.

When Legree returned, baffled and disappointed, all the long-working hatred of his soul towards his slave began to gather in a deadly and desperate form. Had not this man braved him – steadily, power-fully, resistlessly – ever since he bought him? Was there not a spirit in him which, silent as it was, burned on him like the fires of perdition?

'I *hate* him!' said Legree, that night, as he sat up in his bed; 'I *hate* him! And isn't he MINE? Can't I do what I like with him? Who's to hinder, I wonder?' And Legree clenched his fist and shook it as if he had something in his hands that he could rend in pieces.

But then Tom was a faithful, valuable servant; and, although Legree hated him the more for that, yet the consideration was still somewhat of a restraint to him.

The next morning, he determined to say nothing, as yet; to assemble a party from some neighbouring plantations, with dogs and guns; to surround the swamp, and go about the hunt systematically. If it succeeded, well and good; if not, he would summon Tom before him, and – his teeth clenched and his blood boiled – *then* he would break that fellow down, or – there was a dire inward whisper, to which his soul assented.

Ye say that the *interest* of the master is a sufficient safeguard for the slave. In the fury of man's mad will, he will wittingly, and with open eye, sell his own soul to the devil to gain his ends; and will he be more careful of his neighbour's body?

'Well,' said Cassy, the next day, from the garret, as she reconnoitred through the knot-hole, 'the hunt's going to begin again, today!'

Three or four mounted horsemen were curvetting[285] about, on the space in front of the house; and one or two leashes of strange dogs were struggling with the negroes who held them, baying and barking at each other.

The men are, two of them, overseers of plantations in the vicinity; and others were some of Legree's associates at the tavern-bar of a neighbouring city, who had come for the interest of the sport. A more hard-favoured set, perhaps, could not be imagined. Legree was serving brandy profusely round among them, as also among the negroes, who had been detailed from the various plantations for this service; for it was an object to make every service of this kind among the negroes as much of a holiday as possible.

Cassy placed her ear at the knot-hole; and, as the morning air blew directly towards the house, she could overhear a good deal of the conversation. A grave sneer overcast the dark, severe gravity of her face, as she listened, and heard them divide out the ground, discuss the rival merits of the dogs, give orders about firing, and the treatment of each in case of capture.

Cassy drew back; and clasping her hands, looked upward, and said, 'O great Almighty God! we are *all* sinners; but what have *we* done, more than all the rest of the world, that we should be treated so?'

There was a terrible earnestness in her face and voice as she spoke.

'If it wasn't for *you*, child,' she said, looking at Emmeline, 'I'd *go* out to them; and I'd thank any one of them that *would* shoot me down; for what use will freedom be to me? Can it give me back my children, or make me what I used to be?'

Emmeline, in her childlike simplicity, was half afraid of the dark moods of Cassy. She looked perplexed, but made no answer. She only took her hand, with a gentle, caressing movement.

'Don't!' said Cassy, trying to draw it away; 'you'll get me to loving you; and I never mean to love anything again!'

'Poor Cassy!' said Emmeline, 'don't feel so! If the Lord gives us liberty, perhaps He'll give you back your daughter. At any rate, I'll be like a daughter to you. I know I'll never see my poor old mother again! I shall love you, Cassy, whether you love me or not!'

The gentle, childlike spirit conquered. Cassy sat down by her, put her arm round her neck, stroked her soft brown hair; and Emmeline then wondered at the beauty of her magnificent eyes, now soft with tears.

'Oh, Em!' said Cassy, 'I've hungered for my children, and thirsted for them, and my eyes fail with longing for them. Here! here!' she said, striking her breast, 'it's all desolate, all empty! If God would give me back my children, then I could pray.'

'You must trust him, Cassy,' said Emmeline; 'he is our Father!'

'His wrath is upon us,' said Cassy; 'He has turned away in anger.'

'No, Cassy! He will be good to us! Let us hope in Him,' said Emmeline. 'I always have had hope.'

The hunt was long, animated, and thorough, but unsuccessful; and, with grave, ironic exultation, Cassy looked down on Legree as, weary and dispirited, he alighted from his horse.

'Now, Quimbo,' said Legree, as he stretched himself down in the sitting-room, 'you jest go and walk that Tom up here, right away! The old cuss is at the bottom of this yer whole matter; and I'll have it out of his old black hide, or I'll know the reason why!'

Sambo and Quimbo both, though hating each other, were joined in one mind by a no less cordial hatred of Tom. Legree had told them at first that he had bought him for a general overseer in his absence; and this had begun an ill-will on their part, which had increased in their debased and servile natures as they saw him becoming obnoxious to their master's displeasure. Quimbo, therefore, departed, with a will to execute his orders.

Tom heard the message with a forewarning heart; for he knew all the plan of the fugitives' escape, and the place of their present conceal-ment. He knew the deadly character of the man he had to deal with, and his despotic power. But he felt strong in God to meet death, rather than betray the helpless.

He set his basket down by the row, and, looking up, said, 'Into Thy hands I commend my spirit![286] Thou hast redeemed me, O Lord God of truth!' and then quietly yielded himself to the rough, brutal grasp with which Quimbo seized him.

'Ay, ay!' said the giant, as he dragged him along; 'ye'll cotch it, now! I'll boun' mas'r's back's up high! No sneaking out, now! Tell ye ye'll get it, and no mistake! See how ye'll look, now, helpin' mas'r's niggers to run away! See what ye'll get!'

The savage words none of them reached that ear – a higher voice there was saying, 'Fear not them that kill the body, and, after that, have no more that they can do.'[287] Nerve and bone of that poor man's body vibrated to those words, as if touched by the finger of God; and he felt the strength of a thousand souls in one. As he passed along, the trees and bushes, the huts of his servitude, the whole scene of his degrada-tion, seemed to whirl by him as the landscape by the rushing car. His soul throbbed – his home was in sight – and the hour of release seemed at hand.

'Well, Tom!' said Legree, walking up, and seizing him grimly by the collar of his coat, and speaking through his teeth, in a paroxysm of determined rage, 'do you know I've made up my mind to kill you?'

'It's very likely, mas'r,' said Tom, calmly.

'*I have*,' said Legree, with grim, terrible calmness, '*done – just – that – thing*, Tom, unless you'll tell me what you know about these yer gals!'

Tom stood silent.

'D'ye hear?' said Legree, stamping, with a roar like that of an incensed lion. 'Speak!'

'*I han't got nothing to tell, mas'r*,' said Tom, with a slow, firm, deliberate utterance.

'Do you dare to tell me, ye old black Christian, ye don't *know*?' said Legree.

Tom was silent.

'Speak!' thundered Legree, striking him furiously. 'Do you know anything?'

'I know, mas'r; but I can't tell anything. *I can die!*'

Legree drew in a long breath; and, suppressing his rage, took Tom by the arm, and, approaching his face almost to his, said, in a terrible voice, 'Hark'e, Tom – ye think, 'cause I've let you off before, I don't mean what I say; but, this time I've *made up my mind*, and counted the cost. You've always stood it out agin' me – now I'll *conquer you or kill you*! – one or t' other. I'll count every drop of blood there is in you, and take 'em, one by one, till ye give up!'

Tom looked up to his master, and answered, 'Mas'r, if you was sick, or in trouble, or dying, and I could save ye, I'd *give* ye my heart's blood; and, if taking every drop of blood in this poor old body would save your precious soul, I'd give 'em freely, as the Lord gave his for me. Oh, mas'r! don't bring this great sin on your soul! It will hurt you more than 'twill me! Do the worst you can, my troubles'll be over soon; but if ye don't repent, yours *won't* never end!'

Like a strange snatch of heavenly music, heard in the lull of a tempest, this burst of feeling made a moment's blank pause. Legree stood aghast, and looked at Tom; and there was such a silence, that the tick of the old clock could be heard, measuring, with silent touch, the last moments of mercy and probation to that hardened heart.

It was but a moment. There was one hesitating pause, one irresolute, relenting thrill, and the spirit of evil came back with sevenfold vehemence; and Legree, foaming with rage, smote his victim to the ground.

Scenes of blood and cruelty are shocking to our ear and heart. What man has nerve to do, man has not nerve to hear. What brother-man and brother-Christian must suffer, cannot be told us, even in our secret chamber, it so harrows up the soul! And yet, O my country! these things are done under the shadow of thy laws! O Christ! thy church sees them, almost in silence!

But, of old there was One whose suffering changed an instrument of torture, degradation and shame, into a symbol of glory, honour, and immortal life; and, where His Spirit is, neither degrading stripes, nor blood, nor insults, can make the Christian's last struggle less than glorious.

Was he alone, that long night, whose brave, loving spirit was bearing up, in that old shed, against buffeting and brutal stripes?

Nay! There stood by him ONE – seen by him alone – 'like unto the Son of God'.[288]

The tempter stood by him, too, blinded by furious, despotic will, every moment pressing him to shun that agony by the betrayal of the innocent. But the brave, true heart was firm on the Eternal Rock. Like his Master, he knew that, if he saved others, himself he could not save; nor could utmost extremity wring from him words, save of prayer and holy trust.

'He's most gone, mas'r,' said Sambo, touched, in spite of himself, by the patience of his victim.

'Pay away, till he gives up! Give it to him! give it to him!' shouted Legree. 'I'll take every drop of blood he has, unless he confesses!'

Tom opened his eyes, and looked upon his master. 'Ye poor, miserable critter!' he said, 'there an't no more ye can do! I forgive ye, with all my soul!' and he fainted entirely away.

'I b'lieve, my soul, he's done for, finally,' said Legree, stepping forward to look at him. 'Yes, he is! Well, his mouth's shut up at last, that's one comfort!'

Yes, Legree; but who shall shut up that voice in thy soul – that soul, past repentance, past prayer, past hope, in whom the fire that never shall be quenched is already burning?

Yet Tom was not quite gone. His wondrous words and pious prayers had struck upon the hearts of the embruted blacks who had been the instruments of cruelty upon him; and, the instant Legree withdrew they took him down, and, in their ignorance, sought to call him back to life – as if *that* were any favour to him.

'Sartin, we's been doin' a drefful wicked thing!' said Sambo; 'hopes mas'r'll have to 'count for it, and not we.'

They washed his wounds – they provided a rude bed of some refuse cotton, for him to lie down on; and one of them, stealing up to the house, begged a drink of brandy of Legree, pretending that he was tired, and wanted it for himself. He brought it back, and poured it down Tom's throat.

'Oh, Tom!' said Quimbo, 'we's been awful wicked to ye!'

'I forgive ye, with all my heart!' said Tom, faintly.

'Oh, Tom! do tell us who is *Jesus*, anyhow?' said Sambo; 'Jesus, that's been a standin' by you so, all this night. Who is he?'

The word roused the failing, fainting spirit. He poured forth a few energetic sentences of that wondrous One – His life, His death, His everlasting presence, and power to save.

They wept – both the two savage men.

'Why didn't I never hear this before?' said Sambo; 'but I do believe! – I can't help it! Lord Jesus, have mercy on us!'

'Poor critters!' said Tom, 'I'd be willing to bar' all I have, if it'll only bring ye to Christ! O Lord! give me these two more souls, I pray!'

That prayer was answered![289]

CHAPTER XLI

The Young Master

TWO DAYS AFTER, a young man drove a light wagon up through the avenue of China trees, and, throwing the reins hastily on the horse's neck, sprang out and enquired for the owner of the place.

It was George Shelby; and to show how he came to be there, we must go back in our story.

The letter of Miss Ophelia to Mrs Shelby had, by some unfortunate accident, been detained for a month or two at some remote post-office, before it reached its destination; and, of course, before it was received, Tom was already lost to view among the distant swamps of the Red River.

Mrs Shelby read the intelligence with the deepest concern; but any immediate action upon it was an impossibility. She was then in attendance on the sick-bed of her husband who lay delirious in the crisis of a fever. Master George Shelby, who, in the interval, had changed from a boy to a tall young man, was her constant and faithful assistant, and her only reliance in superintending his father's affairs. Miss Ophelia had taken the precaution to send them the name of the lawyer who did business for the St Clares; and the most that in the emergency could be done was to address a letter of enquiry to him. The sudden death of Mr Shelby, a few days after, brought, of course, an absorbing pressure of other interests, for a season.

Mr Shelby showed his confidence in his wife's ability, by appointing her sole executrix upon his estates; and thus immediately a large and complicated amount of business was brought upon her hands.

Mrs Shelby, with characteristic energy, applied herself to the work of straightening the entangled web of affairs; and she and George were for some time occupied with collecting and examining accounts, selling property and settling debts; for Mrs Shelby was determined that everything should be brought into tangible and recognisable shape, let the consequences to her prove what they might. In the meantime, they received a letter from the lawyer to whom Miss Ophelia had referred them, saying that he knew nothing of the matter; that the man was sold at a public auction, and that, beyond receiving the money, he knew nothing of the affair.

Neither George nor Mrs Shelby could be easy at this result; and, accordingly some six months after, the latter, having business for his mother down the river, resolved to visit New Orleans in person, and push his enquiries, in hopes of discovering Tom's whereabouts and restoring him.

After some months of unsuccessful search, by the merest accident, George fell in with a man, in New Orleans, who happened to be possessed of the desired information; and with his money in his pocket, our hero took steamboat for Red River, resolving to find out and repurchase his old friend.

He was soon introduced into the house, where he found Legree in the sitting-room.

Legree received the stranger with a kind of surly hospitality.

'I understand,' said the young man, 'that you bought, in New

Orleans, a boy named Tom. He used to be on my father's place, and I came to see if I couldn't buy him back.'

Legree's brow grew dark, and he broke out, passionately: 'Yes, I did buy such a fellow – and a hell of a bargain I had of it, too! The most rebellious, saucy, impudent dog! Set up my niggers to run away, got off two gals worth eight hundred or a thousand dollars apiece. He owned to that, and, when I bid him tell me where they was, he up and said he knew, but he wouldn't tell; and stood to it, though I gave him the cussedest flogging I ever gave nigger yet. I b'lieve he's trying to die; but I don't know as he'll make it out.'

'Where is he?' said George, impetuously. 'Let me see him.' The cheeks of the young man were crimson, and his eyes flashed fire; but he prudently said nothing, as yet.

'He's in dat ar shed,' said a little fellow, who stood holding George's horse.

Legree kicked the boy, and swore at him; but George, without saying another word, turned and strode to the spot.

Tom had been lying two days since the fatal night; not suffering, for every nerve of suffering was blunted and destroyed. He lay, for the most part, in a quiet stupor; for the laws of a powerful and well-knit frame would not at once release the imprisoned spirit. By stealth, there had been there, in the darkness of the night, poor desolate creatures, who stole from their scanty hours' rest, that they might repay to him some of those ministrations of love in which he had always been so abundant. Truly, those poor disciples had little to give – only the cup of cold water; but it was given with full hearts.

Tears had fallen on that honest, insensible face – tears of late repentance in the poor, ignorant heathen, whom his dying love and patience had awakened to repentance, and bitter prayers, breathed over him to a late-found Saviour, of whom they scarce knew more than the name, but whom the yearning ignorant heart of man never implores in vain.

Cassy, who had glided out of her place of concealment, and, by overhearing, learned the sacrifice that had been made for her and Emmeline, had been there, the night before, defying the danger of detection; and, moved by the few last words which the affectionate soul had yet strength to breathe, the long winter of despair, the ice of years, had given way, and the dark, despairing woman had wept and prayed.

When George entered the shed, he felt his head giddy and his heart sick.

'Is it possible? – is it possible?' said he, kneeling down by him. 'Uncle

Tom! my poor – poor old friend!'

Something in the voice penetrated to the ear of the dying. He moved his head gently, smiled, and said –

> 'Jesus can make a dying bed
>   Feel soft as downy pillows are.'[290]

Tears which did honour to his manly heart fell from the young man's eyes, as he bent over his poor friend.

'Oh, dear Uncle Tom! do wake – do speak once more! Look up! Here's Mas'r George – your own little Mas'r George. Don't you know me?'

'Mas'r George!' said Tom, opening his eyes, and speaking in a feeble voice; 'Mas'r George!' He looked bewildered.

Slowly the idea seemed to fill his soul; and the vacant eye became fixed and brightened, the whole face lighted up, the hard hands clasped, and tears ran down the cheeks.

'Bless the Lord! it is – it is – it's all I wanted! They haven't forgot me, It warms my soul; it does my old heart good! Now I shall die content! Bless the Lord, O my soul!'

'You shan't die! you *musn't* die, nor think of it! I've come to buy you, and take you home,' said George, with impetuous vehemence.

'O Mas'r George, ye're too late. The Lord's bought me, and is going to take me home – and I long to go. Heaven is better than Kintuck.'

'Oh, don't die! It'll kill me! – it'll break my heart to think what you've suffered – and lying in this old shed, here! Poor, poor fellow!'

'Don't call me poor fellow!' said Tom, solemnly. 'I have been poor fellow, but that's all past and gone now. I'm right in the door, going into glory! Oh, Mas'r George! *Heaven* has come! I've got the victory! – the Lord Jesus has given it to me! Glory to be His name!'

George was awestruck at the force, the vehemence, the power with which these broken sentences were uttered. He sat gazing in silence.

Tom grasped his hand, and continued – 'Ye mustn't, now, tell Chloe, poor soul! how ye found me; 'twould be so dreeful to her. Only tell her ye found me going into glory; and that I couldn't stay for no one. And tell her the Lord stood by me everywhere and al'ays, and made everything light and easy. And, oh, the poor chil'en, and the baby – my old heart's been most broken for 'em, time and agin. Tell 'em all to follow me – follow me! Give my love to mas'r, and dear good missis – and everybody in the place! Ye don't know. 'Pears like I loves 'em all! I loves every creatur', every whar! – it's nothing *but* love! Oh, Mas'r

George! what a thing 'tis to be a Christian!'

At this moment Legree sauntered up to the door of the shed, looked in with a dogged air of affected carelessness, and turned away.

'The old Satan!' said George, in his indignation. 'It's a comfort to think the devil will pay *him* for this some of these days!'

'Oh, don't! – oh, ye mustn't!' said Tom, grasping his hand; 'he's a poor mis'able crittur. It's awful to think on't! Oh, if he only could repent, the Lord would forgive him now but I'm feared he never will.'

'I hope he won't!' said George. 'I never want to see *him* in heaven.'

'Hush, Mas'r George! it worries me! Don't feel so! He an't done me no real harm – only opened the gate of the kingdom for me; that's all!'

At this moment, the sudden flush of strength which the joy of meeting his young master had infused into the dying man gave way. A sudden sinking fell upon him; he closed his eyes; and that mysterious and sublime change passed over his face that told the approach of other worlds.

He began to draw his breath with long, deep inspirations; and his broad chest rose and fell heavily. The expression of his face was that of a conqueror.

'Who – who – who shall separate us from the love of Christ?'[291] he said, in a voice that contended with mortal weakness; and with a smile, he fell asleep.

George sat fixed with solemn awe. It seemed to him that the place was holy; and as he closed the lifeless eyes, and rose up from the dead, only one thought possessed him – that expressed by his simple old friend, 'What a thing it is to be a Christian!'

He turned: Legree was standing, sullenly, behind him.

Something in that dying scene had checked the natural fierceness of youthful passion. The presence of the man was simply loathsome to George; and he felt only an impulse to get away from him, with as few words as possible.

Fixing his keen dark eyes on Legree, he simply said, pointing to the dead, 'You have got all you ever can of him. What shall I pay you for the body? I will take it away, and bury it decently.'

'I don't sell dead niggers,' said Legree, doggedly. 'You are welcome to bury him where and when you like.'

'Boys,' said George, in an authoritative tone to two or three negroes, who were looking at the body, 'help me lift him up, and carry him to my wagon; and get me a spade.'

One of them ran for a spade; the other two assisted George to carry the body to the wagon.

George neither spoke to nor looked at Legree, who did not countermand his orders, but stood, whistling, with an air of forced unconcern. He sulkily followed them to where the wagon stood at the door.

George spread his cloak in the wagon, and had the body carefully disposed of in it, moving the seat so as to give it room. Then he turned, fixed his eyes on Legree, and said, with forced composure –

'I have not as yet said to you what I think of this most atrocious affair; this is not the time and place. But, sir, this innocent blood shall have justice. I will proclaim this murder. I will go to the very first magistrate, and expose you.'

'Do!' said Legree, snapping his fingers scornfully. 'I'd like to see you doing it. Where you going to get witnesses? – how you going to prove it? Come, now!'

George saw at once the force of this defiance. There was not a white person on the place; and, in all Southern courts, the testimony of coloured blood is nothing. He felt, at that moment, as if he could have rent the heavens with his heart's indignant cry for justice; but in vain.[292]

'After all, what a fuss, for a dead nigger!' said Legree.

The word was as a spark to a powder magazine. Prudence was never a cardinal virtue of the Kentucky boy. George turned, and, with one indignant blow, knocked Legree flat upon his face; and, as he stood over him, blazing with wrath and defiance, he would have formed no bad personification of his great namesake triumphing over the dragon.

Some men, however, are decidedly bettered by being knocked down. If a man lays them fairly flat in the dust, they seem immediately to conceive a respect for him; and Legree was one of this sort. As he rose, therefore, and brushed the dust from his clothes, he eyed the slowly-retreating wagon with some evident consideration; nor did he open his mouth till it was out of sight.

Beyond the boundaries of the plantation, George had noticed a dry, sandy knoll, shaded by a few trees; there they made the grave.

'Shall we take off the cloak, mas'r?' said the negroes, when the grave was ready.

'No, no, bury it with him. It's all I can give you now, poor Tom, and you shall have it.'

They laid him in; and the men shovelled away, silently. They banked it up, and laid green turf over it.

'You may go, boys,' said George, slipping a quarter into the hand of each. They lingered about, however.

'If young mas'r would please buy us – ' said one.

'We'd serve him so faithful!' said the other.

'Hard times here, mas'r!' said the first. 'Do, mas'r, buy us, please!'

'I can't! – I can't!' said George, with difficulty, motioning them off; 'it's impossible!'

The poor fellows looked dejected, and walked off in silence.

'Witness, eternal God!' said George, kneeling on the grave of his poor friend, 'oh, witness that, from this hour, I will do *what one man can* to drive out this curse of slavery from my land!'

There is no monument to mark the last resting-place of our friend. He needs none! His Lord knows where he lies, and will raise him up immortal, to appear with him when he shall appear in his glory.

Pity him not! Such a life and death is not for pity! Not in the riches of omnipotence is the chief glory of God, but in self-denying, suffering love! And blessed are the men whom he calls to fellowship with him, bearing their cross after him with patience. Of such it is written, 'Blessed are they that mourn, for they shall be comforted.'[293]

CHAPTER XLII

An Authentic Ghost Story

FOR SOME REMARKABLE REASON, ghostly legends were uncommonly rife, about this time, among the servants on Legree's place.

It was whisperingly asserted that footsteps, in the dead of night, had been heard descending the garret stairs, and patrolling the house. In vain the doors of the upper entry had been locked; the ghost either carried a duplicate key in its pocket, or availed itself of a ghost's immemorial privilege of coming through the keyhole, and promenaded as before, with a freedom that was alarming.

Authorities were somewhat divided, as to the outward form of the spirit, owing to a custom quite prevalent among negroes – and, for aught we know, among whites, too – of invariably shutting the eyes, and covering up heads under blankets, petticoats, or whatever else might come in use for a shelter, on these occasions. Of course, as everybody knows, when the bodily eyes are thus out of the lists, the spiritual eyes are uncommonly vivacious and perspicuous; and there-fore there was an abundance of full-length portraits of the ghost,

abundantly sworn and testified to, which, as is often the case with
portraits, agreed with each other in no particular, except the common
family peculiarity of the ghost tribe – the wearing of *a white sheet*. The
poor souls were not versed in ancient history, and did not know that
Shakespeare had authenticated this costume, by telling how

> the *sheeted* dead
> Did squeak and gibber in the streets of Rome.[294]

And therefore their all hitting upon this is a striking fact in pneumatology,[295] which we recommend to the attention of spiritual media
generally.

Be it as it may, we have private reasons for knowing that a tall figure
in a white sheet did walk, at the most approved ghostly hours, around
the Legree premises – pass out the doors, glide about the house –
disappear at intervals, and, reappearing, pass up the silent stairway, into
that fatal garret; and that, in the morning, the entry doors were all
found shut and locked as firm as ever.

Legree could not help overhearing this whispering; and it was all the
more exciting to him from the pains that were taken to conceal it from
him. He drank more brandy than usual; held up his head briskly, and
swore louder than ever in the daytime; but he had bad dreams, and the
visions of his head on his bed were anything but agreeable. The night
after Tom's body had been carried away he rode to the next town for a
carouse, and had a high one. Got home late and tired; locked his door,
took out the key, and went to bed.

After all, let a man take what pains he may to hush it down, a human
soul is an awful ghostly, unquiet possession for a bad man to have. Who
knows the metes and bounds of it? Who knows all its awful perhapses –
those shudderings and tremblings, which it can no more live down
than it can outlive its own eternity! What a fool is he who locks his
door to keep out spirits, who has in his own bosom a spirit he dares not
meet alone – whose voice, smothered far down, and piled over with
mountains of earthliness, is yet like the forewarning trumpet of doom!

But Legree locked his door and set a chair against it; he set a night-
lamp at the head of his bed; and he put his pistols there. He examined
the catchings and fastenings of the windows, and then swore he 'didn't
care for the devil and all his angels', and went to sleep.

Well, he slept, for he was tired – slept soundly. But, finally, there
came over his sleep a shadow – a horror – an apprehension of
something dreadful hanging over him. It was his mother's shroud, he

thought; but Cassy had it, holding it up, and showing it to him. He heard a confused noise of screams and groanings; and, with it all, he knew he was asleep, and he struggled to wake himself. He was half awake. He was sure something was coming into his room. He knew the door was opening, but he could not stir hand or foot. At last he turned, with a start; the door *was* open, and he saw a hand putting out his light.

It was a cloudy, misty, moonlight, and there he saw it! – something white, gliding in! He heard the still rustle of its ghostly garments. It stood still by his bed; a cold hand touched his; a voice said, three times, in a low, fearful whisper, 'Come! come! come!' And, while he lay sweating with terror, he knew not when or how, the thing was gone. He sprang out of bed, and pulled at the door. It was shut and locked, and the man fell down in a swoon.

After this, Legree became a harder drinker than ever before. He no longer drank cautiously, prudently, but imprudently and recklessly.

There were reports around the country, soon after, that he was sick and dying. Excess had brought on that frightful disease that seems to throw the lurid shadows of a coming retribution back into the present life. None could bear the horrors of that sickroom, when he raved and screamed, and spoke of sights which almost stopped the blood of those who heard him; and, at his dying bed, stood a stern, white, inexorable figure, saying, 'Come! come! come!'

By a singular coincidence, on the very night that this vision appeared to Legree, the house-door was found open in the morning, and some of the negroes had seen two white figures gliding down the avenue towards the highroad.

It was near sunrise when Cassy and Emmeline paused, for a moment, in a little knot of trees near the town.

Cassy was dressed after the manner of the Creole[296] Spanish ladies – wholly in black. A small black bonnet on her head, covered by a veil thick with embroidery, concealed her face. It had been agreed that, in their escape, she was to personate the character of a Creole lady, and Emmeline that of her servant.

Brought up, from early life, in connection with the highest society, the language, movements and air of Cassy, were all in agreement with this idea; and she had still enough remaining with her, of a once splendid wardrobe, and sets of jewels, to enable her to personate the thing to advantage.

She stopped in the outskirts of the town, where she had noticed trunks for sale, and purchased a handsome one. This she requested the man to send along with her. And, accordingly, thus escorted by a boy wheeling her trunk, and Emmeline behind her, carrying her carpet-bag and sundry bundles, she made her appearance at the small tavern, like a lady of consideration.

The first person that struck her, after her arrival, was George Shelby, who was staying there, awaiting the next boat.

Cassy had remarked the young man from her loophole in the garret, and seen him bear away the body of Tom, and observed, with secret exultation, his rencontre[297] with Legree. Subsequently, she had gathered, from the conversations she had overheard among the negroes, as she glided about in her ghostly disguise after nightfall, who he was, and in what relation he stood to Tom. She, therefore, felt an immediate accession of confidence, when she found that he was, like herself, awaiting the next boat.

Cassy's air and manner, address, and evident command of money, prevented any rising disposition to suspicion in the hotel. People never enquire too closely into those who are fair on the main point, of paying well – a thing which Cassy had foreseen when she provided herself with money.

In the edge of the evening, a boat was heard coming along, and George Shelby handed Cassy aboard, with the politeness which comes naturally to every Kentuckian, and exerted himself to provide her with a good stateroom.

Cassy kept her room and bed, on pretext of illness, during the whole time they were on Red River; and was waited on, with obsequious devotion, by her attendant.

When they arrived at the Mississippi River, George, having learned that the course of the strange lady was upward, like his own, proposed to take a stateroom for her on the same boat with himself – good-naturedly compassionating her feeble health, and desirous to do what he could to assist her.

Behold, therefore, the whole party safely transferred to the good steamer *Cincinnati*, and sweeping up the river under a powerful head of steam.

Cassy's health was much better. She sat upon the guards, came to the table, and was remarked upon in the boat as a lady that must have been very handsome.

From the moment that George got the first glimpse of her face, he was troubled with one of those fleeting and indefinite likenesses which almost everybody can remember, and has been, at times, perplexed with. He could not keep himself from looking at her, and watching her perpetually. At table, or sitting at her stateroom door, still she would encounter the young man's eyes fixed on her, and politely withdrawn, when she showed, by her countenance, that she was sensible of the observation.

Cassy became uneasy. She began to think that he suspected something; and finally resolved to throw herself entirely on his generosity, and entrusted him with her whole history.

George was heartily disposed to sympathise with anyone who had escaped from Legree's plantation – a place that he could not remember or speak of with patience; and, with the courageous disregard of consequences which is characteristic of his age and state, he assured her that he would do all in his power to protect and bring them through.

The next stateroom to Cassy's was occupied by a French lady, named De Thoux, who was accompanied by a fine little daughter, a child of some twelve summers.

This lady, having gathered, from George's conversation, that he was from Kentucky, seemed evidently disposed to cultivate his acquaintance; in which design she was seconded by the graces of her little girl, who was about as pretty a plaything as ever diverted the weariness of a fortnight's trip on a steamboat.

George's chair was often placed at her stateroom door; and Cassy, as she sat upon the guards, could hear their conversation.

Madame de Thoux was very minute in her enquiries as to Kentucky, where she said she had resided in a former period of her life. George discovered, to his surprise, that her former residence must have been in his own vicinity; and her enquiries showed a knowledge of people and things in his vicinity; that was perfectly surprising to him.

'Do you know,' said Madame de Thoux to him one day, 'of any man in your neighbourhood of the name of Harris?'

'There is an old fellow of that name lives not far from my father's place,' said George. 'We never have had much intercourse with him, though.'

'He is a large slave-owner, I believe,' said Madame de Thoux, with a manner which seemed to betray more interest than she was exactly willing to show.

'He is,' said George, looking rather surprised at her manner.

'Did you ever know of his having – perhaps you may have heard of his having a mulatto boy, named George?'

'Oh, certainly – George Harris – I know him well; he married a servant of my mother's, but has escaped now to Canada.'

'He has?' said Madame de Thoux, quickly. 'Thank God!'

George looked a surprised enquiry, but said nothing.

Madame de Thoux leaned her head on her hand, and burst into tears. 'He is my brother!' she said.

'Madame!' said George, with a strong accent of surprise.

'Yes,' said Madame de Thoux, lifting her head, proudly, and wiping her tears; 'Mr Shelby, George Harris is my brother!'

'I am perfectly astonished,' said George, pushing back his chair a pace or two, and looking at Madame de Thoux.

'I was sold to the South when he was a boy,' said she. 'I was bought by a good and generous man. He took me with him to the West Indies, set me free, and married me. It is but lately that he died; and I was coming up to Kentucky to see if I could find and redeem my brother.'

'I have heard him speak of a sister Emily, that was sold South,' said George.

'Yes, indeed! I am the one,' said Madame de Thoux; 'tell me what sort of a –'

'A very fine young man,' said George, 'notwithstanding the curse of slavery that lay on him. He sustained a first rate-character, both for intelligence and principle. I know, you see,' he said, 'because he married in our family.'

'What sort of a girl?' said Madame de Thoux, eagerly.

'A treasure,' said George. 'A beautiful, intelligent, amiable girl. Very pious. My mother had brought her up, and trained her as carefully, almost, as a daughter. She could read and write, embroider and sew beautifully; and was a beautiful singer.'

'Was she born in your house?' said Madame de Thoux.

'No. Father bought her once, in one of his trips to New Orleans, and brought her up as a present to mother. She was about eight or nine years old, then. Father would never tell mother what he gave for her; but, the other day, in looking over his old papers, we came across the bill of sale. He paid an extravagant sum for her, to be sure – I suppose, on account of her extraordinary beauty.'

George sat with his back to Cassy, and did not see the absorbed expression of her countenance as he was giving these details.

At this point in the story she touched his arm, and, with a face perfectly white with interest, said, 'Do you know the names of the people he bought her of?'

'A man of the name of Simmons, I think, was the principal in the transaction – at least, I think that was the name on the bill of sale.'

'Oh, my God!' said Cassy, and fell insensible on the floor of the cabin.

George was wide awake now, and so was Madame de Thoux. Though neither of them could conjecture what was the cause of

Cassy's fainting, still they made all the tumult which is proper in such cases – George upsetting a wash-pitcher, and breaking two tumblers, in the warmth of his humanity; and various ladies in the cabin, hearing that somebody had fainted, crowded the stateroom door, and kept out all the air they possibly could; so that, on the whole, everything was done that could be expected.

Poor Cassy! when she recovered, turned her face to the wall, and wept and sobbed like a child – perhaps, mother, you can tell what she was thinking of! Perhaps you cannot – but she felt as sure, in that hour, that God had had mercy on her, and that she should see her daughter – as she did months afterwards – when – but we anticipate.

CHAPTER XLIII

Results[298]

The rest of our story is soon told. George Shelby, interested, as any other young man might be, by the romance of the incident, no less than by feelings of humanity, was at pains to send to Cassy the bill of sale of Eliza; whose date and name all corresponded with her own knowledge of facts, and left no doubt upon her mind as to the identity of her child. It remained now only for her to trace out the path of the fugitives.

Madame de Thoux and she, thus drawn together by the singular coincidence of their fortunes, proceeded immediately to Canada, and began a tour of enquiry among the stations, where the numerous fugitives from slavery are located. At Amherstberg they found the missionary with whom George and Eliza had taken shelter on their first arrival in Canada, and through him were enabled to trace the family to Montreal.

George and Eliza had now been five years free. George had found constant occupation in the shop of a worthy machinist, where he had been earning a competent support for his family, which, in the mean time, had been increased by the addition of a daughter.

Little Harry a fine bright boy had been put to a good school, and was making rapid proficiency in knowledge.

The worthy pastor of the station in Amherstberg, where George had first landed, was so much interested in the statements of Madame de Thoux and Cassy, that he yielded to the solicitations of the former, to accompany them to Montreal, in their search – she bearing all the expense of the expedition.

The scene now changes to a small, neat tenement, in the outskirts of Montreal; the time, evening. A cheerful fire blazes on the hearth; a tea-table, covered with a snowy cloth, stands prepared for the evening meal. In one corner of the room was a table covered with a green cloth, where was an open writing-desk, pens, paper, and over it a shelf of well-selected books.

This was George's study. The same zeal for self-improvement, which led him to steal the much coveted arts of reading and writing, amid all the toils and discouragements of his early life, still led him to devote all his leisure time to self-cultivation.

At this present time, he is seated at the table, making notes from a volume of the family library he has been reading.

'Come, George,' says Eliza, 'you've been gone all day. Do put down that book, and let's talk, while I'm getting tea – do.'

And little Eliza seconds the effort by toddling up to her father, and trying to pull the book out of his hand, and install herself on his knee as a substitute.

'Oh, you little witch!' says George, yielding, as, in such circumstances, man always must.

'That's right,' says Eliza, as she begins to cut a loaf of bread. A little older she looks; her form a little fuller; her air more matronly than of yore; but evidently contented and happy as woman need be.

'Harry, my boy, how did you come on in that sum today?' says George, as he laid his hand on his son's head.

Harry has lost his long curls; but he can never lose those eyes and eyelashes, and that fine, bold brow, that flushes with triumph, as he answers, 'I did it, every bit of it, *myself*, father, and *nobody* helped me!'

'That's right,' says his father; 'depend on yourself, my son. You have a better chance than ever your poor father had.'

At this moment, there is a rap at the door; and Eliza goes and opens it. The delighted, 'Why – this you?' calls up her husband; and the good pastor of Amherstberg is welcomed. There are two more women with him, and Eliza asks them to sit down.

Now, if the truth must be told, the honest pastor had arranged a little programme, according to which this affair was to develop itself; and, on the way up, all had very cautiously and prudently exhorted each other not to let things out, except according to previous arrangement.

What was the good man's consternation, therefore, just as he had motioned to the ladies to be seated, and was taking out his pocket-handkerchief to wipe his mouth, so as to proceed to his introductory speech in good order, when Madame de Thoux upset the whole plan by throwing her arms around George's neck, and letting all out at once, by saying, 'Oh, George! don't you know me? I'm your sister Emily.'

Cassy had seated herself more composedly, and would have carried on her part very well, had not little Eliza suddenly appeared before her in exact shape and form, every outline and curl, just as her daughter was when she saw her last. The little thing peered up in her face; and Cassy caught her up in her arms, pressed her to her bosom, saying, what, at the moment she really believed, 'Darling, I'm your mother!'

In fact, it was a troublesome matter to do up exactly in proper order; but the good pastor, at last, succeeded in getting everybody quiet, and delivering the speech with which he had intended to open the exercises; and in which, at last, he succeeded so well that his whole audience were sobbing about him in a manner that ought to satisfy any orator, ancient or modern.

They knelt together, and the good man prayed – for there are some feelings so agitated and tumultuous, that they can find rest only by being poured into the bosom of almighty Love – and then, rising up, the new-found family embraced each other, with a holy trust in Him who, from such peril and dangers, and by such unknown ways, had brought them together.

The notebook of a missionary among the Canadian fugitives, contains truth stranger than fiction. How can it be otherwise, when a system prevails which whirls families and scatters their members, as the wind whirls and scatters the leaves of autumn? These shores of refuge, like the eternal shore, often unite again, in glad communion, hearts that for long years have mourned each other as lost. And affecting beyond expression is the earnestness with which every new arrival among them is met, if, perchance, it may bring tidings of mother, sister, wife, or child, still lost to view in the shadows of slavery.

Deeds of heroism are wrought here more than those of romance, when, defying torture and braving death itself, the fugitive voluntarily threads his way back to the terrors and perils of that dark land, that he may bring out his sister, or mother, or wife.

One young man, of whom a missionary has told us, twice recaptured, and suffering shameful stripes for his heroism, had escaped again; and in a letter which we heard read, tells his friends that he is going back a third time, that he may, at last, bring away his sister. My good sir, is this man a hero, or a criminal? Would not you do as much for your sister? And can you blame him?

But to return to our friends, whom we left wiping their eyes and recovering themselves from too great and sudden a joy. They are now seated around the social board, and are getting decidedly companionable; only that Cassy, who keeps little Eliza on her lap, occasionally squeezes the little thing, in a manner that rather astonishes her, and obstinately refuses to have her mouth stuffed with cake to the extent the little one desires, alleging, what the child rather wonders at, that she has got something better than cake, and doesn't want it.

And, indeed, in two or three days, such a change has passed over Cassy that our readers would scarcely know her. The despairing, haggard expression of her face had given way to one of gentle trust. She seemed to sink at once, into the bosom of the family, and take the little ones into her heart as something for which it long had waited. Indeed, her love seemed to flow more naturally to the little Eliza than to her own daughter; for she was the exact image and body of the child whom she had lost. The little one was a flowery bond between mother and daughter, through whom grew up acquaintanceship and affection. Eliza's steady, consistent piety, regulated by the constant reading of the sacred word, made her a proper guide for the shattered and wearied mind of her mother. Cassy yielded at once, and with her whole soul, to every good influence, and became a devout and tender Christian.

After a day or two, Madame de Thoux told her brother more particularly of her affairs. The death of her husband had left her an ample fortune, which she generously offered to share with the family. When she asked George what way she could best apply it for him, he answered, 'Give me an education, Emily; that has always been my heart's desire. Then, I can do all the rest.'

On mature deliberation, it was decided that the whole family should go, for some years, to France; whither they sailed, carrying Emmeline with them.

The good looks of the latter won the affection of the first mate of the vessel; and, shortly after entering the port, she became his wife.

George remained four years at a French university, and, applying himself with an unintermitted zeal, obtained a very thorough education.

Political troubles in France at last led the family again to seek an asylum in this country.[299]

George's feelings and views, as an educated man, may be best expressed in a letter to one of his friends.

> I feel somewhat at a loss, as to my future course. True, as you have said to me, I might mingle in the circles of the whites, in this country, my shade of colour is so slight, and that of my wife and family scarce perceptible. Well, perhaps, on sufferance, I might. But, to tell you the truth, I have no wish to.
>
> My sympathies are not for my father's race, but for my mother's. To him I was no more than a fine dog or horse; to my poor heartbroken mother I was a *child*; and, though I never saw her, after the cruel sale that separated us till she died, yet I *know* she always loved me dearly. I know it by my own heart. When I think of all she suffered, of my own early sufferings, of the distresses and struggles of my heroic wife, of my sister, sold in the New Orleans slave-market – though I hope to have no unchristian sentiments, yet I may be excused for saying I have no wish to pass for an American, or to identify myself with them.
>
> It is with the oppressed, enslaved African race that I cast in my lot; and, if I wished anything, I would wish myself two shades darker, rather than one lighter.
>
> The desire and yearning of my soul is for an African *nationality*. I want a people that shall have a tangible, separate existence of its own; and where am I to look for it? Not in Haiti; for in Haiti they had nothing to start with. A stream cannot rise above its fountain. The race that formed the character of the Haitians[300] was a worn-out, effeminate one; and, of course, the subject race will be centuries in rising to anything.
>
> Where, then, shall I look? On the shores of Africa I see a republic[301] – a republic formed of picked men, who, by energy and self-educating force, have, in many cases, individually, raised themselves above a condition of slavery. Having gone through a preparatory stage of feebleness, this republic has at last become an acknowledged nation on the face of the earth – acknowledged by both France and England. There it is my wish to go, and find myself a people.
>
> I am aware, now, that I shall have you all against me; but, before you strike, hear me. During my stay in France, I have followed up, with intense interest, the history of my people in America. I have noted the struggle between Abolitionist and Colonisationist, and have received some impressions, as a distant spectator, which could never have occurred to me as a participator.

I grant that this Liberia may have subserved all sorts of purposes, by being played off, in the hands of our oppressors, against us.[302] Doubtless the scheme may have been used, in unjustifiable ways, as a means of retarding our emancipation. But the question to me is, Is there not a God above all man's schemes? May He not have overruled their designs, and founded for us a nation by them?

In these days, a nation is born in a day. A nation starts now with all the great problems of republican life and civilisation wrought out to its hand; it has not to discover, but only to apply. Let us, then, all take hold together, with all our might, and see what we can do with this new enterprise, and the whole splendid continent of Africa opens before us and our children. *Our nation* shall roll the tide of civilisation and Christianity along its shores, and plant there mighty republics, that, growing with the rapidity of tropical vegetation, shall be for all coming ages.

Do you say that I am deserting my enslaved brethren? I think not. If I forget them one hour, one moment of my life, so may God forget me! But, what can I do for them here? Can I break their chains? No, not as an individual; but, let me go and form part of a nation which shall have a voice in the councils of nations, and then we can speak. A nation has a right to argue, remonstrate, implore, and present the cause of its race, which an individual has not.

If Europe ever becomes a grand council of free nations – as I trust in God it will – if there serfdom, and all unjust and oppressive social inequalities, are done away; and if they, as France and England have done, acknowledge our position – then, in the great congress of nations, we will make our appeal, and present the cause of our enslaved and suffering race; and it cannot be that free, enlightened America, will not then desire to wipe from her escutcheon that bar sinister which disgraces her among nations, and is as truly a curse to her as to the enslaved.

But, you will tell me, our race have equal rights to mingle in the American republic as the Irishman, the German, the Swede. Granted, they have. We *ought* to be free to meet and mingle – to rise by our individual worth, without any consideration of caste or colour; and they who deny us this right are false to their own professed principles of human equality. We ought, in particular, to be allowed *here*. We have *more* than the rights of common men – we have the claim of an injured race for reparation. But, then, *I do not want it*; I want a country, a nation, of my own.[303] I think that the African race has peculiarities yet to be unfolded in the light of civilisation and Christianity, which, if not the same with those of the Anglo-Saxon, may prove to be, morally, of an even higher type.

To the Anglo-Saxon race has been entrusted the destinies of the world, during its pioneer period of struggle and conflict. To that mission its stern, inflexible, energetic elements, were well adapted; but, as a Christian, I look for another era to arise. On its borders I trust we stand; and the throes that now convulse the nations are, to my hope, but the birth-pangs of an hour of universal peace and brotherhood.

I trust that the development of Africa is to be essentially a Christian one. If not a dominant and commanding race, they are, at least, an affectionate, magnanimous, and forgiving one. Having been called in the furnace of injustice and oppression, they have need to bind closer to their hearts that sublime doctrine of love and forgiveness through which alone they are to conquer, which it is to be their mission to spread over the continent of Africa.

In myself, I confess, I am feeble for this – full half the blood in my veins is the hot and hasty Saxon; but I have an eloquent preacher of the Gospel ever by my side, in the person of my beautiful wife. When I wander, her gentler spirit ever restores me, and keeps before my eyes the Christian calling and mission of our race. As a Christian patriot, as a teacher of Christianity, I go to *my country* – my chosen, my glorious Africa! – and to her, in my heart. I sometimes apply those splendid words of prophecy, "Whereas thou hast been forsaken and hated, so that no man went through thee; I will make thee an eternal excellence, a joy of many generations!"[304]

You will call me an enthusiast: you will tell me that I have not well considered what I am undertaking. But I have considered, and counted the cost. I go to *Liberia*, not as to an Elysium[305] of romance, but as to *a field of work*. I expect to work with both hands – to work *hard*; to work against all sorts of difficulties and discouragements; and to work till I die. This is what I go for; and in this I am quite sure I shall not be disappointed.

Whatever you may think of my determination, do not divorce me from your confidence; and think that, in whatever I do, I act with a heart wholly given to my people.

GEORGE HARRIS

George, with his wife, children, sister and mother, embarked for Africa, some few weeks after. If we are not mistaken, the world will yet hear from him there.

Of our other characters we have nothing very particular to write, except a word relating to Miss Ophelia and Topsy, and a farewell chapter, which we shall dedicate to George Shelby.

Miss Ophelia took Topsy home to Vermont with her, much to the surprise of that grave deliberative body whom a New Englander recognises under the term '*Our folks*'. 'Our folks', at first, thought it an odd and unnecessary addition to their well-trained domestic establishment; but, so thoroughly efficient was Miss Ophelia in her conscientious endeavour to do her duty by her *élève*,[306] that the child rapidly grew in grace and in favour with the family and neighbourhood. At the age of womanhood she was, by her own request, baptised, and became a member of the Christian Church in the place; and showed so much intelligence, activity and zeal, and desire to do good in the world, that she was at last recommended, and approved, as a missionary to one of the stations in Africa; and we have heard that the same activity and ingenuity which, when a child, made her so multiform and restless in her developments, is now employed, in a safer and wholesomer manner, in teaching the children of her own country.

PS It will be a satisfaction to some mother also to state that some enquiries which were set on foot by Madame de Thoux have resulted recently in the discovery of Cassy's son. Being a young man of energy, he had escaped some years before his mother, and been received and educated by friends of the oppressed in the North. He will soon follow his family to Africa.[307]

CHAPTER XLIV

The Liberator

GEORGE SHELBY had written to his mother merely a line, stating the day that she might expect him home. Of the death scene of his old friend he had not the heart to write. He had tried several times, and only succeeded in half-choking himself; and invariably finished by tearing up the paper, wiping his eyes, and rushing somewhere to get quiet.

There was a pleased bustle all through the Shelby mansion that day in expectation of the arrival of young Mas'r George.

Mrs Shelby was seated in her comfortable parlour, where a cheerful hickory fire was dispelling the chill of the late autumn evening. A supper table, glittering with plate and cut glass, was set out, on whose arrangements our former friend, old Chloe, was presiding.

Arrayed in a new calico dress, with clean, white apron, and high, well-starched turban, her black polished face glowing with satisfaction, she lingered, with needless punctiliousness, around the arrangements of the table, merely as an excuse for talking a little to her mistress.

'Laws, now! won't it look natural to him?' she said. 'Thar – I set his plate just whar he likes it – round by the fire. Mas'r George allers wants de warm seat. Oh, go way! Why didn't Sally get out de *best* teapot – de little new one, Mas'r George got for missis, Christmas? I'll have it out! And missis has heard from Mas'r George?' she said, enquiringly.

'Yes, Chloe; but only a line, just to say he would be home tonight, if he could – that's all.'

'Didn't say nothin' 'bout my old man, s'pose?' said Chloe, still fidgeting with the teacups.

'No, he didn't. He did not speak of anything, Chloe. He said he would tell all, when he got home.'

'Jes like Mas'r George; he's allers so ferce for tellin' everything hisself. I allers minded dat ar in Mas'r George. Don't see, for my part, how white people gen'lly can bar to hev to write things much as they do – writin's such slow, oneasy kind o' work.'

Mrs Shelby smiled.

'I'm a thinkin' my old man won't know de boys and de baby. Lor'! she's de biggest gal, now, good she is, too, and peart, Polly is. She's out to the house, now, watchin' de hoe-cake. I's got jist de very pattern my old man liked so much, a-bakin'. Jist sich as I gin him the mornin' he was took off. Lord bless us! how I felt, dat ar morning!'

Mrs Shelby sighed, and felt a heavy weight on her heart at this allusion. She had felt uneasy, ever since she received her son's letter, lest something should prove to be hidden behind the veil of silence which he had drawn.

'Missis has got dem bills?' said Chloe, anxiously.

'Yes, Chloe.'

' 'Cause I wants to show my old man dem very bills de *perfectioner* gave me. "And," says he, "Chloe, I wish you'd stay longer." "Thank you, mas'r," says I, "I would, only my old man's coming home, and missis, she can't do without me no longer." There's jist what I telled him. Berry nice man, dat Mas'r Jones was.'

Chloe had pertinaciously insisted that the very bills in which her wages had been paid should be preserved to show to her husband, in memorial of her capability; and Mrs Shelby had readily consented to humour her in the request.

'He won't know Polly – my old man won't. Laws, it's five year since they tuck him! She was a baby den – couldn't but jist stand. Remember how tickled he used to be, 'cause she would keep a fallin' over, when she sot out to walk. Laws a me!'

The rattling of wheels now was heard.

'Mas'r George!' said Aunt Chloe, starting to the window.

Mrs Shelby ran to the entry door, and was folded in the arms of her son. Aunt Chloe stood anxiously straining her eyes out into the darkness.

'O *poor* Aunt Chloe!' said George, stopping compassionately, and taking her hard black hand between both his; 'I'd have given all my fortune to have brought him with me, but he's gone to a better country.'

There was a passionate exclamation from Mrs Shelby, but Aunt Chloe said nothing.

The party entered the supper-room. The money of which Chloe was so proud was still lying on the table.

'Thar,' said she, gathering it up, and holding it, with a trembling hand, to her mistress, 'don't never want to see nor hear on't again. Jist as I knew 'twould be – sold, and murdered on dem ar' old plantations!'

Chloe turned, and was walking proudly out of the room. Mrs Shelby followed her softly, and took one of her hands, drew her down into a chair, and sat down by her.

'My poor, good Chloe!' said she.

Chloe leaned her head on her mistress' shoulder, and sobbed out, 'Oh, missis! 'scuse me, my heart's broke – dat's all!'

'I know it is,' said Mrs Shelby, as her tears fell fast; 'and *I* cannot heal it, but Jesus can. He healeth the broken hearted, and bindeth up their wounds.'

There was a silence for some time, and all wept together. At last, George, sitting down beside the mourner, took her hand, and, with simple pathos, repeated the triumphant scene of her husband's death, and his last messages of love.

About a month after this, one morning, all the servants of the Shelby estate were convened together in the great hall that ran through the house, to hear a few words from their young master.

To the surprise of all, he appeared among them with a bundle of papers in his hand, containing a certificate of freedom to everyone on the place, which he read successively, and presented, amid the sobs and tears and shouts of all present.

Many, however, pressed around him, earnestly begging him not to send them away; and, with anxious faces, tendering back their free papers.

'We don't want to be no freer than we are. We's allers had all we wanted. We don't want to leave de ole place, and mas'r and missis, and de rest!'

'My good friends,' said George, as soon as he could get a silence, 'there'll be no need for you to leave me. The place wants as many hands to work it as it did before. We need the same about the house that we did before. But, you are now free men and free women. I shall pay you wages for your work, such as we shall agree on. The advantage is that in case of my getting in debt, or dying – things that might happen – you cannot now be taken up and sold. I expect to carry on the estate, and to teach you what, perhaps, it will take you some time to learn – how to use the rights I give you as free men and women. I expect you to be good, and willing to learn; and I trust in God that I shall be faithful, and willing to teach. And now, my friends, look up, and thank God for the blessing of freedom.'

An aged, patriarchal negro, who had grown grey and blind on the estate, now rose, and, lifting his trembling hand, said, 'Let us give thanks unto the Lord!' As all kneeled by one consent, a more touching and hearty Te Deum[308] never ascended to heaven, though borne on the peal of organ, bell and cannon, than came from that honest old heart.

On rising, another struck up a Methodist hymn, of which the burden was –

> 'The year of Jubilee is come –
> Return, ye ransomed sinners, home.'[309]

'One thing more,' said George, as he stopped the congratulations of the throng. 'You all remember our good old Uncle Tom?'

George here gave a short narration of the scene of his death, and of his loving farewell to all on the place, and added –

'It was on his grave, my friends, that I resolved, before God, that I would never own another slave while it was possible to free him; that nobody, through me, should ever run the risk of being parted from home and friends, and dying on a lonely plantation, as he died. So, when you rejoice in your freedom, think that you owe it to that good old soul, and pay it back in kindness to his wife and children. Think of your freedom, every time you see UNCLE TOM'S CABIN; and let it be a memorial to put you all in mind to follow in his steps, and be as honest, and faithful and Christian as he was.'

CHAPTER XLV

Concluding Remarks

THE WRITER HAS OFTEN BEEN ENQUIRED of, by correspondents from different parts of the country, whether this narrative is a true one; and to these enquiries she will give one general answer.[310]

The separate incidents that compose the narrative are, to a very great extent authentic, occurring, many of them, either under her own observation, or that of her personal friends. She or her friends have observed characters the counterpart of almost all that are here introduced; and many of the sayings are word for word as heard herself or reported to her.

The personal appearance of Eliza, the character ascribed to her, are sketches drawn from life. The incorruptible fidelity, piety and honesty of Uncle Tom, had more than one development to her personal knowledge.[311] Some of the most deeply tragic and romantic, some of the most terrible incidents, have also their parallel in reality. The incident of the mother's crossing the Ohio river on the ice is a well-known fact. The story of 'old Prue'[312] (Chapter XIX) was an incident that fell under the personal observation of a brother of the writer, the collecting-clerk to a large mercantile house in New Orleans. From the same source was derived the character of the planter Legree. Of him her brother thus wrote, speaking of visiting his plantation, on a collecting tour: 'He actually made me feel of his fist, which was like a blacksmith's hammer, or a nodule of iron, telling me that it was "calloused with knocking down niggers". When I left the plantation I drew a long breath, and felt as if I had escaped from an ogre's den.'

That the tragical fate of Tom, also, has too many times had its parallel, there are living witnesses, all over our land, to testify. Let it be remembered that in all Southern States it is a principle of jurisprudence that no person of coloured lineage can testify in a suit against a white, and it will be easy to see that such a case may occur wherever there is a man whose passions outweigh his interests, and a slave who has manhood or principle enough to resist his will. There is, actually, nothing to protect the slave's life but the *character* of the master. Facts too shocking to be contemplated occasionally force their way to the public ear, and the comment that one often hears made on them is more shocking than the thing itself. It is said, 'Very likely such cases may now and then occur, but they are no sample of general practice.' If the laws of New England were so arranged that a master could *now and then* torture an apprentice to death, without a possibility of being brought to justice, would it be received with equal composure? Would it be said, 'These cases are rare, and no samples of general practice'? This injustice is an *inherent* one in the slave system, it cannot exist without it.

The public and shameless sale of beautiful mulatto and quadroon girls has acquired a notoriety from the incidents following the capture of the *Pearl*. We extract the following from the speech of Hon. Horace Mann,[313] one of the legal counsel for the defendants in that case. He says: 'In that company of seventy-six persons, who attempted, in 1848, to escape from the District of Columbia in the schooner *Pearl*, and whose officers I assisted in defending, there were several young and healthy girls, who had those peculiar attractions of form and feature which connoisseurs prize so highly. Elizabeth Russel was one of them. She immediately fell into the slave-trader's fangs, and was doomed for the New Orleans market. The hearts of those that saw her were touched with pity for her fate. They offered eighteen hundred dollars to redeem her; and some there were who offered to give that would not have much left after the gift; but the fiend of a slave-trader was inexorable. She was despatched to New Orleans; but, when about halfway there, God had mercy on her, and smote her with death. There were two girls named Edmundson[314] in the same company. When about to be sent to the same market, an elder sister went to the shambles[315] to plead with the wretch who owned them, for the love of God to spare his victims. He bantered her, telling what fine dresses and fine furniture they would have. "Yes," she said, "that may do very well in this life, but what will become of them in the next?" They, too, were sent to New Orleans; but were afterwards redeemed, at an enormous ransom, and brought back.' Is it not plain from this, that the histories of Emmeline and Cassy may have many counterparts?

Justice, too, obliges the author to state that the fairness of mind and generosity attributed to St Clare are not without a parallel, as the following anecdote will show. A few years since, a young Southern gentleman was in Cincinnati, with a favourite servant, who had been his personal attendant from a boy. The young man took advantage of this opportunity to secure his own freedom, and fled to the protection of a Quaker, who was quite noted in affairs of this kind. The owner was exceedingly indignant. He had always treated the slave with such indulgence and his confidence in his affection was such that he believed he must have been practised upon to induce him to revolt from him. He visited the Quaker, in high anger; but being possessed of uncommon candour and fairness, was soon quieted by his arguments and representations. It was a side of the subject which he never had heard – never had thought on; and he immediately told the Quaker that, if his slave would, to his own face, say that it was his desire to be free, he would liberate him. An interview was forthwith procured, and Nathan was asked by his young master whether he had ever had any reason to complain of his treatment, in any respect.

'No, mas'r,' said Nathan; 'you've always been good to me.'

'Well, then, why do you want to leave me?'

'Mas'r may die, and then who get me? – I'd rather be a free man.'

After some deliberation, the young master replied, 'Nathan, in your place, I think I should feel very much so, myself. You are free.'[316]

He immediately made him out free papers; deposited a sum of money in the hands of the Quaker, to be judiciously used in assisting him to start in life, and left a very sensible and kind letter of advice to the young man. That letter was for some time in the writer's hands.

The author hopes she has done justice to that nobility, generosity, and humanity, which in many cases characterise individuals at the South. Such instances save us from utter despair of our kind. But she asks any person, who knows the world, are such characters *common* anywhere?

For many years of her life, the author avoided all reading upon or allusion to the subject of slavery, considering it as too painful to be enquired into, and one which advancing light and civilisation would certainly live down. But, since the legislative act of 1850, when she heard, with perfect surprise and consternation, Christian and humane people actually recommending the remanding of escaped fugitives into slavery, as a duty binding on good citizens – when she heard on all hands, from kind, compassionate and estimable people, in the free states of the North, deliberations and discussions as to what Christian duty could be on this head – she could only think these men and Christians cannot know what slavery is; if they did, such a question could never be open for discussion. And from this arose a desire to exhibit it in a *living dramatic reality*. She has endeavoured to show it fairly, in its best and its worst phases. In its *best* aspect, she has, perhaps, been successful; but, oh! who shall say what yet remains untold in that valley and shadow of death that lies the other side?

To you, generous, noble-minded men and women, of the South – you, whose virtue, and magnanimity, and purity of character, are the greater for the severer trial it has encountered – to you is her appeal. Have you not, in your own secret souls, in your own private conversings, felt that there are woes and evils in this accursed system far beyond what are here shadowed, or can be shadowed? Can it be otherwise? Is *man* ever a creature to be trusted with wholly irresponsible power? And does not the slave system, by denying the slave all legal right of testimony, make every individual owner an irresponsible despot? Can anybody fail to make the inference what the practical result will be? If there is, as we admit, a public sentiment among you, men of honour, justice and humanity, is there not also another kind of public senti-ment among the ruffian, the brutal and debased? And cannot the ruffian, the brutal, the debased, by slave law, own just as many slaves as the best and purest? Are the honourable, the just, the high-minded and compassionate, the majority anywhere in this world?

The slave-trade is now, by American law, considered as piracy. But a slave-trade, as systematic as ever was carried on on the coast of Africa, is an inevitable attendant and result of American slavery. And its heart-break and its horrors, *can* they be told?

The writer has given only a faint shadow, a dim picture, of the anguish and despair that are, at this very moment, riving thousands of hearts, shattering thousands of families, and driving a helpless and sensitive race to frenzy and despair. There are those living who know the mothers whom this accursed traffic has driven to the murder of their children; and themselves seeking in death a shelter from woes more dreaded than death. Nothing of tragedy can be written, can be spoken, can be conceived, that equals the frightful reality of scenes daily and hourly acting on our shores, beneath the shadow of American law, and the shadow of the cross of Christ.

And now, men and women of America, is this a thing to be trifled with, apologised for, and passed over in silence? Farmers of Massachu-setts, of New Hampshire, of Vermont, of Connecticut, who read this book by the blaze of your winter-evening fire – strong-hearted, generous sailors and ship-owners of Maine – is this a thing for you to countenance and encourage? Brave and generous men of New York, farmers of rich and joyous Ohio, and ye of the wide prairie states, answer, is this a thing for you to protect and countenance? And you, mothers of America – you, who have learned, by the cradles of your own children, to love and feel for all mankind, by the sacred love you bear your child; by your joy in his beautiful, spotless infancy; by the motherly pity and tenderness with which you guide his growing years; by the anxieties of his education; by the prayers you breathe for his soul's eternal good – I beseech you, pity the mother who has all your affections, and not one legal right to protect, guide, or educate, the child of her bosom! By the sick hour of your child; by those dying eyes, which you can never forget; by those last cries, that wrung your heart when you could neither help nor save; by the desolation of that empty cradle, that silent nursery, I beseech you, pity those mothers that are constantly made childless by the American slave-trade! And say, mothers of America, is this a thing to be defended, sympathised with, passed over in silence?

Do you say that the people of the free states have nothing to do with it, and can do nothing? Would to God this were true! But it is not true. The people of the free states have defended, encouraged, and participated; and are more guilty for it, before God, than the South, in that they have *not* the apology of education or custom.

If the mothers of the free states had all felt as they should, in times past, the sons of the free states would not have been the holders, and proverbially, the hardest masters of slaves; the sons of the free states would not have connived at the extension of slavery in our national body; the sons of the free states would not, as they do, trade the souls and bodies of men as an equivalent to money in their mercantile dealings. There are multitudes of slaves temporarily owned and sold again, by merchants in Northern cities; and shall the whole guilt or obloquy of slavery fall only on the South?

Northern men, Northern mothers, Northern Christians, have something more to do than denounce their brethren at the South; they have to look to the evil among themselves.

But, what can any individual do? Of that every individual can judge. There is one thing that every individual can do, they can see to it that *they feel right.* An atmosphere of sympathetic influence encircles every human being; and the man or woman who *feels* strongly, healthily, and justly, on the great interests of humanity, is a constant benefactor to the human race. See, then, to your sympathies in this matter! Are they in harmony with the sympathies of Christ? or are they swayed and perverted by the sophistries of worldly policy?

Christian men and women of the North; still further, you have another power; you can *pray!* Do you believe in prayer? or has it become an indistinct apostolic tradition? You pray for the heathen abroad, pray also for the heathen at home. And pray for those distressed Christians whose whole chance of religious improvement is an accident of trade and sale – from whom any adherence to the morals of Christianity is, in many cases, an impossibility, unless they have given them from above the courage and grace of martyrdom.

But, still more. On the shores of our free states are emerging the poor, shattered, broken remnants of families, men and women, escaped, by miraculous providences, from the surges of slavery, feeble in knowledge, and, in many cases, infirm in moral constitution, from a system which confounds and confuses every principle of Christianity and morality. They come to seek a refuge among you; they come to seek education, knowledge, Christianity.

What do you owe to these poor unfortunates, O Christians? Does not every American Christian owe to the African race some effort at reparation for the wrongs that the American nation has brought upon them? Shall the doors of churches and school-houses be shut upon them? Shall states arise and shake them out? Shall the Church of Christ hear in silence the taunt that is thrown at them, and shrink away from the helpless hand that they stretch out; and, by her silence, encourage the cruelty that would chase them from our borders? If it must be so, it will be a mournful spectacle. If it must be so, the country will have reason to tremble, when it remembers that the fate of nations is in the hands of One who is very pitiful, and of tender compassion.

Do you say, 'We don't want them here; let them go to Africa?'

That the providence of God has provided a refuge in Africa, is, indeed, a great and noticeable fact; but that is no reason why the Church of Christ should throw off that responsibility to this outcast race which her profession demands of her.

To fill up Liberia with an ignorant, inexperienced, half-barbarised race, just escaped from the chains of slavery, would be only to prolong for ages the period of struggle and conflict which attends the inception of new enterprises. Let the Church of the North receive these poor sufferers in the spirit of Christ; receive them to the educating advantages of Christian republican society and schools, until they have attained to somewhat of a moral and intellectual maturity, and then assist them in their passage to those shores where they may put in practice the lessons they have learned in America.

There is a body of men at the North, comparatively small, who have been doing this; and, as the result, this country has already seen examples of men, formerly slaves, who have rapidly acquired property, reputation, and education. Talent has been developed, which, considering the circumstances, is certainly remarkable; and for moral traits of honesty, kindness, tenderness of feeling, for heroic efforts and self-denials, endured for the ransom of brethren and friends yet in slavery, they have been remarkable to a degree that, considering the influence under which they were born is surprising.

The writer has lived, for many years, on the frontier-line of slave states, and has had great opportunities of observation among those who formerly were slaves. They have been in her family as servants; and, in default of any other school to receive them, she has, in many cases, had them instructed in a family school, with her own children. She has also the testimony of missionaries, among the fugitives in Canada in coincidence with her own experience; and her deductions, with regard to the capabilities of the race, are encouraging in the highest degree.

The first desire of the emancipated slave, generally, is for *education*. There is nothing that they are not willing to give or do to have their children instructed; and, so far as the writer has observed herself, or taken the testimony of teachers among them, they are remarkably intelligent and quick to learn. The results of schools founded for them by benevolent individuals in Cincinnati fully establish this.[317]

The author gives the following statement of facts, on the authority of Professor C. E. Stowe,[318] then of Lane Seminary, Ohio, with regard to emancipated slaves, now resident in Cincinnati; given to show the capability of the race, even without any very particular assistance or encouragement.

The initial letters alone are given. They are all residents of Cincinnati.

'B—. Furniture maker; twenty years in the city; worth ten thousand dollars, all his own earnings; a Baptist.

'C—. Full black; stolen from Africa; sold in New Orleans; been free fifteen years; paid for himself six hundred dollars; a farmer; owns several farms in Indiana; Presbyterian; probably worth fifteen or twenty thousand dollars, all earned by himself.

'K—. Full black; dealer in real estate; worth thirty thousand dollars; about forty years old; free six years; paid eighteen hundred dollars for his family; member of the Baptist church; received a legacy from his master, which he has taken good care of, and increased.

'G—. Full black; coal dealer; about thirty years old; worth eighteen thousand dollars; paid for himself twice, being once defrauded to the amount of sixteen hundred dollars; made all his money by his own efforts – much of it while a slave, hiring his time of his master, and doing business for himself; a fine, gentlemanly fellow.

'W—. Three-fourths black; barber and waiter; from Kentucky; nineteen years free; paid for self and family over three thousand dollars;

worth twenty thousand dollars, all his own earnings; deacon in the Baptist church.

'G. D—. Three-fourths black; whitewasher; from Kentucky; nine years free; paid fifteen hundred dollars for self and family; recently died, aged sixty; worth six thousand dollars.'

Professor Stowe says, 'With all these, except G—, I have been, for some years, personally acquainted, and make my statements from my own knowledge.'

The writer well remembers an aged coloured woman, who was employed as a washerwoman in her father's family. The daughter of this woman married a slave. She was a remarkably active and capable young woman, and, by her industry and thrift, and the most persevering self-denial, raised nine hundred dollars for her husband's freedom, which she paid, as she raised it, into the hands of his master. She yet wanted a hundred dollars of the price when he died. She never recovered any of the money.

These are but few facts among multitudes which might be adduced to show the self-denial, energy, patience, and honesty, which the slave has exhibited in a state of freedom.

And let it be remembered that these individuals have thus bravely succeeded in conquering for themselves comparative wealth and social position in the face of every disadvantage and discouragement. The coloured man, by the law of Ohio, cannot be a voter,[319] and, till within a few years, was even denied the right of testimony in legal suits with the white. Nor are these instances confined to the State of Ohio. In all states of the Union we see men, but yesterday burst from the shackles of slavery, who, by a self-educating force, which cannot be too much admired, have risen to highly respectable stations in society. Pennington, among clergymen, Douglas and Ward[320] among editors, are well known instances.

If this persecuted race, with every discouragement and disadvantage, have done thus much, how much more they might do, if the Christian Church would act towards them in the spirit of her Lord!

This is an age of the world when nations are trembling and convulsed.[321] A mighty influence is abroad, surging and heaving the world, as with an earthquake. And is America safe? Every nation that carries in its bosom great and unredressed injustice has in it the elements of this last convulsion.

For what is this mighty influence thus rousing in all nations and languages those groanings that cannot be uttered for man's freedom and equality?

O Church of Christ, read the signs of the times! Is not this power the spirit of HIM whose kingdom is yet to come, and whose will is to be done on earth as it is in heaven?

But who may abide the day of his appearing? 'For that day shall burn as an oven: and he shall appear as a swift witness against those that oppress the hireling in his wages, the widow and the fatherless, and that *turn aside the stranger in his right*: and he shall break in pieces the oppressor.'[322]

Are not these dread words for a nation bearing in her bosom so mighty an injustice? Christians! every time that you pray that the kingdom of Christ may come, can you forget that prophecy associates, in dread fellowship, the *day of vengeance* with the year of his redeemed?

A day of grace is yet held out to us. Both North and South have been guilty before God; and the *Christian Church* has a heavy account to answer. Not by combining together, to protect injustice and cruelty, and making a common capital of sin, is this Union to be saved – but by repentance, justice and mercy; for, not surer is the eternal law by which the millstone sinks in the ocean, than that stronger law, by which injustice and cruelty shall bring on nations the wrath of Almighty God!

NOTES

I strongly recommend readers of this edition to use the notes sparingly during a first reading, so as not to interrupt the flow of the novel. My notes are indebted to the annotations of Elizabeth Ammons (Norton Critical Edition) and Jean Fagin Yellin (Oxford World's Classics). All biblical references are to the Bible: Authorised King James Version, with Apocrypha (Oxford World's Classics, 1997). *Key* signifies Stowe's *A Key to Uncle Tom's Cabin* (1853). For full citations see the Bibliography, pp. xxvii–xxxi. The novel contains several references to money and the financial worth of the slaves; for a modern equivalent, we need to multiply by at least fifty.

1 (p. xxxv) *Preface*   written for the first edition (1852)

2 (p. xxxv) *good-will to man*   Luke 2:14

3 (p. xxxvi) *What personal knowledge . . . in its time*   A reference to her current work on the *Key*. 'The greater part of this material was gathered after *Uncle Tom* was published. She brought it together, not to indicate to the doubtful reader that she had been working from pre-assembled facts and drawing on documentary evidence, but rather to corroborate with data from other sources the authenticity of the scenes she had depicted' (Kirkham, p. 80).

4 (p. xxxvi) *When an enlightened . . . shores of Africa.*   Stowe supports the policy of the American Colonisation Society (founded in 1816) which renounced any intention of interfering with slavery in the United States and advocated the return of the blacks in America to Liberia in West Africa. (See Goodman, pp.11–25.) In 1834, Mrs Stowe witnessed at first hand the famous 'Lane Debates', when Lane Seminary in Cincinnati (whose first president was her father, Lyman Beecher) was almost destroyed by an eighteen-day forum, organised by Theodore Weld, over the respective merits of the abolitionist and colonisationist positions. Lyman Beecher tried in vain to argue that he was both an abolitionist and a colonisationist. The students led by Weld voted overwhelmingly for immediate abolition and most of them walked out of Lane and went to the rival, more militant, Oberlin College. By 1851, Colonisation was a marginalised and largely redundant programme.

5 (p. xxxvi) *Egypt to the Israelites* The latter were enslaved in Egypt by Pharaoh until Moses delivered them (Exodus 1–14). Both the first Puritan settlers and later the African-American slaves drew heavily upon this 'type' story as a prefigurement and endorsement of their own liberation. Stowe recruits both the biblical analogy and 'Him' to support Colonisation.

6 (p. xxxvi) *He shall not fail . . . His sight* See Isaiah 42:4 and Psalm 72:12, 14.

7 (p. 3) *Grammar* Lindley Murray's popular *English Grammar* (first published 1795)

8 (p. 4) *camp-meeting* held outdoors (often in tents) by evangelical Christian sects and often lasting for several days

9 (p. 4) *Orleans* New Orleans, the major southern port, situated in south-east Louisiana where the Mississippi River enters the Gulf of Mexico

10 (p. 4) *Cincinnati* a city in south-west Ohio on the Ohio River across from Covington, Kentucky. Lying on the Mason-Dixon line, on the border between slave and free territories, it was also in the mid-nineteenth century the gateway to the West. Stowe lived there from 1832 to 1849.

11 (p. 4) *Canada* In 1834, as in Great Britain, slavery had been abolished in Canada. Especially after the passage of the Fugitive Slave Law (1850), which gave slave-owners the right to pursue and reclaim fugitives, it became for slaves their nearest point of refuge.

12 (p. 4) *Ah . . . I couldn't!* In her *Key* Stowe cites *The Life of Josiah Henson* (1849) as the source of this anecdote. See Kirkham for an entertaining and thorough account of the ways Henson subsequently exploited his claim to be the original Uncle Tom (pp. 88–98).

13 (p. 4) *quadroon* a person of one-quarter African heritage

14 (p. 5) *Jim Crow* derogatory stereotype for a black person, especially a clown, singer or minstrel, derived from the comic caricature performed by the white minstrel T. D. Rice, who performed in black face. From the 1880s through to the 1960s the laws enforcing racial segregation and black disenfranchisement were called 'Jim Crow' laws.

15 (p. 6) *neatest* In the first of only nine pages of holograph (i.e. in Stowe's hand), the dress is 'of the closest possible fit' (Kirkham, p. 204), adding an even more unsavoury dimension to Haley's 'gaze'.

16 (p. 7) *Wilberforce*   William Wilberforce (1759–1833), the English statesman and most prominent leader of the British movement to abolish slavery

17 (p. 8) *Natchez*   a city in south-west Mississippi on the river

18 (p. 10) *oft-fabled . . . and all that*   a sarcastic reference to Southern writers who idealised plantation life and fostered legends of the chivalry and gallantry of the Old South; such as, perhaps, John Pendleton Kennedy (1795–1870), William Alexander Carothers (1802–46) and William Gilmore Simms (1806–70)

19 (p. 10) *the work-stand*   a small table with draws for needlework, etc.

20 (p. 12) *bagging factory*   one that manufactures coarse fabrics such as burlap

21 (p. 12) *Whitney's cotton-gin*   In 1793, Eli Whitney (1765–1825) patented the cotton gin which mechanically separated cotton from its seeds. Stowe's note that a young coloured man was really the inventor, or first had the idea, is probably true; the patent law, of course, did not apply to slaves.

22 (p. 16) *dray-horse*   a horse used to pull a cart; still used by local breweries today

23 (p. 18) *down river*   the lower Mississippi where slave conditions were notoriously bad

24 (p. 19) *I'll be free, or I'll die*   a pointed echo of Patrick Henry's, 'I know not what course others may take; but as for me, give me liberty or death!' in a speech in Virginia Convention, 23 March 1775

25 (p. 20) *four-o'clocks*   the plant *Mirabilis Jalapa* or Marvel of Peru

26 (p. 20) *Aunt*   and Uncle were generic terms of address for older black women and men

27 (p. 20) *corn-cake*   cornmeal

28 (p. 21) *General Washington*   George Washington (1732–99), commander-in-chief of the Continental Army during the War of Independence and the first president of the United States.

29 (p. 21) *daguerreotype*   early type of photograph, produced by an impression taken upon a silver plate sensitised by iodine

30 (p. 23) *pone o' bread*   small oval loaf of cornbread

31 (p. 23) *flecky paste*   dough containing a large proportion of lard

32 (p. 24) *hornbug*   a stag beetle, June bug

33 (p. 25) *Old Virginny* Virginia, one of the original thirteen states comprising the United States

34 (p. 27) *Come, saints and sinners, hear me tell* from the Methodist hymn, also known as 'Heavenly Union'. The verse continues 'The wonders of Immanuel/Who snatch'd me from a burning hell,/ And brought my soul with him to dwell,/To dwell, in sweetest union.' Frederick Douglass ends his *Narrative* (1845) with a superb parody of this hymn written by a Methodist preacher disgusted by the morals, manners and piety of slaveholders.

35 (p. 28) *berage* usually *barége* (Fr.); a light, gauze-like fabric, or a dress made from it

36 (p. 28) *Die . . . Glory in my soul* a version of the hymn 'Die in the Field' by Samuel Wakefield: 'Firmly, brethren, firmly stand, / All united heart and hand, / One unbroken valiant band, / Dauntless, brave and true' – followed by the chorus, 'Die in the field of battle [x 3], / Glory in your soul.'

37 (p. 28) *Oh, I'm going . . . everlasting day?* A spiritual similar to 'Bound for the Promised Land': 'I am bound for the promised land [x 2], / Oh, who will come and go with me, / I am bound . . . ' etc.

38 (p. 28) *Jordan's banks . . . Canaan's fields . . . New Jerusalem* The River Jordan marked the boundary of the land promised by God to the Israelites after their flight from Egypt (Deuteronomy 11:31); Jehovah 'established my covenant with them, to give them the land of Canaan' (Exodus 6:4), the promised land, the land of freedom; and the New Jerusalem was the holy city promised to Christians after the Last Judgement (Revelation 3:12).

39 (p. 29) *Oh, Canaan . . . land of Canaan* from John Wesley's hymn 'Bound for the Land of Canaan': 'How happy is the pilgrim's lot! / I am bound for the land of Canaan.'

40 (p. 29) *Revelation* the last book of the New Testament, depicting the punishment of sinners and the reward of the redeemed

41 (p. 29) *morale* moral or mental faculties (Fr.)

42 (p. 30) *Its done!* Shelby's musing repetition of Haley's words indicates that he recalls Christ's last words on the cross: 'It is finished' (John 19:31).

43 (p. 33) *Abolitionist* Generically anybody who sought the emancipation of all slaves; but Shelby's shocked tone suggests the radical wing of the American Anti-Slavery Society founded by William

Lloyd Garrison in 1831 who advocated through his journal *The Liberator* the immediate, unconditional, uncompensated abolition of slavery. See Lowance, *Against Slavery*, pp. 92–108.

44 (p. 40) *one answer for him*   i.e. a duel

45 (p. 41) *'It's . . . a fact'*   an amusing version of, 'Not the ill wind which blows no man to good.' (2 *Henry IV* 5, 3)

46 (p. 41) *grand as Cuffee*   Cuffee or Cuffy was a name given to black men in the South; the phrase is a variant of the patronising 'proud as Cuffy', used of gaudily-dressed Africans.

47 (p. 41) *cut stick*   departed hastily

48 (p. 43) *suitor . . . St James's or Washington*   i.e. a political careerist. The Palace of St James in Westminster had been the royal residence from 1697–1837 and Washington is the capital of the United States.

49 (p. 45) *Coeur De Lion*   Richard Lion-Heart, King Richard 1 of England (1157–99)

50 (p. 51) *de novo*   anew (Latin)

51 (p. 51) *Ravelations . . . the altar*   a reference to Revelation 6 which describes the opening of the seven seals on Judgement Day by the Lamb of God (Christ): 'And when he had opened the fifth seal, I saw under the altar the souls of them that were slain for the word of God . . .' (verse 9)

52 (p. 58) *constitutional relations*   an ironic reference to the Fugitive Slave Law that made it a crime to assist runaways

53 (p. 62) *shines*   mischief

54 (p. 62) *whist*   quiet

55 (p. 62) *his doggish nature*   aptly, this is said of Satan in John Bunyan's Protestant allegory, *Pilgrim's Progress* (1678)

56 (p. 64) *justices . . . quite reasonable*   the Fugitive Slave Law empowered commissioners to investigate suspected fugitives. In her *Key*, Stowe answered charges that 'the plan for kidnapping Eliza' was a 'gross caricature' by citing the case of one of her own servants who feared that she would be kidnapped by the son of the woman who freed her. Calvin Stowe assisted in her escape (pp. 22–3).

57 (p. 65) *Shelby County*   a county in north-central Kentucky

58 (p. 66) *underground . . . Sandusky*   This city on Lake Erie, north-central Ohio, was a point of departure for fugitives, most of whom had been assisted by the 'underground railroad', an illegal system organised by abolitionists.

59 (p. 66) *Mobile*   seaport in south-west Alabama

60 (p. 67) *summerset*   somersault

61 (p. 70) *prodigal son himself*   a light-hearted reference to Christ's parable of the prodigal son (Luke 15:11–32)

62 (p. 70) *olla podrida*   a stew with a variety of ingredients (Spanish)

63 (p. 72) *vinegar upon nitre*   'As he that taketh away a garment in cold weather, and as vinegar upon nitre, so is he that singeth songs to an heavy heart' (Proverbs 25:20).

64 (p. 73) *camphor-bottle*   derived from the camphor tree, it was used to relieve colic or as a stimulant

65 (p. 78) *bombazine*   a twilled dress-material, composed of silk and worsted, cotton and worsted, or worsted alone

66 (p. 81) *Van Trompe*   According to the *Key*, the original of Van Trompe was John Van Zondt, and 'a brother of the author, with Professor Stowe, performed for the fugitive that office' performed by Senator Bird (p. 23). Cf. Note 56. In *Men of Our Times* (1868), in her essay on Salmon P. Chase, who lost the case brought by slaveholders against Van Zandt for helping escaped slaves, Stowe recorded that the fine was so heavy that the latter was ruined 'scot and lot' and died 'broken-hearted' (Kirkham, p. 112).

67 (p. 81) *Columbus*   the capital of Ohio

68 (p. 82) *And, O mother . . . has not been so*   One of Stowe's children, Samuel Charles Stowe, died in infancy of cholera in Cincinnati on 24 July 1849. Mrs Bird's grief reprises Mrs Stowe's in a letter of 2 December 1850: 'I shall never love another [child] as I did him – he was my *"summer child"* – I cannot open his little drawer of clothes now without feeling it thro my very heart – Is there a peculiar love given us for those that God wills to take from us – ' (quoted, Kirkham, p. 111).

69 (p. 83) *a little newspaper picture*   Advertisements offering rewards for the return of runaway slaves were placed in newspapers.

70 (p. 85) *Orson of a fellow*   In the nineteenth century, the French medieval romance *Valentine and Orson* (first translated into English about 1550) was rewritten as a children's story and as 'a grand melodrama in two acts'. Valentine and Orson are twin sons of a Greek king separated at birth; and Orson, raised by a bear, is eventually tamed by Valentine.

71 (p. 88) *Testament*   Bible

72 (p. 88) *lifted up her voice and wept* a common biblical phrase; see Genesis 21:16, 27:38

73 (p. 90) *That undiscovered . . . No traveller returns* i.e. death, *Hamlet* 3,1,56–7

74 (p. 91) *ball* usually wooden, used to hold fabric taut when darning socks

75 (p. 92) *dat ar old limb* of the devil; so a wicked person

76 (pp. 92–3) *Haley whipped . . . before he returned* Kirkham notes that this passage was added to the novel to account for Mr Shelby's convenient absence from this scene (p. 174).

77 (p. 94) *dollar* a dollar coin, probably silver

78 (p. 95) *'Member . . . o' yer youth* Ecclesiastes 12:1

79 (p. 97) *chapeau* hat (Fr.)

80 (p. 98) *bonhomie* goodwill (Fr.)

81 (p. 100) *free papers* certificates given to freed slaves as proof of their manumission

82 (p. 100) *feu de joie* victorious rifle salute (Fr.)

83 (p. 102) *en passant* in passing, incidentally (Fr.)

84 (p. 102) *much tumbled . . . in his mind* said of Christiana and Mercy when faced with a fierce dog (*Pilgrim's Progress*, Part II)

85 (p. 103) *Hagar . . . Onesimus* Hagar fled into the wilderness when mistreated by Sarah, Abraham's wife (Genesis 16:6–8); for Onesimus see the Epistle of Paul to Philemon 10–16.

86 (p. 103) *Let everyone . . . called* a slight misquotation of 1 Corinthians 7:20

87 (p. 104) *consent of the governed* From the Declaration of Independence of the United States (1776): 'We hold these truths to be self-evident, that all men are created equal, that they are endowed by their Creator with certain inalienable Rights, that among these are Life, Liberty, and the pursuit of happiness – that to secure these rights, Governments are instituted among Men, deriving their just powers from the consent of the governed.'

88 (p. 104) *sheriff's sale* a public sale of property conducted by a sheriff

89 (p. 109) *righteousness . . . His throne* Psalm 97:2

90 (p. 109) *In Ramah . . . comforted* a free version of Jeremiah 31:15

91 (p. 110) *We have here ... a city*　In Hebrews 13:14–16, Paul advises the Hebrews to spread the word beyond the borders of their own towns.

92 (p. 110) *despair*　At this point, Stowe cut a paragraph from the serial: 'I mention this, of course, philosophic friend, as a psychological phenomenon. Very likely it would do no such thing for you, because you are an enlightened man, and have out-grown the old myths of past centuries. But then you have Emerson's Essays and Carlisle's Miscellanies, and other productions of the latter day, suited to your advanced development' (Kirkham, p. 114). Perhaps Stowe felt that her tart, conservative critique of such liberal views would be thought gratuitous.

93 (p. 110) *Executors' Sale ... Executors*　Weld's *American Slavery as It Is* contains such documentary evidence drawn from newspapers, posters, wills, etc. In the *Key*, Stowe cites several sale notices gleaned from Southern newspapers (pp. 129–30).

94 (p. 113) *La Belle Rivière*　The Beautiful River (Fr.)

95 (p. 114) *they ... mirth*　adapted from Psalm 137:3

96 (p. 115) *Cursed be Canaan ... he be*　Genesis 9:25. Noah's curse of his son Ham, who accidentally saw him drunk and naked and then told his brothers, was a favourite text of pro-slavists who considered Africans Ham's descendants. Douglass in his *Narrative* (1845) mocks this absurd justification: 'If the lineal descendants of Ham are alone to be scripturally enslaved, it is certain that slavery at the south must be unscriptural: for thousands are ushered into this world, annually, who, like myself, owe their existence to white fathers, most frequently their own masters' (Chapter 1).

97 (p. 116) *All things ... even so unto them*　from Christ's Sermon on the Mount (Matthew 7:12).

98 (p. 116) *My friend ... judgement for this*　In her *Key*, Stowe notes that 'this was a real incident' and that she quoted verbatim (p. 48).

99 (p. 117) *a specific*　a drug that mitigates a disease

100 (p. 118) *Louisville*　a city in northern Kentucky on the Ohio River

101 (p. 122) *no evils ... social and domestic life*　Stowe's attribution of this remark to Dr Joel Parker, a Presbyterian minister, so enraged him that he threatened her with a $20,000 libel suit. Stowe dropped her footnote in later editions, but his threat was a major

inspiration for her *Key*, which amply demonstrated clerical support for the pro-slavery case.

102 (p. 122) *Man of Sorrows* Isaiah 53:3. This whole chapter was read as a prophecy of Christ's role and fate.

103 (p. 122) *the year ... come* adapted from Isaiah 63:4

104 (p. 124) *Clarksons and Wilberforces* Thomas Clarkson (1760–1846) with Wilberforce founded in 1787 the Committee to Abolish the Slave Trade. It was outlawed in 1807 and slaves were officially freed in 1834 in Britain's Caribbean colonies. In 1807 Thomas Jefferson signed an Act of Congress banning the importation of slaves from Africa into the United States. Cf. Note 16.

105 (p. 124) *The Quaker Settlement* Quakers or the Religious Society of Friends are a Christian sect that espouses non-violence and pacifism; they were prominent in the American and English abolitionist causes.

106 (p. 124) *brochetelle* usually *brocatelle* (Fr.), a stiff fabric used for tapestry and upholstery

107 (p. 125) *lisse crape* a light silk fabric

108 (p. 130) *green shores ... water* echoes of Psalm 23:2–3: 'He maketh me to lie down in green pastures: he leadeth me beside the still waters.'

109 (p. 130) *cestus* a belt or girdle for the waist, especially that of Venus, the Roman goddess of love and beauty

110 (p. 133) *A young star! ... folded* from *Don Juan* 14:43 by Lord Byron (1788–1824)

111 (p. 133) *Chateaubriand* French writer and statesman (1768–1848); author of 'Les Natchez' (1826), a description of life on the Mississippi

112 (p. 133) *come out ... earth* a reworking of 'For, behold, the Lord cometh out of his place to punish the inhabitants of the earth for their iniquity' (Isaiah 26:21)

113 (p. 134) *stately ... pleasure-grounds* an echo of the opening of Samuel Taylor Coleridge's 'Kubla Khan': 'In Xanadu did Kubla Khan/ A stately pleasure dome decree.'

114 (p. 135) *Let – not ... for – you* John 14:1–2; Jesus consoles his disciples after prophesying his own death.

115 (p. 135) *Cicero* Marcus Tullius Cicero (106–43BC), Roman statesman, philosopher and orator

116 (p. 137) *Pan*   Greek god of shepherds, imaged as a flute player with the legs of a goat

117 (p. 139) *morocco*   fine leather made from goatskin

118 (p. 142) *Huguenot*   French Protestant

119 (p. 143) *Lake Pontchartrain*   a saltwater lake in south-east Louisiana, north of New Orleans

120 (p. 144) *a mind diseased*   an apt echo of Hamlet's 'my wit's diseased' (*Hamlet*, 3, 2, 321)

121 (p. 144) *hartshorn*   smelling salts

122 (p. 145) *the large farmhouse*   Kirkham notes that the whole paragraph 'is reminiscent of Harriet's "Prize Tale" written eighteen years earlier' which described the Beecher house of her childhood in Litchfield (p. 120).

123 (p. 146) *Rollin's History, Milton's Paradise Lost . . . Scott's Family Bible*   All these books and those cited later were Stowe's old favourites from which she frequently quoted. Charles Rollins wrote *Histoire Ancienne des Egytians* (1825); *Paradise Lost* (1667) is a long epic poem by John Milton (1608–74); *Commentary on the Bible* (1788–92) is by Thomas Scott (1747–1821), the English editor and commentator.

124 (p. 146) *Morse's Atlas . . . Flint's Travels in the South and West*   Jedidiah Morse (1761–1826), an American clergyman, wrote the first geography textbook to be published in the United States, *Geography Made Easy* (1784); Timothy Flint (1780–1840), an American missionary and author, wrote *Recollections of the Last Ten Years in the Valley of the Mississippi* (1826).

125 (p. 146) *Sandwich Islands*   now known as the Hawaiian Islands

126 (p. 146) *staunch colonisationist*   See Note 4.

127 (p. 149) *tape-needle*   a needle for inserting strips of fabric used as fasteners

128 (p. 150) *hackman*   cabdriver

129 (p. 151) *come the Green Mountains over us*   impose New England manners. The Green Mountains are in Vermont.

130 (p. 151) *Moorish fashion*   or Islamic architecture of North Africa and Spain

131 (p. 152) *jessamines . . . verbenum . . . aloe jasmines*   Jessamines are exotic plants with fragrant flowers; verbenum is a herb or flowering shrub; aloe is a plant of the lily family whose bitter juice was used as a purgative.

132 (p. 152) *distingué* distinguished in manner or bearing (Fr.)

133 (p. 154) *Queen of Sheba before Solomon* The queen, hearing of Solomon's wisdom, 'came to prove him with hard questions'; after hearing his answers, 'there was no more spirit in her' (1 Kings 10:1-5).

134 (p. 161) *vinaigrette* a small box or bottle with a perforated top, containing smelling salts

135 (p. 161) *Dr Watts . . . idle hands* Isaac Watts, great English hymn writer (1674–1748): 'For Satan finds some mischief still/ For idle hands to do' (*Divine Songs for Children*).

136 (p. 162) *of one blood* God 'hath made of one blood all nations of men for to dwell on all the face of the earth' (Acts 17:26). This was a favourite text of the abolitionists who 'accepted the prevailing view of Enlightenment science that blacks and whites belong to the same species and that physiological differences do not correlate with mental and moral qualities, which, they believed, are the result of environmental circumstance' (Paul Goodman, *Of One Blood*, p. 58).

137 (p. 163) *cowhide* a coarse whip of rawhide or braided leather

138 (p. 163) *calaboose* a local prison

139 (p. 166) *I could . . . own teaching* an adaptation of Portia's words in Shakespeare's *The Merchant of Venice*, 1, 2, 15

140 (p. 167) *Bishop of Carthage* ancient city in North Africa near Tunis. Colonisationalists often appealed to the achievements of the Egyptian, Ethiopian and Carthagian civilisations to prove that repatriated African Americans could thrive in Liberia.

141 (p. 167) *Aladdin's palace* a fabulously rich or magical place, celebrated in 'Aladdin's Magic Lamp', a story in the collection of Arabic tales, *A Thousand and One Nights*

142 (p. 167) *If ever Africa . . . last first* See Note 4. George M. Fredrickson was the first to point out that Stowe probably got the idea of the African as a natural Christian from a series of lectures given in Cincinnati by Alexander Kinmont in 1837 and 1838 and gathered in *Twelve Lectures on the Natural History of Man* (1839).

143 (p. 169) *Evangeline! Rightly named* because derived from Evangelist, one of the names given to the writers of the Four Gospels, Matthew, Mark, Luke and John

144 (p. 170) *He hath . . . in its season*   an adaptation from Ecclesiastes 3:11. This is a most inappropriate text for a racist interpretation because it is not about social orders and distinctions, but about natural activities, all of which are subservient to mutability and time: 'All go unto one place; all are of dust, and all turn to dust again' (verse 20).

145 (p. 170) *Picayune*   the first New Orleans newspaper, founded in 1837; a picayune is a small local coin of little value

146 (p. 172) *cubiculum*   a sleeping chamber; a chapel or oratory attached to a church (Latin)

147 (p. 174) *au-fait*   competent, fully informed (Fr.)

148 (p. 174) *buffalo*   buffalo-hide rug or coverlet

149 (p. 176) *Woe . . . the offence cometh*   a version of Matthew 18:7

150 (p. 178) *But as for me . . . trust in the Lord God*   abbreviated version of Psalm 73:2–28

151 (p. 182) *checker-berry leaves*   wintergreens

152 (p. 183) *we'll fight for our liberty till we die*   Here is another echo of Patrick Henry's famous speech; see Note 24.

153 (p. 184) *Hungarian fugitives . . . applause and welcome*   George does not exaggerate the welcome given to them, following Hungary's failed bid for independence from Austria (1848–9).

154 (p. 188) *Joseph in Egypt*   Joseph was sold by his brothers into slavery in Egypt, but 'the Lord was with' him and he prospered and became a powerful figure in the Egyptian government (Genesis 37–50).

155 (p. 189) *meum and tuum*   a reference to Plautus, *Trinummus*, 2,2 47: '*Quad tuum'st meum'st; omne est autem tuum*' (Latin), 'What is yours is mine, and all mine is yours.'

156 (p. 190) *it biteth . . . adder*   Proverbs 23:32

157 (p. 191) *Magna Charta*   English barons forced a charter of liberties on King John in 1215 and it became a symbol of constitutional (as opposed to monarchal) power.

158 (p. 193) *Muses*   in Greek myth the nine sister goddesses who preside over learning, the arts and sciences

159 (p. 193) *Puseyite*   E. B. Pusey (1800–82), an English High Churchman and a leader of the Oxford Movement, which urged the revival of the sacramental piety and rituals of the seventeenth-century.

160 (p. 193) *articles of vertù*   curious old objects

161 (p. 194) *Madras*   fine cotton fabric named for the Indian city

162 (p. 194) *damask . . . crash*   a rich, patterned, silk fabric named for
the Middle-Eastern city, Damascus; *crash* a coarse fabric used for
towels and table linen

163 (p. 196) *Sisyphus or the Danaides*   Both refer to Greek mythology:
Sisyphus the king of Corinth was doomed to push a heavy boulder
uphill that forever rolled down again; the Danaides were the fifty
daughters of King Danaus of Argos of whom forty nine, at their
father's command, murdered their husbands, and were condemned forever to draw water with a sieve.

164 (p. 198) *Look at . . . for the good of the upper*   Kirkham points out
that St Clare's radical formulation is reminiscent of Orestes
Brownson's discussion of Carlyle's work in 'The Laboring Classes'
(1840), in which he condemns slavery and also 'wage slavery' that
ensures 'men are rewarded in inverse ratio to the amount of actual
service they perform' (pp. 126, 53).

165 (p. 200) *tarletane*   dress made of sheer cotton fabric

166 (p. 202) *sighed heavily*   The end of Chapter xviii marked the end
of the first volume in the original two-volume edition of the novel.

167 (p. 204) *selectmen*   elected town officials in New England

168 (p. 204) *Here is a whole class . . . half of mankind*   This case is central
to Weld's critique of slave-owners in *American Slavery as It Is*.

169 (p. 205) *the Fates*   in classical myth the three goddesses supposed
to determine the course of human life

170 (p. 206) *stay me . . . with apples*   Song of Solomon 2:5

171 (p. 206) *When in the course of human events*   the opening words of
the Declaration of Independence, 4 July 1776

172 (p. 207) *Quashy*   a common name for slaves, derived from *Quassi*,
used in Surinam (Dutch Guyana)

173 (p. 207) *Sodom and Gomorrah*   sinful cities destroyed by the Lord
(Genesis 18:20–33 and 19:1–28)

174 (p. 209) *saints arrayed . . . clean and white*   Revelation 3:5

175 (p. 209) *nobody dreamed any harm in it*   A dubious proposition;
Jefferson, for example, wanted to include a strong statement
against slavery in *The Declaration of Independence*, but the Congress
opposed it.

176 (p. 211) *Poland ... Ireland* Poland was thrice divided between Russia, the Austro-Hungarian Empire and Prussia in the last half of the eighteenth century, and independence for Ireland was repeatedly denied in the first half of the nineteenth.

177 (p. 211) *Jesus healing the blind man* John 9

178 (p. 213) *Humbug! ... directing soul of the lower* St Clare rehearses the standard Southern defences of slavery, argued most forcefully by John C. Calhoun and George Fitzhugh. The claim that 'the American planter is "only doing ... what the English aristocracy and capitalists are doing by the lower classes" ', anticipates, as several historians have noticed, the social analysis of Karl Marx – see Stanley M. Elkins, *Slavery*, pp. 213ff.

179 (p. 215) *non sequitur* a statement that does not follow logically from the previous statement (Latin)

180 (p. 216) *dies irae* day of wrath (Latin)

181 (p. 216) *millennium ... Christ should reign* America in the mid-nineteenth century was in the middle of a huge religious revival and the end of the world and 'the kingdom' of Christ was eagerly anticipated: see Revelation 20:7–15; and the Lord's Prayer – Matthew 6:9-13.

182 (p. 217) *African lion ... Scipio* named after Scipio Africanus (234–?183BC), the famous Roman general whose exploits included the final defeat and destruction of Carthage

183 (p. 221) *train in the way she should go* 'Train up a child in the way he should go: and when he is old, he will not depart from it' (Proverbs 22:6).

184 (p. 223) *limb* an agent of Satan, from 'limb of the devil' (*OED*)

185 (p. 224) *land of Diablerie* i.e. Hell; diablerie is witchcraft, devilry

186 (p. 225) *the flood of light ... on education* The Beecher family were committed educationalists in an age dedicated to the reform of schools and Topsy is a test case for the rule of kindness; see Richard H. Brodhead, 'Sparing the Rod'.

187 (p. 229) *laudanum* a medicine derived from opium to relieve pain; it is addictive

188 (p. 231) *raising Cain* causing trouble, from the biblical story of Cain's murder of his brother Abel (Genesis 4:1–16)

189 (p. 231) *India Canton crape* a lightweight, crinkled fabric

190 (p. 233) *Our first parents . . . created* adapted from the catechism printed in the *New England Primer* (first published circa 1690). Ophelia's ideas are indeed 'of the kind that prevailed in New England a century ago' (p. 225).

191 (p. 234) *corps de ballet* the ensemble of a ballet company (Fr.)

192 (p. 236) *Quixotism* extraordinary chivalry or noble and impractical idealism, after the title character of *Don Quixote* by Cervantes (1547–1616)

193 (p. 239) *The Grass . . . the Flower Fadeth* Isaiah 40:7, 1 Peter 1:24

194 (p. 239) *learned . . . content* Philippians 4:11

195 (p. 240) *Revelations and the Prophecies* i.e. the Old Testament books of Joshua, Judges, 1 Samuel through 2 Kings, and all the last seventeen books, except for Lamentations and Daniel

196 (p. 241) *And I saw . . . fire* Revelation 15:2

197 (p. 241) *Oh had I . . . Jerusalem* from the spiritual 'Wings of the Morning'

198 (p. 241) *gates of pearl* Revelation 21:21; another reference to the New Jerusalem

199 (p. 242) *I see . . . they bear* based on Revelation 7:9

200 (p. 242) *a child like Eva* Hedrick is good on the historical and social origins of 'The notion of the "special child" – of whom Little Eva was the apotheosis' (p. 191); cf. Note 68.

201 (p. 243) *soft, insidious disease* tuberculosis, known at the time as consumption

202 (p. 248) *All men . . . free and equal* from the Constitution of Massachusetts (1779) by John Adams, echoing the Declaration of Independence: 'All men are created equal . . .'

203 (p. 248) *canaille* mob, rabble (Fr.)

204 (p. 248) *St Domingo* In 1804 the slaves of the French colony Haiti rebelled and declared their independence.

205 (p. 249) *nobles in Louis XVI's time . . . Austria and Pius IX* The last king of France was guillotined during the French Revolution; in 1848, the Austrian Empire was threatened by revolutions in Vienna, Italy, Hungary and Bohemia; and Pius IX (Pope from 1846–78) was driven out of Rome by Italian nationalists.

206 (p. 249) *Dies declarabit* time will tell (Latin)

207 (p. 249) *sans culottes* generic term for revolutionary political

extremists; literally, 'without knee-breeches', the nickname given to French Republicans during the Revolution

208 (p. 249) *Anglo-Saxon blood will lead on the day*   as was the case, most notoriously, with Nat Turner, a mulatto, who led (in 1831 in Virginia) the most successful and bloody (if abortive) rebellion against the white slavers in Southern history

209 (p. 249) *As it was . . . took them*   In Matthew 24:37–9, Christ drew upon the scepticism of Noah's friends with regard to the Flood (Genesis 6–9) to warn those who doubt the coming of the Messiah.

210 (pp. 249–50) *circuit rider*   itinerant preacher

211 (p. 250) *They that . . . govern others*   perhaps an adaptation of 'He that would govern others, first should be master of himself', from *The Bondsman* (1, 3) by Philip Massinger (1583–1640)

212 (p. 250) *Mount Etna*   famous volcanic mountain on the east coast of Sicily

213 (p. 252) *Don't the Bible say . . . everybody*   it does; repeatedly in the New Testament (e.g. Matthew 5:43 and Romans 13:9), and once in the Old, Leviticus 19:18

214 (p. 263) *Weep not . . . our eyes*   The opening lines of Thomas Moore's 'Weep Not for Those', *Sacred Songs* (1816)

215 (p. 263) *Parian vase*   made from white porcelain

216 (p. 264) *eldritch*   uncanny, weird

217 (p. 272) *At midnight . . . cometh*   Matthew 25:1–13

218 (p. 273) *It's the trumpet . . . o' day*   from the hymn 'O, thou Almighty Father'

219 (p. 275) *gone for ever*   John Punchard Jewett claimed that he was persuaded to publish *Uncle Tom's Cabin* by 'my noble wife', who read to him from the serial 'the touching death scene of Little Eva, having more than once urged me to write to Mrs Stowe soliciting the story for publication in book form' (cited, Kirkham, p. 143).

220 (p. 275) *This is the Last of Earth*   'I am content!' These were the famous last words of John Quincy Adams (1767–1848), sixth president of the United States.

221 (p. 275) *He giveth to his beloved*   Psalm 127:2

222 (p. 275) *dimness of anguish*   Isaiah 8:22

223 (p. 277) *I am . . . yet shall he live*   Christ's words to Martha, shortly before his greatest miracle, the raising of Lazarus from the dead, John 11:25–6

224 (p. 278) *the weed*   black mourning crape

225 (p. 279) *The heart . . . bitterness*   Proverbs 14:10

226 (p. 279) *even so . . . good in thy sight*   Christ's words, Matthew 11:26

227 (p. 280) *Lord I believe . . . unbelief*   Mark 9:23–4

228 (p. 280) *the love . . . that passeth knowledge*   Ephesians 3:19

229 (p. 281) *Lazarus*   John 11:25–6; cf. n. 223

230 (p. 281) *reveals unto babes*   Matthew 11:25

231 (p. 282) *Goethe*   Johann Wolfgang von Goethe (1749–1832), German poet, playwright, and aesthetician. For Moore, see Note 214; for Byron, Note 110.

232 (p. 286) *doing evil that good may come*   Romans 3:8

233 (p. 287) *In the midst of life we are in death*   from the Burial Service in *The Book of Common Prayer*

234 (p. 288) *When the Son . . . ye did it not to me*   Matthew 25:31–45

235 (p. 289) *Aeolian*   an ecclesiastical mode in music

236 (p. 289) *Dies Irae*   a medieval Latin hymn from the Requiem Mass

237 (p. 291) *Hungarian nobles*   The Hungarian Diet in March 1848 drew up 'The Ten Points', the last of which approved the abolition of serfdom with compensation to the landlords.

238 (p. 291) *is there enough . . . education and elevation*   Stowe, like St Clare, felt 'the unchristian prejudice of the North' vetoed such hopes, thereby fuelling her advocacy of Colonisation.

239 (p. 294) *strong crying and tears*   i.e. like an ideal Christian, Hebrews 5:7

240 (p. 294) *Recordare . . . sedisti lassus*   'Think, kind Jesus / Leave me not to reprobation. / Faint and weary thou hast sought me' – fragments from the Recordare of the Requiem mass

241 (p. 296) *He that dwelleth . . . in him*   I John 4:16

242 (p. 299) *Thy will be done*   from the Lord's Prayer

243 (p. 302) *Tartarus informis . . . ademptum*   Tartarus, in Greek mythology, is the dark abyss in which the wicked are punished – 'frightful, formless, immense, with sight removed' (Latin, from Virgil's *Aeneid* 3, 658).

244 (p. 304) *truck*   odds and ends, rubbish

245 (p. 307) *Whoso causeth . . . depths of the sea*   Christ's words in Matthew 18:6

246 (p. 307) *O, where is . . . in the goodly land*   probably versions of the revival song 'Hebrew Children': 'Where are the Hebrew children? [x 3] / Safe in the promised land.'

247 (p. 308) *Bourse*   exchange or financial market (Fr.)

248 (p. 308) *pavé*   pavement (Fr.)

249 (p. 311) *Red River*   a tributary of the Mississippi

250 (p. 311) *When he maketh . . . cry of the humble*   an abridgement of Psalm 9:12

251 (p. 311) *The Middle Passage*   in the international slave trade, the crossing of the Atlantic from Africa to the New World

252 (p. 312) *taken . . . chattel personal*   from the South Carolina slave code: 'Slaves shall be deemed, sold, taken, reputed and adjudged in law to be *chattels personal* in the hands of their owners and possessors, and their executors, administrators and assigns, to all intents, constructions, and purposes, whatsoever' (*Key*, p. 107). In Chapter xi of the *Key*, 'A Comparison of the Roman Law of Slavery with the American', Stowe quotes extensively from the various racial laws of the South.

253 (p. 313) *Fear not! . . . Thou art* MINE!   Isaiah 43:1

254 (p. 314) *poco moonshine*   an odd construction; perhaps, meaning 'little devil', from *poco* (little, Italian), and *moonshine*, 'smuggled or illicit spirit' (dialect)

255 (p. 317) *The dark places . . . cruelty*   Psalm 74:20

256 (p. 318) *Jerusalem . . . shall*   from 'Song of Mary', a hymn (1601)

257 (p. 319) *China trees*   chinaberry trees, planted for shade in the Southern States

258 (p. 322) *the Inquisition*   the Spanish Inquisition became a byword for the torture of one human being by another

259 (p. 323) *Come . . . and I will give you rest*   Christ's words to 'the multitudes' (Matthew 11:28)

260 (p. 324) *God is . . . that diligently seek Him*   adapted from Hebrews 11:6

261 (p.324) *when thou . . . thy Saviour*   adapted from Isaiah 43:2–3

262 (p. 331) *Servants obey yer masters*   adapted from Colossians 3:22

263 (p. 335) *Father forgive them . . . they do*   Christ's words on the cross, Luke 23:34

264 (p. 337) *yellow fever*   infectious tropical disease, transmitted by mosquitoes, often fatal

265 (p. 339) *Pearl River*   in central Mississippi

266 (p. 342) *And slight . . . darkly bound*   by Lord Byron

267 (p. 344) *brangle*   quarrel

268 (p. 346) *God is . . . fire*   Moses instructs his people not 'to forget the covenant of the Lord your God' for 'thy God is a consuming fire, even a jealous God' (Deuteronomy 4:23–4)

269 (p. 346) *Oh . . . judgement-seat of Christ*   from the spiritual 'Judgement Seat'

270 (p. 352) *I am . . . and morning-star*   Revelation 22:16

271 (p. 352) *crank*   lively, cocky (dialect)

272 (p. 353) *The Lord . . . for this time*   adapted from Daniel in the lion's den, Daniel 6:22

273 (p. 354) *Curran*   John Philpott Curran (1750–1817), Irish Catholic orator and magistrate, pronouncing in 1772 on the famous case of the Jamaican, James Somerset, who arrived in England with his master and asserted his freedom.

274 (p. 354) *touzling*   tossing

275 (p. 359) *husband*   'new-made freeman' in the serial; cf. Kirkham for a discussion of the differences between serial and novel at this point (pp. 177–80)

276 (p. 360) *Thanks be . . . the victory*   i.e. over death, I Corinthians 15:55–7

277 (p. 363) *The earth . . . we first begun*   from John Newton's hymn 'Amazing Grace'

278 (pp. 364–5) *When I can . . . my all!*   Isaac Watts, *Hymns and Spiritual Songs*, Book 2, hymn 65

279 (p. 365) *What have we . . . before the time*   spoken by the 'two possessed with devils' to Christ, Matthew 8:29

280 (p. 368) *love our enemies*   from the Sermon on the Mount, Matthew 5:43–4

281 (p. 371) *a land of darkness . . . death*   Job 10:21

282 (p. 374) *coup d'état*   sudden violent change of government (Fr.)

283 (p. 376) *flambeaux*   flaming torches (Fr.)

284 (p. 378) *Deem not . . . suffer here*   adapted from 'Blessed Are They

That Mourn' by William Culler Bryant (1794–1878), the poet and abolitionist. The first line read, 'Nor let the good man's trust depart.'

285 (p. 380) *curvetting* A curvet is a horse's leap with all four legs off the ground.

286 (p. 381) *Into thy hands . . . my spirit* cf. Christ's last words on the cross, Luke 23:46

287 (pp. 381–2) *Fear not them . . . they can do* a version of Christ's words to his apostles: 'And fear not them which kill the body, but are not able to kill the soul: but rather fear him which is able to destroy both soul and body in hell' (Matthew 11:28)

288 (p. 383) *like unto the Son of God!* Hebrews 7:3

289 (p. 384) *Oh, Tom . . . That prayer was answered!* Stowe adapts the story of Christ and the two thieves crucified alongside Him, one of whom rails against Him and the other pleads 'remember me when thou comest into thy kingdom', to which He replies, 'To day shalt thou be with me in paradise' (Luke 23:39–43).

290 (p. 387) *Jesus can . . . pillows are* a version of the black spiritual, 'Jesus Goin' to Make Up My Dyin' Bed': 'Oh, don't worry 'bout me dyin' [x 3], / Jesus goin' to make up my dyin' bed.'

291 (p. 388) *Who. . . shall. . . the love of Christ?* Romans 8:35

292 (p. 389) *Then he turned . . . but in vain* Kirkham observes that this sequence was added to the novel after the serial (pp. 180–2).

293 (p. 390) *Blessed are . . . shall be comforted* from the Sermon on the Mount' (Matthew 5:4)

294 (p. 391) *the sheeted dead . . . streets of Rome* Hamlet, 1, 1, 113

295 (p. 391) *pneumatology* the study of spiritual phenomena

296 (p. 392) *Creole créole* (Fr.), *criollo* (Sp.); descended from the original Spanish settlers of the states bordering the Gulf of Mexico

297 (p. 393) *rencontre* casual meeting (Fr.)

298 (p. 396) *Results* the narrative jumps five years beyond the novel's publication in 1852

299 (p. 399) *this country* presumably Canada

300 (p. 400) *Haitians* i.e. the French, who are Catholics; hence George's Protestant disdain

301 (p. 400) *On the shores of Africa . . . a republic* Liberia was founded in West Africa by the American Colonisation Society in 1821.

302 (p. 401) *I grant ... against us* Stowe acknowledges that 'our oppressors' (i.e. Southerners) were much keener on Colonisation than both African-Americans and the American Anti-Slavery Society.

303 (p. 401) *But then I ... a nation of my own* Fredrickson relates George's separatist stance to Stowe's acceptance of Alexander Kinmont's view that the African race had a glorious future in 'the Peninsula of Africa' where they would found 'a great civilisation ... and humanity in its more advanced millennial state will reflect, under a sweet and mellow light, the softer attributes of the Divine munificence'. Cf. Notes 4 and 142.

304 (p. 402) *Whereas ... of many generations* Isaiah 60:15

305 (p. 402) *Elysium* any place of ideal happiness; from notions of paradise in classical mythology

306 (p. 406) *élève* pupil (Fr.)

307 (p. 403) *PS ... family to Africa* 'this sloppy and unnecessary additional information appears only in the novel' (Kirkham, p. 182)

308 (p. 406) *Te Deum* 'Te Deum laudamus' (Latin): 'Thee, God we praise', the beginning of a hymn of thanksgiving

309 (p. 406) *The year ... sinners, home* 'Blow Ye the Trumpet', a hymn by Charles Wesley (1707–88)

310 (p. 407) *The writer ... one general answer* Stowe responds here to comments from her readers during the serialisation, anticipating her more systematic response in the *Key*.

311 (p. 407) *The incorruptible fidelity ... personal knowledge* including, as Stowe acknowledges in Chapter VI of the *Key*, 'of the venerable Josiah Henson' (p. 26). Cf. Robin Winks's essay in Charles T. Davis and Henry Louis Gates Jr (eds), pp. 112–46.

312 (p. 407) *old Prue* Cf. Chapter XI of the *Key* (pp. 48–9)

313 (p. 408) *Horace Mann* the important American educationalist (1796–1859), who was the defence attorney at the trial in 1848 of Daniel Drayton, whose conviction for attempting to transport seventy-six slaves to freedom on the schooner *Pearl* greatly outraged Northern as well as abolitionist opinion

314 (p. 408) *two girls called Edmundson* Stowe became personally interested in the girls and aided in their education at Oberlin College (Kirkham, p. 140).

315 (p. 408) *the shambles* the slaughterhouse

316 (p. 409) *An interview . . . You are free* paraphrased from one of Stowe's early stories, 'Immediate Emancipation', which had appeared in the New York *Evangelist*, 2 January 1845

317 (p. 413) *The results . . . establish this* In 1834 a permanent school was organised through Lane Seminary to educate the freed slaves and fugitives who were excluded from white schools in Cincinnati.

318 (p. 413) *Professor C. E. Stowe* Calvin Ellis Stowe (1802–86), Stowe's husband, a preacher and educator who moved to Cincinnati in 1833 to be professor of biblical literature at Lane Theological Seminary; Harriet Stowe's father, Lyman Beecher, was the president.

319 (p. 414) *cannot be a voter* and couldn't until 1870 when the Fifteenth Amendment awarded voting rights to all males; citizenship was granted to ex-slaves in the Fourteenth Amendment in 1866.

320 (p. 414) *Pennington . . . Douglass and Ward* J. W. C. Pennington (1807–70), born a slave in Maryland, was the pastor of a church in Hartford, Connecticut, and a fierce opponent of Colonisation. His slave narrative, *The Fugitive Blacksmith*, was published in 1849. Frederick Douglass (*c.*1817–95) was the most famous black abolitionist of his generation; his autobiographical *Narrative* (1845), recounting his escape from slavery in Maryland to New England, is an American classic. In 1847 he founded the abolitionist weekly *North Star*. Samuel Ringold Ward (1817–*c.*1866), a black abolitionist, orator and journalist, escaped North with his parents in 1820. His *Autobiography of a Fugitive Negro* was published in 1855.

321 (p. 414) *This is an age . . . convulsed* Stowe refers to the revolutions of 1848 in Europe; cf. Note 153 (p. 184).

322 (p. 415) *For that day . . . the oppressor* adapted from Malachai 4:1